A Dark Truth

Jeff Ross

3210 41st Street

Moline Public Library

Moline, IL 61265

orca soundings

ORCA BOOK PUBLISHERS

3 0067 00109 1597

Copyright © 2016 Jeff Ross

All rights reserved. No part of this publication may be reproduced
or transmitted in any form or by any means, electronic or mechanical, including
photocopying, recording or by any information storage and retrieval system now
known or to be invented, without permission in writing from the publisher.

Library and Archives Canada Cataloguing in Publication

Ross, Jeff, 1973–, author
A dark truth / Jeff Ross.
(Orca soundings)

Issued in print and electronic formats.
ISBN 978-1-4598-1327-4 (paperback).—ISBN 978-1-4598-1328-1 (pdf).—
ISBN 978-1-4598-1329-8 (epub)

I. Title. II. Series: Orca soundings
PS8635.06928D37 2016   jc813'.6   c2016-900782-0
c2016-900783-9

First published in the United States, 2016
Library of Congress Control Number: 2016931892

Summary: In this high-interest novel for teens, Riley learns that the color
of your skin does affect how you are treated.

MIX
Paper from
responsible sources
FSC® C016245

*Orca Book Publishers is dedicated to preserving the environment and has
printed this book on Forest Stewardship Council® certified paper.*

Orca Book Publishers gratefully acknowledges the support for its
publishing programs provided by the following agencies: the Government
of Canada through the Canada Book Fund and the Canada Council
for the Arts, and the Province of British Columbia through
the BC Arts Council and the Book Publishing Tax Credit.

Cover image by iStock.com

ORCA BOOK PUBLISHERS
www.orcabook.com

Printed and bound in Canada.

19 18 17 16 • 4 3 2 1

For Luca & Alex, who got me back into skateboarding, the SMC for enabling and encouraging, and Megan for tolerating this madness.

Chapter One

"You have to think about where your shoulders are all the time," Dashawn said. The sun was right above us, glaring straight down, hot and bright. We were two blocks from the skate park and I was already beginning to sweat. I could feel my underwear binding to my skin. The cascade of water building beneath the brim of my hat.

1

"I know," I said.

"Well, if you know, Riley, then start doing it."

"Shut up," I replied. We bumped into one another, arm against arm, then kept moving. Dashawn and I had been best friends since kindergarten. Our mothers used to take us to the same playground to roll around in the sand, but the second they were distracted, we'd be up the play structure and dangling from one of the high bars, laughing our asses off. Four years old and already we required the world to be filled with adventure or boredom settled in.

It was the same need for an adrenaline boost that had us skateboarding when we were ten. We'd tried other things, like BMX or jumping off cliffs into the deep waters of the bay, but those things didn't require the same skill. At least, not the way we were doing them. Skateboarding gave us something different, something we could get better at every day but which, at any time, we could totally ruin ourselves doing.

We bumped into one another again as we turned the corner to the park.

"Ah, shit," Dashawn said. "That is a *lot* of scooter kids." I exhaled slowly. There had to be twenty of them in there. The youngest ones were on those little three-wheeled scooters. The older ones were fourteen or fifteen and were trying to whip the scooters around above their heads after they popped out of the bowl. Everything about scooters depressed me. The handlebars. The whistling noise they made. And the fact that they were in the skate park at all. I mean, they're called *skate parks* for a reason. Anywhere skaters go, we get bothered by security guards or, even worse, the police. No one else has this issue. These kids could ride in the middle of a parking lot and people would think they're cute. There was no reason for them to be here at all. And the worst of it was they didn't understand skate-park etiquette. They'd do circles for twenty minutes in the middle of the space, making it impossible for anyone to set up for a trick or create a line.

"Man," I said. "There's even some of those strider bikes in there."

"That dude's on a mountain bike." Dashawn dropped his board, then popped it back into his hand. This was what he did when he was anxious.

"It is going to be impossible to hit that ledge," I said.

"You give up too easy, bro." He dropped his board again and rolled forward. I did the same, coming up close to him. "The space is there—you just have to make it or take it."

"Make it or take it," I said. "All right. *Or* we could just crash one of them."

"They're little kids, man," Dashawn said. "You're gonna go running over little kids?"

I'd had a hate-on for scooter kids since one of them had cut me off at the last second and I'd seriously sprained my ankle. It had put me out for two weeks. That doesn't sound like much, but it took me another two weeks to get back to where I was actually progressing. I spent that time playing *Skate 3* on my Xbox or watching videos online and just *dying* to get back out again, and all I could see was this little kid on a bright-blue scooter with a stupid grin on his face as he slowly turned into me.

I knew I shouldn't hate all scooter kids because of that one, but it was hard. It didn't seem like any of them really looked out for anyone but themselves. The skate park was nothing more than a place for them to go mess around, whereas kids like Dashawn and me were there to make skateboarding a career.

"Yeah yeah. They're erratic pylons," I said.

"You gotta be kind, bro," Dashawn said. He ollied the curb and rolled into the park. One of the scooter kids wove around him, then cut back down a ramp without a care in the world.

"There's your ledge," Dashawn said. He rolled to the ledge and ollied on, then immediately off.

We were there that day to shoot some clips for our Sponsor Me videos. A lot of people had gone straight to Instagram in an attempt to be seen, but Dashawn and I were old school. We wanted something that you could actually hand out.

The ledge was fairly high. I had an idea for a trick on it, one I totally thought I could get and which would look kick-ass filmed. I needed to practice, though, before anyone filmed me.

I popped an ollie, then rolled around the space, going through my trick list. Shove-it, heelflip, kickflip, hardflip, 180, 360. I did this every time I got to the park. If I could get all those tricks in a row, I knew I was ready to hit something bigger.

By the time I was done, I was wiping sweat from my eyes and breathing heavily.

Dashawn rolled over to me, then dropped his right foot to come to a stop. "I'm going to mess around on the bank," he said.

"I'm getting this ledge."

Dashawn beamed his giant smile at me. "Yeah, you are." He put his fist out before him, and I gave it a bump. "Keep it smooth."

Smooth, I thought as he rolled away. That was Dashawn. Everything he did had a flow to it. Even when he fell, it was with a certain kind of grace.

There were some scooter kids near the end of the ledge. I decided I'd hit it once, just do a 5-0 and pop off, then turn and come right back up to give them the chance to get an idea of the space I was about to take.

Dashawn was on the other side of the park, fist-bumping the only other black skater in the park. He turned just as I was about to push and yelled, "That ledge is yours, bro. Crush it."

I squinted into the sun, waited for a scooter kid to roll away and pushed hard.

Chapter Two

I decided to try the 5-0 without the kick-flip first. A 5-0 is like a manual, only on a ledge, so you have to land with the front of your board in the air and lock into whatever you're sliding on with your back trucks. It's difficult to land this way after doing a kickflip because you have to quickly spot where you need to lock in and then keep the board perfectly balanced beneath you.

I failed the first five attempts. The first four, I just spun off and jumped to the ground. But on the final one I did a full-out Superman onto the concrete and slid a good six feet on my elbows. My head almost cracked against the ground, and I left a wet spot from the massive amount of sweat my shirt was holding. A scooter kid rolled over and asked me if I was all right. I slowly got up, ignoring him.

"Bro, that was a slam," Dashawn said, sliding to a stop beside me. "You aight?"

"That wasn't even with the kick-flip," I said. I tested my body to make certain nothing ached in a broken way. Cuts and bruises I could deal with. Hell, adrenaline did a pretty good job of nulling that. But if something was broken, I needed to lay off right away. You would think a broken bone would be instantly noticeable, but if it's a small fracture of your wrist, say, you might not even know it until the next day when it swells to eight times its normal size, and bright lines of pain flow up your arm.

"You got it this time," Dashawn said. He was always super encouraging. It seemed as though I skated better with him around. When I came to the park on my own, I pretty much endlessly slammed and grumbled about scooter kids under my breath.

"I don't know," I said. The scooter kids seemed to have tripled in number. Six of them were circling the manual pad in the middle of the park, chasing one another and laughing like crazed hyenas.

"Natasha just dropped me a text. She's going to be here in, like, ten minutes."

"Seriously? I thought she was coming closer to six o'clock," I said.

Dashawn held up his watch to show me it was already five thirty.

"She says she'll film this if you want. She was working on your video last night, and somehow you have eight good clips. You're going to need at least twelve."

"I want fifteen," I muttered.

"Then hit that, bro." He clapped my back and set his skateboard down. "I'll see if I can get a good angle from over here so when Tash shows we can both shoot at the same time."

Sponsor Me videos are like calling cards to companies looking to throw products and money at new young skaters. We'd both placed in a contest in August, and a representative for a major company had asked for our videos. We told him we didn't have full clips yet. He said we needed them fast in order to cash in on our contest results, or we'd soon be forgotten. This was all part of skateboarding. Who was in at any moment seemed, in many ways, purely due to luck. There were a lot of great skateboarders out there, so you had to show you had something different to offer. Something no one else had done or done in the same way.

I wanted to skate clean. That was my thing. No wobbles, no flapping arms, always land on the bolts.

Everything I did was smooth. If I landed, that is. I wasn't going to put anything in the video if it wasn't totally smooth and crisp. Dashawn cared less about how smooth he was, but he needed everything to be seriously technical. My video, I hoped, would look amazing on first view. Dashawn's, on the other hand, would likely not seem like much to the untrained eye. But once you rewatched it, you would see that everything he was doing was incredibly difficult and precise. And he did it all with speed.

I lined up the ledge again. Three scooter kids cut in around the end of it.

Two took off while the third stood there and, I am serious here, picked his nose. I was about to yell at him when Dashawn said, "Hey, little dude, would you mind moving?" He pointed at me, and the kid removed his finger from his nose to look. "My friend's trying to hit that ledge." The kid pushed away immediately, then turned around to watch.

"Go, Ry. Full out. Pop, flick, lean, rotate, pop." He held his phone up before him and bent down for the angle. I pushed hard at the ledge, popped and flicked and somehow landed right on the edge of the ledge. I held the manual, feeling my rear trucks grinding along the metal, and then, just as I was rotating my shoulders to try the 180 off, I caught a bright-red blur to my right. I bailed, which was a good thing, because if I'd tried to pop off the ledge, I would have landed right on a scooter kid.

"Goddammit!" I yelled. The kid pushed away, saying sorry over his shoulder. But he'd be right back. That was the problem—they always came back.

Dashawn rolled over to me. "That was sick, man."

"Why are there so many scooters in this world? What are they even doing here? Why can't they watch where they're going or just...*argh!*"

"Chill, man. How was he supposed to know you were coming off there?"

"He would just have to look up now and then and..." The frustration finally boiled over, and I grabbed my board and threw it at a tree. The sound of wood on wood gave me a bit of satisfaction. But the rage built right back up again.

"Bro, get a grip," Dashawn said. "Natasha isn't even here yet. We'll get some guys to really clear the space out when she's filming. No one will cut into you or the shot." He put his hand on my shoulder. "Try to relax. You know, keep calm and carry on and all that shit."

"Man, it doesn't even matter. Have you ever seen a Sponsor Me video that features ten of fifteen clips in a skate park? Anyone can skate this place. That's what it's here for."

"Keep it smooth," he said. "Keep it technical, and it doesn't matter where you are."

"You lose this?"

I turned to find Natasha behind me with my board in her hand. Natasha is about five seven with a giant mass of dark hair and deep-brown eyes. She got into skateboarding when she was about five, but then she busted her arm and was always afraid of reinjuring herself. She didn't want that kind of injury to happen again, and instead of pushing herself to progress, she got into filming.

For the past couple of years she'd been making really sick videos for YouTube and Instagram. A couple of her videos of me were featured on a roundup of clips on the *Ride* website once. The tricks I'd been doing were smooth and sweet, but honestly, it was her editing and the music she'd selected that really stepped the video up.

"Thanks," I said.

"Are we shooting today?" she said. "We're already losing light."

"There are too many kids here," I said. "It's impossible."

"I said we'd clear them out," Dashawn said. "One sec." He stepped away and yelled, "Ryan!"

Our friend Ryan skated over to us.

"Dude, can you get a couple other guys to block the traffic for Riley? He wants to film a clip on this ledge," Dashawn said.

Ryan looked around at the mass of swirling, shifting scooters. "I wouldn't even bother," he said.

"Kickflip to 5-0 to 180 off," Dashawn said. "It's going to be sick."

Ryan looked at me. "It's going to look like you're messing around in a skate park. Is this for Instagram?"

"No," I said. "My Sponsor Me video."

"You have to do those in the real world," he said. He pointed to where his bag was resting against a picnic table in the shade. "Let me show you something I found. I was going to keep it for myself, but if you promise to throw me some gear when you get sponsored, I'll let you in on it."

Chapter Three

Skaters see the world differently. Like, where some people might see a ledge to rest on or a set of stairs to take them from one level to another, a skater is going to see something to grind, slide or jump. Therefore, what Ryan showed us was a pure slice of paradise.

"Where is this?" Dashawn said.

Ryan was flipping through the photos on his phone. They were all taken through what looked like a security fence. Caterpillars and diggers littered the space, and in the background a giant crane shot into the sky like a stairway to the clouds. Everything else was marble, steel, smooth concrete and pavement. There were angles, stairs from three to twenty steps. The building itself was nothing much, just another concrete box jammed in among newly planted lawns. Everything around it, though, was a skater's paradise.

"It's out in the burbs. My aunt lives next door," Ryan said.

"It looks like they're still working on it," I said.

"This was two weeks ago," he replied, flicking to a picture of a smooth, uninterrupted slab of concrete that looked to be around twelve feet long with a perfect four-foot drop at the end.

My mind was already racing with possibilities. "It's done now."

"What do you mean by *done*?" Dashawn said.

"I mean done. All this shit is gone. It's just an empty building with all this around it."

"Are you sure?" Natasha said.

"My aunt is going to start work there in two weeks. It's some kind of high-tech place. Right now there's nothing inside, so I doubt they're even bothering with security. Not on-premise anyway."

"How far out is this?" I said. The ledge, upon closer inspection, had a metal coping along its edge. It was ridiculous. Like someone had designed a skate park around an office building for some reason. It was too perfect to not skate.

"That's the problem. It's out in Westlake. There's only one bus there." Ryan stopped and looked up behind us, where three city buses were idling. "That one," he said.

"The 61?"

"Yeah," Ryan said. "And you likely have about two minutes to get on that bus before it's gone."

I looked at Dashawn, then back at the pictures.

"That right there," I said, pointing at the slab of concrete, "is perfect for the kickflip to 5-0. The building has mirrored windows. From the right angle it would look so sick."

"It would," Ryan said. "You have to go skate it."

I stood and grabbed my board.

"Let's go," I said, pulling at Dashawn's shoulder.

"Hell yeah," Dashawn said, jumping up.

"If you want it filmed, you're going to need me," Natasha said.

"Hell yeah, we need you."

Ryan stood and brushed his pants.

"You coming?" I asked him.

"Nah, I have to get home. I'll text you the address. Get some good clips. And don't forget me when you're huge." He gave me a fist bump. Dashawn, Natasha and I sprinted to the bus.

We grabbed a couple of seats at the back that faced one another.

"What's our security plan?" Natasha asked. She was in a seat by herself, her backpack beside her. She always carried a couple of cameras along with her iPhone. When she was given the right amount of time, she would line up her shots with her iPhone, then start testing levels with her camera, all before we even hit whatever it was we wanted filmed. She was a perfectionist as well, so even when we'd landed something clean and were super stoked about it, she'd find something wrong with the lighting or the angle and send us back to try again.

"Same as always," I said. "Security, we stay where we are and promise to leave and never come back."

"Then we wait them out," Dashawn said.

"Exactly."

"What about police?" Natasha said. We hadn't really had many problems with the police in the past. The only time before, actually, had been when Natasha and I were down on the pier and someone from a fish-and-chip wagon complained about the noise. Two cops showed up and asked us to go somewhere else because we were being too loud, and we left. There'd been a couple of families there that day, and the kids had really seemed to be enjoying watching me endlessly slam on a blunt-to-fakie attempt. But there's no reason to anger the police—after all, they can take you into the precinct and call your parents.

"We run," I said.

"Really?" Natasha said.

"For sure," Dashawn said. "No one wants to mess around with the police."

"Let's have an exit route in mind, okay? It's totally going to depend on how they roll in. But if a cop car shows, let's split in three directions." My phone buzzed, and Ryan's text came in with the address. We were really close. The bus stopped outside a McDonald's. "Meet in there," I said. "No one texts anyone else. No phone calls or anything."

"Every man for himself then, right?" Dashawn said.

"I guess, but not really. If we split up, they can only follow one of us, right? I mean, this is private property, and no matter how careful we are, we're going to leave some marks. Whoever developed this place will be pissed."

"Cool," Dashawn said. "Three separate directions."

25

It was still warm out as we stepped into the gray-blue evening light. The sun was firing up the sky in an explosion of yellow and orange in the distance. Natasha came out with her fingers forming a box, already making decisions about angles.

"It's down here," I said, pointing at a small path in front of us. We looked around as though we were about to commit some kind of horrible crime. We didn't have to walk for more than two minutes before we found it.

"Holy crap," Dashawn said. "It's beautiful."

Everything glowed. The white concrete and marble. Big fat rails and L bars. There were banks and pyramids. One side was on slightly higher ground, so there was even a natural flow from one end to the other. You could push a couple of times and just roll through a line with ease. The fencing was gone, which was good. If we'd climbed over a fence to get to the space, we wouldn't be able to act innocent and ignorant if the building had security guards. We stayed behind a tree and watched to see if there was any security around. The inside of the building and parking lot were totally lit. We waited five unbearable minutes just to see if anything moved.

"It's going to get too dark to shoot soon," Natasha said. She had her camera out and was checking levels.

"I don't see anyone in there," Dashawn said. "There's nothing inside, so there's nothing to protect, right?"

"So do you want to go hit it?" I asked.

"Absolutely. Are you going to try that ledge first?"

"Yeah, in case someone shows. I can totally get that thing. It looks perfect."

Dashawn gave me a fist bump.

Natasha held the camera up. "I'm all set. Practice it right away while I find the right angle."

I inhaled deeply. "Remember the plan if the cops show," I said.

Dashawn pointed at a sidewalk on the other side of the lot. "I'll go that way. Then I'll circle back to the Mickey D's."

"I'll come back this way," Natasha said. "I don't want to run through the trees for any longer than necessary, not with all this stuff. I can ditch my board if I have to and just be some girl waiting for a bus." She pulled a hat out of her bag and tucked her hair up inside it. She instantly looked different.

"Okay," I said. I spotted a trail through the brush that seemed to go into a neighboring suburb. "I'll take that trail, then get on the road back to the McDonald's."

"Change up your clothes at the Mickey D's," Dashawn said. "Stash your board somewhere and chuck your hat or something. Look different."

"That's key," I said. "Look different. Honestly, though, I don't think we're going to get hassled. Let's say we session for forty-five minutes, then leave. That way we might be able to come back."

"We only have about forty-five minutes of light left anyway," Natasha said.

"Then let's hurry the hell up."

Chapter Four

This place was unbelievable. I would have bowed down before the architect if I knew who he or she was. I would kiss his or her dirty boots. I would offer up my first and only A in mathematics if it would please them. They had created, likely without even knowing it, the best skate park in town.

My wheels whistled.

The air rushed across my face.

I felt like I was moving faster and more smoothly than ever before. Without really thinking about it, I landed a backside 50-50 on a low handrail, popping off at the bottom and then cruising up a pyramid and doing a perfect pop shove-it off the side.

"This is so sick!" I yelled.

"Keep it down," Natasha said. She'd popped down a three-step to stand beside me. "Are you going to do one-off shots or a line?"

Looking at the space, it seemed like a line would be best. Ryan's pictures had not done this place justice. There was a little four-step right before the concrete ledge. After the drop there was a bit of space and then a bench that ended on a steep downslope.

"I'm going to tre flip those stairs," I said. "Then kickflip to 5-0 the ledge. I'll try a blunt slide across that bench, then fakie out on the slope. Do you think you can film all that?"

"That's crazy," Natasha said, staring at the little screen on her camera. "Are you sure you can land all of that?" She looked at me seriously.

It *was* a bit much. A tre flip has the board spinning on both axes beneath you. A blunt is when you slide across something on your tail, but your board is straight up in the air. Landing fakie just meant I'd land backward, but even then there was the possibility of wiping out.

Hard.

"DS!" I yelled.

Dashawn had just bailed on a hand-rail. He stooped to grab his board. When he turned to us, his face was glowing. "Yeah."

I held my fingers up like a little skateboarder and pretended to do the line, calling out the tricks along the way.

His eyes lit. "You got that, Ry."

"You think?"

"Just land that tre clean and the rest is yours. Though I still think you want a 180 off the ledge. It just looks so sick."

"Maybe next time." I ran up the stairs. "You ready, Tash?" She gave me a thumbs-up, which meant she'd already begun filming.

It was ridiculously easy to get the speed up for the four-step. It was as if the universe wanted me to move faster. I didn't need to push more than three times, and I was cruising toward the top of the stairs at the perfect speed. I popped the tre flip and somehow landed it cleanly. Right on the bolts. I pushed twice and landed a perfect 5-0 on the ledge and even managed a little pop off the end. Two more pushes and I was set up for a blunt slide across the bench, but my wheels stuck on the surface, and I was tossed straight ahead and down the bank. Natasha rolled past me and did a slow circle, already looking at the screen on her camera.

"Dude," Dashawn said. "You had that."

"We need to wax that bench," I said. "What the hell is that even made of?"

Dashawn skated up the bank and ran a finger along the bench. "It's plastic! But painted silver."

"I totally thought that was metal."

Dashawn started laughing. "This place is ridiculous." He checked his watch. "Half an hour left."

I pulled a block of wax out of Natasha's bag and started working it along the edge of the bench, then farther up, where my wheels would need to slide. A blunt slide is a really difficult trick that requires a lot of balance and, even more so, speed. Plus, if whatever you're hitting isn't slippery, you stop dead. Therefore, you need to spread wax, just like candle wax, wherever your wheels are going to make contact, so they'll slide.

"Go easy on that," Natasha said, putting her hand on mine on top of the wax, "or you'll be launched into space."

"It really stuck that time," I said, finishing the job and handing Natasha the wax. "You set to film again?"

"Go for it."

As I was skating back, I watched Dashawn land a Smith grind down a handrail as if it was nothing. "You have to film him too!" I yelled. "That was awesome."

"In time, bro," Dashawn called back. Our voices echoed off everything, then boomed into the air. Dashawn grabbed his board and ran up the stairs.

I set up in the same spot. I can get pretty superstitious about these things. Everything had worked the first time, I told myself, so if I did it all the same again, only now with the bench waxed, it would be exactly the same. But this time I'd land it.

Three pushes and I was cruising at the four-step. I popped the tre flip but not quite right, and I kicked out. Natasha immediately looked to the screen.

"That was the wind," I said.

"Sure," she replied.

I set up again. Three pushes, pop and a miss. This is skateboarding though. You can land something perfectly once and then not get it again for hours.

"Focus, Ry," Dashawn yelled.

"I got this," I said. One of my big issues is that when something comes easy the first time, I start to think it will always be easy. But the opposite is almost always true. That first try is all about luck and natural ability.

And then your mind kicks in.

Three pushes, and the edge of the stairs was right there. I hit a perfect tre flip and could sense Natasha rolling along beside me as I angled toward the ledge. I popped an ollie to 5-0 on the ledge, and as I came off I could tell a 180 would be doable. But I wanted this line first. Another two pushes and another pop onto the bench. It slid like butter. I managed to pop off but flew at an angle rather than straight, so when I landed I was sideways. I stumbled backward and sat, sliding down the bank to the ground. My board followed me. I grabbed it and started running back up as quickly as possible.

"I had that!"

"We can edit."

"No," I said, running toward Natasha. "It has to be super clean. That's my thing. You have to get me rolling away or it doesn't count." I stopped and pushed against her to look at the little screen. "How are my arms? I'm not flailing, am I?"

"No," she said. "It's tight. You had it."

I pulled my hat off and wiped my face. The heat was seeping out of the air and into the ground, but it was still really warm outside.

"This time," I said, dropping my board and pushing away from her. I waited until she was set up, then did the same three pushes toward the stairs. I managed to land the tre flip, but as I was approaching the ledge, the parking lot erupted in blue and red lights. I put my foot down and came to a stop. Two cruisers had come in, one through the entrance to the parking lot, the other via the exit. They were moving fast.

"Split!" I yelled. I pushed hard, taking a quick look behind me to see Natasha running up the stairs toward where we'd entered the lot. She would be gone in seconds. If she decided to ditch her board and take her hat off, she could instantly look like any girl waiting at a bus stop. I looked up at the top of the stairs but didn't see Dashawn anywhere.

"Cops!" I shouted, then pushed hard and took off across the parking lot. I glanced back once to see a big cop getting out of the car. He was tall and thick with a big, black moustache. I was already in the shadows, so if he saw me I would be little more than a blur. When I got to the far side, I popped my board up and clasped it under one arm. I didn't dare look back. Not even for a second. If I turned around, I might trip on something. The trail cut left, then right. There were roots everywhere, along with fallen branches. Seconds later I was on a suburban street, where I dropped my board, jumped on and pushed harder than I ever had before.

Chapter Five

I came up behind the McDonald's and stopped beside one of the Dumpsters. It was filthy and disgusting, but there didn't seem to be anyone around, and the one light behind the restaurant was shattered. I removed my hat and chucked it under the Dumpster, then kicked my skateboard under before walking as casually as possible to the side door and going in.

It smelled like all McDonald's do and, on a Sunday night at just after six, was pretty busy. I went to the counter and ordered a large drink, filled the cup at the machine and sat down. I kept pushing at my hair and wiping at my forehead to try to stem the flow of sweat. Luckily, I'd sat down right beneath an air-conditioning vent, and soon enough I was cool—cold even.

I didn't see Natasha come in. She had removed her hat and slung her back-pack over one arm. She dropped the backpack on the floor and slid in across from me at the table.

"That was crazy," she said.

"Did you see Dashawn?"

"No," she replied. "I booked it. There was a bus stopped at the corner, and I hopped on, then got off a couple of blocks east. What about you?"

"I went through the woods, then skated straight here. I don't think anyone was following me."

Natasha reached across and grabbed my drink, then took a long pull from it. "I heard them yelling though," she said.

"Me too."

"What were they saying?"

"I don't know. But they came in the way D was going to leave," I said. "He likely had to go around the other side to get away."

"Text him," Natasha said.

I gave her my stone-cold look. "We discussed this before. No texts. I wouldn't give you guys up if I got busted, and Dashawn won't either. But if we start texting each other, the police will have our names and start looking for us. They would just have to get a hold of his phone."

"He didn't get busted," she said. "That would seriously suck. If he got busted."

"He's fast. He will have gotten away. Anyway, I think the cops just pulled in to scare us. They likely didn't even get out of the cruisers."

"Two carloads? That was four cops," she said, throwing herself back in her seat. "They seriously have to have something better to do. Aren't there any real crimes being committed around here?"

"Apparently not." She grabbed my drink again, and I pulled it away from her.

"What?" she said, letting go. "Fine, I'll get my own."

As she was waiting in line, a cruiser pulled up, and two cops got out. They came inside, looking left and right, scanning the place. I slid the straw into my mouth and pulled my cell from my pocket. As the one cop's eyes passed over me, I dropped my cell on the table and opened the Facebook app. The cops split up, one moving to the other side of the restaurant, the other coming right toward me.

I noticed Natasha returning from the counter. I flicked my eyes toward the door, and she walked outside without stopping. The cop slowed as he passed me, making a really big show of glancing down at my phone. I was flipping through posts as though I had been there forever and had nothing but time on my hands. I didn't even look up, because looking up might engage the cop. He might suddenly want to have a conversation. He might even start asking me questions, and then I'd be sweating all over the place and, very likely, confessing to crimes I didn't commit.

The cops did a full circle of the restaurant, then went back out to their car. I had to wait them out. They were sitting in the cruiser, the interior light on. I had no idea what they were doing out there. Finally they flicked the light off and pulled away. A minute later Natasha came in, wearing my hat, and sat down across from me again.

"You would think we just knocked over a bank," she whispered.

"Were those the same cops?"

"I have no idea, but they were in here looking for someone."

"What the hell is with this? We were just skating."

Natasha took a long drink, then tied her hair into a ponytail. "We need to get the bus back home," she said, looking at her phone. "It's Sunday, and the last one goes at seven."

I picked up my phone and discovered I was shaking. It was six thirty.

"We can't leave until right before it comes," I said. "Two kids standing around with skateboards at the bus stop are going to stand out."

"We have to leave our boards here," she said.

"No way. That's a brand-new setup!"

"Riley, those cops were serious. We can't be seen with decks right now. I moved them around under the bushes. We can come back first thing tomorrow and get them."

"Tomorrow is Monday. We'll be in school."

"I'll come get them, then. The first bus out here is at, like, six thirty."

"This is crazy," I said. "We were just skateboarding." I didn't want to leave my deck somewhere overnight. I kept it in my room with me all the time. It had its own spot, where its dirty wheels had lovingly smudged up the wall.

"Did they not look serious to you?" she said.

"Yeah, they sure as hell did."

"Then trust me on this. Your board will be fine overnight. I hid it well."

I sighed heavily as Natasha picked up her backpack and stood. I slid out of the booth and sighed some more.

"Shouldn't we wait for D?" I said.

"He'll get back. He might even be on the bus. Who knows?"

I took a last look around the restaurant in case Dashawn had come in and we hadn't noticed. He was nowhere to be found. In fact, I noticed then that everyone in the restaurant was white except for two of the people behind the counter, who were black. I have no idea why I noticed it at that moment— I guess because I was looking for Dashawn. In any case, it seemed odd that the restaurant was entirely filled with white people.

The suburbs, I figured.

I grabbed my hat off Natasha's head and put it on my own.

"At least you saved my hat," I said.

"Like a boss," she said. "Like a freakin' *boss*."

We stood at the bus stop across the street with two older ladies and a couple of middle-school kids. Right before the bus came, the cruiser rolled past. It slowed, and I could feel the cops looking us over.

"Told you it was a good idea to leave our boards," Natasha said. We got onto the bus and found seats. Dashawn wasn't on the bus. For a couple of stops we were hopeful that he'd hop on, but soon we were close enough to the city that if he'd made it that far, he would have just kept going all the way home.

We didn't dare text him. Not that night anyway. My parents didn't notice my lack of a skateboard when I returned home, even though it was pretty much an extra appendage most days. I went to my room, logged on to Facebook and Hangouts and waited for Dashawn to write. When he didn't, I feared the worst—that he'd been busted.

That wasn't the worst.

Chapter Six

I was awakened by a text from Natasha in the morning. It was a photo of our boards together, pushed up against the back of the seat in front of her on a bus.

Thanks, I texted back as I heaved myself out of bed. It was only the second week of school, and already I was done with it. I'd thought I would have some exciting classes, and who knew, maybe they would pan out over the term, but so far everything was as dull as the year before.

I decided it was safe to text Dashawn. He lived three blocks from my place, and I normally picked him up on my way to school. I sent a simple **What's up?** and left it at that. But a growing sense of dread was creeping in as I ate my breakfast and listened to my parents talk. No matter what, Dashawn would text back. Unless he was in jail. But no one goes to jail for skateboarding. I kept waking my phone up, hoping a text had come in and something had just kept the phone from ringing.

Somehow, neither of my parents noticed that I walked out the front door instead of rolling through the garage and down the driveway. I went at a normal pace at first, but soon I noticed my feet were moving quicker than ever.

Dashawn's house looked empty. I rang the doorbell anyway but wasn't surprised when no one came. I sat on his porch and texted Natasha.

Have you heard from D?

The response was almost immediate.

No.

WTF he's not @ his house.

Jail?

No, I texted back, but I wasn't certain. I waited another ten minutes and then stood up to go to school. I would keep texting him all day, I decided, until I found out what had happened to him.

As I was stepping from the porch, Dr. Reed's BMW pulled into the driveway. I could see Dashawn in the backseat, his mother in the front passenger seat. The car came to a stop, but for some reason I didn't feel the urge to dart over to it. I was stuck in that spot. I had a strange feeling that I couldn't place right that moment. It hummed around inside me and then settled in my stomach.

The doors opened.

Dr. Reed glanced at me before reaching back into the car for something. Mrs. Reed got out of the car and opened the rear door. Dashawn slid out of his seat. Before I noticed anything else, I saw him wince. Then it came in a flood.

His arm in a sling. Black eyes, and a long bruise down his cheek. When he took a step, it was short and hobbled. He raised a hand toward me, but his face showed no sign of pleasure at my presence.

Mrs. Reed went around the side of the house as Dashawn's father took a call on his cell phone, leaving Dashawn and me alone for a moment.

"What the hell, D?" I said. "What happened?"

He couldn't seem to look at me. Finally, staring at his feet, he said, "The police."

"What do you mean?"

He raised the arm that was in a sling. "They did this."

"What are you talking about?"

Dr. Reed was yelling at someone on his phone. He was a big man, six foot six or so, and thick. A surgeon at the local hospital.

It all came out in one long sentence then. The words tripping over themselves, like if they were said quickly enough, they wouldn't count as being real. As words actually representing something that had happened.

"When I tried to run, one of the cops tripped me, and I had my phone in my pocket and when I reached for it another one of the cops stomped on my hand, and then they just started yelling things at me, and before I knew it they were hitting me with batons, and one of them jumped on my back."

"The cops beat you?" I said. "They did this to you?"

"Yeah, man, like I said."

"For skateboarding?" I said.

"No, not for skateboarding."

I shook my head. "Are you saying four cops beat you?"

"No, just two. The other two took off after you guys. Did they catch you?"

"No—I mean, they found us at the Mickey D's, but they didn't know it was us. We stashed our boards like we'd planned. Then Tash and I took the bus back and left our boards there. She just went and got them now."

"Good," Dashawn said.

"Good? What is good about any of this? They can't just do that," I said.

Dashawn finally looked at me. There was something new in his face.

Something that hadn't been there before. "Well, they did."

"What are your parents going to do?"

"Nothing."

"Nothing?" I said. "They can't just do nothing."

"The cops said I bailed skating and that's why I'm all messed up."

"But that's not the truth," I said. Nothing he was telling me made any sense. You couldn't just get beat up for no reason, or just for skating, and nothing happened to the police. I twisted at my waist because my stomach suddenly felt awful. I looked out across the lawn.

"That's their truth, and it's the only one that matters."

"You told your parents exactly what happened?"

"Yeah, and they believe me."

"So they have to press charges, right? Those cops are going to pay for this."

Dashawn inhaled deeply. "There were no cameras in the area, Ry. No one filmed anything. It's their word against mine, and my word is not going to win."

"Dude, they cannot—"

"They can, Riley. They can. They do it all the time. Don't you watch the news?"

"No," I said. Because I didn't believe it—not really. I heard things now and then, and sometimes someone would post a news story about a police beating, but I didn't see it in our city. I'd never expected it would happen here.

"They can do what they want, Ry. That's the point. I got busted somewhere I shouldn't have been, and they decided to teach me a lesson. That's what they said." His voice had gone quiet. "When they were hitting me, the guy on my back told me I'd learn a lesson about what I was and wasn't allowed to do in his city."

"His city?"

"Yeah. That's what he said."

"D," I said. But I had nothing else. "This can't happen."

"Well," he said, "it did."

Chapter Seven

Dashawn's father was suddenly standing beside us, pocketing his cell.

"They can't do this to him," I said. The sickening sensation I had in my stomach had changed to an anger I didn't even see coming.

"Oh yes they can," Dr. Reed said. "And they proved it. I went straight to the chief of police. He already had the officer's story, and that was all he needed. The official story is that the officers responded to a call of intruders on private property. They discovered three youths skateboarding." He looked me in the eye. I felt myself sink a little. We'd run. It wouldn't have happened if we hadn't run.

"At this time they witnessed Dashawn attempting to slide down a handrail. Do you notice my tone, Riley? Tone is very important in these reports. One must make certain to sound official so people won't be swayed by other ideas."

"Okay," I said.

"The report goes on to state that 'a black youth' slipped, fell, crashed down half a dozen stairs, smashed into a ledge and then twisted his arm violently. His injuries were the direct result of a skateboarding accident. The kind-hearted police officers helped the black youth to their cruiser, and instead of bringing him to the police station, they delivered him to the hospital. There were no signs of destruction to any of the property in question, and therefore the black youth would not be charged for trespassing or destruction of property. The chief of police informed me that the police officers in question should be thanked for their assistance when they could have been much less kind."

"That's what they told you?"

Dr. Reed bent down slightly. "That's what happened, Riley. That's the truth because it came from the mouths of two white cops rather than one black kid. Oh, the black kid has a different story. That he didn't fall. He didn't crash. But instead that these officers of the law beat him with their batons, kicked him with their boots, *jumped on his back*. But that's not the truth. The truth is what the white cops say it is."

"But it isn't," I said. I'd never felt uncomfortable in or around Dashawn's house. Not once in all the years we'd hung out. But right then I felt as though I'd rather be anywhere else.

"I know it isn't, you know it isn't, Dashawn and his mother know it isn't, and every black man and woman who hears this story will know it isn't. But that doesn't matter because the truth is in that report those officers submitted."

I didn't know what to say. Dashawn sat on the porch. I wanted to leave. It was awful. Dashawn couldn't look at me. His father was growing more and more angry. I took a step away. Dr. Reed grabbed my arm and held it lightly.

"They put their hands on my son, Riley. They beat him because they knew they could get away with it. They beat him to put him in his place. They beat him to put fear in his heart. Not as a kid. Not as a skateboarder. But as a black man. And now that they've done this, they know they can do it again. People out there hear about this—I mean, white people hear about this? They'll say it was awful, but a lot of them are going to believe the police. Others might not—they might believe Dashawn's story. But then they think he must have been doing something more. He was reaching for a weapon. Resisting arrest. He'd been destroying property or stealing. He didn't *deserve* to be beaten, but then again, he didn't really *not* deserve it. This wasn't just wrong place, wrong time, some people will think. This was a kid who'd done something and was punished. Most people will think the punishment didn't fit the crime, but on the other hand, there was a crime, and there was punishment."

"But he was just skating," I said.

"He was black and skating. That's a different crime, Riley, than being white and skating." He let go of my arm. "Same as being black and stealing some cigarettes is different than being white and stealing some cigarettes. Being black and walking down the damn street is a completely different act than being white and walking down that same street. And now that they've done it once, they know they can do it again. Dashawn isn't safe here any longer. Not at all."

He was about to say something else when his phone rang. He put it to his ear and walked into the house, leaving Dashawn and me alone on the porch.

"This is messed up, man," I said.

"So we're moving," Dashawn replied.

"What? Why?"

Dashawn looked at the ground some more. I couldn't tell if he was crying. Thinking back, I'd never seen Dashawn cry. Not once. Not even when we were kids. But I sensed that that was exactly what he was doing.

"You heard him. It's not safe here."

"It's totally safe here," I said. "It's, like, ridiculously safe."

"Not for me," he said. "Not anymore." He shifted slightly. It looked like every movement hurt. "My parents have been thinking of it for a while. We have a lot of family down in Atlanta, and my dad's been offered a good spot at a hospital there. He could become head surgeon someday. There are just way more opportunities."

"You can't move," I said. I was thinking of myself then.

"I don't really have a choice, Ry," he said. "And anyway, after last night…"

"It's not that," I said.

"What?"

"It didn't happen because you're black. There's just no way."

"It did, Riley." He looked up at me and wiped his eyes with the back of his hand. There was no question in his voice.

"We never should have split. If we'd been there…"

"It wasn't your fault, man," he said. He stood and walked over to me. He kind of leaned into me and gave me a one-armed hug. "You've been a good friend, man." He stood back. "I gotta go lie down. Talk soon, okay?"

"Okay," I said. "You have to figure out a way to stay."

"That's not going to happen."

He went inside, his father's voice leaking out as he yelled into his phone. When the door shut, I was left standing in the same neighborhood I had walked through for years. The same birds and passing cars. The same wind rushing across my face. But none of it was really the same. Not the birds or cars. Not the wind.

Nothing.

Chapter Eight

Dashawn didn't go to school that week.
I would skate to his house after last bell
and we'd work on flatland tricks on his
driveway. It wasn't until Thursday, when
I had a spare last period, that we returned
to the skate park. We were the only ones
there. Some of the old Dashawn came out
as he breezed around the park, although
he was pretty cautious. I expected some

of it was his arm, which was still in a sling. But whenever a car came toward the park, he would jump a little and watch it go past. Just before we were about to leave, he tried a hardflip up the bank and landed it dead on the bolts. It was the first time I'd seen him smile since that night at the new building.

"I'm moving on Monday," he said while we rested beneath a tree and drank some water.

"This Monday?"

"Yeah."

"Shit," I said. I didn't say anything more. I couldn't ask him to stay. I didn't need to tell him how much it would suck. We both knew exactly what was happening.

I'd been thinking all week about what Dashawn's dad had said. How black people needed to be more cautious. How some people placed others on a different level based entirely on the color of their skin. At first I'd been certain he was wrong. That it didn't happen anymore. Those days were gone. But then I'd remembered a few things that had happened over the years. Things I'd never talked to Dashawn about.

Like this one summer when our parents had forced us to play soccer so that we could see what being on a team was like. Most of the games were fine. We were an okay group, and we won a little more than we lost. Then we played an out-of-town team. Those guys rode Dashawn hard the whole game. Tripping him, elbowing him—everything that makes soccer a horrible sport. At first I'd thought it was because Dashawn was one of our best players. But in the handshake line, one of the kids leaned over to Dashawn and said as quietly as possible, *We'll kick your ass next time, nigger.*

I'd thought I misheard him. Dashawn looked shocked. I shoved the guy right away, and he shoved me back. He said something into my face. Something else with that offensive word another couple of times. A ref came over and separated us, and later, in the locker room, our coach talked to me about behavior and sportsmanship. I didn't tell him what the guy had said because Dashawn seemed so embarrassed by it. As if it were, in some way, his fault.

Then there was Mr. Wells, our history teacher. It was well known that he sized up his students based on their first assignment and then gave out the same grade, paper after paper. He never gave tests, which made it difficult to prove anything. I always received a B+. I did the work I had to do, and maybe it just happened to always deserve a B+. Dashawn kept receiving Cs or even C–. When Dashawn would ask Wells about his grades and how he could improve, Wells would tell him he had to dig deeper into the topic. And work on his grammar. So Dashawn would try harder. He would study more, use multiple sources for his papers, and still he'd get the same mark—*C– work harder.*

Mr. Wells also had a horrible memory. Over the years students had often resubmitted an older sibling's paper to him. So when I got my hands on a paper from a student who'd passed through the school three years before, I gave it to Dashawn. It had been given an A+. And it really was an A+ paper. I read it, and what the guy had written was better than anything I'd read in any of our textbooks. Dashawn decided to hand it in, just to see if an A+ was actually an A+.

When he got it back, it didn't even appear to have been read. The pages were flat. The space around the staple uncreased. The only evidence of actual human involvement with it was an

As I said, Dashawn, you need to dig deeper into the research. C–

The bibliography was three pages long.

Of course, we couldn't say anything. Dashawn had handed in someone else's work, after all.

I remembered seeing the same look on his face that day, and after the soccer incident, as what seemed to live there permanently since the night with the police.

"My dad has a good job lined up in Atlanta," Dashawn said, capping his water bottle. "My whole family is down there as well. Both sides. I have, like, twenty cousins."

"That's cool."

"Yeah, we never see them. Same with my grandparents. I know my mom's been wanting to live closer. So, I mean, it's not just…" He inhaled and looked at the sky for a second. "It's not just

71

what happened. This has kind of been in the works for a while."

"Yeah," I said.

"I'm going to miss this place."

"This place is going to miss you," I said.

"Not likely."

"You know, without you here, there is a very high likelihood of my murdering a scooter kid."

"Nah, you're cool with them."

"I am not. They wreck this place. I mean…" I was getting to yelling about it already, even without a scooter in sight.

Dashawn tapped my arm. "They're just enjoying the space as well, bro."

"Yeah," I said. "I guess."

A vanload of middle-school kids arrived. Dashawn grabbed his board and stood up.

"Let's split," he said.

We walked back to his house, talking about random stuff. Girls, I guess. Videos we'd watched. Tricks we wanted to land before it got too cold to skate.

"There's a bonus right there," I said. "It doesn't get cold in Atlanta. You'll be able to skate year-round."

"Damn," he said. "You know what? I never thought about that."

"You'll be pro in a year."

"You think that long?" he said. "I'll be thinking of you when I'm out hitting a bowl on Christmas Eve."

We'd reached his house. I put my fist out for a bump. Instead, he stepped up to me and gave me a hug. A man hug, for sure, with all the back patting and thumping, but he didn't seem to want to let go. Neither did I.

"So, bro, I kind of lied," he said, stepping back.

"About what?"

"Moving on Monday. I mean, it's kind of true. The movers are coming Monday. We're leaving tomorrow."

"Seriously?"

"Yeah." He looked at his feet, then dropped his board and popped it back into his hands. "I just wanted one last good skate with you, you know? Without all that hanging over us."

"I hear you," I said. "It was cool."

"Say goodbye to Tash for me, would you?"

"For sure."

"I always kind of thought she and I would end up getting married."

"Seriously?"

"No." He laughed. "Tell her that though. I want to hear what she says in reply." He put his fist out and I gave it a bump, and then he walked inside. I dropped my board and pushed toward home, feeling more empty than I thought possible.

Chapter Nine

In the weeks after Dashawn left, I spent a lot of time with my parents. I still went to the skate park and tried to hit other locations with Natasha. I mean, I needed my freedom, and that's what skateboarding was for me. Complete freedom. But it wasn't the same without Dashawn. There was no one there to push me. No one to pick me up after a bad slam. No one to get pumped up with.

Two weeks after Dashawn moved, I was watching the news with my parents. There was a story about a man, a black man, who'd died when a couple of cops jumped on him and held him to the ground. They crushed him to death. There was a video of it as well. The man had a pack of cigarettes in his hand. Apparently he'd stolen them. The police kept yelling "Stop resisting!" at him, though the man couldn't resist. He couldn't even move.

My father shook his head at the story. But my mother was different.

"Why does he keep resisting?" she said.

"He isn't," I replied.

"He must have been before the video started. That's the problem with all these videos—we don't see everything."

"He's not even moving, and the cops are still on him," I said.

"They knew who he was, right, Dan?" she said to my dad. "That's how the story began. He was known to police. You can't be a law-abiding citizen who is known to police. There are all kinds of things we don't even know about, I bet."

I couldn't believe what she was saying. The video showed a man being murdered for a pack of cigarettes. His last words were "I'll give them back."

"So he deserved to die?" I said.

"Well, no, of course not."

I was enraged. I could feel the fury inside me rising. "He deserved to die for taking a pack of cigarettes? That's not even a real crime. At worst, you'd get a fine."

"I didn't say he deserved to die, Riley. I just said that if he was known to police, then he must be a criminal of some sort."

"The reporter said he had no prior convictions."

"Well," Mom said. There was a tone attached. A weary *You don't understand the world* tone.

"Well, *what*?"

"Riley, don't yell at your mother. What's this all about?"

"That guy didn't do anything dangerous at all and now he's dead," I said. "Two cops decided that stealing cigarettes was a crime worthy of the death penalty. And it means nothing to you guys."

"What do we have to do with this?" Mom said. She pointed with both hands at the television. The report was from a place way west of us. For her it was as if this man was in a different world altogether.

Which, I was beginning to think, he was.

"Nothing," I said. "That's the thing. We have nothing to do with this." I wasn't even making sense to myself, but my words still felt true. "None of it has anything to do with us, but because of that it has *everything* to do with it. I mean, how fucked up is this country that something like this can happen and we let it go?"

"Language, Riley," Mom said.

"Yeah, that's what's important. Cuss words. People die for stealing cigarettes or being in the wrong place at the wrong time, but that doesn't bother anyone around here. On the other hand, one swearword and I'm—"

"Riley, you're yelling at us," Dad said.

"Nothing is going to happen to those cops," I yelled. "I bet they're back on the street next week. They killed someone! That guy had kids and a family and—"

"It was likely an accident," Mom said. "They couldn't have meant to do it. The police don't go around killing innocent people, Riley."

I didn't want to argue any longer. I would only get more angry. So I left the living room, grabbed my board and went outside.

It was dark and cold. Leaves were blowing down the street. I went to the curb where I'd first started skateboarding and began slamming down grinds and slides. I hit that curb as hard as I could whenever I landed. It rang out through the neighborhood like shots. A few cars passed, their lights illuminating me for a moment. But that was it. No one cared that I was out there. No one said a word.

The idea that the man in the news story must have been guilty of something bothered me. And I knew why. Because if that's what it was for him, then it had to be the same for Dashawn. Dashawn had been beaten by the police, though I'd never told my parents this. He'd been taught a lesson. The guy in the news story was the same. The police were trying to teach him a lesson. A lesson in who had the power.

I slammed down a 50-50 and fell forward onto the lawn. I was sweating even though it was cold outside. The neighborhood was silent except for the few remaining crickets and the gentle hum of cars on the nearby interstate.

What Dashawn and I had been doing that night was illegal. Skateboarders don't want to destroy property, and a lot of the time we don't. I mean, other people do the tagging and graffiti at skate parks, and we get blamed for it. Concrete chips, sure, but a truck backing into a ledge will do the same thing. We leave black marks with wax and paint tearing from the graphics on our boards, but that can be washed away. Nothing is permanent.

Most people don't know this though. They see the skaters, hear the noise and think we're wrecking everything. Those cops might have believed that. It still didn't warrant the beatdown they gave Dashawn. But when they said those words to him, that they were going to teach him a lesson, maybe they were saying it to him as a skater and not because he was black.

I wanted to believe this so badly that night. Not because it could bring Dashawn back to town. That would never happen. I wanted it because I'd known Dashawn since we were little kids and he was my best friend, and to think that some people considered him lesser than me because of the color of his skin made me sick.

I decided there was only one way to find out for certain. I was going to have to go back to the building and skate that spot.

Chapter Ten

The trees had lost more of their leaves. The building looked even more stark and gray. It seemed that people had moved into the offices. Computers flashed in the dim light, and the fluorescent lighting burned on all but one of the floors. I waited behind the same tree Dashawn, Natasha and I had hid behind before. I hadn't told Natasha what I was doing. She had wanted to film some clips that night, but I'd told her I was busy. I'd been blowing her off a lot since Dashawn left. We were still good friends, but it had felt before like skating was all about the three of us, and with Dashawn gone it seemed wrong to be out filming clips with Natasha. I hadn't even told her about Dashawn's fantasy of their future life together.

When it came to skating this spot, I wouldn't have told her about it anyway. I couldn't have anyone else around. I needed to be found there. I needed to get busted. I needed to know what would happen after the police arrived.

I waited for fifteen minutes, watching the building for security. No one came, and seeing as it wasn't that large a place, I had to assume that if someone was protecting the property, he or she would have made at least one round during that time. No one was inside either. Not that I could see anyway. The thing was, I didn't want to get busted by a security guard. That would mean nothing. Security guards just tell you to leave, or they threaten to call the cops. They have no more power than a regular citizen.

I was nervous, I'll say that much. Maybe more than nervous. There was every possibility that I was going to receive a beating at the hands of an adult. It seemed bizarre to even consider. The worst part of it was that I wanted it to happen. I wanted so badly to be held down and kicked and hit, but at the same time I was terrified of it happening.

The first ollie sounded like an explosion. It echoed off the walls of the building and came back at me even louder. I popped another couple and then did a quick 180 down a two-step. For the first ten minutes or so, I kept an eye out for the police. But then I got into a groove. I found a flow and started going for higher and faster tricks. I nailed the kickflip to 5-0 and pulled a 180 off the ledge, knowing Dashawn would be proud. I waxed the bench and worked on the blunt slide to fakie. I slammed a few times, but that only meant there was some serious satisfaction once I landed it.

Then I climbed the stairs to the front door and eyed the handrail. There were deeper shadows against the building. It was getting dark, although it wasn't even 7:00 PM yet. I rolled up to the handrail and stopped where I would have to pop to hit it. I figured a board slide would be safest. Just get the front trucks over and glide down on the middle of the deck. There was less precision involved, though the danger of totally sacking myself was much higher.

It took two tries before I committed and landed on the rail. When I did, I instantly understood why Dashawn had been hitting it so hard. It was perfectly smooth, bottomed out with enough space to turn off and had a very sweet roll away. There were no cracks in the pavement anywhere, so the whole ride was just about as smooth as could be.

I decided to try a 50-50 down it. I needed a new angle for this. I had to fly slightly farther out and get that much higher to lock my trucks in on the rail. I bailed the first time and slammed to the ground, knocking the air out of myself.

While I was sitting up to try to breathe again, I noticed that there wasn't a ledge at the bottom of the stairs. I'd never doubted Dashawn. Not even for a second. But seeing that the roll away was clear for a very long way made me that much angrier. If anyone had even come out here and looked, they would have known the cops were lying. No matter how Dashawn had fallen, there was no way he could have been so badly banged up.

I checked my body to make certain I hadn't broken anything and then ran up the stairs again. I thought I'd figured out what I had to do differently. I'd been looking at the end of the rail as I was trying to get onto it rather than where I wanted to land. That is always a recipe for failure. You need to spot your landing, whether it is onto or off of a rail.

I ran with my board, dropping it and giving one push before prepping for the ollie. I got my foot tweaked on the tail, bent my knees and popped. It all seemed to be going perfectly, but I went a little high and passed right over the rail. I jumped away from my board and landed half on and half off a step. I managed to spin around as I fell so I was going forward rather than backward, but I still fell. I jittered down three steps, and my leg bent back strangely on the flat.

I was sitting there with my ankle in my hand and my board still rattling down the steps when the first cop car pulled in. I didn't run—actually, I couldn't have run even if I'd wanted to. My ankle was throbbing, and though I figured it was fine, it hurt too much to put any weight on.

The cops turned their headlights toward me, then came to a stop. I recognized the first one. He was the big, thick cop I'd seen get out of the cruiser the night Dashawn was roughed up. His partner was a younger guy. Rake thin with golden yellow hair. They came out as though they had all the time in the world. I stood, testing my ankle, and hobbled to where my skateboard sat against a wall.

Chapter Eleven

There was a big, ugly black mark on the bench at the bottom of the stairs. The combination of wax, paint, dirt and motion had turned what had been a shining silver to a dull black. I stood right beside it, my board in one hand.

"That looked like a nasty fall," the big cop said.

"Missed," I said. I was shaking. I mean, my whole body was quivering. Sweat was drying on my skin, and the early fall breeze was leaving me cold. I was also really thirsty. I hadn't brought water, for some reason. I took off my hat and wiped at my forehead. Then, just to see what would happen, I reached into my pocket and pulled out my cell.

They didn't move.

"You alone here?" the big cop asked. He seemed bored by the whole thing.

"Yeah," I said.

"You can't be here." He pointed at the marks. "The developer doesn't want everything destroyed."

"I wasn't destroying anything."

The cop rubbed at his mouth. He still didn't seem irate at all. "Nevertheless, things get banged up. You have some ID?"

"No," I said.

"You sure of that? Student card? Driver's license?"

"I didn't bring anything with me."

"What's your name?"

"Jim Riley," I said, using the fake name we always used when we got hassled by security guards. Jim was a kid who'd moved away in first grade, so we always figured it was safe enough to claim to be him.

The cop sniffed and pointed at my board. "Well, Jim, don't you have anything better to do with your time?"

"What?" I said, wanting to make this situation as difficult as possible. I wanted the cops to hate me. To *need* to teach me a lesson.

"Jumping down stairs. Sliding on benches." He shook his head some more. "It's a waste of time, son. You need to learn some things to get ahead in this world. Math and science is the way.

Everyone tells me the world is all about computers now."

"I do fine in school," I said. Everything was so casual that it was bothering me. I mean, it was like we were having a friendly conversation. A couple of old friends.

"I did all right too," the cop said. "What about you, Mark?"

"Yeah, I did good," the other cop said. He was sitting on a ledge, his eyes half closed against the setting sun. "Wouldn't have caught me dead on one of those, that much I can tell you."

"Yeah, me neither." The big cop laughed at the idea. "Either way, you can't be here, Jim. The neighbors hear the banging and they call us, and then we have to come here and kick you out. *We* have better things to do." Officer Mark was already on his way back to the cruiser, where the radio was squawking.

The big cop waved at the street and said, "So don't come back or we'll have to call your parents, and if they're anything like mine were, you'll be in a world of trouble."

They sat in the cruiser while I limped away. I wanted to turn around and scream at them. I almost did. But they were gone by the time I got to the path leading up to the bus stop.

A bus was waiting there, but I walked on by. It was miles to my house. I didn't care though. I started pushing. I went into the street, onto the sidewalk. My ankle throbbed, but I kept pushing as hard as I could. I skimmed rocks, popped over curbs. Ran red lights.

I kept pushing.

I bombed a hill, and when I got to the bottom, sweating, worn and exhausted, I kept pushing.

I knew I'd gone there to get a beat-down. I'd done all I could to force the police to teach me a lesson, and they'd walked away. When I got home, I had trouble holding back the tears. What had happened to Dashawn had nothing to do with him being a skateboarder and everything to do with the color of his skin. I hadn't wanted to believe it, but it was true.

"Were you at the park, Ry?" Dad asked in his happy, casual voice when I came in the door. He had always been really supportive of my skating. I thought back to all the times that Dashawn had been at our house and Dad had treated him like a son. So had my mom.

"No," I said. "This other spot."

"Yeah? Where?" He was drying dishes. The radio was tuned to the classic-rock station he always listened to.

"A new tech building in Westlake."

He put the glass down and leaned against the counter. "That's a long way away," he said. "Were you alone?"

"This time, yeah," I said.

"This time?"

"Tash, Dashawn and I went there right before he moved."

"I see."

I inhaled, feeling everything building inside me. The fury and anger and confusion. "The police showed both times."

"Riley," he said. "If it's private property, you shouldn't—"

"The first time, they got a hold of Dashawn, and they beat him, Dad. They hit him with their batons. They stomped on his hand. They kicked him in the face."

"What? I thought he'd fallen!"

"That's what the police said. That's the truth they made. But he didn't fall. Dashawn never falls. Not like that."

"And tonight?"

"It was just me. Nothing happened. They told me to go home and not come back." I let that sink in. "I just walked away."

"Riley, why would they…" He stopped and picked a glass up and started drying it. "You can't go back."

"It's not fair, Dad."

"I know."

"He never did anything to anyone. He's a kid just like me."

"I know."

"But they could just do that," I said.

"It happens, son," Dad said. I waited for more, but he had nothing to offer.

"They got away with it. And now he's gone." I wanted to scream. I wanted to take my board and smash something. But the anger I had wasn't like that. Nothing that had happened had really happened to *me*. I'd lost my friend, sure, but as I stood there watching my father dry a glass, put it away and pick up another one, totally unable to say anything at all, I felt as if I'd lost much, much more.

Chapter Twelve

"What did Tash say?" Dashawn asked. The Skype connection was clear for once. I could see Dashawn as if he were sitting beside me. He was smiling, and the late-afternoon sunshine burned through the window behind him.

"I haven't told her about your unrequited love yet," I said.

"Bro, come on. Actually, you know, hold on to that. I've met a nice girl out here. A friend of my cousins. I'm like a little celebrity down here, man. Apparently people don't move into this area all that often."

"Why not?"

"I have no idea. It's amazing. I can walk to two different skate parks from here. I'm getting into some vert stuff now as well. It's not all that hard."

"What about the scooter kids?" I said.

"They're everywhere," he replied, laughing. "A necessary evil." Someone passed behind him. A black kid with an Etnies hat and *Thrasher* T-shirt.

"Who's that?"

"That's my cousin Harold."

Harold leaned down and waved. "Who's this?"

"My oldest friend, Riley. I was telling you about him."

"Cool." Harold held his fist up to the camera, and I did the same. Then I watched as he grabbed a deck and left the room.

"Harold can't skate for shit, but he's got right into the culture. He hangs at the park with me. I'm trying to get him to do some flat-ground stuff, but he's about as coordinated as a goat. We'll see what happens."

"Awesome," I said.

Dashawn sat back in his chair. "How are things there?"

"About the same. The park is still overrun with scooter kids. I think I have enough clips now to send to that guy at Volcom."

"Oh, shit, Ry, I forgot to tell you. I got my video finished as well." Dashawn shot forward and started hammering on the keys. A second later a YouTube link popped up on my screen.

"This is the whole thing?" I said as I clicked it.

"Fifteen clips. Ten one-offs and five lines. One of my cousins here does all kinds of video editing. He put it together for me."

I clicked the link, and the video began to play. It was weird how the setting changed. From the lush green of our town to the sandy brown of Atlanta. The parks he was skating there looked like pieces of art. Everything was skate-able though. The final line was outside a building that looked a lot like the one here in town where he'd been busted.

"Where's that last shot?"

"Downtown," he said. "If you go on Sundays, the security guy is a skater. He was actually out there with us. It was so bizarre. He was, like, on the lookout for security guys who cared. I mean, it's his job, right? We'd get kicked out, but he'd get fired. Still, he was over-the-top excited watching us. It was sick."

"That's awesome," I said. "It looks like you're loving it there."

"Yeah, mostly. It's all right. The best thing is it isn't going to get cold. You need to come visit. I'd suggest, like, February."

"That'd be sweet," I said. "I'll come for the rest of my life."

"Listen, Ry, I gotta go. Harold is all jacked up to start skating, and if he gets cooled down it just doesn't happen. We'll be on the couch eating Doritos and watching football or something. Peace."

"Peace," I said, then disconnected.

I grabbed my board from its spot against the wall. With Dashawn's voice in my head, I banged out the door and onto the street. I pushed to the skate park and picked my board up when I got to the dirt path. I could almost feel Dashawn knocking against me as I moved through the tight part of the trail. A late Sunday afternoon and the park was, somehow, mostly empty. Natasha was at the picnic table, fiddling with her equipment. She looked up when I blocked the sun in front of her.

"One more clip," I said.

"A line or a one-off?"

"A line," I said. I pointed at the ledge. "Kickflip, 5-0, 180 off."

"Okay," she said. She got down into position as I rode to the top of the ledge. Someone had waxed it, which was fine. I wanted to move fast. I wanted to slide forever on it. I gave her a thumbs-up, received one in reply and pushed hard toward the ledge.

Skateboarding Terms

5-0: a grind on a ledge or rail where only the back trucks are touching

50-50: a grind on a ledge or rail where both trucks are touching

180: a spin of 180 degrees

360: a full 360-degree spin

blunt: a slide where only the back of the board is in contact with the rail or ledge

deck: the wooden part of a skateboard

fakie: riding backwards

flatland tricks: tricks that take place on flat ground rather than in a ramp or on an obstacle

grind: to slide along an obstacle such as a ledge or rail on the trucks or deck of your board

hardflip: a kickflip and shove-it performed at the same time so that the board spins and rotates on both axes

heelflip: a trick where the board is spun over itself one full rotation by kicking it in the air with your heel

kickflip: a trick where you kick the board so that it spins 360 before landing

manual: riding on two wheels

ollie: the most basic move, where you pop the back of the board and jump into the air, bringing the skateboard with you

shove-it: a trick where you rotate the board 180 or 360 degrees beneath you

slam: to wipe out

Smith grind: the most difficult, basic grind. The back truck grinds a rail while the front truck hangs over the side.

tre flip: a combination of a kickflip and shove-it

vert: any ramp or angle

Jeff Ross is an award-winning author of a number of novels for young adults. He currently teaches scriptwriting and English at Algonquin College in Ottawa, Ontario, where he lives with his wife and two sons. For more information, visit www.jeffrossbooks.com.

orca soundings

For more information on all the books
in the Orca Soundings series, please visit
www.orcabook.com.

He lifted up her hback, his eyes still

Rosie closed her eyes, loving the feeling of the touch of his lips on her skin. But she wanted more. As if her hand had a mind of its own, it turned over and lightly stroked his strong jawline. Her gaze moved to his lips. Those full, sensual lips. She imagined what it would be like to be kissed by him.

Tingling erupted on her lips and she gave a small moan. She caught her bottom lip with her teeth, slowly raking them across the skin, to stop any more telltale reactions.

Alexander's hand gently surrounded her wrist. Their eyes locked. Heat surged through her as she registered the hunger in his dark eyes, a hunger both exciting and unnerving.

Time froze. Every inch of her body tensed as she waited for him to act. Her breath caught in her throat. She stared up at him, waiting to see what he would do next. Would he kiss her? Oh, how she wanted him to kiss her.

Author Note

ori tessix yltripil ers

The late nineteenth and early twentieth century saw many wealthy young American women married off to members of the British aristocracy.

These young women came from families who wanted to advance their position in society by attaching themselves to the British aristocracy. The aristocrats were often facing financial ruin and were after the American dollars that came in the form of a dowry.

The plight of these so-called Dollar Princesses has long fascinated me. These young women were not only fabulously wealthy, they were often lively and spirited, and their antics shocked some members of the British establishment.

In *Beguiling the Duke*, Rosie Smith is the poor ward of a wealthy man. She's determined to save her friend Arabella from an arranged marriage and to have as much fun as she can while doing so. But there's one thing she hasn't expected—that she will fall in love with the handsome Alexander Fitzroy, the Duke of Knightsbrook, herself.

I hope you enjoy reading *Beguiling the Duke* as much as I enjoyed writing it. My next book will feature Arabella, Rosie's friend, who is in danger of falling in love with a duke of her own.

EVA SHEPHERD

Beguiling the
Duke

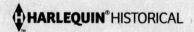
HARLEQUIN®HISTORICAL

If you purchased this book without a cover you should be aware that this book is stolen property. It was reported as "unsold and destroyed" to the publisher, and neither the author nor the publisher has received any payment for this "stripped book."

Recycling programs
for this product may
not exist in your area.

ISBN-13: 978-1-335-63544-0

Beguiling the Duke

Copyright © 2019 by Eva Shepherd

All rights reserved. Except for use in any review, the reproduction or utilization of this work in whole or in part in any form by any electronic, mechanical or other means, now known or hereafter invented, including xerography, photocopying and recording, or in any information storage or retrieval system, is forbidden without the written permission of the publisher, Harlequin Enterprises Limited, 22 Adelaide St. West, 40th Floor, Toronto, Ontario M5H 4E3, Canada.

This is a work of fiction. Names, characters, places and incidents are either the product of the author's imagination or are used fictitiously, and any resemblance to actual persons, living or dead, business establishments, events or locales is entirely coincidental.

This edition published by arrangement with Harlequin Books S.A.

For questions and comments about the quality of this book, please contact us at CustomerService@Harlequin.com.

® and TM are trademarks of Harlequin Enterprises Limited or its corporate affiliates. Trademarks indicated with ® are registered in the United States Patent and Trademark Office, the Canadian Intellectual Property Office and in other countries.

Printed in U.S.A.

www.Harlequin.com

After graduating with degrees in history and political science, **Eva Shepherd** worked in journalism and as an advertising copywriter. She began writing historical romances because it combines her love of a happy ending with her passion for history. She lives in Christchurch, New Zealand, but spends her days immersed in the world of late Victorian England.

Beguiling the Duke **is Eva Shepherd's gripping debut for Harlequin Historical!**

Visit the Author Profile page
at Harlequin.com.

To Julia Williams, Bryony Green and the editorial team at Harlequin, for their support, guidance and encouragement.

Chapter One

London 1893

Rosie Smith raised the delicate bone china cup to her lips, took a sip of the fragrant Darjeeling tea and sighed with contentment.

Despite being a penniless orphan, with no prospects worth mentioning, here she was, dressed in the latest fashion, taking tea at the Ritz, surrounded by Britain's elite.

Her feet, encased in soft kid leather boots, were aching after spending all day walking around the shops and sights of London. She was still tired from the gruelling trip across the Atlantic from New York. And yet she couldn't be happier.

She sighed again and looked across the lace-covered table at her friend, who was smiling with equal contentment.

'What shall we do tomorrow?' Rosie took a cucumber sandwich from the top layer of the three-tiered cake stand and placed it on her rose-patterned plate. 'More shopping? Or shall we take in some art galleries and museums?'

'Art galleries and museums, I think.' Arabella placed a scone on her plate and smothered it with jam and clotted cream. 'After all, I'm sure Father would want us to absorb as much culture as we can while we're in England.'

The two girls giggled conspiratorially.

Rosie lifted a finger and waggled it in Arabella's direction. '"What good is art, my dear? You don't get a decent return on sculptures. Nobody ever got rich from culture."'

Arabella clapped her hands and laughed loudly. 'You do such a brilliant impersonation of Father. It's you who should be on the stage, Rosie, not me.'

Their jubilation drew the attention of the women sitting at the next table, who glared down their imperious noses with looks that might have withered the spring buds on the tree. Rosie was tempted to poke out her tongue. Instead she lifted her head and returned their looks of disapproval. Although she suspected being glared at down a small button nose wouldn't have quite the same impact.

'Humourless old biddies,' she whispered. 'Have they never heard anyone laugh before?' She smiled at Arabella. 'So, tomorrow it's art galleries and museums—perfect.'

The two girls sipped their tea and sighed simultaneously.

A waiter approached the table and bowed low. Arabella smiled her thanks, removed the folded letter from his silver tray and read its contents. Her smile dissolved. Her hand shot to her mouth and her shoulders slumped.

'What is it? What's wrong, Bella?' Rosie reached across the table and touched her friend's arm.

Arabella's hands trembled as she passed her the letter. Rosie quickly scanned the elegant handwriting. It was an invitation from the Dowager Duchess of Knightsbrook, inviting Arabella to a weekend party at her estate in Devon.

'Oh, this is too, *too* terrible, Rosie.' Arabella took a lace handkerchief from her embroidered clutch purse and dabbed at her eyes. 'It's from the mother of that horrid man Father expects me to marry.'

'It's disgusting!' Rosie threw the letter down on the table. 'They think they can buy you. That all they have to do is dangle a title and you'll come running, and then they can get their greedy hands on your father's money. Disgusting!'

'I know… I know. I don't want to go. And I especially don't want to go that weekend. It means I'll miss the opening night of Oscar Wilde's play. I'll miss the opportunity to meet the great man himself.'

'Then don't go.' Rosie thumped the table, making the teacups jump and rattle in their saucers. 'You can't possibly miss the opening of that play. That's one of the main reasons we came to England.'

Her raised voice drew another scowl from the next table. This time Rosie didn't hold back. She screwed up her face, poked out her tongue and let the women know just what she thought of their disapproving looks.

Their gasps and bulging stares would have made Rosie laugh if she had felt like laughing.

Arabella lowered her handkerchief. 'Well, no…the main reason we're here is because Father wants to marry me off after that…' She tilted her head and lightly bit her upper lip. 'After that scandal.'

'Scandal? That was no scandal. Your appearance on the New York stage as Lady Macbeth was a triumph and should be celebrated as such. Your father just doesn't understand your passion for acting.'

Arabella sent her friend a shaky smile. 'Thank you, Rosie. But I'll still have to go, Father will never forgive me otherwise.

'And I'd never forgive myself if you missed that play. There *has* to be a way out of this.'

Rosie drummed her fingers on the table and looked around the room for inspiration. There had to be a way out of this dilemma; there was always a way out of every problem.

'I'll go instead.' She smiled in triumph.

Arabella twisted her handkerchief in her lap. 'You'll what?'

'I'll go in your place. The Dowager and the Duke have never met me. If I tell them I'm Arabella van Haven how will they ever know the difference? We've both got black hair and blue eyes, and everyone always says we look like sisters. They'll see a fashionably dressed young woman, and all they'll be thinking about is getting their hands on your father's money. They'll never suspect I'm not you.'

'Oh, Rosie, you can't… Can you?'

'Of course I can.'

Arabella screwed her handkerchief into a tighter ball. 'But, Rosie, you might get caught.'

'Nonsense. It's a perfect plan. And when has one of my plans ever gone wrong?'

Arabella frowned in concentration. 'Well, there was that time you said Cook wouldn't notice the missing cakes if we moved those remaining around the pantry. And there was the time you said that if we dressed as boys and went to the local fair we'd be able to get work on the sideshows. And then there was that time you were certain that if we told our tutor we knew everything there was to know about—'

Rosie held up her hand to stop the flow of words. 'Those were mere childish pranks. This time it's serious—and, really, what choice do we have? You don't want to go to this party, do you?'

Arabella shook her head.

'You don't want to miss the play's opening, do you? You don't want to marry this Duke, do you? You don't want to end up living out in the countryside, miles away from the nearest theatre, do you?'

Arabella shook her head more emphatically.

'Right, then leave it to me. You said it yourself. I'm almost as good an actress as you.' She stabbed her finger at the abandoned letter. 'This horrid Duke of Knightsbrook will be completely fooled.'

'Well, I suppose you *could* pretend to be me...' Arabella chewed her lip again, as if not wholly convinced.

'Of course I can. And I'll have fun doing it. This stuffy Duke will think he's wooing the wealthy, beautiful Arabella van Haven. Instead he'll be wasting his energies pursuing a penniless, plain, charmless ward. And it will serve him right.'

'You might be penniless, Rosie, but no one could ever describe you as plain or charmless. You're beautiful, kind, funny and the best friend I could ever—'

Rosie held up her hand again, to stop Arabella's praises. 'Whether that's true or not, I can't say—but I certainly won't be appearing charming in front of the Duke. After all, it might be your father's wish that you marry a titled man, but that's not what *you* want, is it?'

Arabella straightened her spine. 'It certainly is not.'

'So I'm going to have to convince this stuffy Duke that

the last thing he wants to do is marry the appallingly behaved and completely unacceptable Arabella van Haven,
despite her father's fortune.'

Arabella smiled and placed her handkerchief back in
her purse. 'You're so clever, Rosie.' She paused, her purse
half closed. 'Except…'

'Except what?'

'I've just thought of a big flaw in your plan. Aunt
Prudence was going to accompany me as my chaperon.'

Rosie rolled her eyes. 'Aunt Prudence is too sick to
go anywhere. Or at least she thinks she is. I suspect she
won't be over her imagined seasickness until it's time to
go back to New York.'

Arabella covered her mouth to stifle a giggle. 'Poor
Aunt Prudence—she *is* a bit of a hypochondriac. But
you can't go without a chaperon. They'd get suspicious
if a young unmarried woman of twenty arrived at their
estate unaccompanied.'

Rosie would not be deterred. 'Then I'll take Nellie.
I'll need a lady's maid anyway, and Nellie enjoys a good
caper as much as we do. When I tell her we're doing it
so we can make sport of a family of greedy aristocrats
there'll be no stopping her. Nellie will be the perfect
chaperon.'

'This is *so* good of you, Rosie. You're always so kind
to me.'

Rosie waved her hand in front of her face to dismiss
the compliment. Arabella's happiness meant everything
to her.

Rosie drew in a deep breath and ran her hand down the
soft pink silk of her stylish gown. Arabella had saved her
from a life of poverty and loneliness. Without her, Rosie
couldn't imagine how hard her life might have been. She

closed her eyes and shuddered. But she was not alone any more. Thanks to Arabella she had not been forced to try and survive on the streets of New York with no money and without a friend.

There was nothing she wouldn't do for the friend who had saved her from such a life. And she hated to see Arabella sad.

Her friend had been so kind to her, had always treated her as an equal, and she had such little happiness in her life. Rosie saw it as her job to keep her friend happy, so she might be distracted from the neglect she felt over her father's constant absences.

Spending the weekend with a stuffy aristocratic family to save her from an unwanted marriage was nothing compared to the enormous debt she owed her friend. And at least poverty had one compensation. While Arabella's father was determined to marry her off to a titled man for his own social advancement, he had no such concerns when it came to Rosie. Nobody, including Rosie herself, expected anyone to want to marry a penniless orphan who didn't even own the clothes she was wearing.

She smiled and pushed away her unpleasant thoughts. What was the point of dwelling on such things? Today was all that mattered. Having fun was all that mattered. Not what had happened in the past, and not what the future might bring.

'Honestly, Bella. I want to do this. I'll get to have fun putting a stuffy duke in his place, and you'll get to see the play. And when I return I'll be able to regale you with tales of my exploits. It's perfect.'

Rosie smiled. She picked up a smoked salmon sandwich and placed it on her plate.

'Oh, yes, the Duke of Knightsbrook is going to regret ever thinking he can buy Arabella van Haven.'

Alexander FitzRoy, Lord Ashton, Eighth Duke of Knightsbrook, stifled a yawn and gazed over at the ormolu clock ticking on the marble mantelpiece. His mother, the Dowager Duchess, was in full voice, enumerating the seemingly exhaustive list of fine qualities that Arabella van Haven allegedly possessed.

'And I hear she's also accomplished on the banjo, and can recite large passages of Shakespeare from memory.'

His mother looked up at him with wide-eyed expectation. It seemed she had finally run out of accomplishments with which to tempt him.

Alexander uncrossed his legs and stretched. 'That's as may be, Mother, but I still have no intention of marrying the girl—no matter how many tunes she's capable of strumming on the banjo, or how many Shakespearean sonnets she can rattle off.'

'Don't be so hasty, Alexander. I know she's American, and that her father's a *banker*, of all things.' The Dowager grimaced. 'But they are minor drawbacks that I'm sure we can overlook. We need to focus on her finer qualities and not think about her background. After all, she is known for her beauty, and I've heard she possesses exquisite taste in—'

'Surely you have forgotten to list her most attractive attribute?' he interrupted, before his mother could start on another interminable list.

She cocked her head and smiled. 'And what would that be?'

'Her money.'

The Dowager spluttered, gripped the black lace at her

neckline and sent him her sternest look. 'Don't be vulgar, Alexander. You're talking like a common tradesman.'

'Vulgar or otherwise, isn't that what this is all about? She has it—we don't. You want me to marry her and give her a title in exchange for her father's money.'

His mother's pursed lips drew into a thin line and her nostrils flared. It was an expression Alexander was familiar with—the one she had when she heard something she didn't like.

'You don't need to put it so crudely, but you can't deny it would solve all our problems.'

That was indeed something Alexander could *not* deny. The American heiress's money would solve their immediate financial needs, but it was a solution he would not demean himself even to consider.

His grandfather and his father had brought the once wealthy Knightsbrook estate to the brink of financial ruin, but their problems ran deeper than the merely financial. He could almost forgive them squandering excessive amounts of money on gambling, partying and women. *Almost.* But what he could not forgive was them bringing the family's once noble name into total disrepute.

He intended to restore the family's fortune by hard work and modernisation. He also intended to restore the family's tarnished name—and that would not be achieved by selling the title Duchess of Knightsbrook to the highest bidder.

'You're right, Mother. Her father's money *would* provide a short-term solution to our money problems.'

The Dowager smiled and rose from her chaise longue.

'But it would be only that. A short-term solution. What is required is a long-term plan of action.'

The Dowager sank back onto her seat and sighed.

'Really, Alexander, sometimes you can be so tedious. Why don't you just marry the girl and be done with it?'

'Because if the estate is to return to its former glory we need to modernise. We're on the brink of the twentieth century and we're still using farming methods from the eighteenth century. That has to change.'

The Dowager flicked open her fan and waved it rapidly in front of her face. 'Not this again. You and your plans to modernise will be the death of me. If you marry the American you won't have to worry about silly steam trains and traction engines. I want to look out on people using scythes to bring in the harvest—not horrible pieces of wheezing and coughing machinery.'

'That's as may be, Mother, but I'm sure the tenants would rather live on a prosperous estate, where their homes and livelihoods are protected, than in poverty in what *you* see as a picturesque setting.'

'Oh, pish-posh.' The Dowager waved her fan more rapidly. 'Anyway, you're twenty-eight now. It's time you married. You shouldn't let that unfortunate incident with Lydia Beaufort put you off marriage for ever.'

Alexander clenched his jaw so tightly it began to ache. *Unfortunate incident.* Was that how his mother described something that had all but devastated him?

He inhaled deeply to release the tension gripping his neck and shoulders. 'Lydia Beaufort has nothing to do with me not wanting to marry the American. And that, Mother, is my final word on the subject.'

It might be his final word, but he knew from experience it would not be his mother's.

She frowned her disapproval and looked around the room, as if seeking further support for her argument.

She spotted Charlotte, sitting quietly in the corner reading a book.

'What about your sister?'

Charlotte looked up. 'What *about* me?'

'Well, you're going to need a husband soon. Heaven only knows no man is going to want to marry a girl who reads as much as you do and is always getting involved in these ridiculous social causes unless she comes with a decent dowry. Your brother wouldn't be so selfish as to deny you the happiness of marriage.'

Charlotte slammed shut her book. 'For your information, I have no intention of—'

Alexander shook his head slightly, giving his younger sister a silent signal that now was not the time to fight that particular battle with their mother.

Charlotte scowled at her mother and forcefully opened her book again, breaking the spine. She frowned at what she had done, and then went back to reading.

'I will make sure Charlotte is well provided for,' Alexander said.

'Yes, and you can make sure she is well provided for by marrying Arabella van Haven.'

Alexander shook his head and sighed audibly.

'Anyway,' the Dowager continued, undeterred. 'It's all arranged. I've invited her to a house party this weekend. You'll be able to discover for yourself just how ideal a bride she will make and how lucky the man will be who marries her.'

Alexander sprang to his feet. 'You've done *what*?'

'Oh, sit down, Alexander, and don't glare at me like that. I've invited her for the weekend. It will give you a chance to get to know her.'

'Mother, haven't I told you often enough that we need to economise? We cannot afford to host lavish parties.'

The Dowager flicked her fan at him. 'It's just a small house party—nothing too elaborate. And you can see it as an investment in the future. Isn't that what you're always going on about? Well, meeting Miss van Haven will be an investment in your future.'

She sent him a victorious smile.

'Putting aside the complete lack of logic in your argument, you've invited her here under false pretences. I won't lie to her. I will make it clear at the first opportunity that I will not be marrying her.'

'Oh, you and that overblown sense of honesty. You were just as bad when you were a boy, but I would have thought you'd have grown out of it by now.'

'Would you prefer it if I told lies, the way Father and Grandfather did?'

The way Lydia Beaufort did.

His mother's lips tightened, but she made no reply.

'Our family has lost just about everything. Surely you don't expect me to lose my belief in the importance of honesty as well? And if Arabella van Haven is as virtuous as you say she is then I'm sure she will also believe in the value of honesty and will want to know the truth.'

'Oh, yes, I've heard she *does* value honesty in all things. I've also heard she's modest, gentle, demure, and temperate in all areas. And they say that she...'

Alexander sat down and sighed as his mother went back to listing the litany of virtues possessed by the apparently saintly Arabella van Haven.

It seemed his mother would not be stopped in her plan to make her the next Duchess of Knightsbrook, and he was going to have to endure the company of the title-seeking heiress for the weekend. But eventually his mother and the American would both realise his mind was made up, and Arabella van Haven would have to pursue some other duke, earl or marquess desperate for American dollars—because the position of his wife was not for sale.

Chapter Two

It was magnificent. Simply magnificent.

Rosie stood just inside the entrance of Knightsbrook House and looked up at the ornate domed window in the ceiling, shedding a soft light over the two-storey entrance hall. She tried to settle her breathing as she took in the opulence and grandeur of it all.

The coach trip through the estate's parklands had been no less spectacular, with its seemingly endless parade of trees festooned with spring foliage. When the trees had cleared and she'd first seen the expansive four-storey house standing proudly beside a large lake, dominating the landscape around it, her resolve had faltered. Arabella's father was a man of immense wealth, but this was something more than just wealth. The house seemed to proclaim that here was the home of one of England's oldest and noblest families—one that was reverently referred to as 'old money'.

Rosie inhaled slowly and deeply. She would not be overawed by her surroundings. Nor would she be daunted by the stern looks of the ancestors staring down at her from the oil paintings that lined the walls of the expan-

sive hall. Arabella's happiness depended on her keeping her nerve.

She just had to remember who these people really
were. They were a stuffy aristocratic family who had
fallen on hard times. They were people so arrogant that
they thought all they had to do was dangle a title in front
of a rich American and then they could continue to live
in splendour, despite having lost all their own money.

Well, they were about to find out that not all Americans were quite so easily bought. They needed to be
taught a lesson, and she was just the woman to do it.

A man and a woman appeared at the top of the grand
staircase and began the long descent.

'That must be them, the rascals.' Nellie scowled beside her. 'Go teach them a lesson, Rosie.'

Rosie tried to calm her breathing and stifle her fluttering nerves. She just had to remember that she was no
longer poor Rosie Smith. She was Arabella van Haven,
daughter of a wealthy and influential banker. And she
was a young woman whose tendency to misbehave in
polite society made her a decidedly unsuitable bride for
a member of the aristocracy.

'Right...' She gave Nellie a pointed look. 'It's time for
Arabella to put on a show.'

Rosie spread out her arms wide, smiled and started
twirling. Round and round she went, faster and faster,
down the length of the entrance hall, her satin skirt
spreading out around her in a pale blue circle.

The black and white marble floor tiles merged into
one swirling mass. Priceless Chinese urns whooshed past
her face. She whirled past statues, past the paintings of
the ancestors, all the while emitting a loud *whoo-whee*

noise. Dizzier and dizzier, she kept spinning—until she reached the bottom of the staircase.

Stopping abruptly, she looked up to see what impact her entrance had made. The room continued to spin, twirling in front of her eyes as if she were locked inside a child's spinning top.

She reached out, tried to grasp something—anything to stop the room from moving. With both hands she clasped the thin stand of a nearby pedestal, clinging to it as if her life depended on it. The Chinese vase sitting on top of the pedestal wobbled. It tilted. It began to fall.

Rosie let out a loud squeal and dived forward to catch the delicate vase before it crashed to the floor. Her hands gripped the vase. Her feet slid out from beneath her and she tumbled forward.

Before she hit the floor strong hands had surrounded her waist, lifted her up and set her back on her unsteady feet.

Still clasping the vase, Rosie closed her eyes briefly, to try and halt her spinning head and still her pounding heart. She opened them and stared into the eyes of her rescuer. Then closed them again immediately.

It couldn't be.

This astonishingly handsome man could *not* be the stuffy Lord Ashton.

Rosie opened her eyes and blinked a few times, but his appearance became no less stunning.

While he had the haughty, reserved demeanour she had come to expect from the British aristocracy, he had the symmetrical good looks, chiselled cheekbones and full sensual lips she had seen on statues of Greek athletes at the British Museum.

He also had that air of masculine vitality those Greek sculptors had captured so well in their subjects.

Rosie looked down at the floor and gulped, remembering another anatomical feature the sculptures of naked Greek athletes possessed. But she most certainly would not think of that now.

Instead she looked back up and focused on how his dark brown hair brushed the edge of his high collar, and how, unlike most Englishmen she had met, his olive skin was clean-shaven.

And, unlike those Greek statues she wasn't thinking about, he was appropriately attired in a tailored grey three-piece suit, with a silver and grey brocade waistcoat.

Rosie coughed to clear her throat. 'Hello, I'm Arabella van Haven,' she said, hoping she didn't sound as foolish as she felt as she bobbed a curtsey, still clutching the vase to her chest.

He gave a formal bow and reached out his hands. Rosie stared at those long fingers, at the crisp white cuffs of his shirt contrasting with his skin, then looked up into his eyes. Brown eyes…so dark they seemed to absorb all light…eyes that were staring down at her, their accompanying black eyebrows raised in question.

'May I?'

'Oh, yes, of course.' She thrust the tightly clasped vase in his direction.

His fingers lightly touched hers as he removed the vase from her grip, setting off a decidedly unfamiliar reaction in her body. Her hands tingled and burned, as if she had held them too close to the fire. A strange sensation raced up her arm, across her chest, hitting her in the heart, causing it to pound in a wild, untamed manner.

He replaced the vase on its pedestal and turned back

to face her. Her head continued to spin, her heart continued to dance—but surely that had nothing to do with his touch or his stunning good looks. It had to be due entirely to her whirling entrance.

'Miss van Haven, allow me to introduce myself. I'm Alexander FitzRoy, Duke of Knightsbrook, and may I present my mother, the Dowager Duchess of Knightsbrook?'

Rosie bobbed another curtsey, inhaled a quick breath and turned to face his silver-haired mother, who was wearing the strangest expression she had ever seen.

While Lord Ashton was giving every appearance of being unaffected by her unusual entrance, the same could not be said of his mother. Her contorted mouth was presumably meant to be smiling, but a frown kept taking over, causing her lips to twist and turn as if pulled by a puppet master's invisible strings.

It seemed she might have to work a bit harder to shock Lord Ashton, but the Dowager was going to be easy prey.

It was time to have some fun.

'Pleased to meet you, Your Grace.' She reached down, grabbed the Dowager's hand and pumped it in a manly handshake.

Those invisible strings gave her mouth a firm tug. The frown won, and the Dowager's nostrils flared as if she could smell something unpleasant.

Rosie bit the inside of her upper lip to stop herself from laughing as the Dowager finally forced her lips into a smile, her face contorting as if she were undergoing a painful dental procedure.

'I am pleased to make your acquaintance, Miss van Haven,' the Dowager replied, trying discreetly to rub the hand that Rosie had just crushed.

Rosie controlled the giggle bubbling up inside her. 'I'm really sorry about nearly breaking your vase—but it looks like it's a really old one, so perhaps it wouldn't have mattered.'

All three turned and looked at the offending porcelain ornament, now safely restored to its pedestal.

'Yes, it is rather old…' The Dowager sniffed. 'Ming Dynasty, I believe.'

A small giggle escaped Rosie's lips before she had a chance to stop it. 'Oh, as old as that? Well, then, it wouldn't have mattered if I'd broken it. It would have given you a good excuse to replace it with something nice and new.'

The Dowager's eyes grew wide, her tight lips compressed further, and she signalled to a footman to remove the vase, as if concerned that Rosie was about to commit a wanton act of vandalism.

They waited in silence as the footman gently picked up the vase and carried it reverently away in his gloved hands. When he'd safely left the room the Dowager exhaled slowly.

'I'm afraid you've arrived a little earlier than we were expecting, Miss van Haven. We usually greet our guests formally at the entrance,' the Dowager said.

'Oh, I like to take people by surprise. You never know what mischievous acts you'll catch them in.' Rosie winked at the Dowager and received a wide-eyed look of disapproval in response.

'Yes, quite…' she said, flustered.

Rosie looked over at the Duke, hoping to see an equally disapproving look. Instead he stared back at her with unflinching dark eyes, neither smiling nor frowning. Rosie's grin died on her lips and heat rushed to her cheeks.

What was happening? She *never* blushed. And she shouldn't be blushing now. She had to remain in character if she was to convince this man that she was a most unsuitable duchess. Just because he was sublimely handsome it did not mean she should let him unnerve her. She had to remember who he was and what he wanted to do. He wanted to marry Arabella to get his hands on her father's money.

'I imagine there's been a lot of mischief in these halls,' she said, trying to keep her voice light-hearted to disguise the disquiet the Duke was arousing deep inside her. 'I'm sure those ancestors could tell a tale or two.' She threw her arms up in the air and gestured wildly to the paintings lining the wall.

The Dowager took a step back to avoid Rosie's flying arms, while the Duke continued to stare down at her, his face implacable. She lowered her arms. It seemed that bad behaviour wasn't going to upset his demeanour. She would have to try another means of attack.

'Judging by all those portraits, your family has been wealthy for many generations. I suppose you realise that my father was born in poverty? His father was a miner, and his father's father was a mule driver.'

Let's see how the snobby aristocrats react to that!

The Duke nodded slowly. 'Yes, your father's history is well-documented. And he is to be commended for rising so quickly from such humble beginnings to become one of the wealthiest men in America. He's obviously an enterprising man and clearly believes in hard work.'

Rosie fought not to grimace. Was *nothing* going to annoy this man? Surely he couldn't be that rare entity, a member of the British aristocracy who wasn't a snob? Or was he just blinded by the thought of Arabella's substantial dowry?

'You're right. He does believe in hard work—in earning money rather than expecting a hand-out.'

Hopefully this Duke wouldn't be able to miss her thinly veiled disapproval at his plans to marry Arabella for her money.

'Another thoroughly commendable trait.'

Damn. Either he didn't understand that he had just been insulted, or he didn't care.

'It's a shame your father couldn't accompany you this weekend,' the Dowager said. 'I was looking forward to meeting him in person.'

'No, he's too busy back in America.'

Making the money you're so desperate for.

'But meeting me is just like meeting him. I'm a chip off the old block, as they say.'

'Do they? How delightful...' the Dowager said through pinched lips.

Rosie supressed a smile at the Dowager's discomfort. A seed of doubt had definitely been planted in her mind after Rosie's entrance and behaviour. Now all she had to do was water that seed with continued bad behaviour and watch it grow until the FitzRoys realised they couldn't possibly countenance this marriage and sent her on her way.

Alexander almost felt sorry for his mother. This peculiar American woman was most definitely not what she had expected—of that there could be no doubt. But it seemed the thought of Mr van Haven's vast fortune was enough for her to swallow her astonishment and put on a brave face.

With forced politeness his mother led Miss van Haven back down the entrance hall she had just danced up, pausing at each painting and explaining which ancestor it depicted and what great exploit each was famous for.

It was fortunate for his mother that paintings of his father and his grandfather did not adorn the hall. He suspected even *she* would have had trouble finding anything with which to commend those two reprobates, and Miss van Haven's term 'mischievous' was far too tame to describe the damage that those two men had done to the family and to the estate.

Following the two women, Alexander had the opportunity to observe this odd American. His mother had been right about one thing: she certainly was attractive. With her raven-black hair and sparkling blue eyes she was nothing less than radiant. Nor could he deny that her creamy skin with the hint of blush on her cheeks gave her a delicate beauty. And that slightly upturned nose was rather appealing.

His mother was possibly right that she could play the banjo and recite long passages of Shakespeare—although he had no desire to discover whether either of those claims were true or not. But he suspected that nothing else about this young woman was what his mother had hoped for in a future daughter-in-law.

As his mother continued her boastful monologue Miss van Haven nodded furiously, perhaps unaware that her hat had become dislodged as she had flung herself down the hall. It was now sitting at a precarious angle, causing her to look like a very pretty pantomime clown.

Alexander suspected a clown was also not what his mother had had in mind for the next Duchess of Knightsbrook.

Despite her feigned politeness, his mother couldn't stop herself from shooting nervous glances in Miss van Haven's direction. She was no doubt worried that the young lady would suddenly break into a polka, trip over one of the Queen Anne chairs, or send some other priceless antique flying.

There was no question that her performance had certainly been unexpected—but it was quite obviously just that: a performance. While her grandfather might have been a miner, and his father a mule driver, *she* had been raised among America's wealthiest elite. The rules of etiquette and manners were just as strict in New York society as they were in England. And men like her father, who were newly wealthy, tended to follow those rules even more rigidly than those who had been born to wealth.

Miss van Haven had no doubt been given instructions from a very young age on the correct way to behave in every situation—and that wouldn't have involved insulting her hosts by acting in such an outrageous manner.

Why she felt the need to behave in such a way Alexander could not fathom. Perhaps she felt her father's wealth meant she did not have to abide by even the most basic principles of politeness. But, whatever the reason, he had more pressing issues to deal with than the bad behaviour of a frivolous American heiress.

The sooner he could tell Miss van Haven that she would not be the next Duchess of Knightsbrook the sooner they could end this tedious ritual and he could get back to his work of transforming the family estate into a productive, financially viable farm.

She turned and looked in his direction and he realised he had been staring at her. Despite himself, he held her gaze, unable to look away from those stunning blue eyes. The colour was so intense—like a cool lake on a warm afternoon. And, also like a lake, they seemed to contain hidden depths—as if there was a deep, unfathomable sadness behind all her game-playing.

Her excessive grin faltered slightly, and a blush tinged her cheeks before she turned her attention back to his mother and once again resumed her frantic nodding.

They reached the front door, where her maid was still standing, her arms crossed defiantly.

'Now that I've introduced you to our family's history, perhaps Alexander will escort you round the gardens while I attend to my other guests? Your maid can be your chaperon.'

The maid folded her arms more tightly, shot Miss van Haven a questioning look, and received a quick nod in reply. Alexander wondered at the silent exchange, which seemed more like one between equals than maid and mistress.

His mother nodded to Arabella, sent Alexander a stern look—which was no doubt an admonition to do his best to charm the heiress—and then departed.

Alexander suppressed a huff of irritation. Escorting this title-seeking American around the estate was not exactly how he had intended to spend the day, but at least it would give him an opportunity to set her straight. To let her know that she would *not* be the next Duchess of Knightsbrook.

Chapter Three

Alone with the Duke—well, alone apart from Nellie—Rosie knew she had to keep her guard up. She could not let him see how much he unnerved her. She had to keep reminding herself that he was after Arabella's money. That was all that mattered.

She sent him what she hoped was a confident smile and got a familiar stern look in return.

'If I am to escort you round the gardens, can I make one request?'

She shook her head slightly. 'A request?'

'Yes—would you please stop this charade?'

One hand shot to her stomach; the other covered her mouth to stop a gasp from escaping. This was a disaster. He could *see* it was all an act. He *knew* she wasn't Arabella. Her plan was ruined before it had begun.

She looked out through the glass doors to the gardens. Could she escape? No, that was ridiculous. She was in the middle of the Devon countryside, many miles from London. What was she going to do? Walk? All the way back to the train station?

No, she was going to have to bluff her way out of this.

She scanned the entrance hall. Her mind spun with half-formed excuses and explanations.

'Charade?' she squeaked.

'Yes—this play-acting. You may have been able to shock my mother but it won't work on me, Miss van Haven.'

Rosie released the breath she'd been holding and slowly lowered her hand from her mouth. He didn't know she wasn't Arabella. All was not lost.

'Oh, yes. I'm sorry about that…' She gestured around the entrance hall, her hand twirling in imitation of her entrance. 'Just my little joke.'

His dark eyebrows drew together. He frowned slightly. 'Really? Are you in the habit of making fun of your hosts?'

'No, I…' She stopped.

Why make excuses? After all, she didn't *want* Lord Ashton to like her. She had to be completely unlikable if she was to convince him just what a thoroughly unacceptable duchess she would make.

'Well, yes. I do it all the time. I love making fun of people. Don't you?'

His frown deepened. 'No, I don't. Everyone deserves to be treated with respect, no matter who they are.'

Momentarily chastened, Rosie was tempted to agree with him—but she couldn't. The one thing she did not want was to be was agreeable.

'I guess we just see things completely differently. I think everyone is here for my entertainment and I like to have as much fun as possible. If people get offended and think I'm laughing at them—well, that's hardly my fault. Is it?'

He stared at her for a moment longer, as if observing

a strange animal on display at the zoological gardens. 'I'm afraid I can't answer that.'

The response was vague, but Rosie could read his intent in his rigid body language. She had her wish. The Duke disapproved of her.

'Well, don't you worry if you don't know the answer. I'm sometimes not that smart either.'

'I don't doubt that, Miss van Haven.'

Rosie smiled. That almost sounded like an insult.

He offered her his arm. 'Mother would like me to show you the gardens. Shall we…?'

She placed her hand on his forearm and resisted the temptation to give the muscles a little squeeze, just to see how they compared to a marble statue.

They walked out through double French doors, down some sweeping stone stairs and into the gardens, which looked just as magnificent at ground level as it had when she had driven through it in the carriage, with an abundance of trees, lush grasslands and a stunning lake adorned with ornate fountains.

As they strolled along a tree-lined pathway the soft green spring leaves rustled in the light breeze and small birds chirped and flitted between the branches. Rosie breathed in deeply and savoured the fresh country air. She had loved every moment of her time in London, but it was a joy to be in such beautiful, peaceful surroundings.

'I don't know how much you know about Knightsbrook, but this garden was designed for my great-great-grandfather in the mid-eighteenth century, by the famous landscape gardener Capability Brown,' the Duke said, playing the role of dutiful host.

Rosie nodded. When she had first arrived she had

wondered whether the garden was a Capability Brown
design, as it had the natural look the landscape gardener
was famous for.

She gave a small cough. 'Capable who?'

'Capability Brown—he designed some of the most
beautiful and highly regarded gardens in England.'

'Did he always plant so many trees? Trees are quite
frightful, don't you think?'

He stopped, turned to face her, and frowned. 'You
don't like *trees*?'

'No—awful things. They shed their leaves, making
an unsightly mess all over the place. Not to mention all
the terrible birds they attract. And as for the mess *those*
frightful creatures make—well, the less said about that
the better. I think the world would be much better off
without so many trees.'

He looked along the path, then back towards the house.
'Then there's probably little point continuing our walk
along this path, as it leads to a woodland area that contains some of the most established specimens of English
trees to be found in the country.'

'Oh, no. I wouldn't want to see *that*.' Rosie gave a
fake shudder. 'Has this estate got anything other than
trees to look at?'

He stared at her for a moment, his brow furrowed.
'Perhaps you'd prefer to walk alongside the lake?'

She sighed, as if to say that if a lake was all he had to
offer, then a lake it would have to be.

He led her to the gently curving serpentine lake that
wound its way around the house. As they strolled slowly
along its edge Rosie admired the centrepiece sculpture
of Neptune, and the array of carved sea creatures that
appeared to be frolicking in the waters. When the foun-

tain sent water cascading high into the air, Rosie was tempted to clap her hands with delight at its playfulness.

'Is the lake more to your taste, Miss van Haven?

She forced her face to remain impassive. 'Lakes are all right, I suppose. But it's a shame it's got all those sculptures in it. Art is so distracting, don't you think?'

'You don't like art either?'

She shook her head vigorously and scowled. 'No—art is so *wasteful*, don't you think? All those galleries, and museums...theatres and whatnot. I'm sure they could all be put to much better use. Don't you agree?'

'Miss van Haven, you're...' He paused and looked around, as if struggling to find the right words.

Rosie smiled and waited for an appropriately disparaging comment that would seal her fate as a completely unacceptable future bride.

'You're quite unusual—aren't you, Miss van Haven?'

Quite unusual. It wasn't nearly as insulting as she would have liked, but it would have to do.

'Unusual? Me? No, I don't think so. I think it's the rest of the world that's unusual. All those people who like culture...plays, books, art, sculptures... They're the unusual ones.' She shuddered, as if the mere thought of art was abhorrent to her.

'In that case I suspect there will be little point showing you the family's collection of Old Masters.'

Rosie abruptly stopped walking and screwed up her face as if in pain. *No.* She had gone too far. Nothing would please her more than to see the FitzRoy art collection. One of the few things she knew about the family was that they had been collecting art for generations and had one of the finest collections outside the national art galleries. And now she had deprived herself of the opportunity to view some of the world's finest masterpieces.

She bit lightly on her tongue, to stop herself from crying out that she would give just about anything to see the collection. Anything, that was, except betray her promise to Arabella to make sure the Duke had no interest in marrying her.

'Yes, I suspect you're right—it would be a complete waste of time to show me *any* pictures,' she said through clenched teeth.

'Perhaps, then, we should sit awhile?'

He led her to a seat on the stone bridge that curved over the lake. While they looked out at the water and the woodland backdrop Rosie tried to think of a scheme that would convince Lord Ashton that, despite her claim to detest art, it would still be a good idea for him to show her the collection.

'Miss van Haven, there is something I must tell you. I hope you won't be offended, but it is essential that I tell you the truth.'

'I'm sure nothing you say will offend me, Your Grace.' After all, Rosie was the one who was trying her hardest to be offensive.

'You were invited here for the weekend under false pretences and I must let you know the true situation.'

She tilted her head. This was intriguing. 'False pretences?

'It was my mother's idea to invite you. I believe she has given you and your father the impression that I am interested in meeting you with the intention of looking towards a possible marriage. That is not the case. You're a very pretty young lady, Miss van Haven, and I'm sure you will one day make some man very happy, but I'm afraid that man won't be me.'

Had she heard him correctly? 'You don't want to marry me?'

'I'm sorry, Miss van Haven. As I said, I mean no offence. I don't wish to marry anyone. I don't know if you are aware that your father and my mother have put this scheme together without my approval, or even my knowledge. So, my apologies for the gross deception, but I don't want to marry you.'

Rosie clapped her hands and laughed with delight. 'That's wonderful news!'

With his eyebrows knitted together, he once again looked at her as if she were a curiosity. 'Wonderful? Am I to assume that you don't wish to marry either?'

She shook her head vigorously, still smiling and clapping. 'No, I most definitely do not. Why else do you think I put on that performance when I first arrived? Why else do you think I said that trees are horrid? Who thinks *trees* are horrid? No one! I was trying to make you dislike me so you wouldn't want to marry me.'

She had expected him to laugh as well, but he continued to frown. It seemed an inability to smile was another thing he had in common with those statues of Greek athletes.

'None of what you said was true?'

'Of course not.' She shook her head at his obvious statement.

'*Why* did you feel the need to put on such an act?'

'So you wouldn't want to marry me, of course.' Rosie was beginning to wonder if the handsome Duke was perhaps a bit dim-witted.

'You've been lying and pretending since the moment you arrived?'

Her smile faltered. 'Um… Well, yes, I guess I have. But I had to.'

The furrow in his brow deepened. 'Would it not have been easier to have told the truth—that you didn't wish to marry?'

'Well, perhaps, but it might have got complicated if you had been determined to marry *me*.'

'And play-acting *isn't* complicated? Lying *isn't* complicated?'

Rosie shrugged, unsure how to answer.

He looked out at the lake and sighed deeply. 'I've always found that lies inevitably cause complications, and often have far-reaching consequences for too many people. Telling lies might benefit the liar, but it almost always causes a great deal of problems for everyone else.'

Rosie wondered at his reaction, which seemed to be about something more than just her deceptive behaviour. His face looked so solemn, even melancholy, almost as if he was recalling some past hurt, some previous act of deception that had wounded him.

Her immediate impulse was to put her hand on his arm—to comfort him the way she often longed for someone to comfort her. She knew what it was like to have suffered in the past, to feel the need to hide your internal wounds from the world. But she did not know this man—would never really know him. So instead she did what she always did. She kept smiling.

He turned his attention back to her. 'Is anything you've said today been the truth?'

'Um…well, I'm definitely American.' She gave an embarrassed laugh.

'Anything else?'

Rosie looked out at the lake, bit the edge of her lip and struggled to find anything to say.

'In that case, shall we try and sort the truth from the lies?'

Rosie shook her head, then nodded, unsure whether telling the truth was a good idea or not.

'Let's start with trees. What do you think of trees?'

She laughed lightly with relief; that was something about which she was happy to tell the truth. 'I *love* trees. And I love the gardens designed by Capability Brown. I've seen many sketches of his work and I was hoping I'd get a chance to see some of his gardens while I was in England. I love the way he combines a natural look with little whimsical features—like the fountains and sculptures. It's quite stunning.'

The furrow in his forehead disappeared and he looked at her as if seeing her for the first time. 'And I take it you don't object to birds either?'

She laughed again. 'Who wouldn't love birds? Of course I love birds—*and* all other animals.'

'And art, sculptures, plays, books, paintings?'

'I'm not a complete philistine. I *love* art, sculptures, books, paintings, plays…all forms of culture.'

'In that case I suspect you *would* enjoy seeing the family's art collection?'

Rosie clapped her hands again. She had got her wish. 'Oh, yes. Yes, please. I'd love to.'

'Then I'd be delighted to show you. But I think there is one thing that I must do first.'

As he moved towards her along the bench Rosie's breath caught in her throat. What was he doing? What was happening?

'Your hat became dislodged when you spun your way down the entrance hall and is now sitting at a somewhat comical angle. Please allow me to set it right.'

Still holding her breath, she forced herself not to gasp when his fingers lightly brushed her temples as he attempted to remove her hatpin.

The whisper of his hands on her cheeks as he gently pulled the hat straight was as light as a feather, but the sensation was all-consuming. Fire erupted within her. Her cheeks burned and her heart pounded so loudly she was sure he must be able to hear its furious drumbeat.

He was so close she could feel the warmth of his body, could sense his physical strength, and she had to fight hard against the invisible force that was tempting her to move even closer towards him.

He gave the hat a final tug and leaned back to observe his handiwork. 'There—that's much better.'

Rosie released her breath and gasped in another, trying to relieve her light-headedness. Instead she breathed in the masculine scent of leather and musk and her heartbeat increased its ferocious tempo.

She swallowed several times and tried to breathe slowly, to regain the composure that his touch had so easily stripped away.

This would not do. This would not do at all. It didn't matter how handsome he was. It didn't matter what effect his touch had on her. The Duke was not for her. He didn't want to marry Arabella. And if he had no interest in Mr van Haven's daughter—a woman from New York's elite society, a woman with a substantial dowry and the prospect of an enormous inheritance—he certainly wouldn't be interested in Mr van Haven's impoverished ward.

It was foolish even to think such things, and any such illusions had to be put out of her head immediately. She was here for one purpose only: to save Arabella from an unwanted marriage. To be bedazzled just because the Duke had touched her would be madness. She had to stay focused on her task.

No, the Duke was certainly not for her. And if she was to stop herself acting inappropriately in any unintended way she had to remember that at all times.

Alexander gazed down at the puzzling Miss van Haven. Her cheeks had once again turned a pretty shade of pink, and her bright blue eyes glistened as she gazed back at him.

Yes, puzzling was the only word he could use to describe her. From her unconventional arrival to her confession that she had no more desire to marry than he did, she presented one big puzzle.

It seemed that telling lies was part of her nature, and that was something he would never countenance. If he had learnt one lesson from Lydia Beaufort it had been about the destructive nature of lies. Lydia had once been a young woman of great promise, but lies had ruined her life and her downfall had all but destroyed him in the process. Miss van Haven's lies might be less destructive than Lydia's, but they were lies all the same.

And Arabella's reason for lying—that it was less complicated than telling the truth—was no excuse. It appeared that Miss van Haven could challenge his mother when it came to a lack of logical thinking.

But there was something about her that he found undeniably attractive. Something he couldn't define. He rubbed his fingers together and could almost feel the

touch of her silky-smooth skin, like a soft, creamy mag-
nolia blossom.

But it wasn't that. Nor was it her pretty face or her
slim-waisted figure. It wasn't the way she laughed so
readily, nor the way she smelled of delicate spring flowers
after a rain shower. Nor was it the unfathomable depths of
her blue eyes. But there was definitely *something* about
her. Why else would he have felt compelled to straighten
her hat, when merely informing her that it had become
dislodged was all that had been required.

He realised he had been staring at her for longer than
propriety would allow, so quickly looked away and out at
the lake. What did it matter if she was a beautiful young
woman? Lydia had also been pretty and sweet, with a
charming laugh...

'So, Miss van Haven,' he said, as soon as he had resumed his usual sense of equanimity. 'We've established
that you like nature and art. Am I now seeing the real
Arabella van Haven?'

'Oh, yes!' She gave a light, tinkling laugh. 'What you
see is what you get.'

'No more lies.'

She coughed slightly, and her cheeks turned a deeper
shade of pink. 'No more lies.'

Her assertion did nothing to unravel the puzzle. She
claimed to be telling the truth now, but her tightly held
smile and rapidly blinking eyes appeared to make a
mockery of that claim. She was still holding something
back, but what that was Alexander had no idea.

Surely it was of no matter what Miss van Haven might
or might not be holding back. She was not Lydia Beaufort. He was not going to marry her. Her lies could not
hurt him.

And he had achieved his goal. He had informed her that they would not be marrying, and on that he and Miss van Haven were in complete agreement. That was all that mattered.

It was time to put all speculation about this unusual American heiress to one side. Now that their awkward conversation about marriage was behind them, he could relax and simply play the role of good host.

He stood up and once again offered her his arm. 'If the real Arabella van Haven is interested in seeing the art collection, then I would be delighted to show her.'

She clapped her hands in a genuine show of bubbly excitement. 'Oh, yes, please! I've heard you have a Rembrandt that is reputed to be his best work, and a Vermeer, and several Gainsboroughs that are said to be exquisite.'

She stood up and placed her hand on his arm.

'Then shall we?' he said. 'It will also get you away from these horrid trees.'

Alexander found himself unexpectedly pleased when she playfully patted his arm in response to his teasing.

He looked around for the trailing maid, but she was nowhere in sight. 'We seem to have lost our chaperon,' he said.

'Oh, yes, Nellie. She's probably found something more entertaining to do than watch us. I hope you don't mind?'

He shook his head. Surely it should be *she* who should mind, not him. Yes, she was quite a puzzling young lady...

They retraced their steps along the path. Then he led her through the house to the gallery that contained many of the family's major paintings—including the Rembrandt she had remarked upon.

When she saw the self-portrait she stopped. Her hand went to her neck and he heard a quick intake of breath.

'It's beautiful. It's literally breathtaking,' she whispered, transfixed by the painting.

Alexander nodded. He had seen the self-portrait countless times, but its beauty still affected him deeply. He was inexplicably pleased that it had the same effect on Miss van Haven.

They stood, side by side in silent admiration.

'His sensitivity is superb,' she murmured. 'He's painted himself smiling, but he's still managed to capture a sense of tragedy in his eyes,'

Alexander looked down at Miss van Haven, impressed by her insight. It was exactly what he had thought when he first saw her—that there was a sense of tragedy behind her smiling eyes.

Rembrandt had gone from poverty to wealth and back to poverty, and had suffered deeply as a result. Arabella van Haven had been born into privilege and lived the life of a wealthy daughter of a prominent New York banker. And yet she had the look of one who had quietly suffered. Alexander couldn't help but wonder why.

He led her to a painting on the other side of the gallery, to avoid any further contemplation of what had caused Miss van Haven's sad eyes. 'The Vermeer is slightly more cheerful, but no less powerful.'

She gazed as if enchanted at the portrait of a beautiful young woman playing a lute. 'It's wonderful. He's really captured how a woman looks when she's absorbed in her performance. It reminds me so much of a friend of mine who loves to act.'

'Who might that be?'

She shook her head. 'Just a friend in New York.' She

looked up at him and smiled. 'She often looks like that when she's performing—completely lost in the part, as if the real Ara—as if she no longer exists.'

Alexander led her slowly around the gallery, stopping at the paintings by Gainsborough and at the portraits of his ancestors painted by Sir Joshua Reynolds.

'I think if I lived here I would never leave this room. You're so lucky, Your Grace.' She looked up at him, her eyes sparkling with the pleasure and passion that great art clearly evoked in her.

'Alexander—please call me Alexander. Your Grace sounds so stuffy,' he said, surprising himself with his lack of formality.

She gave another musical laugh. 'In that case you must call me...' She hesitated. 'You must call me Arabella.'

'Arabella.' He savoured the name. 'You're right, Arabella, and it is a room in which I spend a great deal of time. Unfortunately many of these paintings are going to have to be sold to pay my father's debts. We will have to enjoy them while they're still here.'

Her eyes grew wide. 'Surely not? It would be terrible if they were lost to the family—especially the ones that are portraits of your ancestors.'

'Yes, it is unfortunate.' Alexander exhaled to try and drive out his annoyance.

Those paintings would indeed have to be sold to cover his father's debts. Paintings that had been in his family for generations would be sold off because of that man's lying, cheating and irresponsible behaviour.

'It's unfortunate, but I intend to sell them to public art galleries, so they can be enjoyed by as many people as possible.'

'Good.' She nodded her approval. 'The more people

who can see these exquisite artworks and experience the kind of pleasure I have today the better.'

As she stared at the painting she chewed lightly on her lower lip and tipped her head to one side.

'But it would still be better if they could remain in the house—especially the portraits of your ancestors. It's a shame you can't open the house to the public. Then people could pay a small entrance fee and enjoy the gardens and the woodlands, the lake and the art. It would be a lovely day out.'

Alexander stared at her, taken aback by the unusual and progressive suggestion of opening the house to the public. 'Yes, it's a nice idea—but I can't see my mother tolerating anyone except invited guests in the house. Even when I invite engineers and other professional people Mother can barely tolerate their presence. And these are people who are going to help transform the estate and make it profitable—not people just having "a lovely day out".'

She wandered over to the portrait of his great-great-grandmother, painted by Sir Joshua Reynolds. 'Well, she tolerated me and my antics when I first arrived. Perhaps she's more adaptable than you think. And it would mean all these wonderful paintings could stay in the house, where they belong.'

'I suspect Mother would tolerate anything from you if she thought there was a chance we might be married.'

The edges of her lips pulled down in mock concern. 'Oh, dear. She's not going to take kindly to hearing we have agreed that neither of us wants to marry.'

'Unfortunately, Miss van Haven...

She raised her finger in admonishment.

'Sorry—Arabella. Unfortunately, Arabella, my mother

is not one to give up easily. You will have to prepare yourself for some concerted matchmaking from her this weekend. I urge you to be resolute.'

'Oh, I can be resolute, Alexander—believe me.' She smiled at him.

He did not doubt it. Arabella was obviously a woman who knew her own mind. She might have some unusual ways of getting what she wanted, but there was no denying she had admirable determination.

They continued their slow movement around the gallery, admiring each painting in turn, until they halted in front of a pastoral scene of two lovers embracing, their naked bodies entwined under the canopy of a sweeping oak tree.

Alexander had seen the painting many times, but never had it affected him so powerfully. With the memory of Arabella's silky skin still imprinted on his fingers he could all but feel the soft, yielding flesh of a woman's naked body against his own. He could imagine looking down into Arabella's eyes as she looked up at him with the same intensity as the woman in the portrait. Her lips would be parted, waiting for his kiss, her body responding to his caresses.

He coughed to chase away the inappropriate image that had invaded his thoughts. Then coughed again to clear his throat.

'It's stunning, isn't it?' he said, his voice strangled despite his repeated coughs. 'It's by an unknown artist. My great-grandfather bought it while he was on his grand tour of Europe as a gift for his future bride.'

'It's beautiful. She must have felt truly desired,' she murmured, her fingers lightly touching her own lips.

It seemed she too was deeply affected by the passion

in the painting. He noted that her breath was coming in a series of rapid gasps, her face and neck were flushed, and she was gazing at the painting as if enraptured.

Alexander forced himself to lead her away until they reached a much more suitable work to show a young lady—one that would have a less disturbing effect on his own equilibrium too.

But as he stared at an etching of Knightsbrook House made not long after it had been extended, with the west wing added in the early eighteenth century, all he could think of was the previous painting of those lovers entwined, of naked flesh, of parted lips waiting for a kiss...

He drew in a deep breath and exhaled loudly. This was ridiculous. He had no interest in Miss van Haven. No interest at all. He did not want to marry her. He did not want to marry anyone. And he most certainly did not want to marry an American heiress. He would *not* have the world thinking he married purely to restore the family's fortune. And if he did not have any interest in marrying her then, as a gentleman, he had no right to be thinking of her lying naked in his arms.

He coughed again. No, he could not—would not think of her in that way. She was a delightful young woman with whom he was having a pleasant time. That was all.

Perhaps it was simply that it had been such a long time since he had enjoyed the company of a young woman as much as he was enjoying himself now. Perhaps that was why his thoughts had gone off on tangents better reserved for the bawdy houses of London.

Whatever the reason, it would not do.

They moved on to the next painting, which was of the estate's garden, and he saw her smile at the small children depicted playing beside the lake. Seeing her delighted smile, he couldn't help but wonder why it was that such an attractive young woman was so set against marriage. He knew why *he* didn't wish to marry, but she must want marriage, children, a family of her own… For some reason it was a question he wanted answered.

'Arabella, when you said you didn't want to marry, you never told me the reason why.'

She looked up at him, her expression startled, then quickly turned back to look at the painting, her hands pulling at the lace on the cuffs of her sleeves. 'I…well. I… It's because…um…it's because I…um…' She blinked rapidly. Her gaze moved around the room, then settled on the painting of the two lovers. 'It's because I'm in love with another man—we're all but betrothed.'

As if punched in the stomach, Alexander winced. It was not the answer he'd expected but surely it was the most logical one. She was beautiful, sweet and funny. Of *course* she would have numerous men wanting to marry her. And for many men her father's fortune would only add to her appeal.

He drew in a series of quick breaths. What was *wrong* with him? The fact that she was in love with another man was of no matter. In fact it made things easier. There would be no difficulties in convincing his mother what a hopeless cause it was, trying to get them to marry.

He should be happy for Miss van Haven. And he *was* happy for her. Why wouldn't he be?

And, that aside, he had much more important things to think about than the romantic entanglements of an American heiress.

He turned from the painting. 'I believe it is time we joined the other guests.' He placed his hand gently on her back and led her towards the gallery door.

'Yes, I suppose you're right,' she mumbled, still blushing inexplicably, but nevertheless following his lead out through the door and into the corridor.

Why she should be blushing over her admission of being in love with another man he had no idea, but the reasons for Miss van Haven's blushes were of as little consequence to him as her romantic attachments.

He had done his duty as host. Now he had work to do. He had a devastated estate to rescue. It was that which demanded his full attention.

Only a fool would allow himself to get side-tracked by the frivolity of a visit by an American heiress, and one thing Alexander knew about himself: he was no fool.

Chapter Four

Why had she said that? Of all the excuses she could have come up with why had she said she was in love with another man?

Usually she could think much faster than that when put on the spot. Instead she had said the first thing that had come into her head and invented a non-existent lover to explain why an American heiress would not be interested in marrying the eminently suitable Alexander Fitz-Roy, Lord Ashton, the handsome and charming Duke of Knightsbrook.

But she could hardly have told him the truth, could she? She couldn't tell him that the real Arabella van Haven didn't want to marry because her one and only true love was the theatre, and she was determined to dedicate herself to pursuing a career on the stage.

Nor could she tell him that she, Rosie Smith, had long ago resigned herself to remaining unmarried. As the ward of a wealthy man, she knew that none of the men who moved in Mr van Haven's circles would be interested in marrying a woman who had no money of her own and no dowry. How could she tell him that a man like him, who could trace his family back countless generations, was so far out of reach it would be a joke for her even to contemplate marriage to such a man.

And she certainly couldn't tell him that she wasn't Arabella van Haven. She had promised Arabella she would help her and her goal had been easily achieved. But she still couldn't reveal that secret without Arabella's knowledge. It would be a betrayal of her promise to her friend—something she would never do.

Instead she had lied to Alexander. Again.

She should have thought more clearly. She should have come up with a better reason—one that was closer to the truth than her invention of a beau for Arabella. Why had she done that? It must have been because that image of the two entwined lovers was still in her mind. That beautiful painting had made her realise that such passion would be something she would never experience. But it had still been a dim-witted thing to say, and Rosie could kick herself for her lack of clear thinking.

She would have to keep her head and her emotions in check for the rest of the weekend, so she didn't say or do anything so foolhardy again.

She took one last glance over her shoulder at the art works she would never see again as Alexander hurried her out of the gallery. Such a shame. She could have spent the rest of the day and the evening looking at the paintings, but it seemed Alexander had different ideas. It appeared he'd had enough of the gallery. Or he'd had enough of her company.

They rushed down the hall as if they were late for an important appointment, his hand on her back hurrying her forward. It was apparent that now Alexander had done as his mother had commanded—had shown her the gardens and done his duty to his guest—he wanted rid of her.

Rosie tried hard not to be offended. It hardly mattered, really. So he was suddenly tired of her company and wanted to end their time alone together? It mattered not one jot.

And yet previously he had been so attentive to her. Right up till the time she had told him she was in love with another man. But there could be no connection between them; that would be too ridiculous. He had no interest in her. He had said so himself. And yet...

Rosie dismissed such scatter-brained thoughts. Even if his change in demeanour had come about because she had told him about the man she supposedly loved, it was the man American heiress Arabella van Haven loved— a woman from a respectable wealthy family. Not poor orphaned Rosie Smith.

Whatever his reason for such haste, trying to figure it out was pointless speculation.

As they rushed down the corridors towards the drawing room Rosie told herself she would not be offended by his determination to be rid of her. After all, what did it matter? She had got what she'd come for. Arabella was safe from an unwanted marriage. She had seen a beautiful garden, and viewed some exquisite paintings that few people got to see. That was a memory she would treasure always. Her plan had worked—not in the way she had envisaged, but it had still worked. Surely that was a satisfying conclusion?

All she had to do now was relax and enjoy the rest of her weekend in this grand home.

She glanced up at Alexander. His handsome face was set like stone as he focused straight ahead. It was as if he had one purpose and one purpose only: to end his time with Rosie as quickly as possible.

They reached the drawing room and she almost expected him to push her in, slam the doors behind her and make his escape. Instead he stood politely behind her, waited for the footman to open the doors, then followed her in.

The stately room was filled with the murmur of polite conversation as the assembled guests took afternoon tea. Fires crackled in several fireplaces, struggling to warm the expansive room, which held a slight chill despite the mild spring afternoon.

Rosie quickly scanned the room and took in every aspect of its opulence—from the large crystal chandelier suspended from the soaring engraved ceiling down to the intricate silk carpets that adorned the polished oak flooring. More of the family's art collection was on display here. The walls were filled with paintings, and every surface seemed to be decorated with artefacts and antiques—presumably collected by Alexander's many wealthy ancestors.

Rosie could only hope she would have an opportunity during the weekend to admire them more closely.

The Dowager was engrossed in conversation with a group of elderly women. When she saw Rosie and Alexander she instantly excused herself, rose from the chaise longue and with a purposeful swish of her black satin skirt walked over to join them.

Her gaze quickly moved from Rosie to Alexander and back again, giving her every appearance of making an assessment as to just how close her plan of marrying off her son to a wealthy heiress was to completion.

'There you two young people are,' she said. 'You were away so long I thought perhaps you had eloped!'

Alexander's body stiffened beside Rosie. She looked up and could see his lips drawn into a tight grimace.

'No, Mother, you are quite wrong. Yet again.'

'Oh, well, never mind,' the Dowager continued, ignoring the note of censure in Alexander's voice. 'I'm pleased you have had a chance to get better acquainted. Did you enjoy your tour of the grounds, Miss van Haven? I hope Alexander showed you just how beautiful Knightsbrook is—particularly when the trees are in blossom. Although *I* think it's beautiful in every season of the year.'

Rosie smiled politely. Now that the issue of marriage had been settled between her and Alexander there was no need to try and shock the Dowager with her bad behaviour. She could be herself. Well, not quite herself. She still had to be Arabella. But she didn't have to pretend to be a completely unacceptable potential bride who posed a constant threat to priceless heirlooms.

'Oh, yes, he did—and you're right. It is beautiful. I'm sorry we took so long, Your Grace, but Alexander also showed me your family's magnificent collection of paintings in the gallery, and I'm afraid we lost all sense of time.'

The Dowager beamed a delighted smile. 'I see you two have become quite familiar and are on first-name terms already. I'm very happy to hear it.'

Alexander returned his mother's smile with a frown. 'I apologise, Mother, for keeping Miss van Haven from the other guests.' His expressionless voice was a stark contrast to his mother's enthusiasm.

'So, how much of the estate did you get the chance to see, Miss van Haven?' the Dowager asked, drawing Rosie's attention away from the frowning Alexander. 'No doubt Alexander told you we have more than five thousand acres of land and that our gardens are among the finest in England?'

Alexander sighed loudly. 'You're starting to sound like a salesman, Mother.'

'Don't be vulgar, Alexander.' The Dowager's smile faltered slightly, before returning, just as large as before, as she focused her attention back on Rosie. 'I hope he told you that the FitzRoys have lived on this land since the fifteenth century? The house is reputed to be one of the most elegant in the country, with more than two hundred rooms. Not that I've counted them, of course. That includes the summer and winter parlours and two formal dining rooms, as well as the breakfast room, three drawing rooms, the ballroom, and countless bedchambers to accommodate as many guests as you could possibly wish to entertain. Do you like to entertain, Miss van Haven?'

Rosie forced herself not to smile as she watched Alexander roll his eyes. Instead she nodded non-committally.

'And every part of this house is desperately in need of extensive and very expensive renovation work,' he said.

The Dowager's lips drew into a tight line and her nostrils flared. She sent Alexander a quick, narrow-eyed glare then resumed smiling at Rosie. 'And you say that Alexander showed you the gallery? Indeed, it contains many priceless works of art—but it houses only a fraction of the family's collection, which can be found in every room of the house.'

Alexander's frown deepened further. 'And many of those works of art will have to be sold to cover our mounting debts.'

'Oh, Alexander, you can be such a bore sometimes,' the Dowager snapped.

Rosie looked from Alexander to the Dowager and back

again. It was as if she were watching a tennis match, played by two equally determined and equally matched opponents.

The Dowager continued to frown at her son, and then, as if remembering herself, she smiled at Rosie. 'Not that he's a bore, *really*. This is most unlike him. Usually he's not in the least bit serious. Oh, yes, Alexander *loves* to have fun and live life to the full.'

Rosie bit the edge of her top lip to stifle a giggle. The supposedly fun-loving Alexander his mother was describing was as far from the serious, disapproving man standing beside her as it was possible to get.

'Really, Your Grace?' Rosie tried hard not to laugh. 'In that case I look forward to seeing Alexander perform a few party tricks.'

The Dowager flicked a nervous look in Alexander's direction, her smile twitching at the edges. Alexander glared back at her, as if challenging his mother to try and talk her way out of her outrageous claim.

Instead of attempting the impossible, she took Rosie's arm. 'There will be plenty of time for that later, but now our other guests are anxious to meet you.'

They swept their way around the large room and Rosie was introduced to Lord This and Lady That, the Countess of This and the Earl of That. If the assembled guests were anything to go by it seemed the FitzRoys really did mix in exclusive society. There was not a Mr or Mrs among them, with everyone in the room bearing a title from Duke down to Baron.

And each guest, no matter what their title, reacted in exactly the same manner when they were introduced to Rosie—with enthusiastic delight, as if they really were meeting the future Duchess of Knightsbrook. She was greeted with smiles, nods of approval, and even the occasional curtsey from the assembled aristocrats.

It seemed the Dowager was so convinced she was going to marry Alexander that she had all but announced the engagement already.

Alexander was right. The Dowager was a very determined woman. But unfortunately for her she was going to discover that both Rosie and Alexander were equally resolute that they would not be wed.

Their circuit of the large room took them to the last guest, a rather severe elderly woman standing by the fire. The Dowager seemed to hesitate, her smile quivering slightly, before she smiled and made the introductions.

'Lady Beaufort, may I introduce Arabella van Haven? She is our guest from America.'

Lady Beaufort's straight posture grew more rigid and her nose rose higher in the air as she tilted back her head and raked her gaze over Rosie from head to toe, then back again. 'So you're the banker's daughter?'

Rosie's fists clenched at her sides. Since her father had lost all his money through no fault of his own, reducing their family to a state of poverty, Rosie had been forced to endure being snubbed, insulted and belittled by people who had once treated her family with respect.

Through bitter experience she had learnt to let such behaviour wash over her. So she did what she always did in such circumstances: breathed in deeply, forced herself to relax her tensely gripped hands and smiled her sunniest smile.

'That's right. I'm the banker's daughter—Arabella van Haven. How do you do?'

She received the expected glare in return, which only caused Rosie to smile more brightly.

'I hear you're seeking a titled husband?' Lady Beaufort said after a prolonged silence.

Several guests nearby gasped at this blatant breach of the rules of polite conversation, but their shock didn't stop them from leaning forward, eager to hear more of this exchange.

'Oh, come, come, Lady Beaufort,' the Dowager said with a false laugh. 'Miss van Haven is here to enjoy our hospitality. If she and Alexander should happen to fall in love, well...'

'I'm just pleased my dear daughter Lydia is not here to see this shameless behaviour.'

The Dowager's mouth opened and closed as she gasped for something to say.

'And now that I've met the banker's daughter who is trying to buy herself a title I think I'll take my leave.'

Lady Beaufort swept past Rosie, causing her to jump out of her way to avoid getting trampled in her bull-like progress.

But Rosie had failed to notice one of the couples who had moved closer to hear the conversation. She stepped back on to the listening man's foot, causing him to cry out and send his teacup clattering to the ground.

The sound of shattering china brought all conversation to a sudden halt as every head turned in their direction.

'Oh, look what the clumsy little thing has done!' Lady Beaufort said as a young maid scrambled on the floor to retrieve the pieces of broken porcelain. 'It's a shame these Americans don't know how to act in polite society.'

'Lady Beaufort, I think you should leave. Now.'

Rosie heard Alexander's commanding voice behind her.

'Oh, don't worry. I'm leaving. I'm quite particular

about the company I keep. Thank goodness Lydia was saved from seeing this appalling display.'

She gave Rosie another disapproving look and swept out of the room, her exit watched by every one of the assembled guests.

'I think our guests are in need of a drink somewhat stronger than tea,' Alexander announced, and signalled to the servants, who began pouring glasses of port.

Conversation instantly erupted in the room, but it was no longer the murmur of polite chatter. The assembled guests were talking loudly, all at once, and judging from the repeated glances in Rosie's direction they were all speculating on what had just happened.

Alexander leaned down and whispered in her ear. 'Would you like to take some air, Arabella?'

She nodded rapidly. She most certainly did want to escape. The last thing she felt like doing was remaining in the drawing room while a group of gossiping lords and ladies discussed that bizarre outburst.

Rosie had been snubbed by some of New York's finest snobs, and she had smiled through every subtle and not so subtle insult. But she was decidedly shaken by Lady Beaufort's outburst.

Why this woman should hate her was unfathomable. Surely being a banker's daughter was not so shameful? Particularly when that banker was one of America's wealthiest men and therefore, by extension, one of the world's wealthiest men. And why was Lady Beaufort so concerned about her daughter not being exposed to someone like Arabella? And why should she care whether she married Alexander?

This was clearly more than just good old-fashioned snobbery.

Chapter Five

Alexander led Arabella out through the drawing room towards the French doors. Voices fell silent as they passed, and each guest turned and attentively followed their progress as they walked across the room. He'd leave his guests to their gossip and speculation, and he was sure there would be an excessive amount of that. All that was important was to get Arabella away from the wagging tongues.

As he closed the doors behind them every gleeful face turned in their direction, all eyes peering out of the large sash windows with insatiable curiosity.

He exhaled with impatience. No doubt talking about that incident would keep them entertained for many weeks to come. It was a pity they did not have more to occupy their time, but with wealth and a multitude of servants came plenty of free hours to gossip.

For once Alexander was grateful that he had such an enormous task ahead of him in saving the estate.

They walked down some stone stairs and across a gravel pathway to a wooden bench in front of the garden.

Arabella seated herself, then looked back over her shoulder at the house. 'Well, that was certainly strange.'

'Strange' was an understatement. Alexander gazed at her, amazed at her composure. But her lack of distress was neither here nor there. She should not have been exposed to Lady Beaufort's wrath.

Alexander had difficulty understanding why his mother had invited her to an event such as this. It was inevitable that Lady Beaufort would be offended by the possibility of Alexander being betrothed to another woman when he had once been betrothed to Lady Beaufort's daughter.

He could only assume his mother had invited her because Lady Beaufort remained a doyen of society, despite Lydia's fall from grace, and it would be thought a folly to slight her. But whatever his illogical mother had been thinking she had caused upset to Arabella, and that was unacceptable.

The American heiress had done nothing to deserve such treatment. She had been set up for a marriage she didn't want by her father and his mother, and invited into this house under false pretences. And now she had been insulted by one of the guests.

Alexander was unsure why he felt such a strong need to protect her—whether it was just a natural instinct or something stronger. Whatever it was, he did not want her subjected to such outrages again.

'I'm sorry. I hope you are not too distressed by Lady Beaufort's rudeness. Unfortunately she has suffered some major disappointments in her life, and that has turned her into a rather unpleasant woman. But she had no right to take it out on you.'

Arabella shook her head. 'That's usually the way, isn't it? When people are unhappy they tend to lash out. And, no, of course I'm not upset.' She looked over her shoulder at the house. 'I'm a bit confused, but not upset.'

Alexander shook his head, dragged in a long, unsteady breath and tried not to think of what had caused that outburst. He did not want to think of how he had been betrayed by Lydia Beaufort, or of how she had caused him so much pain that he had sworn that he would never allow himself to be hurt like that again.

'Lady Beaufort's daughter Lydia was a lovely young woman and we were betrothed to be married.'

Arabella's eyes grew wide. He obviously had her full attention.

'But you are not any more?' she asked, her voice barely audible.

'No, not any more. Lydia…' He dragged in a deep breath. 'Lydia changed. She did things that caused her to be shunned from society.'

He paused again. Arabella did not need to know the full extent of why Lydia had suffered such a fate. Nor did she need to know how she had almost destroyed him in the process. She merely needed an explanation for Lady Beaufort's outburst.

'Her family is one of the best-connected in England, but even that couldn't save her when she chose to live a life that has shocked many people,' he said, hoping that would suffice.

'And Lady Beaufort blames *you* for this?'

He exhaled a ragged breath and nodded. 'Yes—but she has no right to blame you.'

'I'm sorry, Alexander. Is this something you'd rather not talk about?'

He shook his head. 'It is of no matter,' he said, with as much nonchalance as he could muster. 'I'm used to

being on the receiving end of Lady Beaufort's misdirected rage. But you should never have been subjected to
it, and I am truly sorry. If I had known she would behave
like that towards you I would have insisted my mother
not invite her.'

Arabella shrugged. 'You've got nothing to apologise
for. And I can't really criticise anyone's bad behaviour—
not after my somewhat unconventional arrival. At least
your mother was standing right next to me. She could see
that it wasn't my fault that the teacup was shattered. I
wouldn't want her to think breaking porcelain is my special party trick.' She gave a little laugh and patted him
on the arm. 'Let's just forget about that horrible Lady
Beaufort and pretend it never happened.'

Alexander could hardly believe it. He should be comforting *her*; instead she was patting his arm in a reassur-
ing manner and making light of the incident. She really
was quite remarkable. An experience like that would have
had most woman reaching for the smelling salts, but she
was completely calm. He wondered what had given this
young woman such resilience—something usually lacking in the gently reared women of his class.

'You will not have to worry about her being rude to
you again. After that outburst I will make it clear to her
that she is not welcome in this house.'

'Oh, you don't have to do that. A few insults aren't
going to ruffle me. I'm made of stronger stuff than that
and I have learnt to cope with much worse.'

Alexander looked into her deep blue eyes, curious to
know why a woman who had lived the pampered and
protected life of an heiress would need to be strong. 'And
why is that? Why do you need to be strong, Arabella?'

Once again he saw that sadness come into her eyes,

before she shrugged her shoulders and smiled at him. 'Perhaps it just comes naturally to someone whose grandfather was a mule driver,' she said, in her now familiar flippant tone.

It seemed he was not going to get a serious answer to his question. He was not going to find out why that small shadow of sadness seemed to cloud her otherwise sunny disposition.

'Perhaps you are right. Although I suspect there is more to you than you like to reveal to the world.'

Her cheeks burned a brighter shade of red, and she blinked repeatedly before giving a dismissive laugh. 'No, there's nothing more to reveal. I'm just your average young lady with no hidden depths.'

Her words contradicted her look of discomfort. It was obvious to Alexander that Arabella was anything but average. It was also obvious that she was not going to reveal anything to him. And he ought to leave her with her secrets. After all, what business was it of his?

'Well, no doubt that inner strength is going to be called upon soon, when we have to face the guests again. I'm afraid that after Lady Beaufort's outburst you will undoubtedly be the main topic of conversation for quite some time. You will need to prepare yourself for some curious looks at the very least, and no doubt some very impertinent questioning.'

'Oh, that doesn't worry me.' She looked over her shoulder, back at the house. 'It won't be long before someone else makes an inexcusable faux pas—such as using the wrong knife for the fish course—and then they'll be so scandalised that they'll move on from discussing me to some other unfortunate victim.'

It seemed Arabella had the same low opinion of the ridiculous foibles of the gentry as he did himself.

Growing up, he had spent as much time as he could away from this house. His father's riotous gambling parties had often gone on for weeks at a time, and he and Charlotte had taken refuge in the welcoming cottage of Annie, the wife of a tenant farmer, who worked in dairy. It was during his time with Annie and her husband that he had learnt how hard the tenants worked, tilling the soil and making the money which his father and his friends squandered. In contrast to Annie's warm and welcoming ways, the excesses, rituals and snobbery of his own class had seemed absurd, but it was unusual to meet someone who thought the same way as him.

'You must cause quite a stir amongst New York society with that attitude,' he said.

She shrugged her shoulders and shook her head slightly. 'Well, perhaps—but it's an attitude I tend to keep to myself and only share with my closest friends.'

'Your closest friends? Does that include this man you are in love with? Does he share your irreverent attitude to society?'

Damn. He had vowed to ask her nothing about the man, but the questions had come out before Alexander had realised he was asking. Questions that seemed now to hang in the air between them.

Hadn't he told himself he did not want or need to know anything about the man? And yet at the same time he wanted to know everything there was to know about this man Arabella loved. He wanted to know what she felt for him and how he made her feel. And did this man know the reason for the sadness that cast a shroud over her bright blue eyes?

But why should it matter? She was a woman who was in love with another man, and he was unlikely to see her again after this weekend.

And yet it did matter.

His body tensed as he waited for the answers he both did and did not want to hear.

Chapter Six

Rosie squirmed uncomfortably on the wooden bench. How was she supposed to answer such a question? *Did* she share such thoughts with her non-existent lover? *Would* she share such things with him? Probably. Wasn't that what people in love did? But how was Rosie supposed to know? She had never been in love. Never expected to be in love.

She glanced in Alexander's direction. Yes, she could imagine that a woman who was in love would want to tell her man about herself, about her thoughts, her feelings. They would surely want to share their troubles and offer each other comfort and support. A woman in love with a man would also want to hear *his* thoughts, *his* feelings, and to know everything there was to know about him.

If a woman was in love with a man like Alexander she was sure that was how she would be feeling.

She turned to look straight ahead. But she had never been in love—not with this imaginary man, and certainly not with Alexander.

Rosie started. Where had *that* thought come from? Of

course she wasn't in love with Alexander. The mere idea of it was ludicrous.

She gave a little laugh, and took another quick sideways look in Alexander's direction. He was staring at her, waiting for her to answer. An uncomfortable silence stretched out between them. Her cheeks burned hotter. She had to say something. *Anything.*

'Oh, you know...we talk of this and that. And I suppose he's a bit like me when it comes to not taking things too seriously.'

Would that be enough to satisfy his curiosity?

He looked down at her, then stared out at the garden and clasped his hands tightly together. 'What sort of man is he, this man you are in love with?'

Rosie winced. It seemed Alexander wasn't satisfied with her vague answer, and wasn't going to let the subject drop. She cast another quick look in his direction and wondered why he was so curious about her imaginary beloved. He had reacted so strangely when she had first told him, and now seemed to want to know all about him.

But it didn't matter what *he* was thinking. She needed to concentrate. Needed to answer his question. So, what sort of man would he be, this fictional lover of hers? Rosie had no idea, but she had to say something.

'Oh, you know. He's just a man.'

Alexander turned and looked down at her, his eyebrows knitted together. '"Just a man"? He's the man you say you are in love with—the man you're all but betrothed to—and you dismiss him as "just a man"?'

Why was he interrogating her like this? Was he trying to make her feel uncomfortable? If that was his intention then he was succeeding. But it seemed he was uncomfortable too. He was staring down at her, his jaw tense, his hands tightly clasped together as he waited for her answer.

Could he be jealous?

Rosie shook her head slightly. No, she was being ridiculous. He was curious, that was all, and she should be thinking of an answer to his question—not letting her mind drift off to wistful fantasies.

She shrugged as she struggled to find one. What could she say? Especially as the man wasn't even that. He wasn't *just a man*—he wasn't a man at all. He was a figment of her imagination.

'He must at the very least have a name?'

'Of course he's got a name.' Rosie gave a light, dismissive laugh.

He raised his eyebrows.

A name...a name. What on earth would her beloved be called?

She quickly scanned the garden, looking for inspiration. She focused on a statue of Pan, playing his pipes. Pan? Was that a good name? No. Pan might be suitable for a Greek god, but not for a young man in love with the daughter of an influential New York banker.

She spied a ginger cat, curled up and sleeping at Pan's feet.

'Tom—his name is Tom. Thomas, actually, although I call him Tom...sometimes Tommy.' She all but shouted her answer.

'And does Tom, Thomas, sometimes Tommy, have a surname?'

A surname? Yes, he probably would have a surname. But what could it be?

Her gaze shot to the other sculptures. She was desperate for inspiration. Hercules? No. Neptune? No.

She looked at the garden instead, at the sea of daf-
fodils stretched out in front of them, their yellow heads
bobbing in the slight breeze. Tom Daffodil? No. She took
in the sculpted topiary. Then her frantic gaze shot to the
rose garden, laden with multi-coloured buds, ready to
burst forth. She looked up to the line of rustling oak trees.

Still no name occurred to her.

An elderly man pushing a squeaking wheelbarrow
packed high with weeds and dead branches appeared
from behind the line of oak trees and began walking up
the path, his boots crunching on the gravel.

'Gardener. His name is Thomas Gardener.'

She slumped back on to the bench in relief. Thank
goodness for that. Now he had a name the subject could
be dropped and hopefully never mentioned again.

'Thomas Gardener…' Alexander said slowly, as if considering the name. 'And I take it your father does not approve of this Thomas Gardener? Or he would not have
sent you across the ocean in pursuit of a husband. What
exactly is wrong with him? Why doesn't your father wish
you to marry him?'

Rosie sat up straight. Why, indeed? Why would Mr
van Haven not want a woman who was not his daughter to marry a non-existent man who was named after a
sleeping cat and an elderly man with a wheelbarrow? It
was a difficult question to answer.

'Um…he doesn't approve of him because…' Once
again she looked around the garden for inspiration. 'Because…' The garden refused to reveal a suitable reason.

She turned to the house and quickly scanned up and
down its four-storey exterior. She spotted the balconies
on the second floor, and the last play she had seen before
sailing for England jumped to mind.

'Because he's the son of my father's sworn enemy, who is the head of a rival New York banking family.'

It was a bit melodramatic, but it would have to do. Normally Rosie prided herself on being able to think under pressure, but the pressure she was feeling now was far greater than any she had felt before. It was as if all Alexander had to do was raise a questioning eyebrow and she lost all ability to think clearly.

'Oh, so you're like Romeo and Juliet? A couple of young star-crossed lovers whose fathers will never countenance the marriage?' His words dripped with derision.

Rosie pulled at her collar, which seemed to be getting tighter and tighter as she dug herself deeper and deeper into a pit of lies.

She stared straight ahead, hoping his disparaging comment hadn't been made because he had seen her staring at the balcony and made the connection with Shakespeare's famous romantic tragedy.

'Well, not really.' She gave a light laugh, which she hoped didn't sound as false to Alexander as it did to her. 'It's not quite so romantic. After all, they're boring bankers and we're not living in Verona.'

'And is it because of your father's disapproval of this Thomas Gardener's family that he sent you to England? Is that why he's trying to marry you off to someone else?'

'That…and because he wants his daughter to have a title; he wants her to be a duchess.'

Rosie smiled. Didn't it feel good to finally be saying something that was true? Well, almost true. Mr van Haven didn't care a fig whether Rosie married or not, but he most certainly wanted *Arabella* married, and married to a man with a title—the higher up the social strata the better. A daughter with a title would place him well above the rest of the New York elite—not just in money, but also in social status.

'So it seems your father is going to be disappointed?'

'Mmm, I suppose he will…'

In more ways than one—especially when he finds out that Arabella has not only refused to give up her aspirations of becoming an actress, but has arrived in England with the intention of pursuing a career on the London stage.

But that was a problem they would deal with at a later date.

'What about you, Alexander? Why don't *you* want to marry?'

Rosie tried to keep her question flippant. After all, she had merely asked the question to save her from telling more lies. Hadn't she?

If Alexander wanted to marry someone else that would mean Arabella was most definitely safe from an unwanted marriage. But the thought of Alexander in love with another woman, wanting to marry another woman, was doing strange things to her nervous system. Her stomach had clenched itself into a tight knot. Her breath was caught in her throat. And an odd light-headedness was making her dizzy.

It was so *wrong* for her to be feeling like this. What was causing her such pain? Could it be jealousy? Ridiculous. How could she feel jealous over a man she couldn't have? Or be jealous of a woman he might or might not be in love with, who might or might not exist?

No, it couldn't be jealousy. That was too ridiculous. But whatever it was she had to stop feeling like this. She had to stop it *now*.

'I have more important things to occupy my time. I

have an estate to save,' he finally answered, his words brusque.

Rosie tilted her head slightly and cast him a sideways glance. His answer was curious. He claimed to abhor lying and yet his words had been so terse. That, along with his clenched jaw and pressed lips, suggested he was not telling the entire truth.

Rosie knew she should just leave it there. What did it matter why he didn't want to marry? The fact that he didn't want to marry Arabella should be enough. But, like an open wound she couldn't stop prodding, she felt incapable of leaving the subject alone.

'Can't you save the estate and be married at the same time? They're not mutually exclusive activities.'

'My father has left substantial debts,' he said, his brow furrowed, his jaw tightly held. 'I would rather wait until I've cleared all those debts and the estate is once again capable of supporting the family. Then I would have something to offer a wife.'

Rosie was tempted to tell him he already had a lot to offer any woman. He was handsome, charming, kind and loyal. In every aspect he was the perfect man, and it was unlikely that she was the only woman to realise that.

'Surely that wouldn't matter if you met the right woman?' she said quietly.

Alexander made no response and Rosie mentally chastised herself. She had to stop asking these questions—especially as every question and every answer was causing that knot in her stomach to tighten another notch.

She took in a few deep breaths to try and loosen its grip and reminded herself that it didn't matter whether Alexander met any woman, the right one or not. It was none of her concern whether he wanted to marry, as long as he didn't want to marry Arabella. If he wanted to wait until he had saved the estate and restored the family's fortune then all the better. That meant it would be a long time before he considered taking a wife, and by then she and Arabella would be gone.

'Not all women think like that, Arabella—and certainly not aristocratic women,' he said finally. 'They and their families want a marriage that not only improves their position in society but also guarantees they will continue to live in the manner to which they are accustomed. My title is attractive on its own merits, but I am a long way from being able to guarantee the second. And I won't consider marriage until I can provide sufficiently for my wife.'

Rosie looked out at the expansive gardens and parklands, then back at the sweeping four-storey house behind her, with, as the Dowager had claimed, at least two hundred rooms, many of which contained priceless art works and treasures.

'And this wouldn't be enough?' she murmured in disbelief.

'No—a bankrupt estate with ever-mounting debts would *not* be enough. A backward estate that has not been managed properly for generations would not be enough. It needs to change. It needs to be modernised. Perhaps when that has been achieved I'll have the luxury of thinking about such things as marriage.'

'The right woman wouldn't care about any of that,' she said quietly. 'The right woman would want to work *with* you to make the estate viable. She would want to make your load lighter, not expect you to do all the work on your own and then hand it to her on a silver platter.'

He looked down at her and gazed deep into her eyes,

as if trying to read her thoughts. 'Not all women are like you, Arabella,' he murmured.

Rosie swallowed away her embarrassment. No, not all women *were* like her. They didn't all lie. They didn't all pretend to be someone else. They didn't all tell tall tales about imaginary men and fake betrothals. And surely most women would be sensible enough to stop talking about something that made them feel so intensely uncomfortable? But then, as he'd said, Rosie was not like most women.

'You deserve to meet the right woman, Alexander. A woman who wants to marry *you*—not your title or your money, but *you*.'

There was so much more to Alexander than his title and his estate, and surely Rosie would not be the only woman to see this?

He gave a small, humourless laugh.

'You should marry a woman who wants to work with you to achieve your dreams,' she went on.

If Rosie had been in love with Alexander, and if he had been in love with her, that was what she would want. Not that there was any possibility of either of those laughable things ever happening.

He continued to gaze down at her, his deep brown eyes burning into hers. 'Thomas Gardener is a lucky man to have a fiancée who believes in supporting her future husband the way you do.'

His words were kind, but his captivating eyes contained an intensity that caused heat to burn through her body.

She swallowed, looked away, and fought to compose herself. *And the woman who eventually becomes the*

Duchess of Knightsbrook is even luckier, she wanted to say, but knew she never would.

They sat in silence for a few moments, seemingly both absorbed in their own thoughts.

Rosie wondered what was going through Alexander's mind. Surely his thoughts couldn't be as confused as hers? *Nobody's* thoughts could be as confused hers.

It wasn't supposed to be like this. The plan had been so simple. But then, when she had come up with this plan over tea at the Ritz, she hadn't expected the Duke to be anything like Alexander. She hadn't expected him to be handsome. Nor had she expected him to be a proud, honest man who was determined to solve his financial problems without resorting to marrying for money.

And she hadn't expected him to make her feel things she should not be feeling—emotions she could hardly understand, even less put names to.

If only he had been a stuffy duke, set on marrying Arabella for her money, then she would have been in her element. She would have had enormous fun at his expense. Instead she was unsure what she was supposed to do, how she was supposed to behave, how she was even supposed to feel.

All she knew was that she shouldn't be feeling the way she was now.

The discreet cough of a footman broke the silence. 'Her Grace wishes to make you aware that it is time you dressed for dinner,' he said, and bowed then left.

'It looks as if we are going to have to face the gossips,' Alexander said, standing and taking Rosie's hand. 'As uncomfortable as this might be, as you are the guest of honour I fear it would be cause more of a stir for you not to appear at tonight's dinner. But of course if you'd rather not then I will tell my mother that you are indisposed.'

Rosie rose from the bench. She doubted his guests could make her feel any more uncomfortable than she did right now. 'No, it's of no mind. They can gossip about me as much as they like. I'm happy to be their source of entertainment.'

They retraced their steps up the path to the stairs.

'At least you won't have to worry about my mother matchmaking. You'll be saved that annoyance. When I tell her about Thomas Gardener even she will have to back down.'

Rosie halted. 'No, please don't do that,' she blurted out, gripping his arm with both hands. She could not have anyone else knowing about Arabella's non-existent beloved. If news of it got back to Mr van Haven it would cause huge problems for Arabella, and Rosie would never allow that to happen.

He raised a questioning eyebrow.

'If it got back to my father…' Rosie said desperately.

Alexander gently patted her hand. 'I understand, Arabella. If you want to keep your Mr Gardener a secret, it will not be revealed by me.'

A mixture of relief and shame swept over Rosie. Relief that she would not be causing any problems for Arabella, and shame that once again she had lied to an honourable man who deserved better.

But what else could she do? It seemed she was trapped inside a complicated story of her own invention—a story she seemed to make more complex every time she spoke.

'Thank you,' she mumbled, releasing her grip on his arm, and hoping she had told her last lie to Alexander.

Chapter Seven

'So, what's the gossip below-stairs?' Rosie sat on the embroidered stool in front of the mirror and looked up at Nellie's reflection.

It was a relief to be in the company of someone who knew who she really was. She could relax, because she didn't have to be constantly on her guard in case she said or did anything that would give her away.

She waited in expectation. Rosie knew that the best way to find out about anything that was happening was through the servants. Their outward appearance remained impassive as they went about their duties, but they saw and heard everything.

Nellie picked up a brush and ran long strokes through Rosie's hair in preparation for curling, braiding and threading it with ribbons, so it would look stylish for tonight's dinner.

More a friend than a servant, Nellie had been with the van Haven family since she'd emigrated to America from Ireland when she was fourteen years old and had been hired as a scullery maid. Intelligent and talented, she'd quickly risen through the ranks to become a lady's maid.

Arabella was very much aware of just how lucky she was to have Nellie, and her abilities as a hairstylist had seen many of the New York society ladies try to lure her away—but to no avail. And Rosie knew that Nellie harboured ambitions that didn't involve spending the rest of her life as a servant.

'Well, the servants are all atwitter about you, so they are.' Nellie frowned as she teased out a knot in Rosie's hair. 'They're all in agreement that you'll make an excellent duchess. Even the ones who thought it wasn't appropriate to have an American have come around.'

'Except I'm Rosie. Remember? And the real Arabella doesn't want to be a duchess. That's why I'm here.'

Nellie shrugged, divided Rosie's hair into several sections and began rolling one of the long tresses. 'Of course I remember. I'm just repeating what the servants said. And they're all in agreement that they're looking forward to having you as their new mistress.'

'Well, it's good that it's not up to the servants to decide who the Duke is to marry, or they'd have me up the aisle in no time at all. Fortunately the Duke himself isn't the slightest bit interested in marrying me.'

Nellie stopped what she was doing and stared at Rosie's reflection. 'That's not what I heard.'

'Why? What did you hear?' Rosie turned on the stool to face Nellie, who frowned, placed her hands firmly on Rosie's shoulders and turned her back towards the mirror.

She picked up the fallen tress of hair and resumed rolling. 'They all think the Duke is completely smitten with you.'

'They *what*?' Rosie started to turn again, then saw Nellie's frown and remained facing forward. 'They think *what*? No, they're wrong. He's not interested in me in any way whatsoever.'

'Well, all the servants who were in the drawing room when you were being introduced to the other guests said he couldn't take his eyes off you. That he was watching you the whole time. And when that horrible Lady Beaufort had her outburst he was at your side immediately, being all protective, like.'

'He was?' Rosie tilted her head, only to have it straightened by Nellie. 'Well, I'm sure it means nothing. He was just being a gentleman.'

'Hmm…' Nellie said, her mouth full of hairpins and her hands occupied with threading silver ribbon through Rosie's hair. She stood back and admired her handiwork. 'And the footman said he hadn't seen His Grace so taken with a young lady since Lydia Beaufort.'

Rosie's gaze shot up to Nellie's reflection. 'What did they say about Lydia Beaufort?

Nellie frowned and put to rights a silver ribbon that Rosie's sudden movement had dislodged. 'I don't know. All I know is when her name was mentioned all the servants looked very serious—as if the footman had mentioned a forbidden topic. But Jennie, the parlour maid, said she thought you were prettier than Lydia anyway, and much nicer. Before she was shushed by the housekeeper.'

'Oh, she did, did she? She said I was prettier?' Rosie patted the side of her hair and tilted her head slightly to admire her reflection. 'Well, that's something, I suppose. So was there any other gossip?'

'No, but Jennie said that she thought you were smitten too. In fact, she said she'd never seen anyone look so dewy-eyed.'

Rosie looked up at Nellie's laughing reflection, then

back at her own blushing face. 'Dewy-eyed? Me? Non-sense.'

'Hmm...'

'There's no "hmm" about it. Stop staring at me like that and help me into my dress.'

Flustered, Rosie rushed over to the wardrobe, removed the gown from the hanger and began pulling it over her head.

'Stop doing that. You'll ruin your hair. And I think you're going to be needing this first.'

Rosie turned and saw Nellie holding up her corset. She exhaled loudly, handed the dress to Nellie and waited while she wrapped the corset around her waist, tied the laces tight and helped her into her bustle.

'Um...there's something I probably should tell you...' Rosie said, her cheeks still burning.

Nellie stopped brushing down the cambric fabric of Rosie's petticoat and waited.

'The Duke believes we're not going to be married be-cause Arabella is in love with another man.'

Nellie's eyes grew wide. 'She's *what*? When did this happen? Arabella never told me she was in love.'

'She's not really, but I had to make something up to explain why Arabella wouldn't be marrying the Duke. So I said that I am—or she is, really—in love with a man called Thomas Gardener, who is the son of Mr van Ha-ven's arch enemy from a rival banking family.'

'Oh, Rosie, no—you didn't!' Nellie released a frus-trated sigh. 'You always complicate things. You come up with a plan which seems to be simple and then you go and make it complicated. It was just the same when you and Arabella snuck off to the fair dressed as boys, so you could get work on the sideshows. You almost got away with it until you told the sideshow owner you had just returned from the sea, danced that silly jig and your hat fell off—revealing your hair. He nearly hog-tied the pair of you. And then there was that time you tried to trick your tutor by...'

Rosie held up her hands to stop the criticism. 'This is nothing like that. I was put on the spot. I had to come up with *something*.'

'Couldn't you just have said that you want to remain single and have no interest in marrying anyone? Why did you have to invent this Thomas Gardener? And why make him Mr van Haven's arch enemy? Did you *have* to get so overly dramatic?'

Rosie shrugged. 'I was flustered. But what's done is done. Anyway, it's supposed to be a secret. I've asked Alexander not to tell anyone. I just thought I'd tell you in case one of the servants finds out. I didn't want you to be taken by surprise.'

'Hmm...' Nellie frowned in disapproval as she lowered the dress carefully over Rosie's head and began doing up a row of buttons at the back.

'So, what else did the servants say about Lady Beaufort's outburst?' Rosie asked, changing the subject away from her blunder.

'Well, not much. Jennie was annoyed that she had to scramble around her feet to retrieve all those tiny pieces of shattered porcelain, and the housekeeper was worried about the damage the tea had done to the rug, but that was about it.'

Rosie shook her head in disbelief. 'What? No one thought it was odd? No one had any comments or opinions?'

'Apparently she's been a bit odd since Lydia got into

some sort of trouble. The servants all wonder why the
Dowager continues to invite her, but she's fabulously
wealthy, so I suppose everything else gets forgiven.'

'What sort of trouble did Lydia get into?'

Nellie shrugged, scanned Rosie's appearance, nodded
her approval, then turned Rosie around to face the mirror.

When Rosie saw her reflection all questions died on
her lips. She could hardly believe what she was seeing.
Arabella's evening gown was so flattering on her, with
its pinched-in waist, sleeveless top and low-cut neckline.
Rosie had never looked more beautiful.

She gave a small twirl and watched the gorgeous silver
material spread out around her, its embroidered threads
shimmering as they caught the light. She stopped and
smiled at her reflection, gently touching the side of her
head.

Nellie definitely had a magic touch when it came to
hairstyles. She turned her head from side to side and admired the transformation. It was easy to see why so many
of the New York society ladies were determined to lure
Nellie away from Arabella.

She looked down at the beautiful gown, still smiling, then a shadow of doubt crossed her mind and she
frowned slightly.

'Do you think I'm perhaps showing a bit too much
flesh?' She pulled up the plunging neck of the gown,
only to have her hand swatted away by Nellie.

'Nonsense. It looks wonderful. And it took me hours
to iron all that material, so we're not changing now.'

'Has anyone ever told you you're a very impertinent
maid.'

'Yes, Arabella has, many times. And I take as much

notice of her as I do of you. Now, m'lady, shall we put on a bit of rouge?'

Rosie batted at Nellie's arm with her gloves. 'Less of the "m'lady", thank you. And, no, I don't want any rouge.'

Rosie had blushed more since she had arrived at Knightsbrook than she had in the rest of her twenty years combined. The last thing she needed was any help to make her cheeks even redder.

'In that case I think you're done. I've been told my services as your chaperon won't be required tonight. So off you go.'

'Mmm...' Rosie replied absentmindedly, still admiring her dress and her exquisite hairstyle. 'So what will you be doing to occupy yourself? Flirting with the footman or flirting with the coachman?'

'There won't be no flirting,' Nellie said, handing Rosie her fan. 'I went exploring the house while you were wandering round the garden, and I discovered the most wonderful library. I wouldn't want all those books to go to waste, would I? Plus, the Duke's valet is a bit of a bookworm himself, so he might be hiding out there tonight.'

Rosie smiled. 'So you'll be indulging in your two favourite pastimes? Flirting and reading.'

Nellie spent all her free hours back in New York in Mr van Haven's library—which was more than Mr van Haven himself did. He had bought the books in a mortgage sale because he had heard that a gentleman always had a library, but he'd never had any intention of actually reading any of them himself. He took as dim a view of reading as he did of all other art forms.

'Well, they're a bit difficult to do at the same time, but I'll try my best. After all, a bit of harmless flirting never hurt anyone,' Nellie said. 'And I imagine you'll be doing a bit of flirting yourself tonight.'

'Of course I won't. I don't flirt. I *never* flirt.'

That was she had never flirted before—had never wanted to. But then she had never met a man like Alexander before. Suddenly she could see the attraction of fluttering the occasional eyelash or doing a bit of pouting.

Soon she'd be seeing him again, and she'd be attired in a dress just made for flirting…

Soon she'd be seeing him again.

The thought hit her like a thunderbolt. Her stomach turned a series of somersaults and her chest constricted as if Nellie had tied her bodice laces too tight.

She wanted to see Alexander again, but felt ridiculously jittery at the prospect. This was not how she should be feeling. She wasn't here to flirt with the Duke. She wasn't supposed to have any feelings whatsoever for the Duke. She was here to make sure he had no interest in marrying Arabella, and she'd already achieved that. Now she just had to get these foolish emotions under control. Emotions she should not be feeling.

But how was she supposed to tell her heart to stop beating so fast? To stop her stomach from jumping every time his name was mentioned?

Rosie breathed deeply, her hand on her stomach in an attempt to calm her riotous body. Her body was refusing to listen to reason.

Alexander FitzRoy, Duke of Knightsbrook, was not for her, she reminded her foolishly pounding heart. He didn't want to marry Arabella, the daughter of a fabulously wealthy man. He didn't want to marry Lydia, who was from a well-connected wealthy family. Under normal circumstances he wouldn't even *look* at someone like Rosie.

So just settle down, she ordered her jittering nerves. A command her nerves chose to ignore.

'Well, stop staring at yourself,' Nellie said. 'Go on, then. Get moving. You're the guest of honour—they'll all be waiting for you.' Nellie gave her a gentle nudge towards the door.

'Oh, well, here goes nothing,' Rosie said, adopting her bravest demeanour.

She took hold of the door handle, then stopped, as if incapable of turning it. This was not like her. She gripped the door handle more tightly. This was ridiculous, she admonished herself. She had no reason to feel nervous. It was all settled. She would not be marrying the Duke. He didn't want to marry her. She didn't want to marry him. There was nothing to worry about. All she had to do was enjoy a lavish dinner at a beautiful country estate. Perfect.

So why was she finding it so hard to actually leave her room?

'Go on—away with you,' Nellie said, removing her hand and turning the handle for Rosie. 'And mind you be careful. Don't complicate things even further by doing something stupid and going and falling in love with the Duke.'

Rosie rolled her eyes. 'As if I would.'

She left the room and headed down the corridor, with Nellie's words still ringing in her ears like an ominous warning bell.

Chapter Eight

'You can stop staring at the door, Alexander,' the Dowager Duchess said, and gave a little laugh. 'Your future fiancée will be here soon.'

Alexander sighed with exasperation. 'I'm not staring at the door, Mother.' He turned from the door and surveyed the other guests having pre-dinner drinks in the drawing room. 'And do I really need to repeat myself? We will not be getting married.'

'You can try and fool yourself, Alexander, but you can't fool your mother.'

'Arabella and I are in complete agreement: I do not want to get married and she does not want to marry me. The only person who wants this match is you, Mother.'

'Me, her father and your heart, Alexander.' She laughed and patted him lightly on the arm with her folded-up fan. 'I've seen the way you look at her. I've seen the way she looks at you. It's as if wedding bells start to chime every time you make eye contact.'

Alexander gave his mother a long, considered look. Such lyrical descriptions were not like her. It seemed the thought of getting hold of Arabella van Haven's generous dowry was making her poetic.

The door opened. Alexander and his mother turned to see who was being announced. A sense of disappointment swept through him as one of his mother's elderly friends entered the room.

Quashing down that ridiculous reaction, he turned to face his mother. 'Despite the noises you're hearing in your fevered imagination, we are *not* getting married, so let that be an end to it.'

'We'll see, Alexander. I'm sure before this weekend is over we will be announcing your engagement.'

'Mother, there will be no such announcement. You can put that idea right out of—'

He was interrupted by the footman announcing Miss van Haven's arrival.

Alexander turned and saw Arabella standing in the doorway. She looked stunning. And stunned was exactly how he felt. Her day dress had covered her from her neck to her toes, but in her evening gown he was treated to the sight of the creamy skin of her neck, her arms and a tempting décolletage. Her hair was no longer covered by a hat, and he could see it was not raven-black as he had first thought, but had copper threads running through it, which glimmered as they caught the light.

He swallowed to try and relieve his suddenly dry throat and could almost hear those bells his mother had alluded to. He shook his head to chase away such fanciful ideas.

Pull yourself together, man.

She looked in his direction and gave him a small, shy smile. At least it appeared to be a shy smile. Alexander wondered if he had been mistaken. A shy smile was not what he would expect from a young woman as confident as Arabella. Nothing about her suggested shyness. And yet she was still standing in the doorway, still looking in his direction from under lowered lashes, still with that small smile on her lips.

Perhaps the events of this afternoon had unnerved her after all. She had disguised her discomfiture at Lady Beaufort's outburst well, but perhaps she had not been unaffected. And now she had to face a room full of strangers—strangers who no doubt had been gossiping about her all afternoon.

No wonder she looked uncomfortable, and he was a fool to think it had anything to do with him.

Alexander stepped towards Arabella, but was stopped by his mother's hand firmly grasping his arm. 'Don't look so anxious, Alexander, or so desperate. I shall look after our guest.'

'I am neither anxious nor desperate, Mother. I merely intend to be polite.'

'Yes, Alexander, I'm sure that's all it is. Well, go and "be polite" to some of our other guests. I want to talk to my future daughter-in-law.'

'She's not—'

His mother walked away and joined Arabella at the doorway, placed her arm through hers and began leading her around the room, so she could exchange a few polite words with each of her fellow guests.

Arabella appeared to be chatting politely, and his fears that she was nervous about how the other guests would receive her following Lady Beaufort's scene abated. She looked completely unfazed as she walked around the room, confidently and majestically.

If things had been different she would indeed have made an excellent duchess and would have done the family name credit.

Shocked by that ridiculous thought Alexander headed for the sideboard, poured himself a brandy and knocked it back.

He looked over at Arabella again. She looked in his direction and once again sent him a small, seemingly shy smile, contradicting her otherwise confident manner. He refused to read anything into those smiles. He was the only person she knew. Of course she would be smiling at him. And if Thomas Gardener was here, no doubt her smiles would all be reserved exclusively for that man.

Alexander knocked back a second brandy and leant against the sideboard, determined not to speculate on what this Thomas Gardener might be like. Arabella had said he was "just a man"—but he was a man with whom she was in love. That made him a lot more than *just a man.*

He poured yet another brandy and swirled the rich brown liquid around the bottom of the glass balloon. No, he would *not* speculate about him. He placed the glass back on the sideboard with a decisive clink. Nor would he think about those shy smiles that Arabella was sending in his direction.

His mother had led Arabella to the corner where Charlotte was standing, her face a blank expression of boredom. She was pretending—not too convincingly—to listen to Lady Richmond, Dowager Duchess of Pemborne, who was no doubt retelling the story of her daughter's success during last year's season. Charlotte found their mother's parties even more dreary than he did, and he felt for his sister, who had fewer opportunities than he to escape the stultifying atmosphere.

The two young women bobbed curtseys and then Arabella took Charlotte's arm, leading her to a seat by the fire. Whatever she was saying to Charlotte, it was eliciting some surprising reactions from his usually serious sister. Charlotte's eyes grew wide. She bit her lip and then smiled slightly, as if she were doing something almost sinful.

As Arabella continued to talk Charlotte's smile grew wider, less guarded, and then she covered her mouth and laughed. Then, much to Alexander's amazement, she began talking animatedly, gesticulating wildly with her arms. When Charlotte finished what she was saying the two women laughed loudly, causing heads to turn in their direction. Remarkable.

'Damn fine woman you've got there.'

Alexander hadn't realised that Lord Darby was standing beside him.

'Yes, indeed,' he answered, before fully taking in what Darby had said. Arabella was *not* his woman.

'And I hear she's an heiress to boot. Capital. You can't go wrong with beauty and money.' The man gave a small chuckle and helped himself to a large brandy.

Alexander felt his nostrils flare as he fought to stifle his rising anger. Wasn't this exactly what he'd expected when his mother had suggested he marry an American heiress? That everyone would assume the marriage was a way for the FitzRoys to save their estate? That they had found an easy and convenient way to get out of debt?

'I have no interest in Arabella van Haven's fortune,' Alexander said through gritted teeth.

'Of course you don't, old boy. Marry for love…that's the ticket.' His Lordship winked as if they were sharing a private joke, slapped him on the back, and, smiling, walked off drinking his brandy.

Alexander looked over at Arabella. That was what everyone would think if he did marry Arabella. That he had married her for her dowry. The proud name Knightsbrook, which had been so tarnished by his father and his grandfather, would be further sullied. And that was something he would not do. He wanted to restore the name— not degrade it further.

It was good that Arabella was not interested in marriage to him. It was good that she was in love with another man—this Thomas Gardener. It made things simple. They would not be marrying. And that meant there was no need for him to get annoyed by comments made by men like Lord Darby.

But Lord Darby was certainly right about one thing. Arabella was most definitely a beautiful woman. She had an enchanting natural grace and ease of manner. And he had never met a woman who enjoyed herself so much. Her joyfulness seemed to infect everyone she met.

When was the last time he had seen Charlotte laugh and look so relaxed? It was hard to remember. And she certainly never laughed at a party hosted by his mother. A scowl or a look of resigned boredom were her more common expressions. Yet here she was, talking and laughing with Arabella as if they were already the best of friends. Yes, she was a beautiful woman, with a rare beauty that went beyond her pretty face.

The gong rang for dinner and Alexander strode over to the fireplace. 'May I accompany the two most attractive women in the room in to dinner?'

Charlotte smiled and stood up, but before she could take his arm Nicholas Sinclair, Lord Richmond, the errant son of his mother's best friend, was at Charlotte's side, bowing and offering his arm.

Nicholas had recently inherited the title Duke of Pemborne and his own vast estate, but the responsibility had done nothing to subdue his intemperate behaviour.

Charlotte stared up at Nicholas and could not suppress her look of disapproval, but good manners prevailed and with a resigned sigh she took his arm. Alexander had no doubt that Charlotte would have no interest in such a man—one whose reputation as an idle rake was as legendary as Charlotte's for being sensible and serious.

Arabella placed her hand lightly on his arm. 'It looks like Charlotte has made a conquest.'

Alexander scowled as Charlotte and Nicholas walked away together. 'I very much doubt if Charlotte would want to conquer a reprobate like him.' He made no attempt to keep his voice low, not caring whether Nicholas heard his low opinion or not.

They joined the procession into the dining room.

'You and Charlotte seemed to be enjoying yourself,' Alexander said, curious to know how she had managed to get Charlotte to laugh so freely.

'Your sister has a delightfully dry sense of humour.'

Alexander looked down at Arabella. He had heard many characteristics attributed to his sister—compassion for the less fortunate, a studious nature and a quick intelligence. But a sense of humour, dry or otherwise…? No, he hadn't heard that before.

'What were you two talking about?'

Arabella gave a tinkling laugh. 'Don't worry—we weren't talking about you.'

They arrived at their assigned places and the footmen pulled out their chairs.

'We were talking about the season and the extremes

mothers go to in finding suitable husbands for their daughters.'

Alexander nodded, surprised that his sister should find anything in that banal tradition to laugh at. 'For Charlotte the season is something to be endured, not enjoyed. Mother has had to drag her kicking and screaming to the few balls she's attended this season, and I doubt if she'll attend any more.'

'Maybe she won't have to. His Grace seems quite taken with her.'

Alexander looked down the table to where Nicholas was sitting next to his sister, whose stern countenance and stiff posture did not support Arabella's assumption. 'I think a snowball has more chance in hell than Nicholas, Lord Richmond, has of wooing my sister. A more unlikely beau I can hardly imagine.'

'Hmm… I guess we'll have to wait and see.'

He looked at Arabella, who was wearing a knowing smile. He had no desire to inform her again that she was completely wrong. He knew his sister well. She most certainly would not be interested in a notorious rake like the new Lord Richmond. They might have been friends once, but that had been a long time ago. They had since grown into adults who could not be more different.

And why should it matter to Arabella anyway?

He took hold of his napkin before the footman could reach it, shook it vigorously and placed it on his lap. In the highly unlikely event that something should develop between Charlotte and Nicholas, Arabella would be long gone. Out of their lives and back to New York—back to Thomas Gardener.

Chapter Nine

Rosie looked down the table at Charlotte and smiled to herself. Alexander's sister was trying hard to act as if she wasn't interested in Nicholas, Lord Richmond, but nothing could disguise the flush on her cheeks or the quick, shy glances she kept flicking in his direction. They were obvious signs that she was interested. More than interested. She was attracted to her dashing companion.

Rosie touched her own warm cheeks. That was due to the heat coming from the many candles in the silver candelabra that adorned the centre of the dining table. It had nothing to do with Alexander. Nothing at all. And it certainly had nothing to do with what Nellie had said about the way she and Alexander had been looking at each other. Dewy-eyed, indeed.

She did not get dewy-eyed. Had never got dewy-eyed over any man. And she was certainly not going to get dewy-eyed over a man she couldn't have.

Rosie blinked several times to make sure her eyes were completely free of all dew.

At least one body part wasn't reacting inappropriately to Alexander sitting beside her. The same could not be said of her skin, her heart, her stomach… And her toes seemed to have curled themselves inside her silk evening slippers. And the least said about the strange tightening that was happening in her lower regions the better.

'You're very quiet, Arabella. That's not like you,' Alexander said as a footman began ladling soup out of silver tureens into porcelain bowls. 'What are you thinking about?'

Rosie blinked again, rapidly, and her mind went blank. She could hardly answer his question truthfully. She couldn't tell him she was taking an inventory of her various body parts, all of which were reacting in such a peculiar and disturbing way to being in such close proximity to him.

'Um…oh, nothing, really. I was just thinking how lovely the table setting is and how beautiful the women look in the candlelight.' Rosie released her breath, pleased that she hadn't blurted out something completely inappropriate.

The table did look wonderful, with an artful centrepiece of delightfully scented flowers, crystal glasses and silverware reflecting the candlelight, and the gilt mirrors adorning the walls shone with light to give a sense of intimacy. And the women seated around the long oval table, dressed in the lastest fashions, added to the sense of opulence. Their wealth was displayed in the diamonds, rubies, emeralds and other precious jewels that adorned their necks, wrists, ears and hands.

'None looks as lovely as you, Arabella. You look beautiful tonight. That colour suits you.'

Rosie's heart seemed to stop beating, and her breath caught in her throat as she took in the implication of what he had just said.

Beautiful...he thinks I'm beautiful.

An explosion of intense heat suddenly rushed to her face. Her stilled heartbeat sprang back to life, hammering furiously within her chest. A tingling pleasure coursed through her body and she smiled with unbridled joy. She did indeed feel beautiful. Nellie had worked magic on her hair, and Arabella's dress, with its cinched waist and plunging neckline, was designed to flatter her figure.

Tonight she felt every inch the society lady—almost as if this was where she belonged.

She had once lived a privileged existence. As a child she'd had expensive clothes, a room full of toys, and had been indulged by a loving mother and father. She had thought her life would always be like that. But then everything had changed. Her father had lost all his money. Her lovely mother had been reduced to working as a governess, and Rosie had become dependent on the reluctant charity of Mr van Haven and the kindness of Arabella.

Arabella did her best to ensure she never felt as if she was anything less than her equal, but her lack of money and security was something Rosie was always aware of.

However, tonight she was like Cinderella at the ball, seated next to her handsome prince, and it felt wonderful.

And, more than that, Alexander had noticed her appearance. He was still noticing—still looking at her—and under his gaze she felt as if she had dressed exclusively for him, so he would look at her, admire her, even desire her.

Alexander looked every bit the dashing Duke, dressed in a black dinner jacket, with a crisp white shirt and tie contrasting with his olive skin. Every man at the table was similarly attired, but Alexander wore it so much better. But then, a Greek athlete would, wouldn't he?

Rosie breathed in deeply, then exhaled slowly through pursed lips. 'Thank you, Alexander,' she murmured, feeling strangely tongue-tied as once again she reminded herself not to think of those naked Greek statues.

When he gazed back at her with those dark brown eyes her cheeks burned even hotter, her heartbeat pounded faster and her breath came in quicker and shallower gasps. Rosie was sure if her cheeks got any hotter she would ignite the table setting. She had to get herself under control.

Stop it...stop it right now, she admonished her traitorous body. A polite compliment should not make her feel this way. It should not cause her face to burn, and her skin to tingle as if it was being lightly caressed, or that disconcerting tightening between her thighs.

She moved slightly on her chair to try and release the tension that was gripping her, then coughed, pulled off her gloves and laid them beside her plate. She picked up a silver spoon and took a tentative sip of her mock turtle soup.

These strange reactions had to stop. Right now. It did not matter whether Alexander thought she looked beautiful or not. She looked the part. That was all that was important. She was fitting in with the elegant women at the table. Whether or not she looked beautiful to Alexander was of no matter.

She paused, her spoon halfway to her mouth. But he *did* think she was beautiful. A man like Alexander Fitz-Roy, Lord Ashton, Duke of Knightsbrook, thought she was beautiful.

No man had ever said that to her. Usually men didn't even look at her. On the odd occasion when she was allowed to appear at one of Mr van Haven's gatherings it was always made obvious that she was just the ward, a woman of no account, and all the men present treated her as such. She had never felt beautiful before.

Rosie sipped her soup although she tasted nothing, her mind awhirl, her body agitated.

She was being ridiculous—she had to get herself under control. So he'd called her beautiful? It meant nothing. In two days she would be back in London and this would all be over. She would not be marrying a handsome duke. The only reason she was seated at this table was because the Dowager Duchess thought she was an heiress and a good catch for her son—which she most decidedly was not.

'So, have you told your mother yet that we will not be getting married?' Rosie asked, reminding herself of her reason for being at this dinner table as much as asking a question.

'Repeatedly. But, as I've said, she's a very determined woman.

'Perhaps I need to start misbehaving again so she realises just how inappropriate a duchess I would make?'

Alexander looked at her over his wine glass and sent her a smile. And, oh, what a smile. It lit up his face and made those dark brown eyes shine with warmth. Warmth that sent shivers of delight coursing through her already agitated body.

Oh, yes, that was a sight Rosie hoped to see much more of.

'What do you plan to do? Throw some of the wine glasses against the wall? Or perhaps you could swipe the table clear and send the dinner service crashing to the ground?'

'Why, Your Grace, I do believe you're teasing me!'

Rosie laughed. 'I am capable of misbehaving in many other ways.'

'That, I believe,' he said, still smiling that heart-stopping smile.

'I thought I might do a dance down the middle of the table. Do you think that would convince the Dowager that I'm not duchess material?'

Alexander nearly choked on his wine. 'I don't think even that would put my mother off. Unfortunately your father's fortune is so vast I suspect there's nothing you could do to offend her. Although I'd love to see you try. Shall I give you a hand up onto the table?'

Rosie swatted his arm lightly with her napkin. 'I'll save my table dance for the dessert course.'

The soup finished, the footmen removed their bowls and served the fish course, and Rosie reluctantly turned to talk to her other neighbour, as etiquette demanded. As he talked to her about the last shoot he had attended, and how many pheasants, ducks and other small creatures he had bagged, Rosie inclined her head in Alexander's direction and tried to hear what he was discussing with his own dinner companion.

To no avail. The murmur of the twenty-four people seated around the long oval dining table blocked out all voices but one—the man sitting beside her, boasting of his prowess with a shotgun.

The fish plates were removed and replaced with the meat course. With relief, Rosie turned back to Alexander. Her heart gave a little flutter when he smiled, suggesting that he too was pleased to be talking to her once again.

A *flutter*? She reminded herself that she was not supposed to be having a flutter, but she was incapable of suppressing it.

Especially when he continued to smile at her. A smile that was made more special because it happened so rarely. A smile that was even more of a treat because it was directed at *her*.

'I hope you're not going to tell me how many things you've killed lately?' She smiled back at him.

He shook his head in question. 'Killed?'

'My other dinner companion has just been telling me about all the ducks and pheasants whose lives he has prematurely snuffed out.'

'I see. No, I don't take part in the shoot. Nor do I ride to hounds.'

'Good. So, what was *your* other dinner companion talking about with such enthusiasm?' Rosie leaned forward and looked at the attractive blonde woman sitting to his left. Her smile faded and her jaw clenched before she forced herself not to be so ridiculous.

Why do I feel jealousy over a man who is not mine— who will never be mine?

'I don't know about enthusiasm, but she knew my father. She was lamenting that he had been missed at Royal Ascot last season and asking if I'll be taking his place this June.'

'Royal Ascot?'

'The race course. My father was very fond of gambling. *Too* fond of gambling.' He stabbed at a green bean, his smile disappearing. 'That's why the estate is in such a sorry mess.'

Rosie looked up from the impaled bean. 'Oh, so I take it you won't be attending Royal Ascot?'

'No, I won't.'

He cut up his roast beef with such vehemence Rosie almost felt sorry for it.

'I certainly will not be squandering what little funds we have left at the races.' He stilled his knife and drew in a deep breath. 'But there's no point getting angry about that. It's all in the past.'

Rosie nodded her agreement. Like him, she tried hard—*very* hard—not to focus on the sorrows of the past, or to worry about what the future might bring.

Sometimes that could be hard. Sometimes memories of her mother and father came crashing in when she least expected it. Sometimes the vulnerability of her situation would overwhelm her. But then she would push that thought away and keep smiling. Even if sometimes that smile was not always as genuine as she would like it to be.

She had decided when she was still quite young that if she couldn't change the past, and the future was uncertain, then the present was the only time worth focusing on. And right now, sitting here, next to this handsome man, the present was rather pleasant.

'What about you, Arabella? Do you or your father like "a flutter"—as gamblers so innocuously describe losing a fortune at the card table, casino or race course?'

Rosie stilled her knife and fork and thought for a moment. Getting involved with Mr van Haven had been a gamble—a gamble her father had lost. He had once been a wealthy man. A successful engineer, he had built up a thriving company, installing modern electrical lighting in more progressive towns and businesses. His life had been comfortable. He had been married to the woman he loved, and living a contented life.

That was until Mr van Haven had encouraged him to borrow more money, to vastly expand his business throughout the country. When a few ventures hadn't worked out, and he hadn't been able to make his loan repayments, like a shark circling its prey, Mr van Haven had moved in. He had taken possession of the business and merged it with his own considerable portfolio.

Rosie's father had died prematurely, a broken man. As a supposed act of charity Mr van Haven had hired Rosie's mother as a governess and allowed Rosie to live in the house as a playmate for his daughter. Then her mother had died, leaving Rosie alone in the world.

She shuddered and blinked away the tears she would not shed. She did not want to dwell on such misfortune. And, anyway, it wasn't *her* father Alexander was asking about. It was Arabella's.

'No, I never gamble—and neither does my father. All he does is work. And when he wants to relax he works even harder. I can't imagine him doing something so friv-olous as gambling, and he most certainly would never squander money.'

'It's an example I wish my father had followed.' Alex-ander lifted his glass to the invisible Mr van Haven and took a sip of red wine. 'But if he's working all the time I doubt you see much of him?'

Rosie nodded at the understatement. Mr van Haven saw virtually nothing of Arabella. She suspected that was one of the reasons Arabella had argued with such passion to have Rosie taken on as his ward after Rosie's mother had died. Otherwise Arabella would have been left alone in that enormous house on Washington Square, with only her new, rather stern governess for company.

Mr van Haven was rarely at home, and when he was he was buried away in his study. He had little idea of what went on in the house. The girls were often left with minimum supervision, and over the years their friendship had grown and intensified, so they were now closer than many sisters.

Arabella's own mother had died not long after Arabella was born, and Rosie's mother had been more like a mother to her than a governess. When Rosie's mother had also died, Arabella had argued with her father, had thrown tantrums and threatened to run away, until Mr van Haven had finally relented and taken the fourteen-year-old Rosie as his ward.

'You're right. I see very little of my father. He's too busy making more and more money—as if no amount of money can ever be enough,' Rosie answered, as she imagined Arabella would.

'That must be very hard for you?'

She shrugged. 'Perhaps. But there are worse things in life than living in luxury with your every need catered for.'

That was something Rosie was well aware of. Thanks to Arabella, she did live in luxury, and did have her every need catered for. Without Arabella it might have been so different. She might have learnt first-hand what it was like to live in abject poverty, to be cold, to go hungry, to be vulnerable and alone.

Alexander took another sip of his red wine and gave her a considering gaze. 'That's true, but I suspect it is only your material needs that are catered for,' he said softly.

Rosie held his gaze, unable to look away. It was as if he were looking into her very soul and seeing the pain that she tried hard to bury, the past hurts she tried to forget, the vulnerability she hid behind a sunny smile.

'Oh, Arabella, I didn't mean to upset you,' he murmured. His hand moved across the table and gently covered hers. It was a feather-light touch on her naked skin, but it sent a burst of fire coursing up her arm, consuming her in its blaze. She looked down at her small hand, covered by his strong, elegant fingers. That tender gesture had ignited a tempest within her—a tempest she felt incapable of quashing. She looked back at him. His dark eyes burned into hers and she gasped in a quivering breath as her body pulsated to the rapid beat of her heart.

The voices of the assembled guests seem to fade away. It was as if they were alone, no longer under the scrutinising gaze of society, and she longed for him to do more than just touch her hand—longed for him to take her in his arms so she could feel the strength of his body against her own. She ached to be held in those powerful arms, to give herself to his strong body, to have him complete her.

They held each other's gaze. Rosie hadn't noticed till now, but his dark brown eyes contained small gold flecks, like the last rays of sun on a summer's day. When she'd first seen him she had thought his eyes had a dark intensity, as if they absorbed all light. But she had been wrong. They contained warm lights. And now those lights were drawing her in, making her feel safe and protected.

She could gaze at those lovely warm eyes for ever… drown in them…forget everything else…

As if emerging from a trance she blinked several times and slowly slid her hand from underneath his. With shaking hands she took a sip of her wine, clutching the delicate stem of her glass as if it provided a lifeline back to reality, away from such fanciful thoughts.

She gave a light laugh that sounded false even to her own ears. 'No, you didn't upset me. As I've said before, I'm much stronger than I look.'

* * *

Her smile was false. There could be no doubt about that. And Alexander could hear sadness in her attempt at cheerfulness. He wanted to comfort her, to drive away that sadness behind her happy smile and her sunny disposition, to take her in his arms and make her safe.

'So what has made you so strong, Arabella?' he asked quietly.

'Oh, you know... I guess it comes from having a father who grew up in poverty. It puts iron in the soul.'

She took another sip of her wine and he could see her hand was shaking slightly, making a lie of her flippant response. He resisted the almost overwhelming urge to take hold of those trembling fingers. But she was not his to comfort—would never be his.

'I can tell you are a strong woman, Arabella. But even the strong need people to care for them and support them.'

She lowered her wine glass and looked up at him, her deep blue eyes capturing his gaze, capturing *him*. He couldn't have looked away even if he'd wanted to, and he didn't want to.

He had only known Arabella for one short day, but it was as if they had connected on a level he had not thought possible. He didn't know what it was that drew him to her. Was it her laughter, or the sadness in her eyes? Was it her vulnerability, or her resilience? Whatever it was, there was something infinitely attractive about this complex young woman—something that was drawing him to her.

'And is it the same for you, Alexander? Do you need someone to care for you and support you?' she asked, her voice barely a whisper.

Alexander shook his head, dismissing the idea. He

had never expected support. After all, it was he who supported other people.

He had provided seemingly endless support for Lydia. She was a woman who knew only how to take, not to give. She had taken money to fund her gambling habit and taken from him emotionally, leaving him drained, with nothing left to give. He had thought he loved Lydia, but look where love had led him. And when she had finally left he'd known the only way to protect himself from such emotional demands was never to allow himself to get into such a position again.

So, yes, he had to be strong. He had his family to support, plus the tenants who all depended on him.

But in Arabella's eyes he could see such compassion, such warmth, such tenderness. He could imagine what it would be like to have such a woman by his side. A woman who would not only support him, but was also beautiful, delightful and captivating.

He shook his head again to drive away that fanciful idea. It didn't matter how beautiful Arabella van Haven was—she was in love with another man.

He gave a false laugh of his own. 'And is that what you offer Thomas Gardener? Your support?' Alexander could hear the bitterness in his voice and mentally chastised himself for such pettiness.

Arabella blushed a deeper shade of pink and took another sip of her wine, seemingly reluctant to discuss it.

'I should like to think that the man I love would always know he could rely on me to be by his side.'

She continued to toy with the stem of her wine glass. Once again her words seemed a contradiction of the emotion she was expressing. It was such a loving, positive statement, and yet she looked so sad—as if it was something she would like but knew would not happen.

Slowly she raised her gaze and looked into his eyes. For a moment he could almost believe she had been talking about *him*. The softness in those blue eyes spoke of a depth of emotion that almost left Alexander breathless.

He gripped his own wine glass tightly, to stop his hand from reaching out and caressing her soft cheek. His gaze moved from her eyes to her lips—full pink lips which parted slightly under his gaze. Like him, she was taking in quick breaths, and she leaned in towards him as if mesmerised.

If only they were alone... Then he could do more than just gaze at that beautiful face.

The discreet cough of a footman drew him out of his trance and he saw the dessert course being placed on the table. Alexander waved the plate away and with the greatest reluctance turned towards his other dinner companion.

He hardly heard a word Lady Aubrey said. All he could think of was how Arabella had looked at him. Desire had sparked in her crystal blue eyes. Her lips had parted invitingly, as if waiting for his kiss. Like him, she seemed to have lost herself, forgotten who she was...

He had claimed he was strong and he was going to have to be. He could not succumb to temptation. She belonged to another man. *That* was what he had to think about when he looked at her—not how her raven hair caught the light, nor how plump her full lips were, nor how beautiful she looked when she sent him those shy smiles from under lowered lashes.

Quaffing a long draught of his wine, he reminded himself yet again. *She belongs to someone else.*

* * *

The dessert plates were removed and cheese and fruit platters were laid out on the table. Rosie turned back to Alexander, her heart beating fast, hoping he would look at her again with such intensity, with such longing.

Instead he gave a small, polite nod. It seemed the sensitive man she'd glimpsed had once again disappeared beneath a stern, aristocratic exterior.

'So, what were we discussing?' Rosie asked, not really caring about words, just hoping he would once again look at her with affection and warmth.

'You mentioned that your strength comes from having a father who was born in poverty.'

'Oh, yes, so I did. But what about you, Alexander? Did you get your strength from your father or your mother?'

Alexander gave a sudden humourless laugh. 'I don't know if I'd describe either of them as *strong*. My father and grandfather thought only of their own pleasure. They thought the family coffers were bottomless and they could spend and spend without a thought to the future, or the future of the tenants who depend on the success of the estate for their livelihoods. My mother is much the same. She brought a sizable dowry with her when she married my father, but he soon managed to squander that. There was no love between them, which perhaps made it easier for her to live with such a man. Having had a loveless marriage herself, she has no reservations about trying to get me to marry a wealthy heiress. All she can see is a way to save the estate. Hence your presence here this weekend. And no doubt when she finally accepts that we are not going to wed she will be in pursuit of some other heiress to throw in front of me.'

She had been acting like a woman who was being courted by a man she adored—a woman who was loving every minute of it. And, worst of all, it had not been an act. She had thoroughly enjoyed being in Alexander's company. Had loved the way he looked at her. Had loved him touching her…had wanted more, much more.

What was *wrong* with her? Her friend was depending on her. Her best friend. The friend who had saved her from a life of penury. The friend to whom she owed so much and for whom she claimed she would do anything. Was she such a terrible person that she would allow her head to be turned by a handsome man and forget her promise to her friend? It would seem so. There was only one reason for her visit to Knightsbrook House: to save Arabella from an unwanted marriage. Nothing else.

Rosie wanted to hang her head in shame. Instead she turned before she left the room, for one last look at Alexander. He smiled at her and her foolish heart did a somersault.

The door closed behind the train of women and Rosie shook her head slowly from side to side.

No, this would not do at all. She could not go on behaving like this. She was sending out all the wrong messages. It was time she stopped acting like an infatuated debutante at her first ball of the season. And if she couldn't trust herself with Alexander then it was best if she spent no more time in his company.

The women entered the drawing room, where coffee was being served. Rosie took a delicate white china cup from the parlour maid, sat beside the fire and sipped the rich, nutty drink. Charlotte soon joined her, flopping down in the adjoining wing chair and exhaling loudly.

'Thank goodness that's finally over. These dinner par-

Rosie's heart lurched, and the bubble of exhilaration inflated by that look finally burst.

Another heiress.

Maybe the next heiress his mother threw in front of him would be a real one—one who actually wanted to marry Alexander. Maybe she'd be someone Alexander was interested in. Maybe she'd be someone he *wanted* to marry.

She stabbed her cheese knife into a piece of Stilton. There was no 'maybe' about it. Eventually Alexander was going to meet someone he wanted to marry. Someone who wasn't just pretending to be an heiress. Her prodding reduced the wedge of Stilton to a pile of mush and she moved on to massacre a slice of Wensleydale.

But surely it would be a *good* thing if he met and married a real heiress. Surely she should want him to be happy. After all, she didn't want him to remain single, did she? He should find himself a wife—someone he could love and who would love him in return.

'Are you planning on eating that cheese, Arabella? Or are you just going to cut it into smaller and smaller portions?'

Rosie gave a small fake laugh. 'I think I've had enough.' She placed her knife down. Yes, she'd had enough food. And, more than that, she'd had enough of this play-acting and enough of being caught up in the moment and thinking she could mean something to Alexander.

She had felt like Cinderella at the ball, wearing her beautiful gown and sitting next to her handsome prince. But this was just another fairy tale—one she had foolishly allowed herself to think was reality. But in the real world the pauper didn't get the prince.

What did it matter how he gazed at her? What did it matter how often he touched her hand? What did it matter if he said she looked beautiful?

It didn't. And she was a fool to think otherwise.

A crushing heaviness suddenly descended on her, sweeping away the sense of lightness and excitement that came from talking and laughing with Alexander.

She had been trying to fool Alexander and his mother by pretending to be Arabella and she had succeeded, but in the process she had managed to fool herself. Fool herself that she could be part of this world, could have a man like Alexander really wanting her, little Rosie Smith, a no-account orphaned ward, with no money, no position—nothing. She didn't even own the beautiful gown she was wearing.

Yes, she had been a fool—a deluded fool.

All she wanted now was for this evening to end, so she could drop this pointless pretence and get back to reality. A reality that did not contain handsome but unattainable dukes or dreams that were far above her expectations.

Chapter Ten

'Ladies, shall we adjourn and leave the men to their port and cigars?' The Dowager stood up before anyone dared to answer her rhetorical question.

Footmen rushed forward to pull out the chairs of the assembled female guests and the women immediately fell into line, as if under orders from a commanding officer.

Rosie joined the brightly coloured trail of well-dressed woman exiting the room to the accompaniment of rustling silk and satin. Mixed emotions coursed through her as she left the dining room…left Alexander's side.

She wanted to spend more time with him, but knew she had to get away. Her behaviour during dinner had been inappropriate—and not in the inappropriate manner she had intended when she had concocted her plan over tea at the Ritz.

Instead of presenting herself as a thoroughly unacceptable future bride she had been giving him long, lingering looks. Instead of making absurd and discourteous statements to prove what an unacceptable duchess she would make she had been sharing an intimate conversation with him. Instead of acting unimpressed and dismissive she had been getting all dewy-eyed, just as Nellie had said.

ties are always such a bore,' Charlotte said, and took a decisive bite of her Florentine biscuit.

'Really? You seemed to be enjoying His Grace's attention.' Rosie couldn't help herself. She had to tease the girl.

'No, I was not.' The quick and vehement reply made a lie of Charlotte's answer.

Rosie raised her eyebrows and Charlotte shrugged. There was obviously more to this story than Charlotte was telling.

'Nicholas and I were friends once, but he's changed so much,' Charlotte said. 'All he cares about now is enjoying himself and chasing after—' Her cheeks reddened slightly and her lips pinched with disapproval. 'Chasing after women. He really is quite frightful—and he had so much promise when he was young.'

'But you still find him attractive?'

Charlotte shrugged and stared into the fire. 'Only his appearance is attractive. The things he does and the way he lives his life are anything but attractive.' She sat up straighter in her chair and turned to face Rosie. 'But what about you, Arabella? You and Alexander seemed to be completely absorbed in each other, talking quietly with your heads so close together they were almost touching.'

Rosie took another sip of her coffee while she composed her response. 'Your brother is an interesting conversationalist,' she said, in her most nonchalant manner.

Charlotte's eyes grew wide. 'Really? Alexander? Most of the ladies who attend Mother's dinner parties describe him as taciturn and complain that they can hardly get a word out of him. Not that I blame him. Who wants to spend an evening making small talk about the weather, the last ball they attended or the next ball they plan to attend? Certainly not me, and certainly not Alexander.'

She took another bite of her biscuit and chewed it thoughtfully while watching Rosie.

'So, if you weren't talking about the weather or this season's balls, what *were* you talking about?'

'Oh, I can't really remember. This and that.'

'It must have been a very interesting "this and that". I've never seen Alexander so engrossed in a conversation with a woman. Not since…' Charlotte took a sip of her coffee and looked into the fire, then back at Rosie. 'Not for a long time. And I can hardly remember the last time I saw him laughing. But when he's with you he seems to laugh and smile a lot. I think you're really good for him, Arabella.'

Rosie cringed at the sound of her friend's name. She was *not* Arabella. Whether Rosie made Alexander laugh or not was of no importance. In a few days she would be gone and would never see the FitzRoys again.

'So?' Charlotte said, looking down at her coffee cup and turning it round in the saucer. 'Were you and Alexander discussing your wedding plans?'

Rosie almost spluttered on her coffee. 'No, we weren't discussing *any* wedding plans. I'm afraid Alexander and I will not be getting married. We've discussed it, and neither of us wants it. It was a plan concocted by my father and your mother, without the approval of either of us.'

Charlotte's lips drooped into a pouting frown. 'But you seem to be getting on so well. You seem so right for each other. You were looking at each other as if…' She shook her head slightly and sighed. 'Can't you at least get to know each other a bit better before you decide? You might change your minds. My mother might, for once in her life, be right.'

Rosie shook her head. 'I'm sorry, Charlotte. It's not

possible.' She could not tell this lovely young woman that it was impossible because she wasn't really Arabella.

Charlotte gave another heavy sigh and stared into the fire, her shoulders slumped.

Rosie doubted it was possible to feel any worse. This was not how her plan was supposed to work out. She was not supposed to actually *like* the FitzRoys. They were supposed to be a stuffy, snobby family, grasping after Mr van Haven's money. They were supposed to be people she would not have any qualms about making fun of. Instead the Duke was handsome and charming and his sister was a lovely young woman who was honest, trusting and extremely likeable.

The only person who was despicable was Rosie herself. Despicable for playing this trick on such good people, despicable for lying to Alexander, and despicable for not sticking to the plan she had agreed with the real Arabella over tea at the Ritz. No, she couldn't feel much worse than she did right now.

Charlotte turned from the fire and gave Rosie a sad smile. 'But *we* can still be friends, can't we? Even if you don't marry Alexander?'

Rosie slumped in her chair. She had been wrong. It *was* possible to feel worse. Now she was going to have to lie to Charlotte.

She nodded her head and cringed inwardly. 'Of course we can.'

Another lie, to add to the long list of lies she had already told. Obviously she could not be friends with Charlotte after she left Knightsbrook, as they would never see each other again. And it was unlikely Charlotte would want to be friends with Rosie if she discovered the truth and found out that she had been so shamefully deceived.

'Good. And who knows? Maybe eventually you and Alexander will realise it's not such an impossible match after all and we'll be more than just friends. We'll be sisters!'

Rosie's inward cringe became an outward wince as she gritted her teeth and tried to smile through her embarrassment.

Smiling with satisfaction, Charlotte picked up her coffee cup, lifted it to her lips, then put it back in the saucer. 'I'm sorry, Arabella. I've just realised I'm behaving exactly like my mother. She wants you and Alexander to marry and she cares little for what you two want. And I'm doing exactly the same. I would love it if you got married, but obviously you have to make your own decisions and nobody should force you to do anything you don't want to do.'

'Thank you, Charlotte. But you have nothing to apologise for.'

And that was definitely the truth. If anyone should be apologising it was Rosie.

'But you don't need me putting on the pressure. You're going to have enough of that from Mother—and, believe me, she is a master at putting on the pressure.'

'Is she pressuring you to marry as well?' Rosie was curious to know, but also desperate to change the subject, away from herself and Alexander, or at least form Arabella and Alexander.

'Yes, it's already started.'

Rosie listened while Charlotte detailed the plans and schemes her mother was putting in place to try and get Charlotte married off to Nicholas, Lord Richmond. While Rosie commiserated, a small part of her was grateful that

Charlotte was passionately diverted from discussing any future plans of Arabella and Alexander.

The drawing room door opened. Several men carrying brandy glasses entered along with the waft of cigar smoke. Full of bonhomie, they joined the ladies and the volume of conversation in the room rose markedly. Servants began arranging card tables and the lid of the grand piano was lifted. It seemed the party was not about to end any time soon, and a range of entertainments had been organised for the evening.

Rosie's stomach tightened as if the coffee had been far too strong. It seemed she would be expected to spend more time with Alexander, and to continue pretending for a while longer yet.

Her confusion mounted. What was it she was actually pretending to be? Was she pretending to be interested in Alexander, or not interested in him? Was she not interested, but pretending she was, or interested but pretending she wasn't?

Another smiling man entered the room and Rosie quickly looked up, her stomach clenching. It was not Alexander, and Rosie was both pleased and disappointed. She wanted to see him again, but knew it was wisest not to. And if she was going to avoid seeing Alexander now was the time to take action—because once he entered the room she was unsure whether she would have the will-power to walk away from him.

'I'm starting to get a slight headache,' Rosie told Charlotte—something which did have a kernel of truth to it. All this confusion over what she did and didn't want was starting to make her head spin. 'I'm also a little tired after such an eventful day.'

'Oh, of course—you must retire for the evening if you

aren't well. But Mother will be disappointed. She was expecting you to give us a performance on the banjo tonight. She purchased one especially for the occasion.'

The banjo? Why on earth would the Dowager expect her to play the banjo? Rosie played the piano, not the banjo.

Then suddenly she remembered, and gave a small laugh.

'You *do* play the banjo, don't you, Arabella? You're looking somewhat surprised, but we were told you had been playing since you were a child and are quite brilliant.'

Both Rosie and Arabella had learnt the banjo briefly, when they were in their early teens, when they'd harboured dreams of running off and joining a group of travelling performers. But that dream had died a sudden death, as had so many of their outlandish youthful plans for travel and adventure, and the banjos had been consigned to the attic to gather dust.

Mr van Haven paid such little attention to his only child that he presumably thought Arabella had continued with her banjo lessons and had claimed it as one of her accomplishments.

'I afraid that is one talent I suspect has been greatly exaggerated. So I think it might be best if I do retire early, if I'm to avoid ruining the evening and subjecting the guests to that particular torture.'

She bade Charlotte goodnight, then approached the Dowager, her brow furrowed with fictitious pain.

'I'm sorry, Your Grace, but all the excitement of the day and the journey has left me quite fatigued, and I can feel a terrible headache coming on.' She placed the back of her hand on her forehead to emphasise the point. 'My apologies, but I fear I must retire for the evening.'

It might be another lie, but it was in a good cause. She would be saving the guests from her lack of finesse on the banjo, not to mention saving herself from having to cope with the strange, tumultuous emotions that Alexander elicited in her.

The Dowager smiled and patted her arm. 'Of course, my dear. You must rest. Then you'll be fresh tomorrow. I know Alexander is very keen to show you the rest of the estate; he was talking about it earlier and quite bubbling with enthusiasm.'

Alexander? Bubbling?

It seemed Rosie wasn't the only one capable of stretching the truth.

'I'm sure no one bubbles quite like Alexander,' she couldn't stop herself from saying, before giving a tired smile, bobbing a quick curtsey and retreating as quickly as she could without looking too energetic.

The door closed behind her with a decisive click and she walked as quickly as decorum allowed down the tiled entranceway towards the staircase.

The dining room door opened, releasing a group of smiling men, all talking loudly. She nodded greetings as she passed, determined to escape before she saw Alexander again.

Reaching the staircase, she fought the temptation to run up the stairs. That would hardly fit in with her claim to be tired and have a headache coming on.

'Arabella, are you retiring early?'

His deep, velvety voice was behind her. She froze, then slowly turned to face him, her hand tightly gripping the bottom of the carved banister. He was standing at the dining room doorway, a brandy balloon in his hand, and Arabella's breath left her chest. He looked even more magnificent than when she had first seen him.

Was that even possible?

A shiver ran through her. Her hand clasped her stomach, to still the riotous storm of nerves that had erupted deep within her, and her gaze wandered over the sublimely handsome man staring back at her.

Yes, it seemed it was possible.

With his strong body filling the doorframe, he was a picture of masculine strength and virility. Rosie gasped in a quick breath and slowly exhaled as her gaze moved down his body to those long, lean legs, and the muscles delineated through the black fabric of his trousers. Oh, yes, her original assessment had been right. He was the very image of a Greek statue.

Her gaze moved back up to his face, to his dark brown eyes. Eyes that were sparkling with the reflected candle-light of the large chandelier. Eyes that were drawing her in and holding her tight with the intensity of his gaze. Part of her was frightened by the power of that gaze, but most of her wanted to surrender herself to the strong tidal pull that was sweeping her towards him.

She coughed lightly. 'Yes, I'm feeling a little tired, so I thought I'd retire.'

And I need to escape from you before I make even more of a fool of myself than I already have, she added truthfully to herself.

He placed the brandy glass on a nearby table, the amber liquid swirling in the balloon-shaped glass, and crossed the entranceway. 'Yes, you look pale, Arabella. Is there anything I can do?'

You can stop being so handsome. You can stop being so charming. You can stop making my heart skip every time I see you. Then I wouldn't be looking so pale. Then I wouldn't be feeling so shocked at seeing you again.

'No, nothing. I think I just need an early night.'

'Then allow me to accompany you up to your room. Shall I call my sister to act as a chaperon?'

Rosie shook her head. 'No, don't disturb her. And there's no need to accompany me. Nellie will be waiting for me. She can see to my needs.'

Another lie. Only Alexander would be able to see to the need that was surging up within Rosie. A need to be taken in his arms. A need to be held by him. A need to feel those full, sculpted lips pressed against hers.

Rosie closed her eyes and blinked several times to try and clear that image from her mind. But when she opened her eyes she was staring straight at those sculpted lips...lips that were saying something...something that the pounding of her heart prevented her from hearing.

'I beg your pardon? What did you say?'

'I was offering you my arm so I can help you up the stairs.'

'Oh, yes. Of course.'

Rosie was sure that touching him right now was the worst thing she could do, but what could she say? *No, I don't want to take your arm? If I take your arm I don't think I'll be able to trust myself not to do something so inappropriate that even I'll be shocked by it?*

He held out his arm and Rosie drew in a series of steadying breaths. She commanded her fingers to un-clench themselves from the banister and lightly placed her hand on his forearm.

She briefly closed her eyes, registering the touch of

her skin on his muscular arm, and tried to ignore the tingling sensation burning its way up her arm to her chest and taking over her body.

As they ascended the stairs she could hear him making polite conversation, but what he said she had no idea. All she could do was react to the closeness of his warm body and the wonderful scent of him…pure, heady masculinity.

Rosie followed where he led, sure that if she had been trying to find her way down the maze of corridors with their array of paintings and sculptures adorning the walls she would have got completely lost, her mind was so befuddled.

They'd reached her door.

He paused, removed her hand from his arm and took it in both of his. He smiled gently down at her. 'It seems you are starting to feel a bit better, Arabella. Colour has returned to your face,' he said, his voice concerned.

Rosie didn't doubt that she was blushing—the heat radiating from her burning cheeks was making that very clear. And it was not just her cheeks that were burning. Rosie was sure her entire body must be blushing. It was pulsating fiercely as her heart thumped within her chest, as if she'd just undertaken some kind of furious exercise.

'Th-thank you,' she stammered, unsure what she was thanking him for.

'Well, I will leave you to your rest.'

But he remained staring down at her, once again capturing Rosie with the intensity of his brown eyes.

'Goodnight, then,' Rosie murmured, unable to move herself.

He lifted her hand and lightly kissed the back of it, his eyes still burning into hers. Rosie closed her eyes, loving the feeling of the touch of his lips on her skin. But she wanted more.

As if her hand had a mind of its own it turned over and lightly stroked his strong jawline. Her gaze moved to his lips. Those full, sensual lips. And she imagined what it would be like to be kissed by him.

Tingling erupted on her lips and she gave a small moan. She caught her bottom lip with her teeth, slowly raking them across the skin to stop any more tell-tale reactions.

Alexander's hand gently clasped her wrist. Their eyes locked. Heat surged through her as she registered the hunger in his dark eyes…a hunger both exciting and unnerving.

Time froze. Every inch of her body tensed as she waited for him to act. Her breath caught in her throat. She stared up at him, waiting to see what he would do next. Would he kiss her? Oh, how she wanted him to kiss her.

In answer to her silent plea his lips met hers, his kiss crashing over her like turbulent water escaping from a ruptured dam. As his skin rasped against her cheek she inhaled the lemon scent of his shaving soap. Then a stronger, underlying masculine scent and taste filled her senses like a powerful narcotic, taking her over, intoxicating her, leaving her incapable of thought.

But now was definitely not the time for thinking.

Her lips parted wider, to savour more of that musky masculine taste and the delicious hint of brandy. To her surprise his tongue entered her mouth. Was this how men and women kissed? It was her first time, so how could she be sure—but, oh, how good it felt.

His tongue continued to lick and probe, tasting her until she was sure she would collapse from the heady pleasure of having it so intimately inside her mouth. But she couldn't collapse—not with his arms holding her close, so close she could feel the muscular imprint of his strong chest against her breasts, feel his long, lean thighs against hers, feel his hard arousal against her stomach.

Rosie gasped, realising what was pressing against her, his unmistakable need for her.

What would happen now?

Rosie had no idea. She had often wondered whether a man would ever kiss her and, if so, if she would know what to do. But it seemed all she had to do was surrender herself to Alexander and he would guide her. With him to lead her she was free to give herself over to the wild, primitive need building up inside her. The insatiable need for *him*.

Tendrils of hair became dislodged from her carefully constructed coiffure, tumbling around her naked shoulders, intensifying that glorious sense of abandon.

Her tongue took a few tentative licks at his lips, then entered his mouth. Their tongues engaged in an erotic dual, causing him to release a soft moan of pleasure. Exhilaration surged through her. She had made him moan— moan for *her*. Oh, yes, this felt so right. She wanted more of this. Wanted to explore his strong masculine body… wanted to discover just how much pleasure she could experience and how much pleasure he could give her.

Encircling his neck, she ran her hands up through his thick brown hair. She growled with pleasure as his kiss deepened. Her body moved to its own rhythm as his hands ran down her spine, cupping her buttocks and pulling her firmly against his body.

Oh, yes, she definitely wanted more of this. She wanted him never to stop kissing her, never to let her go.

Without thinking, just reacting to the needs of her body, she rubbed her swollen breasts against his hard chest, her tight nipples pressing through the soft fabric of her gown and aching to be touched. To be touched by *him*.

His lips left hers, but her disappointment was quashed when he kissed a line slowly down her neck. Rosie tilted back her head, loving the touch of his lips on her exposed skin as every kiss sent waves of pleasure rippling through her body.

When he reached the base of her neck she mentally urged him to go further. His lips obeyed.

He slid the neckline of her dress off one shoulder, then the other, his lips kissing a tantalising line across her skin. Rosie's breath came in faster and faster gasps, her heart pounded loudly in her chest, and a throbbing pleasure erupted deep within her core.

'Oh, Arabella, you're so beautiful,' he murmured, then kissed her neck, his husky voice almost unrecognisable.

Rosie froze.

Arabella. He had called her Arabella.

She was not Arabella. She was Rosie Smith. And what was she doing? Kissing a man who thought she was Arabella. She was tarnishing Arabella's good reputation. How could she *do* that? What sort of woman *was* she?

She closed her eyes and took a few deep breaths to bring herself back to reality. When she opened her eyes he too had changed. His posture had become rigid, his face stern. Her hesitation seemed to have broken the spell that had captured them both. He appeared to be emerging from a trance, as if he were suddenly registering just what they were doing.

'I beg your pardon, Arabella. Please forgive me.'

She shook her head. He had nothing to be sorry for. It

was she who should be sorry. She was the one who had forgotten who she was—the one who had betrayed her best friend's good name.

He coughed, inhaled deeply, then released his breath slowly. 'I took advantage of you. I'm so sorry.'

She stared at him as if he were talking an unknown foreign language. What did he mean? Took advantage of her? How?

In a daze, she watched as he pulled up her dislodged neckline and retrieved her abandoned hairclips from the floor.

'Kissing you was unpardonable, but I hope you can one day forgive me?'

'No. I mean yes. I mean, you've done nothing that needs my forgiveness.'

Rosie touched her lips. That kiss had been the most wonderful thing that had ever happened to her. How could he say it was unforgivable?

He looked down at his hands, now clenched into fists around her hairclips. 'I have. I took advantage of you and I am sorry.'

Rosie shook her head again. He was so wrong. She had wanted him to kiss her. She still wanted him to kiss her. To hold her. To caress her. Even now that she knew it was wrong and could never happen again.

'My behaviour would be unforgivable under any circumstances, but it is especially reprehensible that I took advantage of a woman who is all but betrothed to another.'

What was he talking about? *All but betrothed?* Then with a sinking feeling she remembered Thomas Gardener. The non-existent Thomas Gardener. He thought he was betraying a non-existent man, when it was Rosie who was betraying a real person—her best friend, the friend who had saved her from poverty, the friend who had always treated her like a sister.

'Please, I implore you, do not feel you have in any way wronged me.'

'You are an admirable young woman, Arabella. It seems that is another virtue to add to the long list.' He handed her the retrieved hairclips.

She took them from his outstretched hands and stared down at them as if unsure what they were, once again shamed by her actions. Admirable? Nothing about her was admirable. And if she actually did possess any virtues she couldn't think of a single one right now.

No, there was nothing admirable about the lies she had told him—was still telling him. Nothing admirable about what she had just done. To satisfy her own longings she had put her friend's reputation at risk. The only admirable person was the man standing before her, begging for her forgiveness.

And there was certainly nothing admirable about her wish that he would kiss her again. Even now—now that she realised just how wrong it had been—she still wanted it. How could she want something that was so wrong so badly? No, there was nothing admirable about Rosie Smith.

'Perhaps we should put it down to the heat of the moment,' she said, as much to excuse her own bad behaviour as to make him feel less remorseful. 'We must put it behind us and pretend it never happened.'

Although she knew that was yet another lie. There was no way she would ever forget the touch of Alexander's lips on hers, nor how it had felt to be encased in his arms. That feeling would stay with her for ever.

He bowed. 'You are very gracious. I wish you good-night, Arabella.'

Graciousness—that was another virtue she doubted she actually possessed.

'Goodnight, Alexander,' she murmured.

She remained rooted to the spot, watching his back as he retreated down the corridor. When he disappeared around the corner she inhaled deeply and placed a steadying hand on her rapidly beating heart. She entered her bedroom, leaned against the closed door and slid to the floor, her body suddenly too heavy for her to remain standing.

With her head in her hands she vowed that it would never happen again. If she could not trust herself in the Duke's company she must never allow herself to be alone with him. *Ever.*

Chapter Eleven

That should not have happened. That most definitely should not have happened. What had he been *thinking*? That was the problem. He hadn't been thinking—just reacting.

He had felt so close to her over dinner. They had laughed together, talked together, shared a closeness that he had not felt for a long time, and it had affected his ability to reason clearly. And then, when he had seen her looking up at him, desire sparking in those big blue eyes, the last vestige of reason he'd possessed had been trampled under his need to take her in his arms.

He had ignored the small voice in his mind that had warned him it was wrong because he'd wanted her so much.

Alexander slammed shut the door and paced his bedroom floor. With his blood pumping, his body tense and his throbbing lust for Arabella straining his breeches, he desperately needed release from this pent-up desire. He had to free himself of this demanding need for her, for the feel of her, the taste and smell of her.

And that wasn't going to happen if he continued to

think about what she'd looked like with her hair tumbling loose around her naked shoulders, her red lips wet and plump, her full breasts arching towards him invitingly and with that look in her eyes—a look that had mirrored his own insatiable desire.

No, it should never have happened. He should never have taken her in his arms. The moment he'd given in to that temptation he had been incapable of stopping, incapable of resisting the need to kiss her, to caress her warm, silky skin.

Balling his hands into tight fists at his sides, he tried to erase the feel of her, tried to chase away the fresh scent of spring flowers that still filled his senses, tried to drive out the image of her gazing up at him with hooded eyes, her lips parted, the mounds of her breasts rising and falling in her tight bodice as she waited for his kiss.

That he was falling for the beautiful Arabella van Haven there could be no denying. He slammed his fist against the wall. He was a fool—a damn fool. After Lydia's betrayal, the next woman he'd fallen for was someone betrothed to another. Was he a glutton for punishment? Had Lydia not hurt him enough with her lies, her tricks?

Because of Lydia he had vowed never to let a woman affect him ever again. But he had let his guard down because Arabella was not like Lydia. She didn't lie. She didn't deceive others for her own ends. She was an innocent young woman. And that only made his behaviour worse.

Lydia had been betrothed to him and had been seduced away by another. Now he had almost done to Arabella what that rake had done to Lydia. He had tried to have his way with a woman who was in love with someone else, who planned to marry someone else. At the time he had despised the man who had seduced Lydia, and yet now he had shown himself to be no better—to be just as much a reprobate as that man had been, a man driven only by his lust for a beautiful woman.

He paced backwards and forwards, rubbing his now bloodied hand, his breath coming in a series of rapid gasps.

Lydia had given herself to that man and followed him into a life of debauchery. Her position in society had been ruined for ever. And now *he* was set on ruining the reputation of a lovely young woman all because he'd wanted her so badly he had forgotten himself—had forgotten all sense of propriety, all sense of decency.

He could only be grateful that she had come to her senses and stopped him. Her sudden withdrawal from his touch had allowed the memory of her telling him that she was in love with another man to invade his fevered brain.

If she hadn't come to her senses he would have been incapable of stopping at just a kiss. He would have taken her to his bedroom and torn off her restricting clothing. He would have freed those enticing breasts, released the tight, sensitive nipples so he could take them in his mouth, kiss them, nuzzle them, lick them until she was senseless with lust for him.

She would now be lying beneath him, writhing under his touch as he kissed every inch of her body. Her legs would be wrapped tightly around his waist as she gave herself to him, opened herself up for him so he could enter her. She would be calling out his name, desperate for the pleasure he would give her, the pleasure she would give *him*.

He slammed his bloodied fist against the wall, leaving a red smear on the cream paper. Yes, he was a fool.

A damn fool. He should not even be *thinking* such things. She belonged to another man. She was in love with another man. Yes, she had kissed him back. Yes, she had responded to his touch. But she was an innocent. It was he who should have known better than to take her into his arms. It was unforgivable.

He had been so desperate to satisfy his own consuming lust for her that all he had cared about was satisfying his own needs. But it wasn't just her body that was driving him mad with desire. He could not remember the last time he had enjoyed a woman's company more. Talking to her had made his mother's unbearable dinner party more than just bearable—it had been entertaining.

It was wrong—and yet for one moment it had felt so right. It had felt as if she was his. When she had been in his arms it had felt as if she belonged there, belonged to *him*. But it was not where she belonged. She was not his. She was in love with another man—all but betrothed to another man.

Explosive energy continued to pump through his veins. He would go mad if he remained in this room, pacing like a caged tiger.

With unnecessary force he pulled open his bedroom door and slammed it shut behind him. He had to get out of the house, out into the open. He needed to feel the cold night air on his face.

He ran down the stairs and out through the front door, ignoring the startled looks of the servants. He crossed the lawn, bathed in the soft light spilling out through the house's large windows, ripping off his jacket, his waistcoat and his shirt. When he reached the lake he pulled off his boots and his trousers and tossed them to the ground. Naked, he dived in.

The cold water hit him like a punch—the punch he needed...the punch he deserved.

But the cold water was not enough to douse his burning lust for Arabella. He swam the length of the lake, his arms rapidly slicing through the water. When he reached the opposite edge he turned and swam back, again and again.

The lights from the house did not reach the lake, and the dark moonless sky made it almost impossible to see his way as he raced up and down in the inky black water. But he had swum this lake many times. He knew it so thoroughly he could navigate his way without sight, without thought. And that was what he needed. Not to think. To exhaust himself.

His body finally began to tire, but he pushed himself on, forcing himself to continue despite his fatigue. Finally, his energy completely spent, he came to a halt. He flicked the water out of his hair and held on to the stone paving at the edge of the lake, his breath coming fast, his heart thumping with the exertion.

He looked up at the house, now in complete darkness. While he'd been swimming the guests, his family and even the servants had all retired for the night. Arabella was no doubt now asleep.

An image of Arabella in her four-poster bed invaded his mind, with her long black hair spread out across a white pillow, her lithe body lying in repose. Her delicious curves would be visible through a linen nightdress...

He slapped at the water. Why did he have to think of that? Why did he have to torture himself? All that strenuous exercise had been for nought if it hadn't driven thoughts of Arabella from his mind.

He forced himself to swim one more length of the lake.

Slowly he ploughed through the cold water, his muscles screaming out for him to stop. He reached the end, but his mind still reeled with images of Arabella.

This was insufferable. His fatigue was so intense that if he swum another length surely he would drown. It seemed if he was ever to be free he was going to have to exercise strenuous control over his mind, not just his body.

Summoning up every last ounce of strength, he dragged himself out of the lake, grabbed his trousers and pulled them over his wet body. He picked up his boots and crossed the lawn to retrieve his discarded shirt, waistcoat and jacket, now damp from the night-time dew. Slowly he retraced his steps up the path to the dark house, returned to his room and fell onto his bed in complete exhaustion.

He stared up at the ceiling and made a solemn vow. Even if the opportunity arose, and even if the temptation was overwhelming, he would not succumb to his feelings for Arabella van Haven. He would never again take her in his arms. Never again would he kiss her. He would exercise stringent self-control.

He just had to keep reminding himself that she would never be his. Her heart belonged to another. Whatever he might feel for her, she was not his. He had to be strong and never touch her again, never kiss her again. *Ever.*

Chapter Twelve

Drawing in a deep, steadying breath, Alexander paused outside the breakfast room. He nodded to the footman to indicate that he wasn't yet ready to enter, and spent some time composing himself.

It was time to put his resolve into action—to stay true to the promises he had made to himself last night. His muscles ached slightly, reminding him of his new determination. Arabella van Haven was simply a guest in his home. A guest who would be leaving tomorrow. A guest from whom he would keep his distance. He would not get too close to her, either physically or emotionally. Getting close contained too many dangers. That was all he had to remember.

Forcefully he turned the door handle and strode into the room. The three people sitting at the breakfast table looked up at him and smiled simultaneously: his mother, Charlotte and Miss van Haven.

Seated with her back to the large sash windows, Arabella was bathed in morning sunlight. Alexander almost suspected his mother of placing her where her beauty would be displayed at its most advantageous. The sunlight glinted off the copper strands in her otherwise black hair, her skin appeared luminescent and a golden glow surrounded her—as if she were a maiden in a Renaissance painting.

He nodded a greeting to the three women and turned his back—ostensibly to serve himself from the silver tureens arranged along the sideboard, but in reality to regain his equilibrium and remind himself once again of his resolve. It didn't matter how beautiful she looked in the morning sunlight—not in the slightest. He would not let that or anything else undermine his determination.

Standing straighter, he walked to the table without looking at Arabella, sat down, whipped open his napkin, placed it on his lap and stared down at his food. Why had he served himself a full breakfast when he didn't feel like eating?

He coughed lightly to clear his throat. 'I trust you slept well, Miss van Haven?' he asked, for politeness' sake. From now onwards it would be formality only. She would be Miss van Haven. No more of this calling each other by their first names. After all, look where adopting the more informal American ways had got them. No, he did not wish to go there again.

'I slept very well, thank you, Your Grace.'

Good. She too had the sense to see the necessity of formality. On that it seemed they were in complete agreement.

His mother, however, had raised her eyebrows and was looking from one to the other of them with curiosity. But what his mother thought hardly mattered. It was his mother who had created this problem in the first place, inviting the American heiress into his home without his knowledge or his permission.

'And you, Your Grace? I hope you also slept well.'

Alexander nodded once, quickly, in response to Arabella's enquiry. Yes, he had indeed been able to sleep—but only because he had exercised so furiously he had been in a state of complete physical exhaustion. Without that rigorous swim he doubted he would have been able to chase away thoughts of kissing her, of her soft lips on his, of her pliant body crushed against his, her soft breasts and tight nipples pushing into his chest...

He coughed again as heat flooded his body, then shook his napkin vigorously to drive out those treacherous thoughts and set about carving up his breakfast.

'Well, now that we've established you both slept well, perhaps we can discuss what activities you have planned for the day,' his mother said. 'Alexander, I think it would be a splendid idea if you showed Miss van Haven more of the estate. That is, once you've finished decimating that defenceless kipper.'

Alexander stopped and looked down at the mash of white flesh spread across his plate, then pushed away his uneaten breakfast. 'I'm not sure what Miss van Haven has planned for today, but I intend to inspect the marshlands at the bottom of the estate. The engineers are coming next week, to begin draining the area so it can be turned into viable farmland. I'm sure that would be of no interest to our guest.'

'Oh, I'm sure Miss van Haven would be delighted to accompany you.'

Alexander inhaled a deep, exasperated breath. Would his mother's infernal meddling never cease? He knew the answer to that. No, of course it would not. Not until Miss van Haven was in her carriage, heading for the railway station and moving out of his life.

'I very much doubt if the marshland would be of any interest to a lady—it's swampy underfoot, and hardly suitable for a leisurely stroll,' he said, hoping that would be the end of the matter.

'Well, if—'

'Nonsense,' his mother answered, cutting off Arabella before she could express her opinion. 'It will give you a chance to show Miss van Haven the parts of the estate she hasn't yet seen—and who knows? She might be interested in your plans for modernisation.'

His mother's lips turned down and her nostrils flared, as if the very idea of anyone being interested in such a subject was extremely unlikely.

'Well, if His Grace would rather—'

'Or you could stay inside all day, Miss van Haven,' his mother interrupted again, a mischievous look sparking in her eyes. 'Our parish priest, the Reverend Truebridge, is an amateur historian, and he has volunteered to give us a talk on the history of Devon—starting with the Bronze Age and working forward to the present day, covering each period in the minutest detail. He can be a little tedious at times, I must admit, and he does tend to go on and on, but he is certainly enthusiastic about his topic. Do you think you might prefer that?'

Arabella's polite smile started to falter, while his mother's smile grew more gleeful.

'After that, some of the older ladies in the party and I are planning on playing cards. Poor Lady Cathridge is having such problems with her lumbago, so we're hoping to discuss that—and many of the other ailments the ladies have suffered with so much over the winter. Aged bodies can be such a trial... The card game will be a good chance for us to catch up and discuss our aches and pains. You're most welcome to join us for that as well, Arabella.'

She smiled with mock innocence at Arabella and waited for her reply. Arabella stared at the Dowager, her brow now deeply furrowed and her lips pinched— like a prisoner watching the iron gates being slammed shut behind her.

Alexander knew he had to offer a reprieve. 'Or if you prefer you can, of course, accompany me. The marshlands may be a bit unsightly, but the walk there will take us through the woodlands and across the farm areas, which are very pleasant at this time of year.'

'Oh, yes, thank you!' she gasped, in obvious gratitude. Recovering, she smiled at his mother. 'And thank *you*, also, Your Grace, for your kind invitation, but I would like to get some fresh air.'

The Dowager smiled in triumph. 'Think nothing of it, my dear. You young people go off and enjoy yourselves.'

'But we must take a chaperon with us.' Alexander stated emphatically.

'Oh, yes—most definitely.'

Arabella's quick response cut Alexander to the quick. She obviously feared being alone with him.

'Nellie will accompany us,' she said.

'That's all settled, then.' His mother smiled. 'And don't feel the need to hurry back—unless, of course, you want to catch some of Reverend Truebridge's talk.'

Alexander glared at his mother. It seemed she had won. Yet again.

Alexander paced backwards and forwards, his boots scrunching on the gravel path, as he waited at the bottom of the stairs for Arabella. A quick walk around the farmlands and back to the house would suffice. That way there would be no danger of them being alone together. They would be in the presence of the tenant farmers through much of the walk, and he was hardly likely to act inappropriately with an audience.

And there would also be Nellie. That should solve both their problems. It would save Arabella from his mother's threat of a torturous death by boredom without the risk of him being alone in her company. Then he could get back to what he'd originally intended for the day: a survey of the marshlands. There was nothing to worry about.

So why did he feel so agitated? He pulled in a few quick breaths to quash the gnawing feeling in the pit of his stomach. This was ridiculous. He did *not* get anxious. And certainly not because of a pretty face.

'Hello, there. I'm ready.'

He turned to see the owner of the pretty face that was causing all this perturbation standing at the top of the stairs, accompanied by her maid. The pretty face was wearing an attractive blue hat that made her crystal-blue eyes even more enchanting.

He coughed to drive away such nonsense. She had a blue hat on which happened to match her eyes. That was all. There was no need to make more of it than that and become absurdly poetical.

'Miss van Haven.' He nodded a terse greeting as she skipped down the stairs.

'Your Grace.' She bobbed a curtsey.

For politeness' sake he offered her his arm, and refused to allow himself to react when he felt the pressure of her gloved hand.

They walked along in silence and Alexander knew that he should make conversation. But what should he say to the woman whom he had taken in his arms and kissed with an intensity as if his very life depended on it? Should he ask about her health? Should he mention how warm it was for this time of year?

No words came, and once again he coughed lightly. This was not like him. He *never* felt awkward. But he was feeling increasingly awkward in her company. Like an adolescent boy unused to the company of the opposite sex. Ridiculous.

'I hope you're not feeling at all worried about what happened last night,' she said, finally breaking the prolonged silence.

About to say he was not worried in the least, he pulled himself up. That would be an outright lie. Of course he was worried by his behaviour. How else should he feel when he had taken advantage of a vulnerable woman for his own lustful purposes?

'I'm very sorry it happened. I can assure you it will never happen again.'

She stopped walking and looked up at him. 'I said last night that you had nothing to be sorry for and I meant it. I would hate what happened to come between us.'

Beseeching eyes stared up at him. Alexander's stern countenance slipped as he stared down at her and he almost forgot his resolve.

He forced himself to look away from those blue eyes and into the distance. 'It is perhaps a bit too late for that.'

'It doesn't have to be, Alexander.' She gripped his arm with both hands, forcing him to look at her. 'You did nothing wrong. I am not offended. The only thing that upsets me is that it has caused a rift between us. I wish we could go back to how we were before the kiss.

Then we could be friends again and comfortable in each other's company.'

'But it *did* happen.'

'Well, I can pretend it never happened if you can.'

Was that possible? Alexander doubted he would ever forget what it had been like to take her in his arms, but he nodded his agreement.

'If that is what you wish, Miss van Haven.'

'It is. And I also wish that you would stop being so formal. Call me Arabella again.'

Not for the first time he realised what a remarkable woman she was. She had every right to be offended, to be upset, to be angry, but she was none of those things. Thomas Gardener was most definitely a very lucky man.

He clenched his jaw at the thought of that man—the man who would have what he could not. He dragged in a deep prolonged breath to drive away the ridiculous thought. Jealousy was something else he did not experience, and he wasn't about to start experiencing it now.

'As you wish, Arabella,' he said, through clenched teeth.

Strolling with him arm and arm, Rosie could almost convince herself that things were just the same between her and Alexander. Almost. But she could sense the tension in his body, feel the unease in her own.

While she might not be able to forget that kiss, she knew she had to pretend it had never happened. They had one more day to spend together and she wanted them once again to be relaxed in each other's company. And that wouldn't happen unless they did indeed try and pretend nothing had changed…that they had not experienced that moment of passionate intimacy.

But she most certainly had no intention of trying to forget that kiss. It was the most wonderful thing that had ever happened to her. Yes, it had been wrong—so wrong—but it was something she would always treasure…something she would savour when she was alone.

Kissing him was so completely outside her original plan as to be almost unbelievable. After all, she had arrived with the intention of making the Duke dislike her. She had intended to behave in a manner that would make her a thoroughly unacceptable bride. Instead she had caused this sublimely handsome, imminently eligible man to desire her.

A thrill of excitement ran through Rosie's body. Who would ever have thought it possible that poor little Rosie Smith, an impoverished ward whom nobody ever noticed, would be kissed with such intensity by such a man? But she *had* been.

She ran her tongue along her bottom lip, where his lips had touched, and shivered at the delicious thrill of it all.

'Are you all right, Arabella?' His look was solicitous. 'You're not too cold?'

'Not in the slightest. It's a beautiful day.'

And so it was. The sun was shining in a bright blue sky dotted with puffy white clouds. She was walking through lush green pastures filled with bleating sheep and sweet baby lambs accompanied by a sublimely handsome man. It was indeed a most beautiful day. And her shiver had nothing to do with the temperature, which was delightfully warm.

Rosie gave a contented smile. As long as they remained in public, surely there was no harm in indulging in a little fantasy that she was taking a lovely stroll on the arm of the man who was courting her? It was a fantasy that would come to an end when she left Knightsbrook, and as long as Rosie did nothing to act on it no one would get hurt.

And with Nellie as her chaperon she was safe.

She looked over her shoulder and saw Nellie lagging behind in the distance. It seemed she had already become distracted and oblivious to her duties.

'Do keep up, Nellie!' she called out.

Nellie stopped staring at the farmhands and rolled her eyes at Rosie in a most un-servant-like manner, but she walked a little faster to catch up.

They resumed their walk, which now took them along the side of a furrowed field, where a line of men and boys were casting seeds from sacks on their backs. As they passed by the men all lifted their cloth caps to Alexander and he shouted out hellos, addressing many by name.

'You seem to know everyone well,' Rosie said, surprised at their informality.

Alexander smiled. 'Yes, I suppose so—but I grew up with them. I almost spent more time with the farmhands as a child than I did with my own family.'

His smile died and he looked out at the tenants, his face solemn.

'Those times were among the happiest of my childhood. My father saw our tenants as a mass of people who worked the land and brought in the revenue that he spent. But I learnt to see each and every one of them as an individual. I could see that they were hard-working people who deserved to be treated with respect.'

He sent her a melancholy smile and she gave his arm a small squeeze.

'Well, it's certainly a beautiful estate to have grown

up on. It's so picturesque. Watching the men work is like seeing a painting by Constable come to life,' Rosie said, breathing in the earthy smell of freshly turned soil.

'Yes, my mother would certainly agree with you on that.'

Rosie tilted her head. 'You don't approve?'

'The tenants aren't here to be "picturesque". They want to make a good living—they want the land to be productive. They should be using machinery to plant out the crops and machinery to bring them in. Not doing it by such intense physical labour. If my father had spent as much money updating the estate as he did at the card table these people would not still be involved in such back-breaking toil. And that is something I intend to change.'

Rosie looked at the men labouring over their work and had to agree. She would hate to have to work that hard—especially when there was machinery that could do the work more quickly.

'Oh, yes. You should. If you used steam engines for ploughing the land and bringing in the harvest, it would free up men and you could farm more intensively and diversify your crops.'

He had stopped walking and was now staring down at her, that wonderful smile once again lighting up his face.

'Exactly. That's *exactly* the sort of modern equipment I want to buy. It will transform the estate.'

Rosie smiled back at him. 'If you brought electricity to the estate then the dairy and the shearing sheds could be made much more productive. And if the train came as far as the estate you'd be able to sell produce in London. And once it reaches London, who knows? With refrigeration you could export to Europe and even farther afield. Oh, the possibilities are endless for making this estate really modern and efficient!'

He was still staring down at her, no longer smiling, but looking at her with wide eyes, his eyebrows raised. Rosie suspected she had been babbling.

'I'm sorry. My father was—' She halted as she remembered who she was supposed to be. 'My father has worked with electrical engineers and I think it has instilled in me a love of all technological advances.'

Rosie had only been a young girl of eight when her father had died, but she could still remember the passion in his voice when he'd talked of the progress being made in America, and how electricity was transforming the lives of so many people. Alexander's enthusiasm reminded her of those happy times.

He shook his head and sent her another of those lovely smiles. 'You truly are a remarkable woman, Arabella, and I applaud the fact that you are so enthusiastic about modernisation. Most people of my class are content to continue living as they have for centuries, just sitting back and letting the money roll in from their land. They don't realise that times are changing—that we're being overtaken by the more progressive farming techniques used in America and the Antipodes. But I, for one, am determined not to be left behind. I want to be ready for the twentieth century and all the modern advances it has to offer.'

Arabella smiled, feeling warm inside.

'But unfortunately it will take money—which, thanks to my father, I don't have.'

The tone of his voice had dropped from excitement to pain and anger, and a stab of guilt pierced Rosie's heart. If she hadn't come up with her plan to trick Alexander...if the real Arabella were here instead of her, and if they had actually fallen in love…maybe Arabella's dowry could have been used to settle those debts and modernise the estate. Then the tenants would have had security and Knightsbrook would have been saved.

'So Ara—so my father's money would have gone to good use?' Rosie asked, feeling guilty bile rise up in her throat.

Alexander shook his head. 'It might have been a short-term solution, but it was never something I was prepared to consider. I intend to raise the money through bank loans and make the necessary changes to ensure the estate becomes profitable once more. I want it to be a place where both my family and the tenants feel proud to live. I want the name of Knightsbrook to be an honourable one once again—a name associated with industry, innovation and enterprise. And that won't happen by taking a hand-out from your father.'

Rosie could hear the passion and determination in his voice and she swelled with admiration. He was most definitely a proud man, and she was honoured to be in his company—even if it *was* under false pretences.

The path had reached a stone fence with a wooden stile. Alexander quickly climbed over, then offered his hand to her. She didn't really need his help—she was used to fending for herself—but it was nice to feel his hand in hers again, even if it was through her linen glove.

She stepped over, and was about to jump down when he placed his hands on her waist and lifted her gently off the wooden step. Her feet touched the ground lightly and his hands remained on her hips, his body close to hers. He stared down into her eyes. She looked up at him expectantly. A gasp escaped her lips and for a hopeful moment she thought he was going to kiss her again.

What she wouldn't give for another kiss…what she wouldn't sacrifice to feel his lips on hers!

His lips drew into a tight line and he removed his hands from her hips. It wasn't to be.

Disappointment, guilt and shame waged a war inside her as they continued their walk in silence, with Nellie trailing along behind. How could she want him to kiss her so much when she knew the harm it would cause? How could she feel so disappointed when she knew they must not kiss? How could she be such a shameful, terrible person?

She cared for Arabella more than she cared for anyone in the world—even more than herself. She would do nothing to hurt her, to tarnish her good name. And yet she still wanted Alexander to take her in his arms, to kiss her. It was beyond reprehensible.

Their walk took them towards a group of thatched cottages nestled together beside a small stream, smoke rising from their chimneys.

'I hope you don't mind,' said Alexander, 'but I can't pass by this way without visiting Annie.'

'Annie?'

Alexander smiled. 'You'll love Annie. She was like a second mother to me and to Charlotte when we were children. More than a second mother.'

A group of women were sitting in a circle outside the cottages, chatting and laughing while they darned socks and mended clothing. When they saw Alexander and Rosie approaching they stopped what they were doing and stood up.

One woman started walking towards them, her arms

outstretched. Although her lined, weathered face suggested she was elderly, the woman still had a youthful agility to her movements and a healthy glow on her round cheeks. Her welcoming smile caused Rosie to warm to her immediately, as if she too was being welcomed home by a loving grandmother.

'This is Annie,' Alexander said, his smile growing as wide as the older woman's.

'Alexander!' Annie said, reaching up and embracing him. 'Or should I say Your Grace? I keep forgetting you're all grown-up now. It's so good to see you again.'

'To you, Annie, I will always be Alexander. And it is very good to see *you*—you're looking younger than ever.'

Annie waved her hand at him, as if refusing to take any flattery, but her smile showed how much she enjoyed it. 'And who's this lovely young lady?'

'This is Arabella van Haven—a visitor from America. I'm showing her around the estate.'

'Oh, indeed? So *you're* the young lady from America. Well, well… I'm pleased to meet you, m'lady.'

Annie made a low curtsey, causing Rosie to laugh.

'Please—there's no need for formality with me. I don't have a title.'

Annie's eyebrows rose and she looked sideways at Alexander. 'Not yet, perhaps—but if what the servants up at the big house are saying is right you'll have a title soon enough.'

Rosie waited for Alexander to counter her claim but he merely shrugged, as if to apologise, indicating that even if he didn't agree he wasn't going to contradict Annie.

'So, tell me what's been happening on the estate, Annie?'

'I'll let you know all the gossip—but, please, come inside. I'm sure you'd like tea.'

'Nothing escapes Annie's notice,' Alexander said, still smiling as they followed her inside. 'She knows everyone who works on the estate, and all the people in the village, and everyone knows her.'

Rosie looked around to see where Nellie had got to but she was nowhere in sight. It seemed the call of the library had been too great and she had deliberately hung back once again.

They entered Annie's tidy cottage and were greeted by the welcoming aroma of freshly baked bread. The cottage was simply but pleasantly decorated, with handwoven rugs on the wooden floor, spring flowers in pottery vases and old but comfortable-looking furniture.

Alexander breathed in deeply and smiled. 'That's the smell of my childhood—bread fresh out of the oven.'

They sat down at a scrubbed pine table while Annie put the kettle on the stove and poked some wood into the firebox.

'Charlotte and I spent many hours here at this cottage, gorging ourselves on Annie's cooking and playing in her garden. We probably spent more time here than we did in our own home.'

Rosie could see why any child would want to visit Annie's cottage. It was much more welcoming than the opulence and formality of Knightsbrook House, and there was a caring warmth to Annie that no child would be able to resist.

'Poor Lady Charlotte,' Annie said as she poured hot water into a brown teapot. 'She's such a lovely girl, but so serious. She needs a good man in her life.'

Alexander gave a mock frown. 'Don't let Charlotte hear you say that. She's determined to remain single.'

'Oh, don't worry—I've already told her. She gave me that look she always gives when she hears something she don't like—just like your mam.' Annie pinched her lips together and flared her nostrils, causing Alexander to laugh. 'But I'm very happy *you've* found someone special, Alexander—and such a pretty girl as well.'

Again, Rosie expected Alexander to disabuse Annie, but still he said nothing.

Annie took a golden loaf of bread out of the oven, and Rosie stood and offered to help. But she was shooed away with a smile and the wave of a tea towel.

'I can already tell she's a good influence on you, Alexander. The last time I saw you, you seemed to be carrying the weight of world on your shoulders and I could barely get a smile out of you.'

She placed the bread on the table, along with the teapot and three teacups. Rosie inhaled the mouth-watering, yeasty aroma. Was there anything more irresistible than freshly baked bread? Rosie doubted it.

'Oh, yes,' Annie continued. 'You need a good woman who'll not only share your burdens but will make you laugh, make you see the joy and wonder in the world. And by look of this pretty young thing she's just the one to do it.'

Annie turned to face Alexander, as if daring him to disagree, but it was a dare that Alexander was apparently reluctant to accept.

When the tea was deemed sufficiently brewed Annie poured. 'You'll be wanting some cheese to go with your bread, won't you, Alexander? Well, you know where it's kept.'

Alexander crossed the small cottage in three steps and

took some cheese out of the cupboard while Annie cut doorstop-sized slices of bread.

'As a child I think Alexander lived on my bread and cheese,' Annie said to Rosie. 'I sometimes wondered whether they ever fed him up at the big house.'

'That's because the cook there could never make bread as good as yours, and there's no better cheese anywhere in the country than the cheese made in your dairy, Annie,' he said as he placed the cheese dish on the table. 'One day soon, when the railway comes through here, I'm hoping that people throughout England will be able to taste the wonderful cheese made in the Knightsbrook dairy under the watchful eye of Annie.'

Annie smiled proudly, cut some generous slices of cheese, and handed plates to Alexander and Rosie.

Rosie took a bite of the still warm bread and murmured her agreement. The cheese had a nutty flavour that was simply delicious. 'I think you're right. This will be very popular. I'm sure it will fetch high prices in London and the other main cities. It's wonderful!'

Alexander took another bite of his own bread and cheese and nodded. He seemed to be enjoying the simple fare much more than the lavish feast that had been served last night in the ornate dining room.

'So, what's been happening on the estate?' Alexander asked again as he served them both another slice of bread and cheese.

Rosie listened as Annie told him all the gossip about the other tenants—about couples who had married, others who were having difficulties, what their children had been up to and who had fallen out with whom.

All the while Annie was talking Rosie watched Alexander. He was smiling, laughing and commiserating about these people he obviously knew well and cared for deeply. The man she was watching was a different man from the one she had first met. He was so much more relaxed sitting in this plain cottage than he was in Knightsbrook House.

Rosie could imagine him as a young boy, running around the fields, playing with the other children on the estate and then, when he was tired and hungry, retreating to Annie's warm, comfortable cottage and the arms of this loving woman.

When she had first met him it would have been impossible for her to imagine that such a commanding man could ever have been a child. He had exuded such authority and been so aloof as he'd glared down at her while she acted the fool.

When Annie finally ran out of gossip Alexander cleared the table, took the plates and cups to the bench and placed the kettle back on the stove to heat up some water for the dishes.

'Oh, be gone with you,' Annie said, flicking a tea towel in his direction. 'I'm not so infirm that I can't wash a few dishes. You take this young lady on that walk you promised her and leave me to my chores.'

Alexander smiled, then bent down and kissed Annie on the cheek. 'Thank you, Annie. It's been lovely to see you. I'll see you again soon.'

'Mind you do. And tell Charlotte she's due for another visit.'

'I will—I will!'

Annie escorted them to the door and took Rosie's hands in hers. 'I hope to see much more of you too. You'll always be welcome at my cottage.'

Rosie smiled her thank you, even though she knew she would never see this warm, wonderful woman again...

Chapter Thirteen

The world always seemed like a better place after a visit to Annie's cottage. But his conversation with her had also reinforced in Alexander's mind his duty to the tenants. All those people she had talked about depended on Alexander. He had their livelihoods to protect. He needed the estate to survive and prosper as much for their sake as for the sake of his own family.

Annie had said he was like a man with the weight of the world on his shoulders. It wasn't quite the weight of the world he carried, but it was the weight of so many people's futures—futures that his feckless father had put in jeopardy. It was a weight that he had no option but to bear.

Annie had also said that Arabella was the woman who could share his burden, lighten his load and make him laugh. During her short time at Knightsbrook Arabella had most definitely made him laugh. Before her arrival he could hardly remember the last time he had laughed, but in the last two days he had laughed often. She was a woman full of fun, who shared her joy of life with everyone she met. It was a rare and valuable quality that he seemed to be lacking.

He suspected she was also a woman who would gladly share the burdens of the man she loved. Most women of his class expected to live a life of cossetted privilege after they married, in which their burdens were no more exacting than keeping up with the latest fashions and admonishing the servants.

He certainly could not see that in Arabella's future. He imagined that her marriage would be a partnership—that she would ease her husband's burdens, not contribute to them. But whether he was right on that count or not, he was destined never to discover.

Annie had also been right in saying that Arabella was a very pretty young woman. That was something he had been aware of from the moment he had seen her spinning down the entrance hall of Knightsbrook House, and every time he looked at her she seemed to grow more beautiful.

Sitting in Annie's cottage, he had been struck once again by how enchanting she was. It had nothing to do with her fine clothes or her stylish hair; she would be just as beautiful in a simple dress with no adornments. Nor was it her bright blue eyes and creamy skin, fetching though they might be. It was an indefinable inner quality that made her quite radiant.

He smiled at her now and she returned it.

Yes, quite radiant.

They retraced their steps back through the fields. The men all tipped their caps as they passed, and one even called out a greeting to Miss van Haven. Alexander shook his head in disbelief—although he really had no reason to be surprised. Gossip spread faster than wildfire on the estate. No doubt one of the women seated outside Annie's cottage had told the men of their visit, and had informed them about the young woman Alexander was escorting.

They had also, no doubt, been told that Arabella was the likely future Duchess of Knightsbrook.

Well, on that, they were going to have to accept disappointment.

Despite her radiant good looks, despite her ready laugh and despite the way she made him feel, she was not for him. She had all the qualities that would make his perfect duchess, but it was not going to happen.

Annie had said he needed a woman who would lighten his burdens, but his burdens seemed even heavier now that he had met Arabella. Yes, it had been a long time since he had laughed—and he suspected that when Arabella left, when she returned to Thomas Gardener, she would take the laughter with her.

They walked on along the tree-lined path down to the river, then halted together to take in the tranquil scene. This had always been his favourite spot on the estate when he was a child, and it looked particularly beautiful at this time of year. Weeping willows bearing their bright green spring foliage dipped in the gently running water, and multi-coloured wildflowers dotted the long grass.

'It's lovely—and so peaceful,' she murmured

It was indeed. All they could hear was the gentle babbling of the river running over mossy rocks and the sound of birds chirping in the foliage.

He led her along the edge of the river until they reached a stone seat beside the old, now abandoned mill.

'I spent hours here as a child,' Alexander said almost to himself as he took a seat beside Arabella. 'It was a place to play but also my sanctuary—somewhere to escape from "the big house", as Annie insists on calling it.'

'A place for a child to get dirty and have adventures?' she said with a laugh.

'Indeed.'

'I can just imagine you as a small boy, your knees muddy, trying to catch fish and skimming stones across the river.'

Alexander smiled as memories came back to him. When he'd got away from the house and played on the estate with the tenants' children his childhood days had been almost carefree.

'My record was eight bounces.'

She gave a little laugh. 'Really? Prove it.'

Alexander turned to face her. 'What? You don't believe me?'

Smiling, she shook her head.

'Well, then…' Alexander stood, took off his jacket, rolled up his shirtsleeves and looked around for a suitable stone. 'It's been a long time, and I'm somewhat out of practice…'

'Oh, excuses, excuses.'

To his surprise she stood up, picked up her own stone and stood beside him.

'I challenge you to a duel!' she said.

'You're on.'

Side by side, they bent their knees, leant back and flicked their stones across the river's surface. Alexander had no idea how many times his own stone skipped because he was watching Arabella's stone fly across the river, bouncing once, twice, three times.

'Well done!' he exclaimed in amazement. It was obviously not the first time she had skimmed stones.

'But not good enough. You beat me by one.'

'Well, I do have the home advantage.'

She let out a delightful tinkling laugh. 'Ever the gentleman. So, are you ready for a rematch? Then I'll be able to find out if you're as much of a gentleman in defeat as you are in victory.'

'I accept your challenge,' he said, and immediately began searching for appropriate stones.

Caught up in the game, he lost count of the number of stones they threw, or who was winning—he just knew it was a long time since he'd enjoyed such childlike pleasure

Having skimmed all the flat stones they could find, they collapsed, laughing, onto the stone bench.

'I think we should declare it a draw,' Alexander said.

Arabella nodded her agreement. 'That was fun. Do you come down here often?'

'This is where I first met Annie. Charlotte and I had escaped from the house because Father was hosting another one of his week-long gambling parties and Mother had taken to her rooms, supposedly with one of her headaches. Charlotte was crying and I was trying to comfort her. Annie found us, took us back to her cottage, fed us and let us stay the night. After that, every time there was a house party the two of us would immediately escape and spend time at Annie's. She saved us from what would have been a miserable childhood.'

'She's a lovely woman,' said Arabella quietly. 'You were lucky to have someone so warm to comfort you as a child.'

Alexander nodded. 'But I haven't been back here for years. Not since...'

He paused and began thinking back to when he had last sat here by the river. He certainly hadn't been since his father had died and he had taken control of the near-bankrupt estate. The moment the lawyers had informed him of the state of the accounts had heralded the end of all frivolity. It must have been some time before that.

Whenever it had been, it was a considerable time ago, but exactly when he could not recall.

'Not since Lydia?'

Her voice was quiet but her words hit him like a cannon ball, knocking the wind out of his lungs.

'I'm sorry, Alexander.' She placed her hand gently on his arm. 'I shouldn't have mentioned her name—not if it pains you.'

Alexander shook his head. 'No, it doesn't pain me.' And he realised that it was true. Not so long ago his grief over Lydia had been so intense he'd preferred to try and forget she had ever existed, had ever been part of his life. Now he had no objection to talking about her.

'Lydia was the love of my life. She was the woman I intended to marry.'

Arabella nodded but said nothing.

'She was a cheerful and loving young woman.' Alexander sighed, remembering what Lydia had been like when they were young. 'But she changed. And that, too, was my father's fault. He ran regular card evenings at the house. They were not sociable events, like the ones my mother hosts, where gossip is more important than winning or losing. These were serious gambling events, where fortunes could easily be lost. And reputations.'

He stopped talking for a moment and looked out into the distance.

'Usually I was able to protect Lydia from the excesses of those weekends, but she visited one weekend when I was away and met one of my father's gambling companions…'

He paused again, and considered how much he should reveal about that debauched man to a woman as innocent as Arabella. He was a notorious rake—a man who loved corrupting innocent young women. And that was exactly what he had done to Lydia.

'She thought she was in love with him and that he was in love with her. She fell in with his lifestyle—the parties, the gambling... Gambling and that man became all she lived for. Then she started to lose. A lot. That was when the real change happened. She borrowed money. She lied to everyone she knew—including me—to get more. She even started to steal from people to pay her gambling debts. I tried to help her...to encourage her to stop... But nothing I did worked. *Nothing.*'

They sat in silence for a moment, both staring into the gently burbling river.

'Where is she now?' Arabella asked, her voice almost a whisper.

'Her debts grew so big she eventually fled to the Continent. I believe the wastrel left her and moved on to his next conquest. The last I heard she was working as a—'

But Arabella did not need to know the extent of Lydia's downfall. She didn't need to know that Lydia had attached herself to a series of wealthy but increasingly disreputable men in order to support her gambling habit, until she'd been reduced to selling herself in order to fund her desperate lifestyle.

'The last I heard she was working at a gambling establishment in Italy.'

An establishment where the women dealt more than just cards.

'It must have been painful for you,' said Arabella.

Alexander nodded. 'It was very painful to watch someone I cared about change and be powerless to do anything about it. It was painful to hear her constant lies. Eventually it was as if every word that came out of her mouth was a lie. She lied about the extent of her debts. She lied about how much money she had lost. And she lied about how she had managed to repay those debts.' Alexander shook his head. 'I sometimes wonder if she was so lost that she no longer knew when she was telling the truth and when she was lying.'

He sighed deeply. It was the first time he had told anyone about Lydia's downfall. It had always been too painful to remember it before, and certainly too painful to talk about it. At the time he had done everything he could to help her. Tried endless ways to keep her away from that man, from the card table and the gaming houses, and in the process of trying to save Lydia he had lost part of himself. He had lost his trust in people, and lost his ability to relax and enjoy himself.

He shook his head, picked up another stone and tossed it into the river. The reality was that there was nothing more he could have done for Lydia. For years he had tortured himself with guilt. Had believed that if only he had been at home that weekend Lydia might never have met that terrible man. Had thought that perhaps there were things he could have done to turn her away from her downward spiral.

But Lydia's path was one she had chosen for herself. Continuing to torture himself about what he might have done, what he might have said to stop her would help no one—not him, and not Lydia.

He sighed again, then smiled at Arabella. 'In answer to your question, I don't remember the last time I visited this spot on the river, but I'm pleased I brought you here today.'

She smiled sadly and nodded. 'So am I.'

It seemed Annie was right again: talking to Arabella

had lifted the weight of the guilt and remorse over Lydia that he had been carrying for many years, and he felt much lighter for it.

Thomas Gardener was a lucky man to have a woman like Arabella in his life. She was indeed a woman who could lighten a man's burdens and take away his worries. He could only hope the man appreciated what a treasure he had. A woman who was not only beautiful, but also clever, funny and supportive.

But this would not do. He had originally decided to take a quick stroll around the estate to save Arabella from the ordeal of a dreary talk by the Reverend Truebridge and the horror of playing cards with his mother and her cronies. Instead he had lost all sense of time.

He looked up at the sky. The sun was heading towards the horizon and there was a slight chill in the air. It must be late-afternoon. He picked up his jacket and pulled his fob watch out of the pocket. Yes, he was right. Time had got away from them, and instead of a quick stroll they had been away all day. It seemed that in Arabella's company he even forgot the passage of time.

His mother would certainly be pleased, and would no doubt read much more into their absence than it warranted.

He stood up, took her hand and helped her to her feet. It had been a delightful day but it was time to bring it to an end.

'I suspect my mother and her friends will have finished their card game, and that every ache and pain will have been discussed in exhaustive detail, so it should be safe to return to the house.'

She gave a light laugh and rolled her eyes. 'Oh, yes—I

haven't thanked you for saving me from that ordeal, have I? It's been a lovely day, Alexander.'

He draped his jacket over one shoulder, dangling it from his thumb, and took Arabella's arm in his. Slowly they walked back along the river, as if neither was in any hurry to return to the house. White swans sailed majestically past them, ducks dived in the water and birds flitted between the trees, fully occupied with finding food for their offspring and oblivious to the couple walking in companionable silence beneath them.

For the first time in many years Alexander enjoyed the simple pleasure that nature brought and the soothing effect it could have on the soul.

They followed the path from the river and walked under the canopy of the tree-lined path that led back to the house. A light, rustling breeze shook the trees, and Arabella lifted her hands and laughed as a cascade of spring blossoms showered them, falling like pink confetti.

She took hold of her skirts and gave them a shake, sending tiny flowers skittering in all directions, while Alexander brushed the blossoms off his shoulders.

'Leave them,' she said, laughing. 'Pink really suits you.'

'I'm not sure about that, but the blossoms adorning your hair are certainly fetching.' He laughed too, and picked a few of the flowers off her hat.

Leaning over her, he could feel the warmth of her body, could almost feel her soft curves, almost taste her silky skin. He closed his eyes and breathed in deeply, inhaling the remembered scent of fresh flowers.

This could not be happening. He had to resist temptation. He could not take her in his arms again. He could not kiss her again. Even if her feminine scent was overwhelming his senses...even if every inch of his body longed to take her in his arms. Even if his throbbing desire was telling him how much he wanted her. This could not happen.

He had to remember his vow. He had to remember his aching muscles, remember his plunge into cold water, how hard he'd had to exercise last night to try and free himself from his desire for her.

Opening his eyes, he discovered his hand was suspended in mid-air above her head, clasping a pink blossom. Despite his self-admonition on the dangers of touching her, he ran his hand down her soft cheek.

Her breath caught in her throat as she stared up at him, her pink lips parted tantalisingly. Even while words of warning rang in his head, he took hold of her chin, tilted it towards him and leant in closer.

How could he not kiss her again? How could he deny himself such temptation? How could he not do what his body was commanding him to do?

But his mind knew better than his body. She was not his. She would never be his.

He released her chin, stood up straight and looked off into the distance.

'We can't do this.' He heard the formality in his voice, so at odds with how he was feeling. 'Don't you agree?'

He looked down and saw her blink a few times, as if unsure she had heard him correctly.

'Don't you agree?' he repeated. Surely she, even more than he, could see the folly of their actions.

'I agree,' she said, in a barely audible whisper.

Once again they walked in silence, although now that sense of companionship had evaporated, to be replaced with a tense uneasiness.

Alexander knew he deserved to feel uncomfortable. He had allowed his desires to overcome his good sense. Wasn't that exactly why he had wanted to avoid being alone with Arabella? And hadn't he been proved correct?

They entered the house and he bowed to her formally, as if their encounter had never happened…as if he hadn't almost kissed her…as if he hadn't unburdened his soul and shared with her intimate details of his relationship with Lydia.

'It is nearly time to change for dinner. I'll bid you farewell till then.'

He bowed again, and then, like the coward he knew himself to be, retreated to his rooms.

Chapter Fourteen

'Ooh, lovely—a bath. Thank you, Nellie, that's exactly what I need.'

Rosie stripped off her dress and undergarments and lowered herself into the warm water of the freshly drawn bath. She slid down until only her head was above the water and rested her head on the soft towel Nellie had kindly draped on the edge of the bath for that purpose. Perhaps Nellie was feeling guilty for abandoning her duties as chaperon, but this bath more than made up for it.

A small fire flickered in the tiled fireplace of the chamber adjoining her bedroom, making the room warm and cosy, and Rosie issued a small sigh of complete contentment.

This was perfection itself. A chance to lie back and have a long, leisurely soak. She picked up the soft sponge and the rose-scented soap, worked up a lather and gently ran the sponge over her body while her mind wandered to the day's events.

And what a day it had been.

It was possibly the happiest day she had ever experienced, and even Alexander's formal parting could not detract from her joy. A few days ago Rosie would not have thought it possible that she could spend such a wonderful day with a man as charming as Alexander Fitzroy, Duke of Knightsbrook.

After her treatment by every man who had ever entered the van Haven home, being snubbed was all Rosie had known. It was a role she had accepted—the poor ward who had no prospects and was of no interest to any man. But not any more.

A man who was head and shoulders above all those men—literally and figuratively—had spent the day with her, had laughed with her, played games with her, unburdened his troubles to her. He had treated her as an equal—more than an equal—and as someone whose views he respected and admired. And, what was more, he had almost kissed her. *Again.*

Rosie wiggled her toes above the warm water and closed her eyes as images of everything that had happened ran past her mind's eye—from Alexander's stiff greeting in the breakfast room through to their enjoyable lunch at Annie's, from their playful encounter by the river to his revelations about Lydia, and then to that almost-kiss under the blossoms.

She squeezed the sponge and released a stream of scented soap bubbles into the water. Oh, yes. It had been quite a day. Within the space of a few hours she had seen so many sides to Alexander. The stern man at the breakfast table. The loving man in Annie's cottage. The childlike man who had skimmed stones on the river. The serious, almost melancholy man who had talked of Lydia. And the passionate man whose hungry eyes had burned into hers when he had nearly kissed her again.

So many men—and she adored them all. Even the

stern Alexander. She knew where *that* man came from. As Annie had said, he carried the weight of the world on his shoulders—the responsibility for his family, for his tenants, and his need to undo the damage his father had done to the family name.

And he also carried the weight of wanting to do the right thing when he was with her. She was sure it was only the non-existent Thomas Gardener that had stopped him from taking her in his arms this afternoon and kissing her.

Rosie squeezed the sponge again and let soapy water run over her shoulders and down her chest as she contemplated how she could get rid of pesky Thomas Gardener. Perhaps she could tell Alexander that she had just had news that the unfortunate man had suddenly dropped dead, or had decided to become a monk instead of marrying her, or had set off for an expedition to deepest Africa and was unlikely to be seen again.

She sighed and rubbed the sponge slowly across her shoulder and down her arm. None of those stories had the slightest chance of being believed. It seemed the imaginary Thomas Gardener was going to have to stay healthy, alive and working at his family's bank for a few days more.

And at least he did serve one valuable purpose. If Thomas Gardener hadn't stopped Alexander from kissing her, Rosie doubted if anything else would have—certainly not her. She sighed again. She was a terrible friend. She knew she had to protect Arabella's reputation, and yet she seemed to forget all about that whenever there was a chance that Alexander might kiss her.

It was as if she was powerless to stop the way she felt about him.

Rosie stopped rubbing her arm and dropped the sponge, then sat up straighter in the bath and gasped.

The way she felt about him?

It was obvious how she felt about him. She had fallen in love with him.

Her hand covered her mouth, as if she must stop herself from blurting out this shocking revelation. But it was true. She had to face the facts. She had fallen in love with Alexander, Lord Ashton, the Eighth Duke of Knightsbrook.

She lowered her hand, picked up the floating sponge and clasped it to her chest. This had most certainly not been part of the plan she had devised over tea and scones at The Ritz just a few days ago. No, falling in love had been the last thing on her mind. Less than the last thing. It had been so unlikely that she had never even considered it.

But that was before she had met Alexander. She sighed loudly and shook her head. How could she *not* fall in love with a man like Alexander?

'There's an awful lot of sighing going on in there,' Nellie said, poking her head around the corner, a clothes brush in her hand. 'Are you all right? Is the water too hot? Too cold?'

'No, it's perfect.'

'So what's all this sighing about?'

'It's just been rather a confusing day, that's all.'

'Don't worry,' Nellie said, heading back into the bedroom. 'Only one more evening and we'll be back in London. This will all be over.'

Rosie couldn't stop herself from sighing once again. This time in frustration. One more evening. That was all. After that she would never see Alexander again. She would have to live without him in her life.

How was she going to be able to bear that?

And it was obvious that Alexander felt something for her as well. That look on his face when he had almost kissed her... He felt it too. Could it be that the Eighth Duke of Knightsbrook *would* consider marrying someone like plain Rosie Smith?

She squeezed hard on the sponge. Oh, what would it be like to be married to Alexander? Bliss. That was what it would be. Pure bliss.

She sighed again and sank down into the water.

But he didn't even know Rosie Smith.

She shot back up.

He thought she was Arabella van Haven. How would he react when he realised she wasn't the daughter of a wealthy banker but an orphan without a penny to her name?

She dragged herself out of the bath and wrapped herself in the soft white towel. Alexander wasn't a snob. He didn't want Arabella's money. Didn't want to marry an heiress. Wasn't it possible he *might* want to marry her, the real Rosie Smith, a woman with no money? Was she being unrealistic to think that he would consider someone of her background as a potential bride? Was that just too ridiculous?

Well, there was only one way to find out.

Rosie padded on bare feet through to her bedroom, where Nellie had laid out her undergarments and the pale blue gown she was to wear that evening.

She would just have to tell him who she really was and see how he reacted. Only then would she know how he felt about the real her, Rosie Smith. That was exactly what she would do.

She sat down at her dressing table, nodded at her reflection, then frowned. But she would have to tell Arabella first. After all, Arabella had agreed to a plan in which Rosie behaved so abominably that the Duke would not *want* to marry her. She had not agreed to a plan in which Rosie pretended to be Arabella and then, when it suited her, let the cat out of the bag and announced to everyone that she wasn't Arabella after all.

No, she owed it to Arabella to let her know first. And then she would tell Alexander.

Yes, that was a much better plan. It was all settled.

With a light step she skipped down the stairs and entered the dining room, to find the family already seated.

Alexander stood up and a footman ushered her to her seat.

'What happened to the other guests?' Rosie asked as she took her seat.

The footman shook out her napkin with a practised flourish and placed it on her lap, and Rosie smiled her thanks.

'The other guests were invited only for yesterday evening so they could meet you,' the Dowager said, signalling to the footman to begin serving the soup. 'Tonight it's family only.'

'Family and one guest,' Alexander added.

It seemed formal Alexander was back again. Rosie smiled at him. She loved even formal Alexander, the honourable man who was so determined to do the right thing.

'Quite right, Alexander.' The Dowager raised her wine

glass. 'To our honoured guest, Arabella van Haven, who already feels like part of the family.'

Alexander glared at his mother and received an equally reproving glare in return, before she turned her attention back to Rosie. 'So, Miss van Haven, did Alexander show you the rest of the estate. It's magnificent, isn't it?'

'Oh, yes. We met some of the tenants and had a lovely walk along the river. It really is quite beautiful.'

The Dowager smiled her approval. 'Indeed it is. And it's so lovely to see the tenants working on the land in the same way they have for generations. So much nicer than horrid steam engines. Steam is diabolical, don't you think?'

Rosie bit her lip to stop her smile as Alexander continued to glare at his mother. 'Well, a "diabolical" steam train brought me here from London. And an even more diabolical steam ship meant I could cross the Atlantic in seven days in considerably more comfort than I would have had I travelled by sailing ship. So, if it weren't for steam I doubt I'd be here this evening.'

'Well, there's that, I suppose...' the Dowager conceded reluctantly. 'But there should be limits to all this modernisation.'

Alexander shook his head and exhaled loudly.

'Did you have a chance to meet Annie?' Charlotte asked, interrupting what Rosie suspected was a familiar argument between the Dowager and Alexander.

'Oh, yes—she made us tea and served us some freshly baked bread and the most delicious cheese I've ever tasted.'

Charlotte smiled and nodded. 'I must go down and visit her tomorrow. Perhaps we could go together in the morning? It would be lovely if we had a chance to spend some time together before you return to London.'

Rosie smiled at the young woman, touched by her offer of friendship. 'I'd enjoy that very much.'

Polite conversation continued throughout all the courses, with just the occasional black look from Alexander when his mother alluded to the topic of marriage or the horrors of the modern world.

'I hear you're an accomplished banjo player, Miss van Haven,' the Dowager said when the meal was almost over. 'Perhaps you can entertain us after dinner? I bought a banjo especially for this weekend.'

Rosie almost choked on her chocolate mousse, and took a sip of water while she recovered herself. 'I suspect my abilities on the banjo have been greatly exaggerated. Unless you enjoy the sound of cats being strangled it might be best to keep me away from that particular instrument.'

The Dowager's lips pinched slightly. 'Then perhaps you would care to recite some verses for us from Shakespeare?'

Oh, dear. She had helped Arabella learn her lines for various Shakespeare plays, but unfortunately had retained none of them.

'I'm afraid in that area too my talents may have been exaggerated.'

The Dowager's already pinched lips tightened further. 'What *are* your accomplishments, my dear?'

'Well, I have some talent on the piano, and I have taken singing lessons.'

'Wonderful.' The pinched lips turned into a smile. 'The piano is so much more cultivated than the banjo, anyway. After dinner you can play for us.'

'I'd be delighted.'

Rosie smiled. There were so many accomplishments Mr van Haven could have attributed to his daughter—but the *banjo*? What had he been thinking? Well, he hadn't been thinking... It seemed he rarely thought of his daughter and didn't know anything about her.

Their meal finished, they rose from the table and all followed the Dowager into her private drawing room, where a grand piano took pride of place.

Rosie sat at the piano and shuffled through the sheets of music until she found one of her favourite pieces, while the family seated themselves and turned towards her with expectant faces.

The piano had been a means of escape for her ever since she was a little girl, and she soon lost herself in the music, forgetting about her game-playing, forgetting about the way she was deceiving the friend she loved, even for a moment forgetting about Alexander.

When she came to the end of Beethoven's 'Moonlight Sonata' she turned to face the family. The room remained silent. Had she done something wrong?

Then Charlotte, the Dowager and Alexander stood as one and applauded enthusiastically.

'It seems you have been hiding the truth,' Alexander said as he continued to clap his hands.

Heat rushed to Rosie's cheeks. He had finally found her out. But how? And which of the many lies she had told was he referring to?

'You have more than *"some talent"*. You're a virtuoso,' he continued. 'I don't think I've ever heard that piece played with more beauty and more warmth.'

Her cheeks grew hotter—but from pleasure, not discomfort. 'Thank you,' she murmured, and turned back to the piano.

His praise had touched her deeply. It seemed there was another Alexander she was also in love with. The one who looked at her with tender admiration.

Chapter Fifteen

She was continually amazing him. Beautiful, funny—
and now it seemed she was also talented. He watched
her shuffle through the music sheets, looking for another piece to play, her pretty forehead furrowed in concentration.

She was not the way his mother had described her
when she had first been trying to convince him that he
should marry an American heiress. And it seemed her
claim that she played the banjo was wrong—thank goodness. But his mother was right in that the man she married would be very lucky indeed.

It was just a shame it wouldn't be him.

If it wasn't for Thomas Gardener he would have no reservations about courting her, despite her father's fortune.

Yes, he'd always had objections to marrying anyone—
and an American heiress in particular—but whether that
was due to pride, his worry that people would assume he
had married for money, or because Lydia had put him off
love and marriage for ever, he couldn't say. Whatever it
was, all those reasons were losing their hold.

When it came to her father's fortune there would be

options. An astute businessman like Mr van Haven would surely prefer to invest his money in the estate and be paid a healthy return rather than merely hand over money in the form of a dowry. And if people thought he had married Arabella for her father's money, so what? He couldn't possibly be so shallow that he would let what others thought of him dictate his actions.

He did care about restoring the nobility and prestige of the family name, but that was in order to honour his ancestors' hard work and the sacrifices they had made. And a respected name was something he wished to pass on to future generations of FitzRoys. It wasn't because he cared what others thought of him personally.

And as for the pain that Lydia had caused him—well, that was fading into a distant memory. It was no longer an obstacle when it came to thoughts of marriage. And Arabella was nothing like Lydia, with all her lies and complications.

But all that was neither here nor there. Arabella was in love with Thomas Gardener. She wanted to marry Thomas Gardener—not him.

He was sick to death of Thomas Gardener.

Arabella replaced the sheets of music on the piano stand, turned around on the piano bench and smiled. 'If you'll indulge me, I think I'll play a tune that I've learnt just recently. When I was in New York I bought a book of contemporary English songs and fell in love with them. I'm playing from memory, so please excuse any mistakes.'

'Oh, I'm sure it will be wonderful,' his mother said, beaming with pleasure. 'Play on...play on.'

Arabella gave a cheeky grin and began playing the opening bars of the music hall song 'Champagne Charlie'.

Alexander suppressed a smile as he watched his mother to see how she would react to such a low-class form of entertainment being performed in her private drawing room?

When Arabella sang the first few lines in a false Cockney accent his mother's smile quivered, but then it returned even wider and she started clapping along to the tune.

Unbelievable. Arabella had got the wife of the Seventh Duke of Knightsbrook clapping along to a music hall song. Simply amazing.

When she repeated the chorus—*Champagne Charlie is me name, Champagne drinking is me game*—the Dowager and Charlotte even joined in, leaving Alexander so stunned his mouth literally fell open.

'Oh, that was so funny!' his mother said when Arabella had finished, wiping away a tear. '"*Champagne Charlie is me name...*" Oh, yes, very funny.'

Arabella smiled. 'What would you like next? More Beethoven or more music hall?'

'Music hall! Music hall,' his mother and Charlotte chanted together.

Alexander shook his head in surprise and admiration. Anyone who could get Charlotte to laugh so easily and his mother and sister to enjoy each other's company really was special. He was beginning to wonder whether he should let Thomas Gardener have things all his own way.

After all, wasn't all fair in love and war? And he was most certainly falling in love with Arabella van Haven...

She began a round of music hall songs, many of which Alexander had heard before, and he noticed she skipped the bawdier verses. A wise decision. It was surprising enough to see his mother enjoying something she would normally dismiss as common; if she knew the true lyrics Alexander suspected it would be a step too far.

Arabella finished and turned to her appreciative audience.

Clapping enthusiastically, his mother stood up and approached the piano. 'That was marvellous, Arabella. Just marvellous. Thank you so much. I can't remember the last time I enjoyed myself this much. But I'm getting tired, so I think I'll retire.' She gave Charlotte a pointed look. 'And I believe *you* were hoping to get an early night as well—weren't you, Charlotte?'

'No.' Charlotte shook her head, then noticed her mother angling her head in Alexander's direction. 'Oh, yes... I was.' Charlotte gave a fake yawn. 'I'm rather tired also, so I think I'll retire early as well.'

Charlotte joined her mother at the piano and kissed Arabella's cheek. 'Thank you so much. For once Mother and I are in total agreement. That was the most fun this family has had for a long time.'

'Yes, yes, it was wonderful,' his mother said, leaning over to kiss Arabella's cheek, and jutting out her elbow in the strangest manner as she did so. Her arm caught the edge of the pile of sheet music and sent the pages scattering to the floor. 'Oh, dear, I beg your pardon. Alexander, help Arabella pick up that music—and come on, Charlotte. It's time we retired.'

She grabbed Charlotte's arm and hurried her out of the room. When the door had closed he could hear the two women giggling and humming the last tune as they headed up the stairs.

Alexander shook his head, still looking at the door. It was an unsubtle move on his mother's part to leave them alone together, but then subtlety had never been his mother's strong suit.

He turned to face Arabella. The room suddenly seemed very quiet. He remained standing in the middle of the room, staring down at Arabella, feeling uncharacteristically awkward. Then he bent down and picked up the scattered sheets and handed them to her.

She shuffled them into an orderly pile, placed them on the music stand, then picked them up again and gripped them in tight hands. It seemed she too was nervous now that they were alone.

And perhaps she was right to be nervous. If she knew what he was about to do...

He sat down beside her on the piano bench and heard the breath catch in her throat. Had he deliberately sat so close that his leg was touching hers? Perhaps. Or had he wanted to be close so he could surround himself in that beautiful floral scent? Whatever it was, being so close to her was intoxicating his senses and making him forget what he wanted to say.

'Thank you for that, Arabella,' he said finally. 'Charlotte was right. That was the most fun our family has had in a long time. You have certainly brought laughter into this house. And I've never seen Charlotte and my mother leave a room together singing. I would never have thought such a thing possible. You really are a remarkable woman.'

'Oh, I'm pleased they enjoyed it.'

She shuffled the music sheets again, put them on the stand, then picked them up once more.

'You really *are* a remarkable woman, Arabella,' he repeated.

She sent him a small smile. 'Well, I love to play the piano and I enjoy singing.'

'It's more than that.' He took the sheets of music from her hands, placed them on the music stand, then took her hands in his.

She looked down at her small hands, encased in his larger ones, then back up at him, her blue eyes sparkling in the candlelight.

'You are truly exceptional, Arabella. You're funny, clever, kind, sweet…and now it seems you're talented as well. You're the most wonderful woman I have ever met.'

'Oh!' she gasped.

'And, what's more, I think I've fallen in love with you.'

Her eyes momentarily grew larger, then she blinked rapidly. 'You think you've…?' She closed her eyes, as if trying to absorb this surprising admission.

'No, I'm wrong. I don't *think* I've fallen in love with you.'

Her eyes sprang open.

'I *know* I've fallen in love with you.' He smiled, feeling buoyant, as if his declaration had cut loose the weights that were tying him down. 'Nothing would give me more pleasure than to court you, one day to marry you.'

'But I…' She swallowed, her breath coming in gasps. 'I…um…'

'I know. I know,' he interrupted, desperate to put her at her ease. 'I've put you in an impossible position. You're already in love with another man—all but betrothed to Thomas Gardener. But I could not let you leave this house without telling you how I feel.'

Her blinking became more rapid. 'Oh, Thomas Gardener… Yes. Him.' She chewed lightly on her lower lip.

Not for the first time Alexander cursed the man's existence, and ungraciously wished that some accident might befall him and take him out of Arabella's life. Or, better still, that Arabella would decide she no longer loved him, making the path easier for Alexander.

But what was the chance of that happening?

Alexander had to know whether he was chasing an impossible dream.

'And I could not let you leave without finding out how you felt about me. I know you said you were in love with him, but do I stand any chance of winning your affections?'

Alexander held his breath and waited for her answer. She was looking down at their hands. He followed her gaze and saw her small hands were clenched into fists inside his larger ones.

She hadn't spoken, but that gesture had given him an answer. It was not one he wanted, but it was one he would abide by.

'Forgive me, Arabella.' He released her hands. 'I've spoken out of turn. I've embarrassed you and made you feel uncomfortable.'

'No, no—not at all.' She took hold of one of his hands in both of hers, clasping it tightly. 'It's just complicated. I need to return to London. There are people I need to talk to before I can tell you how I feel. All I can say is that you have done nothing for which you need to beg my forgiveness. You have not embarrassed me nor made me feel uncomfortable. Quite the contrary.'

He brushed a stray curl back from her face. 'Thank you, Arabella. Thank you for giving me hope,' he murmured.

She angled her head as he ran his hand along her soft cheek. Closing her eyes, she parted her lips slightly, her breath turning to a quick gasp.

His gaze lingered on those soft lips, parted so invitingly. She had given him hope—hope that she would one day be his. Surely that was enough? But those lips...those beautiful, full pink lips...how could he resist?

Perhaps just one small kiss?

He leant forward, unable to fight the fierce urge building up inside him. His lips lightly touched hers. A sound escaped her mouth. Was it a gasp or a moan? Whatever it was, it caused her lips to part further, and they remained parted, seemingly asking him to intensify the kiss.

If that was what she was asking, then it was a request he was more than happy to grant.

He pulled her into his arms and kissed her harder, more deeply. Her sigh of pleasure as he used his tongue to open her mouth told him he had not misread her actions. And when her hands encircled his neck he had definitive proof.

She wanted this as much as he did. And he most certainly wanted this kiss—desperately wanted it, and much more.

A powerful need was driving him on, and he licked those sweet lips, desperate to devour her feminine taste, to devour *her*. Her need matched his own, and she ran her hands through his hair, clasping him close, seemingly urging him on. Then, to his immense pleasure, her tongue entered his mouth, tasting, probing, teasing.

She was just as lost as he was. He would make her forget Thomas Gardener...make her surrender herself to the pleasure he was giving her...make her think only of him.

He clasped her slim waist and pulled her in, closer towards him, impatient to feel those soft breasts against his chest. Even through the silk of her gown her nipples pushed hard, and he could feel the fast beating of her heart.

Her arousal was driving him almost insane with desire, and he kissed her neck, savouring the taste of her soft, warm skin. He heard her purr with pleasure as his lips trailed a line across the naked skin of her chest and along the soft mounds of her breasts, which were rising and falling with each rapid breath.

His hunger for her was rising to an almost insatiable level, and he was tempted to tear open the delicate fabric of her gown, to feast himself on her beautiful body. But he would not compromise the woman he loved.

He withdrew from her and bit down hard on his lip, hoping the pain would distract his mind and his body. He would do nothing to harm her or compromise her. Instead he would lovingly recall every erotic detail of their encounter when he was alone in his room—the touch and taste of her skin, her intoxicating feminine scent, and that look of sensual abandonment on her face.

She remained in his arms, her eyes closed, her lips parted, her face flushed. His erection was almost unbearable now, but that was a price he had to pay.

'So, can I take it from your reaction that I have a chance against Thomas Gardener?'

She slowly opened her eyes and blinked a few times. 'Oh, you most certainly do,' she said, her voice husky. 'After a kiss like that I'm beginning to think that Thomas Gardener is just a figment of my imagination. It's as if he doesn't exist at all.'

That was exactly the response Alexander wanted.

With final victory now close at hand, he took her in his arms and kissed her again.

Chapter Sixteen

Was there ever a more wonderful day? Rosie stretched luxuriously in the four-poster bed. It was as if her entire body was smiling with contentment. Today she would return to London. She would recount to Arabella every delightful, delicious detail of what had happened over the weekend. Then, with Arabella's blessing, she would pen a letter to Alexander and confess all.

In her letter she would tell him that she loved him, loved everything about him, and most of all loved the way he made her feel. All would be revealed—who she really was, what her silly scheme had been about, and the reasons why she had been pretending to be Arabella—and then everything would be put to rights.

She stretched again, her smile turning into a sigh of pure pleasure. It was a perfect plan and one she could hardly wait to put into action. It certainly wasn't her original plan, but this new plan was so much better.

Everything had turned out perfectly. Arabella was saved from an unwanted marriage and could now pursue her real love—the theatre. And Rosie had met a man who had swept her off her feet and changed her life for ever.

She had received a declaration of love and had been given a delightful taste of what it would be like to be loved by a man like Alexander FitzRoy. It was all perfect.

Sweeping back the covers just as Nellie arrived to help her dress for the morning, Rosie all but danced across the room, threw open the curtains and looked out at the grey cloudy sky, edged with threatening black rain clouds lining the horizon.

'Have you ever seen a more beautiful day, Nellie?' She beamed a smile at Arabella's lady's maid.

'Well, *you're* certainly in a good mood,' Nellie said, giving her a sideways glance.

Rosie did a twirl in front of Nellie. 'Indeed I am. Oh, Nellie. It's all too exciting. Last night Alexander declared his love for me. Well, at least he declared his love for the woman he knows who goes by the name of Arabella. But as soon as I let Arabella know what's happened he'll be declaring his love to a woman who goes by the name of Rosie,' She pointed to her chest. 'Me!'

Nellie stared at her, her face closed. It was not the re-action Rosie had expected. Surely Nellie should be more excited and happy for her?

'Yes, I know who you are. I just hope the woman called Rosie knows what she's doing. The Duke may have fallen for you—I don't doubt that—but here you're Arabella: an heiress, the daughter of one of America's wealthiest men. Not a woman with no family and not a farthing to her name.'

Rosie frowned at Nellie, then shook her head, her smile returning. 'No, Nellie, you're wrong. Alexander's not like that. I *know* him. You don't. He didn't want to marry Arabella precisely *because* she's an heiress. He's too proud to take her father's money. He's a proud, honourable man.'

He was also handsome and could turn her to jelly with his kisses, she wanted to add as a shiver of remembered pleasure rippled through her body.

'Oh, Rosie, just don't get your hopes up too high—otherwise when you come crashing down to reality the fall might be more than you can cope with. Men like the Duke do *not* marry women like Rosie Smith.'

Rosie shook her head vehemently. 'No, you're wrong. He loves me. *Me.*' She pointed to her chest again. 'And that's all that matters.'

Nellie was wrong. Rosie knew it. She had seen how Alexander had looked at her last night. That had been the look of a man in love. In love with *her.* It hadn't been just passion she'd seen in his eyes, and it hadn't been just lust. It had been love. Real love.

Nellie sighed and shook her head slowly. 'Well, that's as may be, but hold still now while I get you dressed. Stop spinning round like a top.'

Rosie tried to remain still while Nellie helped her out of her nightdress and into her clothes, but it was too hard—she just wanted to dance and sing in celebration of the night before and the day that was to come.

Her desire to see Alexander again was overwhelming. She desperately wanted the day to begin so she could see his handsome face. But she also wanted the day to be over, so she could return to London as soon as possible and be set free from pretending to be Arabella, return to being Rosie Smith. Then Alexander could get to know the *real* Rosie—the Rosie that he had fallen in love with, the Rosie he had kissed, the Rosie he had caused to writhe in pleasure under his touch.

Then it really would be perfect.

There was no sign of Alexander in the hushed dining room. Only the Dowager and Charlotte were sitting at the highly polished walnut table, with matching grim expressions on their faces. It seemed last night's good grace between them had come to an end and they were once again adversaries.

Never mind. Rosie would talk to Charlotte when they spent time together this morning, and try and make things better between them. After all, wasn't she the breath of fresh air the servants said the family needed?

'Good morning...good morning,' she trilled, and headed towards the sideboard.

It seemed it was self-service this morning, as none of the usual bevy of servants were in attendance.

She lifted the lids of the silver tureens and was greeted by the delicious aromas of crisply fried bacon, scrambled eggs, fried mushrooms and tomatoes. The food looked delicious, and she had never been so hungry. It must be the excitement. Or perhaps being in love stimulated the appetite. Whatever it was, she needed food. Lots of it. Instead of her usual toast and marmalade, this morning she would treat herself to a full English breakfast.

Her plate piled high, she joined her future family at the table. Smiling, she removed her napkin from the engraved silver napkin ring and placed it on her lap. 'Isn't it a beautiful day?'

No greeting came from either woman. Instead the Dowager picked up the newspaper and gripped it tightly, as if frightened that it would fly out of her hands, and Charlotte stared down at her half-eaten plate of food, her shoulders slumped.

Rosie's smile faded. What was wrong? This was

'But... But...' Rosie called out to the now closed door. 'But I didn't mean any harm,' she said quietly, and then slumped down on to a dining chair, the crumpled newspaper still clutched in her hand.

more than their usual ill humour towards each other. Had something happened to Alexander?

Rosie waited, looking from Charlotte to the Dowager and back again, but it seemed neither women felt compelled to enlighten her.

'A beautiful day, is it? I don't think so.' The Dowager finally snapped, her long bejewelled fingers twisting at the paper. 'Perhaps you'd like to explain *this*.'

The Dowager sent the newspaper skidding across the table in Rosie's direction. Rosie's hand shot out to stop it before it fell off the edge, and she looked down at the headline: *New Oscar Wilde Play a Resounding Success.*

'Is that not good news?' she asked, but got a scowl from the Dowager in response.

Perhaps the Dowager didn't approve of Oscar Wilde. Rosie had heard that some people objected to his somewhat flamboyant lifestyle, and the Dowager was hardly likely to be familiar with the ways of theatrical people.

'You have no shame, have you?' the Dowager shot back through clenched teeth.

Rosie sent the Dowager a questioning look, then continued reading the article, which discussed the intricacies of the storyline, the wonderful performances of the cast, and mentioned the series of standing ovations the play had received.

When she got to the bottom of the page she read a paragraph about the notable people who had attended the opening, including American heiress Arabella van Haven, who had dined with the playwright.

So Arabella had got her wish. She had attended the opening night of an Oscar Wilde play and had not only got to meet the great man himself but had actually dined with him. Wonderful.

Smiling, she looked up at the scowling Dowager and the frowning Charlotte—then looked back down at the newspaper.

'Oh,' she squeaked. 'I see…'

'Oh, indeed,' the Dowager said, standing and glaring down at Rosie.

'I can explain…'

Rosie bit the edge of her bottom lip. But what was she going to say? She could hardly tell them she was here taking her friend's place because Arabella would rather go to an Oscar Wilde play than attend their weekend house party, even if it *had* been hosted in her honour.

'Who are you? You're obviously not Arabella van Haven,' the Dowager thundered.

'Um… I'm…'

Where should Rosie begin? What could she possibly say to explain herself?

The Dowager Duchess held up her hands and turned her face away, as if repelled by even looking at Rosie. 'No, I don't want to know. You've lied to us already—as if I would believe anything you would say now. You come into my house…make a fool of me and my guests…insinuate your way into my son's affections… And now you think you can talk your way out of it. You're shameless.'

Rosie stood up, still clutching the newspaper. 'No—no, I didn't…'

She gripped the edge of the table, her mind spinning, her body feeling weak. She wanted to entreat the Dowager, to convince her that she'd meant no harm, but what could she say without betraying Arabella?

'The servants are packing your bags. I would not be so uncivil as to throw you out without your break-fast, but once you have finished eating *our* food—' scowled at Rosie's laden plate '—the carriage will be ready to take you to the railway station. And that will be the end of it.'

'But Alexander? Where's Alexander? I need to speak to him.'

'As if my son would want to talk to a woman like *you*.'

'But I need to tell him—'

'You will tell him *nothing*. And if you have the slightest shred of decency you will tell no one about the way you have made complete fools of this family.'

The Dowager turned and walked towards the door.

'I didn't mean any harm!' Rosie called out to the retreating ramrod-straight back. 'It's just that I… The plan wasn't going to cause any harm… It was just to… I didn't mean to…'

Her hand on the doorknob, the Dowager stopped and turned back to Rosie. 'Stop talking, you thoughtless girl. I don't want to hear any more of your lies. Be thankful that I care about the good name of FitzRoy and want to avoid a scandal. If I didn't I would have you arrested for your fraudulent behaviour. Instead of catching the train home you would be spending the night in jail. And instead of eating that hearty breakfast you'd be dining on bread and water.'

'But I need to talk to Alexander—'

'Don't push me, girl. I can still change my mind and call for the constabulary. My son does not want to talk to you. *No one* wants to talk to you. Now, come, Charlotte, let's leave this criminal to fill her belly with *our* food.'

With that she left the room, followed by an obviously distressed Charlotte.

Chapter Seventeen

It was all over. How could Alexander not hate her now?
The Dowager had said he didn't want to talk to her. This
was as bad as it could get.

How had everything gone so horribly wrong? Her plan
had been simple enough: save Arabella from an unwanted
marriage and have some fun at the same time by making fools of a greedy duke and his snobbish family. Then
she would return to London with a funny story to tell
Arabella—something that would amuse her just as so
many of Rosie's antics had amused Arabella in the past.

But instead of making a fool of a stuffy duke, it was
she who was the fool. Instead of having a joke at their
expense, *she* was the joke.

She gripped both sides of her lowered head and released a deep sob. And now she would go home in disgrace. It was all too, too terrible. And, worse than that,
she had caused the man she loved to despise her—had
caused his family to think she was a fraudster instead of
merely a silly, foolish girl who thought it was amusing
to play tricks on people.

'Damn, damn, *damn*,' she cursed under her breath.
And the worst thing of all: her behaviour had hurt Al-

exander. His lasting memory of her would be as a liar, a woman up to no good, not a woman who loved him, a woman he had held in his arms and who had surrendered herself to his touch, to his kisses.

No, that could not happen.

Rosie stood up quickly, nearly toppling over the chair. She had to do something. She could not just sit there, wallowing in despair. There was no time to waste in self-indulgence. The carriage would be taking her away soon—taking her away from Alexander. Despite the Dowager's threats, she had to find him. She had to try and explain herself.

Even if it resulted in her being thrown in jail, she couldn't leave without talking to Alexander.

She ran out of the dining room, down the corridor, out through the entrance hall, and then halted at the top of the stairs, looking in every direction. Over the vast estate, at the gardens, the woodlands, the green pastures dotted with sheep.

Where would he be?

The door opened quietly behind her and she turned expectantly. But instead of Alexander it was Charlotte, her mouth turned down in a frown, her shoulders slumped.

Intense shame swept over Rosie. Charlotte was hurt too. It had never been her intention to hurt anyone. But she had.

'Oh, Charlotte, I'm so sorry.' She reached her hands out towards the distressed young woman who had shown her nothing but friendship.

Charlotte took a step backwards, as if shocked by the gesture. 'It is unforgivable that you betrayed Alexander. He did not deserve to be betrayed again...to be lied to again.'

Tears filled Rosie's eyes. 'I know. I *know*. I want to

apologise to him. I want to try and explain to him what I did and why I did it. Please, Charlotte, can you tell me where he is?

Charlotte released a long sigh. 'I don't know who you are, or why you are here, but I do know my brother has fallen in love with you, and I do believe you have fallen in love with him. So if you want to talk to him you'll find him down by the river. There's a favourite place of his he used to go when he was a child. It's—'

'I know where it is!' Rosie called out, running down the stairs. 'And I'm sorry for everything I've done,' she shouted over her shoulder, while running along the pathway, her shoes crunching on the gravel.

Her mind spinning with half-formed explanations and excuses, she ran as fast as she could down the tree-lined path towards the river. How could she explain her behaviour? What could she say to him without betraying Arabella?

No answers came, but she had to think of something— had to say something. Had to make him see that she had meant no harm.

Surely when he saw her he would forgive her? After all, he had said he loved her, wanted to court her, even to marry her. And she was still the same woman he had declared his love for. That hadn't changed. Nothing had changed. Not really. It was just that she was not called Arabella and didn't really have a fortune, a rich father or a dowry.

Reaching the river, she came to an abrupt halt and stopped, giving herself time to catch her breath. As she approached the spot where yesterday they had skimmed stones with such child-like joy, she saw him sitting on the stone bench, staring into space.

In profile, his handsome face looked morose, and his body was rigid. Rosie's stomach clenched tightly with guilt. It was her fault he was in such pain. She had to put it right.

It had to be possible to change his mood. Wasn't that what she was good at? Making people laugh? Making them happy? She had spent most of her life entertaining Arabella, making her laugh when she was sad, lightening the mood in Mr van Haven's otherwise gloomy home. It was what she was best at.

But how?

For once she had no plan.

He turned his head slowly and stared up at her. His expression changed from sadness to impassiveness, as if he was shutting down all emotions. It was the same look she had seen the day they'd first met. Gone was the warmth in his brown eyes…gone was the loving look, the friendly smile.

Slowly, she walked towards him, her steps tentative, as if entering an ice-cold stream. When she was close to the bench he stood and faced her, his body tense, his face as harsh and bleak as a winter's storm.

'Oh, Alexander, I can explain…' She reached out to him.

He looked down at her hands, which remained suspended in mid-air between them, then back at her face, his eyes granite-hard. 'I'm sure you can, Miss van Haven—or whatever your real name is. I'm sure you have a very good explanation for why you deceived me, my family and our guests. You no doubt have a very plausible reason for your lies. Unfortunately for you I have been taken in by your lies once and I will not do it again.'

She slowly lowered her hands to her sides. 'Rosie—my name is Rosie.'

A sneer of contempt curled his lips. 'Rosie, Arabella—it makes no difference. Whoever you are, you are no longer welcome here. It is fortunate that your lies were exposed before the full extent of whatever crime you had planned was carried out.'

A gasp escaped Rosie's lips. 'No—*no!* There was no crime. You must believe that. Yes, I lied about who I am, but I meant no harm, and I was certainly never intending to commit a crime.'

Alexander glared down at her through narrowed eyes. 'How can you possibly think you would cause no harm? How could you possibly think that telling such lies, acting in such a manner, would not cause harm? Are you insane as well as deceitful?

Cringing at the insult, she reminded herself that he had every right to be angry with her. She would be angry if she thought he had lied to *her*. But she had to make him see that there had never been any ill intent behind her actions—quite the opposite. Perhaps her plan had been flawed, but how was she to have known that the stuffy, greedy Duke would be someone she would fall desperately in love with? If she had known that she would never have lied to him.

'I'm sorry. So very sorry. I know it was stupid of me. And I'm very, very sorry. I intended telling you the truth—just not yet.'

He shook his head and laughed—a harsh, mirthless laugh. 'Oh, I *see*. Well, that makes everything all right, doesn't it? How could I possibly object if you were planning on telling the truth one day. So, when would that have been? When would you have told the truth? After we had married? When our first child was born? Or were you planning a deathbed confession?'

His sarcasm stung and she grew smaller under his withering stare. He could not think that of her. This had to be put right. But how?

Silently she asked for Arabella's forgiveness. There was no choice now but to tell Alexander who she really was. He already knew she wasn't Arabella, so it was time to tell the whole truth.

'I had intended to write to you after I got back to London, but I will tell you who I am now.'

He shook his head and gave a snort of sarcastic laughter. 'I can hardly wait...'

She forced herself to ignore the barb. 'My name is Rosie Smith. I'm Mr van Haven's ward and Arabella's friend. I'm not an heiress. In fact, I have no fortune of my own. I'm all but penniless.'

He stared at her for a moment, his disdain obvious. 'Yes, that I *do* believe.'

Rosie exhaled in relief and smiled slightly. He believed her. Thank goodness for that. Perhaps now they could put all this unpleasantness and these accusations behind them and return to the way they had been.

'An impoverished ward with ambitions to become a duchess? Yes, that makes perfect sense,' he sneered.

Her smile dissolved. 'No, I never had ambitions to—'

'It explains everything. Unfortunately, Rosie Smith, I have no interest in marrying an impoverished ward who uses such chicanery to advance her position in society. And I certainly have no respect for a woman who would use her *obvious* charms...' his dark eyes raked up and down her body '...to catch herself a titled husband.'

Rosie recoiled as if struck, blood rushing to her face,

her heart pounding violently against the wall of her chest. 'How dare you?' she seethed through clenched teeth. 'How dare you accuse me of—?'

'I dare quite easily, Miss Smith. You have used the oldest tricks known to woman in order to ensnare a man. And I must say you are particularly adept at it.'

Rosie stared at him, uncharacteristically speechless, hardly able to believe what he was accusing her of. This was worse than his mother calling her a criminal. This was too bad.

How could he think that of her? He had ruined everything—tainted what had happened between them and reduced their affection, their passion and their love, to something sordid.

'No! *No!* It wasn't like that,' Rosie cried, barely able to hear her own voice above the sound of blood pounding in her ears. '*I'm* not like that,' she said, her voice rising. 'I wasn't trying to—'

Alexander glared down at her, his merciless eyes burning into hers, his lips a thin, disgusted line. 'That's exactly what it was like, Miss Smith. That's exactly what you were trying to do, and that's exactly the sort of woman you are. But this time you failed. Perhaps you'll have better luck next time and you'll be able to get some other hapless aristocrat to drag you out of the gutter and give you a title.'

Rosie felt her eyes grow wide and her mouth drop open. It seemed Nellie was right. Now that he knew who she really was he thought he was too good for her. As Nellie had said, men like him did not marry women like her. But that did not mean he had the right to insult her.

She closed her mouth, tilted her chin and glared back at him. 'You are an appalling man. You might be a duke but you are most certainly not a gentleman if you think you can speak to a lady like that. How I ever could have thought you were honourable and kind, I don't know.'

'Honourable? Kind?' He gave another humourless laugh. 'I don't think *those* were the attributes you were after. A title and a position in society? Weren't those the qualities you were looking for in a man?'

'I couldn't care less about your title,' Rosie fired back. 'I couldn't care less if you can trace your family back to the Stone Age. But it seems you do care. You think that because you've got a title, all this land and your fancy house, that you're better than me and you can talk to me any way you want.'

'I'm afraid, Miss Smith, your behaviour this weekend has shown that I *am* better than you. You're a liar and a charlatan who isn't above using her body for financial gain. And there are some *very* unpleasant names to describe a woman like that.'

'You—! You—!' Pain surged through Rosie as she clenched her hands so tightly her nails dug into her palms. She stared up at him, attempting to catch her breath as she tried to think of a way to wipe that arrogant sneer off his face.

Forcing herself to unclench her hands, she looked down at the ground and took a few steadying breaths. Slowly she raised her head, pulled herself up to her full height and stared him straight in the eye.

'Perhaps I have told a lie or two, but you're rude, insulting and a snob,' she hissed.

She had hoped her insult would affect him, but he stared back at her with eyes as cold and dark as a winter sky.

'And *you*, Miss Smith, are a liar and a wh—'

'I am no such thing!' Rosie interjected, even though

it meant lying again. Of course she had lied—but that wasn't the point, was it? It didn't mean he could talk to her in such a disrespectful manner or question her morality.

'All right—all right, I lied. And I've said I'm sorry about that. But you have no right to accuse me of…to accuse me of…'

'To accuse you of being a tart? A strumpet? A hussy? What word is it that you're searching for, Miss Smith? There are so many words available to describe a woman who uses her body to get what she wants.'

Her jaw and hands clenching tightly, Rosie glared up at his arrogant face. 'You contemptible man. To think I actually thought that I was in love with you. How could I have been so stupid as to think I loved a man as detestable as you? If I never see you again it will be far too soon.'

'Well, it seems there is one thing on which we are in complete agreement. I suggest you leave immediately and stop wasting my time.'

Rosie stared at him, her face burning, every muscle in her body clenched. There was so much more she wanted to say to him—so many more insults she wanted to fling in his direction. But what was the point? His arrogance was impenetrable. Nothing she could say would make any difference to his low opinion of her.

Summoning up as much dignity as possible, she turned abruptly and strode up the path, her skirts whipping around her ankles. As she walked quickly towards the carriage waiting outside the house a light rain started to fall, the raindrops merging with the tears of anger, shame and remorse running down her cheeks…

Chapter Eighteen

Pebble-sized circles formed on the river as raindrops hit the water, but Alexander was oblivious to the change in the weather. Nor did he hear the burbling river as it raced over the mossy rocks. With his mind shrouded in a fog of anger everything around him was all but silent and invisible.

Yes, he was angry. Angry with Miss Rosie Smith, or whoever she was, but he was even more angry with himself.

Angry that he could be so gullible. He had fallen for her lies, for her beauty, for her play-acting. Hadn't he learnt his lesson with Lydia? It would appear not. The next pretty liar who had come his way had bewitched him and he had fallen again—fallen even harder this time.

He picked up a willow stick and whipped it against the nearest tree, trying to beat out the pain that had overtaken him. His pain over Lydia's betrayal had been intense, but it had been nothing like this. It had not been so all-consuming.

He had trusted her, this Miss Rosie Smith. He had believed her. Believed her lies. He had let down his guard—

the guard that Lydia had taught him was essential if he was to avoid being betrayed again. And this was how his trust had been repaid.

Pain and anger continued to wage a war inside him as he walked up and down the edge of the river, determined to quash down all emotion. Anger he could cope with. Almost. But the pain—that was unbearable.

And he had a right to be angry. Everything about her had been a lie. She had even had the audacity to attempt to explain her actions. As if *anything* could explain her lies, her betrayal. And he had almost been taken in by them. For one fateful moment when he had seen her standing beside the river looking so forlorn he had wanted to *comfort* her.

He was a fool—a complete fool.

He hit the stick against the tree—harder. He knew what it was to be lied to repeatedly. Hadn't Lydia used exactly the same tricks? Hadn't Lydia said anything, done anything, to try and free herself from the web of lies she had woven around her? And he had believed her again and again, until it had been impossible to believe one more lie.

Well, not this time. Miss Rosie Smith had lied. She was a liar. That was all he needed to know. He did not need to know why she had lied or what her intentions had been. She was a liar. And he had been betrayed. *Again*.

Lydia's betrayal had been a mere bee-sting compared to the knife in the heart inflicted by Miss Smith. With Lydia he had never felt such all-consuming passion—a passion he could have drowned in, that could have taken him over and swept him away, so all he could think about was her, a woman he didn't even really know.

Yes, he was a fool. He had fallen in love with a chimera—a woman who didn't really exist. A woman who had been created as a device to ensnare him.

And she had almost succeeded.

Who she really was, what she was really like, he would never know. Never wanted to know.

An image of her laughing face and sad eyes entered his mind and his anger subsided slightly. He had never learnt why there was such sadness behind her laughter. Perhaps it was simply because she was poor and wanted a position in society.

He grabbed both ends of the willow stick and broke it in two. No, he did not need to know about her sadness. Did not need to know anything about her. She was gone and he had been saved from making even more of a fool of himself than he already had.

And yet here he was, standing by the river like some love-struck youth. He just had to remember that the woman he'd thought he loved did not exist.

Alexander tossed the sticks into the stream, watched them float away with the current, then turned and walked back towards the house. It was time to put this entire unfortunate incident behind him. He had work to do, and he had allowed himself to become distracted for far too long.

He should not be wasting time wallowing in self-pity. He should not be thinking about that woman—should not be remembering how she'd looked in the candlelight, or how her lips had felt on his, or what it had felt like to hold her in his arms. No, he should not think of such things. And he wouldn't ever again. Nor would he remember the sweet taste of her soft pink lips, the way she smelt of spring flowers, or how she looked when she lost herself in the passion of their embrace.

Instead he would write to the engineers tomorrow.

They would begin draining the marshlands and that ne-glected area would be converted to farmland. He would arrange a loan with the bank to buy a steam-driven har-vester, so the next harvest could be brought in more effi-ciently. He would contact the owners of the local railway company and begin discussions on bringing the line through his land. He would even investigate the possibil-ity of introducing electricity to the dairy and woolsheds.

He stopped walking. Hadn't electrification been *her* suggestion?

Dragging in a deep breath, he strode off towards the house. It was of no matter where the idea had come from. He had much more important things to occupy his mind than thinking about that woman, or dwelling on such fripperies as her beauty, or how she played the piano with such passion, or how lovely her singing voice was.

He increased his walking pace. No, he would not think of such frivolous things—not when he had so much work to do.

As he neared the house Charlotte raced out to meet him, clutching a large black umbrella, her face contorted with worry.

She handed the umbrella to Alexander and he gripped the curved cane handle in a tight fist, sheltering his sister from the increasing downpour.

'Oh, Alexander, I'm so sorry. I know she meant so much to you.'

Anger continued to simmer inside him. That woman had also caused pain to his sister—a woman who had never hurt anyone.

He took her arm and patted her hand gently. 'It's all right, Charlotte. I'm all right. Please, I think it best if we just try and pretend none of this ever happened.'

'But what did she *say*? Why did she pass herself off as an American heiress? What was it all about?'

Charlotte clutched his arm, her questions coming in a rush, her eyes pleading with him.

'I have no idea, Charlotte. I'm just pleased that she has gone,' he said, his words more clipped than he intended.

'But didn't you ask her? Didn't you want to know? Didn't you *need* to know?'

Alexander released a sigh and looked over Charlotte's head into the distance. 'No, I didn't ask her. I neither needed nor wanted to know why she tried to trick me into marrying her. She's gone. There's no more to be said about it.'

Charlotte inhaled deeply, then slowly released her breath. 'You asked her to marry you? You really were in love with her, weren't you, Alexander? Oh, Alexander, surely you need to know why she did it?'

Alexander gripped the umbrella more tightly, his teeth clenched so firmly his jaw ached.

'If only you had asked, Alexander—asked her why she lied. Perhaps there was a good reason,' Charlotte said, her voice softening.

He looked down at his sister, her face pinched with concern. But it was misdirected concern. Like him, Charlotte needed to forget all about Miss Rosie Smith.

'There can be no good reason to excuse her lies, her deception,' he said, keeping his voice even so his anger would not upset her.

Charlotte shook her head. 'I can't accept that, Alexander. She was here for only two days, and in those two short days she changed you. Because of her you opened up your heart—a heart that had been closed since Lydia left. Please, Alexander, don't just dismiss her...don't close down your heart again. You deserve to be happy—and Arabella, or whoever she is, made you happy.'

Alexander shook his head and exhaled loudly. His ever-perceptive sister was right. Thanks to Miss Rosie Smith he had opened his heart—and look what had happened. For that, he would never forgive her. He had felt so many emotions over the last two days—emotions he'd thought he had forgotten how to feel. And now all he was left with was anger and pain.

Charlotte released her grip on his arm and lightly patted it. 'Perhaps when you calm down you should contact her and find out why she lied to us.'

'No, Charlotte,' he said through gritted teeth, to stop himself from shouting. 'I will *not* be contacting her, and I forbid you from having anything to do with her.'

Charlotte tilted her head and raised her eyebrows.

Alexander knew he had made a mistake. The best way to get Charlotte to want to do something was to forbid it.

'I'm sorry, Charlotte,' he said, his voice softening. 'I did not mean to lose my temper with you. But I entreat you to leave this alone. Nothing good will come of contacting that woman.'

Before she could formulate any other arguments he took her arm and walked her towards the house. He knew he would have to speak to Charlotte again on the subject at a later date because, like his mother, once her mind was made up it could be a monumental challenge to get her to change it.

And the last thing he wanted was for her to have any contact with Miss Rosie Smith.

Chapter Nineteen

Being a strong and resourceful woman was something Rosie had always prided herself on. She'd had to be strong when her father had died. She'd had to be even stronger when her mother had died and she'd been left all alone in the world. She'd had to be strong to endure being poor in a world of extreme wealth, and she'd had to be strong to cope with being completely dependent on Mr van Haven's reluctant charity.

Now she had to be even stronger. She had to be brave and to appear unaffected by the reality that she had fallen in love with a man who now despised her…who thought she was an immoral, gold-digging con woman.

When she'd returned to London she had resolved to keep what had happened a secret from Arabella. All her friend needed to know was that she was safe and did not have to marry the Duke. Arabella did not need to be upset by the painful details.

All her life Rosie had tried to repay her debt to Arabella by entertaining her, keeping her happy, distracting her from the sense of neglect she felt as a result of her father's constant absences. And that was what she intended to do now.

Arabella was trying to establish her career on the stage and that was all that mattered. Rosie would force herself to be happy, to smile, to laugh. After all, wasn't that what she always did? Kept smiling no matter what. Even if her heart was breaking.

Her tea whirled round and round in her cup as she continued to stir long after the sugar had dissolved, the spoon clinking against the fine bone china. Yes, she had to be strong for herself and also for Arabella.

Things were going so well for Arabella. While Rosie took afternoon tea Arabella was attending an audition for a play being staged by a small, newly formed London theatre. She was so close to achieving her dream of becoming an actress, and Rosie would not burden her with her own problems.

She was happy for her friend—very happy. And once that vicarious happiness would have been enough. Not long ago all she had ever wanted was for her best friend to achieve her dreams. She owed so much to the kind and generous young woman who had saved her from a life of poverty and vulnerability on the streets of New York. Just a few short days ago she had been prepared to dedicate the rest of her life to being Arabella's companion, and that ambition had been more than enough for her.

That was until she had met Alexander FitzRoy, Lord Ashton, the Eighth Duke of Knightsbrook. He had turned her world upside down and had changed everything.

Now she had to fight so hard to keep smiling that her cheeks often ached with the strain. It was becoming increasingly difficult to stop the edges of her lips from trembling, to stop her misery breaking through the veneer of joy she was determined to maintain.

Rosie released a quiet sigh. She lifted the teacup to her lips, then lowered it again, un-tasted, and tried to take comfort in the fact that her plan had actually succeeded. At least she had achieved her goal, she thought with sardonic humour.

She had arrived at Knightsbrook with the intention of behaving so badly that Alexander and the FitzRoys would eventually drive her out of the house, never wanting to see her again. And she had succeeded.

She lifted the cup once more to her lips, took a sip, but tasted nothing of the now cold tea. Yes, she deserved the pain she was feeling. Her actions had been appalling. She had lied to Alexander, betrayed his trust and the trust of his family. Charlotte had been right. Alexander did not deserve to be treated in such a manner. Another deep blush of shame swept over her. He deserved someone so much better than her.

Arabella entered the Palm Court at The Ritz, her charming demeanour and pretty face causing every head in the room to turn in her direction. She made her way between the tables, her face a beaming smile, her eyes sparkling.

Rosie forced herself to sit up straighter and to adopt her sunniest smile.

'I got the part! I can't believe it, but I did it—I got the part. I'm going to appear on the London stage!' Arabella nodded her thanks to the waiter who was pulling out her chair and sat down, still smiling. 'It's just a small part, but it's mine, and I appear in virtually every scene.'

'Oh, Bella, that's wonderful news,' Rosie said, clapping her hands together. 'Congratulations! You deserve it. You really are very talented.'

Arabella signalled to the waiter for afternoon tea, pulled off her gloves, clasped her hands together and placed them on the table. 'So... I think I've given you enough time,' she said, her face becoming serious. 'If you're not going to volunteer to tell me, then I'm just going to have to ask you. What's wrong, Rosie? Why are you so unhappy?'

Rosie shook her head and forced her smile to grow even larger. 'Nothing's wrong. I—'

'Don't tell me that nothing's wrong, Rosie. You've been miserable since you came back from Knights-brook. I know you think it's your role to be the happy one, to entertain me. You've always been like that since we were young girls. But I don't want any more of your fake smiles and pretend joyfulness. What happened? Were they really mean to you?'

Rosie's mouth turned down and she shook her head. 'No, they were lovely.'

'Oh... Was the Duke stuffy and unbearable?'

'No, no... He was actually rather nice. Handsome, kind, honourable—not stuffy at all.'

Arabella gave her an assessing stare and Rosie's cheeks burned more fiercely.

'Oh, Rosie. Is that what the problem is? Was he *very* nice, *very* handsome, *very* kind and honourable?

Rosie nodded.

'And has he captured your heart?'

She nodded again.

'And was he uninterested because you have no money of your own?'

Rosie shook her head, then remembered what Nellie

had said about aristocratic men not marrying out of their class and nodded. But she was sure Nellie was wrong, so she shook her head again.

'I don't think such things matter to Alexander.'

'Then what went wrong? Why was he uninterested? Is the man a simpleton? You're beautiful, funny, charming. If you set your mind to it no man could resist you.'

'Oh, Bella. You're so kind.' Tears welled up in Rosie's eyes. 'But it's not that straightforward. He *was* interested. In fact he said he loved me, said he wanted to marry me—but that was when he thought I was *you*.'

Arabella tilted her chin and narrowed her eyes. 'So it *was* money he was after. Well, you're better off without him.'

'No, no, Arabella. You don't understand. He never wanted to marry you—well, at least he never wanted your money…never wanted to marry for money. He's a fiercely proud man, and even though the FitzRoys have lost their wealth he wants to restore the family fortune and their good name through hard work—not by marrying an heiress.'

'Well, there's no problem, then.' Arabella gave a little laugh. 'You have no money of your own. You're exactly what he's after.'

Rosie shrugged and sighed. 'Except he's also an honourable man. When he found out I'd lied to him by pretending to be someone else he was furious. He saw what I'd done as unforgivable.'

'But surely when you told him *why* you were lying he must have understood? Surely an honourable man would know that if you're lying to save someone else then it's not an unforgivable action.'

Rosie looked down at her teacup and then back up at

Arabella. 'I didn't tell him why I was pretending to be you. At first it was because I didn't want to betray you. And then I got so angry… I said some terrible things to him that just confirmed all the bad things he thought about me. And then he got angry with me and said some awful things back. And then we both said we never wanted to see each other again. And then I left.'

'Oh.'

'Yes. *Oh.*'

The waiter served Arabella's tea. She spooned several sugars into her cup and began stirring. 'So what's your plan? How are you going to win him back?'

Rosie stared wide-eyed at her friend. 'What? I have no "plan". Well, the only plan I have is to forget all about it eventually. i'm sure when enough time has passed I won't even remember what he looked like.'

Rosie gave a tentative smile and placed a smoked salmon sandwich on her plate, although eating was the last thing she felt like doing.

Arabella stopped stirring and placed her teaspoon on her saucer, her pretty mouth turned down. 'Hmm… You really are in a bad state, aren't you? When have you ever *not* had a plan? You're a fighter, Rosie. You don't give up easily. You never have before and this is not the time to start.'

Rosie shrugged again. 'You can't *make* someone love you, Bella. All I seem to have done is a very good job of making Alexander hate me.'

'I'm sure that's not true,' Arabella said, shaking her head. 'If he said he loved you once then I'm sure you can make him see that he still loves you—even if you're not who you said you were, and even if you did tell him a few innocent fibs.'

Rosie held up her hands. It was time to end this uncomfortable conversation. 'I know you mean well, Bella, but there's nothing to be done. Alexander is in the past, and I think it would be best if that's where he stays.' She forced another smile. 'So, tell me about this play—what part did you get? Let's start reading lines together after tea, so you're word-perfect for the first rehearsal.'

As long as she kept her mind occupied Rosie was certain that eventually, in time, Alexander would stop monopolising her daytime thoughts and her night-time dreams.

Arabella stared at her for a moment, her brows drawn together in question. 'Right...and once we've done that we'll get down to formulating a plan to recapture the Duke's heart.'

Rosie stifled a sigh. Arabella had the best of intentions, but this time there would be no plan. It was time to admit defeat. It was time to forget Alexander. It was time to move on.

Alexander looked out at the marshlands. After many days' work alongside the engineers and workmen the trenches had been dug and draining the area would soon commence, so that it could be turned into productive farmland. It should be a satisfying sight. He had secured good terms with the bank to pay for the work and had finally started on his plans to transform and modernise the estate.

And yet he was far from satisfied. Discontent racked his mind, and despite his tired muscles his body continued to be in a state of agitation.

He had laboured hard beside his tenants, digging from sun-up to sun-down, trying to exhaust his body so he would fall into a dreamless sleep at night. But still thoughts of a raven-haired beauty had invaded his dreams. And she was constantly on his waking mind, no matter how many distractions he placed in his own way.

He walked along the edge of the marshland, his boots squelching through thick mud. Their final encounter played over in his head once again. How he regretted his cruel words. He should never have flung those insulting names at her. He had no real evidence that she was an immoral woman.

He stopped and stared out at the boggy land. If he could take those harsh words back he would—in a second. But he couldn't undo what had been done. He'd thought of sending her an apology, but he had vowed to himself that he would have no contact with her, and he doubted she'd want any contact with him.

Anyway, what would be gained by an apology?

What would be gained by making contact?

And if he did apologise what would he say?

How could he explain that he had lashed out like an injured animal, thrashing about without thought, only aware that he was in pain and that he would do anything, say anything, to make the pain stop?

He picked up a stick and poked it into the damp earth.

But there had been one good outcome of her visit. She had been right about those plans to diversify. It had been that which had convinced the bank to lend him a substantial amount of money. They had been able to see the good business sense in producing a diversity of crops that could be transported by rail around the country and even abroad. And it had been her suggestion of electrification that had sealed the deal.

He had hoped that the whole unfortunate incident

would put his mother off her quest to find a future duchess with a substantial dowry, but it had not been the case.

His mother was wasting her time. Alexander could not see himself taking an interest in any other woman— not when he found it impossible to get Rosie Smith out of his mind. He would always compare all others to her, and he could not imagine meeting another woman who was as funny, as pretty and such a delight.

Although how much of her charm had been real and how much of it pretence he had no way of gauging. But the woman she had pretended to be—the one who had made him laugh, who had made him forget himself and his troubles—was one he had so easily fallen in love with.

It seemed Rosie Smith had ruined his chances with any other woman. He had fallen in love with a charade, and no real woman would ever be able to match her.

He pulled the stick out of the sucking mud and threw it into the marshland. It was time to be true to his commitment and force himself to excise her from his mind. It might take a while to get her out of his thoughts, but that was what he must do. And hopefully one day, some time in the distant future, he would have forgotten what she even looked like, forgotten her voice and the pretty laughter that came so easily, forgotten those disconcertingly sad blue eyes.

He had plenty of other things to occupy his thoughts. His negotiations with the railway were going well, and preparation of the land where the tracks would be laid would soon start. Once again he planned to join in with the men and help in the clearance of the land. He enjoyed the easy camaraderie of his tenants, and the feeling of pushing himself with hard physical labour.

He turned and headed back to the house. His muscles

ached from the hard day's work, and that at least gave him some satisfaction. Tomorrow would be another day of constant activity, and tonight he would bury himself in plans for the railway. As long as he was making plans for the estate and throwing himself into hard physical toil he could hopefully keep all invading thoughts of a pretty, tormenting, deceitful American at bay.

At least, that was the plan.

Chapter Twenty

Rosie needed time—that much she knew. But how much time?

That was a question she couldn't begin to answer. How long did it actually take for a broken heart to mend? Perhaps she should consult a doctor, because no one else seemed to know. And while that elusive amount of time was passing what was she supposed to do to ease her pain? How was she supposed to remove the constant memory of her last encounter with Alexander from her mind? How was she supposed to stop recalling all those other bittersweet memories of how he looked, how he talked, how his face changed when he laughed and, most painful of all, how his lips felt on hers?

She wandered aimlessly around the hotel suite, picked up a pen from the writing desk, twirled it in her fingers, then put it down again. She moved to the floor-to-ceiling windows. Outside there was a bustling city, just waiting for her to explore.

She pulled back the chintz drapes and looked down at the smartly dressed men and women walking along the pavement below, at the roads congested with horses and carts delivering goods to the many stores, and the carriages and omnibuses ferrying busy people to their destinations. Strains of music from the organ grinder at the street corner reached her.

There was so much activity just outside the front door of her hotel and she should be a part of it—not merely staring down at it from on high, like some miserable princess trapped in a tower.

Yes, she had to move on. Like the organ grinder's handle, the world kept on turning—so she should get out, leave the hotel and join in with that world.

She released the curtains, the mere thought of it draining her of energy.

The door burst open and Arabella swept in, waving tickets above her head. 'Right, you've been moping too long. It's time we went out and enjoyed ourselves. I've got tickets to the Gaiety Theatre on Saturday night. Rumour has it that Lillie Langtry is going to be putting in a guest appearance, so that is one performance we cannot miss. Nellie's going to make us both look beautiful, and Aunt Prudence says she's recovered and can accompany us—so no excuses. You're going to have some *fun*.'

Rosie forced her lips to smile. 'That's wonderful, Bella, how exciting,' she said, with more enthusiasm than she felt.

Just a few short weeks ago the idea of going to the Gaiety Theatre would have filled her with genuine excitement. And actually seeing the famous actress and socialite Lillie Langtry on stage would have been a dream come true. But now she was having to force herself to summon up even a modicum of enthusiasm.

She looked at her smiling friend and realised Arabella was right. She had to shake off this wretched misery, if for no other reason than she didn't want her sadness to make Arabella unhappy as well.

'In the meantime there's shopping to be done,' Arabella continued. 'We'll both need new gowns, new shoes, new hats, new evening bags—new everything if we're to attend the theatre. Plus, we've been very remiss in our exploration of London. We haven't yet visited any of the department stores. I've been dying to see inside the new Harrods. They say it's been rebuilt in spectacular fashion since the fire. It's the largest store in Europe, so it should have everything we could possibly need, and more, all under one roof. We can spend the day there, buy everything we need, and then when we're exhausted with shopping we can take afternoon tea to replenish ourselves for more shopping!'

Rosie smiled her first genuine smile for many days. It was usually her job to make Arabella feel happy, to entertain her friend—not the other way around. But her dear friend was doing everything she could to divert Rosie from her sorrows. Arabella truly was a good friend. The best friend a woman could ever have.

'Thank you, Bella, that sounds wonderful.'

'Oh, don't thank me. Just get ready and join me down in the foyer as quickly as possible. We're on a mission. There's much to do, many items to buy, and no time to waste.'

The two girls stepped down from their hansom cab, stood in front of Harrods and stared up at its seven-storey exterior. It was indeed spectacular, combining the modern American concept of a department store with a British sense of elegance. Adorned with cherubs and its new modern Art Nouveau windows, it seemed to draw them in with the promise of luxury and indulgence.

Inside it was no less spectacular, and the two girls were instantly absorbed into the hubbub of excited shoppers. As they rushed from counter to counter, trying on hats, gloves and scarves, sampling perfumes and watching elegant models display the latest fashions, Rosie was almost able to forget her sadness. *Almost.*

It was just unfortunate that she kept seeing Alexander among the bustling crowd, and then realising she was wrong. The breadth of one man's shoulders reminded her of Alexander's strong physique, but when he turned round it wasn't his handsome face she saw but that of a complete stranger. Another man held his head erect in just the same manner as Alexander, but when he looked her way she was again disappointed.

This was silly, she reminded herself. Alexander was in Devon. She would never see him again and she had to put him out of her mind.

Which was an equally silly idea. Rosie knew she would *never* be able to put Alexander out of her mind.

But at least she could keep trying. Even if she failed again and again and again.

After a whirl of shopping—broken only by a stop for afternoon tea—a hansom cab was summoned to take them back to the hotel, along with their many carefully wrapped packages.

Rosie had expected to return to the hotel suite to have a much-needed rest. But Arabella had other ideas. It seemed she had prepared a full itinerary of activities to keep every minute of Rosie's day and evening occupied.

Her friend knew her so well. Without these activities Rosie knew she would sink back into her morose state. So

Arabella had deemed that there would not be a minute left for Rosie to sit staring out of the window of her London hotel, dwelling on what had happened with Alexander.

'Look what I've got.'

Alexander raised his head, tearing his eyes away from the sorry tale told by the estate's financial ledgers, and gazed at his smiling sister. She was standing at the door of his office, holding a torn envelope and waving two pieces of paper.

'I've got tickets to the Gaiety Theatre on Saturday night.'

'I'm very pleased for you,' he said absentmindedly, placing his hands on the desk and returning his attention to the dilemma of how to save costs on the estate's expenditure without losing any workers.

'They're for us. We need to get out of this dismal house for a few days. We need to go up to London for the weekend. We need to have some fun for a change.'

Frowning, Alexander scrutinised his sister. *Fun?* This was not like Charlotte. The only time she went up to London was when she was visiting one of her charities, or attending a political meeting. When had she ever wanted to do something frivolous like seeing a play? Next thing she would be saying she actually *enjoyed* going to balls.

'I'm far too busy, Charlotte. And we can't spend money on plays and trips to London. We need to cut back on expenses—not waste money.'

Charlotte entered the room, slammed the tickets down on the desk and furrowed her brow.

Startled by this uncharacteristic display of anger, Alexander looked up at her.

'You're not too busy, and it won't cost us much. We

can stay at our London townhouse. It will be good to make use of it one last time before you sell it. And you'll only be away for a few days. You deserve a break after all your hard work and everything you've been through.'

'No, Charlotte.'

'*Yes, Charlotte.* That's the response you're meant to give. If you won't do it for yourself then do it for me. You've been such a misery to live with these past few weeks. You might enjoy being miserable, but I don't like being subjected to all this gloom and doom. I need cheering up as well, you know. So do it for me.'

He stared at his sister. What was happening to her? Was she having a kind of personality change? Insisting on having fun one moment and admonishing him the next. Perhaps his miserable countenance *had* been adversely affecting her, causing her to behave strangely. And she did deserve to have some fun after Miss Smith's betrayal and the uncertainty of their financial woes.

'All right,' he said slowly. 'I suppose one weekend won't hurt. And if you're prepared to waste your allowance on tickets to the theatre, then I suppose I can waste a bit of money on train tickets to London.'

'Good—that's settled.' Charlotte walked away, humming the chorus of 'Champagne Charlie'.

Alexander shuddered at the sound of the tune Miss Smith had entertained them with. He did not need reminding of her. He did not need reminding of all the damage she had caused. He did not need reminding of the pain he had felt—the pain he had been forced to crush down inside him until it sat in his stomach like a lead weight.

He turned back to his ledger, found the figures swirling before his eyes. He had to concentrate. He could not let her invade his mind again and distract him from the important work he had to do. She had taken up too much of his time and his thoughts already.

He would not think of her. He would drive all memories of her from his head. He closed his eyes, took in a deep breath, then stared back at the accounts, forcing himself to concentrate. He could not be distracted—especially if he was going to waste an entire weekend on a visit to London…

Arabella was bubbling with eager anticipation as they headed towards the Gaiety Theatre, and Rosie couldn't help but get caught up in her excitement. Even Aunt Prudence seemed to have brightened up a bit. After spending several weeks in bed, recovering from her imagined sea sickness and then a bout of hay fever, followed by an unidentified malaise, she had finally dragged herself out of her sickbed to fulfil her role as chaperon.

Rosie watched the busy London streets pass them by as the carriage clip-clopped along the cobbled road. Lit up by the gas lamps and the soft white light of a full moon, London looked spectacular.

When they arrived at the Gaiety Theatre their driver jostled with other coach drivers, all dropping off their cargo of excited theatregoers. With careful manoeuvring he managed to find a spot right outside the covered front entrance, so the ladies could disembark comfortably.

'Oh, dear. It's very noisy, isn't it?' Aunt Prudence complained as they entered the foyer. 'I hope it doesn't bring on one of my headaches.'

Rosie and Arabella looked at each other and giggled. *Everything* tended to bring on one of Aunt Prudence's imagined headaches.

But she was right about one thing. The crowded foyer presented a wall of sound, with a mass of bejewelled women and men in formal evening wear talking loudly, laughing and greeting their friends. There was a palpable buzz of excitement, and the rumour that Lillie Langtry might be making a guest appearance had obviously spread, because every group they passed seemed to be talking of her.

The girls made their way up the wide, richly carpeted stairs, along the corridors, and found their box. When they entered their own exclusive little room the noise of the crowd dimmed slightly.

Rosie seated herself and looked out on the assembled audience. The patrons in the stalls below bustled and jostled as they found their seats. In the rows of boxes across from them wealthy patrons entered at a more leisurely pace and settled themselves in for the night's entertainment.

'If Lillie Langtry is going to be on stage, then perhaps the Prince of Wales will attend as well,' Arabella said, scanning her programme. 'They say that she's his mistress, and he *is* rather partial to actresses. Perhaps when I become a famous actress I should become his mistress. I wonder what Father would prefer? Me being the future King's mistress or the wife of an aristocrat.'

Rosie looked at her giggling friend. It wasn't like Arabella to make fun of the way her father was using her to advance his own social status. She was obviously in a very good mood tonight.

The door to their box opened.

Rosie and Arabella turned as a smiling Charlotte Fitz-Roy entered. Rosie shook her head in bewilderment, as if an apparition had suddenly appeared, and then her heart plummeted to her stomach when she heard a familiar deep voice.

'Charlotte, what are you up to? I don't believe your meagre allowance could possibly stretch to taking a box. Are you sure our tickets aren't for the stalls?' said Alexander as he followed his sister into the box, looking down at the tickets and scowling.

When he looked up and saw Rosie staring at him he halted, his face wary, like a man suddenly aware he was entering an ambush. And that was exactly what this was.

Rosie looked from Charlotte to Arabella, then back again. They were wearing identical smiles. This encounter was obviously not a bizarre coincidence. It was something Arabella and Charlotte had concocted.

'Hello, I'm Arabella van Haven—the real Arabella van Haven,' her friend said, standing and smiling like Alice's Cheshire Cat. 'Rosie you already know, and may I present my aunt? Miss Prudence van Haven.'

Alexander stared at them for a moment, as if too stunned to talk, then his well-conditioned manners took over and he bowed to all three women. 'And may I present my sister? Lady Charlotte.'

'It's a pleasure to meet you, Lady Charlotte,' Arabella said, taking Charlotte's arm and leading her to a seat beside her.

The two women commenced chattering enthusiastically, as if oblivious to the tense atmosphere that had now descended on the box.

Rosie remained frozen in her seat, staring up at an equally stunned Alexander. For several painful seconds they remained motionless, like prey caught in a snare and unable to make any move to get free without fear of ensnaring themselves further.

'I'm sorry about this, Alexander,' she said finally, her voice a small croak. 'I didn't know a thing about it. I know you think I'm a liar, but you have to believe me. This is not my doing.'

'Oh, I do believe you. I can see the hand of my sister at work here.'

Rosie nodded. 'And my friend Arabella. The real Arabella. But you're here now. You might as well enjoy the play.'

He cast an annoyed glance at his sister and entered the box.

Rosie had almost forgotten how very handsome he was. Tall, and with such wide shoulders and dark good looks that he was nothing short of stunning. And seeing him again had certainly left *her* stunned.

But as he approached she became aware of a change in his appearance. There were dark rings under his eyes, and a sallowness to his olive skin that hadn't been there when she had visited Knightsbrook. He gave every appearance of a man who had not been sleeping properly.

Had he been working too hard? Worrying about the estate? Whatever had caused this change in him Rosie wanted to help, to soothe away his worries, to brush back the dark brown hair from his furrowed forehead. But caring for the Duke was not her role. It never had been and never would be.

He hesitated, then walked towards the one remaining seat—the seat beside Rosie.

Time seemed to slow down. The tension between them grew. The very air seemed heavy, and Rosie struggled to breathe. The noisy crowd fell silent. It was as if every member of the audience was aware of Rosie's embarrassment and discomfort, and were waiting with bated breath to see what happened next.

Arabella patted her arm. 'Rosie, stand up. The Prince of Wales is here.'

Rosie turned in her seat and as if through a haze of confusion saw a portly gentleman with a full beard enter the royal box. She gathered herself and stood up as Alexander reached his seat and stood beside her.

Someone in the crowd shouted out, 'Three cheers for His Royal Highness,' and they all joined in on three hearty 'hip-hip-hoorays'. All except Rosie and Alexander, whose somewhat muted responses were fortunately drowned out by the happy crowd.

How could Rosie be expected to cheer when she was in a state of shock? When her skin was tingling with nerves and her throat was so constricted she suspected she was incapable of speech?

The band struck up a lively tune and the audience took their seats again. Rosie closed her eyes to try and regain some composure. But how was she supposed to do that in this impossible situation? The man she had thought she would never see again was now sitting close beside her. The man she had treated so badly, the man she had lied to and insulted, the man she had fallen in love with, was now just a few inches away from her.

Rosie wriggled slightly in her seat to try and move away from Alexander, but the arrangement of the chairs allowed no room. A chill ran through her, as if the temperature had suddenly plummeted in the warm theatre. The naked skin of her arms and shoulders tingled, and she was aware that she was all but brushing up against his arm and shoulder. Her leg was so close to his they were almost touching.

She looked down at his legs and could see the muscles under the fabric. Then she quickly looked up again. She must not look at his legs. She must not even think about his legs, nor any other body part. Not the arms that had held her, not the chest that she had pressed herself against, and not his lips. Definitely not his lips. She did not want to think of them most of all.

But how was she supposed to stop her mind from thinking of such things when they were so close it would be easy to reach out and take hold of his hands? Hands that were clenched together between his knees—clenched so tightly that the whiteness of his knuckles was showing.

Oh, yes, it would be easy to touch him. Easy and yet an impossibility.

Throughout the performance Rosie hardly heard a word the actors said, and nor could she follow the plot—which seemed far too complex for a simple musical comedy. Even when Lillie Langtry came on stage, to the accompaniment of rapturous applause and cheers, it seemed to pass her by in a blur. All she could think about was the silent man sitting beside her.

Like her, he sat ramrod-straight in his chair, as if attending a solemn funeral service, not a light-hearted comedy. When the audience laughed, he remained rigid. When they clapped enthusiastically at the end of each scene he gave a brief token applause.

To say he was not enjoying the play would be an understatement. He was obviously hating every minute of the performance. And she knew that was not the fault of the actors, the band, the writer or the director. There was only one person responsible for Alexander's bad mood. And that was her.

After an interminably long time the intermission arrived. At least this ordeal was halfway over. But that was of small comfort. With the lights now raised Rosie could no longer hide behind the darkness of the blackened auditorium. No longer could she pretend to be distracted by the performance.

She might have to make conversation with Alexander.

The prospect caused her already thumping heart to increase its tempo, and her skin to burn as if the theatre had suddenly turned into an inferno.

Charlotte and Arabella stood up and rushed out, saying something about getting refreshments.

Rosie sent a pleading look towards the door they had so hastily departed through, silently begging them to return and save her from this intolerable situation. But the door remained firmly shut. The girls did not return.

She turned to stare straight ahead. They were now alone. All alone except for Aunt Prudence, who seemed to have dozed off at some time during the performance.

Alexander also stared ahead, his body still rigid, his face implacable.

With her heart beating to a frantic rhythm and her breath coming in short, shallow gasps, Rosie scrambled for something to say. Anything to break this uncomfortable silence. But nothing came to her befuddled mind.

'Are you enjoying the play, Your Grace?' she finally asked, her voice barely audible.

'Yes,' was his terse reply.

They slipped back into silence.

'And did you have a good trip up from London?'

He exhaled loudly. 'Oh, for goodness' sake, Miss Smith. After all that has happened between us are we *really* going to indulge in meaningless polite conversation?'

Rosie bit her lip. Even thinking of polite conversation

had required the concerted effort of all her mental capabilities. How was she supposed to think of anything more interesting to say when her mind was completely distracted by the close proximity of the man sitting beside her? A man who had once kissed her, had once told her he loved her, had even said that he wanted to marry her.

Rosie swallowed to ease her dry throat and tried not to think such things. She was supposed to make interesting conversation, not polite chatter. She most certainly did not want to say anything that would allude to what had happened between them at Knightsbrook. But what could she say?

She took a quick glance at Alexander, who was staring straight ahead. He wasn't much help. It was obvious he had no intention of making any conversation at all. At least she was trying—and all she had got for her trouble was a reprimand.

'Well, if you prefer we can sit here in embarrassed silence, staring at the walls and pretending we're somewhere else.'

He breathed in deeply and exhaled slowly. 'Forgive me—that was rude of me.'

Rosie shook her head. She did not want to argue with him. 'No, you have no need to apologise. This is awkward for both of us. I'm sure Arabella and Charlotte meant well, but I more than anyone should know that sometimes you should not interfere with people's lives.'

'Hmm…' came his monosyllabic reply.

Once again they sank into silence.

Alexander crossed his legs, uncrossed them, then crossed them again. Arabella wondered if he too was struggling to think of something to say. She wished that in his agitation he would remain still. All his crossing and uncrossing was once again drawing her attention to his legs—and all the other parts of that magnificent body she was not going to think about.

Rosie swallowed again, her throat still stubbornly dry, and joined him in staring straight ahead.

'So Miss van Haven knew what you had done, I take it? She was in complete agreement with you pretending to be her?' he finally asked, breaking the protracted silence.

'Oh, yes,' Rosie nodded. 'It was a silly plan, I know. But Arabella—the real Arabella—didn't want to go to Knightsbrook because she didn't want to marry you, and she especially didn't want to go that weekend. She wanted to see the opening of Oscar Wilde's new play. So I came up with the plan, which she agreed to. If I pretended to be her and misbehaved terribly then you wouldn't want to marry her—or me, I mean.'

'You're right. It *was* a silly plan. But it looks like you succeeded.'

Rosie closed her eyes, his words like a stab to her heart. Yes, she had succeeded. Succeeded in saving Arabella from an unwanted marriage and succeeded in destroying her own chance of happiness with the man with whom she had fallen in love. But then, had Rosie Smith—the real Rosie Smith—ever had a chance of marrying the Duke or had she deluded herself?

'Well, that's something, I suppose,' she murmured, before they sank back into a tense silence.

Charlotte and Arabella bustled back in, their cheeks pink with excitement, matching smiles on their lips, and the curtain was raised for the second act.

Rosie could not be angry with her friend, nor with Charlotte. The two women had meant well, but they were trying to achieve a hopeless goal. Alexander despised her. That was undeniably evident to her, if not to them. He had made his feelings about her perfectly clear before she'd left Knightsbrook, and he was making them clear now. And even if he didn't despise her, the best she could hope for from Alexander was indifference. He was a duke and she was a nobody—a nobody he could now hardly bear even to speak to.

Once again she returned to staring at the stage, seeing nothing and hearing nothing of the performance, and waited anxiously for the whole embarrassing episode to be over.

Alexander had never felt like a victim before. But, sitting in The Gaiety Theatre, it seemed to him that was exactly what he was. The unwitting victim of a female conspiracy.

He had no doubt that this ridiculous situation was all down to Charlotte and Miss van Haven's scheming. While they had both looked as pleased as Punch when he and Charlotte had entered the box, Miss Smith had looked as shocked as he had felt. Her stilted conversation and awkward demeanour had made it abundantly clear that she would rather be anywhere than confined in this small theatre box watching this seemingly endless play.

He had never expected to see Rosie again. Had hoped he would never see her again. Now, with her sitting next to him, so close he could easily take her in his arms, everything about their weekend together came crashing over him, like a furious wave smashing against a rocky coastline.

The scent of spring flowers filled the air and the soft skin of her naked arms and shoulders seem to offer an all but irresistible temptation. An image of folding down the delicate straps of her gown and kissing a line along the skin of those slim shoulders invaded his mind.

He coughed discreetly and crossed his legs.

Yes, he really was a victim. A victim of Charlotte and Arabella's scheming and a victim of his own foolish desires. And he was going to have to fight those desires with the full might of his strength if he was to maintain his resistance and stop this woman from once again tearing out his heart.

She had hurt him. There was no denying that. And only a masochist would subject himself to continued pain. He was no masochist. As soon as this play was over he would leave, and then he would never have to experience the turmoil of such unwanted emotions ever again.

Finally the play finished, and the sound of hundreds of gloved hands applauding erupted in the theatre. Charlotte and Arabella instantly started chatting enthusiastically about everything they had just seen, while Rosie and Alexander maintained their now familiar uncomfortable silence.

'Right,' said Miss van Haven, standing up and picking up her shawl. 'We're staying at the Savoy and I've booked a table in the restaurant for supper. It will be my treat. It's the least I can do for you, Your Grace and Lady Charlotte, after the appalling trick I played on you.'

Alexander quickly stood up too. 'Not at all, Miss van Haven. You owe us nothing, and Charlotte and I would not dream of imposing.'

'Oh, please, Alexander,' Charlotte entreated him. 'I've never been to the Savoy and I'd love to see it. I'm sure you would as well. It's got electric lighting, you know, and a wonderfully modern contraption called a lift car that carries you up from one floor to another and then back down again.'

She stared at him, wide-eyed, as if the thought of seeing modern innovations should be enough to counter his severe reluctance to spend any more time in the company of Rosie Smith.

'That's as may be, Charlotte, but—'

'Oh, please, Alexander,' Charlotte said again, her eyes pleading. 'We don't get up to London often, and who knows when we'll come again? I would enjoy it so much.'

'Oh, all right, Charlotte. Fine,' he agreed through clenched teeth, sending her a silent message that they would not be staying long.

Charlotte clapped her hands together and beamed at him. It was obvious that it wasn't the thought of supper at the Savoy or of being able to travel by an electric lift from floor to floor that was causing so much excitement, but the fact that she had succeeded in forcing him to endure even more time with Miss Smith.

He escorted the ladies out through the noisy milling crowd and hailed a cab to take them to the Savoy.

As they travelled towards the well-known London landmark Alexander had to admit that Charlotte was right to be enthusiastic about the way the Savoy had embraced modernity. Like a beacon, it shone out in the London night sky, with electric lighting illuminating every room. The carriage pulled up into the courtyard and he helped the ladies down.

Rosie waited till last, and seemed to take a moment to compose herself before she took his offered hand. She placed one foot on the carriage steps and their eyes met.

Despite his attempted resistance to her charms, he had to admit he had never seen her look more beautiful.

Her blue eyes sparkled with reflected light, capturing his gaze, and he stood in front of her as if transfixed.

It wasn't until she lowered her eyes and a blush came to her creamy cheeks that he remembered himself. He took her hand in his and forced himself to recall who she was and what she had done. Even with her gloved hand in his he would not lose his composure—he would not react to the light touch of her fingers that was burning into his hand.

Her touch brought memories flooding back...of taking her in his arms and kissing her with such passionate intensity it had seemed to shake his world off its axis.

Do not think of that—and for goodness' sake, man, pull yourself together.

But even this admonition couldn't stop him from noticing that one tendril of black hair had become dislodged from her coiffure and now curled temptingly around her neck, across her shoulders and down to her beautiful cleavage...

They entered the restaurant and the head waiter ushered them to a table by the French doors, overlooking the balcony and garden.

'Would you like to see the electric lift?' Arabella said to Charlotte, ignoring the waiters who were holding out their chairs.

Before anyone else could respond the two girls had rushed off, leaving Alexander, Rosie and their elderly chaperon standing at the table.

They seated themselves in the plush red leather chairs and a bottle of champagne arrived, unordered. It seemed Miss van Haven's arrangements extended beyond merely getting Alexander and Rosie together. She wanted to make this a celebration as well. But this evening had more in common with a wake than it did a festive occasion.

Alexander made polite conversation with Miss van Haven's elderly aunt, who suddenly announced that all the excitement of the evening had brought on one of her headaches and decided to retire for the evening.

It was a complaint Alexander could have made himself. The tension of the evening was starting to leave its mark on him, in the form of tight shoulders and a stiff neck.

He offered to escort the aunt to her suite, but she waved him away with her fan and bustled off towards the stairs. It seemed that the elderly aunt, like his mother, abhorred modern apparatus such as electric lifts and would prefer to walk up to her room.

He lifted the champagne out of the ice bucket and poured it into two glasses.

'Champagne? Although I'm not entirely sure what we're meant to be celebrating. Perhaps we're supposed to offer up a toast to my sister for discovering the devious side of her personality?'

He handed a champagne flute to Rosie.

'I'm equally surprised by Arabella putting this plan into action,' she said, taking the champagne glass from his hand but carefully avoiding touching his fingers. 'I knew she had received a lot of letters lately that had made her very happy. I'd assumed they were from the theatre she's about to perform with, but they must have been from Charlotte.'

'Hmm… So you and Miss van Haven in the habit of concocting devious plans?'

She screwed up her pretty face and her shoulders rose

up to her ears. 'Yes, I'm afraid we are. But I've learnt my lesson—even if Arabella hasn't.'

'She thought she'd be helping you by getting us together, and you thought you'd be helping her by passing yourself off as a badly behaved American heiress?'

She shrugged again. 'I suppose so...yes.'

He considered her for a moment as she blushed under his gaze. 'So the only reason you did it was to help your friend?'

'Well, no, that wasn't the only reason.' She bit her bottom lip. 'I also wanted to have some fun at the expense of a group of stuffy aristocrats. I thought you were just greedy people who didn't want to work for your money... I thought you deserved to be made sport of. I was wrong and I'm sorry. I know now that I shouldn't have. I shouldn't really make fun of anyone.'

Alexander looked down into his glass at the bubbles rising up through the straw-coloured liquid and bursting when they hit the surface as he absorbed this piece of information.

'Perhaps... But your main reason was to help your friend. You had honourable intentions, even if you were misguided,' he said.

He looked over at her. Despite his conciliatory words her blush had not subsided.

'You're very kind to say that,' she mumbled. 'But I still shouldn't have done it and I beg your pardon.'

He shook his head. 'No, it seems you have nothing to apologise for. You were helping a friend. I jumped to the conclusion that you were up to no good—that you were playing games with me or performing some sort of confidence trick on my family. I judged you unfairly. I should have known there would be a reason for your behaviour and I didn't give you a chance to explain. For that I am sorry.'

Alexander suspected his reaction had also been influenced by his history with Lydia Beaufort. He had been lied to before, cheated before, tricked before, and that had coloured his assessment of Rosie Smith. But Rosie was not like Lydia. Lydia had lied to achieve her own disreputable ends—not to help a friend.

'No, no, no.' Rosie shook her head emphatically. 'You most definitely have nothing to apologise for. My behaviour was terrible—and not in the way it was meant to be terrible. When I came up with my plan I didn't think about the people I would be deceiving. I just wanted to save Arabella and have some fun in the process. It really was quite appalling.'

'No, Miss Smith. I should be the one to apologise. I said some awful things to you. I was rude and offensive, and you did not deserve that.'

Alexander cringed as memory came flooding back—all those accusations he had made, all those harsh words he had said. It really had been unforgivable—especially now that he knew she had not been lying to him for her own sake, but to help her friend.

She held up her hands to stop his words. 'You were angry. And you had every right to be after the way I acted. I came into your home, I was rude to your mother, I tricked you and Charlotte. It was disrespectful. You said when we first met that everyone deserves to be treated with respect. You most certainly do—as does Charlotte, and even your mother...' She gave a little laugh. 'Well, perhaps your mother deserves to have tricks played on her...' She pulled her face into a more serious expression. 'No, even dowager duchesses deserve to be treated with respect.'

It was lovely to see that smile again—that beautiful, radiant smile—even if it was only for a fleeting moment. Alexander took a moment to bask in its remembered glow before asking a question that had been tormenting him since he had found out she was not really Arabella van Haven.

'And what of Thomas Gardener. Was he in on this game?'

She bit the edge of her bottom lip again. 'Oh, him. Yes, about him… I…um… I sort of…well, I made him up.'

He stared at her as she sent him a tentative smile. 'So there is no Thomas Gardener?'

She shook her head.

'Why on earth did you invent him? What did *he* have to do with your plan?'

Her flushed cheeks coloured a darker shade of pink. 'Well, you put me on the spot when you asked why I didn't want to marry. I couldn't think of any reason why I wouldn't want to marry a man like—' She bit that poor lip again. 'I couldn't think of any reason why I wouldn't want to get married, so I invented a beau. I named him Thomas after a sleeping ginger tomcat, and Gardener after an elderly man pushing a wheelbarrow.'

He stared at her in disbelief as she smiled through her embarrassment, and then laughter exploded within him. He had tormented himself with jealousy over a cat and his aging gardener.

'Oh, Rosie, you really are—' He stopped suddenly, his laughter dying. 'I'm sorry. Miss Smith.'

Her smile grew wider. 'Oh, no, call me Rosie, please.

It is my real name, after all. And I'm so sorry I lied about having a beau.'

'As I've said, you have nothing to apologise for. Now that I know the full story it seems it is only I who needs to apologise. I should have given you a chance to explain. I should not have jumped to conclusions. You say you have behaved terribly, but you were doing so for honourable reasons. I have no such excuse for my own unreasonable behaviour.'

She sent him a small smile. 'Oh, well…perhaps we should just agree that we're both really terrible people?'

Alexander laughed again. 'Yes, we're terrible people who deserve each other!'

He placed his hand over hers, and then, suddenly realising the easy level of informality he had slipped into, removed it, picked up his champagne and drained the glass.

'So, perhaps you'd like to tell me about the real Rosie Smith.' He placed the now empty glass back on the table. 'I know she plays the piano exquisitely, that she loves nature and that art enraptures her. I know she's funny, and that she is a good and loyal friend to Miss van Haven. But what else can you tell me about the real Rosie Smith?

She shrugged. 'There's not much to tell, really. As I already told you, I'm Mr van Haven's ward. I have been since I was fourteen.'

That familiar sadness washed over her deep blue eyes. It had intrigued him from the first time he had seen her. A sadness so at odds with her ready smile and easy laughter.

'But I once did have my own family.' She smiled as if lost in her memories. 'My father was an electrical engineer, and he ran a successful company installing electricity in towns and businesses throughout New York State. Mr van Haven convinced him to expand, but unfortunately it didn't work out. He lost money on bad debts and other misfortunes. He couldn't repay the money he owed to Mr van Haven's bank, so the bank took over his company. Not long after that he died. I think he died of a broken heart. He was certainly a broken man. Mr van Haven then employed my mother as a governess for Arabella. I don't know if that was an act of charity, guilt because of what he had done to my father, or because he knew my talented and accomplished mother would make the perfect governess and substitute mother for Arabella. And, being a cunning businessman, he knew she was desperate to find work and a place to live—somewhere she could keep her child with her. That meant she wouldn't object to the low wages he paid. My mother died when I was fourteen, but thanks to Arabella Mr van Haven took me on as his ward. That's why I owe so much to Arabella; she's the best friend a girl could ever have.'

Alexander could now see why such sadness clouded her otherwise sunny disposition. She had lost her father and her mother at an early age—had gone from a secure family life to one of insecurity, dependent on a man who seemed to have little regard for other people. He could also see why she was such a resilient young woman. She'd had to be, if she was to survive under such conditions.

He had been right in his original assessment: she really was a remarkable young woman.

'I'm sorry, Rosie. That must have been very hard for you,' he said, gently patting her hand.

She sent him a sad smile. 'It was. But I always had Bella.'

'I can see you two are very close.'

She nodded and they slipped into silence, both staring into their glasses.

Her life had been so hard, he thought, and yet she continued to smile and laugh, even through her sorrow. She was clever, witty, loyal and so beautiful it could take his breath away. How could he ever have doubted her? And why had he wasted so much time and so much energy feeling pain and anger towards her? It had to be due to what had happened between him and Lydia Beaufort.

But Lydia was in his past. Rosie was here, now, and very much part of his present. And the two women couldn't be more different.

He looked up at her and smiled. 'Your father was an electrical engineer?'

Rosie beamed a smile back at him. 'Yes, I'm sure you two would have got on well. He would have loved your plans for modernisation and would have had many ideas to contribute.'

'And he also produced a rather lovely, rather clever and innovative daughter as well,' he said, causing that delightful blush to tinge her creamy cheeks once again. 'I would have been honoured to meet him. It's men like your father who will transform this country. Not the old aristocracy who are still clinging on to their old ways, desperate to preserve a class system that is rapidly becoming outdated.'

She looked at him sideways, no longer smiling. 'Don't let your mother hear you say that. She thinks a title means everything, and that finding you a woman from a wealthy family who thinks the same way will save Knightsbrook.'

Alexander exhaled loudly. 'My mother knows exactly what I think of that. I've told her often enough. I don't care about my title and I care even less about other people's titles. The estate I have inherited means more than the title. What I have inherited is the responsibility of running it well, and improving it—not just for my family, but for everyone who depends on the estate for their livelihood. My mother and many like her think a title gives you privileges, but the title of Duke and Duchess should go to people who take their responsibility seriously.'

'Really?' Rosie gave him another sideways glance. 'You don't care about titles, class, background...? All that sort of thing?'

'There are more important things—like character, personality, resilience.'

He was about to add other frivolous attributes, such as beauty, a ready laugh and a lovely smile, when he was interrupted by the two co-conspirators, returning arm in arm.

Alexander suspected they had been hiding just out of sight and watching all that had unfolded between him and Rosie, waiting until their differences had been resolved before they made their reappearance.

Over the meal they discussed the play—although Alexander could contribute little, having seen virtually nothing of it, his mind having been occupied elsewhere. They also talked of what the girls had seen in London, and Arabella's ambitions as an actress. Uncharacteristically, Rosie did not say much, but she smiled a lot, particularly when she looked at Alexander, and that warmed his heart.

The crowd at the Savoy Restaurant began to thin, until they were the only people remaining at their table. Alexander had so thoroughly enjoyed the company of these young women, and the pleasure of once again being comfortable in Rosie's company, he had failed to notice how late it was getting.

He looked over at the waiters, who were not too successfully stifling yawns, and reluctantly decided it was time to call it a night. But he knew it would not be the last time he would see Rosie Smith. They had a lot of time to make up—time they had wasted in foolish misunderstandings and unnecessary pain and anguish.

Arabella was the first to stand, and she asked Charlotte to accompany her to her suite. 'It will give you one more chance to play on the electric lift,' she said. And the two girls rushed off together, leaving Alexander and Rosie alone to say their goodbyes.

Alexander stood and held out his hand to Rosie. With a shy smile she placed her hand lightly on his and stood. They gazed at each other for a moment.

'It has been lovely to see you again,' he said, knowing his words were inadequate to express what he was feeling.

'And you too, Alexander.'

Charlotte was suddenly at his side, still beaming the smile that had not left her lips all evening. Rosie kissed Charlotte on the cheek and thanked her for everything she had done, before sending Alexander another smile and departing.

As Charlotte and Alexander waited for their hansom cab to take them back to their townhouse, curiosity got the better of him.

'I have to ask you,' he said. 'How did you manage to organise all this?'

Charlotte gave a little laugh. 'Oh, it was surprisingly easy. I wrote to the newspaper that reviewed the Oscar Wilde play—the one that mentioned Arabella van Haven. I asked them to forward a letter on to her. They did. She wrote back and explained what Rosie had done, and why.

I knew there was no point just telling you—you'd never listen…'

Alexander had to nod his agreement. He was so stubborn he had refused to listen to Rosie when she had tried to explain herself by the river, and he would no doubt have refused to listen to Charlotte. He had been so caught up in his own anguish he had become completely unreasonable.

'Arabella and I decided the best thing to do was to get you two together so you could talk it out yourselves. So we did. And it seems we were right.'

Alexander smiled at his sister. Normally he would be annoyed with anyone trying to interfere in his life— after all, didn't he get enough of that from his mother? But this time, he had to admit, a little interference had been a great success.

Chapter Twenty-One

Alexander stared at his reflection as his valet brushed down his jacket, removing every last speck of dust so it was immaculately clean. Although such meticulous attention to detail was wasted. He would be returning by train to Knightsbrook this morning, and no doubt when he arrived he would be speckled with the smuts emitted from the steam train's funnel.

He hadn't wanted to come to London—had not wanted to waste time on such frivolity. It was only Charlotte's insistence that had dragged him away from his work. He had been annoyed by the interruption, but now he couldn't be more grateful to Charlotte for insisting he accompany her to the theatre.

She had also been right that he'd needed to find out why Rosie had deceived him. He had tried to convince himself that it didn't matter, but in reality he had been tormenting himself with unanswered questions. Possible reasons to explain why someone who had seemed so lovely could behave so treacherously had been spinning round and round in his head.

And now he knew the answer. She was not treacherous, and she was not deceitful. She was an honourable, lovely and lively young woman.

He smiled to himself at the memory of how she had looked as they'd dined at the Savoy. Then further images entered his mind. Her twirling her way down the entrance hall at Knightsbrook...her talking and laughing with Annie...her playing the piano with such passion and virtuosity.

Yes, he owed a debt of gratitude to Charlotte for tricking him and overcoming his stubborn resistance to meeting Rosie again.

He thanked his valet, picked up his hat and gloves and headed downstairs. Charlotte was waiting for him, her trunk and hat box stacked by the front door, ready for their departure.

They were going home—back to Knightsbrook. Away from London...away from Rosie. Alexander knew he must pen a letter to her immediately, before they left town. He had to inform her of how much he had enjoyed their reunion and how much he was looking forward to seeing them again.

He called for some pen and paper.

Or, better than a quick farewell note, perhaps he should extend an invitation to Rosie, Arabella and Aunt Prudence to spend some time at Knightsbrook. That would provide an opportunity to re-do their time together— this time with no pretence, no artifice, and no barriers put in place by him.

The pen and paper arrived and he dipped the pen in the ink, watched over by a very interested Charlotte. He put the pen to the paper, then hesitated.

'What's wrong, Alexander?' Charlotte asked, her brow furrowed.

'I've changed my mind.'

The furrow grew deeper.

'I believe we deserve a longer break in London. Perhaps we should invite Miss Smith and Miss van Haven to accompany us on a drive around Hyde Park? I'm sure the air would do us all some good.'

Charlotte's furrowed brow smoothed. She clapped her hands together and smiled. 'That's a marvellous idea, Alexander.' Then her smile disappeared and she placed the back of her hand theatrically on her brow. 'Oh, but I think you might have to go by yourself... I can feel a terrible headache coming on.'

Alexander shook his head and smiled at his sister. 'If that's your best performance, then I don't think you should consider a career on the stage. And you don't need to feign a headache. I'm sure Miss Smith and Miss van Haven would be delighted to see you again.'

'Well, perhaps—but I can see them another time. I hope there will be many more times we will all spend together. So, off you go.'

Alexander grabbed his hat and gloves and hailed a hansom cab to take him to the Savoy. There, standing at the reception desk, he penned a note to the Misses Smith and van Haven, inviting them and their chaperon for a drive in Hyde Park.

As he waited for their reply he paced up and down the foyer, feeling ridiculously nervous, like a young man waiting for his beau.

He heard the clanking of the electric lift behind him, turned and saw Rosie emerging. Dressed in a dark blue skirt, with a blue and white striped blouse, she looked a vision. Could she have become even more beautiful overnight? Was that even possible? He could have sworn it was a fact. And she was smiling at him—that radiant smile that seemed to light up the room.

'Alexander,' she said when she reached him, still beaming that smile.

He nodded a greeting, unable to stop himself from smiling his own foolish smile.

She looked back at the stairs. 'I'm afraid we're going to have to wait for Aunt Prudence. She refuses to take the electric lift as she says it is a new-fangled contraption.' Rosie bit the top of her lip, as if suppressing a giggle. 'And Arabella says she can't join us because she has a headache.'

Alexander laughed. 'There seems to be a lot of that going around. Charlotte, too, seems to have been struck down suddenly by a mysterious headache.'

Aunt Prudence joined them, and Alexander took both ladies' arms and led them to a waiting carriage.

The carriage took them through the grand entrance to Hyde Park, where they joined the parade of locals exercising their horses and riding in carriages along the path, under the canopy of lightly rustling trees.

'Oh, let's walk, Alexander!' Rosie said, patting his arm. 'You know how much I love trees and nature.'

Alexander laughed, but told the driver to stop. 'From memory, I think you said trees were horrid and those terrible birds were even worse.'

Smiling, Rosie patted him on the arm again. 'I never said that. That was Arabella.'

He helped the two ladies down from the carriage and took each one by the arm. They walked in silence for a few moments, before Aunt Prudence released his arm and headed for the nearest bench.

'You two young people go ahead. I can feel another one of my headaches coming on.'

Alexander rushed to the older woman's side. 'Shall I summon the carriage?'

'No, no. I'll just sit here under the trees until I start to feel better. You two young people carry on with your walk.'

Rosie sent him a small wink.

'Did you know that would happen?' Alexander asked.

'You can almost set your clock by Aunt Prudence's headaches, so I knew if we decided to walk it wouldn't be long before she claimed another imaginary headache and then we'd be able to spend some time together.'

He laughed as she raised her eyebrows and tried to look innocent. 'You really are quite devious, aren't you?'

'I thought you would have realised that by now, Alexander,' she said, and laughed as she took his arm.

They strolled along the path together. Alexander was suddenly strangely tongue-tied—unsure what to say now that all barriers between them had been lowered.

'I hope you enjoyed last night's play,' he said, to break the silence.

'Oh, yes, it was marvellous,' she responded, and then gave one of her now familiar tinkling laughs. 'No, I'm sorry, Alexander. That's not true. I can hardly remember any of the play. I wasn't concentrating. I was so distracted by seeing you again.'

He had to smile at her response, which was so unguarded. 'I was the same, I'm afraid. But apparently it has had good reviews, so it seems we missed an excellent play.'

'Well, we might have missed an excellent play, but I for one think it was still a great night.'

He squeezed her arm lightly in agreement.

Their walk took them past a pond, where groups of young boys were playing with boats on the water. The miniature flotilla included vessels of all sizes, from simple boats of sticks and cloth to elaborately carved sailing vessels.

'Shall we stop and watch for a while?' Rosie asked.

'I'm so pleased we talked last night,' he said as he led her to a nearby park bench. 'I feel we now have a chance to start all over again, and for me to get to know the real Rosie Smith.'

'Oh, I'm afraid the person you've already met is mostly Rosie Smith. I might have been lying about my name, but almost everything else about the person you met at Knightsbrook was the real me.'

She tucked her skirt underneath her and sat down.

'Sadly, the person who twirled down the entrance hall at Knightsbrook, and the person who sang inappropriate songs in the Dowager's drawing room, is the real Rosie Smith.'

Alexander smiled as he remembered her unusual entrance and the look of horror on his mother's face. 'I'm pleased to hear that.' He sat down beside her on the bench and looked out at the busy children. 'And I wouldn't have it any other way. Your twirling entrance was priceless.'

She patted his arm again and smiled. 'That wasn't my intention. I was supposed to be shocking you, not impressing you. You were supposed to conclude that I was entirely unacceptable.'

'I don't think it would be possible for me to think that the real Rosie Smith is unacceptable.'

She sent him a shy smile and a delightful blush tinged her cheeks.

'And I was the one whose behaviour was unacceptable. You said you expected to meet a stuffy aristocratic family, and after my reaction that must have been exactly what you thought of me. A delightful young woman had come into my home, bringing laughter and joy, and I reacted by being disapproving and stern.'

'Oh, no—no.' She turned to him, shaking her head, with a deep furrow in her brow. 'You are most definitely not stuffy, and you were nothing but polite. I mean, the first time we met you saved me from falling to the ground.'

Alexander smiled again at the memory of Rosie, diving across the room to save the Ming vase. It was strange, but even then he had been more concerned for her welfare than for an irreplaceable valuable vase.

'And if you were sombre at times—well, you had reason to be,' she said in a quieter voice. 'You've had all those problems with your father, with the estate, and then there's Lydia…'

Lydia. The name caused no reaction in Alexander whatsoever. It was as if some kind of an exorcism had been performed and her spirit no longer haunted him. 'The only problem with Lydia is that she caused me to judge you more harshly than you deserved.'

Memories of what Charlotte had said came back to him—that because of Lydia he had hardened his heart, had shut down emotionally. And yet when he had met Rosie she had managed to find a chink in his armour and he'd begun to open himself up to her. That was why her perceived betrayal had hurt him so much. But now he knew she had not betrayed him. He had been given a second chance.

He smiled at her, and got a beautiful smile in return.

'As for the estate—I've secured sufficient advances from the bank to begin a modernisation programme, and what convinced the bank manager the most was my telling him of your suggestion to diversify and bring electrification to the dairy and the woolshed. He was most impressed with my progressive thinking.'

'*Whose* progressive thinking?' she said, raising her finger and waggling it in front of his face.

'*Your* progressive thinking!' He laughed, taking her finger and giving it a light kiss. 'And for that I thank you—on behalf of my family and all the tenants of Knightsbrook.'

He continued holding her soft hand for a moment, before reluctantly releasing it.

'I'm so pleased, Alexander,' she said quietly. 'I know how much Annie and the tenants mean to you. They're more than just people who work on your land, aren't they? They're family.'

He nodded. 'They are indeed. As a child I often used to pretend to myself that Annie was my real mother, her husband my real father, and the tenant children my brothers and sisters.'

She placed her hand gently on his arm and he smiled at her.

'At least that is something for me to be grateful to my father for,' he said, with a laugh that contained no humour. 'He taught me a valuable lesson: that there are good and bad people in all classes. It doesn't matter what your background is, who your family is, or how much money you have, it's what's in your heart that matters.'

She nodded her agreement.

'And that's something I admire in *you*, as well, Rosie.'

'Me?' she said, pointing to herself.

'You've risen above your circumstances. You might have become bitter or angry, but instead you smile more than some people who have had a good life handed to them on a silver platter.'

She shook her head in disagreement. 'In many ways I think my life has been much easier than a lot of people's. Before things changed I had a very happy childhood, and I have warm, lovely memories from that time. I had a mother and father who loved me, and a home that was full of laughter, joy and music. I think it was that start in life that gave me such resilience and allowed me to rise above misfortune. When my father lost all his money, and then died, it was heartbreaking. But I still had my lovely mother, who was a very strong woman. She tried to protect me as much as possible from what was happening. And when she became Arabella's governess she continued to be a loving mother to me and became a substitute mother for Arabella as well.'

She paused and took in a deep breath.

'When she died...yes, I was devastated, and I felt very frightened and alone. But I had my friend Arabella. We were united in our grief and we supported each other. That's why we're such good friends now.' She sent him a sad smile. 'So, yes, I've had a lot of sadness in my life—but there's also been a lot of happiness and a lot of kindness.'

Alexander's admiration for this remarkable young woman continued to grow. She had been through so much, and yet there wasn't a hint of self-pity, a hint of anger against how unfairly the world had treated her.

'I've said it before but I'll say it again: you really are an impressive young woman.'

She raised her hands in protest. 'Well, perhaps it's as

you said. Life teaches you lessons. Your father's behaviour taught you to value your tenants, and my misfortune taught me to appreciate my friendship with Arabella and all the good things in my life.' She tilted her head and gave another sad smile. 'And my time with you taught me the folly of playing silly games—they can backfire spectacularly.'

'Oh, no, Rosie, don't change a thing about yourself.'

They smiled at each other, then went back to watching the young boys at their carefree play.

'Oh, Aunt Prudence!' Rosie said suddenly, standing up. 'If my timings are correct she should be starting to feel slightly better and will by now feel that she is capable of the arduous journey home. That is as long as the driver doesn't go over any bumps and set off her imagined lumbago.'

They made their way back to the bench where they had left Aunt Prudence, but as they approached Alexander could see they had no need to worry. She had engaged an elderly gentleman sitting at her bench in conversation.

'Well, well, well!' Rosie laughed. 'It looks like Aunt Prudence has found the cure for a headache. Perhaps we should patent it.'

Alexander bowed to the elderly gentleman and they made a round of introductions. While Rosie smiled on, Aunt Prudence blushed and simpered, almost like a young girl. And then the three of them made their way back to the park's entrance, where Alexander hailed a carriage to take them back to the Savoy.

He escorted them into the foyer and Aunt Prudence departed up the stairs. Alexander knew he had to say goodbye to Rosie, but he was reluctant for his time with her to come to an end.

'Lady Jennings is having a ball tonight, and Charlotte and I have been invited. I would be honoured if you, Miss van Haven and Aunt Prudence would join us.'

In fact Alexander had already declined the invitation, as had Charlotte, but he was sure Lady Jennings would have no objection. He rarely attended balls, and had no real interest in attending this one, but he did not want to leave London without seeing Rosie at least one more time. Having to dance and make small talk would be a very small price to pay for one more evening in her company.

She smiled her delightful smile and bobbed a little curtsey. 'Why, Your Grace, I would be honoured,' she said, with mock formality.

Chapter Twenty-Two

The ballroom glittered with reflected candlelight and couples glided round the highly polished parquet dance floor, the women in an array of colourful gowns, and the sound of music filling the air.

Rosie and Arabella paused at the entrance and Rosie took a moment to compose herself. Her heart was beating so hard it was almost drowning out the sound of the music, and her nerves were tingling at the thought of meeting Alexander again.

Their day together in the park had been so special. And now she was going to spend the evening dancing with that wonderful man.

She took in a deep breath and looked around the room. Then she she saw him, standing on the far side of the room, staring straight at her. She gasped in another breath as once again the image of a Greek statue entered her mind. She swallowed. And this Greek statue was walking straight towards her, his dark eyes fixed firmly on hers.

He reached the group and bowed his greetings to Arabella and Aunt Prudence, and then, taking Rosie's hand he formally asked her to dance.

Her heart hammering in her chest, Rosie could only nod her agreement and hope she wouldn't betray her nerves by tripping over the hem of her pink gauze gown or trampling his leather-booted feet.

He took her in his arms and they joined the couples circling the room in a waltz. It was the first time she had been in Alexander's arms since he had kissed her. And now he was dancing with Rosie Smith, a poor orphan, not with the woman he assumed was an American heiress. And he was doing it in front of everyone.

Rosie doubted it was possible to feel happier.

His hand held her waist firmly as he led her round the floor. She suspected the gap that was supposed to be maintained between dancing couples at all times was narrowing scandalously. But Rosie cared not a bit whether anyone was scandalised. All she wanted was to be even closer to this magnificent man. For his arms to be encircling her, for his lips to be kissing hers.

She sighed deeply and moved in even closer, tempted to place her head on his broad shoulder.

The dance ended and he led her off the dance floor. Rosie could see outraged faces looking in their direction, and hear muttered voices. Everyone was wondering who this nobody was that she had captured the attentions of His Grace the Duke of Knightsbrook.

Usually such a reaction would have got Rosie's hackles up—would have caused her to poke out her tongue or do something else outrageous to shock them further. But tonight she was too happy to care how they looked at her or what they were saying about her.

Removing two glasses from the tray of a passing footman, Alexander handed one to Rosie. She was sure her face must be burning red—something she knew young ladies should avoid at all cost. But how could she stop her excitement from being reflected on her cheeks?

Alexander smiled at her—that wonderful smile that had once been so rare, but which she was now starting to see more often—and her cheeks burnt brighter.

'May I write my name on your dance card for the next dance?'

She handed him the card and the tiny pencil, then laughed as he wrote his name in bold letters diagonally across the card, claiming her for himself for the entire evening.

'Why, Your Grace, I don't believe that is entirely appropriate.'

His smile turned to a laugh. 'Why, Miss Smith, being in your company makes me want to behave entirely *inappropriately.*'

Rosie didn't think she could smile more brightly, but she did. 'I'm very pleased to hear it.'

'Shall we?' He offered her his arm to escort her back on to the dance floor for the quadrille.

They danced together throughout the night, only breaking apart when supper was announced, but Rosie knew she was far too excited to eat.

'Would you like to take some air?' Alexander asked, and Rosie nodded gratefully. 'With the doors open Aunt Prudence will be able to see us, so we won't further scandalise the guests.'

They looked over to where Aunt Prudence was seated, talking to the elderly gentleman she had met in the park. It was unlikely that the distracted chaperon would be keeping an eye on her charge, and that suited Rosie just fine.

With as much discretion as possible they left the ballroom for the balcony. She looked out over the dark garden, where the nearby flowering shrubs were lit up by the light cascading out of the ballroom.

Now that they were outside she was hoping the night air would cool her burning cheeks, but there was little chance of that. Not with Alexander standing so close she could feel the warmth of his body and smell that wonderful masculine scent of his.

He gently took hold of her hands and Rosie made a small step closer to him.

'Rosie, thank you so much for coming tonight. It's as if we've been given a chance to start again.'

Rosie sent him a quivering smile. Wild horses wouldn't have stopped her from coming to tonight's ball and the chance of seeing him again.

She nodded her head slightly. 'It's been magical, Alexander,' she murmured.

He pulled her closer, into the shadows, and Rosie eagerly moved with him. He leant down and his lips lightly touched Rosie's. It was the lightest of touches, but it set off a burning on her lips that sparked through her body.

She reached up and put her hands around his neck, wishing he would kiss her the way he had when they were at Knightsbrook.

Her wish came true. He swept her into his arms, holding her tightly. As if a dam had been ruptured his kiss burst over her, swamping her in its passionate embrace. She moulded herself against his strong body as his kiss deepened. It was as if he could not get enough of her, and she knew she could not get enough of him.

Closing her eyes, she surrendered herself to the sensation of his lips on hers, his arms surrounding her, his body pressed up against her. Her lips parted wider as the hunger of his kiss intensified. She moaned with pleasure as his tongue entered her mouth, probing and tasting, filling her up, causing her to lose all sense of where she was. All she could do was give herself over to the powerful sensations rippling through her.

His hot, hungry lips kissed a line down her neck before returning once again to her demanding lips. She ran her hands through his thick hair, holding him closer, kissing him harder, loving the feel of his rough skin against her own soft cheeks, loving his masculine scent, loving the strength of his body. Loving *him*.

Music filled the air, as if in celebration of their kiss. And then Rosie realised she was being fanciful. The music signalled that the dancing had recommenced.

Slowly, Alexander broke from their kiss. 'Oh, Rosie. You are the most beautiful woman I have ever met,' he said, his voice cracking. He drew in a deep breath and looked towards the open doors. 'The dancing has recommenced. I believe we should return to the ballroom. We've already set tongues wagging, and our absence will be noted. If nothing else I wouldn't want to embarrass Aunt Prudence with our behaviour.'

Reluctantly, Rosie had to agree, and they re-entered the ballroom.

For Rosie the rest of the evening went by in a magical whirl of dancing and laughing. It really was a fairy tale come true, and she was the beautiful Cinderella on the arm of her handsome prince.

But when the evening came to an end she did not have to flee at midnight. Instead Alexander escorted her to the waiting carriage, which most definitely had not turned into a pumpkin.

He bowed formally, before helping her into the carriage. 'I'm afraid commitments are forcing me to return home tomorrow, but I would love you to visit Knightsbrook again soon.'

Rosie could hardly speak—could only nod, repeatedly.

'I will send a note with the arrangements. And of course Miss van Haven and Aunt Prudence are invited as well.'

Rosie raised her eyebrows. 'You aren't worried that your mother will try and matchmake you with Arabella?'

'In that case we will just have to invite Thomas Gardener as well,' he said, then laughed and kissed her hand.

Rosie's heart was singing as she rode home with Arabella and Aunt Prudence. He had invited the real Rosie Smith to Knightsbrook. He would be introducing her to his mother. Rosie knew this could only mean one thing: Alexander was officially courting her—Rosie Smith, a penniless orphan. It really was like a dream come true.

He had not yet declared his love for her, the way he had at Knightsbrook, and nor had he made any suggestion of marriage. But surely that was only a matter of time.

Oh, yes, it was almost too wonderful to believe.

But there was one thing Rosie did believe. Her excitement was so great she would not be sleeping that night.

Chapter Twenty-Three

Rosie was waiting anxiously for his letter to arrive. That had been her main occupation for the past week. With Arabella away at rehearsals she had little else to occupy her time. So she waited. And waited.

Apart from the wonderful affectionate note he had sent before he'd returned to Knightsbrook the day after the ball nothing had arrived from him, and it had been a whole week. A whole week of waiting.

The happiness that had filled her heart was ebbing away, to be replaced by increasing anxiety.

She paced backwards and forwards, up and down her hotel suite. Should she contact him? Would that be too forward? But what if something had happened to him? What if he was ill? Wouldn't he be expecting to hear from her? But if he wasn't ill, what would he think then? Should she just be content to wait until he contacted her? After all it had only been a week.

One whole week.

Once again she went down to the foyer, to ask the receptionist if there was any mail for her. This time surely there would be something waiting for her.

Making enquiries at Reception was something she

did several times a day, even though she knew that if any letters did arrive they would be immediately sent up to her room.

As she approached the desk the receptionist shook his head sadly before she even had a chance to ask. She returned to her room, that fleeting bubble of optimism once again bursting, and leaving her deflated.

After being so loving and attentive, there had to be a good reason why he hadn't contacted her.

Rosie sat down at the desk and took out a piece of stationery. She was being silly. She should just write to him. A casual letter of enquiry about his health.

She wouldn't ask why he hadn't contacted her. She wouldn't ask why he hadn't written to her. And she would not mention that she was still waiting for her invitation to Knightsbrook. No, she wouldn't mention that. She would make sure her anxiety did not come through in any of the words she wrote.

And she most certainly would not accuse him of being remiss, of letting her down, causing her to go over and over their conversations, looking for something she might have said or not said that had given him offence. Something that might have caused him to change his mind and decide not to contact her again, as he had promised.

She dipped her pen in the ink pot and put it to the paper. Yes, she would write a casual, friendly letter, just enquiring after his health.

She stared at the blank page, her mind equally blank. Instead of writing she stood up and paced the room some more, wondering if any mail had arrived and whether she should take another trip down to the reception desk

A knock on the door sent her rushing across the room. It had arrived. The much-awaited letter had finally arrived.

She pulled open the door and clapped her hands together with glee when she saw a porter, bearing a silver tray containing the most valuable treasure Rosie could ever want. A crisp white envelope embossed with the Knightsbrook crest.

Rosie held it to her chest and sighed loudly. *Finally.* Finally he had contacted her. She savoured the moment and forced herself not to rip it apart to get to its contents. Instead she walked to the desk and picked up the silver letter opener, and with trembling hands slipped it under the edge of the envelope.

It was then that she saw the address. It wasn't for her. It was addressed to Arabella van Haven.

She stared at it. It had to be a mistake. Or was it a joke? Was Alexander playing a joke on her? Calling her Arabella instead of Rosie. That had to be it.

But until Arabella came home she would just have to wait and find out.

She placed the envelope on the desk, leaning it against the shelves, and stared at it.

She walked to the window and turned back to stare at the letter from across the room.

She looked over at the clock, ticking on the mantel. It would be another hour before Arabella was back from rehearsals. Could she hold out that long? Or would she succumb—do the unthinkable and open her friend's mail.

She walked over to the desk, picked up the letter, scanned both sides of it, then placed it down again. Picking up a book, she slumped down in an armchair, determined to divert herself as she waited for Arabella.

But her eyes kept leaving the book she wasn't reading and staring across the room at that letter.

After what seemed like the longest hour in Rosie's life Arabella returned. Before she had time to remove her hat and gloves—before she even had time to say hello—Rosie rushed across the room and grabbed the letter.

'There's some mail for you,' she said, thrusting the letter and the letter opener in Arabella's direction.

Arabella looked at Rosie's reflection in the mirror, one hand on her hat, the other removing a hatpin. She took off her hat and placed it on the sideboard, then took the letter from Rosie's outstretched hand and slit open the envelope while Rosie watched on anxiously.

Rosie waited, her anticipation mounting, as Arabella read the contents. Arabella placed her hand across her mouth. Not a good sign. She looked up at Rosie, her eyebrows pinched together, her mouth turned down in a frown, then back at the letter. Definitely not a good sign.

'What is it? Is Alexander ill? Is it worse?' *Oh, please God, do not let it be worse.*

'He's… He's…' Arabella handed her the card. 'I'm sorry, Rosie. I think you had better read it yourself.'

Rosie took the thick cream card and scanned the contents.

The Dowager Duchess of Knightsbrook
has pleasure in inviting
Miss Arabella van Haven
to Knightsbrook on May the fifteenth, 1893,
to celebrate the engagement of her son,
Alexander FitzRoy, Lord Ashton,
Eighth Duke of Knightsbrook,
to Elizabeth Barclay-Fortescue,
daughter of the Earl and Countess of Suffolk

Time seemed to stop. All sound seemed to evaporate except the pounding of Rosie's heart and the gasping of her breath.

There had to be a mistake.

She read the card again, then turned it over to see if there was anything on the back that would explain this absurdity. Nothing. She turned it over and read it one more time. There was no mistake. Alexander was engaged.

The card dropped from her hand and fluttered to the floor as her legs gave out from beneath her. She dropped to the floor, her voluminous skirts crumpling around her.

'Why would he do this? *Why?*' She looked up, appealing to Arabella, who looked down at her with an ashen white face.

'I am so sorry, Rosie. So very sorry.'

Rosie retrieved the card from the floor. 'Perhaps it was all a cruel game—a trick...a way of getting revenge on me? Perhaps that's what this has been all along. He wanted to hurt me the way I hurt him. He made me think that all was well between us so the shock would be even greater.' She looked questioningly at Arabella. 'Could he be that cruel?'

She looked back down at the card. Rosie had not thought he would be capable of such a thing, but after everything that had happened she no longer knew what to believe.

'Or perhaps he's just succumbed to the reality of his financial situation. He needs money to save the estate, to protect everyone's livelihood. Perhaps he has decided that marrying an heiress is the most sensible, most responsible thing to do after all. And courting a penniless ward was never going to save Knightsbrook. But why didn't he tell me himself instead of letting me find out this way?'

She threw the card onto the floor.

'Oh, Rosie, I'm so sorry,' Arabella repeated, sitting down beside her and taking her in her arms. 'I should not have interfered. Now all I've done is made things worse for you, caused you even more heartache.'

The two friends sat together, holding each other, taking comfort in their friendship in a world that could sometimes be unfair.

Rosie rested her head on her friend's shoulder. 'No, Bella. This is not your fault. It's nobody's fault but mine—setting my sights on a duke, of all things. What was I *thinking*? Men like the Duke of Knightsbrook do not marry poor little orphans like Rosie Smith. They marry women like Elizabeth Barclay-Fortescue, daughter of the Earl and Countess of Suffolk.

'But Alexander did not seem like that to me,' Arabella said quietly.

'Nor to me either, Bella, but that is just the way of the world. I foolishly thought that after I'd explained everything to Alexander and he'd forgiven me we'd have some sort of future together. I'd forgotten one important fact. He's a duke and I'm a nobody. Well, I've remembered it now and I won't make that mistake again.'

'You're not a nobody, Rosie, and if he can't see how special you are then he's a fool.'

Rosie stood up and straightened her crumpled skirts. What was done was done and there was nothing she could do to change it. She knew she just had to get on with her life.

'Oh, well,' she said, with as much good humour as she could summon. 'I've already had practice in putting Alexander out of my thoughts. Now I have even more reason to forget him. He'll be more than out of my reach once he's married—he'll be completely unattainable. So the sooner I start not thinking about him the better.'

Arabella stood, picked up the discarded card, ripped it in two and sent Rosie a tentative smile. 'Yes. Just remember you're a survivor, Rosie. You've survived a lot in the past and you'll survive this as well.'

Rosie smiled at her friend and blinked away her tears. She hoped Arabella was right, but at that moment she felt completely lost, and survival seemed far out of her grasp.

Chapter Twenty-Four

Alexander could hardly believe his mother's treachery. She had sunk to new depths in order to get her way. If he hadn't received a bill for one embossed invitation he would never have known what she was up to.

That she would have the audacity to send out a fake invitation to Arabella van Haven was beyond reprehensible. And then, when he confronted her, it had been to discover that she had been intercepting the mail and removing his letters to Rosie before the servants had had a chance to deliver them. That had left him speechless.

He had to put things right. Taking the train up to London and telling Rosie the truth was the only way. A letter would get there no faster, and he had to ensure that she understood the true situation.

Arriving at Paddington Station, he immediately jumped into a hansom cab and instructed the driver to get him to the Savoy as quickly as possible. He jumped from the cab almost before it had stopped, threw the fare in the driver's direction and ran into the foyer.

'I need to speak to Miss Rosie Smith,' he demanded of the receptionist.

The receptionist looked up from his ledger and shook his head. 'I'm afraid Miss Smith is not here. She left for the docks this morning. I ordered the carriage myself.'

The news hit Alexander like a punch to the stomach. She was leaving. She was going home. He was too late. His mother's plan had worked.

He turned and ran out of the foyer, hearing the receptionist calling out that he had left his hat behind. Running down the road towards the docks, he waved his arm wildly in the air to hail a cab.

Jumping in as soon as one stopped, he ordered the man to drive to the docks as fast as he could.

Unlike him, the driver knew which dock the steam ships departed from for America, and as they approached the Royal Albert Dock he could see a forest of sailing ships' masts and steamer chimneys.

A cacophony of sound hit him as he disembarked from the cab. Sailors of all nations were talking in a babble of foreign tongues, dock workers were yelling at each other as they loaded and unloaded cargo for the waiting vessels, chains clanked as large loads were hauled high in the air, wooden sailing ships creaked and the water lapped against the wooden beams of the docks.

Alexander looked in every direction, trying to see Rosie among the multitude of workers, passengers and merchants milling round the docks. Then he saw her, along with Aunt Prudence, standing beside a mound of trunks and suitcases. Her pretty face looked sad and she stared down at the ground, her usually upright posture slightly stooped.

He started running again. He had to stop her before she boarded the vessel that would take her away from him. He had to explain. He had to stop her leaving.

Reaching her, he came to a sudden stop, completely out of breath.

She looked up at him and gasped.

'Rosie, I...' He panted, trying to get his breath back. 'Rosie, I'm so sorry.'

He reached out his hand to her. She took a quick step back and clasped her hands tightly together, as if his touch was repugnant to her.

'Rosie, I'm sorry. Please let me explain.'

She shook her head and took another step backwards. 'There's nothing to explain. Nothing at all.'

She blinked several times and he could see tears in her eyes.

'Oh, and congratulations on your engagement.'

He stepped towards her. 'I'm not engaged, Rosie. That's what I want to tell you.'

She tilted her head. 'You're not... But I saw the engagement party invitation. It was sent to Arabella.'

He took in a few more breaths so he could speak more clearly. 'No. I am *not* engaged. My mother invented the whole thing. I don't think she expected me to find out, but she forgot that I do all the accounts, and the bill for one invitation was sent to me.'

'One invitation? But...' She shook her head in confusion.

'There was no engagement—no engagement party. Only one card was sent—to Arabella. She was obviously hoping that you'd return to America and we'd never see each other again. And it looks as if she almost succeeded.'

'So you're not engaged?' Rosie repeated, as if unable to comprehend this change of events.

'No, not yet.'

'Oh,' she said, lowering her head

'Not yet because you're going to have to marry me, Rosie. That's the only way I'm going to stop my mother from constantly interfering and matching me up with every passing heiress.'

Rosie's head shot up and her eyes grew wide. 'I'm going to have to *what*?' She gasped.

'Marry me, Rosie. I said you're going to have to marry me. That's the only thing that will let my mother know that her interfering won't work.'

'What?' she repeated, her face a vision of confusion, and he realised what he had just said.

'I'm so sorry, Rosie. I've been running like a madman since I arrived in London, and in my haste that came out all wrong. Let me start again.'

He took in a few deep breaths to try and slow his racing thoughts so he could explain himself better.

'What I mean to say is that if we have a long courtship then it will give my mother too much opportunity to put obstacles in our way. She will be constantly trying to thwart our plans. Even when she fails—which she will—it will be a constant irritation, so I think we should marry as soon as possible.'

She stared back at him, her dazed eyes even wider.

'I'm still doing this wrong...' He dropped down onto one knee and took hold of Rosie's hand. 'Rosie Smith— my darling Rosie. I adore you. I love you. I think I've loved you from the moment I saw you twirling down the entrance hall at Knightsbrook House. I've never seen anyone so free, so full of joy, and I've never experienced such happiness as I do when I'm with you. Without you it's as if there is no daylight—only a long, interminable night. I can't offer you immediate wealth, but I can offer you a title, and my undying love and devotion, and one day I hope to be able to lavish you with all the luxuries that you deserve. Will you do me the honour…the very great honour…of consenting to be my wife?'

'Of course I will,' she said, nodding her head vigorously. 'And I don't want luxuries. I don't even want a title. All I want is you. All I've ever wanted is you.' She looked around at the bustling crowd and laughed. 'Now, get up, will you? People are staring at us, and you know how much I hate making a scene.'

He looked around and saw that she was right. Even among this crowd that had seen virtually everything before, they had caused the bustle to come to a halt and people to stare in their direction.

'Oh, I have a confession to make,' she said as he rose to his feet. 'I'm not departing. We're meeting Mr van Haven. This is his luggage. He and Arabella have gone off to get a carriage. Your mother sent him a telegram, telling him what had happened, and he got the next steam ship over here. Poor Arabella's probably getting a severe telling-off at the moment, and when he comes back he'll probably try and offer you a deal you can't resist so you'll make his daughter a duchess.'

They looked towards where the carriages were waiting and saw Arabella and an older gentleman walking towards them.

'In that case we'll have to convince him that he's wasting his time,' said Alexander.

And with that he took his bride-to-be in his arms, lifted her off the ground and kissed her.

He knew that he had found his perfect duchess. A woman who would love him as deeply and passionately as he loved her, who would stand beside him and share his burdens the way he would stand beside her and share hers, and who would fill his days with love, laughter and happiness.

Epilogue

The wedding was to have been a simple affair: just family, a few friends and the tenants. But Mr van Haven had had other ideas. He was now connected to the aristocracy—albeit through a ward he had never really wanted, and to whom he had never paid more than the most minimal of attention—and he wanted to celebrate the fact. To that end he had arranged a lavish affair, no expense spared, and Rosie had conceded.

After being supported by Mr van Haven's reluctant charity for so many years, she had decided that letting him organise a large wedding at Knightsbrook and allowing him to invite almost every member of the British aristocracy was a small price to pay.

A lavish wedding would also go some way to appeasing the Dowager, who was still struggling to accept the fact that the next Duchess of Knightsbrook came with no dowry. But now that her attention had turned to finding a good match for Charlotte, she was at least leaving Rosie and Alexander alone.

And she wasn't the only one desperately matchmaking. With so many dukes, earls, barons and viscounts assembled in one spot, Mr van Haven was like a child in a candy shop. The wedding was providing him with the ideal opportunity to thrust Arabella in front of as many aristocrats as he could. He still most definitely had ambitions in that direction.

Well, Mr van Haven was in for a big surprise. Marriage did not figure in Arabella's future. She would soon be appearing on the London stage—albeit in a minor role, with a production company that was struggling financially to survive—but Rosie was sure it was the first step in what would be a brilliant career.

Rosie could only hope that Mr van Haven's business concerns would take him back to America before Arabella's opening night. A career on the stage was certainly *not* the future Mr van Haven had envisaged for his only child.

At least Rosie would now be able to act as Arabella's chaperon. After all, what was more respectable than being chaperoned by a member of the aristocracy—a duchess, no less? Aunt Prudence would be able to return to America with Mr van Haven, leaving the girls to enjoy themselves—and enjoy themselves is exactly what they were intending to do.

But they would think of that another day. Today they had a wedding to celebrate. *Her* wedding—something Rosie had never imagined would happen.

'Have I told you how radiant you look today, Rosie?' Arabella asked, joining her friend and linking arms.

'Only about a thousand times.'

'White lace definitely suits you. And it seems being a married woman also suits you. I've never seen you look happier or more beautiful.'

Smiling, Rosie hugged her best friend, who also looked radiant in a pale blue satin bridesmaid's gown.

It was hard to believe. She was now Rosie Ashton, the Duchess of Knightsbrook.

She looked over at her husband, who was in conversation with Annie, a delighted smile on his lovely lips. Alexander had insisted that all the tenants be invited to the wedding and the reception, much to his mother's and Mr van Haven's chagrin. But after much huffing and puffing they had been forced to accept his decision.

Alexander looked back at her. His smile grew larger and once again she was struck by how much he reminded her of a Greek statue—albeit one that now knew how to smile and laugh.

She smiled too, and a shiver of excited anticipation ran through her. Tonight she would finally discover whether he resembled a *naked* Greek athlete in all other respects.

He excused himself and walked towards her, causing her heart to beat faster. This handsome man, dressed in a dove-grey morning suit, his top hat long abandoned, was her husband. The man who had vowed to love and honour her until death did them part.

'I think I'll leave you two alone,' Arabella said with a light laugh. 'I'm sure my father has some man with a sizeable income and a country estate that he's dying to introduce me to.'

Alexander took Rosie's hands and lightly kissed her cheek. 'While the music, the dancing and the champagne are distracting everyone, there is something we really must do,' he whispered in her ear. 'Will you allow me to lure you away from our guests so I can satisfy a demanding urge that's starting to overwhelm me?'

Rosie nodded. Oh, yes, he could lure her away…and he could satisfy whatever urge he had.

He took her hand and led her across the grass, past the tables draped in white linen, laden with food and drink, and up the stone stairs leading to the entrance of Knightsbrook House—her new home. She looked back and saw that he was right. Everyone was distracted…talking, drinking and dancing. No one had noticed their departure. No one would know what they were up to.

He stopped when they entered the house, took both her hands and placed them around his neck, then encircled her waist with his arms.

Rosie's breath caught in her throat in anticipation. She tilted her head back, closed her eyes and parted her lips, waiting for a kiss.

'I know I should wait till our guests leave before doing this, but I've been waiting for so long I can't wait a minute longer.'

Rosie's hammering heart increased its tempo. 'Really? And what might "this" be?' she asked, her voice a breathy whisper.

'This…'

He began twirling, taking Rosie with him. They spun down the entrance hall, Rosie getting dizzier and dizzier. Her laughter joined his as the black and white floor tiles merged into one and the paintings, vases and statues that lined the walls whirled past.

When they reached the staircase they stopped suddenly, but the room continued to spin. He held her tightly, to stop himself from falling and to save her. But neither worked.

They collapsed in a tangled mass of arms and legs at the foot of the stairs.

Rosie continued to giggle—only to have her giggles stifled when his lips found hers. She kissed him back, her heart overflowing with love, passion and deep contentment.

* * * * *

WITHDRAWN

YARRA PLENTY REGIONAL LIBRARY

WITHDRAWN
HOWARD COUNTY LIBRARY

When will Tess know if

She reminded herself that ~~s~~
days, but those days seemed ~~like years. Was it possible to fall~~
in love this quickly?

This man with the chocolate brown eyes and dark hair silvered with early gray, could he be the one intended for her? Maybe, she thought somewhat ruefully, at her age God sped up the clock and ran courtships at breakneck speed. It was probably necessary when you were on the outer fringes of the dating stage of life.

JANET SPAETH figures she has it all, living between the prairies of North Dakota and the north woods of Minnesota. She has been blessed with a loving and supportive family. Her big gray cat, the model for Cora in this story, helped with this book by sleeping on Janet's lap as she wrote. And if her husband just happens to be a bit like all of the heroes she creates. . .

Books by Janet Spaeth

HEARTSONG PRESENTS
HP458—Candy Cane Calaboose

Don't miss out on any of our super romances. Write to us at the following address for information on our newest releases and club membership.

Heartsong Presents Readers' Service
PO Box 721
Uhrichsville, OH 44683

Or visit www.heartsongpresents.com

Angel's
Roost

Janet Spaeth

Heartsong Presents

This book is dedicated to those angels, seen and unseen, who have shaped and changed my life. I am especially grateful to Cleo Rowe, whose faith is constant and unwavering and who believes in angels because they believe in her.

Cleo, this is your book. Thank you for being my friend. You are an angel yourself.

A note from the author:
I love to hear from my readers! You may correspond with me by writing:

> **Janet Spaeth**
> **Author Relations**
> **PO Box 719**
> **Uhrichsville, OH 44683**

ISBN 1-58660-684-0

ANGEL'S ROOST

© 2003 by Janet Spaeth. All rights reserved. Except for use in any review, the reproduction or utilization of this work in whole or in part in any form by any electronic, mechanical, or other means, now known or hereafter invented, is forbidden without the permission of Heartsong Presents, an imprint of Barbour Publishing, Inc., PO Box 719, Uhrichsville, Ohio 44683.

All Scripture quotations are taken from the King James Version of the Bible.

All of the characters and events in this book are fictitious. Any resemblance to actual persons, living or dead, or to actual events is purely coincidental.

PRINTED IN THE U.S.A.

one

Now faith is the substance of things hoped for,
the evidence of things not seen.
HEBREWS 11:1

Yes, her halo was definitely tilted.

Tess leaned into the display and straightened the halo on the three-foot-tall angel that stood inside the door of her store. It was always an eye-catcher, but sometimes it seemed as if it had a mind of its own—kind of a renegade angel.

"There," she said at last, leaning back and admiring the angel, which grinned at her from under its wild raffia hair, not at all repentant. "Now try not to get into any more trouble."

She opened the door that led from the store into the rest of her house. It was nice having the store only footsteps from where she lived. She walked the short distance to the kitchen and put the teakettle, painted with whistling angels, on the stove to boil.

Tea would be nice, she thought, as she shivered in the back room. It was the day before Thanksgiving, and in North Dakota that meant winter had already arrived, no matter what the calendar said. Heat didn't quite penetrate into the far rooms of her old Victorian house, but she wouldn't trade it for the world. The rooms were still alive with precious memories—of Grandma and Grandpa and the very happy childhood they had given her.

The tinkling of the angel chime over the shop door broke her reverie. She turned off the burner and dashed back into the store.

A man, his hat and shoulders dusted with large white snowflakes, stood in silence, looking around the room. Tess

5

smiled. Her store had this effect on many people.

"Welcome to Angel's Roost," she greeted him.

He continued to take silent inventory of the store. "This is incredible!" he said at last, removing his snow-sodden hat and revealing disheveled hair that was mostly black but shot through in places with early silver. He tried unsuccessfully to straighten it. "Hat hair," he said briefly in apologetic explanation before turning his attention back to the store. "Is it all angels? Everything in this store?"

"Every last bit of it."

"This is incredible," he repeated.

"Are you trying to find something in particular? A gift for your wife perhaps?" she asked.

"No wife, not even a girlfriend—sorry to say." He looked at her, and under the droplets of melting snow she saw that his eyes were dark and fringed with long lashes. Gorgeous. Absolutely gorgeous. The kind of eyes she usually saw looking back at her from the pages of magazine advertisements.

Then the corners of those eyes crinkled, and she knew that under the thick muffler he was smiling. "This must be what heaven looks like." He gestured in a sweeping motion at the hundreds of angels of all sizes, shapes, and colors that filled the shelves, tables, and chairs of Angel's Roost.

His motion stopped when he saw the angel with the halo that was, once again, tilted.

He tugged his mittens off and pulled the snowy muffler down under his chin, revealing a face that was not traditionally handsome but already had deep laugh lines etched into it.

"This is a wonderful piece of work," he said as he leaned over and straightened the out-of-kilter halo. "How much is she? I've got to have her—I can just see her greeting my customers as they walk in!"

An odd sensation of possessiveness about the crazy angel washed over Tess. She did some unnecessary neatening of the angel's ecru and pink ruffled skirts.

"She is for sale, isn't she?" the man asked. "She'd look

perfect right inside the front door."

"Her halo won't stay straight," Tess said softly.

"That adds to her charm." He knelt and closely examined the angel's face, studying her mischievous eyes, her tousled hair, her lopsided smile. "Yes, this is an angel that knows exactly what's what in the heavenly realm. Want to bet she's hidden Gabriel's horn more than a few times?"

Tess laughed. His description was perfect.

He stood up and stuck out his hand. "I'm Jake Cameron, by the way."

He said it as if expecting the name would mean something to her. Quickly she ran it through her memory: *Jake Cameron, Jake Cameron.* In the dim recesses of her mind a light began to glow. Food, something to do with food.

"Tell me where the angel will fit into your store," she improvised.

"It's not a store, exactly, although we do sell some items. You've been in Panda's, haven't you?"

Panda's! The upscale coffee bar was a big draw for college students on the far end of town, near the mall. All the new development out there had attracted most retail and new eating establishments when the downtown had fallen out of favor and into disrepair.

It had become a division of the town's loyalties in which sides had been taken, battle lines drawn. Tess was firmly on the side of downtown.

The history of the community itself, a river town established by a long-ago fur and commodities trade, was still evident, preserved in the stately structures that had crowded together in the early days of the Dakota Territory to form a business center that had eventually deserted it.

Tess delighted in it. Its bricks and ornate moldings had much more character than the plastic and glass of the End, as the new area had come to be called.

She'd been in Panda's once, almost a year ago, and she was overwhelmed by the choices. All she'd wanted was a cup of coffee, but she'd ended up with a brownie-type creation and a mocha drink topped with a dollop of whipped cream and a sprinkling of cinnamon. She had to admit that both were wonderful, even if she didn't know exactly what she'd eaten or drunk.

Tess nodded. "I've been there."

He studied her for a moment. "You're not a regular, though. I'm sure I'd remember you."

"To be honest, it's a bit out of the way for me," she responded. "I don't get over to that part of town very often."

She knew she was understating her disdain for the End, but this man was a customer, and she was not about to get into an argument about the town's two diverse business sectors.

"I know what you mean. I don't get downtown much either, or, believe me, I would have been in here before. It's astonishing what all you have in this store. I've never seen so many angels gathered in one place." He looked around curiously and picked up a small packet from a calico-lined basket near the cash register. "What's this?"

"Smell it," Tess suggested.

"Wow! This is great! What is this stuff called?"

" 'Angel's Breath,' " she answered. "Potpourri. The manufacturer calls this little package a sachet, but to me a sachet is something you put in a drawer to scent your clothing, and this is too potent for that. One little packet will scent an entire room. Some people buy it for their cars too."

The potpourri was one of her best-selling items. She even used it in her bedroom.

"Well, it's wonderful, whatever it's called." He put it back and asked her directly, "How do you like being downtown?"

He had touched on one of her favorite subjects. "I love it! It has a special ambiance that, quite frankly, the newer development doesn't have—yet," she added hastily, recalling that was where his business was located. "I really do like it. I suppose it's not for everyone, but it works for me."

He nodded and picked up a terra-cotta angel, which he

studied with casual interest. "But hasn't it gone to street people?"

She warmed to her topic. "Actually, downtown has always catered somewhat to street people. Not too long ago people strolled up and down Main Street, window-shopping even at midnight."

"That's not the same thing."

"You're right. It's not. But what I'm getting at is that the downtown has always had a nightlife that other parts of town haven't had. It's part of the downtown identity. And," she acknowledged, "as time's gone on, those people on the streets at night have changed. That's true."

"It's not safe." His statement was blunt.

"It's not totally unsafe either. But the mayor's renewal project has taken this into account, and I'm hopeful about seeing changes down here."

"You know a lot about this."

"I'm a member of the task force."

"Do you think Panda's would fit in downtown?"

Before she could respond, a large gray cat sauntered in. Its plumed tail waved back and forth, dusting dangerously near a set of fragile china angels that hovered protectively around and over a detailed porcelain nativity set.

She scooped the cat up as it began to weave through the display and affectionately rubbed her face in the cat's fur. "This is Cora."

"Hi, Cora." Jake reached out and scratched the cat's nose. A loud purr rewarded his efforts.

"You must be a cat person," she said as Cora wiggled free to wrap herself in and out of Jake's ankles.

"I adore cats." Cora investigated the puddles of melted snow that had dripped off Jake's coat. He stood still, exhibiting the instinct of a cat lover not to move quickly and startle an investigating cat. "And this one is terrific."

"She's been with me since I moved in here." After two years Tess was finally able to tell the story without tearing up.

"This was my grandparents' house, although I grew up here too. When Grandma died—Grandpa'd died about a year before—she left me this house. I came back here after the funeral, and Cora was waiting. Sunning herself right in this front area, as if she'd always been here."

"Was she your Grandma's cat?"

Tess shook her head. "No. Grandma loved cats, but she'd been living in a nursing home since Grandpa died, and she couldn't have a cat there." As she remembered, she couldn't help smiling. "Grandma always said there'd be a cat waiting for her in heaven, a cat the color of pussy willows."

Jake knelt and stroked Cora's gray head. "The color of pussy willows, huh? What an extraordinary story!"

The cat meowed imperiously and meandered over to the large angel with the rakish halo. Jake watched her. "Cora's got good taste. I truly do want to buy this wonderful angel. Are you going to tell me how much she is?"

She paused, and he pulled out his wallet, clearly misunderstanding her hesitation. "Oh, I suppose it really doesn't matter. I'll take her at whatever price you're asking."

"I really didn't have a price put on her," Tess said. "To be honest, she's been here since I opened, and she's almost a fixture in Angel's Roost." She made some quick mental calculations and named a price she almost hoped was too high.

He didn't flinch. "No problem." He handed her several bills, and Tess tried not to let her eyes widen at the amount of green she saw in his wallet.

Then he smacked his forehead. "I can't take her!"

Tess breathed a mental sigh of relief, and she turned from the old-fashioned cash register.

"Here's your money back, then."

He shook his head. "Oh, no. I still want her in Panda's, but my car is packed with boxes I have to mail. For once in my life I'm ahead of the game with my Christmas shopping. Too bad too, because I see lots of things here that would have been great. My mother, for example, would adore that angel with the emerald green wings, and—"

"Would you like me to deliver the angel?" She tried not to wince as she spoke. Parting with the angel was hard enough; having to take her to her new home was almost unimaginable.

"No. No need to. I've decided I want to come back and do a little more Christmas shopping. When do you close?"

She had to smile. "Around five, but it doesn't matter. I can stay—"

He scratched Cora's neck as he thought. "No. You probably want to get home."

"I am home."

He looked up, startled.

"I live here."

"I didn't realize this was an apartment building," he said.

"It's not. It's a house—my house. As I say, I live here. Well, Cora and I live here."

Cora looked at Tess as if challenging her words. Jake caught the glance too, and his chocolate brown eyes twinkled with amusement.

"I have the feeling that you live here only through her largesse."

"Basically. In exchange for vast amounts of tuna and Cat-Cat Yums, I get all the kitty kisses and snuggles I could ever want."

They exchanged laughing glances.

"In other words she tolerates me."

He grinned as the cat happily scraped the side of her head on the big angel. "She's a character, that's for sure. So may I pick up Faith tomorrow?"

"Faith?" Tess was at a loss.

"That's what I'm naming this angel. Faith. Doesn't it fit her?"

Tess tilted her head and studied the wayward angel. "I don't know. I always thought of faith as being light and airy and pure, not crazy like this one." Mechanically she once again straightened the angel's halo. "But let me think about it."

"When I come back tomorrow, let me know what you've decided. But Faith seems right for her, so Faith she is."

"Well, she is your angel now." The words cost her dearly.

"As a matter of fact, let's put a SOLD sign on her," he said. He took one of the business cards from the angel-wings holder near the cash register and scrabbled in his pocket until he found a pen.

"SOLD!" he proclaimed as he wrote the word on the back of the card. He bent over and tucked the card into the angel's raffia grasp.

As he stood up, he looked out through the prism edges of the piano window that graced the front of the store. "Still snowing. Not that that's any big surprise, right?"

She nodded mutely, relieved he didn't seem to expect much of an answer.

"I'd better be going," he said, wrapping the muffler around his neck again and settling the sodden cap back on his head. "The snow isn't stopping, and I want to get to the post office before it closes."

His warm brown eyes met hers. "By the way, I didn't get your name."

"Tess Mahoney," she said, somewhat breathlessly. Had her heart always beat this irregularly? Maybe she should get a checkup.

"Tess Mahoney," he repeated. "Sounds a bit Irish."

"You've got it right with 'a bit.' The name is Irish, but the rest of me is a mishmash of everything."

"Well, Tess Mahoney, I'm very glad to have met you and your angels, and I'll be back tomorrow to pick up Faith and do some more shopping."

"I'll be here."

With a wave he opened the door and left, the cold November air swirling in to replace the warmth that left with him.

Cora leaped up to the counter and leaned against Tess, her body heat welcome as the chilled early night air invaded the cozy store.

"Well, Kitty-Cat," she said as she locked the store's door and turned off the light, "thanks to Mr. Cameron you'll be in

Cat-Cat Yums for quite awhile."

There was nothing to take her from her snug house that night—no choir practice, no urban renewal meetings, no shopping to be done. So she curled up on the couch under one of the many colorful afghans her grandmother had crocheted, with Cora cozied in beside her and a cup of spiced tea heating her hands.

It had been a long time since she'd gone out with anyone. She smoothed Cora's already silky fur. Thoughts crowded her mind.

He wasn't married. He liked cats. He didn't seem to think her store was silly.

But one major question was still unanswered, and she posed it aloud to Cora: "Does he believe in angels? What does he believe?"

The answer made all the difference in the world.

Cora's even purring became hypnotic, and Tess felt herself drifting off to sleep after she'd downed the dregs of her tea.

Her last thoughts were of Faith. Why would he think Faith was an appropriate name for an angel who seemed to be always challenging her? No, he was wrong. Faith was constant, unchanging, not an angel whose halo refused to stay put.

two

Tess woke as a thought broke into her dreams with the clarity of a fire alarm. She had told Jake Cameron to come back for the angel today. But this was Thanksgiving! She was going to help serve dinner at her church.

She found his phone number in the telephone book and whistled at the address. Panda's must do a fairly decent business, she realized, for him to be able to afford a home in the Pines. It was the newest housing development in town, far down along the river, and houses there began at more than she could make in fifteen years even if she saved every penny she earned.

She waited until ten o'clock to dial the phone. He answered on the second ring, but his voice was thick with sleep.

"Oh, I'm sorry—I woke you up," she said, her words falling over each other.

"No, well, yes, but that's all right. I had to get up now anyway. What time is it?"

"And how do you know you have to get up now if you don't know what time it is?" She couldn't resist teasing him.

"The sun is up," he responded, the grogginess clearing from his voice. "I'm always up at the crack of dawn."

"Well, dawn has cracked. About four hours ago." She grinned at Cora, who lifted one exhausted eyelid in response.

He muttered something she couldn't understand and probably didn't want to. "The roaster blew a bearing last night around midnight. Wouldn't you know it, just as we head into our biggest season. So I stayed up to work on it."

"Did you get it fixed?"

"Oh, I cobbled it together to last until I can get a replacement part." His voice softened. "So how are you today, Angel Lady?"

14

"You recognized my voice!" Tess couldn't hide her astonishment.

"Sure. Even the combined voices of the guy at the post office yesterday, telling me that 'Sorry, Sir, these boxes need extra tape,' and the college student at Panda's, notifying me that 'Hey, Dude, your big machine has just gone blooey,' couldn't erase the memory of your angelic tones. Seriously, I do have a good ear for voices."

His dead-on imitation of the postal worker and the Panda's employee caught Tess off-guard, and she laughed. "Have you considered comedy?"

"Some people say that's what I'm doing at Panda's, but they're just jealous. So how's my angel doing? Is Faith's halo askew again?"

"I don't think it would stay on straight if you glued it on," she said. "It seems destined to go off to the side no matter what I do."

"I'm anxious to get her here."

"That's what I called about. I said you could take her today, but I forgot—this is Thanksgiving."

"Oh, that's right. I guess I could pick her up tomorrow, but I'd kind of hoped to have her already in place when I opened on Friday."

"You could take her this afternoon," Tess suggested, "unless you have other plans."

"No, I don't. I was just going to loll around the house and watch ball games on TV, but now I'll probably go in and tinker with the roaster. I don't want to interfere with your plans."

"Well, I do need to be at the church by three."

"Church? They have services on Thanksgiving afternoon?"

"We serve an open dinner. I'm in charge of salads and desserts this year. Plus I'll be going in to make sure everything is in place and set the tables, put up the chairs, that kind of thing."

"Sounds like fun. Can you use an extra pair of hands?"

"You're volunteering?" Tess couldn't believe her ears. "Of

course we can! But what about your roaster?"

He laughed softly. "It's undoubtedly safer without my hammering and fiddling around on it. I'm not exactly Mr. Handy, unfortunately. All around, the best choice—the wisest choice—is for me to help out at your church. It'll make me feel useful."

"Fair enough. Can you be here at Angel's Roost shortly before three?"

"With bells on."

She hung up the phone and swept Cora up and whirled her around until the cat meowed a clear complaint. "He's coming to my church! He's coming to my church!"

She hugged Cora to her chest and buried her face in the soft fur as her thoughts led into prayer. "Dear God, I sense something is moving here by Your power. Guide me in the way I should go."

She felt the soft glow of prayer heard and answered, and her heart relaxed.

Cora's impatient wriggle reminded her of the earthly demands of a cat that needed to be fed.

The rest of the morning and the early afternoon sped by. Tess had just slipped into her favorite sweatshirt, a bright yellow one festooned with angels in rainbow colors playing musical instruments, when she heard a car pull up in front of the house. She flew to the front door and motioned him around to the side, where the outside entrance to the house was.

He hadn't even reached the door yet, and her heart was already singing. Did he have any idea how happy he was making her this day?

He came into the entryway off the kitchen and stamped the snow from his feet.

"I'm ready," he announced, kneeling and rubbing Cora's waiting ears. "We can take my car. I left it idling so it'd be warm."

A smile curved her lips. "Better turn it off because we're walking."

"Walking? Are you serious? It's freezing outside, and there's this white stuff called snow all over the sidewalks. Say, this isn't one of those 'work up an appetite' ploys, is it?"

"No, Silly. Trust me."

She pulled on her boots and coat and, after saying good-bye to Cora and promising her turkey leftovers, led him back to the sidewalk. He reached inside the late-model sedan, which Tess knew carried a very expensive price tag, and turned off the ignition.

"Okay, let's go!" Tess said. "Just pretend we're arctic explorers. It'll be fun."

"Way cool. Too way cool," he grumbled. "And the pun is definitely intended. We've just met, and already you're trying to kill me for my insurance money. Well, it won't work. It just won't work. Mom's my beneficiary, so there." He glared at her with mock suspicion. "She didn't put you up to this, did she?"

"You nut," Tess answered, poking him with her elbow.

They crossed the street and trudged through half a block of snow-covered sidewalks before Tess tugged on his arm. "Let's go in here."

Jake peered at the white stone church in front of him. "Nativity Church," he read from a sign by the steps. "Why, this is charming!"

"Ah, you're just saying that because you're cold, and if this is our destination, it means you don't have to walk anymore."

"That might color my opinion," he confessed playfully, "but I am truly serious. This is an absolutely delightful church!"

A tall man with thinning hair and an open smile met them inside the door. "Hi, Tess! The others aren't here yet, but if you want to go on down and—oh, in the glare of the sunlight I didn't see your friend." He stuck out his hand toward Jake. "I'm Reverend Barnes."

"Jake Cameron," Jake said, taking Reverend Barnes's hand and shaking it enthusiastically. "I hope you don't mind my coming. Tess said—"

"Everyone's welcome. Glad we could treat you to a hot

meal and some fellowship. Not necessary to explain why," he continued as Jake tried to stop the well-meaning pastor's words. "We all have times when we need a little something. Maybe food, maybe companionship. Certainly in these hard—"

Tess interrupted gently. "Reverend Barnes, Jake's here to help with the dinner."

Reverend Barnes wasn't at all nonplused. He tilted his head back and laughed with a joy that seemed to boom to heaven itself. "Welcome, welcome," he said, grasping Jake's hand again. "Glad to have you with us, Son."

Another couple arrived, and the minister's attention turned to them. Tess guided Jake down the stairs to the kitchen.

"Who comes to this dinner, anyway?" he asked as Tess tossed him a large white apron.

"Well, as Reverend Barnes already said, some people come because this is the only way they'll get a decent meal today. Others come because of the companionship that's offered." Her eyes met his. "I come because it reminds me that one of the things I have to be thankful for is that I am blessed with food and friendship."

His gaze didn't waver. "But shouldn't it be more than that? Those in need—surely their purpose isn't to remind us of our blessings."

His words took Tess by surprise. She'd never thought about it that way. Certainly he had a point. She hadn't examined this closely enough.

"Can you explain?" she asked.

"Not really," he answered, and she appreciated the honesty in his voice. "But it does seem rather egocentric to think the role of the hungry is to make us aware of how good it feels not to be hungry."

"You've posed a good question, Son." Reverend Barnes's deep voice filled the kitchen as he joined them. "Sorry to eavesdrop, but I might be able to help."

"Please do," Jake said.

"Maybe if you flip the picture over, it'll make more sense.

For the hungry what purpose does being fed serve? Rather than thinking of what this does for us, we should be asking what it does for those in need. We should focus on them. Being hungry is a wrong that must be righted. And we here today are simply agents of that change. In serving this food we serve at a greater table."

He smiled benevolently at Tess. "It should make us feel better, helping out today, but it shouldn't make us complacent. For many people hunger is an ever-present enemy of happiness. We need to do what we can to feed the hungry. It's what Jesus wants."

He handed Jake a folding chair and smiled. "Now that I've solved that problem, it's back to work for me. I've got to come up with some inspirational words for tonight's dinner."

"Wow," Jake breathed as Reverend Barnes turned and raced back up the steps, like a man half his age. "It seems to me he's already come up with some incredibly inspirational words."

"He is astonishing," Tess agreed. "He has the ability to see right through to the center of things. Even if I hadn't been a member of Nativity since I was born, I'd be here because of him."

Jake nodded thoughtfully. "Where do I start with these chairs?"

A twinge of concern creased through the satisfaction of the day. He had changed the subject so quickly—but why? He didn't seem to be trying to avoid the matter; yet he certainly didn't seem inclined to pursue it.

Her musings were interrupted by a stream of people carrying foil-wrapped turkeys and mysterious casserole dishes that smelled wonderful. The kitchen exploded with the joy of many hands cooking.

Jake fell into the role of chief chair-placer quite easily. Tess found herself taking pleasure in the relaxed way he became part of the group and the openness with which her church friends accepted him.

She found herself watching him and the way he interacted

with the others. A small movement behind him caught her eye: Reverend Barnes moved toward his wife. For a slice of a moment the minister and his wife glanced at each other, and Tess could tell that volumes passed unspoken—in a muted language only they understood. Then Reverend Barnes sloped his head down and dropped a gentle kiss on his wife's forehead.

A surprising, new hunger washed over Tess. That same degree of closeness and understanding the minister and his wife had—she wanted it, suddenly wanted it, but with whom? Could it be that having Jake there today was bringing this to the forefront? A hole in her life had become a gaping, aching wound of lonely need.

"He's a keeper, I think." The voice belonged to Ellen Smalley, the organist. The tiny woman had always reminded Tess of a wren, small, drab, and twittering but completely harmless. Tess had adored her since she had been a small child in the Carolers' Choir in grade school.

Tess tried to collect her scattered thoughts. "He's not mine to keep."

Mrs. Smalley's brow furrowed. "He's not married, is he?"

"Oh, no." Tess couldn't stop the bubble of laughter that arose at Mrs. Smalley's obvious relief. "I mean he's just a customer of mine. There's not anything going on between us."

Mrs. Smalley nodded, clearly not believing a word Tess was saying. "Give it time, Honey—give it time."

"No, no." Tess tried to object, but the furious heat she felt pouring up her throat was making things worse. Why on earth had God decided to make her a blusher?

To make things worse, Jake chose that moment to look at her and wink. Mrs. Smalley laughed out loud. "You know," she said close to Tess's ear, "there is a phrase 'match made in heaven.' "

This was too much!

But heaven intervened and saved her as the first of the hungry and lonely trickled past on their way to the small dining room.

Thanksgiving dinner had begun.

For the next two hours Tess was too busy to give Jake much thought, although their eyes did meet frequently over steamy bowls of stuffing and corn as she passed them from the kitchen to the serving area.

Eventually, however, the area moved from organized chaos to a diminished roar and then to an exhausted but satisfied calm. The workers drooped into the now-vacant folding chairs, and Tess smiled as Jake collapsed into the one adjoining hers.

"Whew." He ran his fingers through his work-ruffled hair.

A single voice began to sing softly, and soon the others joined in: " 'We gather together. . . .' " Tess's soft alto was joined by Jake's strong baritone, and they smiled at each other as they united in the familiar Thanksgiving hymn.

He sang the hymn from memory. Tess's heart lifted again.

But her hopes were deflated quickly as, when the song ended, he sighed. "I learned that early on. We sang it every year in school at Thanksgiving. I've always loved it."

He learned it in school.

She fought against the disappointment. But before she could phrase a prayer, words of assurance came, this time from Reverend Barnes.

"We've done a good thing here today, but feeding over a hundred people a rollicking good turkey dinner isn't enough. I hope we've done more than send them out with warm food in their bodies. A full stomach doesn't mean a lot if there isn't a full soul to go with it. Let us pray that today we fed those whose souls were already full, and those whose souls were hungry. Let this food be our testimony to Jesus Christ."

She heard several fervent amens.

Reverend Barnes continued as he reminded them of one of Tess's favorite passages from the Bible: "When Jesus said, 'I was hungry, and you fed Me,' was He talking about turkey dinners only? Or should we search for more in His words? What lesson do we take forward with us from this day?"

The group silently considered the minister's words. Tess found herself returning yet once more to Jake's presence today and her role in it. Was he one of those Reverend Barnes had referred to as those with hungry souls? If so, had her words and actions been witness enough?

"Bless you all for what you have done. No matter how small, every effort grows when united with others. Have a blessed Thanksgiving, my friends, and don't forget the leftovers. You've earned them!"

Soft laughter spread through the small gathering, and, one by one, people stood up, stretched, and returned again to the kitchen for one last stop—the take-home containers Tess and Mrs. Smalley had packed during the last minutes of the dinner for each of the workers.

Neither Jake nor Tess spoke until they were out of the church. The night sky overhead was clear and cloudless, and stars sprinkled the deep indigo with dots of silver. If she looked hard enough, she could see all the way to heaven, she thought.

Their breath plumed outward as they stopped, by silent mutual agreement, and took in the view.

"Thanks for inviting me," Jake said at last.

"Actually I didn't. You invited yourself," she teased him.

"So I did." He chuckled softly. "Are you sorry?"

"No. I'm not." Her eyes met his in an honest gaze. "I'm glad you came."

"You know, I'm beginning to rethink my opinion of downtown," he said. "I'm starting to see what you find so appealing here. It does have a life of its own I was never aware of." He chuckled again. "And I don't feel at all threatened by this great long walk at night."

As they started the short trek back to her house, her foot found a slick patch on the walk, and she began to slip. He took her hand to steady her.

He held her hand, mittened fingers closed in mittened fingers, the entire way to her house.

"Thank you again," he said, still holding her hand. "This has been a Thanksgiving I will never forget."

"Nor will I," she agreed.

"Your church is as friendly and warm as you are." His dark eyes seemed to be saying something she couldn't read so she took the plunge.

"You know you're always welcome at Nativity." When he seemed still to be waiting for her to say more, she added, "If you'd like, you can go with me to a service."

"That's an invitation I may take you up on someday," he said, and his fingers tightened around hers before letting her hand go.

He turned and walked away.

Tess stood outside and watched him drive off. His car seemed so big, and so empty.

She went inside her house and gave Cora the leftovers. As the cat gulped down the turkey tidbits, Tess went into the store to double-check the front-door lock. The glow from the streetlight outside caught on a sideways gleam—that of a halo, once again tipped.

Faith. They had both forgotten about her.

He'd be back. He didn't have any choice. She still had his angel, his Faith.

Tess's evening prayer centered around Jake as she sought guidance on living as a witness. The answer was not quite what she had expected: She remembered another Bible verse, this one from Hebrews, that Reverend Barnes could have easily used. "Be not forgetful to entertain strangers: for thereby some have entertained angels unawares."

Could it be? Maybe the one needing the witness had been her? Had she, the expert on angels, been in the presence of some tonight? Which stranger might fit the bill? One of those in need of warm food? One in need of a warm heart?

Jake's image sprang into her mind.

"Flip the picture," Reverend Barnes had advised.

"Wow," breathed Tess. "Wow."

three

Not that Tess thought he was an angel! No, if anything, Jake was on the other end of the celestial spectrum.

Actually, that wasn't fair. He had volunteered to help out at the church dinner, and so far he'd given her no indication he wasn't a Christian. And, that little annoying niggling voice inside reminded her, he'd also given her no indication he was a Christian.

But she was getting off track. "Maybe," she said to Cora, who had finished her feast of turkey leftovers and was cleaning her whiskers with satisfaction, "I should be worrying less about his soul and more about mine."

Cora was too stuffed even to meow, it seemed. Instead she strolled over to her spot beside the heating vent and collapsed in sated ecstasy.

"You glutton," Tess said. "Here I am in moral turmoil, and all you can do is purr."

Cora opened one heavy eyelid and stared at her.

"You're right, as usual," Tess told the cat. "I can't expect God to answer my prayers just like that"—she snapped her fingers—"and in a way I'm necessarily going to like. Maybe what I need to do now is get out of God's way on this and let Him work through me, instead of trying to make Him work through me."

She flopped down beside Cora. "You are the smartest kitty in the world," she cooed as she ran her fingers through the soft fur.

She was certain the cat smiled, just a bit.

❧

The day after Thanksgiving was traditionally the busiest shopping day of the year, and this year was no different. What

24

Tess didn't know as the day began was that the evening news had aired a special about downtown regrowth and the mayor's plan. She hadn't watched the news because she'd been at the Thanksgiving dinner at Nativity when the story ran.

But her first customers told her about it. Angel's Roost had been one of the shops mentioned, and over and over she heard the same comment: "I didn't even know you were down here."

Clearly she needed to advertise. With only the brief mention on the news her business had tripled. What could it do with an effective promotional campaign?

During breaks in the flow of people stocking up on angels for decorations and gifts, she began to sketch out an advertisement.

But, as the afternoon trade died down, so did her enthusiasm.

"I'm no artist," she told Cora. "If I want to get Angel's Roost in the public's mind, I'll have to hire an advertising agency or get on the news every night."

She chose a name at random from the phone book's listing of ad agencies.

Their conversation was short and anything but sweet. "Well, Toots," she informed Cora, "I'd better hope for lots of news coverage because there is no way I can afford a professional advertising agency."

The price of an original ad from an agency wasn't high, but it was more than she could pay right now. Maybe after Christmas she'd look into it. She'd have more time then. Unfortunately, when things were quieter at the store, her bank balance dropped accordingly.

The tinkle of the door chime ended in a crash.

"Uh-oh." Jake picked up the legs of the metallic angel, now separated from her body, which swung freely over the door.

"Poor thing." Tess took the pieces and examined them. "Oh, no problem. I can put them back together. This ring came apart here."

"Whew. I was afraid I was responsible for bringing an

angel earthward. That weighs heavy on the old conscience, you know."

She grinned at him. "You lowly mortal. Don't you know it takes more than a human being to bring down an angel?"

"I'm not going to argue." He held up his hands in mock surrender. "I'm delighted I haven't taken an angel out of more than temporary commission. And speaking of angels"—he patted Faith on her curly little head—"I've come to take this gal with me."

"I'm going to miss her, you know." Tess was surprised at how true that was.

"I don't blame you. But she'll have a good home with us at Panda's. She has her own niche all set up right inside the door."

Tess was struck with a sudden horrible thought. "She's not going to be holding a coffee cup, is she, with a sign at her feet saying something like 'World's Most Heavenly Coffee'?"

Jake looked aghast. "Do you really think I'd be guilty of a cheap trick like that? No, let me assure you. She is going to be there as an angel, not as an advertising gimmick. If she wants to take over as Panda's guardian angel—that is, if one hasn't already been assigned to us—well, that'd be fine with me."

"I'm not sure businesses have guardian angels," Tess said doubtfully.

"But their owners do, don't they?"

"Everybody does." She couldn't resist adding, "And some people must have a whole host of them guarding them. Children, for example. How else do they live through childhood relatively unharmed?"

He chuckled. "I bet I sent at least one angel into early retirement."

She motioned to a famous print of a guardian angel guiding two precious children, a boy and a girl, along a path. "How often do you suppose something like this happens? One angel assigned to two children?"

"If that were a picture of my sister and me, that poor angel would be a nervous wreck. What you don't see is the itching powder the little boy put inside the girl's clothing, and the Kick Me sign she taped to his pants." He studied the picture. "Matter of fact, why don't you wrap that up too? I'm going to give it to my sister for Christmas, just to remind her of how angelic we were as kids."

"Does your family live around here?" Tess asked as she took the painting down and wrapped pink and gold angel-printed tissue paper around it.

"They're all over the country," he said, paying her once again with cash. "Sis and her family are in Mississippi, my two brothers are in New England, and Mom and Dad are in Southern California."

"Will you be seeing them this Christmas?"

He shook his head. "No. The big family gathering takes place every summer at the family cabin in Montana, but I'll try to buzz out and see Mom and Dad later in January." His eyes twinkled. "Right about then I'm ready for some basking in the sun without a parka, and, oh, yeah, it's great to see my parents too."

"Sounds fun."

"It is. They have a big ranch-style house with a swimming pool. It's quite a nice break from the icy depths of winter. Although I have to say it gets harder and harder to go out there to visit, what with Panda's taking so much of my time."

"Being a sole practitioner in business means vacation time is severely curtailed, that's for sure."

"True." He reached down and patted Cora, who had joined them. "Besides, this grand lady might not be as flexible as your customers."

"That's the truth!"

She handed him the package. "Want some help carrying all this to your car?"

"I can get it." As he gathered up the large angel and balanced the print under his arm, he said, "By the way, come out to Panda's soon and see how Faith is doing out there. I think you'll like it."

"I'll try." She held the door open for him. "It was nice doing business with you."

He stopped and turned to look at her. "Oh, I'm not finished yet. I still have more shopping to do. See you later!"

Cora joined Tess at the door but cringed back at the gust of cold air that swept into the small store.

"Brr. You're right, Cora. It's way too cold today." She shut the door and, through the window, watched him struggle with the angel as he tried to wrangle it into the car without bending the wings or totally tearing off the halo.

She grinned as he finally gave up and put it in the front seat, like a passenger.

What was he doing now? She laughed out loud as he stood up and moved away from the door. He'd even fastened her in with the shoulder strap of the seat belt!

He glanced back at the store and, catching her eye through the window, gave a jaunty wave before pulling away from the curb.

He'd no sooner left than another figure loped up the walk to the front of the shop.

"Reverend Barnes!" Tess cried in delight as the minister stooped slightly at the door. "You don't have to duck today. The door angel broke."

"Oh, no." He looked in consternation at the body of the angel still swinging over the transom. "She always seemed to say hello when I visited."

"Oh, she'll be back. It wasn't anything I can't fix. Actually, it's a good sign. I've been so busy today that she got a work-out, the likes of which she's never seen before."

"I heard you had some good coverage last night on the news. It's great that it brought out customers in droves."

"Well, not in droves, exactly. Clusters. That's it. Clusters of customers. So what can I do for you, Reverend?"

"I want to buy Mrs. Barnes a really special angel this year. This will be our thirty-seventh Christmas together, you know."

"Thirty-seventh! I'm impressed. You both deserve angels

for that. What did you have in mind?"

"Something with gold and diamonds and emeralds for putting up with me all these years," he said jokingly.

"Gold and diamonds and emeralds," she mused. "Gold and diamonds and emeralds. Hmm. Let me think what I have in stock right now."

"I'm just teasing!" he protested.

"So am I. Crystal and colored glass, maybe. Hey!" She snapped her fingers. "I have an idea that might work."

She reached high overhead and felt around until her fingers closed around it. "How about this?"

She handed it to him. It was a shining silver bell, a bit dusty now. At the top of it, serving as a handle, was an elaborately sculpted angel's head, her hair made of hundreds of delicate gold wires fused together lightly. The bell was her skirt, a lacy gold mesh network overlaid atop the silver background.

"I could engrave it here"—she pointed to the hem of the gleaming skirt where a band of smooth silver ran along the border—"with whatever you would like. That would personalize it."

"Perfect!" The minister's eyes shone with enthusiasm. "What should I put on it?"

Tess shrugged. "Whatever you want is fine; it just can't be too long, or it won't fit. What would you like to say to her?"

"You know, she's been my angel all these years, but I wonder if she knows it."

"How about 'My Angel'?" she suggested.

"Perfect! How soon will it be done? And this is a secret, you know."

"I'll have it done early next week. And my lips are sealed," Tess promised solemnly.

"And, speaking of secrets, why have you been keeping your young man a secret?"

"What young man? Talk about secrets! I didn't even know I had a young man! Rats. I'm always the last to know." Tess laughed lightly and tried to suppress the telltale flush she knew was edging its way up her neck.

"Don't play coy with me, Tess Mahoney." The minister waggled his finger under her nose. "You know good and well who I'm talking about. I mean that fellow who came to the dinner with you and helped us out so much. That young man. What's the story with him?"

"There really isn't a story, Reverend Barnes." Tess sadly acknowledged to herself that this wasn't an actual lie. "He's a customer. As a matter of fact, he just bought that big angel that's usually there"—she pointed to the empty spot and tried to ignore the twinge in her heart—"and a print, and that's that."

Reverend Barnes studied her shrewdly. "No, that's not that. There's more, but I'm not going to pry. I did promise your grandmother I'd keep watch over you, you know."

"Yes, I know." Tess's heart gentled. "And I am telling you the truth. I've only known him since the day before Thanksgiving. And I do like him—a lot—but there's really no more to the story."

"It's still early," he said.

"He's a customer," she repeated, with slight emphasis on the last word.

"I meant early in the day," he said, his bright blue eyes dancing with impishness. "Why, whatever did you think I meant? Girl, you've got to learn to relax!"

She could not become irritated with him. He was a rascal, and she absolutely adored him. Besides, she knew he had only her best interests at heart.

She made a split-second decision to confide in him. "Reverend Barnes, I do like him. A lot. I like his sense of humor, his thoughtfulness." She struggled for the words. "He even likes Cora."

"More to the point, does she like him?" He was all too familiar with the way the cat ruled the household.

"She adores him. Well, she lets him scratch her ears. And her nose. And her forehead." She pretended to frown. "Reverend Barnes, I do believe the man is courting my cat."

"This sounds like it's getting serious," he answered, and Tess realized he was only partially kidding her. "When a man woos a woman's cat, he's building the base for an all-out campaign to win her heart."

"Do you think so?" Her fingers clasped together so tightly that her ring cut into her palm. "I mean, I almost don't dare to hope, and, let's face it, I'm out of practice with all this. But I do like him."

The minister pried her tensed fingers apart. "Just take it easy, Tess. Let God guide you through this. I'll be praying for you."

"I also wonder if he's a Christian," she said softly. "It does matter, you know."

He patted her hands. "You were born into the faith, my dear, and it's always been part of you, like your red hair and your blue eyes. But even if I didn't know your religious background, I'd have to say I'd be more surprised if I learned that you weren't a Christian than that you were."

"I don't follow."

"I can't say for sure, but I have that feeling about Jake. He's a good man, Tess, at least from what I saw of him last night. Certainly there are consummate actors who can fool you into thinking they're saints when the only view of heaven they've seen is a perfume ad. But I don't sense that about this young man. I think he's all right."

His assessment tallied with hers, she had to admit. Jake did seem ethical, so why was she looking for something to be wrong with him?

"Just let God lead you," the pastor advised. "And let this relationship develop without complicating it early on. Have faith in God's wisdom."

There was that word again. "Faith."

"You're still young," Reverend Barnes continued. "You need to get out, have fun, go to dinner. And, speaking of dinner, I'd better be going. Mrs. Barnes is making her famous stuffed pork chops."

Tess smiled. "World famous, I'd say. She's going to have to give me that recipe."

He shook his head as he pulled up the collar of his overcoat. "Not a chance. That recipe ranks right up there with the CIA's most-secret secret. About the other matter"—he grinned widely—"I'll check back with you later. Meanwhile, try to relax and have a good time. If you get the chance to share your faith, do it, but don't push it too hard too fast."

He winked at her. "Your grandparents raised you to be a good Christian girl, and your faith shows through you like a beacon. That alone does more to move a seeking soul than a year of my sermons. Why, I'll bet that right now your faith is having a nice visit with that young man, Jake What's-His-Name."

She stared after him, her mouth agape. How did he do that? She looked at the empty spot where Faith had stood. Nice visit, indeed. Sometimes that man was downright spooky.

The phone rang, interrupting her contemplations. She picked it up and held it to her ear, still absorbed in the minister's words.

"Hello? Hello?" A disembodied voice floated from the telephone receiver. "Tess?"

"Angel's Roost," she answered, snapping back to reality. "May I help you?"

"Tess, this is Jake." The connection spit and crackled. "Sorry. This car phone is giving me all sorts of problems. Anyway, I wanted to know if you had plans for tonight."

"No, no." The minister's words revisited her: *"Have fun—go to dinner. Easy for him to say,"* she thought. "No, I don't have any plans."

"How'd you like to go to dinner tonight?" Jake asked. "Tess? Tess?"

How did that man do it?

four

Tess pawed through her closet one more time. Well, there was nothing to be done at this stage: She'd wear her green silk. She slipped into it and preened at her reflection in the hall mirror. She had to admit it. No matter that the dress was four years old; it did look good on her.

She told herself she was cool, calm, and collected. She pulled back her shoulders, tilted her chin upward, and tried for a haughty look, like a lady of society.

A furry shadow moved into the mirrored image, sniffed Tess's ankles, and twitched her tail crossly, as if angry that her owner would be leaving her alone on a cold winter night.

"Don't worry, Sweetie. I'll only be gone awhile," Tess crooned, smoothing Cora's already silky gray coat. "It's just a date."

Just a date. Her stomach flipped up and flopped down.

A slight whisk of makeup, a quick brush through the tousled auburn curls, and she was ready. She'd just sprayed on a light spritz of cologne when she heard a knock at the back door.

Jake whistled as he saw her. "You, my friend, are a knock-out!"

"Why, thank you!" she responded, trying not to smile too much. A knockout! No one had ever called her a knockout before. She felt ridiculously flattered.

He helped her into her coat and then paused as she opened the door. "I hate to be making fashion suggestions to such an elegant lady, but wouldn't you be more comfortable walking to the car with shoes on?"

"Shoes?" she asked blankly. Then she looked down at her feet and saw her stockinged toes. "Shoes," she repeated.

She must be more flustered than she had given herself

credit for. She dashed up the stairs and pulled a pair of shoes from her closet, making sure they matched. She wasn't taking any more chances!

She said good-bye to Cora, who glared at her through slitted eyes, and they left her house. His car was parked in front, and it was still warm.

"Where are we going?" She settled herself into the leather luxuriousness of his car. The dashboard had more lights than Las Vegas. She didn't have any idea what half of them were for, but she didn't want to ask.

"To Whispering Winds."

Wow. Tess formed the word silently.

"Ever been there?"

"No, can't say I have."

He turned slightly toward her, taking his gaze off the road momentarily. "Guess why I chose it."

"Because it has good food?" she ventured.

"Partially. Guess again."

"Good service?"

"Nope. Keep trying."

She was stumped. Because it was probably the most expensive place in the area? Because he thought she'd probably never eaten there? Because she'd be impressed? No, all those reasons sounded so shallow. She made one last effort.

"Because you own it?"

He burst out laughing. "I wish! No, guess again."

"I give up. Tell me."

"Because it's not downtown and not on the south end. It's middle ground."

That was true. Even as he spoke, they left the city limits and drove on the old highway access toward a darkened county road.

Jake slowed down and peered at the small blue reflecting markers that glowed alongside the road. "If I'm not careful, I'll miss the turnoff. They should mark it better."

He located the road sign and turned down the county road.

Without the street lamps or even occasional lights of the highway, the night sky surrounded them so completely she couldn't tell where sky ended and earth began. Only the headlights of the car cut through the darkness like a searchlight.

"Are you sure this is right?" Tess asked tentatively. "It's really, really dark out here."

"Well, I'm pretty sure," Jake responded, but his words held a trace of hesitancy. "It can be hard to tell out here, though. You get on the wrong road, and you can go miles before you get your bearings. Even during the day. Why, last summer I was out—oh, here it is. I recognize that white-painted rock."

Tess felt the car begin to climb a small rise—almost a hill, if there could be such a thing in eastern North Dakota.

And, sure enough, at the top of the rise, there, spread out before them like a sparkling lake of glittering lights, lay Whispering Winds.

He slowed down and pulled into the expansive parking lot. Even at night Tess could tell the place was spectacular. She had the impression of a ring of pines and spruce edging the parking lot and circling behind the restaurant.

Small trees, possibly maples, although she couldn't tell without their foliage, dotted the freshly snowplowed parking lot. Tiny white lights glittered in the leafless branches.

A young man in a military-style overcoat and hat met the car as Jake pulled into the looping road by the front door of the restaurant. As the keys were exchanged between Jake and the valet, Tess let herself out of the car, over their objections, and stood near the entrance.

She heard a soft murmur as the evergreens brushed against each other in the evening breeze, undoubtedly the source of the poetic name of the restaurant.

"You didn't need to wait outside," Jake said as he joined her, taking her elbow and guiding her toward the restaurant's door. "It's too cold."

She shook her head. "No. I was listening."

"Listening?" For a moment Jake seemed lost; then he

nodded in understanding. "Oh, you heard the whisper. That says a lot, you know. Not everyone can be quiet enough to hear it. Legend has it that only a truly peaceful soul can hear it."

They entered through the massive brass and etched-glass doors. Tess paused and looked around her.

"This is magnificent!" she breathed.

The restaurant was constructed as a great room. The ceiling arched a full two stories overhead. Each table was draped with a pristine white tablecloth, and the chairs were upholstered in a muted mallard green. Over the hardwood floors Oriental rugs of a thousand colors and patterns were scattered, adding an underlay of hues that contrasted with the stark monochromatic vault above them.

They checked their coats and allowed a server to lead them to a table. It was tucked back into the corner, and Tess wondered if Jake had requested it. But every table seemed to be situated with an awareness of privacy, so maybe she was reading too much into it.

"Would you like a cocktail before you order?" the hostess asked.

Jake looked at her, and Tess shook her head slightly. "If they have mineral water, that would be wonderful."

"Mineral water for both of us, please," Jake directed the hostess, and she left.

"You didn't have to skip the drink because I did," Tess said, though she was secretly glad he did.

"I don't drink," Jake said and paused, as if weighing what to say next. "I grew up in a house where drinking was a problem for awhile. My dad was a borderline alcoholic, although he's come around since then."

"I'm sorry to hear your family was in that situation," Tess said, "but I'm delighted to hear it's different now."

"Yes. Dad has changed in a lot of ways. I'm glad the period when he was at rock bottom was brief. Still, it's something that stays with me, and I consider it every time I'm offered a drink."

Once again Jake rose in her estimation. If there were a ladder to measure his standing, he'd be climbing it steadily, rung by rung.

"Thank you for sharing that," she said softly. "You didn't have to, you know."

"Oh, I'm sorry." He reached across the table and covered her hand with his. "I didn't mean to get too personal."

"Don't worry. It didn't offend me. I just realize how painful personal topics can be to disclose."

"It's not a subject I usually chat about, but something about you makes me want to tell you everything about me." His look was intense and a bit unsure. "But, to be honest, we're edging into an area that makes me uncomfortable."

He might as well have dumped the crystal pitcher of ice water in her lap. Her face must have registered her shock, because he explained quickly: "I'm afraid this conversation is going to give you the wrong impression of my family and me. I had a very happy childhood, all in all. This one stage was blessedly short-lived, but memorable. I like to think it made me stronger. I know it served that function for my father."

"Well, I also had a pleasant childhood, although it was, at the time, unconventional. My parents were both killed in an automobile accident—"

"Oh, I'm sorry," he murmured sympathetically.

"Thank you, but I wasn't even two at the time, so I don't have anything but vague unshaped memories. My grandparents stepped into the breach and took over, never letting me have a moment that wasn't filled to overflowing with love."

She smiled as the memories washed over her. They were wonderful people, her grandparents. She wished they could have met Jake, and she said so aloud.

"I can see their love in you still," he said, his gaze resting softly on her face.

It was the best thing he could have said. Tess felt their legacy daily, the strong basis of faith and trust they had instilled in her early.

The waitress chose that moment to appear at their table and take their orders. Tess quickly studied the menu and selected the salmon pasta in pesto sauce.

"That does sound good," Jake said. "Maybe I'll switch my choice from the filet mignon."

The waitress stood by patiently while they sorted through the side dishes and salads that accompanied their entrees, leaving them in solitude at last.

The conversation took a lighter turn, as they discussed television shows they enjoyed. Both admitted to liking half-hour situation comedies, and when Jake allowed that his favorites were the late-night reruns of the old black-and-white shows, Tess agreed happily.

They ran through some of the more memorable *I Love Lucy* episodes and were just reliving the famous assembly-line sequence in the chocolate factory when their salads arrived.

Tess didn't know it was possible to do such wonderful things with a salad. The heated dressing was heavenly, and the butter flavored with sun-dried tomato and a hint of Parmesan cheese was exquisite on the warm rolls, clearly fresh from the oven.

"You know, I could have a whole meal of this alone," she said at last. "I'm going to try adding seasoning to butter at home, but I doubt I can do this justice. This is scrumptious!"

"I'm glad you're enjoying it. You said this is your first time here?" he prompted.

She nodded. "I've been meaning to come for a long time, but I've never gotten around to it. Do you come out here often?"

"Not as often as I'd like," he confessed. "Panda's keeps me pretty busy." He pushed his salad plate to the side and lowered his voice. "I'd like your feedback on something. But first I need your promise that this will stay confidential."

"Sounds pretty serious."

"It is."

"Then I can't promise." At his look of surprise she explained.

"I decided a couple of years ago not to put myself in morally compromising spots. And part of that was not making promises that make me uneasy. This one does that."

"There's nothing morally compromising in this!" he protested.

"But I don't know that," she reminded him gently. "You haven't told me anything. For all I know, you may be about to tell me your plans to rob First Central Bank next Wednesday."

"Rob a bank!" His words rang out loudly, and several diners turned to him with surprised looks on their faces. He grinned sheepishly and waved his hand apologetically to them.

"Well, now that they all think I'm a master criminal—"

"Hardly a master criminal," she interrupted. "I don't think a master criminal would announce his plans to a crowded restaurant."

"That's true. But what I want to talk to you about isn't criminal or anything like that. It's business," he said.

She laughed. "A master criminal you're not, and a master businessperson I'm not. Why on earth would you ask my opinion about a business matter?"

"Here's the deal. I'm thinking about moving Panda's downtown."

She sat up straight. "You're kidding me! Panda's downtown?"

"Sssh!" He glanced around the crowded dining room, but no one seemed to have heard. "I'm not sure yet. I'm just tossing the idea around."

"Well, a coffeehouse downtown would be welcomed by the business owners—I can assure you of that," she said, trying to sound calm when in fact she wanted to shout with anticipation. The idea was spinning cartwheels in her head.

Panda's downtown! The contribution that move would make to economic regrowth was nearly unfathomable. If Panda's moved, other trendy restaurants and shops in the south end might follow. It could be the initial step in a trend that signaled the necessary revitalization of the historic downtown!

"So you do think it's a good idea?" he persisted cautiously.

"What do I have to do—a wild dance of joy?" She grinned at him.

"That would be interesting but unnecessary, I think. No, I'm serious. What do you think?"

"I love it! Do you have a location selected yet? There are some wonderful old buildings that would be ideal. There's one down on the riverfront with a wide span of a back wall. You could break through it—I'm sure the owner would allow construction—and be able to serve in the back, alfresco, in the summer."

She warmed to her subject, becoming more enthusiastic by the minute. When she finally began to run down, she realized he was staring at her, his chin cupped in his hand. "Wow," was all he said.

Tess fussed unnecessarily with her napkin. "Well, it is a topic near and dear to my heart. I'm a downtown girl, you know. I honestly don't see what the appeal is in the south end. Not a single tree grew there naturally, except for some old homesteader's shelterbelt trees that escaped the ax, and they exist only through the good graces of who knows what."

"The End is safer. It's cleaner. We have a lot more traffic out there. I see an excitement there that I honestly don't sense downtown."

She had done it. She had unwittingly insulted him and his original business decision. She quickly tried to make amends. "I'm sorry. I don't get over there very often—" She bit her tongue to keep from speaking the rest of the thought, that she purposely avoided that part of town.

"That's all right. I know there's a solid division in the city between downtown and the End. Each thinks it has the advantage over the other."

She nodded. "Considering how you feel about the End, why are you considering bringing Panda's downtown?"

The vigor came back into his demeanor. "I do appreciate the historic setting of downtown. And I like the mayor. If anyone can make this new project work, she most certainly can.

It would be exciting to be part of it."

"But—?" she prompted.

"But I have no assurances—and a lot of questions. What if she loses the next election? What if she can't get the rest of the business community behind her? What if, despite the city's best intentions, the whole thing flops? What then?"

They weren't questions she hadn't heard and fielded a hundred times, but for once, the ready, pat answers wouldn't serve. It became real, this chance they were asking business-people to take. Invest in downtown. Invest their money. Probably most of it. And with nothing to promise in return.

Now the doubt had a face and a name. Jake's. And her answer became vitally important. She sent a quick prayer heavenward, asking for guidance in what she was about to say to him.

She chose her words carefully. "Beginning your business in the End was a risk. You had no guarantee it'd go."

He shook his head. "No. It was a risk, but not a great one. There was no other coffeehouse, and the time was right. The only risk now if I stay there is that the appeal may fall off in a few years. But then the challenge would be to adapt."

"Okay," she conceded. "Let's talk about moving Panda's."

"On the downside," he said, "I risk losing my established customers."

"No," she argued, "they'll follow you."

"Maybe, but a great number of them will simply move to another place in the End. I no longer have the monopoly on coffeehouses out there."

"But you would downtown," she pointed out. "No other place there is like Panda's."

"And, on the other hand," he continued, "although I might lose some in the move, a significant number downtown would come to Panda's, not just businesspeople like you, but those who live there."

"What you want is a guarantee," she stated at last, sensing an impasse. "You don't lose anything, but you gain substantially."

He grinned. "Well, that would be nice. Is the downtown commission by any chance offering something like that?"

"Nice try, but no."

"So what do you say to me, to make me bring Panda's downtown?"

She deliberated before she spoke. "I say, follow your heart. You're right—it's going to be exciting for the downtown in the next couple of years. If you want to be part of that excitement, then join us. But don't do it if your heart isn't in it 100 percent. This is going to be a long-range commitment, and you need to be willing to be in it for the duration. About the last thing this project needs is people who will fall away as it begins rolling along."

"I understand all of that," he said uneasily, "but is it enough for me to be committed to the project? Isn't there more to it? I do have my own financial future to consider. I don't have a wife and children now, but I hope to someday. I don't want to go into that relationship in debt."

The thought of him married and with a family brought a shimmer to Tess's heart.

"I guess," she said at last, "it's like a lot of things in life. You've got to have faith. There are no guarantees about how things will turn out, but there you have it. Faith. That's what it's going to take."

His dark eyes met hers. "I bought her at your store, remember?"

She smiled at him, glad for the way the tone of the conversation had quickly lightened. "How could I ever forget?"

"I'm wondering if Faith belongs downtown or if there's a place for her out on the End."

She heard the seeking in his words. "Faith can be anywhere, Jake. Anywhere."

"Even in a coffeehouse on the other end of town? Guarding a roaster that's held together by a wire coat hanger and duct tape?"

"Even there," she said.

five

Tess put aside her turmoil-bound thoughts and turned her attention to her dinner. The pasta was just as wonderful as she'd hoped it would be, the sauce perfectly spiced with basil and a hint of garlic, and an array of pine nuts sprinkled over the top.

The server brought a tray laden with desserts of all kinds: caramel cheesecake dripping with honeyed sauce, apple pie with a crust that flaked at the slightest motion, and the pièce de résistance: something called chocolate truffle elegance. Neither Tess nor Jake could resist it, but their stomachs ached in protest at the thought, so they agreed to share a slice.

Soon it arrived, a heart-shaped deep chocolate concoction, which Tess realized was exactly the color of Jake's eyes, dusted with pale pink-tinted powdered sugar and drizzled with an even darker chocolate sauce. Atop it were two cherries perched on a pure white cloud of whipped cream.

"How many calories do you suppose this bite has?" Tess groaned as she reluctantly destroyed the picturesque presentation. "Thousands and thousands?"

"Like you care," Jake retorted, his eyes dancing. "You probably won't have to spend the next month at the gym doing penance for this."

"Well—"

"If you're about to tell me about the lucky metabolism you inherited, can it, Lady." He growled menacingly at her. "I inherited a metabolism meant to carry me through the endlessly harsh winters of my prairie ancestors when there wasn't anything to eat but a buffalo tail and a dust bunny. Why, I could live on this little snack alone for a month or two, if I didn't move too much."

" 'Little snack'? I can't eat another bite, although it does seem criminal to leave even a crumb. It's so good."

He leaned over and whispered conspiratorially, "Wrap it up in the napkin and put it in your purse."

"That does it!" Tess wiped her mouth and leaned back, trying to stop the laughter that bubbled up.

He signaled to the server, and when she came over he murmured some low words to her that Tess didn't catch. Undoubtedly something about the bill.

As they stood up to leave, the server returned with a small foil package shaped like a heart. "No way!" Tess cried. "You didn't."

"Maybe I did, and maybe I didn't," he said, guiding her toward the door where the valet was pulling up with his car. "Just keep that pretty little nose out of it."

A few people were outside, their voices carrying clearly in the night air. Somewhere in the distance, a cow mooed, and Tess laughed. "A not-so-subtle reminder that we are not alone," she said to Jake as he held open the car door for her. "No matter how elegant the surroundings, no matter how fluffy the whipped cream atop the chocolate truffle elegance, there will be a reminder that somewhere a big old cow is responsible for that whipped cream!"

Once they had topped that slight rise that constituted the county hill, they were again left in the pool of absolute night sky. Jake drove for a few minutes before pulling over to the side.

"What's wrong?" Tess couldn't keep the alarm out of her voice.

"Not what's wrong—what's right. Come on—let's go." Jake turned off the motor of his car.

"Go? I'm stuffed, Jake! I can't walk anywhere!"

"We're not going anywhere. Come on!" He opened his door and stepped out.

"Okay." Tess undid her seat belt and joined Jake at the side of the car.

"Look at this," he said, his arm sweeping around them. "Is this magnificent or what? Just look at all those stars. How many are there? We don't know. All we know is there are lots of them and they're beautiful, and that's enough."

He was right. The stars had never glittered so brightly, she was sure, as they did that night. There were stars behind stars, and the more she looked, the more she saw.

"There's Orion," he said, pointing to the row of three stars that made up the hunter's belt. "And the Big Dipper, and the Little Dipper, of course. And there's Cassiopeia, right over that big tree—can you see it? The celestial queen on her throne."

She leaned against him as the frigid air crept in around her coat.

"Cold?" he asked.

"A bit."

"Good." Jake grinned as he held her closely to him. With his arm wrapped around her, she basked in the warmth of their togetherness.

The sensation of absolute romance swept over her and through her. She felt light-headed, almost giddy, ready to dance, to sing.

How was he feeling right now? She stole a glance at him and discovered he was already looking at her.

"I really want to kiss you," he said softly.

"Then do."

Meteor showers probably fell that evening. That would explain the brilliant flashes and fireworks Tess saw, even through closed eyes.

"We'd better go," Jake said at last as the kiss finally broke. She nodded, trying unsuccessfully to keep her teeth from chattering as the cold reasserted its icy grip.

He led her around to the passenger's side of the car, and when she got in, he leaned over and fastened her seat belt.

"One more," he said. "Just one."

And he reverently laid a light kiss on her lips.

Conversation seemed unnecessary on the way back to town.

He selected a radio station that played mellow orchestral music, which fit her mood precisely, and she rested her head against the glove-leather seat.

He had kissed her.

Over and over her mind replayed the scene, and with each replaying it just got better.

He had kissed her!

She was so engrossed in her happiness that she was surprised when the car came to a stop.

"Home, Sweetheart." His voice shook her back to reality.

He opened the car door for her and walked her to the side door of her house. He waited patiently as she fumbled in her purse for the key. On the other side of the door came a plaintive meow and frantic scratching.

"I think somebody missed you," he said, his voice low in her ear.

"Usually she's not this crazed," Tess said as her fingers finally closed around the elusive key. "I hope nothing's wrong."

She opened the door, and the cat launched herself—not at Tess, but at Jake.

"What in the world is up with her?" Tess wondered aloud. Cora had never acted like that. She reached out to prevent the cat from attacking Jake, but to her astonishment Cora was rubbing against his arms and shoulders.

"Here, I'll try to pry her off you," she said. "She's usually not like this. Actually she's never been like this. I don't know what's gotten into her."

He tossed her the foil-wrapped package from the restaurant. "Maybe it's something she's hoping to get into her."

"Chocolate?" Tess asked. "She's a cat. She can't have—"

Cora jumped down from his grasp and pawed at Tess's knees.

Tess opened the package and laughed. It held bits and pieces of salmon. "Would you by any chance like some salmon, Sweetie?"

"They're fillets that fell apart before cooking and couldn't be used," Jake explained, "so I asked them to save them."

"That's amazing. I didn't know they'd do something like that."

"Well, I may not own the place, but I do know the owner, and he's a cat lover from way back. He saves these portions all the time. You just have to know to ask for them."

He was extraordinary, no doubt about it.

"This is so sweet of you," she said to him.

Jake cooed at the cat as he fed her the scraps. "Nothing but the best table scraps for this exquisite cat, right, Cora?"

The cat gazed lovingly at Jake.

Tess had to smile. "I have never seen that cat look so googly-eyed before, not even with a major dose of catnip under her belt."

"I'm just trying to buy her affections. She's an amazing cat, you know. I think she has definite celestial connections, and, let's face it, we can use all the help we can get on that end."

"I prefer to get my help through more traditional means," Tess said quietly.

"More traditional means? Like what?" The question seemed almost throwaway; he asked it so offhandedly.

"Prayer." The single word was barely more than a whisper.

"Ah." He nodded but didn't volunteer anything else. He toyed with Cora's ear thoughtfully.

"It works." She sounded more defensive than she had intended to so she tried to soften it. "It really does, you know."

"Oh, I believe that."

"I'm still somewhat befuddled," she confessed. "Are you telling me you're a Christian?"

"Of course I am," he said. "I've been baptized, confirmed, the whole nine yards. I can still recite the Apostles' Creed from memory. We had to learn it in membership classes in sixth grade."

Her mind spun. She'd never been challenged like this before. Usually her conversations about religion were with people from Nativity, where everyone agreed on their terms.

"Are you active in your church?" she asked, teasing a salmon-stuffed Cora into activity with a fuzzy ball.

"No. Much of weekly trade comes from the post-church crowd, which begins early and lasts until shortly after lunch. I couldn't make it to any of the services in town, I'm afraid, and definitely not to the ones at the church I grew up in."

She asked which church that was, and when he named the largest, wealthiest church in town, she nodded. It was known for the strength of the pastoral care and its outreach projects specially designed to reach generally underserved groups; those targeted to college students, young parents, and single mothers were the best known among their many programs.

She had met the minister several times and had been impressed with the care he expressed about his congregation. She'd never seen him be depressed or sad for long; he was a man truly uplifted with joy by his knowledge of Jesus Christ.

"Don't they have midweek services there too?" she ventured as a faint memory floated to the surface of her mind.

Jake shrugged. "I suppose so. I just don't get over there very much."

She didn't respond.

"Okay," he said, "I haven't been there for a long time. This Thanksgiving at Nativity was the first time I've set foot inside a church—any church—in probably fifteen years."

"You're right—that is a long time," she agreed.

As much as she longed to scold him for not going to church, she didn't. Perhaps if she kept quiet, he would lead himself back into the church. And, sure enough, he continued to talk.

"I liked what I saw of Nativity," he said, filling the unbearable silence, "and Reverend Barnes seems like a very inspiring person. What are your services like?"

She told him about the structure of a traditional Sunday service at Nativity and gave him a brief overview of the congregational belief.

"I don't know," he said. "I'll have to think about it."

"Come to church with me," she offered. "We'd all be delighted to have you join us for worship."

"Thanks. Maybe someday I'll take you up on that." He rubbed Cora's nose.

"I was raised in Nativity," she said, quietly remembering Sunday schools with dedicated teachers who painstakingly taught her the Ten Commandments, the Lord's Prayer, and, yes, the Apostles' Creed.

"We—Grandma, Grandpa, and I—would dress in our finery every Sunday morning and walk the half block to Nativity. Grandma carried her white leather Bible, Grandpa his great black one, and I'd proudly tote my pink one with my name on the front. My grandparents got that for me the Christmas I turned five."

"May I see it?" he asked, his question catching her by surprise.

"Honestly, no. I don't have it anymore." She raised her eyes as she spoke.

He leaned back, clearly shocked by her revelation. "Why not? I'd think someone as religious as you are and as admiring of your grandparents would hold on to that Bible until you died."

"I gave it away."

"You what?"

"A woman and her two children came into our church one very cold, very wintry day about two years ago. Their home had burned to the ground, with all their belongings in it. Poor woman. She was a widow whose husband had been shot during a convenience-store robbery, and she was trying so hard to hold it together for those dear children."

She smiled a bit at the memory. "Reverend Barnes made her a little apartment downstairs at Nativity—actually, the dining area where we served Thanksgiving dinner—until she could put her life back together."

"And the Bible. . . ?" Jake asked.

"The little girl sat by me on Sundays and called it the pretty pink book. She liked to look through it during the service and study the pictures. Her favorite was the one of Jesus surrounded by the children."

"So you gave it to her."

"Sure. Why not?"

He shook his head in amazement. "It still astounds me. Couldn't you have given her another Bible, maybe a new one? That would have worked as well."

"No, Jake, it wouldn't have. I wasn't just giving her a book. I was giving her more than that. See, the mother had decided to go into church service, and this was my way of supporting them when I wasn't there to give them a hug or read them a story." The more she tried to explain it, the muddier it sounded to her. "I was giving her my love, my confidence in her, my support."

"It's wonderful," he said. "I think that Bible has gone deeply into places no other book, no other copy of that book, could go. I'm sure it went directly into their hearts and souls and took up residence. And," he added softly, "the greatest compliment they could give you would be to give the Bible away again, right?"

"I occasionally have twinges of nostalgia about that sweet old Bible. But now I carry Grandma's when I make my weekly pilgrimage to church, and Grandpa's is in the place of honor in the house, over the mantel in the living room."

Out of nowhere a yawn overtook her. With great embarrassment she covered her mouth and tried to stop it, but it was too late.

"It's almost midnight," he said. "It's time for me to go anyway."

He ran his hand over Cora's smooth fur as the cat slept peacefully between them, her stomach distended with the salmon scraps.

"She's snoring!" he said softly.

"She does that when she's overindulged herself," Tess said lovingly.

"Well, here's to a snoring night for all of us," he said, standing up. "I don't know about you, but I'm still stuffed."

"Me too."

She handed him his coat. "Thanks for taking me to dinner. I apologize for the conversation getting so serious here at the end."

"No need to apologize. I'm just delighted to be getting to know you."

He touched her cheek with his fingertips. "Good night, sweet angel. I'll call you later." His lips barely brushed the top of her head before he turned and left.

She couldn't help herself. She yawned widely and openly.

It had been a wonderful and strange night. And it was clear to her that she was falling for this man more quickly than she had ever imagined possible.

Did people fall in love this rapidly? It was one question too many for her overworked brain.

"Come on, Cora," she said to the slumbering cat. "Race you to bed."

Even stopping to brush her teeth and wash her face, Tess won the race easily. Cora didn't, in fact, try. Instead Tess padded downstairs in her robe and slippers, picked up the slumbering cat, and carried her upstairs.

The two ladies slept, their tummies full of gourmet salmon. And both snored softly.

six

Saturday. Tess was usually up and around every day of the week by seven, but this morning Cora had to notify her the day had begun without her breakfast. Some loud meows in her owner's ear and a few well-placed swats with a thick furry paw, and the situation was well on its way to being remedied.

Tess was awake—sort of.

She ambled downstairs in her robe and fuzzy slippers, yawning in the bright sunshine that flooded the dining area as Cora followed her, reminding her of her very important errand.

She dumped a can of Meow Meals into Cora's bowl and was met with disdain. Had the cat actually sniffed with haughty contempt over her food?

"Come on, Cora—you've had Meow Meals every morning for three years. Are you all right?" Suddenly filled with concern, she knelt and put her hand on the cat's brow. Maybe that wasn't the way to test a cat for a fever. She'd never seen a veterinarian do that, at any rate.

The cat gave her one long annoyed look and, turning her back to Tess, began to scratch the floor around her dish as she pretended to bury the food.

"Oh, Cora, this is really too much." She tried to pick up the cat, but Cora slithered out of her grasp and leaped to the floor with a thump.

"I can't figure out—oh, wait a minute—yes, I can." She remembered the silvery heart filled with salmon scraps from the night before.

Tess retrieved the package, now considerably smaller, and emptied it onto Cora's plate. "I can't believe my weirdo cat has a better memory than I do," she told Cora, who was now gobbling the fish with relish, her earlier bout with hunger averted.

She nudged the cat's side with the tip of her slipper. "Just don't get used to it. When that's gone, it's back to Meow Meals and Cat-Cat Yums for you."

She yawned and stretched. Coffee, that's what she needed. The thought that Jake must have wonderful coffee every morning popped into her mind. He probably had all sorts of exotic varieties at his fingertips, and a grinder too, she thought as she measured the store-brand coffee from the can. She did appreciate good coffee, freshly ground and brewed, but what she needed right now was immediate coffee.

A shriek sprang from her lips as she noted the clock over the stove. It was nearly nine!

Her toe caught in the rug, and she stumbled over Cora, who didn't so much as twitch a hair. Nothing was going to move her from her salmon breakfast.

A quick shower and speed dressing got her in the store in half an hour. She flipped the sign on the window from Closed to Open and unlocked the door.

Saturday mornings were generally slow, times when she dusted the inventory and wiped down the display cases and shelves. She tried to keep up with it on a catch-as-catch-can basis through the week, but she relied on Saturdays to do a more thorough job.

She took all the birthstone crystal angels off their shelf for detailed cleaning with the tiny brush she used specifically for the delicate items. A slight movement startled her.

It took a moment for her to identify the source of the motion—Cora had plopped herself in the spot vacated by Faith's departure.

Tess thought about how easily she had moved into calling the angel Faith, although the logical part of her still considered it foolish and misguided. But something about the zany angel made the name fit. It didn't make sense.

Neither did the fact that she missed the angel. The hole it left was more than in the display area. How many times had she greeted it when opening? How often had Cora blissfully rubbed up against the rough grain of it, as if brushing herself on the textured robe? And straightening the wayward halo was part of the daily ritual.

Rats. She wanted to see Faith again.

The bell on the door tinkled a welcome as Jake walked in the front door.

"Are you always as hungry as I am the morning after a big meal?" he asked without preamble, sliding a bakery box across the counter to her.

"Oh, you didn't need to," she answered. The most delicious aroma wafted from the box to her nose, and her stomach replied with a loud growl that startled Cora out of a sound sleep. "But I'm glad you did," she added hastily, tearing into the box.

What met her eyes was a true sweet tooth's delight indeed. The selection of doughnuts and other pastries was astonishing. It was enough to stop any diet dead in its tracks. Twisted cinnamon rolls were nestled next to white frosted cake doughnuts sprinkled with tiny decorations.

He picked one up and held it out to her proudly. "Check it out."

The little candies were white angels! "I've never seen these," she marveled. But, even as she spoke, the businesswoman in her was taking note. "I wonder where they came from. I should—"

He pulled a slip of paper from his pocket and handed it to her. "Here. I already asked. And I called my distributor—he's making a delivery to us on Monday—and he said if you want him to bring some then, he sure can do that."

"To sell? For me to sell?" she asked numbly, feeling as if the morning had suddenly gone into fast-forward—but she hadn't.

He nodded. "They sell them in large bags for bakeries, but he said he thought they might have some in smaller packets for retail sale."

"Wow." That was all she could manage as he moved in a blur. Maybe she was still too groggy from sleep to keep up with him.

"You look like you could use some coffee," he said sympathetically. "I didn't know what you had here so I also brought—ta-da!—a thermos from Panda's. It's a blend called Spice of the Season. It has some cinnamon in it and nutmeg, ginger and a few other mysterious ingredients I couldn't divulge to anyone, including my own dear mother. Trade secret."

He had even brought cups.

She pulled out two chairs from a wrought-iron table set and pushed the display of angel-animal beanbags on the tabletop out of the way. "We can sit here."

Cora was over like a silver flash.

"Is it okay if I feed her?" he asked as the cat looked lovingly up at him.

Tess could see her having to feed Cora only gourmet food and pastries for the rest of her life, and she fought it as hard as she could. Her cat needed healthy food, not this table-scraps stuff.

But the fight was lost as soon as she saw Cora's goo-goo gaze resting adoringly on Jake. "Sure, go ahead," she heard herself saying.

She took a sip of the coffee and almost choked. It was twice as strong as the way she usually drank it.

"Don't you like it?" Jake asked as her eyebrows shot up at the bitterness.

"It's a bit thick," she said.

"It is?" He poured himself a cup. "I haven't tried it yet, but we try to keep it at a constant level of strength."

He took a sip and sighed. "No, this is right. Try it again."

She did, and to her surprise she liked it.

"I guess I'm not used to tasting the coffee flavor so much, but I do like it."

"How late are you open today?" he asked.

"Five-ish. Why?"

"Would you be interested in seeing Panda's? I know you've been there already, but I'd like to show you the roaster and the back rooms. It's really quite an operation."

"Do I get to sample?"

"Everything."

"Only if I can have decaf. If I drink coffee after four in the afternoon, I get wired and will be up all night."

"Decaf?" He said the word with scorn. "That's like artificial coffee." But then he grinned at her to let her know he was teasing. "We have decaf. And it's pretty spectacular if I do say so myself. And if you want to, we can eat supper at Panda's too."

"I didn't know you served dinner," Tess said.

"We do now. A woman moved here from Santa Barbara who does incredible things with sun-dried tomatoes and sprouts that will set your tongue singing."

He'd hit upon her second food weakness, sun-dried tomatoes. A day with sun-dried tomatoes and angel-decorated pastries was almost too good to be believed.

He picked her up at five o'clock sharp.

Panda's was larger than she'd remembered. The grounds were landscaped now with small trees draped with lights. "At dusk they'll come on. During the Christmas season each tree has a different color of lights. Otherwise, when the leaves are off the trees, they're all white."

She looked at the trees curiously. "What color are they?"

He began pointing them out. "That one is purple, that one turquoise, and that one green. That one is gold."

"Not exactly the traditional Christmas colors," she noted.

He nodded. "But at night, when they're all glowing, the scene is rich and spectacular. Those colors remind me of the three kings—now here I go getting sentimental about Christmas, but I remember three gigantic Wise Men Mom always had inside the front door. One had a turquoise robe, one a purple robe, and one a green one. And each was highlighted with gold."

"So these colors remind you of those Wise Men?" she asked.

"They sure do." His mouth broke into a wry grin. "Then one memorable Christmas my sister and I came flying in the front door, covered with snow. As soon as our boots hit the tiled floor, the rest of us hit the floor too. We crashed right into the display. Broke Melchior's head off, gave Balthasar a ding in his elbow, and took a chunk out of Gaspar's foot."

"What did your mother do?"

He laughed. "Replaced those plaster statues with brass ones. She said the next time we did something like that, we'd be the ones with the gouges."

"She sounds like a neat lady," Tess commented.

"She is."

She could smell the coffee even before they reached the door. She wrinkled her nose, and he chuckled.

"The aroma is a bit strong when the roaster's going. For some it's better than perfume. Others would rather have a face-to-face encounter with a skunk."

He guided her inside the store. The building was made of rosy brick and smoked glass, a combination that shouldn't have worked but did. She said as much.

"I wish I could take credit for it, but it has to do with an argument between the contractor and the architect. I don't know all the details of it, but it sure did make for a striking building," he explained.

The interior picked up the same color themes, pink and gray, she noted as her eyes began the slow adjustment to the dimmed lights after the bright sunlit glitter of the snow outside.

And there she was. Faith. Looking just as zany and happy as she had in Angel's Roost. Tess was relieved to see she wasn't holding a sign advertising "World's Most Heavenly Coffee."

He hadn't lied when he said Panda's had a place for her. In a little sheltered alcove off to the side of the entrance, she held court. Her nook was lined with pink and green flowered tiles that matched the colors in her face and dress exactly.

And below it, a discreet card with carefully written letters done in a flowing calligraphic hand that said merely "Angel's Roost" and her address.

"Oh, you didn't have to do that," she protested. "You own her."

"As much as one can, I guess. We had the card made, and I'm glad we did because we get many comments on the angel and questions about where we found her. Having the card there frees up my staff from those endless questions about where we got her, are there others like her, what kinds of things are at Angel's Roost, and on and on."

"I wish!"

"Truly Faith has generated a sizable interest since she arrived. We're delighted she's here."

She walked over and straightened Faith's halo, which was once again tilted. "I miss the old girl," she said. "And I think Cora does too. She used to wrap around Faith when the late-morning sun poured in through the window and take her morning snooze. Now she just sprawls in the space."

"Maybe she's enjoying having it all to herself," he suggested.

"Who knows what Cora thinks? Her mind doesn't operate the same way mine does, that's for sure. I think her brain operates mainly on a need basis: 'I need food; I need a nap.'"

He led her back through the dining area. Most of the seats and booths were filled. Mixed in with the college crowd were families, people on their breaks from work, and some older women sharing a chocolate concoction that looked as if it had a week's worth of calories.

As they went through the swinging doors into the kitchen area, a tall, gangly young man stopped Jake. "Dude, I've got five finals this week. I cannot believe it. Cannot. So I've got to, like, cut back on my hours this week. Majorly. Is that cool?"

Tess bit her lip to avoid laughing. This youth was obviously the same one who had told Jake, "Your big machine has gone blooey." Jake had nailed the student's inflections down to the very last detail.

She glanced around while Jake and Todd, as his name turned out to be, hammered out the workweek schedule. The kitchen was spotless. Chrome and glass gleamed. The cups were neatly aligned inside glass-fronted cupboards, and the countertops sparkled like those on television advertisements.

"So what do you think?" Jake asked, rejoining her after having finished talking with Todd.

"Is it always this clean and shiny back here?"

"Todd. He is an absolute clean freak so I let him sanitize his little heart out. Panda's always earns top ratings by the health department, and I value that highly."

She nodded. She'd seen the scores published in the newspaper, and it always made her cringe when one of her favorite eateries was given a low mark.

He led her to a large barrel-shaped machine. "This baby is the roaster. I'm the only shop in town that has one of these. It used to be that if you offered freshly ground coffee, you were on the cutting edge. That's old news. Now people are discovering how rich and tasty freshly roasted coffee is, and that's one of my major attractions here—besides Faith, of course."

"Of course," she murmured.

She walked around the impressive machine. "Is it fixed now?"

"Yes. Cost me an arm and a leg. I had to fly the certified repairman in, but it was cheaper than packing the machine up and freighting it to Minneapolis for warranty work. Besides, then I wouldn't have it while it was on its way, being fixed, and sent back."

"I didn't realize how competitive this business is." She frowned. "To have your entire business revolve around a roaster. . ."

"Well, I like to think it's more than that. Panda's offers some terrific food too, especially desserts and now sandwiches. Speaking of which, are you ready for dinner?"

"Thought you'd never ask."

Her sandwich was a masterful creation of sun-dried tomatoes, sprouts, and some interesting cheeses she'd never heard of before. He insisted that she try a new dessert, chocolate cake drizzled with pastel-blue mint syrup.

He disappeared into the kitchen with it and came out a few moments later, bearing it as if it were a royal gift of gold.

She smiled as she saw what he had done. Topping it was a sprinkle of those tiny white angel candies.

"Give me your opinion, please," he begged as she ate the first forkful. "Do the angels add anything to it?"

She gave him her response, which was enthusiastic. He sat back in the seat, satisfied.

"I'm glad you like it," he said. "I hope now I'll see more of you here."

"I'll certainly try harder. But the problem is I just don't get down to this part of town very often."

"I know what you mean." He crossed his arms over his chest and lapsed into unhappy thought for awhile. "This is part of my problem."

"That I don't get to this part of town?"

"Well, sure, but I mean the way this town is divided into two clear business parts." He motioned to the others seated around them. "I don't know if I can give all of this up. I don't know if I should. Panda's is doing well here, but can it sustain itself? What if someone else gets a roaster?"

"Oh, it can't be as simplistic as that," she protested. "There's an ambiance here. And you said yourself that you've developed a clientele."

"Sure. But look at them. For the most part this is their section of town. Maybe the college students would follow me downtown since the university is as close to downtown as it is to the End. But maybe not."

He pushed his chair back and stood up. "But the fact of the matter is that it's been a bright and beautiful winter day, and I'm with a bright and beautiful woman, and I don't want to talk about anything that is not bright and beautiful. Let's go!"

She hastily swallowed the last of her coffee and wiped her lips. "Where are we going?" she asked as she shrugged into her coat.

"Shopping!"

seven

She tried to object as he bustled her into the car. "But I don't have any money with me. I'm not ready to do my shopping. I haven't given it any thought. I don't want to go to the mall on a Saturday."

The truth was that the last reason was the real one. She abhorred going to the mall on the weekend, especially when it was busy. And the first Saturday after Thanksgiving, the mall was going to be wild, especially as people began their Christmas shopping in earnest.

He apparently didn't hear anything she was saying, or he chose to ignore it. Instead he began singing "The Twelve Days of Christmas" as loudly as he could.

" 'Six geese a-laying—' "

"I said I don't want to go sho—"

" 'Five goooooooolden rings!' "

She gave up and glared out the window. She hated the mall, absolutely, completely, totally hated it. She had to carry her coat because she was too hot with it on. And if she bought anything, then she had to carry that as well as her coat and her hat and her mittens and her purse. Her arms ached at the thought.

And her feet got sweaty in the mall, and then she'd climb into her unheatable van where her toes froze into ice chunks on the way home because they'd been wet inside her boots.

She couldn't believe her eyes. He drove right past the mall.

"Um, Jake, the mall—?"

" 'Four calling birds,' " he warbled. " 'Three French hens—' "

"You went by it already. Jake, Jake." She tugged on his sleeve. "It was back there."

" 'Two turtle doves and a parrrrrtridge in a pear tree.' " He

61

flung his right arm out in a triumphant finale. "Sorry, Tess—did you say something?"

"The mall was back there. You drove past it."

"You wanted to go to the mall?"

She could have throttled him. "You said you wanted to go shopping," she reminded him, her words measured and spoken with a calm she didn't feel.

"You don't strike me as the mall type," he said. "Do you want to go? I can turn around, although I must admit this surprises me. This is a side of you I've not seen before."

She couldn't tolerate it any longer. She growled at him. Bared her teeth and snarled.

"Okay," he said, whistling through his teeth. "We won't go to the mall."

She rolled her eyes so hard she thought she'd pulled some kind of eye muscle. He was infuriating.

But he put on his turn signal and swung off onto a frontage road.

Her curiosity got the better of her. "What's out here?"

He pulled into the parking lot of a large brick building. It seemed nondescript until he drove close enough for her to see the front of it clearly.

"Welcome to the Animal Kingdom," she read. "Oh, I've heard of this. It was mentioned in the paper, but I've never been here before."

"You have to get out more often," he said as he switched off the ignition and opened his door.

His comment stung a bit. She was a downtown businesswoman as well as a member of the mayor's task force on rejuvenating the city's heart. Not only didn't she have the time to visit every business in town, but her loyalties were firmly on the side of downtown. Whenever she could, she patronized those businesses in the heart of the city.

She knew there was truth in what he said, though. It was almost too easy to let herself cocoon in the downtown district, what with Nativity half a block away and a grocery store only a few blocks past that. Most of her clothes she bought from mail-order catalogs and had them delivered to her home. She was well on her way to becoming a hermit if she didn't watch it.

She trailed after him as he strode across the lot. Snow that hadn't been scraped off by the plow crunched under her feet.

Just as a few well-chosen words were about to escape concerning men who walked ahead of their companions, he stopped and waited for her to catch up. "I thought you were right beside me! This is embarrassing—I've been talking away to you, and here I am, jabbering to myself. I'm sorry. I didn't realize you weren't with me. I'll be more considerate—I promise."

The words died on her lips. He was too good.

She stopped to read the sign on the door: "We do not sell animals here. We recommend you visit your local humane society." Below that, the address of the animal shelter was lettered in neatly.

"That's great!" she said, feeling more enthusiasm for the visit. She was an avid supporter of the humane society.

Her eyes widened at the sight that met her inside. It was a warehouse of pet supplies that stretched wall to wall and floor to ceiling.

Jake clutched her hand. "Help me pick out some gifts for a very special young lady."

She fell easily into his game. "Tell me something about her."

"Well, she's about this big—" He carved in the air a shape the size of a small calf. "And she has lovely gray hair and white whiskers and an attitude that tells me she doesn't suffer at all from low self-esteem."

"I see. And you were thinking of getting her—?"

"Something edible."

They located the cat section, and Tess's eyes widened at the aisles of cat treats. They lined the shelves in bags and boxes and cartons of many differing sizes and shapes, and they came in an even greater variety of flavors.

"Fish Medley. Poultry Delight. Beefy Bouquet. Halibut Hearties," he read. "Whatever happened to tuna, chicken, and beef?"

"Well, it's not that easy. Apparently combo meals have come to kitty land. You've got choices here of tuna and liver"—she shuddered—"or salmon and chicken on this row, or, ooh, now this sounds good: mackerel and cod with cheesy cheddar bits."

"Actually they do sound appealing." He picked up a foil packet and studied it. "Hey, this one even cleans their teeth. Like dog bones but for cats, I guess. Wouldn't that be neat, if you could just eat a snack, and you wouldn't have to get up and brush your teeth because the snack's already done it for you?"

"Now there's something for your cook to work on!" she said.

"Which do you think Cora would like the best?" He walked a bit farther down the aisle and picked up a diamond-shaped package. "Here are some herbal treats."

"Trying to predict what Cora will like is folly. She's fond of anything expensive. That much I know."

"These are $12.59."

"That's expensive, I'll grant you, but I don't think herbal anything will fly with the lady, unless it's catnip, of course. In which case, she'll fly."

He picked up a basket from the end of the row and began throwing packets into it. She tried to intervene, but he continued until he had an assortment that filled half the basket.

"Now to the toys."

They found the section with cat toys. Jake gave each one serious consideration and eventually selected several felt-covered, catnip-stuffed mice, some soft spongy balls covered with fuzzy metallic threads, and a windup mouse that Tess was sure Cora would bat into the wall and destroy within seconds.

Then he chose an elaborate contraption that allowed the human to dangle a stuffed glittery toy from the end of a flexible stick. But more than that, a system of pulleys and relays changed the height and sway of the toy.

He didn't stop there. He added a scratching post, since Cora still had her claws, and a special tray for enjoying her catnip without spreading it all over the house. And, of course, a bag of catnip, guaranteed to make her a very happy kitty cat.

Tess watched in amazement as the bill was totaled. "All this for Cora?" she asked. "I mean, I love her dearly myself, but this is too much!"

He flashed her a grin as he signed the credit slip and returned his wallet to his pocket. "I like doing this. One day maybe I'll have a cat of my own, and chances are I'll spoil him or her instead. But for now, if it's all right with you—and Cora—I'll pamper her. Indulge me. I'm having fun."

She shrugged. "Well, okay. But you know she's going to be awfully mad when all the treats come to an end."

"Why would they?" He thanked the salesclerk and picked up the bag.

As they walked to the parking lot she tried to choose the words that would convey what she meant.

"Well, someday you'll, uh, I'll, uh, we. . ." Her voice trailed off. The day he wouldn't be stopping by every day to see her, surprising her in some way or another, was bound to come eventually. Putting it into words was painful, and the syllables caught in her throat like dry shreds of paper.

He stopped and faced her squarely. "At this moment, Tess Mahoney, I plan to continue seeing you as long as I can. Yes, I'm growing very fond of you, and I do hope, fervently, that this relationship will grow and develop into something permanent. There. Does that explain it to your satisfaction?"

Tess had the unshakable impression she was standing in the parking lot of the Animal Kingdom, her mouth open as if she were waiting for an out-of-season fly to come along. She tried to shut her mouth, but it wouldn't cooperate.

"Is that all right with you?" he asked.

She tried to speak again, but she could only nod. She knew how she was feeling about him, and she knew how she hoped he was feeling about her, but this declaration was so sudden that she was caught off guard.

He smiled. "Okay, then. Let's go wrap these for Cora. We'll

go to my house since she'll probably insist on watching the whole operation if we try to do it at your house, and that would spoil the surprise."

He chattered the entire way to his house about this and that, items in the news, the sweater he had bought his father for Christmas, the prospects for his favorite team, the Minnesota Vikings. He didn't mention his proclamation in the parking lot, but that was all right.

She had heard, and now she knew, and that was all that was necessary.

He turned into the development known as the Pines. Some of the downtowners called it Snooty Acres, poking fun at the people who lived there. It was heavily populated with doctors, lawyers, and car dealers.

He pulled into the driveway of one of the smaller homes. It was a tidy brick colonial, its pristine white shutters marked now with the deep forest green of wreaths that adorned the side of each window. The sidewalk and entrance were neatly cleared of snow.

The front door opened into a large antechamber with a bench and coat tree. She sat on the bench to pull off her snow boots and tried not to envy him for this.

The two entrances to her house led directly into the store and into her kitchen. Whatever people had on their shoes or boots followed them in. It was an unavoidable problem unless she remodeled, and even then that would steal some precious space from the room.

A stack of drywall leaned against the closet door, and beside it were a can of paint and a brush. "The basement was pretty much unfinished when I moved in," he explained, "so I'm having some work done on it. The theory is there'll eventually be a guest room downstairs, but it's going so slowly I've about given up hope."

He showed her through the house. It was larger inside than it appeared, and it was amazingly clean. It was so spotless it looked almost unlived in.

She began to get nervous. She was anything but a neatness nut. The store she had to keep in shape, and she managed that by a strict cleaning schedule she adhered to.

But her own living quarters were another matter. She shuddered at the thought of the upstairs, where her bedroom and what she used as a den were. Some people decorated with antiques. She decorated with clothes. And books. And a lot of unclassifiable stuff.

So far Jake had seen only the downstairs, which stayed fairly neat by virtue of the fact that she didn't use it. If he were really this neat—she saw trouble ahead.

He offered to take her coat, and she hugged her arms to herself after she gave it to him. The house was chilly.

He noticed. "Let me turn up the heat." He paused, as if trying to remember where the thermostat was, before excusing himself to turn it up.

Could it be this was not his home? Why would he pretend it was? A photograph sat on the fireplace mantel, and she studied it. The couple in the picture was posed in front of a boat, their arms draped over each other's shoulders. The man's grin was familiar; it must be Jake's father.

He entered the room and confirmed the identification. They were his parents, standing in front of their new boat. The snapshot had been taken only a few months ago.

His arms were filled with two rolls of wrapping paper, some tape, and a bag of bows.

"Let's do this in the dining room."

The large table was cleared. "Wow," said Tess. "I didn't know you could see an entire tabletop anywhere but in a furniture store."

As soon as she said it, she wanted to bite back the words. They sounded horrid and critical.

But he didn't seem offended. Instead he offered an apology. "I'm really not here very often. I spend most of my waking hours at Panda's, and I come here only to sleep and shower. I don't even eat here generally. I do that at the restaurant too."

He looked around as if seeing it for the first time. "It doesn't feel like home, you know? That's one of the reasons I'm doing the remodeling downstairs. Maybe if I can put my own touch in here. I don't know. What do you think?"

She decided to stay noncommittal. What she thought was that it had all the warmth of a model home on display for a builder, but she didn't want to say that. "You probably need to stay here for awhile. Sit in the furniture. Read a book in bed. Have pizza in front of the television. That kind of thing."

He nodded miserably. "But I hate to be alone." The admission cost him dearly, she could tell.

"I could come out, and we could sit in front of the television and eat pizza. Make cookies in the kitchen." She grinned. "Trust me. I can slob up a place in seconds flat. If there were an Olympic competition for uncleaning a house, I'd win the gold medal."

"I'm going to take you up on that offer," he declared. "Sometime this week let's rent a video and pop popcorn—the whole shebang."

"Sounds good to me." She rubbed her hands together. "I can feel it starting to warm up now. Let's get wrapping."

After they had finished, she started to pick up the scraps of wrapping paper and throw them away. He put his hand on her arm and stopped her. "I like the way it looks now—lived in. Like people have been here and had a good time. Leave it."

He picked up the packages and piled them in a corner of the living room. "This is where I'm going to put the tree," he said. "And these presents will be a good reminder to buy one."

"I need to get one too," she said. "A school down the street from Nativity is selling trees. The profits go to the school library so I thought I'd get mine there."

"It's kind of late," he said, glancing at the clock. "Almost nine. Won't they be closed?"

She shook her head. "They're open another half hour on the weekends."

"Let's go then." He sprang up from the pile of presents and

retrieved their coats from the entryway. He waited while she pulled her boots back on.

"How are we going to fit two trees in this car?" she asked.

"We'll go to Panda's and pick up the delivery van. And we'll be buying three trees—Panda's needs one too, don't you think?"

"I think everybody needs a tree," she said, that wonderful sense of bliss settling over her again.

After a quick stop at Panda's to switch to the van, they were headed back downtown. Jake found the school easily; they had a series of CD players hooked together playing Christmas carols full blast.

Because it was still early in the season, the selection was wide. It was as if a mini-forest had sprung up alongside the playground equipment.

Tess had the search narrowed to two candidates: a blue spruce that was full and elegant and a Douglas fir that was tall and narrow. She leaned them both up against the school wall and paced back and forth between them, comparing them.

"I don't know which to choose," she said as Jake rejoined her. "I like them both."

"Then buy them both. We'll figure out later which one goes where. I need your help. I can't decide either. I found this one flocked tree that is either incredibly gorgeous or incredibly awful, and I don't know which. I can't take my eyes off it."

"I don't really care for flocked trees," she began, but the words died in her throat as he stopped in front of the most amazing tree she'd ever seen. It was thickly flocked in dazzling white, and the ends of the branches were tipped in gold.

"Oh, wow," she breathed.

"So tell me, good or bad?"

"This tree defies the usual value system of a simplistic good or bad," she said at last. "It exists totally outside that realm."

"Well, should I get it? And for my house or for Panda's?"

"I can't make that decision for you, but I'm terribly afraid if you don't take it, I will. Wait. I wonder if Cora would eat flocking. With her appetite I'd better not take the chance. It might hurt her. I suppose I should pass on it then. I don't want to take any chances." She leaned her head to one side and studied the tree. "What an incredible tree."

"Okay. Here's my suggestion. We take these three trees and sort them out later."

She nodded. "That sounds fair. I want all three of them, but that's overkill. And there's no room in the store. But this white and gold tree would be an eye-catcher in there, wouldn't it? Couldn't you see it all decorated with angels? And a large gold and white angel on the top—you know, I have one that would work perfectly."

He looked at her, an idea clearly dawning in his mind. "I think I have it. Let's put this in Panda's and have you decorate it with angels from Angel's Roost. Can I hire you to decorate it?"

"Oh, I'll do it for free," she said, but he shook his head.

"No, it's a paying deal, or it's no deal. It'll look super with Faith there and the lights outside."

His enthusiasm was infectious.

"It won't be too garish, will it?" he asked, his voice suddenly worried.

"Well, no one's ever going to accuse you of being overly subtle, but this is campy garish, I think. And with the angels it'll be wonderful. You don't need to worry about it."

"When can you set it up?" he asked.

"How about Monday night? I'll have to go through my stock first and see what I have left after this weekend." The day after Thanksgiving had been so busy she'd lost track of what was left.

He smiled happily. "Terrific. If you have everything selected and boxed up and ready to go, I'll pick you up after you close, and we can come down to Panda's and set the tree up."

He reached out and took her hand. "Something is happening to me, Tess Mahoney, and it all has to do with you." He kissed her lightly on her nose. "Thank you."

It had to happen eventually. Her heart exploded with joy.

eight

She slipped into the red choir robe the next morning in the small anteroom at Nativity, mindless of the Christmas chatter that surrounded her—who had finished their shopping, who had the impossible person to buy for, what would someone else give his boss.

If only Jake had decided to join her in church this morning. She berated herself for not extending the invitation again, but she had twice already, and he hadn't taken her up on it.

"If only God believed in phone calls."

She didn't realize she'd spoken aloud until one of the other members of the choir, a teenage girl with baby blue fingernails that matched her eye shadow, looked at her curiously.

"Well," Tess explained, "if God would call me and tell me exactly what to do, life would be so much easier. Right?"

The girl looked at her with much the same disdain Cora had shown that morning when Tess had delivered a plate of Meow Meals instead of gourmet salmon. "But if He did that," she drawled, "your friends would never get through. The line would be busy all the time. Unless He has call-waiting."

Tess stared at her. What on earth—? Then it struck her, and she let the laughter roll out from deep inside her, cleansing her from her worries.

"What's so funny?" the girl asked, her pastel-painted eyes wrinkled in a frown.

"I think I just got a call from God," Tess said, wiping tears of laughter from her eyes.

The girl stepped back from her. "Whatever."

But the message had been clear. Stop. Enjoy. Rejoice.

Tess's heart was light and free when she entered the sanctuary. The first sight of the Christmas decorations always took her breath away. She was never quite prepared for it.

She sang the processional, "O Come, All Ye Faithful," with gusto. It was one of her favorite hymns, especially the line, "Born the king of angels."

Reverend Barnes invited one of the children up to the front. A little boy, his red hair slicked into place, joined the minister at the pulpit.

"Do you know what Advent is?" Reverend Barnes asked the young lad.

"Yes, Sir. It's the time of the coming. Jesus is coming. In four weeks and three days. That's 'til Christmas Eve. Four weeks and four days, and it's Christmas morning. We're going to Aunt Edie's, unless Uncle Ned has to work, and then she'll come here, and we'll drive out to Grandpa's. He gots horses, you know. Six of them, but they don't all have shoes. But a horse's shoe isn't like a person's shoe. It doesn't go on with Velcro."

The congregation was roaring, but the little boy didn't hear, so intent was he upon his story. He had the minister's entire attention, and he wasn't about to let it go. Tess couldn't hear his words anymore, but she saw one hand make a little fist and pound it on the sole of his sneaker, obviously exhibiting how a horse was shod.

Reverend Barnes regained control by offering to let the little boy light the first candle. "We light the candle of Hope today," he said as he guided the boy's hand to the wick. "And what are we hoping for? This week I want you to focus on that in your prayers and meditation time. Let this be a week of crystallizing your priorities."

The little boy looked at him, puzzled, so Reverend Barnes clarified. "Deciding what's really important. What are you hoping for this year?"

"I want a race car," the boy said loudly. "Not a toy one, but a real one. I want to drive it—vroom! vroom!—to my sister's school. I could drive real fast if I had a race car. I would—"

His mother, red-faced but laughing, held her arms out for

her child, and he happily went to her, wrapping his arms around her neck.

"At least he knows why he wants a race car," Reverend Barnes said, smiling at the little boy as he settled between his parents. "Let's take a lesson from him and examine our own wishes and motives—not just for Christmas, but for all aspects of our lives."

Tess pondered his words as he ended the sermon and moved into the announcements. She listened only vaguely as he ran through the notices of meetings, Sunday school outings, and special projects.

"If any visitors are among us today, we invite you to stand and introduce yourself so we might greet you and welcome you after the service." It was his traditional ending for the announcements, and Tess automatically looked up to see which family had visiting relatives.

To her astonishment Jake stood up. "I'm Jake Cameron. I was invited by Tess Mahoney, and I'm delighted to be here with you."

In one motion the entire congregation turned and looked at her. Tess cringed as the dreaded flush crept up her neck and spread onto her face.

Reverend Barnes beamed at her, then Jake, and told the congregation, "This young man helped us with the Thanksgiving dinner on Thursday. We've already come to enjoy him, and we look forward to his presence again among us. Welcome, Son."

Jake nodded and stuck the visitor's label the usher handed him onto his jacket.

Tess didn't know whether to be ecstatic or furious at Jake. Why hadn't he told her he was coming—or even that he was considering it?

But, her mind argued back, what difference would it have made?

None.

Tess was discovering something about herself—she was a busybody, always wanting to know why people did what they

did and preferably knowing what they were going to do
before they did it.

Well, maybe not everyone.

Maybe just Jake.

But at this moment that was more than enough.

From across the sanctuary, his gaze caught hers. He met her
still-surprised eyes with a smile, almost as if he were proud of
himself for being at Nativity on a Sunday morning. Actually,
she was proud of him too, or she would be as soon as she
could get over her astonishment at seeing him there.

For the rest of the service she kept stealing glances at him.
He seemed genuinely interested and followed along closely
with the bulletin and the hymnal.

He was here! She allowed herself to revel in the knowledge. He was here!

The analytical part of her wouldn't leave it alone without
pestering her purely emotional side with questions. Why was
he here? Was it because he had been impressed with Nativity
and Reverend Barnes on Thanksgiving evening? Or was it
because he had felt a tugging on his soul to give himself to the
Lord? Or was he here because he knew it would please her?
And which one meant the most to her?

She recalled the situation in the choir room before church
began, and once again she took the Lord at His word. She
would relax and let Him do His work. All the Lord was asking of her was that she welcome each movement that brought
a hungry soul closer to His presence.

Keeping her attention on the remainder of the worship was
difficult, at best. When Reverend Barnes pronounced the
benediction, she was almost glad.

She left the choir area—Nativity was too small to have a
true loft—and instead of returning to the music room to hang
up her robe, she hurried over to him.

"It's great to have you here!" she said, trying to strike a
median note between gushing with happiness and sounding
accusatory. "I didn't expect to see you here, though. You didn't

say anything yesterday about coming to church."

"It was a spur-of-the-moment thing. I got up, showered and shaved, and was ready to head out the door to Panda's when I thought I'd give this a try instead." One of the men he had worked on the dinner with stopped to greet him, and Tess was impressed by how easily Jake spoke with him although he had met him only briefly that one evening.

Tess didn't hear the first part of their conversation, but she caught the later words, when the man asked if Jake was going to start coming to Nativity.

"This is a wonderful church, and I've certainly enjoyed it," Jake replied, and Tess noted, with a heart that sank just a notch, that he didn't really answer the man's question.

She reminded herself that she had known him only a few days, but those days seemed like years. Was it possible to fall in love this quickly?

This man with the chocolate brown eyes and dark hair silvered with early gray, could he be the one intended for her? Maybe, she thought somewhat ruefully, at her age God sped up the clock and ran courtships at breakneck speed. It was probably necessary when you were on the outer fringes of the dating stage of life.

"This is all too grand," the birdlike voice of Ellen Smalley twittered in Tess's ear as she fluttered in place, adjusting the lace collar on her nut-brown dress, and tucking an escaping strand of faded brown hair back into the bun at the nape of her neck. "You know, you can go sit with him after the choir sings. Many couples like to do that. Then they're together for the rest of the service. It can be so cozy."

Jake was still in conversation with the man, but Tess saw him watching her curiously as she spoke with the organist. As much as she loved the woman, she wanted her to do nothing more than go away and forget she ever saw Jake Cameron.

It was clear that Ellen Smalley had no intentions of going away, and she certainly wasn't going to forget Jake. "I believe I'm remembering correctly"—flutter, flutter, adjust sleeves, tap hair—"that he has a splendid singing voice. A baritone, as I recall."

"I'm sorry. I don't know," Tess replied, trying to smile serenely although her teeth were clenched so tightly that her latest round of dental work was in serious peril.

"We could use a strong baritone in the choir. Well, we could use any strong male voice in the choir. Ted Walman is the only loudish voice we have, and"—the organist's voice sank to a whisper that everyone in the narthex could hear—"he can't sing for a hill of beans."

Tess smiled her fake smile at those who lingered nearby, obviously eavesdropping on their conversation. She fervently hoped none of them was a friend of Ted Walman.

"He's visiting," Tess said. "He's a member of another church elsewhere in town."

Mrs. Smalley drew back in reproof, her arms crossed over her plump bosom that did, for all the world, round out into a shape that looked like a bird's chest. "You're not thinking of leaving us and going there, are you?" she asked bluntly.

"No!" Tess's sharp reply turned heads.

"Well—" Mrs. Smalley said with a sniff, turning her attention to Tess's clothes and plucking a stray thread from the sleeve of her choir robe—"I hope not. We love you here at Nativity, and we want you to stay with us forever and ever and ever."

Tess hugged her. "I won't leave. Don't worry." Her heart melted as she realized how much she cared for the organist, even if the woman did often drive her crazy with her snoopiness.

"I'm glad to hear that," Mrs. Smalley replied, brushing some invisible dust from a nearby tabletop. "He seems like a good fellow."

Jake had finished his conversation with the man and moved back closer to Tess. Seeing her opportunity to make her getaway, she told him, "I need to put away my robe."

"Oh, Honey, let me do that," Mrs. Smalley chirped, holding out her arms. "I don't want to be the one who stands in the way of love's progress."

"We're not—" Tess started to object. But Jake took her elbow and smoothly interjected a "Thank you" to the organist and steered Tess out of the church as if she were a small canoe.

"There's no arguing with people like that," Jake said. "Bless their souls—they care so deeply for others they can't quite separate what's helping and what's meddling. I'm going to have to watch my p's and q's in this church; they love you so very much."

They walked to her house together, not saying much because it was too cold to do more than walk home as quickly as possible. Although the temperature was barely above zero, the sun had never been brighter, the sky bluer, or the clouds fluffier than they were that morning.

Nor any cat hungrier. Cora meowed loudly at both Tess and Jake as they walked in the door. When she realized Jake hadn't brought her any food, she stalked away, her tail twitching angrily.

"A cat the color of pussy willows," Jake mused. "What was your grandmother like?"

Tess laughed. "Well, she certainly wouldn't have gone off in a huff just because you hadn't brought her food! No, Grandma was a very mannerly, very polite, very gentle, and sweet woman."

Jake knelt and tried to lure Cora out from under the Hoosier cabinet with his key chain. "Cora is a lot more like my grandmother. Now there's a personality fit."

"You're kidding!"

"When I was a teenager, Grandmother had advanced diabetes and kept trying to bribe me into bringing her chocolates, if you can believe it. And not sugar-free ones either. No, they had to be those expensive specialty ones."

"Did you?"

"No! I loved the lady. I didn't want her to die, and I certainly didn't want to be the angel of death for her. But she kept trying to get me to do it, and I kept refusing, and she kept getting angry."

"That must have been hard." Her heart melted with sympathy for the young man whose grandmother asked such a difficult task of him. "Didn't it hurt to be put in that position with her?"

"Well, I loved her. Besides, she was sick, and that probably wasn't making her mind work all that great. What hurt the most was seeing her like that, not the way she treated me. I could go out and do something to take my mind off my problems, but she was her own problem, and she couldn't get away from that."

"Wow. Pretty deep thinking for a teenager," Tess commented. "I'm impressed!"

"Mom counseled me through it. It was during Dad's rough patch, so we were all having a hard go then. Mom would put her arm around my shoulder, give me a little hug, and tell me, 'This too shall pass,' and it did."

She was filled with admiration for the woman who held together the family when members of it were falling apart. What a remarkable person she must be.

Cora finally succumbed to curiosity and strolled over to investigate Jake's keys. She took her time, though, as if saying to him she was in no hurry to look at the keys, but if it would make him happy, she'd humor him and bat them around for awhile.

"This is a wonderful cat, you know," he said to Tess as he teased Cora with the ball on the key ring.

"Why don't you have one?" she asked. "You seem to be crazy about cats."

"I moved from a no-pets apartment to my house about a year ago, and I've been having some more construction done on it. I thought I'd wait until that was done, since the workers were in and out all day long with the doors open. Not good for a kitten."

"How do you like living in the Pines?" She felt as if she were being as curious as Cora, asking all these questions, but she really wanted to know the answers. "Aside from going to your house, the only time I ever get out there is to look at the

Christmas decorations at night."

He grinned as Cora swatted the key ring, trying to get the ball free from the keys. "Done your sightseeing, or should that be light-seeing, yet this year?"

When she shook her head no, he stopped playing with Cora and looked up at her, his dark eyes gleaming with an idea. "Tonight we can drive through town and check out the Christmas lights. It's still a little early in the season, but down in the Pines a few folks have put up some pretty elaborate displays."

It sounded like fun. She hadn't yet made the annual Christmastime circuit of town, gawking at the lights that brightened the winter nights, and going with him sounded even more fun.

Especially if they went in his car. Not only were the leather seats incredibly comfortable, but his heater actually warmed the car. This was a wonder to her. Her old van's heater vaguely blew out tepid air, only neutralizing the icy interior. She couldn't stay in it long in the heart of winter, not without losing the feeling in her fingers and toes.

He gave Cora one final loving nose rub and stood up. "I'll come back around six-thirty. We can do the grand tour of the lights and then have a late supper. How does that sound?"

Cora looked up at him and meowed sweetly.

"Sorry, old girl—you need to stay home and guard the angels. If you're a good kitty, I'll bring you a treat," he told her.

"You are going to make that cat as big as a barn," Tess interrupted. "She's already the size of a shed."

Cora's tail switched once in haughty disdain before she walked away.

"Guess you've been told," Jake said laughingly.

"Oh, I never listen to anything she says," Tess responded, sniffing with contempt. "Cora is always so—oh, how can I say this—catty?"

nine

True to his word, Jake appeared at Tess's house at six-thirty. He reached into his pocket and pulled out a package. "Cora, Sweetie, want a treat?"

"Jake, you're going to make it so that she'll never eat Meow Meals again. She's going to expect only gourmet food and special snacks pretty soon. Already she's getting snooty about Cat-Cat Yums, and she used to be wild about them."

"You're right." He looked properly chastised. "Well, I can't very well go back on my offer now. I'll have to give her these."

She grinned. "Indeed, you are a man of honor. I suppose it'll be all right this last time, but you've got to go slower, or she'll be the size of a horse and eat about as much too."

Cora watched him somewhat suspiciously.

He tore open the bag and sniffed it heartily. He grimaced and gagged. "How on earth can this be a treat? It smells like someone was sick in it!"

He had Cora's interest, and she trotted over. She batted the bag out of his hands, and the treats sprayed across the floor.

Tess quickly covered her nose. "They're horrible! What are they?"

Cora, however, gobbled them up quickly from the floor, and within seconds the offending treats were gone, safely inside her stomach.

He picked up the bag and, holding it at arm's length, read the label. " 'Giblet Niblets.'" He shuddered. "I wonder if they all smell this bad."

"If they do, Cora gets one chance to eat them, and if she doesn't snarf them down the way she did these nasty things, out they go. I think I'll flush them. Are you sure they weren't bad or something?"

"I think they were okay."

"Maybe they were spoiled. Come here, Sweetness—come to me." Cora ambled over and climbed lazily on Tess's knee. "I wonder if they were okay. I hope she won't get sick."

The cat looked up at her and yawned happily. Tess turned pale. "I hope her breath will smell better by the time we come back, or else she's sleeping outside."

Cora's eyes drooped, and Tess put her on her blanket by the heat register. "I think she's okay. She probably just has horrible taste in food, no pun intended."

Jake quickly mapped out his plan for the rest of the evening.

"We'll do the Pines and then the End. By the time we finish with that, the memory of Giblet Niblets should be gone, and I'll be ready to eat again without gagging. Sound okay to you?"

"Sure." It sounded heavenly to her, spending this much time with him.

"Do you have any suggestions about dinner?" he asked her.

"How about Stravinski's? We'll be late enough that we probably won't need reservations. I like it because you can get a salad or pasta or whatever. The food is wonderful there."

They agreed on Stravinski's and bundled up again to face the inevitable cold. After a quick trip into the coffeehouse on a mysterious mission, he returned with a familiar white box, a thermos, and two cups.

"I can't understand why you don't weigh four hundred pounds," she grumbled as she investigated the contents of the box. "Ooh, look at this! And this! I don't know what it is, but it's chocolate, so it has my attention."

"They're cookies and fudge," he said. "We're offering ready-made tins filled with them for people who need quick Christmas gifts. The thermos is filled with hot chocolate, and here's a bag of marshmallows and a can of whipped cream," he added as he reached in his pocket, pulled them out, and laid them on the console of the car.

"Chocolate to eat, chocolate to drink. And Christmas lights to look at. Life is good, very good," she commented happily.

As they left, Jake drove around to the front of Panda's so she could see how it looked with all the trees lit up.

It was an amazing sight. The rich tones he had chosen were strikingly beautiful. She could see why the hues he had chosen reminded him of the three Wise Men and their camels. The jeweled hues were majestic.

The Pines was aglow with Christmas lights. Jake pointed to one house on the first block they visited. Full-size snowmen made out of wire and colored bulbs guarded the front yard. On the roof a Santa and sleigh were parked—not the usual plywood cutout, but a real sleigh and a mannequin to portray Santa.

He pulled over to the side so she could see it better. "Look," she said, pointing to Santa, "he seems so real." She nearly passed out from shock when Santa got out of his sleigh and waved at them.

Jake laughed. "That's Mike Summers up there. He does this every evening between six and seven. Great fun, isn't it?"

One yard had an elaborate nativity scene with animated animals. "Mary and Joseph look chilly out there in the snow with only their robes on," Tess said.

Jake agreed. "Makes you want to throw some coats on them, doesn't it?"

In a neighboring yard the owners had used the snow to sculpt a three-dimensional scene of Bethlehem in white that extended the length of their property. It was backlit with a soft blue light. Over one section a bright golden light shone, signifying the star that led the shepherds to the stable.

Another house was wrapped entirely in lights, like a gigantic present.

Tess quickly picked her favorites. The Bethlehem scene showed great creativity, she said, and Jake nodded. "The owner is a doctor with no creative ability at all except in healing, but he's very religious. He hired some college students to do it."

Knowing that took nothing away from her enjoyment of it.

As they drove through the area, large white flakes began to fall.

"Look at that. It's truly the Christmas season," she said as she cradled her hands around the warm mug of hot chocolate.

"I can't imagine living someplace where it was warm at Christmas," he said. "As much as I complain about the snow, this is one time when I want to see it."

"Isn't it interesting that we do depend upon it to bring us to the season?" she asked. "Like for us, anyway, there are cues. Would it be Christmas without the snow and the lights and the trees?"

"Yes," he said reflectively, "it would be, but would we truly feel it? I hear people all the time saying they don't have the Christmas spirit or they're not in the mood right now for Christmas."

"I wonder about that because it's true. I know I've felt it myself. Why do we need these cues? I've even heard children say it, so it's not because we're jaded or shopworn."

"Could it be that this is not a solitary holiday, that we need to share it with others? There's such a universal joy surrounding this time of year. Maybe that's it. We pick up on other people's droopiness." He shrugged. "I never really thought about it, but you're right. It is an intriguing phenomenon."

"I've been giving Reverend Barnes's sermon this morning some thought. Remember how he asked us to focus on what we want?"

"Yes."

"I'm glad he did."

"And what have you decided?" he asked, his head cocked as he listened carefully.

"I don't know yet. But it is a challenge. It's like shopping in the world's biggest candy store. What do I want? About the only thing I'm sure of is that I know I want more than a racing car." They both laughed at the memory of the little boy who had amused the congregation that morning.

"There is so much I want. The usual good things like health

and happiness for my family and friends," he said, "but I think Reverend Barnes means more than that. What do we want for ourselves?"

"It's a hard thing to know and even harder to put into words. But I think that's part of what he was getting at," she mused thoughtfully, watching the Christmas lights as he continued to drive slowly.

"The minister who taught our confirmation class many years ago said our prayers are a good way of finding out what's truly important to us. What matters enough to pray about? And do we care enough to take whatever action we can?" Jake slowed down to avoid a cat that dashed across the road.

"Can you explain?"

"Well, he gave the example of someone who is in a nursing home. We may care enough to pray about that person, but do we care enough to leave the comfort of our homes and visit him? And then he also said we should ask how God must feel about our priorities. A good exercise might be to compare ours to His."

"It's a wonderful concept," she said softly. "I'll have to keep that in mind as I work through my wish list this week."

"Unfortunately," he continued, as they left the Pines and traveled back toward the rest of the End, "this doesn't do much good when my most fervent prayer is something like, 'Oh, God, please let this roaster work,' or, 'If You let my car start, I will love You forever.' Selfish little things like that. I wonder sometimes if God gets a bit annoyed with me."

She chuckled. "Well, God is probably annoyed with 99 percent of the population then. I do that all the time, pray dumb things like that. Sometimes I catch myself trying to make deals with God: 'God, if You'll let the pilot light on the furnace ignite on the first match, I'll pray more each day.' "

"Does it work?" Jake asked, tilting his head and smiling.

"Of course not! Actually, my grandparents trained me well enough that I almost always catch myself in the act of praying that way, so I'm not too bad in that realm. I have more problems with the flat-out, spur-of-the-moment demands on God's powers: 'Let this person buy this angel because then I can pay the utility bill.' Or worse, 'Please let these pants fit.' "

"I can't imagine you doing that," he said, reaching across the car and patting her hand. "First of all, you're much too pious—"

"Pious!"

He had the grace to look embarrassed. "Well, what word would you use?"

"Not pious. Faithful, maybe. Devoted. True. Loyal. Trusting."

"That's better? That list makes you sound like a cocker spaniel."

She laughed. "Maybe we should all be like cocker spaniels. I'm a cat person, but I have to admit that cocker spaniels are the epitome of loving adoration mixed with exuberance."

"Good way to phrase it."

"Maybe they're good spiritual models for us. And maybe even earthly models."

"I guess the greatest danger would be that people would feel compelled to pat your head and give you nice meaty bones to chew on."

"And make you eat snacks like Giblet Niblets. There is undoubtedly something similar for dogs that is just as stinky as that stuff." She shuddered again at the memory of the fetid treats.

"I had a black Lab when I was a kid, and I can tell you from past experience, dogs will eat anything. I won't go into details. Just be a good dog and trust me."

"Or I could be a good cat and ignore you," she teased in return.

They entered a section of the End where small houses sat next to each other, no two exactly alike but not entirely different, like brothers and sisters.

Each house was decorated with what was apparently an obligatory string of lights along the lower edge of the roof. In the yards were illuminated plastic snowmen or Santa Clauses.

"This is low-income housing," he told her. "The End's Community and Business Organization, CBO, discovered that the people who live here really wanted to decorate their houses but couldn't afford it. So we gathered together donations and bought Christmas lights for anyone who wanted them. The only hitch was they had to put them up themselves."

He stole a glance at her. "What was truly heartwarming about this story is every single house accepted them, and every single house put them up. We heard that in houses where elderly people lived, their neighbors volunteered to put the lights up."

"This is truly a neighborhood where the Christmas spirit abounds," she whispered, seeing new meaning in the gleaming colors that stretched ahead as far as she could see like an endless rope of light, all at roof level, and all indicating a unified neighborhood celebrating the extraordinary joy of this holiday season.

She stared out the window of the car, drinking in the view as if it were water for a hungry soul.

"Stop!" she cried.

Jake slammed on the brakes, and the car fishtailed on the frost-slicked road before coming to a stop.

"Sorry," she said. "Didn't mean to startle you. But look!"

She pointed to a figure in the yard. It was a snowman, obviously fashioned by children, and around its neck hung a hand-lettered sign.

She had to struggle to make out the letters through the thickly falling snow. "Jake, look at that," she said in delight as she figured it out. "It's a birth announcement. Listen!"

Jake leaned forward as she read the words aloud: " 'Born December 25. Name: Jesus. Parents: Mary, Joseph, and God. Weight: Our endless sin and His forgiveness. Length: Eternity. Welcome, Jesus!' "

Her throat closed up as she fought back tears. Whoever had written this had captured the true sentiment of the season perfectly.

She had heard the downtowners referring with scorn to the End and particularly to this part of town, the assisted housing. She'd always imagined it to be like the housing projects she'd seen on the news, ill-kept and overrun with who-knew-what. She'd never expected to see the pride and care evidenced by the vista she now beheld.

"You seem taken by this all." His voice revealed his surprise.

"I've never been out here before," she confessed, "and what I'm seeing is totally at odds with what I'd envisioned it would be like."

"It's nice, isn't it?"

"Very nice. As a matter of fact, I wish many places downtown were maintained as well as this neighborhood."

He drove to another section of the End. Here middle-class families had bedecked their homes with several strands of lights, and the yard scenes were larger. Wreaths hung from every house, and many sported electric candles shining from curtained windows.

Then the houses became much larger and the decorations more ostentatious. On many houses were rooftop displays, although none of these Santas stepped out of the sleigh to wave.

Some arrays were downright garish.

Tess blinked as one house came into view. The owners had obviously decided to spare no expense, and their electric bill would surely show it.

The house was entirely wrapped in lights. Animated elves climbed up and down the walls, bringing toys to Santa's workshop, which was stationed on the housetop. A relay system must have run down the back of the house because the elves worked in an endless loop, bringing dolls and baseball bats up the wall and climbing back down for another load.

The yard itself had been turned into a candy-cane garden. Nearly fifty candy canes, seven feet tall, sprouted through the snow, and Tess and Jake watched as children played tag through the maze.

Over it all a loudspeaker played "Jingle Bells" continuously, as gigantic cutout silvery jingle bells swung back and forth over the garage doors, not quite in time to the music.

"That's, well, that's—" Tess was at a loss for words. All she could do was stare at the display.

"Bizarre?" Jake suggested.

"At least. What do you suppose their neighbors think of it? It would drive me absolutely bonkers in one night. By Christmas I'd be a basket case."

"Well, his closest neighbor is the president of the electric company."

"Ohh." She nodded understandingly. "I see. And so does he, I suppose. I bet every time he looks out his window he sees a bonus in his future."

"And the person who lives in this house is also a business owner." Jake named the largest electric equipment supply company in the northern region. "So you can probably write this scene off as part wild Christmas spirit and part economic grandstanding."

"I've certainly done my share of goofy decorating blunders, but that place is downright tacky. I can't imagine living there."

"Hey!" Jake protested laughingly. "This is prime real estate."

"It's definitely prime something. All I know is after seeing that I need chocolate. I need some fudge, and I need it quick!"

"Chocolate will make you like that house better?" he asked her.

"No, but I do like fudge. Almost anything is bearable if you're eating fudge."

"Oh." He nodded in mock seriousness. "That explains chocolate's mass appeal."

They drove farther down the street where the houses sprawled a bit more and the decorations became as expansive as the property allowed. These houses had grounds, not yards.

One house was technically perfect. The pristine white front of the three-story Edwardian was lit with soft cream lights. Evergreen ropes wrapped around the columns in precise twists. The polished brass fixings of the entrance reflected the light and offset the deep green wreath that was easily five feet across. Tess tried to determine if the musical instruments tied to the wreath were real. They certainly looked that way.

There were no garish lights here, no animated displays of the North Pole. It looked like a picture from a Christmas card, especially with the snow continuing to fall, light and fluffy, but it felt hollow and icy. This house seemed to be on the other end of the spectrum from the electrical extravaganza down the street.

And both were, in their opposing ways, pretentious.

"That's about the extent of the Christmas-lights tour of the End," Jake announced as he pulled away from the final house. "So what did you think? Of course it'll all be beefed up in a week or so. Lots of folks went out of town this weekend for Thanksgiving."

"You know what my favorite was?"

"The Electric Elves visit Candy Cane County?" he guessed.

"Wrong-o. Although that one will live in my memory forever," she said dryly, "kind of like those Giblet Niblets."

They grimaced in unison.

"And to think they both happened on the same night. That's a bit too much coincidence for me," he said, shaking his head. "I'm not a superstitious guy—don't believe in it—but let's hope these things don't come in threes. So which of these holiday houses was your favorite, although I think I already know?"

"My favorite was the section with only the string of lights and the handmade decorations. Especially the snowman holding the birth announcement."

He nodded. "I hadn't seen that before, but it's wonderful."

"I'm going to call Reverend Barnes tomorrow and tell him to go take a look at it." She glanced sideways at him, chagrined. "But I don't know where the house was. Can you write down the directions for me?"

"I'll go you one better," he promised. "I'll call him and tell him. And if he wants, I'll drive him over there to see it."

"You're a nice guy, Jake." And he truly was. Over and over

he was showing her his compassion for others, a kind streak that ran a mile wide and a mile deep.

"Do nice guys finish last?" His eyes were twinkling like the lights they'd seen.

"Not at my table. And speaking of finishing last and eating, let's go to Stravinski's."

"But we haven't seen the downtown lights," Jake protested.

She was grateful for the darkened interior of the car so he couldn't see the betraying flush that was creeping up her neck and washing over her cheeks. She could feel the heat from it.

"I'm hungry, okay?" It came out more defensively than she'd intended.

He saluted. "Yes, Ma'am!"

She softened her approach. "There's one thing you'll learn about me, or maybe you already have. I think it's probably hereditary, a defect I was born with."

He glanced over at her with concern. "What is it, Honey?"

"Where some people have a stomach, I have a bottomless pit."

"You scamp! You had me worried there!" he threw back at her, but she could tell he wasn't angry. The edges of his eyes turned up with amusement. "I thought it was something serious."

"It is when I'm hungry. Then everybody had better watch their step!"

"Luckily for me I own a restaurant," he muttered playfully. "It's closer than Stravinski's. Should we go there instead?"

She shook her head emphatically. "While I loved Panda's, my stomach is all set for Stravinski's Caesar salad and white northern soup."

"And I wondered where Cora got her appetite." He winked at her. "Are you two related?"

"Close. By a whisker."

He groaned. "That was bad, Tess. You had me feline real, real awful."

She smiled impishly. "Ah, just drive, Mr. Cameron. No more puns. I want the rest of this evening to be absolutely, totally purrfect."

ten

An hour later Tess wiped her mouth with her napkin and sighed in satisfaction. "I am stuffed."

The server walked over, balancing a tray with one hand. He lowered it enticingly near Tess's face, close enough that she could see and smell the mouthwatering aromas of the elaborate desserts.

"But no one can be too stuffed for a serving of tiramisu," she amended after the server left with their orders. "I've been on a tiramisu binge since October when I first tasted it."

"I like tiramisu, but I'm going for that cheesecake concoction—what did he say it was? Cherry almond? It sounds wonderful." He sipped his coffee and grinned. "It's hard for me sometimes to enjoy a dinner at a different restaurant because I'm always comparing everything to Panda's, like this coffee."

"This decaffeinated is good." The brew was so rich and full she couldn't tell it was decaffeinated.

"It should be. They buy it from us. We bring a fresh roast over every other day, sometimes every day. It's one of the areas we've been branching into, doing wholesale to restaurants."

"Really. I didn't know that, but it makes sense. This coffee is terrific."

"Thanks. See, having a local roaster makes all the difference. I hope this is a wise move, moving into wholesale, but it's hard to know. I can only do so much before I burst. I'm wondering when my limit will come and what will happen."

"Are you trying to do all this without an assistant?" she asked, suddenly concerned. She was hearing an exhaustion in his voice that either hadn't been there before or she had missed.

"I'm trying to be conservative about this while it's in the trial phase. I'd hate to get someone involved and then have

91

the whole thing fall down around our heads like a pack of cards. It's my risk now. It has to be, until I know if it'll be a success or not. Then, and only then, will I hire someone."

"But if you need the help now—," she said, feeling protective of him.

"Tess," he said earnestly, "I can't in good conscience hire someone only to have to let him or her go within a couple of weeks. I want to be able to offer that person a good job, a stable job. And I'll wait until I can."

"I admire that, Jake—I really do. I can't help but think you've chosen a suicide course, though." She couldn't keep the concern from entering her voice. "The human body can do only so much, you know."

"I know. That's one of the reasons I spend so much time at Panda's and hardly any at my home. Every waking minute I spend down there. Until I get established enough, until I feel confident in this new venture, that's the way it'll have to be."

A wave of suspicion washed over her. "You've spent most of today with me. This morning you were in church. How much time have you spent at Panda's today?"

"Some."

"How much?" she demanded. "In hours and minutes. How much?"

His brow furrowed. "Well, I went in early—"

"How early?"

"Five-ish."

"Five in the morning?" She couldn't keep the amazement from surfacing in her voice. "I'm just starting to dream deeply at that time. Okay. You went in a little after five—"

"Uh, before five." He spoke almost guiltily.

"Before five. Which means you got up at—?"

"Four or so."

"And you went to bed when?"

"Around midnight." At her glare he modified it. "All right, twelve-thirty."

She totaled it up. "So you've had a whopping three-and-a-half hours of sleep. Jake, that stinks. Big time. And now you've spent the day with me when you could have been catching a nap."

"But I'd rather be with you."

"Sweet, and I appreciate it, but that's not the point." A new worry struck her. "We're still supposed to tour this part of town and check out the lights. And then what—what are you going to do?"

"I didn't have any particular plans." He avoided meeting her eyes and toyed with the linen napkin, folding it first one way and then the other.

"You were going back to Panda's and work, weren't you?"

When he didn't answer, she repeated the question. "Tell me the truth, Jake."

His chin lifted. "Yes."

She touched his hand and took the napkin from his edgy fingers. "Do me a favor," she pleaded. "Take the rest of the evening off. Let's go for our drive, and then we'll go to my house and make sure Cora hasn't starved to death in our absence. We'll sit and talk, and then you will go home—do you hear me?—go home and get in your jammies and go to sleep."

"But they expect me at Panda's," he objected. "What if something needs my attention?"

"I have a phone at my house. Hey, you even have a phone in your car. Call Panda's. See how things are going. Who's in charge right now?"

"Well, I guess that would be Todd."

"He's capable, right?" she persisted.

The uneasiness began to fade from his face. "Yes. He's good, a little flaky but good."

"Do you trust him?" She felt as if she were leading him, step-by-step, along this path.

"Sure." He shoved back his chair. "I know where you're going with this, and I get your point. But you know what it's like to own a business."

"I know that since I've owned Angel's Roost I've been the

strictest boss I've ever had. I understand what you're feeling, but, Jake, you need to take care of yourself, or all you've accomplished won't matter."

He stared at her, and she watched as the challenge drained from his face. When he spoke at last, his words were so quiet she had to strain to hear him.

"You're right."

The relief that flooded through her body made her weak. "Let's pay our tab then and go. More Christmas lights await us."

Main Street had been decorated earlier the week before. Great ropes of silvery lights and green garlands looped across the road, hooked onto the old-fashioned street lamps that lined the street.

A few businesses had decorations in the windows or a strand of lights draped over a door. But for the most part their only bow to the season were signs advertising loans to help with Christmas shopping or a holiday sale on washers and dryers.

She saw it for the first time through new eyes. "If it weren't for the city's decorations, this whole area would be bland, bland, bland."

"Maybe they need some encouragement," he suggested. "Like what we did out in the End, but modified, of course. I'm not trying to say the downtown merchants and businesses are low income, but maybe if they had some incentive. . . ?" He left the sentence hanging.

"What a great idea. We do a lot with First Night, but even that doesn't involve too much decoration of individual stores. It's not a business festivity, so many aren't really involved."

"Are you going to First Night?" he asked, referring to the city's gala downtown celebration of New Year's Eve. This would be the fourth year the town and its businesses, churches, and offices had put on the nonalcoholic festival as a way to salute the change of the year, and it had already become a treasured tradition throughout the community.

"Wouldn't miss it for the world. What about you? Do you go?"

"I haven't so far," he confessed. "As you might imagine, that's a fairly busy night for us. People consume a lot of coffee. And the pastries too. It's like the last caloric blowout of the year."

She must have looked disappointed because he added, "But this year I think I'll try to go. It'll depend upon how the help list looks."

When she looked confused, he explained. "The help list is something I use for holidays when we're open, as well as special times. My workers use it to tell me if they can work that night, so I don't have to call through the entire list when I need someone. If enough people are on the help list, I'll take in First Night. . .or at least part of it," he qualified at the end.

They drove to the residential section next to the city center. The houses were small and close together, but they rose tall.

"The houses along here remind me of the people who must have built these houses, needing each other for warmth and companionship, so they huddled together, like these houses. And they're tall because on the prairie you can see forever, but first they needed to see over the trees that lined the riverbanks." She couldn't keep the pride out of her voice as she spoke of her neighborhood.

"Their height may also have made the upper floors, the sleeping areas, easier to heat," Jake commented pragmatically, "because hot air rises. That way they could take advantage of the stored heat from the day's activities. If they'd been spread out, the outer corners would have been icy on a night like this without additional heating and thus cost."

She made a face at him. "I like my version better. It's more poetic."

"It is," he acceded, "but mine is more practical, more realistic about why the houses are built the way they are. Don't you agree?"

She tried not to let her face reveal the truth, that she had never thought of it that way. Her vision of how the community had grown and shaped itself had always been a romantic one. Never once had something as everyday as heating the homes entered her thoughts.

"I'm somewhat embarrassed," she confessed. "Heating was too prosaic, I'm afraid, for my fanciful mind. Of course you're right."

The houses seemed immediately smaller, dingier, grayer, just tall scrawny buildings lining a river.

He glanced at her. "And I'd never seen them with such an artistic eye. These houses suddenly have character, personality, and a quiet steadfastness about them I'd never noticed before. Thank you for sharing this with me."

The holiday decorations were simple on most houses. Some had decorated their homes traditionally, while others had used modern themes and colors, like the one house which was lit with purple and turquoise bulbs.

The fresh snow in the moonlight made the houses that lined the street look homey and Christmassy. Her heart warmed as she surveyed the area where she had lived her entire life.

As Jake pulled up in front of her house, she realized she hadn't put up her own lights this year. She mentioned it to Jake, and he immediately seized upon the opportunity.

"I'll do it."

She took his arm in her mittened hand and pulled him toward her door. "Not tonight. This is our time to relax and take it easy."

Cora met them with a chorus of meows and complaints that let them know she'd been alone the entire evening, it had been horrible, and she had almost starved to death.

While Tess refilled her dish with Meow Meals and replaced her bowl of water, Jake picked Cora up and talked to her. Tess had to turn her face to hide the grin on her face as he cooed to the cat. "You poor baby cat. Were you all alone in this big old house and not a thing to eat? Poor, poor baby cat. Don't worry—Tessie is home now."

She couldn't stop herself. "Tessie? It makes me sound like that Loch Ness monster."

"What's that, Sweetums?" Jake bent his ear to Cora's mouth, then reported, "Cora says you are the Loch Ness monster."

"Cora is a flat-out opportunist who will say anything for a treat. Remember that you're the one who gave her Giblet Niblets. You rank right up there with the guy who invented salmon takeout. In fact, as far as she knows, you might be the guy who invented salmon takeout. I'm getting her some Meow Meals, tuna flavor, by the way, and some water. May I get you anything?"

"Sorry, no. If you have any of those Giblet Niblets left, though. . ." He pretended to look hopeful.

"No, thankfully. The piglet ate them all—bless her little heart. I do have some brownies."

"Okay, you've convinced me."

They went into the living room with the plate of brownies, Cora trailing after them. When she realized she wasn't getting any tasty tidbits from them, she curled up on her blanket in front of the furnace vent.

Jake walked around the room, checking out the decorations there. "These are your grandparents, I assume?" he asked, picking up a black and white photograph of an older couple.

"Yup. Those are the sweethearts. I miss them a lot, but I know they're in good hands in heaven."

He sat down on the overstuffed couch draped with a few of her grandmother's crocheted afghans. "Do you believe in angels?"

Her answer was simple and direct. "Yes."

"Have you ever seen one?"

She weighed his question. Some people asked her the question, searching for the answer as some reliable indicator that a spiritual force was truly at work in human lives. Others asked it with disbelief, their minds already made up that angels were no more real than, say, leprechauns.

What was his motive?

He seemed to be asking it honestly, wanting to hear the answer.

"Yes," she said at last. "Perhaps."

Many would have stopped her there. How could her answer be both yes and perhaps? But he considered her reply and seemed to understand.

"Do you mind telling me more?" he continued.

"I have seen children escape injury by what could only be an angel's hand. I'm talking about suddenly stopping midfall and missing the corner of a table by no possible physical means."

She took a deep breath. "I've heard stories of people who have, during times of stress and spiritual trial, had someone with them who, upon later investigation, could not be verified as existing. The extra nurse in the hospital who talked someone through a difficult recovery. The roommate at the recovery center who kept a fellow from crashing mentally. The woman who pulled a child from a burning car and then vanished."

She paused, studying his face for his reaction. She couldn't read it, but he didn't appear to think she was insane.

"Now none of these instances I've mentioned proves the existence of what we call angels," she went on. "A strong spiritual force is at work in each of these stories, and whether you call them angels or spirits or simply God's intervention, they're visible signs of the strength that comes from God."

"Have you ever seen an angel?" he repeated.

"I've seen a child's fall stopped. Jake, it was the strangest thing. A little boy was standing on a chair in the kitchen at church. It tipped over backward, and suddenly he was falling, the back part of his head aimed right at the sharp corner of the counter. No one could get there fast enough; but apparently someone did because he stopped falling, only a fraction of an inch from the corner. We all watched as his head moved over just far enough to miss the corner, and he fell the rest of the way without hurting himself. He sort of sat down too—he didn't even get a bump."

She shivered at the memory. It was still so real. She had thought they'd be going to the hospital with him, and instead he wasn't harmed at all.

"And there's one other time. This happened when I lived in St. Paul, going to college. I hadn't been to church for awhile—I was in my rebellious period—and I finally decided to go back, to see if it was what I was searching for."

She paused. This too was vivid.

"I walked into the sanctuary, and as I stood at the door, wavering about whether or not I'd stay, an elderly woman said, 'Here—sit by me.' She shared her hymnal, and when she sang, Jake, it was the sweetest sound. I've never heard a voice as clear and sweet and pure as hers was. Her caring made me give church a second chance. And when I tried to find her the next Sunday, to tell her what she had done for me, I couldn't find her. I asked the minister, and he said there wasn't anyone like her in the church. To me, she was an angel."

He didn't speak right away. Then he said, "Those stories are pretty convincing to me. I've never seen an angel."

"That you know of," she said. "My favorite Bible verse is from Hebrews, and it goes: 'Be not forgetful to entertain strangers: for thereby some have entertained angels unawares.' You may have encountered an entire host of angels and not known it."

"I doubt it."

"Think about the dinner on Thanksgiving. Any one of those people could have been an angel. How would you have known it? An angel could be symbolic too, I suppose."

"Explain, please." His head was cupped in his hands, as he waited for her answer.

"I'm not sure about this, but maybe it could be that a human being could act as an angel too. Like that woman in the church in Minnesota for me. Maybe she truly was a human being; maybe she was just visiting, and that's why no one knew her; but she performed God's deeds."

"That's an interesting theory. Actually, that is probably the most logical explanation. Well, except for that falling child thing—but I suppose there could be some theory about reactive neutrons or something."

"Reactive neutrons?" she repeated. "What are reactive neutrons?"

"Made up," he replied cheerfully. "I just made it up. I'm simply saying there might be some physical response we haven't identified. But that's not to deny the possibility of angels."

"You can't quite believe in them."

"But I can't quite not believe in them," he countered. "I think I'm too pragmatic, though, to accept this angels thing totally. I guess I want proof. You know, pictures on the ten o'clock news. Full coverage by *Newsweek* with photographs and scientific capitulation. The *New York Times* carrying the story on their front page with an in-depth explanation that will answer once and for all whether there is such a thing as an angel."

"They exist whether you believe in them or not," she said. "In some form or some fashion they do. Call them what you will, but they exist. They don't flap down with gigantic wings, although that would make identification much easier, and they're not wearing halos nowadays. But I believe in them."

"Are you upset with me?" he asked, his warm brown eyes studying her.

"No." It was true. At the basis of the ability to believe in angels was the ability to believe in God. And she wasn't yet sure of where Jake stood in his faith journey.

"I guess that surprises me," he said. "You know, as heavily invested as you are with angels and all."

"Invested? Financially or emotionally?"

He shrugged. "Both, I guess, but I did mean emotionally. Isn't it all tied in with your religion, whether you believe in angels or not?"

"Considering they're the messengers of God, yes, it would help if you believed in Him first." The words sounded testy, and she immediately regretted them as she saw his face. "Of course, I'd rather you agreed with me 100 percent, but your arguments are valid, I think. They're definitely much more considered than those I usually hear."

The clock bonged softly, and she leaped up.

"It's after eleven! Remember—you were going home early to get some sleep."

He hedged a bit, but she took his face in her hands and turned it so he was looking directly at her. She could feel the stubble of his beard beneath her hands. It felt wonderful.

"How late is Panda's open tonight?" she asked.

"Midnight."

"And Todd can close, right? You could check the till tomorrow, couldn't you, to make sure it balanced? Or ask him to let you know if it's off wildly?"

"Yes."

"Call. See if there's any reason you need to go in." She pushed him toward her phone.

Tess eavesdropped shamelessly.

When he hung up the phone, she confronted him. "I know everything is all right, so you don't need to go there. Go home. Sleep."

"I'm not tired," he protested.

"Yes, you are. You need to remind your body you are. Have a big glass of milk before you go to bed." The image of his cold, unlived-in house came into her mind. "You do have milk, don't you?"

"I can go to Panda's and get some."

"You will do no such thing. Wait here."

She went into the kitchen and retrieved the thermos he had brought on Saturday. As she opened the refrigerator door and took out the carton of milk, Cora padded in to join them.

Tess filled the thermos for Jake and a bowl for Cora.

"Now, both of you, drink up. And go to sleep."

Now that she was aware of it, she could see the little lines that worry and exhaustion had carved into his face. Automatically her fingers strayed up to soothe them.

"Please, for me, get some sleep."

"I am tired," he admitted. "So tired I may kiss Cora and scratch you behind your ears."

But he got it right.

eleven

She took her own advice and went to bed, but sleep was maddeningly elusive. Even when Cora thumped onto the bed and curled up beside her, like a living hot-water bottle, she couldn't stop thinking about the evening.

Had it been only a few days she'd known him? In that short time he'd become very dear to her. And when he acknowledged how tired he was, she'd nearly cried.

He was such a good man, such a good man.

Her thoughts floated around the word *love* but refused to settle on it.

Cora began to snore softly, her mouth open just enough to allow leftover snatches of the aroma of Giblet Niblets to escape. Tess pushed her carefully so as not to awaken her, but so she'd sleep with her mouth facing the other direction.

Cora stirred from her sleep, sighed, and stood up enough to circle three times and resume her earlier spot, breathing happily into Tess's face.

Tess gave up. Maybe she'd get used to it soon. She had other, more pressing problems to deal with.

Something she was seeing in Jake was an emerging pattern of his inability to move into faith. He wanted proof of angels; he wanted numbers to guarantee his move downtown would be successful; he wanted assurances that his new venture into wholesale was going to be prosperous. Proof. He wanted proof.

But he wanted a proof that didn't exist, not the way he envisioned it. Very little in life came with a guarantee—it was a concept so basic it almost seemed cliché. Could he ever make that important step past the necessity of proof and into faith?

Her mind turned it over and over, but fruitlessly. Finally she buried her face in the warm fur of Cora's side, away from the cat's mouth, and slept.

·ᴥ·

Quite a bit of snow had fallen overnight. She'd have to clear the walks before her customers arrived. She cleaned the kitchen after breakfast and pulled on her snow-shoveling outfit, a gray one-piece snowsuit that had been her grandfather's, and arctic lace-up boots in military green and yellow. She waited until the last minute to put on the orange woolen hat with the pull-down mask that covered her face—it itched mercilessly.

She caught a glimpse of herself in the hall mirror. "Stunning. Absolutely stunning."

One advantage of the narrow houses clustered together, the hallmark of downtown homes, was not having much public sidewalk to shovel. But the paths to the doors were another matter.

She cleared the sidewalk of snow and turned her attention to the front walk and steps. The path going to the kitchen could wait. Actually, as cold as she was, it could wait forever. Like until April. Or May if necessary. She could use the front door.

Right now she needed to warm up.

The telephone was ringing as she stepped inside. She flung her snow-crusted mittens off her hands, snatched the phone from the hook, and tried to balance so she could untie frozen laces from her boots.

"Hello!" she shouted. Her lips were frozen into thin blocks of ice, and it was difficult to modulate her voice. "Hello!"

"Tess?" He sounded unsure.

"This is Tess." The phone fell from her icy fingers and clattered onto the floor, startling Cora who had come into the kitchen on her eternal quest for food. "Oh, sorry. Hi, Jake. Cora, in a minute."

"Did I call at a bad time?"

"I was shoveling." She had to say the word three times before she could get it out. Apparently even her teeth were frozen.

"With a snow shovel?" Disbelief resounded through his voice.

"No, with my tongue." Clumps of snow fell from her jacket and began to melt in icy pools on the freshly cleaned floor of her kitchen. Why had she decided to mop before shoveling?

"Don't you have a snowblower?"

"No. Where would I keep it, in my kitchen?" She tried not to sound angry, but she knew she was losing the battle. Shoveling snow, especially when it was frigid like this and blowing icy particles into her face, frustrated her. "My garage is too small, but a shovel fits just fine by my back door, so I shovel."

She tried for a more cheerful attitude. "Besides it's good exercise."

The feeling was starting to return to her fingers and nose. Good. She wasn't frostbitten. She blew on her hands and rubbed them together, trying to speed the warming process.

"Tess, it's seventeen below. That arctic front is here."

"I know it's seventeen below. And with the windchill it's even worse. Believe me, I know. I just spent half an hour in it. Major chunks of my body are frozen and may never recover properly. I see my fingers, but I don't feel them. I haven't checked, but I'm not sure there's anything below my ankles. It's not like I have any other options, though. I have to shovel, or the city fines me. And my customers stay away. Either one of those is too much for me."

He apparently got the idea not to pursue the subject because he changed the topic. "I did what you said. I went home, drank the milk, and you know what? I went right to sleep. Slept until six-thirty this morning. And I stayed away from Panda's until eight!"

She resisted the urge to utter a sarcastic "Congratulations." She knew how difficult this had been for him. And she realized he was doing it for her. She should feel glad, proud, relieved, instead of wallowing in this anger that was misdirected.

So she forced herself to relax and try to feel cordial. It wasn't his fault the cold front had arrived in full force.

"I'm glad. Now don't you feel better already?"

"Actually I do. Although I'll have to be here tonight. I have a very important business meeting, so we'll need to delay setting up the Christmas trees."

He sounded mysteriously vague, and she couldn't help but be interested.

"May I ask what's going on?" she inquired curiously, giving way to the snoopy side of her nature.

Cora licked one of the puddles formed by the snow melting from her boots. "Ick, ick, ick!" Tess said to her, trying to push her away from it without dropping the phone again.

"Well, it sounds as if you're busy so I'll talk to you later," he said cheerfully and hung up, leaving her with her curiosity unsatisfied.

"Humph," she said to Cora. "It sounds like we're on our own tonight. That's okay, though, because there's a good movie on the classics channel. You and I can snuggle up with a bowl of popcorn that's swimming in butter and have girls' night in."

Cora didn't seem too impressed, but she would be when the popcorn made an appearance. Cora loved buttered popcorn.

Tess quickly changed out of her snow-shoveling outfit, and just in time, as the first customer of the day came into Angel's Roost.

She was almost too busy to miss Jake. Almost. There were corners in the day when he'd appear in her mind or moments would replay. And she'd catch herself leaning against something and smiling goofily at the air.

Maybe it was best they take a break from each other. Tonight would be good. It would be difficult, but good. And tomorrow night she had the mayor's commission to go to, and Wednesday night was choir practice. Unless he stopped by the store sometime, she wouldn't see him until Thursday.

He did. The following morning he struggled in with her Christmas tree, the blue spruce she'd finally decided on. He left quickly afterward, pleading short-staffing at Panda's.

She missed him when she struggled to bolt the tree into its holder, when she decorated the branches with her collection of heritage ornaments, when she placed the special piece on top. But she did get to see him. Each day he popped in with some pastries and coffee, and each day she lost a little more of her heart to him.

He wouldn't, however, tell her what the secretive meeting had been about, but it was easy to see he was excited about it. He seemed almost glowing with happiness and anticipation.

She didn't have to wait until Thursday night to see him. He met her at Nativity's church door after choir practice on Wednesday night with the news that he wanted to put up the Christmas trees.

Fortunately she had laid aside some angels for the tree at Panda's, afraid they'd be snapped up by anxious shoppers if she didn't. She dashed inside, got the box, and blew a kiss to Cora, who regarded her sleepily.

"I'll be back in awhile, Punkin," Tess told her. "Christmas calls!"

Jake's house was warmer than it had been before, not just in temperature, but in emotion. She could feel his touch in the rooms, which, she noted happily, were no longer showroom perfect.

He brought her a paper bag imprinted with the name of a local discount store. "Here's the stuff for my tree. What do you think?"

She opened it. "It's all new." She looked up from the sack of boxed multicolor ornaments and tinsel.

He nodded proudly. "I bought it today."

The reality finally sank in. He didn't have any ornaments of his own!

She thought quickly. With some quick juggling she could use a few of the ornaments she'd designated for Panda's and sprinkle them in amidst these sparkling new ones. It should lessen the cold, austere sensation of a tree with all-new decorations.

She presented the idea to him, omitting any mention of her

intent to bring his tree some holiday warmth. "It would be a theme then. If you don't mind angels, of course."

Jake laughed. "Could you do anything else?"

Within an hour of working steadily they had decorated his tree with a melange of old and new. She stood back and admired it. It was astonishing what the angels had done to make the tree less brittle-looking.

They hurried on to Panda's. The decorating was easier there because the branches were so thickly laden with flocking that only gilded tips could carry the ornaments. The angels were suspended, hanging only from slender invisible wires, as if ready to take flight. To finish it off, Tess looped a strand of golden beads through the white and gold branches, balancing the effect of the angels dangling from the outer edges.

Jake contributed a gold-lettered sign: "Decorations by Angel's Roost." He tried to pay her, but she refused his money.

Together they stepped away from the tree and studied the effect.

"It's incredible," Jake said at last. "Who would have thought something as garish as that thing was could ever turn out as, well, celestial as it looks now? Tess, I could kiss you."

She turned to him. "Now that's a payment I can accept."

And she did.

❧

They made a date to go to a movie on Thursday night.

But early in the morning the phone rang.

He started right in. "Tess, have you seen the morning's paper?"

"No," she said sleepily. She hadn't even seen the morning sun.

"What have I done?" Anguish laced his voice.

Immediately she was wide-awake. "What's going on, Jake? Are you in trouble?"

"In a sense, yes. Tess, I need to talk to you. May I come over?"

"Sure. Just give me a few minutes for a quick shower."

"Thanks. I'll be over in half an hour."

She was about to hang up when he said, "Tess, Sweetheart, one more thing. You might want to unplug your phones for awhile."

"Jake! What is going on? Tell me! What? What?" But the only response to her questions was a dial tone. He'd hung up.

Questions abounded as she raced through her shower and tugged on a sweat suit. She didn't bother with makeup. Her hands were shaking too much with worry.

She met him at the door, and he handed her the morning paper. He had folded it open to the business section, displaying one article in particular: "IS PANDA'S AN ENDANGERED SPECIES IN THE END?" The subtitle read: "PANDA'S TO BOLT DOWNTOWN."

She scanned the article: "Panda's, a popular trendy coffee spot in the End, is planning a move downtown, reliable sources say. Jake Cameron, owner of Panda's, will close his south-end restaurant and coffeehouse by April of next year and head downtown where growth initiatives are attractive for business owners. The move will leave a hole in the End's growing economy, but it is expected to be a boon to the city's center. Why this sudden departure from an area which has served him well for the past five years? Perhaps his newest companion, a downtown business owner and member of the mayor's commission, has something to do with it. Whatever the reason, the move is expected to be positively angelic."

Her mouth dropped open in horror. "Can they say that? Is it true? It isn't! It is? You haven't—oh, you have! Oh, Jake, I'm so happy and so furious right now."

She was dimly aware that she was making no sense at all, but it didn't matter—her emotions warred with each other as they jockeyed for prime place in her brain. Her speech was only a mirror of what her thoughts looked like, chaotic and disordered.

He was moving Panda's downtown. That was good. He had told a newspaper reporter before he told her. That was bad. He hadn't told her at all. That was even worse. He had somehow implicated her in it, although weren't people implicated only in crimes? That was bad, but it meant he cared for her—didn't it?—which was good. Wasn't it?

Oh, she was so confused.

"It's true. Somewhat true," he corrected himself. "That's what the big news was I've been so mysterious about. I was going to check into that building you told me about, but I hadn't done anything with it. I don't even know which building it is. All I'd done was make a call to a Realtor, and we played some phone tag. We never did connect so I'm not sure what this is all about."

"Why didn't you tell me?"

"I didn't want you to know," he said glumly. "When it was a done deal, all signed, sealed, and delivered, I was going to make a big production out of it. I thought you'd be surprised."

"Well, it worked. I'm surprised." She handed him back the paper. "I'm delighted with the news, of course, although I am livid over the snide innuendoes that I influenced you."

"You did. If I hadn't met you and talked to you, I wouldn't even have considered moving down here."

"But I didn't make you do something you didn't want to do," she reminded him. "And there's a humongous difference."

"I'm trying to figure out how they got this story. I talked to the real estate agent handling the deal, and he claims he didn't talk to the paper, and I believe him. So who—?" He slapped his forehead. "Stupid, stupid, stupid."

"You figured it out? Who told the reporter?" She leaned forward eagerly.

"I did."

"Jake!" How could someone with his business savvy sabotage his own project? "What on earth are you talking about?"

"People from the newspaper come to Panda's all the time," Jake said, "and I spent a lot of time on the phone with the real estate agent there. The reporter probably overheard us talking about it."

"But, even so, this is still slimy journalism. Did they ever contact you to verify the story?"

He wouldn't meet her eyes, and she knew something was wrong. She persisted until he explained he had cut back his time at Panda's and had missed the reporter every time.

Her stomach rolled over and sank. She was the one who had been encouraging him not to go to Panda's so frequently. He'd been spending a lot of time with her, and yet she had kept him away from the coffeehouse even more by telling him he needed to stay home and not go to work so often.

Had she, in a roundabout way, caused this problem with her misguided interference in his life?

As if he were reading her mind, Jake said, "I don't know if it would have mattered if I'd been there or not. This kind of writing is tabloid trash at best, full of half-baked truth that's more fiction than reality."

He had a point there, and she felt her heart lighten, although her stomach was still in turmoil.

"Still, he shouldn't have run the story without checking it out. And he never asked me anything," she said proudly.

She picked up the paper again and reread the article, forcing herself to go through it slowly. "I guess we can't sue him for slander or libel or anything like that since it's all sort of true in a basic sense. Besides it's not a signed article. It's just in that Shop Talk column, which is really no better than some tabloid coverage of the town's merchants."

"I could easily find out who wrote it," Jake said, "but I'm debating that. My mom always told me, 'Least said, soonest healed,' or something like that. I might just leave it alone and see if it blows over." He tried to smile. "So, Kiddo, do you still want me as a neighbor? I'm probably *persona non grata* in my own neighborhood. They'd no doubt be glad to see me go now."

She dropped the paper and hugged him. "Anyone would be lucky to have you."

He hugged her back, but she could tell his heart wasn't in it. "I'm a member of the Community and Business Organization in the End. This was a terrible way to let them know I was thinking about leaving them, having to read it in the paper, especially in a column like this."

"You're starting to back down now, aren't you?" she asked quietly, holding his hand in hers.

He looked miserable. "I've always prided myself on being civic-minded and a good boss and a caring person. Think how many people feel betrayed this morning, reading this in the paper. I feel lower than a snake's belly."

He stood up and walked over to the window, shoving his hands in his pockets. "So Reverend Barnes wants us to prioritize what we want this week, does he? Why didn't he add the warning: 'Be careful what you wish for—you might get it'?"

She didn't know what to say, if in fact there was anything she could say. With all her being, she wanted to take his pain away, but right now it seemed beyond her power. She felt limp and weak as her helplessness overwhelmed her.

She started in the only way she knew. Silently she began to pray: *Dear Lord, help us pass through this time of trial. Guide us and heal his hurting soul. Take us through this valley of—*

"Are you praying?" His words rang out sharply. "Is that what you're doing? Praying?"

"Yes."

"Well, don't bother."

She stared as his sudden burst of anger contorted his face. "Don't you get this, Tess? This isn't about anything God can help with. He can't take those words off that newspaper page. He can't take them out of the minds of the folks who have read the article. It's done. It's all over. Every bit of it. And don't tell me prayer will help anything. It can't."

He snatched up his coat. "Because if there is a God, He sure has it in for me. How can I believe in a God who doesn't believe in me?"

With a slam of the door he was gone. And with him he took her heart.

❧

She proceeded through the day numbly, smiling mechanically at her customers as she rang up their sales. Her sales didn't seem to have dropped, and she couldn't see any difference in the way people acted today from the way they'd acted all week long.

No one seemed to have noticed the article, and she took courage from that.

That is, until late in the day when the door swung open and Mayor Lindstrom strode into Angel's Roost.

She was wearing her trademark bright yellow wool coat and brilliant red boots, a burst of sunlight in the white of winter. At the commission meetings she had often said she was going to visit Angel's Roost, but this was her first time in the store. Somehow Tess didn't think she was there Christmas shopping.

At first Tess thought her worries were for naught as the mayor commented favorably on the store and the inventory. But then she launched into a discussion of the mayor's commission.

"I've appreciated everything you've done for us. You've been a tireless worker and a valuable asset to the commission. But we're looking at restructuring the committee now." Mayor Lindstrom straightened a rack of bookmarks cut out in the shape of angels, with Bible verses printed on the wings.

"You want me to leave," Tess said flatly.

"No. I don't. And that's why I'm here." The mayor was known and admired—or hated—for her way of speaking directly. "But the question of your way of operating is going to come up." She picked up a ceramic birth angel and studied it casually. "Pretty. You saw the paper, I gather. Did you influence him?"

Tess decided to answer as honestly as she could. "Jake and I have known each other for a very short time. He asked what I thought about whether he should move Panda's downtown, and I admit I was encouraging. But I was not the one to suggest it, nor did I in any way bribe or finagle him into this decision. As a matter of fact, it was a total surprise to me. I learned it by reading it in the paper this morning."

"Tess, it's not quite as simple as it might appear. The End is part of the city too, and if Panda's moves, that'll have an impact on the End's economy just as it will on downtown's." The tension in the mayor's voice was sharp enough to snap.

"I never thought of that," Tess said. She felt like a schoolgirl being called on the carpet by the principal.

Mayor Lindstrom examined a wind chime made of shells carved into the shapes of angels. "The worst part of this situation is that reading about it in the morning paper is a rotten way to let people know. I've had phone calls from the End's CBO members, from Panda's regular customers, from the families of Jake Cameron's employees. It's not as simple as it seems."

Tess agreed with her, and the mayor turned to face her straight on.

"Then why did he choose that way to let us all know? Why didn't he tell us first?"

"He didn't have any control over the story."

"Balderdash," the mayor said bluntly. "He talked to the reporter, didn't he?"

"Actually, no, he didn't." Tess began the explanation, detailing what Jake had told her earlier. When Tess had finished, Mayor Lindstrom was clearly angry. Her face had grown pale with a bright spot of red on each cheek.

When she spoke, each word shot out as if it had been bitten off. "I've never liked that business column to begin with. The use of unsubstantiated rumor and insinuation is irresponsible at best, but this is it. I've reached the end of my patience with that column."

As the mayor swung out of the store, Tess was certain she saw sparks flying from her heels.

twelve

Tess watched the mayor stride down the front walk of Angel's Roost and step into her car.

She certainly didn't want to be the editor of the paper when Mayor Lindstrom arrived, although the snoopy part of her would have loved to be a fly on the wall.

The newspaper was only a few blocks from Angel's Roost, not time enough for the mayor to cool down if she headed straight there from the store. And Tess thought she probably would.

Tess knew the editor would get a piece of the mayor's mind when she arrived. As much as Tess was a nonconfrontational person and dreaded conflict, she was glad Mayor Lindstrom had stepped in. There were lines in ethics that needed to be drawn, and the mayor was the person to do it.

She picked up the phone and called Panda's. When she asked for Jake, the young woman on the other end said, "Um, he's, um, like not here—I don't think. He's, um, in a meeting. . .or something. I could, um, like, take a message if you want."

It did Tess's heart good to hear someone who was so obviously ill at ease with lying.

"He's there, isn't he?" she asked gently.

"Um, I, um, no, not really." The young woman's hedging was getting worse.

"Would you please tell him Tess called and that it's very important I speak with him?"

"Sure. Um, wait a sec, okay?"

The woman must have put her hand over the speaker part of the receiver because the background noise became muted. She could hear some mumbled conversation; then Jake came on the phone.

"Tess, I'm really busy." He sounded tired again and harassed.

"Is your staff fielding your calls?" Tess asked.

"Yes. It was their idea, but I gave in. It's easier this way."

"Phone's been ringing off the hook, huh?"

"Endlessly. People congratulating me on making a good decision. People ready to kill me. People wanting to know who this woman is who influenced me. People suggesting I do all sorts of interesting things I have no inclination for, nor are any of them physically possible—thank you very much."

"Then screening your calls is a good idea," she said.

"What about you?" he asked. "Has there been a lot of backlash at you?"

"I must not be as high profile as you," she said ruefully, "because I don't think anyone recognized who I am. Oh, wait. One person did. Mayor Lindstrom."

"Whaaat?" he asked in astonishment. She had his complete attention.

"Yes, indeed. The mayor finally found the time to stop by Angel's Roost." She was unable to resist voicing what had bothered her since the mayor's visit—that she hadn't found the time to stop by Angel's Roost until there was trouble. She knew the mayor was busy, but Tess didn't like hollow promises.

"And did she buy anything?" he inquired.

"Are you checking into the mayor's purchasing habits, or do you want to know what happened?" An edge of testiness crept into her words, and Tess fought to keep the snappishness away.

"I want to know what happened. Can you tell me?" His voice filled with anxiety and a sprig of hope that seemed to bloom in the winter.

"Not on the phone. I'll tell you tonight," she said.

"Tonight? I can't wait that long. Please tell me now," he pleaded.

"Can't. Won't. Actually I don't know myself that anything happened. You know the mayor. She doesn't abide foolishness, at least not with her town."

"What does that mean?" he asked, thoroughly confused now.

She grinned into the telephone receiver. "Come by around five. By then it may all be old news. And, by the way, bring food." She hung up before he could say more.

She turned to Cora, who had been watching the telephone cord dangle, apparently trying to decide if it was worth her while to get up, cross the room, and try to catch it. Idleness must have won out because the cat hadn't moved at all.

"I hope I'm not getting him over here under false pretenses," she said to Cora, who yawned. "But I've been so concerned about him this week. First he's so tired, almost to the point of exhaustion, and now this. Body and soul can bear only so much, Sweet Pea, and I'm worried. Really worried."

She felt that she needed to be there for him, but what words could she say that would bring comfort, let alone advice? What kind of wisdom did she have, or could she call upon, that would lead her into the right way to address the situations he was facing?

The shop was empty of customers, so she left Cora guarding the store while she popped into the back of the house.

One place she could count on for finding an answer. It was a book that had been her guide for many years now, and it had never let her down.

Just holding her grandmother's Bible brought her an immediate sense of calm. Tess brought it close to her heart and let it soothe her more.

She took it to the store and sat on the chair behind the counter. As she did so, something fluttered to the ground.

It was a thin sheet of paper. The handwriting on it was familiar; she'd seen it a hundred times when her grandmother was alive. She'd never seen this paper, though, and she read it eagerly. It was a list of Bible verses appropriate to certain needs, and her eyes focused on one in particular: "For speaking wisely, read Colossians 4:6."

Quickly she turned to the verse: "Let your speech be alway with grace, seasoned with salt, that ye may know how ye ought to answer every man."

A snapshot memory of her grandmother appeared in her mind: She was standing by the old stove in the kitchen, stirring something warm and spicy and listening to Tess's tearful confession about a teenage spat. Tess had said something about one of her friends, words that had come back to haunt her, and her grandmother had advised her on that long ago day, "Tess, make sure your words are seasoned with salt, as you may have to eat them." At the time it had seemed a curiously old-fashioned thing to say, but now it made sense. How like her grandmother to turn to the Bible for wisdom!

She read it again, just the verse, and then in context. How she wished she could have met Paul! "Walk in wisdom," he said in a nearby line. That was her goal.

She recalled Reverend Barnes's words. She needed to start making her wish list. At the top of it would be those words: "Walk in wisdom."

Jake burst through the door, balancing three take-out trays, a plastic bowl covered with foil, and a drink carrier. "I'm here," he announced breathlessly. "I know I'm early. So shoot me. Have I got news for you."

She flipped the sign on the front door to CLOSED and motioned him toward the back. Cora roused herself from her slumber and, at the sight of the take-out cartons, came to life with amazing alacrity.

The three of them marched into Tess's small dining room. Tess pushed aside the week's accumulation of mail she would get to, someday, and cleared a spot for them to eat.

Cora wound herself in and out of Jake's legs in a frantic figure eight, punctuating her movement with plaintive meows.

He reached down and absently patted her head with his hand, but it had nothing in it to eat. Cora's massive disappointment was clear. Fortunately Tess saw the look and captured Cora's attention with Meow Meals before the cat could snack on Jake's fingers. She'd seen that expression before and knew exactly what it meant. It did not bode well for him.

As she was saving his hand from certain attack, she noticed he seemed almost chipper. The more she watched him, the surer she was. He must have good news.

The take-out containers held a variety of sandwiches and salads, and the bowl was filled with wild rice and cheese soup. Her mouth began to water as she helped him set the food on plates.

The drinks were Italian sodas, and she poured them into clear glass tumblers so they could enjoy the bright colors.

Before he took a bite, she covered his hand with hers. "I've always done this silently, so maybe you don't know I do it, but I say grace before each meal. May I say it aloud this time?"

She dared not breathe as she awaited his answer. He had been so angry at God before, so opposed to her praying, at least for his plight. She had been hoping it was a temporary snap of anger with God and not a revelation of his true feelings. How would Jake react now? Would he let her pray?

"Tess, I must apologize for my angry outburst. There is no excuse for it. I wouldn't blame you if you could not forgive me." He looked down in misery.

"Not forgive you?" She gripped his hand. "How could I not forgive you? Think what Jesus forgave. They killed Him, Jake, and He forgave them. How could I hold this against you? Is your sin worse? No, it isn't. It is up to Him to forgive you, and I think He already has."

"Thank you, Tess." He looked up and smiled shyly at her. "I needed to hear that. And there's more I need to hear. I need to hear you pray. Yes, please, offer grace." He bowed his head in reverence.

She breathed a sigh of relief, and then she began.

"Heavenly Lord, bless this food which You have given us. We ask so much of You, and in return You provide. Thank You, dearest Lord, in the name of Your Son, Jesus Christ, who is indeed the greatest gift of Christmas. Amen."

"Amen." Jake joined with her in response.

Their eyes met, and for a moment Tess saw the oneness

she had been seeking.

The mood was shattered as Cora meowed loudly, indicating it was dinnertime.

"What's your news?" Tess asked Jake as she passed him the plate of sandwiches.

"What's yours?" he countered.

"I don't want to get into one of those who-goes-first battles," she said, "so I'll start since mine is first in line chronologically."

She told him about Mayor Lindstrom's visit, and when she ended her narrative, he leaned back and nodded thoughtfully.

"That goes a long way to explaining my news," he said at last. "I had a call from the editor of the paper, apologizing. The entire situation is bizarre. Here's the story.

"The writer of Shop Talk had written the story before checking with me because his wife was due for a heart transplant, and he was working ahead to be ready. He had written the copy but hadn't intended it to go in yet, pending verification of the story. He'd heard about it from someone who'd heard about it from someone who'd heard about it— one of those long, convoluted stories you can never get to the bottom of.

"Then his wife got the call—there was a donor heart—so they packed up quickly and left for Rochester, where the transplant is being done. Unfortunately he left the copy on his desk as a way to remind him to call me and check out the story when he got back. And his replacement saw it, thought it indicated he wanted the story to run and used it."

"Oh, wow," she breathed. "What an incredible story! Who ever would have thought it would be something like that? How's his wife?"

He stood and hugged her. "Only you, Tess Mahoney, would ask that question right off the bat. You really do care about other people, don't you?"

"Well, how is she?" she persisted. "Heart transplants are more common now, but a grave element of danger is still involved. Is she doing okay?"

He nodded. "So far, so good. She just underwent surgery, so it's early yet. But she's a fighter, they say."

She sent a quick silent prayer heavenward for the woman's safety.

"You know," she commented, "it tells me a lot that you knew the answer. That means you must have inquired about her health."

"I can't imagine," he said softly, "how it feels to know you must risk your life in order to live. And what those around you who love you must go through at the same time. How can they deal with the uncertainty, the not knowing?"

"It's called faith."

"Maybe someday I'll understand." He looked at her, his deep brown eyes liquid with hope.

The light over the table cast severe shadows on his face, and she was once again struck by how tired and worn down he was. It seemed as if the silver threading through his hair was more abundant now, but that had to be a trick of the light.

"Jake, it's there. You just have to reach out with your heart and accept it."

"I want to—I really want to," he said, "but there's this iron-clad part of me that wants proof. And what can I do? Despite all your avowals how can you prove it to me? How can I prove it to myself? Is it even possible, or am I asking the impossible?"

"It is kind of a looping theory," she admitted. "You need to have faith in order to believe in faith or even to understand what it is."

"How did you come to have faith?" he asked. "I really need to hear this."

"I was raised in a family that went to church every Sunday, but more than that, they absolutely believed in Jesus and in God. It was as much a part of our lives as, say, electricity."

"No power failures?" His lopsided smile didn't cover the deep concern she heard in his voice.

"God doesn't have power failures," she stated firmly. "None.

At one time when I was a teenager I tried to outrun God. I couldn't do it. My grandparents wouldn't let me, He wouldn't let me, and when it came right down to it, I wouldn't let me."

"You? You seem as if you've never doubted God at all."

"Wait a minute," she protested. "I never doubted Him. I was a teenager, sure that I knew more than anybody. God was in my life, but I had my priorities jumbled up. Grandma and Grandpa were rock-steady, and with their help I pulled through adolescence with few scars. One of the most important things I learned from my grandparents was that I had to have my own faith, not just a general 'I believe in God,' but a strong current that runs through every hour of my life. My faith is a commitment to Him. I made that pledge when my rowdy time, short-lived though it was, ended. I had the foundation from my family, but when it came right down to it I had to make a personal decision to give my life back to Him."

"I believe in God—I truly do—but I'm beginning to wonder if I have faith," he confessed. "I mean, I look at you, and you have this wonderful trust and assurance that it's all working out fine. While I'm a basket case waiting for the men in white coats to come and take me away to a place with pillows on the walls."

"What's interesting," she said, "is that all the worry in the world isn't going to make the situation better for you. As a matter of fact, it can only make it worse because it robs you of sleep, causes you to neglect your eating habits, and generally makes you a crabby person."

"Have I been crabby?"

"You've had your moments."

He grinned. "I certainly didn't mean to snap at you."

"That's my point. It's not what you intend to do, but it's what you do. How can worry possibly be good for you? Grandma used to say, 'Idle hands are the devil's workshop,' but Grandpa would correct her and say, 'A worrying mind is the devil's workshop.' "

"I wish I could have met them," he said wistfully. "They

must have been great people."

"They were. Not a day goes by that I don't thank God for having given them to me, and I miss them. But they're with Him now, and I know their pains are gone, and their happiness is fulfilled."

Cora jumped up on her lap, and Tess buried her fingers in the soft longish fur around the cat's neck. "And Grandma has her cat the color of pussy willows, and so do I. Right, Cora?"

Cora sniffed meaningfully at the plate where uneaten remnants of Tess's sandwich were.

"I think she smells the seafood salad," Jake said. "It has crab and shrimp in it and some kind of whitefish."

"Definitely more appealing than Giblet Niblets," Tess said, scraping the sandwich filling onto Cora's plate. "And, I hope, a little more conducive to sweeter bedtime breath. That stuff lingered way beyond the normal span. If only they could make perfume that potent and long-lasting!"

"In the kitty world it's probably the equivalent of expensive French perfume. You know, if you rubbed some of it behind your ears, Cora would undoubtedly think you smelled heavenly!"

"I could just go roll in the garbage," she suggested cheerfully. "Maybe that would work instead!"

They chatted a bit longer until Jake said he had to go home.

"Home?" she repeated. "Are you serious? Even after all this, you're not going back to Panda's?"

He shook his head. "You've converted me to this thing called sleep. I sometimes have a little problem convincing my body it's okay to sleep, but I've been using your suggestion of a glass of milk, and it's working great. Last night I added a turkey sandwich and could barely stay awake enough to brush my teeth afterward."

"Oh, yeah, turkey has that stuff in it that makes you sleepy. At least, that's what Grandpa said whenever he slept in the living room after a big turkey dinner. Claimed he couldn't help it; it was nature's way of giving him a well-deserved nap." The old memory brought a smile to her lips.

She walked with him to the door. Cora trailed behind but backed away quickly when she felt the icy draft from under the door.

"The wind is blowing so hard it's coming right through the door frame," he said, putting his hand out to feel the air move. "That's one of the problems with old houses. The wood dries and shrinks a bit, and you get gaps. I can even hear the wind whistling through the cracks."

She patted the wall fondly. "Yes, this old house whistles and creaks and groans, but so will I when I'm this old, I suspect."

"I could seal the cracks and make it stop—in the house, I mean. You're on your own with your personal noises, I'm afraid. It wouldn't take long for me to straighten this right up for you, and I suspect it would save you considerably on your heating bill this winter. Right now you're trying to heat part of the outside, but with this wind it's just getting blown off to who knows where."

"So my leaky house is responsible for global warming?" she teased. "Actually, if you can fix these places where the heat is escaping, I'd very much appreciate it."

"No problem. I used to work for a construction firm special-izing in renovating old houses, so I do know my way around homes like this and the problems they have. If it's warm enough tomorrow, I can hang your lights too, if you have any."

"If I have lights, he says. Of course I have lights. And they're shaped like—?"

"Angels?" he guessed.

"Right!"

With promises to see each other the next day, he slid his arms around her.

Before she fell into the embrace, she saw Cora look up from her station near the heating vent.

She must have been mistaken. It wasn't possible.

The cat looked absolutely smug.

thirteen

The controversy over Jake's moving Panda's downtown blew over with the ease of a prairie wind. When the newspaper published the clarification that it was still tentative and explained the error in the column, the townspeople accepted it.

The Enders thought Panda's would, of course, stay put, whereas the downtowners were sure Panda's was joining them. But each side was so sure it was right that the issue never arose again, much to Jake's relief.

The newspaper even waited an appropriate amount of time for the Shop Talk column to be forgotten and then ran a full interview with Tess about Angel's Roost and what it was like to own and operate a downtown business.

Sales soared, and Jake began to tease her about how she was going to have to hire someone. And to think she'd once worried about how to advertise Angel's Roost.

Jake had fixed the leaking door frame and hung her precious angel-shaped lights that Grandpa had made. They were an intriguing set of small lights set on metal forms he'd fashioned himself. They gave the appearance of a host of glowing angels surrounding her house.

This was the first year Tess was involved with planning the Christmas Eve service at Nativity. As she explained to Jake, her part was simple. She told people, "Stand here and don't move. Now move." And that was it.

She had been placed in charge of the silhouette stable. A large sheet—she wondered where they had managed to get such a huge piece of seamless cloth—was hung across the front of the church. Behind it were the figures from the manger scene: Mary, Joseph, the baby in the manger, plus three shepherds and an assortment of farm animals.

The animals were shapes cut out of plywood, but Mary, Joseph, and the shepherds were portrayed by high school students. The entire scene was subtly lit so that the figures cast large shadows on the cloth.

The students had discussed trying to borrow a real baby to use, but they'd quickly discovered the disadvantages far outweighed the advantages. The youngest one they could find was eleven-month-old Andrew Tyler, a charming child with the lungs of an air horn.

As they explained to his slightly miffed parents, Andrew was a bit too large to be a newborn. In addition to his astonishing lungs, he was already the size of the average two year old.

So instead they borrowed Andrew's sister's Baby Snoozie, which didn't look at all real, but which they hoped would cast a realistic shadow. At least she wouldn't cry.

Andrew's sister Katie had given Tess very detailed instructions on how to make the baby snore, but Tess furtively removed the doll's battery pack. She'd replace it after the program before anyone realized it was missing. All they needed was for Jesus to start snoring during "Away in a Manger."

That was the only time anyone moved. The song was Mary's cue to put the baby in the manger. Tess hoped she would remember but was thankful it didn't matter if she forgot.

Two days before Christmas Jake stopped by the store for some last-minute employee gifts. Tess realized he'd never said what his plans were for Christmas Eve.

"If it's okay, I'll tag along with you and go to the service at Nativity," he said.

"You know you're more than welcome to come with me to church. Always. I'll have to leave during the shadows tableau scene, but other than that we can sit together the entire time."

"What are your plans after that?" he asked. "Are you going somewhere special?"

"Sure. I'm coming back home, and Cora and I will watch *It's a Wonderful Life* and open our presents to each other."

She looked at him carefully. He seemed to be waiting for her to say something. "Would you like to join us?"

"I adore *It's a Wonderful Life*. It has to be the Christmas classic of all times. Is it on television?"

"Ha. Cora and I take no chances with our traditions. We own a copy."

After he left, Tess pondered what had just happened. Bringing someone into a tradition was risky, but leaving him out was not even a consideration.

He had quickly become part of her life.

The day before Christmas was wild at Angel's Roost. Customers swarmed through her store, buying last-minute gifts by the basketful. She ran out of bags by noon and had to dart back into her kitchen and grab some old grocery sacks.

She had promised herself she'd close the store at noon, but it was almost half past two by the time the last customer was gone and she was able to flip the door sign over to CLOSED. The store looked positively picked over, with gaping spots where entire displays had been purchased by the day's spree-shoppers.

She paused by the sunlit spot which Faith, the crazy angel, had once occupied, and she felt a twinge in the region of her heart. She missed the zany angel with the tilted halo.

More than anything she wanted to collapse on the couch with Cora and put her feet up, but she had something else to do first.

It was embarrassing, but she didn't have anything to give Jake for Christmas yet. She hadn't been able to decide what would be an appropriate present.

A sweater seemed too impersonal. A robe, on the other hand, was too personal. Aftershave implied he could smell better than he did.

She strolled through Angel's Roost, rearranging the remaining inventory to fill the gaps left by the day's sales. What could she get him?

Her mind ran through an endless list of no-goes. A gift

certificate. A catcher's mitt. A cassette deck. A fountain pen. A calendar. All her ideas were blah, blah, blah.

Her fingers absently straightened the remaining items left on a far shelf. As she touched one, it made a slight sound.

It was a sterling-silver bell, similar to the one Reverend Barnes had bought, but much less ornate. The only decoration was the set of angel wings etched into the body of the bell.

An idea occurred to her. It might work. It had to work.

She gift wrapped the bell in the remnants of the store's angel-themed paper and scrawled a few words on a card. She proofread it once, paused, and then taped the card to the package and put it under the tree.

She barely had time to get herself ready for the evening.

Jake was prompt. Her breath caught as she saw him outlined by moonlight in the snow. His face had begun to relax and the tension fade. He looked ten years younger and, if it was possible, even more good-looking than he had before.

About two inches of fresh light snow had fallen that afternoon, and the air had turned wonderfully mild, so they decided to walk to church. The town was silent. What few cars had ventured out were muted by the new snow not yet packed on the streets.

The sky had cleared, and overhead the stars were bright and plentiful.

"Did you know some scientists have come up with an explanation of the Christmas star?" Jake asked. "Apparently there was a—"

She laid her mittened hand over his lips. "Stop. I believe in the star. I believe in the birth. Nothing you can tell me will make it any less of a miracle."

"But this article proves it existed," Jake argued. "Wouldn't you like to know for sure the Christmas story is real?"

"I do know it."

"I mean as a fact."

She stopped walking. She'd been through this argument before with other people, and it was a debate she didn't enjoy.

The only way to win it was for the other person to allow change into their lives and to quit resisting the pull of faith.

"Proof. It all comes back to proof for you, doesn't it?" she asked. "There are all kinds of proof; yet you recognize only a few. Jake, I cannot make you believe. I cannot give you faith. All I can give you is my witness that it exists and it works. Beyond that you're on your own."

"I don't mean to bicker with you, especially on Christmas Eve," he said.

"Then let's not discuss it anymore. First we'll have a moving hour of deep religious significance for me. You can take it however you want in your heart, but let me enjoy this. It rekindles me for the next year."

She tried to quell the anger that was burning in her. This was Christmas Eve, the time when Jesus' life saga began anew. It always filled her soul, and she carried that with her into the next year.

He tried to interrupt, but she held up her hand. "Then we'll go back to my house and have a great time, opening our presents and watching Cora explode with happiness over all the things you bought her. Then I'll indulge myself with my annual dive into sentimentality with the movie. That's the way I do Christmas. You are welcome to come with me, but you may not change a thing about it. I need this."

There. She had said it. And now the evening wasn't going at all the way she'd envisioned it. Instead she felt crabby and out of sorts, and he was now probably going to be distant and not at all receptive to the renewing hour ahead of him.

They trudged along in silence, lost in their own thoughts, until they reached the walk leading to Nativity's inviting front door.

Jake took her hand in his and walked with her to the door. "If the animals can speak at midnight on this blessed night," he said softly, "I can try to keep silent."

"You don't have to keep quiet." She couldn't hold back the shakiness from her voice. "I just don't want to get into one of those 'discussions' that force me to say what I believe again and again. You know I give my testimony freely, but once in awhile I like to have some time to reflect upon it."

"Isn't there a line in—help me here, my Bible knowledge is a little rusty—Ecclesiastes, maybe, about 'a time to keep silence, and a time to speak'?"

She nodded. "It's a beautiful passage. It begins, 'To everything there is a season.' "

"Maybe it's my time to be still, to let events unfold as they are meant to." His eyes rested upon her with incredible gentleness.

"You know," she said softly, "it's in the deepest silence that truth is heard most clearly. Maybe instead of analyzing truth and belief and proof and faith, you need to sit back and let it come to you. Let it tell you what you need to know. Maybe faith has proof. Why don't you let it prove itself to you?"

He was about to answer when the door swung open. The merry sounds of laughter rolled out into the night like a golden wave.

"There you are!" One voice detached itself from the others. It belonged to Lena, the young woman who played Mary in the silhouette stable.

Lena flitted down the steps, brushing off Tess's scoldings about not wearing a coat or hat or mittens. "Oh, shoo. I'll only be out here for a sec. Just long enough to tell you that Katie Tyler is screaming mad because she went to show her friends Baby Snoozie, and the stupid doll wouldn't snore."

"Uh-oh," Tess muttered. "Guess I got caught red-handed."

Lena looked confused for a moment but didn't stop. "So she's going around telling everyone you broke Baby Snoozie, and to top it off she's pulling the dumb doll from the play."

"I'd better go in and see what I can do," Tess said. She didn't look forward to it. Katie Tyler was a beautiful but spoiled child and as stubborn as a cat.

"I told her I didn't need her raggedy old doll. I'd just wad up a bunch of towels and use those instead," Lena continued.

"Oh, no!" Tess groaned.

"And then she said, 'Where are you going to get towels, Miss Smarty Pants?' Can you believe it? She actually called me Miss Smarty Pants! So I told her I'd use her coat when she changed into her costume for the kids' play, and now she won't take off her coat, and her costume won't fit, but she won't take off her coat, and she's the star so she has to be in the show, and the choir director's about ready to kill both her and you!" Lena's exciting narrative came to a triumphant and breathless finish.

"And a merry Christmas to you too," Tess said under her breath as she mentally girded her loins to go into the church and do battle with one Katie Tyler over Baby Snoozie's missing snore box.

Katie took one look at Tess's face and, without a word, stuck her arms behind her parka-covered back, protecting Baby Snoozie from the marauding clutches of Tess.

Tess motioned for Katie to follow her, and Katie did, mesmerized by Tess's silence. Neither one of them spoke as they went into the Sunday school room and sat in the minuscule chairs.

It was Katie who broke the wordless standoff. "You killed Baby Snoozie."

Tess pondered how to rectify the situation and do it quickly. She sent up a quick prayer for help and began.

"Katie, I'm sorry I took the battery pack out without telling you. I did it simply because I didn't want the doll to start snoring during the show. Just like you're pretending to be a star tonight, Baby Snoozie is pretending to be Baby Jesus. Think of it, Katie. Your doll is an actor, just like you!"

Tess was sure she saw the girl soften.

"I'll replace the battery pack as soon as the show is over. I promise." Tess leaned forward earnestly. "I promise."

The girl narrowed her eyes and studied Tess. "Okay," she said, shoving the doll into Tess's arms.

"Now please scurry into your star costume."

"Okay."

"Wow, that was fast," Jake said when Tess emerged with Baby Snoozie in tow. "How did you do that?"

"I tried something unheard of today. I told her the truth." Tess grinned at him. "Now I have to return this doll to Lena before she rips Katie's coat off her. Go ahead and find a seat and save one for me. I'll only be a minute."

Lena had calmed down considerably, enough to manage one last sarcastic comment about the doll's face: "If I have to look at the grotesque doll all evening long, I'm going to turn it upside down so I'll be looking at its feet instead."

The tableau was scheduled to be the last presentation of the show. Tess made a mental note to slip out a few minutes before its start.

She had just eased into the seat Jake had saved for her, ignoring the fond glances the rest of the congregation gave them, when Mrs. Smalley switched from the meditative introductory music. The organ notes swelled into the magnificent opening chords of "O Come, All Ye Faithful."

Everyone stood and joined in, most singing the words from memory. It was one of her favorite Christmas carols, so exuberant that it brought the wild joy of Jesus' birth even closer.

Reverend Barnes began straight out with the reading from Luke: " 'And it came to pass in those days. . . .' " As many times as she heard it and read it, Tess could never tire of the words. So simple, so meaningful.

As he read through the story, he paused while the children presented a skit or sang a song. Katie Tyler, Tess saw with satisfaction, portrayed the Christmas star with a brilliance.

She couldn't help stealing a glance at Jake during Katie's play—was he, too, thinking back to their discussion on the way to church?

The stars moved offstage to allow the next heavenly host: the angels. The youngest children looked beatific in their short white robes that belled around them. Someone had gone to great lengths with their costumes. The wings were snowy puffs of feathers that made them look as if they could truly take off and return to heaven at any moment.

Tess almost missed her cue so enraptured was she with the little ones. But she slipped off just in time to corral the teenagers and hustle them behind the curtain, with Baby Snoozie in an upright position.

As she pulled the cords opening the curtain and revealing the sheet, she flipped on the lights. The congregation voiced a unison "Ooooh." Even from the side of the stage it looked impressive. Lena apparently was moved to new thespian heights and gazed at Baby Snoozie with rapture as the children around her sang "Away in a Manger."

Tess stole back to her seat by Jake in time to watch the angels flock to the front of the sheet. One of them kicked a light on the floor, but miraculously it didn't tip over. The angels fluttered around the silhouetted scene as the congregation joined them in "Hark, the Herald Angels Sing."

Then the lights were dimmed, and ushers distributed candles. One by one, the light was passed from person to person while they sang "Silent Night."

The sanctuary at Nativity was small, but in the light of all the candles it looked endless, like a scene of eternity.

Reverend Barnes invited them to keep the light of Jesus burning in their hearts throughout the year and to remember that one little candle can light a world of darkness. As the candles were extinguished and the lights brought up, he smiled at them. "He is born!"

Mrs. Smalley launched into "Joy to the World!" and the churchgoers sang with gusto.

Tess felt tears of happiness and renewal spring to her eyes. As she dug her handkerchief out of her coat pocket, she noticed Jake smiling at her through eyes that were a bit bright too.

"Merry Christmas," he whispered to her as the last notes of the organ sounded.

"And to you," she responded.

She saw Lena signaling madly to her. "Excuse me for a

moment," she said to Jake. "I promised Katie I'd reinstall the battery pack on her doll."

"Take this ugly thing away from me," Lena said, her stage piety totally evaporated. She pressed the doll into Tess's hands. "I don't even want to be in the same room with it anymore. It gives me the creeps."

She spun around on her heel and was several feet away before she stopped and called, "And Merry Christmas, Tess!"

"Merry Christmas, Lena," she answered back. "You were a splendid Mary."

Katie was surrounded by doting relatives, and from the way she was smirking and simpering Tess was fairly sure she'd forgotten about Baby Snoozie. She slipped back into the Sunday school room and reinstalled the doll's battery pack.

Immediately the doll began a chorus of snores that would have made Tess's grandfather proud. A small sound at the door turned her head.

"What on earth is that?" Jake asked.

"This is Baby Snoozie, the source of the earlier battle," she explained. "She belongs to Katie Tyler, the star of the program, no pun intended."

He picked it up and held it at arm's length. "This is possibly the ugliest doll I've ever seen. What's the big deal with her, other than that obnoxious snore?"

"This, my friend, was the best actor of the evening. You hold in your hand tonight's Baby Jesus."

"This thing? You've got to be kidding me!"

"Nope. Baby Snoozie played Baby Jesus. I took her battery pack out in advance, and she did just fine."

Katie arrived with relatives in tow to claim her doll, and Tess was more than glad to hand it over.

As they left the room, Jake bent close to Tess's ear and murmured, "Next time I start to get too mouthy, like tonight, just take out my battery pack, okay?"

fourteen

Cora met them impatiently at the door, letting them know that once again they had inconvenienced her. Her plate was nearly empty, and she led them to it. Their arrival had once more narrowly averted the near-catastrophe of her starvation.

"That cat is obsessed with food," Jake marveled as Tess put more Meow Meals on Cora's plate. "She can't possibly be this hungry all the time."

Tess cooed to Cora and stood up. "Cats overeat for a lot of reasons. Frequently it's because they're bored, which is a major problem with people who overeat too. With Cora, though, I think it's something else."

He watched Cora as she hunched over her dish and ate. "Why do you think she chows down so much?"

"I think something happened to her before she got here. Maybe she was abandoned or a street cat or whatever. The way she acts, sometimes I think her life before she arrived here wasn't good. Remember—I've only had her three years, and she's much older than that. How old, I don't know. I'm guessing she must be around eight or nine, and the vet agrees."

The kinds of things Cora must have experienced always bothered her. Would it be better to know what her earlier life had been like? Or would that be too much to bear, if it were bad?

"Well, she is a precious cat, whatever. When you told me the story about her being here when you moved in, and your grandmother saying there'd be a cat the color of pussy willows waiting for her in heaven, well, I have to confess, I got goose bumps." He rubbed his arms as if experiencing them again.

"Tell me about it. I nearly passed out when I walked in and saw her. I thought for sure it was a sign that Grandma was in heaven. It was definitely a sign that God recognized I needed a little comfort." She smiled at the cat, who was chasing a last nugget of Meow Meals around the plate. "And what a comfort she has been. She is like a rock. A complaining, domineering rock, but a rock just the same."

"I need to run out to my car and get the Rock's presents. I'll be right back."

Cora had captured the last bit of food and watched him leave, too full to be more than vaguely curious. Tess picked her up and fondly buried her face in the soft gray fur. The cat's side vibrated as her purrs reached full throttle.

"Are you going to speak at midnight, Cora?" Tess asked, reminded suddenly of the legend Jake had referred to earlier. "And what would you say?"

Jake was back in before she could finish.

"Wow, that was quick!" she said as he dropped a large sack on the floor beside him.

"It's way too cold to dawdle. I ran," he panted, clutching his chest. "I hope you know CPR—or at least mouth-to-mouth." He leered at her teasingly.

"Cora does the mouth-to-mouth around here," Tess said, "but only after she's had a bag or two of Giblet Niblets. If that won't put air back in your lungs, I don't know what will."

"Ha! It'd probably kill me. So did I interrupt a conversation between you and Cora?"

"We were just discussing if she was going to speak at midnight and what she would say."

"Interesting concept." He shed his mittens and coat and tried to keep Cora away from the bag as he balanced on one leg and then the other, while pulling off his snow boots. "And what did she say?"

"Nothing, Silly. It's not midnight."

"Oh, well, of course."

"Although," Tess conceded, "this is a fascinating theory. If you could speak only once a year, what would you say?"

He looked at Cora thoughtfully. "I don't know. How long do I get to speak?"

She shrugged. "I don't know. Let's say you have five minutes."

"Five minutes for a whole year? Hmm. Let me think."

"I'll bet all the petty, whiny things wouldn't make it. Like who forgot to buy milk or who left the cap off the toothpaste or even carping about the guy at work who borrows your pens and never returns them. Things we spend so much time going on and on about and which are really nothing of importance."

He nodded. "You've got a point. So what would you say?"

"Point of clarification, please," she said. "Who am I talking to?"

"Oh, me, I suppose. And Cora. Yes, let's include Cora."

"And I haven't spoken all year, right?"

"Right."

"This is hard," she protested. "You and I have known each other for only a month."

"Try it."

"You know, if I were an animal, I'd have a whole year to think about it before my big moment came. It's not quite fair to put me on the spot like this." She smiled at him.

"I agree. This would take more consideration than we've given it. Let's come back to it later, okay?"

They moved into the living room where the tree stood. The blue spruce was large and full, and it filled most of one corner.

He crossed to examine the ornaments. "I'm surprised this isn't decorated in angels," he said as he touched a small red knit stocking.

"Decorated by angels," she said. "Most of these ornaments were made by my grandmother and grandfather, and the others came from my parents' collection. Grandma knit that stocking, for example. Grandpa carved that woodcut stable scene. And the blown-glass bulbs, like that one, are from a collection my parents started when they were first married."

He walked around the tree, examining each decoration.

"The tree topper was a difficult decision for me. Star or angel? My parents had an exquisite golden star, and my grandparents had a porcelain angel."

He looked up to see her choice and laughed.

At the top of the tree, an angel triumphantly held a star aloft.

Cora, who had followed them into the living room, plopped down under the tree, as if proclaiming herself the best present of all.

He opened the bag he'd brought and spread the colorfully gift wrapped contents out under the lower boughs. Then, in silent accord, he and Tess waited and watched.

Cora's nose twitched once. Then twice. She rose, her nose now in constant use, and ambled over to the nearest package.

She eyed it from all angles. With a furry paw she batted it tentatively, then with more assurance. Finally she grabbed it with her teeth and front paws and tore at it madly with her hind legs, shredding the paper and most of the container with her powerful claws.

Cora rolled over and over with the catnip mouse, chewing and kicking the toy.

"So much for my cat's snooty decorum," Tess said. "She's absolutely nuts!"

One by one, Cora opened her packages with increasing fervor, until at last she collapsed in a satisfied heap with her catnip mouse tucked in her paws.

"For all the world she looks like a little kid holding a teddy bear," Tess said fondly.

"I think she enjoyed it."

"I'm ready for the movie now," Tess said. "Shall I make popcorn?"

"But I have a present for you," he objected.

"And I have one for you. But right now I want to revel in the memory of Cora's unbridled happiness and get good and teary with *It's a Wonderful Life.*"

As she popped the popcorn, she reviewed the gift she'd chosen for him. Was it appropriate? Would he think it was silly?

"Mmm." Jake tasted the top kernels from the bowl. "This is great popcorn!"

"I made it the old-fashioned way, with a popper and

melted butter and loads of salt." She sat down beside him, balancing the bowl in her lap.

Cora's nose snuffled her awake from sleep, and she sprang from her spot in the middle of the floor, abandoned her catnip mouse, and leaped up onto the couch beside Tess. Tess offered a few of the popped kernels, and Cora sniffed at them.

Apparently even Cora had her food limits. She licked the butter from the kernels and gave up, curling herself into a warm ball beside Tess.

Tess clicked the remote control and started the video. Within minutes she was in Bedford Falls, and the dissension between downtown and the End, faith and proof, and anything else evaporated as she lost herself in the classic movie.

By the end of the video she was leaning against Jake, sniffling openly.

"I love this movie!" she exclaimed. "Love it, love it, love it!"

He agreed with her. "It's timeless. No matter how often I watch it, I still enjoy it. And it doesn't seem to age, either. I'm sure I'll never see this movie as old-fashioned or out-of-date."

She sighed. "Well, we're out of popcorn. I can't believe we ate that whole bowl by ourselves. And we can't blame any of it on Cora. She must be totally wiped out—she not only slept through the movie, but she was too tuckered to do more than lick the popcorn."

"She did make a valiant effort, though," he pointed out.

"True."

After putting the empty popcorn bowl in the kitchen, they returned to the living room. Cora had sprawled even more across the couch, her body occupying one entire cushion and her outstretched feet and head encroaching upon the others.

"I think we've been bumped," Jake said to her, his arm sliding around her shoulder. "Shall we sit in front of the tree instead to open our presents to each other?"

They hadn't turned the lights back on after the movie, and the living room was lit with only the glow of the bulbs on the Christmas tree.

"Christmas music?" he asked, motioning toward the stereo.

"Lovely."

He turned the stereo on, and soon mellow carols filled the air. "I love the music of Christmas," he said as he joined her in front of the tree. "It's hard to decide which carol is my favorite. I'll think I know, and then I'll hear another one, and I'll tell myself, 'Oh, no, that one is my favorite,' and it is— until I hear the next one. And so it goes, on and on."

"I know what you mean. I have never been able to decide, although I like 'O Come, All Ye Faithful.' And 'He Is Born.' And, oh, yeah, 'O Come, O Come, Emmanuel.' And that one about the rose. And. . ." She caught his expression and laughed. "I should quit before I run through the list of every carol I've ever heard. Maybe it'd be quicker to list the ones we don't like."

"Can't. I love them all."

"Me too," she agreed. "Oh, listen! It's 'The Little Drummer Boy.'"

They sang along, helping each other with the words when one stumbled.

She loved Christmas. Something about it made people be at their best. She couldn't imagine anyone actually arguing at Christmas.

She handed him her present to him. He carefully undid the tape on the end of the box.

"You do that any more, and I will scream," she warned him.

"What? What did I do?" He raised his eyes to her in alarm. "I didn't say anything, and I haven't moved except to start opening this."

"Then open it!" She pretended to strangle herself. "I'm too antsy to open a present that slowly."

"Oh," he said, nodding. "Okay, here goes." And he ripped the paper open with an abandon that rivaled Cora's.

"This is wonderful!" he exclaimed as he took the bell from its wrapping and examined it.

"There's a note too," she prompted, willing her stomach to quit roiling. Of course he'd like the gift, she told herself. It was a terrific present. And with the note she hoped she captured what she meant by it.

He read it aloud: " ' "It is a wonderful life." ' I'll always remember tonight, especially watching the movie with you—and Cora, of course—snuggled up with me. Thank you, Tess.' "

He rang the bell and grinned. "Giving an angel a boost."

She smiled at him, relieved that he understood the meaning of the bell. "I'm glad you like it."

He leaned toward her and dropped a sweet kiss on her lips. "It's perfect."

He handed her his present, a small gold-wrapped box with lacy ribbon. Under the wrapping was a box with a well-known jeweler's name emblazoned across it in gilt script, and she held her breath as she opened it.

It was a necklace. The fine gold chain held a cross that not only was a cross but, she realized as she examined it carefully, was also an angel. The two symbols were cleverly merged to form one shape.

His gaze did not leave her face.

"Like it?" he asked at last.

"I don't know what to say. It's way beyond anything I ever. . . I can't. . ." She looked at him. "I don't like it. I love it. Please put it on me."

She turned so he could fasten the necklace around her neck. The cross caught the varicolored lights of the tree and flashed an entire paint box of colors.

From her vantage point on the couch, Cora snored softly in time to the music.

They leaned back and admired the tree, until Tess remembered something.

"Every year I add a new ornament to the tree, chosen to symbolize something about the year that I want to remember. And I hang it on the tree on Christmas Eve. I haven't done that yet."

She stood up and pointed to a cat angel. "This is for the year Cora came to live here. This apple represents the year I planted the tree in the back. And this easel symbolizes the year I took painting lessons. You'll notice none of my paintings is displayed. I had fun but discovered I have absolutely no talent for painting."

She took a white box from the mantel and opened it carefully.

"What is this year's ornament?" he asked, craning his neck to peek inside the box.

"Just wait, Mr. Nosey-Parker."

She carefully lifted the new decoration from the cotton batting that lined the box and held it for him to see.

He squinted his eyes. "I can't quite make out what it is."

She held the flat brass ornament toward the light of the tree.

"It's the skyline of downtown. See? Here's the courthouse, and here's Saint Agatha's, and this, I think, is the bank. An artist on Third Street made it. I couldn't pass it up, since I became a member of the mayor's commission this year."

He was silent for a moment. "I thought we'd avoid that topic tonight."

She paused in the act of hanging the ornament on the tree. "Avoid what topic?"

"Well," he said, just a bit peevishly, "if I can't talk about scientific proof, I don't think it's fair that you talk about the downtown thing."

"Oh, Jake. It's not the same at— No. You're right. It sort of is, isn't it? But I didn't mean it that way."

She finished placing the ornament on the tree and sat back down. "Maybe for you, being active in the community is easy. For me it was extraordinarily difficult. I didn't wait to be asked. I volunteered."

She could tell by his expression that he didn't understand why it had been such a major step for her.

"I'm not a naturally outgoing person." As she said it, she remembered what an effort it had been for her to put her name on the list of applicants for the commission.

She continued, "It took an incredible amount of gathering

my courage and putting my self-esteem on the line. What if the mayor said no? It wasn't like I'm a financial big shot in town. I'm sure most people said, 'Tess who?' and 'Angel's what?' So this symbolizes not so much the commission, but the step forward I took in getting there."

He smiled. "I understand. That's a great tradition. Do you mind if I borrow it?"

"Not at all, but don't you think the decorations are going to be pretty well picked over at this late date?" she asked.

"Well, you may not be a financial wizard, but I sure am. On December 26 I'll be able to shop for my ornament at half price!"

The grandfather clock reminded them time was passing quickly.

They walked to the back door, and she watched as he put on his boots and coat. He motioned her to him, and she went gladly.

"I can't go without my Christmas kiss, now can I?" he asked.

She didn't answer but raised her lips to his.

His arms stayed around her long after their lips had parted. His voice was almost a whisper when at last he spoke. "Have you given any more thought to what you might say if you could speak only on Christmas Eve?"

She nodded. "Have you?"

"Yes," he said huskily. "I would say you are quickly becoming very special to me, and I want you near me throughout the year."

She smiled drowsily. It was so warm and comfortable in the circle of his arms that she could stay there a day, a month, a year.

"So what would you say to me?" he prompted.

"I'd say, 'Kiss me.' "

And he did.

fifteen

The delicious smells of turkey roasting in the oven sent Cora into near fits of ecstasy. She wound herself around Tess's legs again and again, stopping only to meow plaintively.

"Yes, yes, Sweetie-Cat," Tess crooned. "You will have a big chunk of this turkey all to yourself. But right now it has to cook. Be patient."

Patient was a word totally alien to Cora's vocabulary. She meowed even louder, and Tess looked around the kitchen frantically to find something that might appease the cat until dinnertime.

Evaporated milk might work. She had made fudge earlier in the day, and, as always, a bit of milk was left over. Cora inhaled it and begged for more.

Luckily Tess had bought two cans so she brought down the spare from the cupboard. "Okay, Cora, my dear. Drink up, and please, please, please go sleep by the register and leave me alone!"

Thus bribed, Cora wandered off to her spot by the floor heating register where she had the added bonus of mid-morning sunshine flowing in through the window.

Tess smiled benevolently at her cat. "Heat below, heat above. And a full tummy to boot, with the promise of turkey forthcoming. You lead a tough life, Cora-Cat."

She studied the recipe for truffles, her next Christmas expedition into cooking. She'd gotten the recipe from a lady at church who had since moved away. Although her version would never rival the chocolate truffle elegance she'd been served at Whispering Winds, it was impressive enough to have become her signature piece at Christmas gatherings.

Plus it was breathtakingly easy.

She had just combined the ingredients, shaped the chocolate mixture into balls, and begun rolling them in ground nuts when the phone rang.

"Merry Christmas." Jake's voice was a warm embrace on a cold day.

"Merry Christmas to you too," she answered. "Did you sleep well?"

"Like the proverbial log." He chuckled. "Guess that would be the Yule log, huh?"

She smiled. His good humor was one of his best attributes. Suddenly she wanted him there very much.

"When are you coming over?" she asked.

"Soon. I just have to—"

"Where are you?" she asked, as a terrible suspicion surfaced in her mind.

"Um, well, I, um—"

His hedging didn't deter her. "You're at Panda's, aren't you?"

"Tess, Honey." His voice was soft with suppressed laughter. "I stopped by to pick up some coffee for our dinner. You didn't expect me to drink that washy bilgewater you call coffee, did you?"

How could she have thought he'd be at work on a glorious day like Christmas? "I'm sorry," she said, truly apologetic she had doubted him. "But can you pick up a mild blend, please? I don't want to be awake until New Year's Day!"

"Wimp," he bantered back. He ended by saying he'd be at her house in thirty minutes.

Tess took one look around her kitchen where a major war had apparently just been fought. Used dishes were piled in the sink and trailed across the counter.

"Thirty minutes!" she said to herself, pushing her hair back with a hand that was, she realized too late, sticky with chocolate.

"I need a shower and the kitchen needs a—well, I guess it needs a power wash, but vanity wins. Into the shower it is," she said to a snoring Cora, who could have cared less what the kitchen looked like, as long as it produced a turkey at some point in the day.

Her hair was still in damp tendrils when Jake arrived, his arms full of bundles. "Cute," he said, pulling on an escaping curl from behind her ear. "New hairdo?"

"The wet look," she explained, taking the packages from him. "What do you have in all of these, by the way? You know I do have a turkey basting away in the oven."

"Better than wasting away, I guess," he responded, kissing her lightly on the nose. "These boxes are filled with Christmas cookies that will lose their seasonal oomph if we don't eat them sometime soon, so they're my contribution to the day's festivities."

The aroma of the turkey beckoned them back to the kitchen. Jake gave a low whistle at the sight that met his eyes.

"Is this classic or what?"

"What do you mean?" she asked, reminded of the impeccability of Panda's kitchen area.

"Whenever my mom and grandma and aunts and whoever else gathered in the kitchen, they cooked like crazy. There were always a lot of cooks, and none of them, not a one of them, would wash a dish."

"So what did they do, throw them away?" It was a curious idea, but as she glanced around her chaotic kitchen it gained ground as a possibility.

He shook his head. "No. Mom always said if you eat, you clean up." He rolled up the sleeves of his deep turquoise sweater in readiness.

"Oh, no, really, you don't have to," she objected, but not too strenuously as he quickly assumed his post at the sink. She'd always resisted an automatic dishwasher, telling herself it was a useless expense when the only mouths fed there were hers and Cora's. But now it seemed as if it would probably be worth every penny of its cost.

He was remarkably fast, and soon he had the kitchen restored to rights.

The table was laid with an embroidered cloth that had been her great-grandparents', and the china was also three generations old. She felt a sacredness about sitting down to a table thus arrayed, and she identified every piece of table service, every bit of linen, for Jake.

"It's an honor to be seated here," he said reverently as his long fingers smoothed a napkin decorated with fine threads outlining a silhouetted Bethlehem.

He surprised her. He took her hand in his and asked, "Would you say grace?"

"Of course." She smiled, then bowed her head. "Dearest Lord, on this happy day of Your birth we celebrate the gifts of Christmas. First is the greatest gift of all—the gift of life. A baby's arrival is always a time of excitement and anticipation, and it is with shining eyes that we see the gift in the manger. We welcome You, Lord, into our hearts again. Make us as new as Yourself, free to see with eyes that do not know hatred but look ahead only with expectation. Lord, we thank You for the gift of each other, for friendship, for fellowship, and for love. Happy Birthday, Lord, and welcome! Amen!"

"Amen." He raised his head and looked at her, his deep chocolate-hued eyes warm with emotion. "And I also want to thank you for inviting me over today. I'm afraid it would have been a very lonely day for me without this."

"And for me," Tess agreed softly. "Sometimes I rattle around in here by myself—"

Cora meowed loudly from beneath the table, and Tess and Jake both laughed.

"Well, maybe not by myself," Tess corrected herself. "By myself and supervised at all times by my watch cat, the incomparable Cora."

Cora demanded—and received—her allotment of turkey, and after Tess nixed the idea of clearing the dishes, let alone washing them, the three of them plopped onto the couch in the living room.

"There are probably some television programs on that

would be good to watch," Jake said.

"Probably. Do you know of any?" Tess asked, too lazy and stuffed with turkey and other goodies to get up and check the television schedule that lay three inches from her grasp.

"Dunno," came the answer from the other end of the couch. "Do you know, Cora?"

The cat gave a perfectly timed sigh, followed by gentle, even snoring.

"She sounds happy," Jake said, still motionless on his end of the couch.

"Why shouldn't she be? She's transformed us into her idea of perfection. Look at us—we've become cats." She patted her full tummy.

"You're right. I can't move. And I don't care." He groaned.

"Meow." Tess's eyes began to drift shut.

He flung his hand out. "Okay. I'll assert my right as the reigning male here. Give me the remote control."

Jake set the television to a station that was showing *A Christmas Carol* and meandered out to the kitchen to make some coffee.

"Mild," Tess reminded him as she trailed after him. "I want to wake up now, but eventually I do plan to sleep again."

She arranged the cookies he'd brought on a tray and added her truffles. "I don't know why I'm doing this," she said as they took the tray and the coffee into the living room. "I don't have any more room in my stomach."

"I know what you mean," Jake said, nibbling on a sugar cookie. "I'm so stuffed I couldn't eat another bite." He popped one of her truffles in his mouth. "Wow! Where did these come from? These are great!"

"I made them," she said proudly.

"Can I have the recipe for the restaurant?" he asked eagerly. "They'd be a great seller."

She demurred as gently as possible. How could she tell him they were made from canned frosting and a few other common ingredients?

Fortunately his attention was diverted by the television, where the Ghost of Jacob Marley was rattling his chains at a terrified Ebenezer Scrooge.

"I can remember this movie from when I was a kid," Jake said. "I thought it was the scariest thing I'd ever seen."

"Really?" she replied, her mouth full of a delightful Christmas cookie.

"I understood the moral of the story, about appreciating your life, and every time I watched it I'd vow to take more time to remember the past, heed the present, and prepare for the future."

"Wow! That's some heavy thinking for a child," she said, reaching for another cookie. "I was more afraid of the spirits, but I have to be honest and tell you I didn't get the point until I was a teenager, and by then I'd figured out the spirits weren't ghosts as such. Guess I was a slow learner, huh?"

Jake laughed. "You sound like you were a typical teen."

"Probably. I hope I've learned from the story. The only sticky part is that I hope I'm not doing my good deeds now only because I'm selfish enough to want heaven for my future—as if all my actions are an insurance policy of sorts. They're not. I have to believe it in my heart."

"There's the rub," Jake commented. "How do you know if you're doing it right and if you're going to heaven?"

She smiled. "Jesus tells us. A lawyer asked Him what he had to do to have eternal life. And Jesus asked him back what the Scriptures said. The lawyer said, 'Thou shalt love the Lord thy God with all thy heart, and with all thy soul, and with all thy strength, and with all thy mind; and thy neighbour as thyself.' "

"I remember that. Jesus said that was the right answer, didn't He?"

"Yes, He did. So maybe the answer is to do those things, and good works and good deeds will follow as naturally as night follows day."

Jake fell silent. "I wish I had your convictions, Tess. Your faith is so solid and true. I believe—I truly do—but I don't have it as completely as you do. I wish I did."

Her heart opened, and the words flowed out. "Just wanting it is the first step. Let yourself be open to God, Jake. He's there, waiting for you. He's been there all along, in the past, in the present, and He'll be there in the future too. He's never left you, and He will always be at your side. Let yourself be open to Him. Let yourself see Him."

"If only I had proof, it'd be easier to believe."

"Maybe. But would it be in your heart? Or would it be because you don't see another choice?"

"Good point," Jake said. "I don't know what I'd do if I had real proof."

"Actually, Jake, if you want proof, it's there. Look in the face of a newborn baby. It's there. Look in the face of an older person. It's there. I can even see it in Cora's face. God makes beautiful creations. And each one is a gift of proof."

She touched his hand. "The proof was there in the manger, and it was there in the empty tomb. Faith is an amazing thing. It is its own proof, even as it denies proof. I can't explain faith, but I know it is there."

She fell silent. His eyes were focused on hers, searching and seeking for this elusive thing they called faith.

"I need it, especially as I think about the possibility of moving Panda's," he said, breaking the quiet at last. "Maybe it's not the same thing, but I have an intensive need for proof. Give me charts. Give me graphs. Give me statistics."

"Did you build Panda's from a blueprint?" she asked.

He laughed. "Sort of. The conflict between the contractor and the architect gave it its distinctive rose brick and gray smoked-glass look, but basically, yes, we had a blueprint. Why do you ask? Is it really that bizarre looking?"

"No, no!" she demurred. "It's just that you've already invested heavily in faith. When you built Panda's, you did so on a promise—that the building would replicate what the blueprint proposed. Right?"

"Right."

"And did it?"

"Yes."

"But the blueprint didn't have the personality of Panda's. It didn't include all the little details like the cooking, the roaster, even the personnel. Like Todd." She couldn't resist asking. "Todd wasn't in the blueprints, was he?"

"No," Jake admitted, "though he probably should have been. He knows everyone and can keep the place running like a top, unless you want the till to balance."

"And you definitely had a role in it. Your enthusiasm and dedication to Panda's show. My point is that these little things make the entire place come alive."

A slow smile crossed Jake's face. "You know what else wasn't in the blueprints?"

She shook her head. "What?"

"Faith. A crazy angel whose halo will not stay straight. And Faith, Tess Mahoney, is making all the difference in the world. Without Faith I'd never have met you."

She didn't know what to say. And she didn't have to. He said it for her.

"Faith has brought us together. And I'm hoping—no, I'm praying—that Faith will keep us together."

sixteen

Tess grimaced at her reflection. She felt like a sausage, her body snugly encased in a set of thickly knit long johns, a long-sleeved turtleneck, a heavy sweat suit in a bizarre chartreuse she'd never had the nerve to wear before, heavy woolen socks, a bright green parka, her military olive snow-shoveling boots, an emerald and yellow patterned muffler, and an orange hunting hat topped with a fluorescent lime-colored pompom.

Jake's greeting confirmed what she feared: that she looked like an inflated and somewhat eccentric elf.

"I don't want to be cold," she said defensively. It was difficult to be assertive about what she was wearing when underneath it she was sweating like mad.

"Honey, you'd have to be in the Arctic before you got cold in that getup." He batted the pom-pom on her cap playfully.

"But most of First Night is outside," she objected. "It's freezing!"

"It's only eleven below." He grinned at her.

She looked one more time in the mirror. Chartreuse! What an odd color and definitely not for her. Whatever had possessed her to purchase it from the mail-order catalog? She knew the answer, though. The model had looked stunning in it, and the color hadn't been quite so, well, so chartreuse.

"I'll be right back," she said and ducked upstairs to change into jeans and her new sweatshirt that had been her Christmas present to herself. Its snowy white background was crusted with pink rhinestones that spelled out the words *flutter*flutter*flutter* across an outline of angel wings.

"I feel ten pounds lighter," she said as she came back downstairs. "And I probably look it too. After a month of hanging around with you, I need all the help I can get, thanks to your insistence upon feeding me all sorts of gourmet treats."

Cora sashayed into the room and meowed loudly.

"Speaking of gourmet treats," Tess commented, "Cora's girth has increased too. She has a definite bulge now, and the old gal wiggles when she walks."

"Both of you get lovelier every day," he said, dropping a kiss on Tess's head and scratching behind Cora's furry ears. The cat lifted her gray head and drooled blissfully.

Jake watched as Cora waddled off to her spot by the heat register, apparently having had enough attention for the moment.

"That is a splendid cat," he whispered to Tess. "Absolutely splendid."

The First Night festivities were easily within walking distance, and they made their way quickly to the city center. In the town square a tent had been set up as a nuclear gathering spot.

Tess and Jake stopped there first. As Jake gathered the list of locations and events from the table, Tess warmed her hands by the kerosene heater that was almost unnecessary with all the people clustered in there.

"Where do you want to start?" he asked as he rejoined her.

"Ice sculptures, of course!"

Circling the frozen pond in the square was a fantasy display of statues carved of shimmering ice. They glistened in the reflected light of the street lamps like sculpted diamonds and crystals.

"The theme this year is the Winter Garden," she commented as they strolled through the array of sparkling images. "Look! Here's a hyacinth, I think, and over there—oh, I can't believe the detail! It's a prairie rose!"

Jake bent over the cards and read each one aloud. "Yup, once again they're all done by local artists. I keep thinking that some year they'll have to farm this out to a bigger city, but our art community sure can produce some astonishing works! Check out this one: Jack Frost as a master gardener!"

"And each one is carved from a single block of ice," Tess marveled aloud. "With my luck I'd be right at the end, and my little hammer thing or whatever they use would slip just a teensy bit, and, blammo, my statue would be minus an arm. What steady hands they must have!"

They decided to check out the local library's exhibit next. They climbed the stone steps with a host of other revelers.

"Sure are a lot of people out tonight," Jake said, turning back to gaze over the square from the top step of the library. "Look at that!"

The sea of humanity was impressive.

"A lot of people are like us," Tess said. "They don't want to see the New Year in by getting sloshed, and yet they want to celebrate without risking getting killed by someone who's been drinking and driving. That's one of the things I like the most about First Night—that I don't have to drive anywhere. It's all set up within walking distance of the downtown parking lots for those who don't live down here. And for the rest of us it's great to be able to stroll on over!"

More people surged up the steps, and Tess and Jake found themselves propelled into the library.

For the next half hour they were entertained by a team of storytellers from the town, including the children's librarian, a man who wrote poetry, and the mayor herself, who waved at them. The room was filled to capacity, and the temperature soared.

Tess wiped a band of sweat from her brow. It was a good thing she'd changed out of her earlier outfit; she would have been roasting in all those layers. Jake nudged her and indicated the door. They stole out together and stood at the top of the stairs, letting the cold air wash over their heated faces.

"That feels tremendous," he said. "Whew, it was hot in there!"

"Why isn't the sweat freezing on my forehead?" Tess asked. "Scientifically it should, right?"

He shook his head. "Beats me. It must have sizzled off

when we came outside. It was blazing in that room with all those people crunched together like that."

He consulted the schedule. "Hey, if we hustle over to the police station, we might catch a ride on a horse-drawn wagon. Does that interest you?"

"Sounds like fun!"

The line at the police station extended the length of the block and wrapped around the corner. "There'll be a thirty-minute wait," the woman overseeing the rides told them.

"Want to wait?" Jake asked Tess.

"Sure. Look—a guy is selling hot apple cider and doughnuts!" She pointed to a man behind a red-and-gold painted pushcart, which was mostly hidden by the people hunkered around his source of heat—an open fire in an old oilcan.

Jake grinned at her. "Are you always hungry?"

She tried not to be embarrassed. "Well, it's been awhile since dinner, and doesn't that sound good—hot apple cider and fresh doughnuts?"

Jake admitted it did, and they agreed she would hold their place in line while he bought them some food from the vendor.

"There's something special about food served in open air like this," she murmured, gratefully biting into the doughnut. "It seems to taste a whole lot better than it does inside."

"Remind me to transfer all the tables out of Panda's then. At the very least, it'll keep them moving. No one will want to sit very long when it's fifteen below."

The line moved quickly, and they were soon climbing into the wagon. Jake made room for her on the straw bundle closest to the horse and created a circle of warmth around her with his arm. She leaned against him, enjoying the heat his body generated, but mostly reveling in being close to him.

First Night had never been so much fun.

It was only a tickle at first, then a little more, and it quickly mushroomed into a full-fledged itch. She tried to ignore it, but she eventually had to scratch her leg. And then her hip.

And her leg again.

"Problem?" Jake asked her, his mouth tilted with amusement.

"I seem to be allergic to hay," she answered, trying gracefully to reach her hip again. "Or something. Whatever it is, I think this will be my last trip."

The ride seemed to take an eternity. Around the town square the wagon went, up the hill to the high school, around the water treatment plant, alongside the river, over the little footbridge, and back down past the post office to stop again in front of the police station.

She couldn't hop off quickly enough. She scratched and clawed, uncomfortably aware that Jake was finding her actions amusing.

"Do you need to go back home and maybe shower?" he suggested.

Tess pulled herself up to her full height and tried to regain her decorum. "No, I'm quite"—*scratch, scratch*—"fine. I can do that"—*scrape, claw*—"later. Right now let's just enjoy the"—*scratch*—"evening."

They went to an exhibit at the police station about drugs and how to recognize them, examined a display of historic photographs at city hall, and stopped at the school to listen to the junior-senior choir sing hits from the major musicals.

By the end her itching had fairly well abated.

"I love downtown," she mused aloud, giving her hip one final scratch. "For one thing it's a comfortable place to be—well, except for when we have to sit on straw."

"It's nice, but I still don't know my way around here very well, so I can't feel totally at ease yet." He pulled out the schedule again and squinted at a street sign. "Is this Fifth? Or Fourth?"

"It's Perth, and you need glasses," she teased. "You probably feel the same way here that I do when I have to go to the End. I don't know the names of the streets or even what businesses are where. Like the Animal Kingdom. That place is heaven on earth for cats, but I've never been there since it's in the End. And this town isn't all that big. We probably use it as an excuse."

She couldn't believe that she, Tess Mahoney, was saying that. She was an ardent supporter of downtown growth and an adamant opponent of anything having to do with the End. How had she mellowed so quickly? Had she lost her edge? Or maybe her mind?

As she turned to say something else to Jake, she realized the little lines had reappeared around his eyes and mouth, the road map of tension.

Stupid, stupid! she berated herself. *He was finally relaxing, and you've tightened him right back up.*

She sent a prayer upward, so immediate that its words weren't formed, its ideas weren't clear to her, but its focus was true. Jake. He needed the freedom to come to his decision as she had needed the freedom to give away her precious Bible.

And with the prayer she felt her own self lightening, and she realized she had given herself freedom too—the freedom to move away from the old patterns of thinking, the old ways of seeing, and into the new.

So new that she wasn't prepared for what happened next.

An idea roared into her mind with the strength of a tidal wave.

"Come on," she said, tugging on his coat sleeve.

"What? There's nothing down that street," he responded, consulting the now-bedraggled flyer he'd picked up in the tent.

"Maybe there is. Come on," she urged.

"What? What is it?"

She stopped and crossed her arms over her chest. "You are so stubborn sometimes, Jake Cameron."

"What do you mean?" He frowned at her.

"Always wanting to know it all, not trusting that the future might hold something you don't know about and yet you might want or need."

He sighed. "Tess, it's just a street."

"No, it's not 'just a street,' Jake. Have faith. Trust me. Walk down this street with me."

He shrugged. "Okay, but—"

She laid a mittened hand over his mouth. "Sssh. Faith. Trust."

They walked down the darkened street in silence.

Suddenly Tess stopped and pointed. "There. What do you think?"

"Of what?"

"Of that." She waved her hand toward a windowless hulk of a building that was shadowed beyond the streetlight's reach.

"What is it?" He peered at it.

Tess took his hand. "Come on. Take a look."

She pulled him up the unshoveled walk to the front door. "It's locked, of course, but I think this is it. Check out the back."

"This is what?"

She headed around the corner and threw the word back at him. "Panda's."

He hadn't followed her yet, and she had to wait for him to catch up with her. "Panda's? What? I haven't decided to move Panda's down here, and when I do—if I do—I will choose the location according to demographics, tax base, traffic patterns— those sorts of things."

"You want a good reason? Look at this back door," she said, flinging her arm toward the rear of the building.

A large wooden and metal door, nearly half the size of the building itself, opened onto an area cleared of trees and bushes.

"Under all this snow," Tess said, stamping on the ground to make her point, "is a large concrete slab. Imagine tables and chairs back here and deep green umbrellas. Flowers, maybe geraniums—yes, red geraniums—in terra-cotta pots scattered around. A white wrought-iron fence surrounding the patio. And it all overlooks the river."

She couldn't keep the enthusiasm from bubbling up in her voice. She knew she was in severe danger of overstating it and driving him away, but she was caught up in the wonder of her idea, and, as she looked at him, she realized he was too.

He walked evenly around the building, as if pacing off the square footage, while Tess trailed hopefully behind, trying to step in the prints his feet made in the still-drifted snow.

She could see it—she could actually see it. If only he could too!

"I'd have to take a look at the inside, of course," he said at last, stopping so suddenly that Tess, her head tucked down as she tried to match her footprints to his, crashed right into his back. "And check the city code. This might not be zoned for a coffeehouse. What did this used to be—do you know?"

"It's been called the River Exchange for a long time. It was originally used as a place where the barges and merchant shipping vessels could unload and take on new cargo."

He rubbed his chin thoughtfully. "How long has it been empty?"

"Quite awhile," she admitted. "I couldn't tell you the exact date—this was just a spur-of-the-moment inspiration. I hadn't planned on bringing you here—I hadn't even thought about this building as a possible location until God put it in my mind."

"God put it in your mind?" His voice brimmed with disbelief.

"He did."

For a moment he looked at her, not saying anything. Then he asked, "Why? Why would He do a thing like that? Don't you think He has other priorities, like war and famine and crime? Do you really think He's worried about whether a little coffeehouse like Panda's moves downtown?"

It was a common question, and she had heard the meat of it before. But this time it hurt, coming from him.

The answer came forth with a surprising ease. "God cares about you. You are not at war. You are not starving. You are not in the clutches of crime. Yes, for people who are at war, are starving, or are victims of crime, those are His priorities. And I don't pretend to know why God does everything He does. He doesn't answer to me. I answer to Him."

"But why are you saying He gave you the idea and led you down this street? Give yourself some credit here, Tess. It was probably in the back of your mind, and you weren't even aware you were thinking about it. Your subconscious solved it."

"God did it," she insisted. "Because God answers prayer."

He smiled. "Sure. I admit that. But who on earth was praying about this?"

"I was."

His eyes held hers. "You prayed for this? You want me downtown enough that you prayed to God to find me a place for Panda's?"

"Don't be ridiculous. That's not what I prayed for." She tried to look away, but his gaze was arresting.

"Then what did you pray for?"

"Prayer is private communication," she hedged.

He stared hard at her for a moment, then looked away, but not before she saw the expression on his face. It was part annoyance, part anger, and part disappointment.

Reverend Barnes had told her she would have a chance to share her faith. Perhaps this was it.

"I prayed that you'd find a resolution to your dilemma soon, that you could settle your heart about what to do with Panda's. Move here or stay in the End. At this stage all I know is that I care more about you than I do about the downtown commission or any growth statistics about recovering the lost merchantability of the heart of the city. I just want you to be happy."

He turned back, and his face was shining. "You goose. That wasn't your prayer He answered. It was mine."

A curious sensation arose in her chest, and it took a moment to identify it. Yes, it was indeed possible: Her heart was singing.

"You are a very sweet, wonderful man, Jake Cameron. You are kind and considerate and absolutely blessed, and I think you are terrific."

A deep red stain began to creep over the top of his collar and edged up his neck. He was blushing!

At that moment Tess fell deeply and totally in love.

seventeen

Their last stop was Nativity, where an array of brightly twin-kling lights led First Night revelers to the door of the church.

The downstairs had been transformed into a children's craft fair. The dining room was filled with the chatter of children busily constructing masks of canvas, feathers, and glitter.

In the Sunday school area, preschoolers spread large swaths of paint across squares of muslin, happily dripping the plastic-covered flooring with wild splotches of red, green, blue, yellow, and purple.

Reverend Barnes's reedy figure separated itself from the horde and loped over to join them. He greeted Jake with a hearty "Good to see you again, friend!" and Tess with a "We need you—now. Somebody has to set up a secondary project area, because. . ."

His words blurred into the general noise as they left for the resource room. Tess looked over her shoulder and mouthed, "I'll be back in a minute," and Jake waved his acknowledgment.

The room was a delight for Tess. It was filled with orderly shelves lined with paper in a rainbow of colors, woolly pipe cleaners in clear plastic bags, cartons of glue sticks, baskets of scissors, and covered boxes her fingers itched to explore.

"We have more children coming than we can attend to right now. Could you possibly cobble together some other projects for some of them to do? You can set it up in the nursery—I'll dash up and get things arranged there. Thanks, Tess—you're a gem. And so's your young man."

"He's not my young man," she protested, but her heart was not in it.

"Sure, Tess. Give me a holler if there's anything else you need. I'm running up to the nursery now."

Running was undoubtedly the right word, Tess thought as he spun out of the room like a whirlwind. He had more energy than she had ever imagined a man his age could possess.

She shrugged out of her jacket and mittens and dug into the cupboard.

The boxes were a storehouse of wonderful things. She quickly pulled out several sheets of colored tissue paper, some cellophane pieces, construction paper, scissors, and glue sticks. She dumped her treasure trove into an empty box she found neatly stashed in a corner and headed upstairs to the nursery.

Reverend Barnes was just pulling the last chair into place around the table and looked up in surprise as she walked in.

"Are you ready this soon?" he asked.

She nodded and began displaying her treasures on the table. "We'll make stained-glass windows. First we'll cut out shapes from the construction paper and back the holes with tissue or cellophane."

"I remember those," he mused. "Great idea, Tess. I knew I could count on you!"

"Say, where's Jake?" she asked as she divided the materials.

"I don't know. He wasn't in the dining room, and I got only a peep in the Sunday school room."

A group of five children burst into the room, and Tess's career as a craftswoman began.

She had only stolen moments to think about Jake and wonder where he might have gone. There was a steady stream of children for the next hour.

At last Reverend Barnes poked his head in. "I think you can shut down now. It's almost fireworks time, and everybody's abandoning us."

She flexed her fingers, stiff from cutting countless pieces of paper, and tried to flick the dried-on crust of glue off her fingernails. Her pale pink polish was chipped, and what was left was hidden under the glue remnants.

She gathered up the pieces of paper and put them in a stack. She'd come in sometime during the week and straighten up the room with more attention to detail.

The dining room crafts center was closing down, and the Sunday school room had shut entirely. No one she asked had seen Jake, and she wandered back upstairs.

Where could he have gone? Surely he hadn't left already.

At the top of the stairs she could see into the sanctuary. Outlined in one of the middle pews was the shape of a man, not bent in prayer, but facing the large cross suspended behind the pulpit.

Could it be—?

She tiptoed around the side aisle, trying to be as inconspicuous as possible, but the floor creaked and gave her presence away.

Jake turned to her, and when he did, her heart sparked anew.

What she saw was a man transformed.

His eyes shone with a gentle radiance that could mean only one thing. "It makes perfect sense. I have the proof."

She slid into the pew next to him. "Do you want to tell me?" she asked softly, not taking her gaze from his face.

He nodded. "I wandered up here. It was dark so I was fumbling around, looking for the switch to turn on the lights. I remembered what you said about electricity and faith. That started me thinking. I have no proof electricity exists, other than the fact that my coffeemaker works and the lights come on at my house. And, of course, the monumental bill I get every month. But it could be squirrels in little wheels powering the utilities, for all I know. I've never seen what makes my microwave work. It just does. And when I put my nachos in there, I trust it'll work and the cheese will melt, whether or not I understand why it does. That melted cheese is proof enough of electricity's existence. I don't need more."

"Jake, I am 100 percent, completely, totally lost. What do squirrels and nachos and electricity have to do with God?"

"I've always believed in God. Always. But I've prayed for a faith that goes beyond just belief. What I needed was trust, the trust that would let me allow Him into my life. Didn't it make sense that I should trust God at least as much as I trust the power company?"

He turned to her and took her hand. "That's the step I didn't have before. I didn't trust Him, and without trust there really can't be faith. I'm still working it through, and I'm not sure yet that it's making any sense."

"Oh, it is," she whispered.

"I remembered your story about giving away your Bible, and suddenly I understood. I had to come to the point where I was willing to say, 'I believe, and more than that I trust.' "

He shook his head. "It was the hardest thing I've ever had to do—to give myself over completely to Someone I can't see, but who I do know exists. And it was the easiest thing, once it was done. I feel so different—refreshed, healthy, whole."

"Praise the Lord." Her words were barely spoken, but he heard them.

"Yes," Jake said. "Yes."

The song in her soul soared. He was home—she could hear it in his voice, see it in his eyes, feel it in the way his hand gripped hers.

They sat silently, hand in hand, relishing the glory together.

The noise level of the revelers outside increased, and Jake glanced at his watch. "We'd better get outside. It's almost midnight!"

A fresh vigor possessed her as they walked out, side by side, from the sanctuary and into the air that was so cold it snapped.

New faith. What was more beautiful than that, except perhaps the patina of old faith? She pondered this until the blare of a horn startled her back into the present. Whistles clanged, people shouted, and somewhere a band struck up the traditional New Year's Eve song "Auld Lang Syne."

Jake faced her, tilted her chin upward, and said softly, "Happy New Year, Sweetheart."

With lips as gentle as a prayer he kissed her.

The world exploded into a stunning display of golden and

purple glitter, streams of brilliant orange and yellow, a spray of red and silver.

And the earth moved to make room for heaven.

At last his lips left hers, and she opened her eyes. Behind his head a fountain of blue stars shot into the sky far above the horizon, and she laughed shakily.

"Fireworks," she explained. "The city display is on. I thought we were—I mean, when you kissed me, I saw—oh, Jake. . ." Her words trailed off, and she was grateful the dark hid her heated cheeks from his scrutiny.

In the splashes of light that cut through the darkness, she saw him smiling. "I saw them too—the fireworks. Both sets."

For not speaking much they were saying volumes, and the image of Reverend Barnes and his wife flashed into her mind. She remembered looking at them on Thanksgiving and wanting the same closeness of silent language they had. And now, apparently, she had it.

Her heart was full.

"Happy New Year," she said to him, reaching up to touch his cheek with her mittened hand. "It's going to be a great year!"

Especially for someone who had just committed his life to Jesus Christ, she added silently. Jake knew who walked with him every step of his life's way, who had been with him all along, and now was revealed.

The church doors were still open, and the voices of Reverend Barnes, his wife, and some of the First Night team from Nativity floated up from downstairs.

"I'm falling in love with you, Tess. I'm declaring it in front of God Himself because, if you feel the same way, I want His blessing and His guidance on us as we go forward."

Feel the same way? She could only nod, mute with the happiness that flooded her entire being.

It was a wonderful way to end the year and to start a new one.

❧

Jake swung his head back and forth in amazement. "I can't

get over that. You don't strike me as the kind of person to watch a football game at all, especially on New Year's Day."

He was pouring pretzels and chips into a bowl.

"Word of warning," she said, laughing at his expression. "I don't know a thing about football except that if the guy runs the ball to the end of the court—"

"Field," he corrected.

"Field, that it's worth more than if he kicks it down there. If there's logic in that, well, I'll eat a Giblet Niblet."

He grinned. "A Giblet Niblet, huh? That alone would make it worth my time to find out."

"If you want to see me be sick and die, yes, it'd be very entertaining. But to get back to football, the only reason I watch it is so I can sit on the couch and not think except to wonder where the pretzels are."

"Here they are," he said, carrying the bowl to the living room. "I've never been a pretzel fan, so you can have the whole bowl to yourself."

"Nothing like a pretzel when the ball hits the twenty-foot line."

"Yard line. Twenty-yard line. And you probably don't want to hit it, you want to—hey, you really don't know anything about football, do you?"

"Nope," she answered cheerfully. "And I like it that way, so don't even bother trying to explain it to me. My eyes and my ears both will glaze over, and I'll be as catatonic as, well, my cat."

He shook his head. "You are an amazing woman. Truly amazing. So when does the game start?"

"Two."

"When's that?"

"After one and before three."

"Funny woman. Which team are you rooting for?" he asked. Then, noticing her face, he winced. "You're not rooting for a team, are you?"

"No. I have no idea about either one of them. I just shout and yell and hoot and holler and have a ripsnorting good time."

He leaned back and looked at her. "I'm still finding this a total contradiction in you. How can you be so wild about a game you know nothing about?"

"My grandparents had a tradition like the one we're following. I asked Grandma one time why she let Grandpa watch the game and why she sat in with him the entire time, usually doing some sort of needlework. She said her mind wandered all over the place during the game. Even back to when she met Grandpa, after a football game when he was in his uniform and she was selling apples." She smiled at the memory.

"She was a romantic, was she?" Jake edged down the couch, past a sleepily objecting Cora, to put his arm around Tess. "I like that."

"She loved Grandpa, that's for sure," Tess said. "And that, my dear man, is the story of how Tess Mahoney came to her New Year's Day tradition."

The football game took all afternoon. Jake claimed he still couldn't see how Tess could possibly enjoy the game without knowing the rules of play. She knew all she needed to know, she told him.

"There's a football," she said, pointing at the screen. "That guy with the amazing shoulders has it, and everybody else who's wearing different colors wants it."

"They're on the other team," Jake offered helpfully, but he received a withering glance in return.

"I know that. And I also know those aren't the guy's real shoulders, that they're pads and not really paddy pads but big plastic jobbers that'd probably jar your teeth out if you ran into him face on, which is why the other guy's wearing a cage on his head."

"Helmet," Jake said helplessly.

"And that one end of the, um, the big football place—"

"Field."

"Belongs to one side, and the other belongs to the other side, and the players want to kick the ball and make a goal."

"Touchdown." His voice was weak.

She shrugged. "So what's the big deal with rules? What I don't understand is why they run right into each other and pile on top of one guy. I mean, it's clear he's not going to slither out from under this heap of, what, nearly a ton of sweaty men, right?"

"A ton?" Jake looked confused.

"Well, there are ten of them, right?"

"Um, no, well, yeah, sure. There are ten. Close enough."

"And each one weighs what, two hundred pounds?"

He tried unsuccessfully not to laugh.

She glared at him, and he controlled himself. "You bet. Two hundred pounds."

"So ten of them would weigh two thousand pounds, which is pretty close to a ton in my book," she ended triumphantly.

He stopped and stared at her. "Through all that convoluted logic you've come to what has to be an absolutely correct answer. Amazing."

She smiled happily. "And that, Jake Cameron, is why I love football."

Later, when the team with the green and white uniforms beat the team with the gold and blue ones, as Tess explained it, they sat with the living room illuminated with only the lights from the Christmas tree.

"We need to take that thing down," he said. "It's flinging its needles off with abandon."

"But it's so pretty," she objected. "I like to keep it up until Epiphany."

He stared at her. "Isn't that January 6?"

"Sure is. What's wrong with that?"

"That tree will be nothing but a stem and some twigs by then. You'll have to take it down sometime this week, sorry to say."

"Um-hum," she responded lazily, leaning against him. "Cora's finally used to having her very own tree in the house. You expect me to justify taking it down with the thin excuse that it's dropping needles and it's so dry it's a fire hazard?"

"Take it down while she's sleeping and put a bag of Giblet Niblets in its place. She'll think the Tree Fairy came."

Tess snorted. "Giblet Niblets indeed. I'll send her over to breathe in your face—thank you very much."

Their conversation turned to the events of the night before.

"How many people do you suppose turned out for First Night?" he asked.

"I don't know, but we have a commission meeting next week; so if the paper doesn't have the count, I'll probably find out then." She stretched languidly. "The committee's been on hiatus during the holidays, and I still don't expect there to be much business to report on. So we'll undoubtedly hear every detail about how the New Year's celebration went."

"Next year maybe Panda's will participate in First Night," he said, absently tracing one of her auburn curls with his fingertip.

"Sure! You could have a stand somewhere and probably bring in a ton of money."

A yawn overtook her, and she nearly missed his next words.

"Setting the halo straight."

At least that's what she thought he said. It didn't make any sense, and she was too sleepy to figure out what he meant.

"You're tired, and I need to get home. Happy New Year, dear Tess," he whispered. "I'll lock the door on my way out."

She pulled Cora's warm body up and nestled her cheek against the soft fur and let the Christmas lights blur into dreams.

eighteen

Cora was not impressed with the swirl of red taffeta Tess proudly displayed.

"You don't like it, Cora?"

Tess held it up against herself and swished the dress around her legs. That caught Cora's immediate attention, and a gray ball of fur shot off the bed and attacked the hem of the dress.

"No, no, Cora! You'll rip it!" Tess gently disengaged Cora's extended claws from the fabric and grinned at the expression on her cat's face. "I suppose I shouldn't have teased you with it like that. Sorry, Sweetie-Cat." She rubbed Cora's nose, but the cat glared at her and stalked out of the room.

Tess didn't know for sure where she and Jake were going this Valentine's night. From his hints she assumed it was Whispering Winds. Her mouth watered at the memory of the elegant chocolate dessert she'd tasted there.

As she dressed, she thought about how she and Jake had both changed during the time they'd been together. In such a short period they'd come to know and understand each other.

Since making the step from belief to faith, Jake had grown both spiritually and personally. He attended Nativity regularly and had even joined the choir, much to Mrs. Smalley's delight.

Tess had seen the way his face had relaxed, the way the lines around his eyes and mouth had softened, the easy way he moved, since he'd let Jesus fully into his life. Now that he knew he no longer walked alone, that his burden was shared, he could allow the harmony of being in spiritual balance back into his life.

A glance at the clock told her she had better hurry. He was due to arrive soon.

"Wow!" Jake added a low whistle as she showed off her

new red dress. "You look like a Valentine yourself in that!"

He knelt down to greet Cora, who had padded out to the kitchen to see if by any chance Jake had remembered to bring her some treats.

"Happy Valentine's Day, Cora," he said to the cat, who was already sniffing around the coat pocket he had reached into.

"Those had better not be Giblet Niblets," Tess threatened.

He laughed and took the bag out to prove they weren't. "No, these are plain old Tuna Buddies. See? They're shaped like little fishies, and they even smell like them."

Tess nodded. "So I notice—from way over here. But at least they're not as awful as the dreaded Giblet Niblets. Go ahead. She can have them."

The last words were unnecessary as Cora snatched the bag away from Jake. With one powerful swipe of her claws she had torn it open and was eating the treats before Tess could finish her sentence.

"Now's the time to make our getaway," he whispered to Tess, "while she's still wrapped up in the Tuna Buddies."

She had been right about their destination. They were headed toward Whispering Winds.

The night was cloudless, and the moon was bright. It was a perfect evening, even if it was seven below.

He pulled the car over to the side of the road at a familiar spot. "Do you remember when we first came out here?"

She nodded. How could she forget? The kiss had changed her life.

"And we looked at the stars?"

They had! He had shown her the patterns in the sky, but no shine was as great as the one in her heart that night.

"Well," he continued, "there's a nova I want you to see."

He unfastened his seat belt. "Come on. Let me show it to you."

They stood at the edge of the road. She shivered against him, and he wrapped his arms around her.

"Do you know what a nova is?" he asked.

"Sort of. Fill me in."

"It's a new star being born. I suppose it happens all the time—for angels, it's probably an everyday occurrence," he said, grinning at her. "But for us mortals, seeing a nova is rare."

The sky, away from the glare of the town's lights, glittered with thousands and thousands of stars.

"Each one of those was once a nova," he said. "Even the old stars."

"What does the nova look like? Where is it?" she asked, her eyes scanning the sky. "I can't see it."

"It's here."

"Where?"

"In my hand."

She looked down, startled.

Open in his hand was a jeweler's box with a ring nestled inside it. The diamond caught the reflected light of the stars and glittered wildly.

"Tess Mahoney, I love you. I love you completely, totally, and madly. I think I fell in love with you the minute I walked into Angel's Roost that first day and saw you standing there, looking as if you'd just alighted from heaven yourself."

She tried to speak, but something had happened to her voice. No words came out.

The verse from Ecclesiastes Jake had mentioned on Christmas Eve returned to her: "A time to keep silence." She understood and listened.

He continued. "I come to you as a Christian who has given himself to Jesus, but I need to know one more thing."

Right there, on the edge of County Road Four, Jake Cameron knelt in the snow. "Tess, will you share my life with me? Will you marry me?"

" 'It is not good that the man should be alone,' " she quoted softly, regaining her voice. "Nor is it good that the woman should be alone. Yes. Yes!"

He put the ring on her finger. Overhead the stars, both old and new, danced joyfully as the nova of love twinkled on her hand.

❧

Could an evening ever be more extraordinary? Tess pondered the question over a dinner she barely tasted.

He loved her! That much she had come to know, bit by bit, throughout the time they'd been together. But to hear him say it and to have him commit to her for life—she kept turning it over and over in her mind. No matter how she looked at it, it was spectacular.

"Where should we live?" he asked. "I feel as if your house is more like home to me, but if you'd prefer we can move to the Pines."

"Oh, please, can we stay at Angel's Roost? After all, that's where we met."

"And," he said, his fingers pleating and unpleating his napkin, "it'll be closer for me."

"Closer for what?" she asked idly.

"Work."

She sat up straight. "How can you say that? Panda's is in the End!"

"Panda's South is. But Panda's Downtown is much closer." He looked up and smiled.

She couldn't stop the grin that spread across her face. "Panda's South and Panda's Downtown! It's the perfect solution, but can you do it?"

He nodded. "The River Exchange, the building you chose— the building God chose—is historic, and I'm getting a financial break in the restoration because I've promised to keep it as true to its original glory as possible."

He pulled some papers from inside his coat pocket and unfolded them on the table. "See? Here are some pictures of what it used to look like. I've been working with the county museum, with the special collections department at the library, and with the state historical society to re-create both the interior and the exterior accurately. I want to keep the integrity of that building, but the modern touches will all be removable, should we need to take them out at some time."

She studied the drawings. "Why didn't I know about it?"

"I wanted to keep it a surprise."

"I'm surprised—and so happy, Jake!"

He signaled to the server and whispered in his ear. The server nodded, smiling, and soon returned with a familiar foil-wrapped package.

"For Cora?" Tess asked.

"I need to ask her for your hand in marriage," he said, "and I'm just smoothing the way."

"I think she'll give her consent. If that has what I think it has in it—salmon?—she'd probably let you rob us blind."

"Oh, I think she's more discerning than that," Jake said. "After all, she chose you."

"And she has been a shameless matchmaker ever since she met you," she reminded him. "I'm pretty blessed by that furry girl."

"I have a question I've been meaning to ask," he continued, holding her hand as they left Whispering Winds. "Why is your store called Angel's Roost?"

"I hope it's a place where angels can stop and rest for awhile before they go on to serve." She smiled. "After all, some of those guardian angels probably need a good rest now and again."

"Speaking of resting," he said as they stood outside the restaurant. "I'd like to bring Faith back home."

"But she's so perfect in Panda's!" Tess said.

"I think a certain cat the color of pussy willows would like her friend back."

"Maybe now Faith's halo will stay on straight," Tess commented.

"I hope not." Jake laughed, and Tess remembered his words on New Year's Eve. "I want her there, reminding us how wild and crazy the journey of faith is, and how much fun it's going to be, when we walk along the path with love."

He bent to kiss her, and as his lips touched hers Tess was sure she heard the fluttering of wings.

TESS'S CELESTIAL TRUFFLES

1 12-oz. package semisweet chocolate chips
1 can dark chocolate frosting
¼ cup ice cream topping, such as caramel or butterscotch
1 tsp. cold coffee
Ground nuts

Melt the chocolate chips. Stir in the frosting. Add the topping and the coffee. Chill until the mixture begins to set. Shape into balls (or drop with spoon, if mixture is very sticky, into the ground nuts) and roll in the nuts until the chocolate is covered.

Refrigerate. The truffles firm up when cold.

Note from Tess: If for some unfathomable reason you don't want chocolate, you can try different flavors and combinations of chips, frostings, and toppings with some interesting results. Be creative!

A Letter To Our Readers

Dear Reader:

In order that we might better contribute to your reading enjoyment, we would appreciate your taking a few minutes to respond to the following questions. We welcome your comments and read each form and letter we receive. When completed, please return to the following:

Fiction Editor
Heartsong Presents
PO Box 719
Uhrichsville, Ohio 44683

1. Did you enjoy reading *Angel's Roost* by Janet Spaeth?
   ❏ Very much! I would like to see more books by this author!
   ❏ Moderately. I would have enjoyed it more if

   _____

   _____

   _____

2. Are you a member of **Heartsong Presents**? ❏ Yes ❏ No
   If no, where did you purchase this book? _____

   _____

3. How would you rate, on a scale from 1 (poor) to 5 (superior), the cover design? _____

4. On a scale from 1 (poor) to 10 (superior), please rate the following elements.

   ____ Heroine   ____ Plot
   ____ Hero   ____ Inspirational theme
   ____ Setting   ____ Secondary characters

6. How has this book inspired your life?_____
_____
_____

7. What settings would you like to see covered in future
   Heartsong Presents books? _____
_____
_____

8. What are some inspirational themes you would like to see
   treated in future books? _____
_____
_____

9. Would you be interested in reading other **Heartsong
   Presents** titles?   ❑ Yes   ❑ No

10.   Please check your age range:
          ❑ Under 18   ❑ 18-24
          ❑ 25-34   ❑ 35-45
          ❑ 46-55   ❑ Over 55

Name_____
Occupation _____
Address _____
City_____ State_____ Zip_____
E-mail_____

D0677782

THE
LAST BATTLE

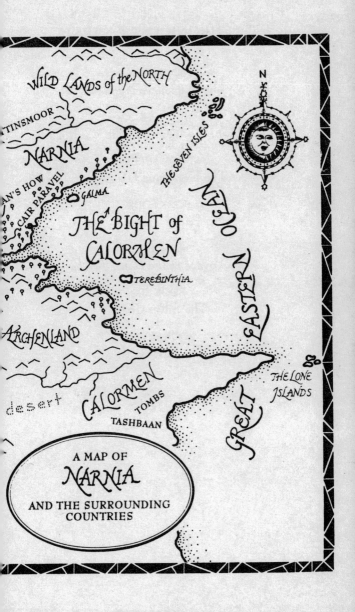

The CHRONICLES *of* NARNIA

The CHRONICLES *of* NARNIA

C. S. LEWIS

BOOK 7

THE
LAST BATTLE

Illustrated by Pauline Baynes

HarperTrophy
A Division of HarperCollins*Publishers*

"Narnia" is a trademark of C.S. Lewis (Pte) Limited.
"The Chronicles of Narnia" is a U.S. Registered Trademark of C.S. Lewis (Pte) Limited.

The Last Battle
Copyright © 1956 by C.S. Lewis (Pte) Limited
Copyright renewed 1984 by C.S. Lewis (Pte) Limited
All rights reserved. No part of this book may be used or reproduced in any
manner whatsoever without written permission except in the case of brief quotations
embodied in critical articles and reviews. Printed in the United States of America. For
information address HarperCollins Children's Books, a division of HarperCollins
Publishers, 10 East 53rd Street, New York, NY 10022.

Library of Congress Cataloging-in-Publication Data
Lewis, C. S. (Clive Staples), 1898–1963.
  The last battle / C. S. Lewis ; illustrated by Pauline Baynes.
    p.   cm. — (The Chronicles of Narnia ; bk. 7)
  Summary: When evil comes to Narnia, Jill and Eustace help fight the great last bat-
tle and Aslan leads his people to a glorious new paradise.
  ISBN 0-06-023493-8. — ISBN 0-06-023494-6 (lib. bdg.)
  ISBN 0-06-447108-X (pbk.)
  [1. Fantasy.]   I. Baynes, Pauline, ill.   II. Title.   III. Series: Lewis, C. S. (Clive
Staples), 1898–1963.   Chronicles of Narnia   (HarperCollins (Firm)) ; bk. 7.
PZ7.L58474Las   1994   93-14302
[Fic]—dc20   CIP
                                                                                    AC

Typography by Nicholas Krenitsky
❖
First Harper Trophy Edition, 1994

CAST OF CHARACTERS

ASLAN. The King, Lord of the whole wood, and son of the Emperor across the Sea. Aslan is the Lion, the Great Lion. He comes and goes as and when he pleases; he comes to overthrow the witch and save Narnia. Aslan appears in all seven books.

DIGORY KIRKE. Digory was there at the very beginning in *The Magician's Nephew*, and he is also in *The Lion, the Witch and the Wardrobe*. If it were not for Digory's courage, we might never have heard of Narnia. Find out why in *The Magician's Nephew*.

POLLY PLUMMER. Polly is the first person to leave our world. She and Digory take part in the very beginning of everything in *The Magician's Nephew*.

JADIS. The last Queen of Charn, which she herself destroyed. Jadis arrives in Narnia with Digory and Polly in *The Magician's Nephew* and has taken over the land as the White Witch in *The Lion, the Witch and the Wardrobe*. Completely evil, she is also very dangerous, even in *The Silver Chair*.

UNCLE ANDREW. Mr. Andrew Ketterley thinks he is a magician, but like all who meddle with magic, he doesn't really know what he is doing. The results are dire in *The Magician's Nephew*.

THE PEVENSIES.

Peter Pevensie, King Peter the Magnificent, the High King

Susan Pevensie, Queen Susan the Gentle

Edmund Pevensie, King Edmund the Just

Lucy Pevensie, Queen Lucy the Valiant

The four Pevensies, brothers and sisters, visited Narnia at the time of the winter rule of the White Witch. They remained there for many Narnian years and established the Golden Age of Narnia. Peter is the oldest, followed by Susan, then Edmund and Lucy. They are all in *The Lion, the Witch and the Wardrobe* and *Prince Caspian*. Edmund and Lucy are also in *The Voyage of the* Dawn Treader; Edmund, Lucy, and Susan appear in *The Horse and His Boy*; and Peter, Edmund, and Lucy appear in *The Last Battle*.

SHASTA. There is a mystery about this adopted son of a Calormene fisherman. He is not what he seems, as he himself discovers in *The Horse and His Boy*.

BREE. This great war horse is also unusual. He was kidnapped as a foal from the forests of Narnia and sold as a slave-horse in Calormen, a country across Archenland and far to the south of Narnia. His real adventures begin when he tries to escape in *The Horse and His Boy*.

ARAVIS. Aravis is a Tarkheena, a Calormene

noblewoman, but even so she has many good points, and they come to light in *The Horse and His Boy*.

HWIN. Hwin is a good-natured, sensible horse. Another slave taken from Narnia, she and Aravis become friends in *The Horse and His Boy*.

PRINCE CASPIAN. He is the nephew of King Miraz and is known as Caspian the Tenth, Son of Caspian, and the True King of Narnia (King of Old Narnians). He is also called a Telmarine of Narnia, Lord of Cair Paravel, and Emperor of the Lone Islands. He appears in *Prince Caspian*, *The Voyage of the* Dawn Treader, *The Silver Chair*, and *The Last Battle*.

MIRAZ. Miraz is a Telmarine from the land of Telmar, far beyond the Western Mountains (originally the ancestors of the Telmarines came from our world), and the usurper of the throne of Narnia in *Prince Caspian*.

REEPICHEEP. Reepicheep is the Chief Mouse. He is the self-appointed humble servant to Prince Caspian, and perhaps the most valiant knight in all of Narnia. His chivalry is unsurpassed, as also are his courage and skill with the sword. Reepicheep appears in *Prince Caspian*, *The Voyage of the* Dawn Treader, and *The Last Battle*.

EUSTACE CLARENCE SCRUBB. Eustace is a cousin of the Pevensie family whom Edmund

and Lucy must go and visit. He finds Narnia something of a shock. He appears in *The Voyage of the Dawn Treader*, *The Silver Chair*, and *The Last Battle*.

JILL POLE. Jill is the heroine of *The Silver Chair*; she goes to Narnia with Eustace on his second Narnian adventure. She also comes to aid Narnia in *The Last Battle*.

PRINCE RILIAN. The son of King Caspian the Tenth, Rilian is the lost Prince of Narnia; find him in *The Silver Chair*.

PUDDLEGLUM. Puddleglum is a Marsh-wiggle from the Eastern Marshes of Narnia. He is tall, and his very serious demeanor masks a true heart of great courage. He appears in *The Silver Chair* and *The Last Battle*.

KING TIRIAN. Noble and brave, Tirian is the last King of Narnia. He and his friend Jewel, a Unicorn, fight *The Last Battle*.

SHIFT. An old and ugly Ape, Shift decides that he should be in charge of Narnia and starts things that he can't stop in *The Last Battle*.

PUZZLE. Puzzle, a donkey, never meant any harm—you see, he's not really very clever. And Shift deceives him in *The Last Battle*.

CONTENTS

BY CALDRON POOL

In the last days of Narnia, far up to the west beyond Lantern Waste and close beside the great waterfall, there lived an Ape. He was so old that no one could remember when he had first come to live in those parts, and he was the cleverest, ugliest, most wrinkled Ape you can imagine. He had a little house, built of wood and thatched with leaves, up in the fork of a great tree, and his name was Shift. There were very few Talking Beasts or Men or Dwarfs, or people of any sort, in that part of the wood, but Shift had one friend and neighbor who was a donkey called Puzzle. At least they both said they were friends, but from the way things went on you might have thought Puzzle was more like Shift's servant than his friend. He did all the work. When they went together to the river, Shift filled the big skin bottles with water but it was Puzzle who carried them back. When they wanted anything from the towns further down the river it was Puzzle who went down with empty panniers on his back and came back with the panniers full and heavy. And all the nicest things that Puzzle brought back were eaten by Shift; for as Shift said, "You see, Puzzle, I can't eat grass and thistles like you, so it's only fair I should make it up in other ways." And Puzzle always said, "Of course, Shift, of course. I see that." Puzzle never complained, because he knew that Shift was far cleverer than himself and he thought it was very kind of Shift to be friends with him at all. And if ever Puzzle did try to argue about anything, Shift would always say, "Now, Puzzle, I understand what needs to be done better than you. You know you're not clever, Puzzle." And Puzzle always said, "No, Shift. It's quite true. I'm *not* clever." Then he would sigh and do whatever Shift had said.

One morning early in the year the pair of them were out walking along the shore of Caldron Pool. Caldron Pool is the big pool right under the cliffs at the western end of Narnia.

The great waterfall pours down into it with a noise like everlasting thunder, and the River of Narnia flows out on the other side. The waterfall keeps the Pool always dancing and bubbling and churning round and round as if it were on the boil, and that of course is how it got its name of Caldron Pool. It is liveliest in the early spring when the waterfall is swollen with all the snow that has melted off the mountains from up beyond Narnia in the Western Wild from which the river comes. And as they looked at Caldron Pool Shift suddenly pointed with his dark, skinny finger and said,

"Look! What's that?"

"What's what?" said Puzzle.

"That yellow thing that's just come down the waterfall. Look! There it is again, it's floating. We must find out what it is."

"Must we?" said Puzzle.

"Of course we must," said Shift. "It may be something useful. Just hop into the Pool like a good fellow and fish it out. Then we can have a proper look at it."

"Hop into the Pool?" said Puzzle, twitching his long ears.

"Well how are we to get it if you don't?" said the Ape.

"But—but," said Puzzle, "wouldn't it be better if *you* went in? Because, you see, it's you who wants to know what it is, and I don't much. And you've got hands, you see. You're as good as a Man or a Dwarf when it comes to catching hold of things. I've only got hoofs."

"Really, Puzzle," said Shift, "I didn't think you'd ever say a thing like that. I didn't think it of you, really."

"Why, what have I said wrong?" said the

Ass, speaking in rather a humble voice, for he saw that Shift was very deeply offended. "All I meant was—"

"Wanting *me* to go into the water," said the Ape. "As if you didn't know perfectly well what weak chests Apes always have and how easily they catch cold! Very well. I *will* go in. I'm feeling cold enough already in this cruel wind. But I'll go in. I shall probably die. Then you'll be sorry." And Shift's voice sounded as if he was just going to burst into tears.

"Please don't, please don't, please don't," said Puzzle, half braying, and half talking. "I never meant anything of the sort, Shift, really I didn't. You know how stupid I am and how I can't think of more than one thing at a time. I'd forgotten about your weak chest. Of course I'll go in. You mustn't think of doing it yourself. Promise me you won't, Shift."

So Shift promised, and Puzzle went cloppety-clop on his four hoofs round the rocky edge of the Pool to find a place where he could get in. Quite apart from the cold it was no joke getting into that quivering and foaming water, and Puzzle had to stand and shiver for a whole minute before he made up his mind to do it. But then Shift called out from behind him and said: "Perhaps I'd better do it after all, Puzzle." And when Puzzle heard that he said, "No, no. You promised. I'm in now," and in he went.

A great mass of foam got him in the face and filled his mouth with water and blinded him. Then he went under altogether for a few seconds, and when he came up again he was in quite another part of the Pool. Then the swirl caught him and carried him round and round and faster and faster till it took him right under the waterfall itself, and the force of the water plunged him down, deep down, so that he thought he would never be able to hold his breath till he came up again. And when he had come up and when at last he got somewhere near the thing he was trying to catch, it sailed away from him till it too got under the fall and was forced down to the bottom. When it came up again it was further from him than ever. But at last, when he was almost tired to death, and bruised all over and numb with cold, he succeeded in gripping the thing with his teeth. And out he came carrying it in front of him and getting his front hoofs tangled up in it, for it was as big as a large hearthrug, and it was very heavy and cold and slimy.

He flung it down in front of Shift and stood dripping and shivering and trying to get his breath back. But the Ape never looked at him or asked him how he felt. The Ape was too busy going round and round the Thing and spreading it out and patting it and smelling it. Then a wicked gleam came into his eye and he said:

"It is a lion's skin."

"Ee—auh—auh—oh, is it?" gasped Puzzle.

"Now I wonder . . . I wonder . . . I wonder," said Shift to himself, for he was thinking very hard.

"I wonder who killed the poor lion," said Puzzle presently. "It ought to be buried. We must have a funeral."

"Oh, it wasn't a Talking Lion," said Shift. "You needn't bother about *that*. There are no Talking Beasts up beyond the Falls, up in the Western Wild. This skin must have belonged to a dumb, wild lion."

This, by the way, was true. A Hunter, a Man, had killed and skinned this lion somewhere up in the Western Wild several months before. But that doesn't come into this story.

"All the same, Shift," said Puzzle, "even if the skin only belonged to a dumb, wild lion, oughtn't we to give it a decent burial? I mean, aren't all lions rather—well, rather solemn? Because of you know Who. Don't you see?"

"Don't you start getting ideas into your head, Puzzle," said Shift. "Because, you know, thinking isn't your strong point. We'll make this skin into a fine warm winter coat for you."

"Oh, I don't think I'd like that," said the

Donkey. "It would look—I mean, the other Beasts might think—that is to say, I shouldn't feel—"

"What are you talking about?" said Shift, scratching himself the wrong way up as Apes do.

"I don't think it would be respectful to the Great Lion, to Aslan himself, if an ass like me went about dressed up in a lion-skin," said Puzzle.

"Now don't stand arguing, please," said Shift. "What does an ass like you know about things of that sort? You know you're no good at thinking, Puzzle, so why don't you let me do your thinking for you? Why don't you treat me as I treat you? I don't think I can do everything. I know you're better at some things than I am. That's why I let you go into the Pool; I knew you'd do it better than me. But why can't I have my turn when it comes to something I *can* do and you can't? Am I never to be allowed to do anything? Do be fair. Turn and turn about."

"Oh, well, of course, if you put it that way," said Puzzle.

"I tell you what," said Shift. "You'd better take a good brisk trot down river as far as Chippingford and see if they have any oranges or bananas."

"But I'm so tired, Shift," pleaded Puzzle.

"Yes, but you are very cold and wet," said

the Ape. "You want something to warm you up.
A brisk trot would be just the thing. Besides, it's
market day at Chippingford today." And then of
course Puzzle said he would go.

As soon as he was alone Shift went sham-
bling along, sometimes on two paws and sometimes on four, till he reached his own tree. Then
he swung himself up from branch to branch,
chattering and grinning all the time, and went
into his little house. He found needle and
thread and a big pair of scissors there; for he was

a clever Ape and the Dwarfs had taught him how to sew. He put the ball of thread (it was very thick stuff, more like cord than thread) into his mouth so that his cheek bulged out as if he were sucking a big bit of toffee. He held the needle between his lips and took the scissors in his left paw. Then he came down the tree and shambled across to the lion-skin. He squatted down and got to work.

He saw at once that the body of the lion-skin would be too long for Puzzle and its neck too short. So he cut a good piece out of the body and used it to make a long collar for Puzzle's long neck. Then he cut off the head and sewed the collar in between the head and the shoulders. He put threads on both sides of the skin so that it would tie up under Puzzle's chest and stomach. Every now and then a bird would pass overhead and Shift would stop his work, looking anxiously up. He did not want anyone to see what he was doing. But none of the birds he saw were Talking Birds, so it didn't matter.

Late in the afternoon Puzzle came back. He was not trotting but only plodding patiently along, the way donkeys do.

"There weren't any oranges," he said, "and there weren't any bananas. And I'm very tired." He lay down.

"Come and try on your beautiful new lion-skin coat," said Shift.

"Oh bother that old skin," said Puzzle. "I'll try it on in the morning. I'm too tired tonight."

"You *are* unkind, Puzzle," said Shift. "If *you're* tired what do you think I am? All day long, while you've been having a lovely refreshing walk down the valley, I've been working hard to make you a coat. My paws are so tired I can hardly hold these scissors. And now you won't say thank you—and you won't even look at the coat—and you don't care—and—and—"

"My dear Shift," said Puzzle getting up at once, "I am so sorry. I've been horrid. Of course I'd love to try it on. And it looks simply splendid. Do try it on me at once. Please do."

"Well, stand still then," said the Ape. The

11

skin was very heavy for him to lift, but in the end, with a lot of pulling and pushing and puffing and blowing, he got it onto the donkey. He tied it underneath Puzzle's body and he tied the legs to Puzzle's legs and the tail to Puzzle's tail. A good deal of Puzzle's gray nose and face could be seen through the open mouth of the lion's head. No one who had ever seen a real lion would have been taken in for a moment. But if someone who had never seen a lion looked at Puzzle in his lion-skin he just might mistake him for a lion, if he didn't come too close, and if the light was not too good, and if Puzzle didn't let out a bray and didn't make any noise with his hoofs.

"You look wonderful, wonderful," said the Ape. "If anyone saw you now, they'd think you were Aslan, the Great Lion, himself."

"That would be dreadful," said Puzzle.

"No it wouldn't," said Shift. "Everyone would do whatever you told them."

"But I don't want to tell them anything."

"But you think of the good we could do!" said Shift. "You'd have me to advise you, you know. I'd think of sensible orders for you to give. And everyone would have to obey us, even the King himself. We would set everything right in Narnia."

"But isn't everything right already?" said Puzzle.

"What?" cried Shift. "Everything right?—when there are no oranges or bananas?"

"Well, you know," said Puzzle, "there aren't many people—in fact, I don't think there's anyone but yourself—who wants those sort of things."

"There's sugar too," said Shift.

"H'm yes," said the Ass. "It would be nice if there was more sugar."

"Well then, that's settled," said the Ape. "You will pretend to be Aslan, and I'll tell you what to say."

"No, no, no," said Puzzle. "Don't say such dreadful things. It would be wrong, Shift. I may be not very clever but I know that much. What would become of us if the real Aslan turned up?"

"I expect he'd be very pleased," said Shift. "Probably he sent us the lion-skin on purpose, so that we could set things to right. Anyway, he never *does* turn up, you know. Not nowadays."

At that moment there came a great thunderclap right overhead and the ground trembled with a small earthquake. Both the animals lost their balance and were flung on their faces.

"There!" gasped Puzzle, as soon as he had breath to speak. "It's a sign, a warning. I knew we were doing something dreadfully wicked. Take this wretched skin off me at once."

"No, no," said the Ape (whose mind worked

very quickly). "It's a sign the other way. I was just going to say that if the real Aslan, as you call him, meant us to go on with this, he would send us a thunderclap and an earth-tremor. It was just on the tip of my tongue, only the sign itself came before I could get the words out. You've *got* to do it now, Puzzle. And please don't let us have any more arguing. You know you don't understand these things. What could a donkey know about signs?"

2

THE RASHNESS
OF THE KING

About three weeks later the last of the Kings of
Narnia sat under the great oak which grew beside the door of his little hunting lodge, where
he often stayed for ten days or so in the pleasant
spring weather. It was a low, thatched building
not far from the Eastern end of Lantern Waste
and some way above the meeting of the two
rivers. He loved to live there simply and at ease,
away from the state and pomp of Cair Paravel,
the royal city. His name was King Tirian, and he
was between twenty and twenty-five years old;
his shoulders were already broad and strong and

his limbs full of hard muscle, but his beard was still scanty. He had blue eyes and a fearless, honest face.

There was no one with him that spring morning except his dearest friend, Jewel the Unicorn. They loved each other like brothers and each had saved the other's life in the wars. The lordly beast stood close beside the King's chair, with its neck bent round polishing its blue horn against the creamy whiteness of his flank.

"I cannot set myself to any work or sport today, Jewel," said the King. "I can think of nothing but this wonderful news. Think you we shall hear more of it today?"

"They are the most wonderful tidings ever heard in our days or our fathers' or our grandfathers' days, Sire," said Jewel, "if they are true."

"How can they choose but be true?" said the King. "It is more than a week ago that the first birds came flying over us saying, Aslan is here, Aslan has come to Narnia again. And after that it was the squirrels. They had not seen him, but they said it was certain he was in the woods. Then came the Stag. He said he had seen him with his own eyes, a great way off, by moonlight, in Lantern Waste. Then came that dark Man with the beard, the merchant from Calormen. The Calormenes care nothing for Aslan as we do; but the man spoke of it as a thing beyond doubt. And there was the Badger last night; he too had seen Aslan."

"Indeed, Sire," answered Jewel, "I believe it all. If I seem not to, it is only that my joy is too great to let my belief settle itself. It is almost too beautiful to believe."

"Yes," said the King with a great sigh, almost a shiver, of delight. "It is beyond all that I ever hoped for in all my life."

"Listen!" said Jewel, putting his head on one side and cocking his ears forward.

"What is it?" asked the King.

"Hoofs, Sire," said Jewel. "A galloping horse. A very heavy horse. It must be one of the Centaurs. And look, there he is."

A great, golden bearded Centaur, with man's sweat on his forehead and horse's sweat on his chestnut flanks, dashed up to the King, stopped, and bowed low. "Hail, King," it cried in a voice as deep as a bull's.

"Ho, there!" said the King, looking over his shoulder towards the door of the hunting lodge. "A bowl of wine for the noble Centaur. Welcome, Roonwit. When you have found your breath you shall tell us your errand."

A page came out of the house carrying a great wooden bowl, curiously carved, and handed it to the Centaur. The Centaur raised the bowl and said,

"I drink first to Aslan and truth, Sire, and secondly to your Majesty."

He finished the wine (enough for six strong men) at one draft and handed the empty bowl back to the page.

"Now, Roonwit," said the King. "Do you bring us more news of Aslan?"

Roonwit looked very grave, frowning a little.

"Sire," he said. "You know how long I have lived and studied the stars; for we Centaurs live longer than you Men, and even longer than your kind, Unicorn. Never in all my days have I seen such terrible things written in the skies as there have been nightly since this year began.

The stars say nothing of the coming of Aslan, nor of peace, nor of joy. I know by my art that there have not been such disastrous conjunctions of the planets for five hundred years. It was already in my mind to come and warn your Majesty that some great evil hangs over Narnia. But last night the rumor reached me that Aslan is abroad in Narnia. Sire, do not believe this tale. It cannot be. The stars never lie, but Men and Beasts do. If Aslan were really coming to Narnia the sky would have foretold it. If he were really come, all the most gracious stars would be assembled in his honor. It is all a lie."

"A lie!" said the King fiercely. "What creature in Narnia or all the world would dare to lie on such a matter?" And, without knowing it, he laid his hand on his sword hilt.

"That I know not, Lord King," said the Centaur. "But I know there are liars on earth; there are none among the stars."

"I wonder," said Jewel, "whether Aslan might not come though all the stars foretold otherwise. He is not the slave of the stars but their Maker. Is it not said in all the old stories that He is not a tame lion."

"Well said, well said, Jewel," cried the King. "Those are the very words: *not a tame lion*. It comes in many tales."

Roonwit had just raised his hand and was

leaning forward to say something very earnestly to the King when all three of them turned their heads to listen to a wailing sound that was quickly drawing nearer. The wood was so thick to the West of them that they could not see the newcomer yet. But they could soon hear the words.

"Woe, woe, woe!" called the voice. "Woe for my brothers and sisters! Woe for the holy trees! The woods are laid waste. The axe is loosed against us. We are being felled. Great trees are falling, falling, falling."

With the last "falling" the speaker came in sight. She was like a woman but so tall that her head was on a level with the Centaur's yet she was like a tree too. It is hard to explain if you have never seen a Dryad but quite unmistakable

once you have—something different in the color, the voice, and the hair. King Tirian and the two Beasts knew at once that she was the nymph of a beech tree.

"Justice, Lord King!" she cried. "Come to our aid. Protect your people. They are felling us in Lantern Waste. Forty great trunks of my brothers and sisters are already on the ground."

"What, Lady! Felling Lantern Waste? Murdering the talking trees?" cried the King, leaping to his feet and drawing his sword. "How dare they? And who dares it? Now by the Mane of Aslan—"

"A-a-a-h," gasped the Dryad shuddering as if in pain—shuddering time after time as if under repeated blows. Then all at once she fell sideways as suddenly as if both her feet had been cut from under her. For a second they saw her lying dead on the grass and then she vanished. They knew what had happened. Her tree, miles away, had been cut down.

For a moment the King's grief and anger were so great that he could not speak. Then he said:

"Come, friends. We must go up river and find the villains who have done this, with all the speed we may. I will leave not one of them alive."

"Sire, with a good will," said Jewel.

But Roonwit said, "Sire, be wary in your just wrath. There are strange doings on foot. If there should be rebels in arms further up the valley, we three are too few to meet them. If it would please you to wait while—"

"I will not wait the tenth part of a second," said the King. "But while Jewel and I go forward, do you gallop as hard as you may to Cair Paravel. Here is my ring for your token. Get me a score of men-at-arms, all well mounted, and a score of Talking Dogs, and ten Dwarfs (let them all be fell archers), and a Leopard or so, and Stonefoot the Giant. Bring all these after us as quickly as can be."

"With a good will, Sire," said Roonwit. And at once he turned and galloped Eastward down the valley.

The King strode on at a great pace, sometimes muttering to himself and sometimes clenching his fists. Jewel walked beside him, saying nothing; so there was no sound between them but the faint jingle of a rich gold chain that hung round the Unicorn's neck and the noise of two feet and four hoofs.

They soon reached the River and turned up it where there was a grassy road: they had the water on their left and the forest on their right. Soon after that they came to the place where the ground grew rougher and thick wood came down to the water's edge. The road, what there was of it, now ran on the Southern bank and they had to ford the River to reach it. It was up to Tirian's arm-pits, but Jewel (who had four legs and was therefore steadier) kept on his right so as to break the force of the current, and Tirian put his strong arm round the Unicorn's strong neck and they both got safely over. The King was still so angry that he hardly noticed the cold of the water. But of course he dried his sword very carefully on the shoulder of his cloak, which was the only dry part of him, as soon as they came to shore.

They were now going Westward with the River on their right and Lantern Waste straight ahead of them. They had not gone more than a mile when they both stopped and both spoke at the same moment. The King said "What have we here?" and Jewel said "Look!"

"It is a raft," said King Tirian.

And so it was. Half a dozen splendid tree-trunks, all newly cut and newly lopped of their branches, had been lashed together to make a raft, and were gliding swiftly down the river. On the front of the raft there was a water rat with a pole to steer it.

"Hey! Water-Rat! What are you about?" cried the King.

"Taking logs down to sell to the

Calormenes, Sire," said the Rat, touching his ear as he might have touched his cap if he had had one.

"Calormenes!" thundered Tirian. "What do you mean? Who gave order for these trees to be felled?"

The River flows so swiftly at that time of the year that the raft had already glided past the King and Jewel. But the Water-Rat looked back over its shoulder and shouted out:

"The Lion's orders, Sire. Aslan himself." He added something more but they couldn't hear it.

The King and the Unicorn stared at one another and both looked more frightened than they had ever been in any battle.

"Aslan," said the King at last, in a very low voice. "Aslan. Could it be true? *Could* he be felling the holy trees and murdering the Dryads?"

"Unless the Dryads have all done something

dreadfully wrong—" murmured Jewel.

"But selling them to Calormenes!" said the King. "Is it possible?"

"I don't know," said Jewel miserably. "He's not a *tame* lion."

"Well," said the King at last, "we must go on and take the adventure that comes to us."

"It is the only thing left for us to do, Sire," said the Unicorn. He did not see at the moment how foolish it was for two of them to go on alone; nor did the King. They were too angry to think clearly. But much evil came of their rashness in the end.

Suddenly the King leaned hard on his friend's neck and bowed his head.

"Jewel," he said, "what lies before us? Horrible thoughts arise in my heart. If we had died before today we should have been happy."

"Yes," said Jewel. "We have lived too long. The worst thing in the world has come upon us." They stood like that for a minute or two and then went on.

Before long they could hear the hack-hack-hack of axes falling on timber, though they could see nothing yet because there was a rise of the ground in front of them. When they had reached the top of it they could see right into Lantern Waste itself. And the King's face turned white when he saw it.

Right through the middle of that ancient forest—that forest where the trees of gold and of silver had once grown and where a child from our world had once planted the Tree of Protection—a broad lane had already been opened. It was a hideous lane like a raw gash in the land, full of muddy ruts where felled trees had been dragged down to the river. There was a great crowd of people at work, and a cracking of whips, and horses tugging and straining as they dragged at the logs. The first thing that struck the King and the Unicorn was that about half the people in the crowd were not Talking Beasts but Men. The next thing was that these men were not the fair-haired men of Narnia: they were dark, bearded men from Calormen, that great and cruel country that lies beyond Archenland across the desert to the south. There was no reason, of course, why one should not meet a Calormene or two in Narnia—a merchant or an ambassador—for there was peace between Narnia and Calormen in those days. But Tirian could not understand why there were so many of them: nor why they were cutting down a Narnian forest. He grasped his sword tighter and rolled his cloak round his left arm. They came quickly down among the men.

Two Calormenes were driving a horse which

was harnessed to a log. Just as the King reached them, the log got stuck in a bad muddy place.

"Get on, son of sloth! Pull, you lazy pig!" cried the Calormenes, cracking their whips. The horse was already straining himself as hard as he could; his eyes were red and he was covered with foam.

"Work, lazy brute," shouted one of the Calormenes: and as he spoke he struck the horse savagely with his whip. It was then that the really dreadful thing happened.

Up till now Tirian had taken it for granted that the horses which the Calormenes were driving were their own horses; dumb, witless animals like the horses of our own world. And though he hated to see even a dumb horse overdriven, he was of course thinking more about the murder of the Trees. It had never crossed his mind that anyone would dare to harness one of the free Talking Horses of Narnia, much less to use a whip on it. But as that savage blow fell the horse reared up and said, half screaming:

"Fool and tyrant! Do you not see I am doing all I can?"

When Tirian knew that the Horse was one of his own Narnians, there came over him and over Jewel such a rage that they did not know what they were doing. The King's sword went up, the Unicorn's horn went down. They rushed forward together. Next moment both the Calormenes lay dead, the one beheaded by Tirian's sword and the other gored through the heart by Jewel's horn.

THE APE IN ITS GLORY

"Master Horse, Master Horse," said Tirian as he hastily cut its traces, "how came these aliens to enslave you? Is Narnia conquered? Has there been a battle?"

"No, Sire," panted the horse, "Aslan is here. It is all by his orders. He has commanded—"

"'Ware danger, King," said Jewel. Tirian looked up and saw that Calormenes (mixed with a few Talking Beasts) were beginning to run toward them from every direction. The two dead men had died without a cry and so it had taken a moment before the rest of the crowd knew what had happened. But now they did.

Most of them had naked scimitars in their hands.

"Quick. On my back," said Jewel.

The King flung himself astride of his old friend who turned and galloped away. He changed direction twice or thrice as soon as they were out of sight of their enemies, crossed a stream, and shouted without slackening his pace, "Whither away, Sire? To Cair Paravel?"

"Hold hard, friend," said Tirian. "Let me off." He slid off the Unicorn's back and faced him.

"Jewel," said the King. "We have done a dreadful deed."

"We were sorely provoked," said Jewel.

"But to leap on them unawares—without defying them—while they were unarmed—faugh! We are two murderers, Jewel. I am dishonored forever."

Jewel drooped his head. He too was ashamed.

"And then," said the King, "the Horse said it was by Aslan's orders. The Rat said the same. They all say Aslan is here. How if it were true?"

"But, Sire, how *could* Aslan be commanding such dreadful things?"

"He is not a *tame* lion," said Tirian. "How should we know what he would do? We, who are murderers. Jewel, I will go back. I will give up my sword and put myself in the hands of these Calormenes and ask that they bring me before Aslan. Let him do justice on me."

"You will go to your death, then," said Jewel.

"Do you think I care if Aslan dooms me to death?" said the King. "That would be nothing, nothing at all. Would it not be better to be dead than to have this horrible fear that Aslan has come and is not like the Aslan we have believed in and longed for? It is as if the sun rose one day and were a black sun."

"I know," said Jewel. "Or as if you drank water and it were *dry* water. You are in the right, Sire. This is the end of all things. Let us go and give ourselves up."

"There is no need for both of us to go."

"If ever we loved one another, let me go with you now," said the Unicorn. "If you are dead and if Aslan is not Aslan, what life is left for me?"

They turned and walked back together, shedding bitter tears.

As soon as they came to the place where the work was going on the Calormenes raised a cry and came toward them with their weapons in hand. But the King held out his sword with the hilt toward them and said:

"I who was King of Narnia and am now a

dishonored knight give myself up to the justice of Aslan. Bring me before him."

"And I give myself up too," said Jewel.

Then the dark men came round them in a thick crowd, smelling of garlic and onions, their white eyes flashing dreadfully in their brown faces. They put a rope halter round Jewel's neck. They took the King's sword away and tied his hands behind his back. One of the Calormenes, who had a helmet instead of a turban and seemed to be in command, snatched the gold circlet off Tirian's head and hastily put it away somewhere among his clothes. They led the two prisoners uphill to a place where there was a big clearing. And this was what the prisoners saw.

At the center of the clearing, which was also the highest point of the hill, there was a little hut like a stable, with a thatched roof. Its door was shut. On the grass in front of the door there sat an Ape. Tirian and Jewel, who had been expecting to see Aslan and had heard nothing about an Ape yet, were very bewildered when they saw it. The Ape was of course Shift himself, but he looked ten times uglier than when he lived by Caldron Pool, for he was now dressed up. He was wearing a scarlet jacket which did not fit him very well, having been made for a dwarf. He had jeweled slippers on his hind paws which would not stay on properly because, as you know, the hind paws of an Ape are really like hands. He wore what seemed to be a paper crown on his head. There was a great pile of nuts beside him and he kept cracking nuts with his jaws and spitting out the shells. And he also kept on pulling up the scarlet jacket to scratch himself. A great number of Talking Beasts stood facing him, and nearly every face in that crowd looked miserably worried and bewildered. When they saw who the prisoners were they all groaned and whimpered.

"O Lord Shift, mouthpiece of Aslan," said the chief Calormene. "We bring you prisoners. By our skill and courage and by the permission of the great god Tash we have taken alive these two desperate murderers."

"Give me that man's sword," said the Ape. So they took the King's sword and handed it, with the sword-belt and all, to the monkey. And he hung it round his own neck: and it made him look sillier than ever.

"We'll see about those two later," said the Ape, spitting out a shell in the direction of the two prisoners. "I got some other business first. They can wait. Now listen to me, everyone. The first thing I want to say is about nuts. Where's that Head Squirrel got to?"

"Here, Sir," said a red squirrel, coming forward and making a nervous little bow.

"Oh you are, are you?" said the Ape with a nasty look. "Now attend to me. I want—I mean, Aslan wants—some more nuts. These you've brought aren't anything like enough. You must bring some more, do you hear? Twice as many. And they've got to be here by sunset tomorrow, and there mustn't be any bad ones or any small ones among them."

A murmur of dismay ran through the other squirrels, and the Head Squirrel plucked up courage to say:

"Please, would Aslan himself speak to us about it? If we might be allowed to see him—"

"Well you won't," said the Ape. "He may be very kind (though it's a lot more than most of you deserve) and come out for a few minutes tonight. Then you can all have a look at him. But he will *not* have you all crowding round him and pestering him with questions.

Anything you want to say to him will be passed on through me: if I think it's worth bothering him about. In the meantime all you squirrels had better go and see about the nuts. And make sure they are here by tomorrow evening or, my word! you'll catch it."

The poor squirrels all scampered away as if a dog were after them. This new order was terrible news for them. The nuts they had carefully hoarded for the winter had nearly all been eaten by now; and of the few that were left they had already given the Ape far more than they could spare.

Then a deep voice—it belonged to a great tusked and shaggy Boar—spoke from another part of the crowd.

"But *why* can't we see Aslan properly and talk to him?" it said. "When he used to appear in Narnia in the old days everyone could talk to him face to face."

"Don't you believe it," said the Ape. "And even if it was true, times have changed. Aslan says he's been far too soft with you before, do you see? Well, he isn't going to be soft any more. He's going to lick you into shape this time. He'll teach you to think he's a tame lion!"

A low moaning and whimpering was heard among the Beasts; and, after that, a dead silence which was more miserable still.

"And now there's another thing you got to learn," said the Ape. "I hear some of you are saying I'm an Ape. Well, I'm not. I'm a Man. If I look like an Ape, that's because I'm so very old: hundreds and hundreds of years old. And it's because I'm so old that I'm so wise. And it's because I'm so wise that I'm the only one Aslan is ever going to speak to. He can't be bothered talking to a lot of stupid animals. He'll tell me what you've got to do, and I'll tell the rest of you. And take my advice, and see you do it in double quick time, for he doesn't mean to stand any nonsense."

There was dead silence except for the noise of a very young badger crying and its mother trying to make it keep quiet.

"And now here's another thing," the Ape went on, fitting a fresh nut into its cheek, "I hear some of the horses are saying, Let's hurry up and get this job of carting timber over as quickly as we can, and then we'll be free again. Well, you can get that idea out of your heads at once. And not only the Horses either. Everybody who can work is going to be made to work in future. Aslan has it all settled with the King of Calormen—The Tisroc, as our dark faced friends the Calormenes call him. All you Horses and Bulls and Donkeys are to be sent down into Calormen to work for your living—pulling and carrying the way horses and such-like do in other countries. And all you digging animals like Moles and Rabbits and Dwarfs are going down to work in The Tisroc's mines. And—"

"No, no, no," howled the Beasts. "It can't be true. Aslan would never sell us into slavery to the King of Calormen."

"None of that! Hold your noise!" said the Ape with a snarl. "Who said anything about slavery? You won't be slaves. You'll be paid— very good wages too. That is to say, your pay will be paid into Aslan's treasury and he will use it all for everybody's good." Then he glanced, and almost winked, at the chief Calormene. The Calormene bowed and replied, in the pompous Calormene way:

"Most sapient Mouthpiece of Aslan, The Tisroc (may-he-live-forever) is wholly of one mind with your lordship in this judicious plan."

"There! You see!" said the Ape. "It's all arranged. And all for your own good. We'll be able, with the money you earn, to make Narnia a country worth living in. There'll be oranges and bananas pouring in—and roads and big cities and schools and offices and whips and muzzles and saddles and cages and kennels and prisons—Oh, everything."

"But we don't want all those things," said an old Bear. "We want to be free. And we want to hear Aslan speak himself."

"Now don't you start arguing," said the Ape, "for it's a thing I won't stand. I'm a Man: you're only a fat, stupid old Bear. What do you know about freedom? You think freedom means doing what you like. Well, you're wrong. That isn't true freedom. True freedom means doing what I tell you."

"H-n-n-h," grunted the Bear and scratched its head; it found this sort of thing hard to understand.

"Please, please," said the high voice of a woolly lamb, who was so young that everyone was surprised he dared to speak at all.

"What is it now?" said the Ape. "Be quick."

39

"Please," said the Lamb, "I can't understand. What have we to do with the Calormenes? We belong to Aslan. They belong to Tash. They have a god called Tash. They say he has four arms and the head of a vulture. They kill Men on his altar. I don't believe there's any such person as Tash. But if there was, how could Aslan be friends with him?"

All the animals cocked their heads sideways and all their bright eyes flashed toward the Ape. They knew it was the best question anyone had asked yet.

The Ape jumped up and spat at the Lamb.

"Baby!" he hissed. "Silly little bleater! Go home to your mother and drink milk. What do you understand of such things? But the others, listen. Tash is only another name for Aslan. All that old idea of us being right and the Calormenes wrong is silly. We know better now. The Calormenes use different words but we all mean the same thing. Tash and Aslan are only two different names for you know Who. That's why there can never be any quarrel between them. Get that into your heads, you stupid brutes. Tash is Aslan: Aslan is Tash."

You know how sad your own dog's face can look sometimes. Think of that and then think of all the faces of those Talking Beasts—all those honest, humble, bewildered Birds, Bears,

Badgers, Rabbits, Moles, and Mice—all far sadder than that. Every tail was down, every whisker drooped. It would have broken your heart with very pity to see their faces. There was only one who did not look at all unhappy.

It was a ginger Cat—a great big Tom in the prime of life—who sat bolt upright with his tail curled round his toes, in the very front row of all the Beasts. He had been staring hard at the Ape and the Calormene captain all the time and had never once blinked his eyes.

"Excuse me," said the Cat very politely, "but this interests me. Does your friend from Calormen say the same?"

"Assuredly," said the Calormene. "The enlightened Ape—Man, I mean—is in the right. *Aslan* means neither less nor more than *Tash*."

"Especially, Aslan means *no more* than Tash?" suggested the Cat.

"No more at all," said the Calormene, looking the Cat straight in the face.

"Is that good enough for you, Ginger?" said the Ape.

"Oh certainly," said Ginger coolly. "Thank you very much. I only wanted to be quite clear. I think I am beginning to understand."

Up till now the King and Jewel had said nothing: they were waiting until the Ape should bid them speak, for they thought it was no use interrupting. But now, as Tirian looked round on the miserable faces of the Narnians, and saw how they would all believe that Aslan and Tash were one and the same, he could bear it no longer.

"Ape," he cried with a great voice, "you lie damnably. You lie like a Calormene. You lie like an Ape."

He meant to go on and ask how the terrible god Tash who fed on the blood of his people could possibly be the same as the good Lion by whose blood all Narnia was saved. If he had been allowed to speak, the rule of the Ape might have ended that day; the Beasts might have seen the truth and thrown the Ape down. But before he could say another word two Calormenes struck him in the mouth with all their force, and a third, from behind, kicked his feet from under him. And as he fell, the Ape squealed in rage and terror.

"Take him away. Take him away. Take him where he cannot hear us, nor we hear him. There tie him to a tree. I will—I mean, Aslan will—do justice on him later."

4

WHAT HAPPENED
THAT NIGHT

The King was so dizzy from being knocked down that he hardly knew what was happening until the Calormenes untied his wrists and put his arms straight down by his sides and set him with his back against an ash tree. Then they bound ropes round his ankles and his knees and his waist and his chest and left him there. What worried him worst at the moment—for it is often little things that are hardest to stand—was that his lip was bleeding where they had hit him and he couldn't wipe the little trickle of blood away although it tickled him.

From where he was he could still see the little stable on the top of the hill and the Ape sitting in front of it. He could just hear the Ape's voice still going on and, every now and then, some answer from the crowd, but he could not make out the words.

"I wonder what they've done to Jewel," thought the King.

Presently the crowd of beasts broke up and began going away in different directions. Some passed close to Tirian. They looked at him as if they were both frightened and sorry to see him tied up but none of them spoke. Soon they had all gone and there was silence in the wood. Then hours and hours went past and Tirian became first very thirsty and then very hungry; and as the afternoon dragged on and turned into evening, he became cold too. His back was very sore. The sun went down and it began to be twilight.

When it was almost dark Tirian heard a light pitter-patter of feet and saw some small creatures coming toward him. The three on the left were Mice, and there was a Rabbit in the middle: on the right were two Moles. Both these were carrying little bags on their backs which gave them a curious look in the dark so that at first he wondered what kind of beasts they were. Then, in a moment, they were all standing up

on their hind legs, laying their cool paws on his knees and giving his knees snuffly animal kisses. (They could reach his knees because Narnian Talking Beasts of that sort are bigger than the dumb beasts of the same kind in England.)

"Lord King! dear Lord King," said their shrill voices, "we are so sorry for you. We daren't untie you because Aslan might be angry with us. But we've brought you your supper."

At once the first Mouse climbed nimbly up

till he was perched on the rope that bound Tirian's chest and was wrinkling his blunt nose in front of Tirian's face. Then the second Mouse climbed up and hung on just below the first Mouse. The other beasts stood on the ground and began handing things up.

"Drink, Sire, and then you'll find you are able to eat," said the topmost Mouse, and Tirian found that a little wooden cup was being held to his lips. It was only the size of an egg cup so that he had hardly tasted the wine in it before it was empty. But then the Mouse passed it down and the others refilled it and it was passed up again and Tirian emptied it a second time. In this way they went on till he had quite a good drink, which was all the better for coming in little doses, for that is more thirst-quenching than one long draft.

"Here is cheese, Sire," said the first Mouse, "but not very much, for fear it would make you too thirsty." And after the cheese they fed him with oat-cakes and fresh butter, and then with some more wine.

"Now hand up the water," said the first Mouse, "and I'll wash the King's face. There is blood on it."

Then Tirian felt something like a tiny sponge dabbing his face, and it was most refreshing.

"Little friends," said Tirian, "how can I thank you for all this?"

"You needn't, you needn't," said the little voices. "What else could we do? We don't want any other King. We're your people. If it was only the Ape and the Calormenes who were against you we would have fought till we were cut into pieces before we'd have let them tie you up. We would, we would indeed. But we can't go against Aslan."

"Do you think it really is Aslan?" asked the King.

"Oh yes, yes," said the Rabbit. "He came out of the stable last night. We all saw him."

"What was he like?" said the King.

"Like a terrible, great Lion, to be sure," said one of the Mice.

"And you think it is really Aslan who is killing the Wood-Nymphs and making you all slaves to the King of Calormen?"

"Ah, that's bad, isn't it?" said the second Mouse. "It would have been better if we'd died before all this began. But there's no doubt about it. Everyone says it is Aslan's orders. And we've seen him. We didn't think Aslan would be like that. Why, we—we *wanted* him to come back to Narnia."

"He seems to have come back very angry this time," said the first Mouse. "We must all have done something dreadfully wrong without knowing it. He must be punishing us for something. But I do think we might be told what it was!"

"I suppose what we're doing now may be wrong," said the Rabbit.

"I don't care if it is," said one of the Moles. "I'd do it again."

But the others said, "Oh hush," and "Do be careful," and then they all said, "We're sorry, dear King, but we must go back now. It would never do for us to be caught here."

"Leave me at once, dear Beasts," said Tirian. "I would not for all Narnia bring any of you into danger."

"Goodnight, goodnight," said the Beasts, rubbing their noses against his knees. "We will come back—if we can." Then they all pattered away and the wood seemed darker and colder and lonelier than it had been before they came.

The stars came out and time went slowly on—imagine how slowly—while the last King of Narnia stood stiff and sore and upright against the tree in his bonds. But at last something happened.

Far away there appeared a red light. Then it disappeared for a moment and came back again, bigger and stronger. Then he could see dark shapes going to and fro on this side of the light and carrying bundles and throwing them down. He knew now what he was looking at. It was a bonfire, newly lit, and people were throwing bundles of brushwood onto it. Presently it blazed up and Tirian could see that it was on the very top of the hill. He could see quite clearly the stable behind it, all lit up in the red glow, and a great crowd of Beasts and Men between the fire and himself. A small figure, hunched up beside the fire, must be the Ape. It was saying something to the crowd, but he could not hear what. Then it went and bowed three times to the ground in front of the door of the stable. Then he got up and opened the door. And something on four legs—something that walked

rather stiffly—came out of the stable and stood facing the crowd.

A great wailing or howling went up, so loud that Tirian could hear some of the words.

"Aslan! Aslan! Aslan!" cried the Beasts. "Speak to us. Comfort us. Be angry with us no more."

From where Tirian was he could not make out very clearly what the thing was; but he could see that it was yellow and hairy. He had never seen the Great Lion. He had never seen a common lion. He couldn't be sure that what he saw was not the real Aslan. He had not expected Aslan to look like that stiff thing which stood and said nothing. But how could one be sure? For a moment horrible thoughts went through his mind: then he remembered the nonsense about Tash and Aslan being the same and knew that the whole thing must be a cheat.

The Ape put his head close up to the yellow thing's head as if he were listening to something it was whispering to him. Then he turned and spoke to the crowd, and the crowd wailed again. Then the yellow thing turned clumsily round and walked—you might almost say, waddled—back into the stable and the Ape shut the door behind it. After that the fire must have been put out for the light vanished quite suddenly, and Tirian was once more alone with the cold and the darkness.

He thought of other Kings who had lived and died in Narnia in old times and it seemed to him that none of them had ever been so unlucky as himself. He thought of his great-grandfather's great-grandfather King Rilian who had been stolen away by a Witch when he was only a young prince and kept hidden for years in the dark caves beneath the land of the Northern Giants. But then it had all come right in the end, for two mysterious children had suddenly appeared from the land beyond the world's end and had rescued him so that he came home to Narnia and had a long and prosperous reign. "It's not like that with me," said Tirian to himself. Then he went further back and thought about Rilian's father, Caspian the Seafarer, whose wicked uncle King Miraz had tried to murder him and how Caspian fled away into the woods and lived among the Dwarfs. But that story too had all come right in the end: for Caspian also had been helped by children— only there were four of them that time—who came from somewhere beyond the world and fought a great battle and set him on his father's throne. "But it was all long ago," said Tirian to himself. "That sort of thing doesn't happen now." And then he remembered (for he had always been good at history when he was a boy)

how those same four children who had helped
Caspian had been in Narnia over a thousand
years before; and it was then that they had done
the most remarkable thing of all. For then they
had defeated the terrible White Witch and
ended the Hundred Years of Winter, and after
that they had reigned (all four of them together)
at Cair Paravel, till they were no longer children
but great Kings and lovely Queens, and their
reign had been the golden age of Narnia. And
Aslan had come into that story a lot. He had
come into all the other stories too, as Tirian
now remembered. "Aslan—and children from
another world," thought Tirian. "They have always come in when things were at their worst.
Oh, if only they could now."

And he called out "Aslan! Aslan! Aslan!
Come and help us now."

But the darkness and the cold and the
quietness went on just the same.

"Let *me* be killed," cried the King. "I ask
nothing for myself. But come and save all
Narnia."

And still there was no change in the night
or the wood, but there began to be a kind of
change inside Tirian. Without knowing why, he
began to feel a faint hope. And he felt somehow
stronger. "Oh Aslan, Aslan," he whispered. "If
you will not come yourself, at least send me the

helpers from beyond the world. Or let me call them. Let my voice carry beyond the world." Then, hardly knowing that he was doing it, he suddenly cried out in a great voice:

"Children! Children! Friends of Narnia! Quick. Come to me. Across the worlds I call you; I Tirian, King of Narnia, Lord of Cair Paravel, and Emperor of the Lone Islands!"

And immediately he was plunged into a dream (if it was a dream) more vivid than any he had had in his life.

He seemed to be standing in a lighted room where seven people sat round a table. It looked as if they had just finished their meal. Two of those people were very old, an old man with a white beard and an old woman with wise, merry, twinkling eyes. He who sat at the right hand of the old man was hardly full grown, certainly younger than Tirian himself, but his face had already the look of a king and a warrior. And you could almost say the same of the other youth who sat at the right hand of the old woman. Facing Tirian across the table sat a fair-haired girl younger than either of these, and on either side of her a boy and girl who were younger still. They were all dressed in what seemed to Tirian the oddest kind of clothes.

But he had no time to think about details like that, for instantly the youngest boy and both the girls started to their feet, and one of them gave a little scream. The old woman started and drew in her breath sharply. The old man must have made some sudden movement too for the wine glass which stood at his right hand was swept off the table: Tirian could hear the tinkling noise as it broke on the floor.

Then Tirian realized that these people could see him; they were staring at him as if they saw a ghost. But he noticed that the king-like one who sat at the old man's right never moved (though he turned pale) except that he clenched his hand very tight. Then he said:

"Speak, if you're not a phantom or a dream. You have a Narnian look about you and we are the seven friends of Narnia."

Tirian was longing to speak, and he tried to cry out aloud that he was Tirian of Narnia, in great need of help. But he found (as I have sometimes found in dreams too) that his voice made no noise at all.

The one who had already spoken to him rose to his feet. "Shadow or spirit or whatever you are," he said, fixing his eyes full upon Tirian. "If you are from Narnia, I charge you in the name of Aslan, speak to me. I am Peter the High King."

The room began to swim before Tirian's eyes. He heard the voices of those seven people all speaking at once, and all getting fainter every second, and they were saying things like, "Look! It's fading." "It's melting away." "It's vanishing." Next moment he was wide awake, still tied to the tree, colder and stiffer than ever. The wood was full of the pale, dreary light that comes before sunrise, and he was soaking wet with dew; it was nearly morning.

That waking was about the worst moment he had ever had in his life.

5

HOW HELP CAME
TO THE KING

But his misery did not last long. Almost at once there came a bump, and then a second bump, and two children were standing before him. The wood in front of him had been quite empty a second before and he knew they had not come from behind his tree, for he would have heard them. They had in fact simply appeared from nowhere. He saw at a glance that they were wearing the same queer, dingy sort of clothes as the people in his dream; and he saw, at a second glance, that they were the youngest boy and girl out of that party of seven.

"Gosh!" said the boy, "that took one's breath away! I thought—"

"Hurry up and get him untied," said the girl. "We can talk, afterward." Then she added, turning to Tirian, "I'm sorry we've been so long. We came the moment we could."

While she was speaking the Boy produced a knife from his pocket and was quickly cutting the King's bonds: too quickly, in fact, for the King was so stiff and numb that when the last cord was cut he fell forward on his hands and knees. He couldn't get up again till he had brought some life back into his legs by a good rubbing.

"I say," said the girl. "It was you, wasn't it, who appeared to us that night when we were all at supper? Nearly a week ago."

"A week, fair maid?" said Tirian. "My dream led me into your world scarce ten minutes since."

"It's the usual muddle about times, Pole," said the Boy.

"I remember now," said Tirian. "That too comes in all the old tales. The time of your strange land is different from ours. But if we speak of Time, 'tis time to be gone from here: for my enemies are close at hand. Will you come with me?"

"Of course," said the girl. "It's you we've come to help."

Tirian got to his feet and led them rapidly down hill, Southward and away from the stable. He knew where he meant to go but his first aim was to get to rocky places where they would leave no trail, and his second to cross some water so that they would leave no scent. This took them about an hour's scrambling and wading and while that was going on nobody had any breath to talk. But even so, Tirian kept on stealing glances at his companions. The wonder of walking beside the creatures from another world made him feel a little dizzy: but it also made all the old stories seem far more real than they had

ever seemed before . . . anything might happen now.

"Now," said Tirian as they came to the head of a little valley which ran down before them among young birch trees, "we are out of danger of those villains for a space and may walk more easily." The sun had risen, dew-drops were twinkling on every branch, and birds were singing.

"What about some grub?—I mean for you, Sir, we two have had our breakfast," said the Boy.

Tirian wondered very much what he meant by "grub," but when the Boy opened a bulgy satchel which he was carrying and pulled out a rather greasy and squashy packet, he understood. He was ravenously hungry, though he hadn't thought about it till that moment. There were two hard-boiled egg sandwiches, and two cheese sandwiches, and two with some kind of paste in them. If he hadn't been so hungry he wouldn't have thought much of the paste, for that is a sort of food nobody eats in Narnia. By the time he had eaten all six sandwiches they had come to the bottom of the valley and there they found a mossy cliff with a little fountain bubbling out of it. All three stopped and drank and splashed their hot faces.

"And now," said the girl as she tossed her wet hair back from her forehead, "aren't you going to tell us who you are and why you were tied up and what it's all about?"

"With a good will, damsel," said Tirian. "But we must keep on the march." So while they went on walking he told them who he was and all the things that had happened to him. "And now," he said at the end, "I am going to a certain tower, one of three that were built in my grandsire's time to guard Lantern Waste against certain perilous outlaws who dwelled there in his day. By Aslan's good will I was not robbed of my keys. In that tower we shall find stores of weapons and mail and some victuals also, though no better than dry biscuit. There also we can lie safe while we make our plans. And now, prithee, tell me who you two are and all your story."

"I'm Eustace Scrubb and this is Jill Pole," said the Boy. "And we were here once before, ages and ages ago, more than a year ago by our time, and there was a chap called Prince Rilian, and they were keeping this chap underground, and Puddleglum put his foot in—"

"Ha!" cried Tirian, "are you then that Eustace and that Jill who rescued King Rilian from his long enchantment?"

"Yes, that's us," said Jill. "So he's *King* Rilian now, is he? Oh of course he would be. I forgot—"

"Nay," said Tirian. "I am the seventh in

descent from him. He has been dead over two hundred years."

Jill made a face. "Ugh!" she said. "That's the horrid part about coming back to Narnia." But Eustace went on.

"Well now you know who we are, Sire," he said. "And it was like this. The Professor and Aunt Polly had got all us friends of Narnia together—"

"I know not these names, Eustace," said Tirian.

"They're the two who came into Narnia at the very beginning, the day all the animals learned to talk."

"By the Lion's Mane," cried Tirian. "Those two! The Lord Digory and the Lady Polly! From the dawn of the world! And still alive in your place? The wonder and the glory of it! But tell me, tell me."

"She isn't really our aunt, you know," said Eustace. "She's Miss Plummer, but we call her Aunt Polly. Well those two got us all together partly just for fun, so that we could all have a good jaw about Narnia (for of course there's no one else we can ever talk to about things like that) but partly because the Professor had a feeling that we were somehow wanted over here. Well then you came in like a ghost or goodness-knows-what and nearly frightened the lives out of us and vanished without saying a word. After that, we knew for certain there was something up. The next question was how to get here. You can't go just by wanting to. So we talked and talked and at last the Professor said the only way would be by the Magic Rings. It was by those Rings that he and Aunt Polly got here long, long ago when they were only kids, years before we younger ones were born. But the Rings had all been buried in the garden of a house in London (that's our big town, Sire) and the house had been sold. So then the problem was how to get at them. You'll never guess what we did in the end! Peter and Edmund—that's the High King Peter, the one who spoke to you— went up to London to get into the garden from the back, early in the morning before people were up. They were dressed like workmen so that if anyone did see them it would look as if they'd come to do something about the drains. I wish I'd been with them: it must have been glorious fun. And they must have succeeded for next day Peter sent us a wire—that's a sort of message, Sire, I'll explain about it some other time—to say he'd got the Rings. And the day after that was the day Pole and I had to go back to school—we're the only two who are still at school and we're at the same one. So Peter and Edmund were to meet us at a place on the way down to school and hand over the Rings. It had to be us two who were to go to Narnia, you see, because the older ones couldn't come again. So we got into the train—that's a kind of thing people travel in in our world: a lot of wagons chained together—and the Professor and Aunt Polly and Lucy came with us. We wanted to keep together as long as we could. Well there we were in the train. And we were just getting to the station where the others were to meet us, and I was looking out of the window to see if I could see them when suddenly there came a most frightful jerk and a noise: and there we were in Narnia and there was your Majesty tied up to the tree."

"So you never used the Rings?" said Tirian.

"No," said Eustace. "Never even saw them. Aslan did it all for us in his own way without any Rings."

"But the High King Peter has them," said Tirian.

"Yes," said Jill. "But we don't think he can use them. When the two other Pevensies—King Edmund and Queen Lucy—were last here, Aslan said they would never come to Narnia again. And he said something of the same sort to the High King, only longer ago. You may be sure he'll come like a shot if he's allowed."

"Gosh!" said Eustace. "It's getting hot in this

sun. Are we nearly there, Sire?"

"Look," said Tirian and pointed. Not many yards away gray battlements rose above the tree-tops, and after a minute's more walking they came out in an open grassy space. A stream ran across it and on the far side of the stream stood a squat, square tower with very few and narrow windows and one heavy-looking door in the wall that faced them.

Tirian looked sharply this way and that to make sure that no enemies were in sight. Then he walked up to the tower and stood still for a moment fishing up his bunch of keys which he wore inside his hunting-dress on a narrow silver chain that went round his neck. It was a nice

bunch of keys that he brought out, for two were golden and many were richly ornamented: you could see at once that they were keys made for opening solemn and secret rooms in palaces, or chests and caskets of sweet-smelling wood that contained royal treasures. But the key which he now put into the lock of the door was big and plain and more rudely made. The lock was stiff and for a moment Tirian began to be afraid that he would not be able to turn it: but at last he did and the door swung open with a sullen creak.

"Welcome friends," said Tirian. "I fear this is the best palace that the King of Narnia can now offer to his guests."

Tirian was pleased to see that the two strangers had been well brought up. They both said not to mention it and that they were sure it would be very nice.

As a matter of fact it was not particularly nice. It was rather dark and smelled very damp. There was only one room in it and this room went right up to the stone roof: a wooden staircase in one corner led up to a trap door by which you could get out on the battlements. There were a few rude bunks to sleep in, and a great many lockers and bundles. There was also a hearth which looked as if nobody had lit a fire in it for a great many years.

"We'd better go out and gather some firewood first thing, hadn't we?" said Jill.

"Not yet, comrade," said Tirian. He was determined that they should not be caught unarmed, and began searching the lockers, thankfully remembering that he had always been careful to have these garrison towers inspected once a year to make sure that they were stocked with all things needful. The bow strings were there in their coverings of oiled silk, the swords and spears were greased against rust, and the armor was kept bright in its wrappings. But there was something even better. "Look!" said Tirian as he drew out a long mail shirt of a curious pattern and flashed it before the children's eyes.

"That's funny-looking mail, Sire," said Eustace.

"Aye, lad," said Tirian. "No Narnian Dwarf smithied that. 'Tis mail of Calormen, outlandish gear. I have ever kept a few suits of it in readiness, for I never knew when I or my friends might have reason to walk unseen in The Tisroc's land. And look on this stone bottle. In this there is a juice which, when we have rubbed it on our hands and faces, will make us brown as Calormenes."

"Oh hurrah!" said Jill. "Disguise! I love disguises."

Tirian showed them how to pour out a little

of the juice into the palms of their hands and then rub it well over their faces and necks, right down to the shoulders, and then on their hands, right up to the elbows. He did the same himself.

"After this has hardened on us," he said, "we may wash in water and it will not change. Nothing but oil and ashes will make us white Narnians again. And now, sweet Jill, let us go see how this mail shirt becomes you. 'Tis something too long, yet not so much as I feared. Doubtless it belonged to a page in the train of one of their Tarkaans."

After the mail shirts they put on Calormene helmets, which are little round ones fitting tight to the head and having a spike on top. Then Tirian took long rolls of some white stuff out of the locker and wound them over the helmets till they became turbans: but the little steel spike still stuck up in the middle. He and Eustace took curved Calormene swords and little round shields. There was no sword light enough for Jill, but he gave her a long, straight hunting knife which might do for a sword at a pinch.

"Hast any skill with the bow, maiden?" said Tirian.

"Nothing worth talking of," said Jill, blushing. "Scrubb's not bad."

"Don't you believe her, Sire," said Eustace. "We've both been practicing archery ever since we got back from Narnia last time, and she's about as good as me now. Not that either of us is much."

Then Tirian gave Jill a bow and a quiver full of arrows. The next business was to light a fire, for inside that tower it still felt more like a cave than like anything indoors and set one shivering. But they got warm gathering the wood—the sun was now at its highest—and when once the blaze was roaring up the chimney the place began to look cheerful. Dinner was, however, a dull meal, for the best they could do was to pound up some of the hard biscuit which they found in a locker and pour it into boiling water, with salt, so as to make a kind of porridge. And of course there was nothing to drink but water.

"I wish we'd brought a packet of tea," said Jill.

"Or a tin of cocoa," said Eustace.

"A firkin or so of good wine in each of these towers would not have been amiss," said Tirian.

6

A GOOD NIGHT'S WORK

About four hours later Tirian flung himself into one of the bunks to snatch a little sleep. The two children were already snoring: he had made them go to bed before he did because they would have to be up most of the night and he knew that at their age they couldn't do without sleep. Also, he had tired them out. First, he had given Jill some practice in archery and found that, though not up to Narnian standards, she was really not too bad. Indeed she had succeeded in shooting a rabbit (not a *Talking* rabbit, of course: there are lots of the ordinary kind about in Western Narnia) and it was already skinned, cleaned, and hanging up. He had found that both the children knew all about this chilly and smelly job; they had learned that kind of thing on their great journey through Giant-Land in the days of Prince Rilian. Then he had tried to teach Eustace how to use his sword and shield. Eustace had learned quite a lot about sword fighting on his earlier adventures but that had been all with a straight Narnian sword. He had never handled a curved Calormene scimitar and that made it hard, for many of the strokes are quite different and some of the habits he had learned with the long sword had now to be unlearned again. But Tirian found that he had a good eye and was very quick on his feet. He was surprised at the strength of both children: in fact they both seemed to be already much stronger and bigger and more grown-up than they had been when he first met them a few hours ago. It is one of the effects which Narnian air often has on visitors from our world.

All three of them agreed that the very first thing they must do was to go back to Stable Hill and try to rescue Jewel the Unicorn. After that, if they succeeded, they would try to get away Eastward and meet the little army which Roonwit the Centaur would be bringing from Cair Paravel.

An experienced warrior and huntsman like

Tirian can always wake up at the time he wants. So he gave himself till nine o'clock that night and then put all worries out of his head and fell asleep at once. It seemed only a moment later when he woke but he knew by the light and the very feel of things that he had timed his sleep exactly. He got up, put on his helmet-and-turban (he had slept in his mail shirt), and then shook the other two till they woke up. They looked, to tell the truth, very gray and dismal as they climbed out of their bunks and there was a good deal of yawning.

"Now," said Tirian, "we go due North from here—by good fortune 'tis a starry night—and it will be much shorter than our journey this morning, for then we went round-about but now we shall go straight. If we are challenged, then do you two hold your peace and I will do my best to talk like a cursed, cruel, proud lord of Calormen. If I draw my sword then thou, Eustace, must do likewise and let Jill leap behind us and stand with an arrow on the string. But if I cry 'Home,' then fly for the Tower both of you. And let none try to fight on—not even one stroke—after I have given the retreat: such false valor has spoiled many notable plans in the wars. And now, friends, in the name of Aslan let us go forward."

Out they went into the cold night. All the

great Northern stars were burning above the tree-tops. The North-Star of that world is called the Spear-Head: it is brighter than our Pole Star.

For a time they could go straight toward the Spear-Head but presently they came to a dense thicket so that they had to go out of their course to get round it. And after that—for they were still overshadowed by branches—it was hard to pick up their bearings. It was Jill who set them right again: she had been an excellent Guide in England. And of course she knew her Narnian stars perfectly, having traveled so much in the wild Northern Lands, and could work out the direction from other stars even when the Spear-Head was hidden. As soon as Tirian saw that she was the best pathfinder of the three of them he put her in front. And then he was astonished to find how silently and almost invisibly she glided on before them.

"By the Mane!" he whispered to Eustace. "This girl is a wondrous wood-maid. If she had Dryad's blood in her she could scarce do it better."

"She's so small, that's what helps," whispered Eustace. But Jill from in front said: "S-s-s-h, less noise."

All round them the wood was very quiet. Indeed it was far too quiet. On an ordinary Narnian night there ought to have been noises—an occasional cheery "Goodnight" from a Hedgehog, the cry of an Owl overhead, perhaps a flute in the distance to tell of Fauns dancing, or some throbbing, hammering noises from Dwarfs underground. All that was silenced: gloom and fear reigned over Narnia.

After a time they began to go steeply uphill and the trees grew further apart. Tirian could dimly make out the well-known hilltop and the stable. Jill was now going with more and more caution: she kept on making signs to the others with her hand to do the same. Then she stopped dead still and Tirian saw her gradually sink down into the grass and disappear without a sound. A moment later she rose again, put her mouth close to Tirian's ear, and said in the lowest possible whisper, "Get down. *Thee* better." She said *thee* for *see* not because she had a lisp but because she knew that the hissing letter S

is the part of a whisper most likely to be over-heard. Tirian at once lay down, almost as silently as Jill, but not quite, for he was heavier and older. And once they were down, he saw how from that position you could see the edge of the hill sharp against the star-strewn sky. Two black shapes rose against it: one was the stable, and the other, a few feet in front of it, was a Calormene sentry. He was keeping very ill watch: not walking or even standing but sitting with his spear over his shoulder and his chin on his chest. "Well done," said Tirian to Jill. She had shown him exactly what he needed to know.

They got up and Tirian now took the lead. Very slowly, hardly daring to breathe, they made their way up to a little clump of trees which was not more than forty feet away from the sentinel.

"Wait here till I come again," he whispered to the other two. "If I miscarry, fly." Then he sauntered out boldly in full view of the enemy. The man started when he saw him and was just going to jump to his feet: he was afraid Tirian might be one of his own officers and that he would get into trouble for sitting down. But before he could get up Tirian had dropped on one knee beside him, saying:

"Art thou a warrior of the Tisroc's, may he live forever? It cheers my heart to meet thee among all these beasts and devils of Narnians. Give me thy hand, friend."

Before he well knew what was happening the Calormene sentry found his right hand seized in a mighty grip. Next instant someone was kneeling on his legs and a dagger was pressed against his neck.

"One noise and thou art dead," said Tirian in his ear. "Tell me where the Unicorn is and thou shalt live."

"B—behind the stable, O My Master," stammered the unfortunate man.

"Good. Rise up and lead me to him."

As the man got up the point of the dagger never left his neck. It only traveled round (cold and rather ticklish) as Tirian got behind him and settled it at a convenient place under his ear. Tremblingly he went round to the back of the stable.

Though it was dark Tirian could see the white shape of Jewel at once.

"Hush!" he said. "No, do not neigh. Yes, Jewel, it is I. How have they tied thee?"

"Hobbled by all four legs and tied with a bridle to a ring in the stable wall," came Jewel's voice.

"Stand here, sentry, with your back to the wall. So. Now, Jewel: set the point of your horn against this Calormene's breast."

"With a good will, Sire," said Jewel.

"If he moves, rive him to the heart." Then in a few seconds Tirian cut the ropes. With the remains of them he bound the sentry hand and foot. Finally he made him open his mouth, stuffed it full of grass and tied him up from scalp to chin so that he could make no noise, lowered the man into a sitting position and set him against the wall.

"I have done thee some discourtesy, soldier," said Tirian. "But such was my need. If we meet again I may happen to do thee a better turn. Now, Jewel, let us go softly."

He put his left arm round the beast's neck and bent and kissed his nose and both had great joy. They went back as quietly as possible to the place where he had left the children. It was darker in there under the trees and he nearly ran into Eustace before he saw him.

"All's well," whispered Tirian. "A good night's work. Now for home."

They turned and had gone a few paces when Eustace said, "Where are you, Pole?" There was no answer. "Is Jill on the other side of you, Sire?" he asked.

"What?" said Tirian. "Is she not on the other side of you?"

It was a terrible moment. They dared not shout but they whispered her name in the loudest whispers they could manage. There was no reply.

"Did she go from you while I was away?" asked Tirian.

"I didn't see or hear her go," said Eustace. "But she could have gone without my knowing. She can be as quiet as a cat; you've seen for yourself."

At that moment a far off drumbeat was heard. Jewel moved his ears forward. "Dwarfs," he said.

"And treacherous Dwarfs, enemies, as likely as not," muttered Tirian.

"And here comes something on hoofs, much nearer," said Jewel.

The two humans and the Unicorn stood dead still. There were now so many different things to worry about that they didn't know what to do. The noise of hoofs came steadily nearer. And then, quite close to them, a voice whispered:

"Hallo! Are you all there?"

Thank heaven, it was Jill's.

"Where the *devil* have you been to?" said Eustace in a furious whisper, for he had been very frightened.

"In the stable," gasped Jill, but it was the sort of gasp you give when you're struggling with suppressed laughter.

"Oh," growled Eustace, "you think it funny, do you? Well all I can say is—"

"Have you got Jewel, Sire?" asked Jill.

"Yes. Here he is. What is that beast with you?"

"That's *him*," said Jill. "But let's be off home before anyone wakes up." And again there came little explosions of laughter.

The others obeyed at once for they had already lingered long enough in that dangerous place and the Dwarf drums seemed to have come a little nearer. It was only after they had been walking Southward for several minutes that Eustace said:

"Got *him*? What do you mean?"

"The false Aslan," said Jill.

"What?" said Tirian. "Where have you been? What have you done?"

"Well, Sire," said Jill. "As soon as I saw that you'd got the sentry out of the way I thought hadn't I better have a look inside the stable and see what really *is* there? So I crawled along. It was as easy as anything to draw the bolt. Of course it was pitch black inside and smelled like any other stable. Then I struck a light and—would you believe it?—there was nothing at all there but this old donkey with a bundle of lion-skin tied onto his back. So I drew my knife and told him he'd have to come along with me. As a matter of fact I needn't have threatened him with the knife at all. He was very fed up with the stable and quite ready to come—weren't you, Puzzle dear?"

"Great Scott!" said Eustace. "Well I'm—jiggered. I was jolly angry with you a moment ago, and I still think it was mean of you to sneak off without the rest of us: but I must admit—well, I mean to say—well it was a perfectly gorgeous thing to do. If she was a boy she'd have to be knighted, wouldn't she, Sire?"

"If she was a boy," said Tirian, "she'd be whipped for disobeying orders." And in the dark no one could see whether he said this with a frown or a smile. Next minute there was a sound of rasping metal.

"What are you doing, Sire?" asked Jewel sharply.

"Drawing my sword to smite off the head of the accursed Ass," said Tirian in a terrible voice. "Stand clear, girl."

"Oh don't, please don't," said Jill. "Really, you mustn't. It wasn't his fault. It was all the Ape. He didn't know any better. And he's very sorry. He's a nice Donkey. His name's Puzzle. And I've got my arms round his neck."

"Jill," said Tirian, "you are the bravest and most wood-wise of all my subjects, but also the most malapert and disobedient. Well: let the

Ass live. What have you to say for yourself, Ass?"

"Me, Sire?" came the Donkey's voice. "I'm sure I'm very sorry if I've done wrong. The Ape said Aslan *wanted* me to dress up like that. And I thought he'd know. I'm not clever like him. I only did what I was told. It wasn't any fun for me living in that stable. I don't even know what's been going on outside. He never let me out except for a minute or two at night. Some days they forgot to give me any water too."

"Sire," said Jewel. "Those Dwarfs are coming nearer and nearer. Do we want to meet them?"

Tirian thought for a moment and then suddenly gave a great laugh out loud. Then he spoke, not this time in a whisper. "By the Lion," he said, "I am growing slow witted! Meet them? Certainly we will meet them. We will meet anyone now. We have this Ass to show them. Let them see the thing they have feared and bowed to. We can show them the truth of the Ape's vile plot. His secret's out. The tide's turned. Tomorrow we shall hang that Ape on the highest tree in Narnia. No more whispering and skulking and disguises. Where are these honest Dwarfs? We have good news for them."

When you have been whispering for hours the mere sound of anyone talking out loud has a

wonderfully stirring effect. The whole party began talking and laughing: even Puzzle lifted up
his head and gave a grand Haw-hee-haw-hee-
hee; a thing the Ape hadn't allowed him to do
for days. Then they set off in the direction of
the drumming. It grew steadily louder and soon
they could see torchlight as well. They came out
on one of those rough roads (we should hardly
call them roads at all in England) which ran
through Lantern Waste. And there, marching
sturdily along, were about thirty Dwarfs, all with
their little spades and mattocks over their shoulders. Two armed Calormenes led the column
and two more brought up the rear.

"Stay!" thundered Tirian as he stepped out
on the road. "Stay, soldiers. Whither do you lead
these Narnian Dwarfs and by whose orders?"

7

MAINLY ABOUT DWARFS

The two Calormene soldiers at the head of the
column, seeing what they took for a Tarkaan or
great lord with two armed pages, came to a halt
and raised their spears in salute.

"O My Master," said one of them, "we lead
these manikins to Calormen to work in the
mines of The Tisroc, may-he-live-forever."

"By the great god Tash, they are very obedient," said Tirian. Then suddenly he turned to
the Dwarfs themselves. About one in six of
them carried a torch and by that flickering light
he could see their bearded faces all looking at
him with grim and dogged expressions. "Has

The Tisroc fought a great battle, Dwarfs, and conquered your land?" he asked, "that thus you go patiently to die in the salt-pits of Pugrahan?"

The two soldiers glared at him in surprise but the Dwarfs all answered, "Aslan's orders, Aslan's orders. He's sold us. What can we do against *him*?"

"Tisroc indeed!" added one and spat. "I'd like to see him try it!"

"Silence, dogs!" said the chief soldier.

"Look!" said Tirian, pulling Puzzle forward into the light. "It has all been a lie. Aslan has not come to Narnia at all. You have been cheated by the Ape. This is the thing he brought out of the stable to show you. Look at it."

What the Dwarfs saw, now that they could see it close, was certainly enough to make them wonder how they had ever been taken in. The lion-skin had got pretty untidy already during Puzzle's imprisonment in the stable and it had been knocked crooked during his journey through the dark wood. Most of it was in a big lump on one shoulder. The head, besides being pushed sideways, had somehow got very far back so that anyone could now see his silly, gentle, donkeyish face gazing out of it. Some grass stuck out of one corner of his mouth, for he'd been do-ing a little quiet nibbling as they brought him

along. And he was muttering, "It wasn't my fault, I'm not clever. I never said I *was*."

For one second all the Dwarfs were staring at Puzzle with wide open mouths and then one of the soldiers said sharply, "Are you mad, My Master? What are you doing to the slaves?" and the other said, "And who are you?" Neither of their spears were at the salute now—both were down and ready for action.

"Give the password," said the chief soldier.

"This is my password," said the King as he drew his sword. "*The light is dawning, the lie broken.* Now guard thee, miscreant, for I am Tirian of Narnia."

He flew upon the chief soldier like lightning. Eustace, who had drawn his sword when he saw the King draw his, rushed at the other one: his face was deadly pale, but I wouldn't blame him for that. And he had the luck that beginners sometimes do have. He forgot all that Tirian had tried to teach him that afternoon, slashed wildly (indeed I'm not sure his eyes weren't shut) and suddenly found, to his own great surprise, that the Calormene lay dead at his feet. And though that was a great relief, it was, at the moment, rather frightening. The King's fight lasted a second or two longer: then he too had killed his man and shouted to Eustace, "'Ware the other two."

But the Dwarfs had settled the two remaining Calormenes. There was no enemy left.

"Well struck, Eustace!" cried Tirian, clapping him on the back. "Now, Dwarfs, you are free. Tomorrow I will lead you to free all Narnia. Three cheers for Aslan!"

But the result which followed was simply wretched. There was a feeble attempt from a few dwarfs (about five) which died away all at once: from several others there were sulky growls. Many said nothing at all.

"Don't they understand?" said Jill impatiently. "What's wrong with all you Dwarfs? Don't you hear what the King says? It's all over. The Ape isn't going to rule Narnia any longer. Everyone can go back to ordinary life. You can have fun again. Aren't you glad?"

After a pause of nearly a minute a not-very-nice-looking Dwarf with hair and beard as black as soot said: "And who might you be, Missie?"

"I'm Jill," she said. "The same Jill who rescued King Rilian from the enchantment—and this is Eustace who did it too—and we've come back from another world after hundreds of years. Aslan sent us."

The Dwarfs all looked at one another with grins; sneering grins, not merry ones.

"Well," said the Black Dwarf (whose name was Griffle), "I don't know how all you chaps feel, but I feel I've heard as much about Aslan as I want to for the rest of my life."

"That's right, that's right," growled the other Dwarfs. "It's all a plant, all a blooming plant."

"What do you mean?" said Tirian. He had not been pale when he was fighting but he was pale now. He had thought this was going to be a beautiful moment, but it was turning out more like a bad dream.

"You must think we're blooming soft in the head, that you must," said Griffle. "We've been taken in once and now you expect us to be taken in again the next minute. We've no more use for stories about Aslan, see! Look at him! An old moke with long ears!"

"By heaven, you make me mad," said Tirian. "Which of us said *that* was Aslan? That is the Ape's imitation of the real Aslan. Can't you understand?"

"And you've got a better imitation, I suppose!" said Griffle. "No thanks. We've been fooled once and we're not going to be fooled again."

"I have not," said Tirian angrily, "I serve the real Aslan."

"Where's he? Who's he? Show him to us!" said several Dwarfs.

"Do you think I keep him in my wallet, fools?" said Tirian. "Who am I that I could make Aslan appear at my bidding? He's not a tame lion."

The moment those words were out of his mouth he realized that he had made a false move. The Dwarfs at once began repeating "not a tame lion, not a tame lion," in a jeering sing-song. "That's what the other lot kept on telling us," said one.

"Do you mean you don't believe in the real Aslan?" said Jill. "But I've seen him. And he has sent us two here out of a different world."

"Ah," said Griffle with a broad smile. "So *you* say. They've taught you your stuff all right. Saying your lessons, ain't you?"

"Churl," cried Tirian, "will you give a lady the lie to her very face?"

"You keep a civil tongue in your head, Mister," replied the Dwarf. "I don't think we want any more Kings—if you *are* Tirian, which you don't look like him—no more than we want any Aslans. We're going to look after ourselves from now on and touch our caps to nobody. See?"

"That's right," said the other Dwarfs. "We're on our own now. No more Aslan, no more Kings, no more silly stories about other worlds. The Dwarfs are for the Dwarfs." And they began to fall into their places and to get ready for marching back to wherever they had come from.

"Little beasts!" said Eustace. "Aren't you even going to say *thank you* for being saved from the salt-mines?"

"Oh, we know all about that," said Griffle

over his shoulder. "You wanted to make use of us, that's why you rescued us. You're playing some game of your own. Come on you chaps."

And the Dwarfs struck up the queer little marching song which goes with the drum-beat, and off they tramped into the darkness.

Tirian and his friends stared after them. Then he said the single word "Come," and they continued their journey.

They were a silent party. Puzzle felt himself to be still in disgrace, and also he didn't really quite understand what had happened. Jill, besides being disgusted with the Dwarfs, was very impressed with Eustace's victory over the Calormene and felt almost shy. As for Eustace, his heart was still beating rather quickly. Tirian and Jewel walked sadly together in the rear. The King had his arm on the Unicorn's shoulder and sometimes the Unicorn nuzzled the King's cheek with his soft nose. They did not try to comfort one another with words. It wasn't very easy to think of anything to say that would be comforting. Tirian had never dreamed that one of the results of an Ape's setting up a false Aslan would be to stop people from believing in the real one. He had felt quite sure that the Dwarfs would rally to his side the moment he showed them how they had been deceived. And then next night he would have led them to Stable

Hill and shown Puzzle to all the creatures and everyone would have turned against the Ape and, perhaps after a scuffle with the Calormenes, the whole thing would have been over. But now, it seemed, he could count on nothing. How many other Narnians might turn the same way as the Dwarfs?

"Somebody's coming after us, I think," said Puzzle suddenly.

They stopped and listened. Sure enough, there was a thump-thump of small feet behind them.

"Who goes there!" shouted the King.

"Only me, Sire," came a voice. "Me, Poggin the Dwarf. I've only just managed to get away from the others. I'm on your side, Sire: and on Aslan's. If you can put a Dwarfish sword in my

93

fist, I'd gladly strike a blow on the right side before all's done."

Everyone crowded round him and welcomed him and praised him and slapped him on the back. Of course one single Dwarf could not make a very great difference, but it was somehow very cheering to have even one. The whole party brightened up. But Jill and Eustace didn't stay bright for very long, for they were now yawning their heads off and too tired to think about anything but bed.

It was at the coldest hour of the night, just before dawn, that they got back to the Tower. If there had been a meal ready for them they would have been glad enough to eat, but the bother and delay of getting one was not to be thought of. They drank from a stream, splashed their faces with water, and tumbled into their bunks, except for Puzzle and Jewel who said they'd be more comfortable outside. This perhaps was just as well, for a Unicorn and a fat, full-grown Donkey indoors always make a room feel rather crowded.

Narnian Dwarfs, though less than four feet high, are for their size about the toughest and strongest creatures there are, so that Poggin, in spite of a heavy day and a late night, woke fully refreshed before any of the others. He at once took Jill's bow, went out and shot a couple of wood pigeons. Then he sat plucking them on the doorstep and chatting to Jewel and Puzzle. Puzzle looked and felt a good deal better this morning. Jewel, being a Unicorn and therefore one of the noblest and most delicate of beasts, had been very kind to him, talking to him about things of the sort they could both understand like grass and sugar and the care of one's hoofs. When Jill and Eustace came out of the Tower yawning and rubbing their eyes at almost half past ten, the Dwarf showed them where they could gather plenty of a Narnian weed called Wild Fresney, which looks rather like our wood-sorrel but tastes a good deal nicer when cooked. (It needs a little butter and pepper to make it perfect, but they hadn't these.) So that what with one thing and another, they had the makings of a capital stew for their breakfast or dinner, whichever you choose to call it. Tirian went a little further off into the wood with an axe and brought back some branches for fuel. While the meal was cooking—which seemed a very long time, especially as it smelled nicer and nicer the nearer it came to being done—the King found a complete Dwarfish outfit for Poggin: mail shirt, helmet, shield, sword, belt, and dagger. Then he inspected Eustace's sword and found that Eustace had put it back in the sheath all messy from killing the Calormene. He was scolded for that and made to clean and polish it.

All this while Jill went to and fro, sometimes stirring the pot and sometimes looking out enviously at the Donkey and the Unicorn who were contentedly grazing. How many times that morning she wished she could eat grass!

But when the meal came everyone felt it had been worth waiting for, and there were second helpings all round. When everyone had eaten as much as he could, the three humans and the Dwarf came and sat on the doorstep, the four-footed ones lay down facing them, the Dwarf (with permission both from Jill and from Tirian) lit his pipe, and the King said:

"Now, friend Poggin, you have more news of the enemy, belike, than we. Tell us all you know. And first, what tale do they tell of my escape?"

"As cunning a tale, Sire, as ever was devised," said Poggin. "It was the Cat, Ginger, who told it, and most likely made it up too. This Ginger, Sire—oh, he's a slyboots if ever a cat was—said he was walking past the tree to which those villains bound your Majesty. And he said (saving your reverence) that you were howling and swearing and cursing Aslan: 'language I wouldn't like to repeat' were the words he used, looking ever so prim and proper—you know the way a Cat can when it pleases. And then, says Ginger, Aslan himself suddenly appeared in a flash of lightning and swallowed your Majesty up at one mouthful. All the Beasts trembled at this story and some fainted right away. And of course the Ape followed it up. There, he says, see what Aslan does to those who don't respect him. Let that be a warning to you all. And the poor creatures wailed and whined and said, it will, it will. So that in the upshot your Majesty's escape has not set them thinking whether you still have loyal friends to aid you, but only made them more afraid and more obedient to the Ape."

"What devilish policy!" said Tirian. "This Ginger, then, is close in the Ape's counsels."

"It's more a question by now, Sire, if the Ape is in *his* counsels," replied the Dwarf. "The Ape has taken to drinking, you see. My belief is that the plot is now mostly carried on by Ginger or Rishda—that's the Calormene captain. And I think some words that Ginger has scattered among the Dwarfs are chiefly to blame for the scurvy return they made you. And I'll tell you why. One of those dreadful midnight meetings had just broken up the night before last and I'd gone a bit of the way home when I found I'd left my pipe behind. It was a real good 'un, an old favorite, so I went back to look for it. But before I got to the place where I'd been sitting (it was black as pitch there) I heard a cat's voice say *Mew* and a Calormene voice say 'here . . . speak softly,' so I just stood as still as if I was frozen. And these two were Ginger and Rishda Tarkaan as they call him. 'Noble Tarkaan,' said the Cat in that silky voice of his, 'I just wanted to know exactly what we both meant today about Aslan meaning *no more* than Tash.' 'Doubtless, most sagacious of cats,' says the other, 'you have perceived my meaning.' 'You mean,' says Ginger, 'that there's no such person as either.' 'All who are enlightened know that,' said the Tarkaan. 'Then we can understand one another,' purrs the Cat. 'Do you, like me, grow a little weary of the Ape?' 'A stupid, greedy brute,' says the other, 'but we must use him for the present. Thou and I must provide for all things in secret and make the Ape do our will.' 'And it would be better, wouldn't it,' said Ginger, 'to let some of the more enlightened Narnians into our counsels: one by one as we find them apt. For the Beasts who really believe in Aslan may turn at any moment: and will, if the Ape's folly betrays his secret. But those who care neither for Tash nor Aslan but have only an eye to their own profit and such reward as The Tisroc may give them when Narnia is a Calormene province, will be firm.' 'Excellent Cat,' said the Captain. 'But choose which ones carefully.'"

While the Dwarf had been speaking the day seemed to have changed. It had been sunny when they sat down. Now Puzzle shivered. Jewel shifted his head uneasily. Jill looked up.

"It's clouding over," she said.

"And it's so cold," said Puzzle.

"Cold enough, by the Lion!" said Tirian, blowing on his hands. "And faugh! What foul smell is this?"

"Phew!" gasped Eustace. "It's like something dead. Is there a dead bird somewhere about? And why didn't we notice it before?"

With a great upheaval Jewel scrambled to his feet and pointed with his horn.

"Look!" he cried. "Look at it! Look, look!"

Then all six of them saw; and over all their faces there came an expression of uttermost dismay.

WHAT NEWS
THE EAGLE BROUGHT

In the shadow of the trees on the far side of the clearing something was moving. It was gliding very slowly Northward. At first glance you might have mistaken it for smoke, for it was gray and you could see things through it. But the deathly smell was not the smell of smoke. Also, this thing kept its shape instead of billowing and curling as smoke would have done. It was roughly the shape of a man but it had the head of a bird; some bird of prey with a cruel, curved beak. It had four arms which it held high above its head, stretching them out Northward as if it

wanted to snatch all Narnia in its grip; and its fingers—all twenty of them—were curved like its beak and had long, pointed, bird-like claws instead of nails. It floated on the grass instead of walking, and the grass seemed to wither beneath it.

After one look at it Puzzle gave a screaming bray and darted into the Tower. And Jill (who was no coward, as you know) hid her face in her hands to shut out the sight of it. The others watched it for perhaps a minute, until it streamed away into the thicker trees on their right and disappeared. Then the sun came out again, and the birds once more began to sing.

Everyone started breathing properly again and moved. They had all been still as statues while it was in sight.

"What was it?" said Eustace in a whisper.

"I have seen it once before," said Tirian. "But that time it was carved in stone and overlaid with gold and had solid diamonds for eyes. It was when I was no older than thou, and had gone as a guest to The Tisroc's court in Tashbaan. He took me into the great temple of Tash. There I saw it, carved above the altar."

"Then that—that thing—was Tash?" said Eustace.

But instead of answering him Tirian slipped his arm behind Jill's shoulders and said, "How is it with you, Lady?"

"A-all right," said Jill, taking her hands away from her pale face and trying to smile. "I'm all right. It only made me feel a little sick for a moment."

"It seems, then," said the Unicorn, "that there is a real Tash, after all."

"Yes," said the Dwarf. "And this fool of an Ape, who didn't believe in Tash, will get more than he bargained for! He called for Tash: Tash has come."

"Where has it—he—the Thing—gone to?" said Jill.

"North into the heart of Narnia," said Tirian. "It has come to dwell among us. They have called it and it has come."

"Ho, ho, ho!" chuckled the Dwarf, rubbing

his hairy hands together. "It will be a surprise for the Ape. People shouldn't call for demons unless they really mean what they say."

"Who knows if Tash will be visible to the Ape?" said Jewel.

"Where has Puzzle got to?" said Eustace.

They all shouted out Puzzle's name and Jill went round to the other side of the Tower to see if he had gone there.

They were quite tired of looking for him when at last his large gray head peered cautiously out of the doorway and he said, "Has it gone away?" And when at last they got him to come out, he was shivering the way a dog shivers before a thunderstorm.

"I see now," said Puzzle, "that I really have been a very bad donkey. I ought never to have listened to Shift. I never thought things like this would begin to happen."

"If you'd spent less time saying you weren't clever and more time trying to be as clever as you could—" began Eustace but Jill interrupted him.

"Oh leave poor old Puzzle alone," she said. "It was all a mistake; wasn't it, Puzzle dear?" And she kissed him on the nose.

Though rather shaken by what they had seen, the whole party now sat down again and went on with their talk.

Jewel had little to tell them. While he was a prisoner he had spent nearly all his time tied up at the back of the stable, and had of course heard none of the enemies' plans. He had been kicked (he'd done some kicking back too) and beaten and threatened with death unless he would say that he believed it was Aslan who was brought out and shown to them by firelight every night. In fact he was going to be executed this very morning if he had not been rescued. He didn't know what had happened to the Lamb.

The question they had to decide was whether they would go to Stable Hill again that night, show Puzzle to the Narnians and try to make them see how they had been tricked, or whether they should steal away Eastward to meet the help which Roonwit the Centaur was bringing up from Cair Paravel and return against the Ape and his Calormenes in force. Tirian would very much like to have followed the first plan: he hated the idea of leaving the Ape to bully his people one moment longer than need be. On the other hand, the way the Dwarfs had behaved last night was a warning. Apparently one couldn't be sure how people would take it even if he showed them Puzzle. And there were the Calormene soldiers to be reckoned with. Poggin thought there were about thirty of them. Tirian felt sure that if the Narnians all rallied to his side, he and Jewel and the children and Poggin (Puzzle didn't count for much) would have a good chance of beating them. But what if half the Narnians—including all the Dwarfs—just sat and looked on? or even fought against him? The risk was too great. And there was, too, the cloudy shape of Tash. What might it do?

And then, as Poggin pointed out, there was no harm in leaving the Ape to deal with his own difficulties for a day or two. He would have no Puzzle to bring out and show now. It wasn't easy to see what story he—or Ginger—could make up to explain that. If the Beasts asked night after night to see Aslan, and no Aslan was brought out, surely even the simplest of them would get suspicious.

In the end they all agreed that the best thing was to go off and try to meet Roonwit.

As soon as they had decided this, it was wonderful how much more cheerful everyone became. I don't honestly think that this was because any of them was afraid of a fight (except perhaps Jill and Eustace). But I daresay that each of them, deep down inside, was very glad not to go any nearer—or not yet—to that horrible bird-headed thing which, visible or invisible, was now probably haunting Stable Hill.

Anyway, one always feels better when one has made up one's mind.

Tirian said they had better remove their disguises, as they didn't want to be mistaken for Calormenes and perhaps attacked by any loyal Narnians they might meet. The Dwarf made up a horrid-looking mess of ashes from the hearth and grease out of the jar of grease which was kept for rubbing on swords and spear-heads. Then they took off their Calormene armor and went down to the stream. The nasty mixture made a lather just like soft soap: it was a pleasant, homely sight to see Tirian and the two children kneeling beside the water and scrubbing the backs of their necks or puffing and blowing as they splashed the lather off. Then they went back to the Tower with red, shiny faces, looking like people who have been given an extra good wash before a party. They rearmed themselves in true Narnian style, with straight swords and three-cornered shields. "Body of me," said Tirian. "That is better. I feel a true man again."

Puzzle begged very hard to have the lionskin taken off him. He said it was too hot and the way it was rucked up on his back was uncomfortable: also, it made him look so silly. But they told him he would have to wear it a bit longer, for they still wanted to show him in that get-up to the other Beasts, even though they were now going to meet Roonwit first.

What was left of the pigeon-meat and rabbit-meat was not worth bringing away but they took some biscuits. Then Tirian locked the door of the Tower and that was the end of their stay there.

It was a little after two in the afternoon when they set out, and it was the first really warm day of that spring. The young leaves seemed to be much further out than yesterday: the snow-drops were over, but they saw several primroses. The sunlight slanted through the trees, birds sang, and always (though usually out of sight) there was the noise of running water. It was hard to think of horrible things like Tash. The children felt, "This is really Narnia at last." Even Tirian's heart grew lighter as he walked ahead of them, humming an old Narnian marching song which had the refrain:

> Ho, *rumble, rumble, rumble,*
> *Rumble drum belabored.*

After the King came Eustace and Poggin the Dwarf. Poggin was telling Eustace the names of all the Narnian trees, birds, and plants which he didn't know already. Sometimes Eustace would tell him about English ones.

After them came Puzzle, and after him Jill

and Jewel walking very close together. Jill had, as you might say, quite fallen in love with the Unicorn. She thought—and she wasn't far wrong—that he was the shiningest, delicatest, most graceful animal she had ever met: and he was so gentle and soft of speech that, if you hadn't known, you would hardly have believed how fierce and terrible he could be in battle.

"Oh, this *is* nice!" said Jill. "Just walking along like this. I wish there could be more of *this* sort of adventure. It's a pity there's always so much happening in Narnia."

But the Unicorn explained to her that she was quite mistaken. He said that the Sons and Daughters of Adam and Eve were brought out of their own strange world into Narnia only at times when Narnia was stirred and upset, but she mustn't think it was always like that. In between their visits there were hundreds and thousands of years when peaceful King followed peaceful King till you could hardly remember their names or count their numbers, and there was really hardly anything to put into the History Books. And he went on to talk of old Queens and heroes whom she had never heard of. He spoke of Swanwhite the Queen who had lived before the days of the White Witch and the Great Winter, who was so beautiful that when she looked into any forest pool the reflection of her face shone out of the water like a star by night for a year and a day afterward. He spoke of Moonwood the Hare who had such ears that he could sit by Caldron Pool under the thunder of the great waterfall and hear what men spoke in whispers at Cair Paravel. He told how King Gale, who was ninth in descent from Frank the first of all Kings, had sailed far away into the Eastern seas and delivered the Lone Islanders from a dragon and how, in return, they had given him the Lone Islands to be part of the royal lands of Narnia forever. He talked of whole centuries in which all Narnia was so happy that notable dances and feasts, or at most tournaments, were the only things that could be remembered, and every day and week had been better than the last. And as he went on, the picture of all those happy years, all the thousands of them, piled up in Jill's mind till it was rather like looking down from a high hill onto a rich, lovely plain full of woods and waters and cornfields, which spread away and away till it got thin and misty from distance. And she said:

"Oh, I do hope we can soon settle the Ape and get back to those good, ordinary times. And then I hope they'll go on forever and ever and ever. *Our* world is going to have an end some day. Perhaps this one won't. Oh Jewel— wouldn't it be lovely if Narnia just went on and on—like what you said it has been?"

"Nay, sister," answered Jewel, "all worlds draw to an end, except Aslan's own country."

"Well, at least," said Jill, "I hope the end of this one is millions of millions of millions of years away—hallo! what are we stopping for?"

The King and Eustace and the Dwarf were all staring up at the sky. Jill shuddered, remembering what horrors they had seen already. But it was nothing of that sort this time. It was small, and looked black against the blue.

"I dare swear," said the Unicorn, "from its flight, that it is a Talking bird."

"So think I," said the King. "But is it a friend, or a spy of the Ape's?"

"To me, Sire," said the Dwarf, "it has a look of Farsight the Eagle."

"Ought we to hide under the trees?" said Eustace.

"Nay," said Tirian, "best stand still as rocks. He would see us for certain if we moved."

"Look! He wheels, he has seen us already," said Jewel. "He is coming down in wide circles."

"Arrow on string, Lady," said Tirian to Jill. "But by no means shoot till I bid you. He may be a friend."

If one had known what was going to happen next it would have been a treat to watch the grace and ease with which the huge bird glided

down. He alighted on a rocky crag a few feet
from Tirian, bowed his crested head, and said in
his strange eagle's-voice, "Hail, King."

"Hail, Farsight," said Tirian. "And since you
call me King, I may well believe you are not a
follower of the Ape and his false Aslan. I am
glad of your coming."

"Sire," said the Eagle, "when you have heard
my news you will be sorrier at my coming than
of the greatest woe that ever befell you."

Tirian's heart seemed to stop beating at
these words, but he set his teeth and said,
"Tell on."

"Two sights have I seen," said Farsight.
"One was Cair Paravel filled with dead

Narnians and living Calormenes: The Tisroc's banner advanced upon your royal battlements: and your subjects flying from the city—this way and that, into the woods. Cair Paravel was taken from the sea. Twenty great ships of Calormen put in there in the dark of the night before last night."

No one could speak.

"And the other sight, five leagues nearer than Cair Paravel, was Roonwit the Centaur lying dead with a Calormene arrow in his side. I was with him in his last hour and he gave me this message to your Majesty: to remember that all worlds draw to an end and that noble death is a treasure which no one is too poor to buy."

"So," said the King, after a long silence, "Narnia is no more."

9

THE GREAT MEETING
ON STABLE HILL

For a long time they could not speak nor even shed a tear. Then the Unicorn stamped the ground with his hoof, and shook his mane, and spoke.

"Sire," he said, "there is now no need of counsel. We see that the Ape's plans were laid deeper than we dreamed of. Doubtless he has been long in secret traffic with The Tisroc, and as soon as he had found the lion-skin he sent him word to make ready his navy for the taking of Cair Paravel and all Narnia. Nothing now remains for us seven but to go back to Stable Hill, proclaim the truth, and take the adventure that Aslan sends us. And if, by a great marvel, we defeat those thirty Calormenes who are with the Ape, then to turn again and die in battle with the far greater host of them that will soon march from Cair Paravel."

Tirian nodded. But he turned to the children and said: "Now, friends, it is time for you to go hence into your own world. Doubtless you have done all that you were sent to do."

"B—but we've done nothing," said Jill who was shivering, not with fear exactly but because everything was so horrible.

"Nay," said the King, "you loosed me from the tree: you glided before me like a snake last night in the wood and took Puzzle: and you, Eustace, killed your man. But you are too young to share in such a bloody end as we others must meet tonight or, it may be, three days hence. I entreat you—nay, I command you—to return to your own place. I should be put to shame if I let such young warriors fall in battle on my side."

"No, no, no," said Jill (very white when she began speaking and then suddenly very red and then white again). "We won't, I don't care what you say. We're going to stick with you whatever happens, aren't we, Eustace?"

"Yes, but there's no need to get so worked up about it," said Eustace who had stuck his hands in his pockets (forgetting how very odd that looks when you are wearing a mail shirt). "Because, you see, we haven't any choice. What's the good of talking about our going back! How? We've got no magic for doing it!"

This was very good sense but, at the moment, Jill hated Eustace for saying it. He was fond of being dreadfully matter-of-fact when other people got excited.

When Tirian realized that the two strangers could not get home (unless Aslan suddenly whisked them away), he next wanted them to go across the Southern mountains into Archenland where they might possibly be safe. But they didn't know their way and there was no one to send with them. Also, as Poggin said, once the Calormenes had Narnia they would certainly take Archenland in the next week or so: The Tisroc had always wanted to have these Northern countries for his own. In the end Eustace and Jill begged so hard that Tirian said they could come with him and take their chance—or, as he much more sensibly called it, "the adventure that Aslan would send them."

The King's first idea was that they should not go back to Stable Hill—they were sick of the very name of it by now—till after dark. But the Dwarf told them that if they arrived there by daylight they would probably find the place deserted, except perhaps for a Calormene sentry. The Beasts were far too frightened by what the Ape (and Ginger) had told them about this new angry Aslan—or Tashlan—to go near it except when they were called together for those horrible midnight meetings. And Calormenes are never good woodsmen. Poggin thought that even by daylight they could easily get round to somewhere behind the stable without being seen. This would be much harder to do when the night had come and the Ape might be calling the Beasts together and all the Calormenes were on duty. And when the meeting did begin they could leave Puzzle at the back of the stable, completely out of sight, till the moment at which they wanted to produce him. This was obviously a good thing: for their only chance was to give the Narnians a sudden surprise.

Everyone agreed and the whole party set off on a new line—Northwest—toward the hated Hill. The Eagle sometimes flew to and fro above them, sometimes he sat perched on Puzzle's back. No one—not even the King himself except in some great need—would dream of *riding* on a Unicorn.

This time Jill and Eustace walked together. They had been feeling very brave when they were begging to be allowed to come with the others, but now they didn't feel brave at all.

"Pole," said Eustace in a whisper. "I may as well tell you I've got the wind up."

"Oh *you're* all right, Scrubb," said Jill. "You can fight. But I—I'm just shaking, if you want to know the truth."

"Oh shaking's nothing," said Eustace. "I'm feeling I'm going to be sick."

"Don't talk about *that*, for goodness' sake," said Jill.

They went on in silence for a minute or two.

"Pole," said Eustace presently.

"What?" said she.

"What'll happen if we get killed here?"

"Well we'll be dead, I suppose."

"But I mean, what will happen in our own world? Shall we wake up and find ourselves back in that train? Or shall we just vanish and never be heard of any more? Or shall we be dead in England?"

"Gosh. I never thought of that."

"It'll be rum for Peter and the others if they saw me waving out of the window and then when the train comes in we're nowhere to be found! Or if they found two—I mean, if we're dead over there in England."

"Ugh!" said Jill. "What a horrid idea."

"It wouldn't be horrid for *us*," said Eustace. "We shouldn't be there."

"I almost wish—no I don't, though," said Jill.

"What were you going to say?"

"I *was* going to say I wished we'd never come. But I don't, I don't, I don't. Even if we *are* killed. I'd rather be killed fighting for Narnia than grow old and stupid at home and perhaps go about in a bath-chair and then die in the end just the same."

"Or be smashed up by British Railways!"

"Why d'you say that?"

"Well when that awful jerk came—the one that seemed to throw us into Narnia—I thought it *was* the beginning of a railway accident. So I was jolly glad to find ourselves here instead."

While Jill and Eustace were talking about this, the others were discussing their plans and becoming less miserable. That was because they were now thinking of what was to be done this very night and the thought of what had happened to Narnia—the thought that all her glories and joys were over—was pushed away into the back part of their minds. The moment they stopped talking it would come out and make them wretched again: but they kept on talking. Poggin was really quite cheerful about the night's work they had to do. He was sure that the Boar and the Bear, and probably all the Dogs would come over to their side at once. And he couldn't believe that all the other Dwarfs would stick to Griffle. And fighting by firelight and in and out among trees would be an advantage to the weaker side. And then, if they could win tonight, need they really throw their lives away by meeting the main Calormene army a few days later?

Why not hide in the woods, or even up in the Western Waste beyond the great waterfall and live like outlaws? And they might gradually get stronger and stronger, for Talking Beasts and Archenlanders would be joining them every day. And at last they'd come out of hiding and sweep the Calormenes (who would have got careless by then) out of the country and Narnia would be revived. After all, something very like that had happened in the time of King Miraz!

And Tirian heard all this and thought "But what about Tash?" and felt in his bones that none of it was going to happen. But he didn't say so.

When they got nearer to Stable Hill of course everyone became quiet. Then the real wood-work began. From the moment at which they first saw the Hill to the moment at which they all arrived at the back of the stable, it took them over two hours. It's the sort of thing one couldn't describe properly unless one wrote pages and pages about it. The journey

from each bit of cover to the next was a separate adventure, and there were very long waits in between, and several false alarms. If you are a good Scout or a good Guide you will know already what it must have been like. By about sunset they were all safe in a clump of holly trees about fifteen yards behind the stable. They all munched some biscuit and lay down.

Then came the worst part, the waiting. Luckily for the children they slept for a couple of hours, but of course they woke up when the night grew cold, and what was worse, woke up very thirsty and with no chance of getting a drink. Puzzle just stood, shivering a little with nervousness, and said nothing. But Tirian, with his head against Jewel's flank, slept as soundly as if he were in his royal bed at Cair Paravel, till the sound of a gong beating awoke him and he sat up and saw that there was firelight on the far side of the stable and knew that the hour had come.

"Kiss me, Jewel," he said. "For certainly this is our last night on earth. And if ever I offended against you in any matter great or small, forgive me now."

"Dear King," said the Unicorn, "I could almost wish you had, so that I might forgive it. Farewell. We have known great joys together. If Aslan gave me my choice I would choose no other life than the life I have had and no other death than the one we go to."

Then they woke up Farsight, who was asleep with his head under his wing (it made him look as if he had no head at all), and crept forward to the stable. They left Puzzle (not without a kind word, for no one was angry with him now) just behind it, telling him not to move till someone came to fetch him, and took up their position at one end of the stable.

The bonfire had not been lit for long and was just beginning to blaze up. It was only a few feet away from them, and the great crowd of Narnian creatures were on the other side of it, so that Tirian could not at first see them very well, though of course he saw dozens of eyes shining with the reflection of the fire, as you've seen a rabbit's or cat's eyes in the headlights of a car. And just as Tirian took his place, the gong stopped beating and from somewhere on his left three figures appeared. One was Rishda Tarkaan the Calormene Captain. The second was the Ape. He was holding on to the Tarkaan's hand with one paw and kept whimpering and muttering, "Not so fast, don't go so fast, I'm not *at all* well. Oh my poor head! These midnight meetings are getting too much for me. Apes aren't meant to be up at night: It's not as if I was a rat or a bat—oh my poor head." On the other side of the Ape, walking very soft and stately, with his tail straight up in the air, came Ginger the Cat. They were heading for the bonfire and were so close to Tirian that they would have seen him at once if they had looked in the right direction. Fortunately they did not. But Tirian heard Rishda say to Ginger in a low voice:

"Now, Cat, to thy post. See thou play thy part well."

"Miaow, miaow. Count on me!" said Ginger. Then he stepped away beyond the bonfire and sat down in the front row of the assembled Beasts: in the audience, as you might say.

For really, as it happened, the whole thing was rather like a theater. The crowd of Narnians were like the people in the seats; the little grassy place just in front of the stable, where the

bonfire burned and the Ape and the Captain stood to talk to the crowd, was like the stage; the stable itself was like the scenery at the back of the stage; and Tirian and his friends were like people peering round from behind the scenery. It was a splendid position. If any of them stepped forward into the full firelight, all eyes would be fixed on him at once: on the other hand, so long as they stood still in the shadow of the end-wall of the stable, it was a hundred to one against their being noticed.

Rishda Tarkaan dragged the Ape up close to the fire. The pair of them turned to face the crowd, and this of course meant that their backs were toward Tirian and his friends.

"Now, Monkey," said Rishda Tarkaan in a low voice. "Say the words that wiser heads have put into thy mouth. And hold up thy head." As he spoke he gave the Ape a little prod or kick from behind with the point of his toe.

"Do leave me alone," muttered Shift. But he sat up straighter and began, in a louder voice— "Now listen, all of you. A terrible thing has happened. A wicked thing. The wickedest thing that ever was done in Narnia. And Aslan—"

"Tashlan, fool," whispered Rishda Tarkaan.

"Tashlan I mean, of course," said the Ape, "is very angry about it."

There was a terrible silence while the Beasts

waited to hear what new trouble was in store for them. The little party by the end-wall of the stable also held their breath. What on earth was coming now?

"Yes," said the Ape. "At this very moment, when the Terrible One himself is among us— there in the stable just behind me—one wicked Beast has chosen to do what you'd think no one would dare to do even if *He* were a thousand miles away. It has dressed itself up in a lion-skin and is wandering about in these very woods pretending to be Aslan."

Jill wondered for a moment if the Ape had gone mad. Was he going to tell the whole truth? A roar of horror and rage went up from the Beasts. "Grrr!" came the growls. "Who is he? Where is he? Just let me get my teeth into him!"

"It was seen last night," screamed the Ape, "but it got away. It's a Donkey! A common, miserable Ass! If any of you see that Ass—"

"Grrr!" growled the Beasts. "We will, we will. He'd better keep out of *our* way."

Jill looked at the King: his mouth was open and his face was full of horror. And then she understood the devilish cunning of the enemies' plan. By mixing a little truth with it they had made their lie far stronger. What was the good, now, of telling the Beasts that an ass had been dressed up as a lion to deceive them? The Ape would only say, "That's just what I've said." What was the good of showing them Puzzle in his lion-skin? They would only tear him in pieces. "That's taken the wind out of our sails," whispered Eustace. "The ground is taken from under our feet," said Tirian. "Cursed, cursed cleverness!" said Poggin. "I'll be sworn that this new lie is of Ginger's making."

10

WHO WILL GO
INTO THE STABLE?

Jill felt something tickling her ear. It was Jewel
the Unicorn, whispering to her with the wide
whisper of a horse's mouth. As soon as she heard
what he was saying she nodded and tiptoed back
to where Puzzle was standing. Quickly and quietly she cut the last cords that bound the lion-
skin to him. It wouldn't do for him to be caught
with *that* on, after what the Ape had said! She
would like to have hidden the skin somewhere
very far away, but it was too heavy. The best she
could do was to kick it in among the thickest
bushes. Then she made signs to Puzzle to follow

her and they both joined the others.

The Ape was speaking again.

"And after a horrid thing like that, Aslan—Tashlan—is angrier than ever. He says he's been a great deal too good to you, coming out every night to be looked at, see! Well, he's not coming out any more."

Howls and mewings and squeals and grunts were the Animals' answer to this, but suddenly a quite different voice broke in with a loud laugh.

"Hark what the monkey says," it shouted. "We know why he isn't going to bring his precious Aslan out. I'll tell you why: because he hasn't got him. He never had anything except an old donkey with a lion-skin on its back. Now he's lost *that* and he doesn't know what to do."

Tirian could not see the faces on the other side of the fire very well but he guessed this was Griffle the Chief Dwarf. And he was quite certain of it when, a second later, all the Dwarfs' voices joined in, singing: "Don't know what to do! Don't know what to do! Don't know what to do-o-o!"

"Silence!" thundered Rishda Tarkaan. "Silence, children of mud! Listen to me, you other Narnians, lest I give command to my warriors to fall upon you with the edge of the sword. The Lord Shift has already told you of that wicked Ass. Do you think, because of him that there is no *real* Tashlan in the stable! Do you? Beware, beware."

"No, no," shouted most of the crowd. But the Dwarfs said, "That's right, Darkie, you've got it. Come on, Monkey, show us what's in the stable, seeing is believing."

When next there was a moment's quiet the Ape said:

"You Dwarfs think you're very clever, don't you? But not so fast. I never said you couldn't see Tashlan. Anyone who likes can see him."

The whole assembly became silent. Then, after nearly a minute, the Bear began in a slow, puzzled voice:

"I don't quite understand all this," it grumbled, "I thought you said—"

"*You* thought!" repeated the Ape. "As if anyone could call what goes on in your head *thinking*. Listen, you others. Anyone can see Tashlan. But he's not coming out. You have to go in and see *him*."

"Oh, thank you, thank you, thank you," said dozens of voices. "That's what we wanted! We can go in and see him face to face. And now he'll be kind and it will all be as it used to be." And the Birds chattered, and the Dogs barked excitedly. Then suddenly, there was a great stirring and a noise of creatures rising to their feet, and in a second the whole lot of them would have been rushing forward and trying to crowd into the stable door all together. But the Ape shouted:

"Get back! Quiet! Not so fast."

The Beasts stopped, many of them with one paw in the air, many with tails wagging, and all of them with heads on one side.

"I thought you said," began the Bear, but Shift interrupted.

"Anyone can go in," he said. "But, one at a time. Who'll go first? He didn't *say* he was feeling very kind. He's been licking his lips a lot since he swallowed up the wicked King the other night. He's been growling a good deal this morning. I wouldn't much like to go into that stable myself tonight. But just as you please. Who'd like to go in first? Don't blame me if he swallows you whole or blasts you into a cinder with the mere terror of his eyes. That's your affair. Now then! Who's first? What about one of you Dwarfs?"

"Dilly, dilly, come and be killed!" sneered Griffle. "How do we know what you've got in there?"

"Ho-ho!" cried the Ape. "So you're beginning to think there's *something* there, eh? Well, all you Beasts were making noise enough a minute ago. What's struck you all dumb? Who's going in first?"

But the Beasts all stood looking at one another and began backing away from the stable. Very few tails were wagging now. The Ape waddled to and fro jeering at them. "Ho-ho-ho!" he chuckled. "I thought you were all so eager to see Tashlan face to face! Changed your mind, eh?"

Tirian bent his head to hear something that Jill was trying to whisper in his ear. "What do you think is really inside the stable?" she said. "Who knows?" said Tirian. "Two Calormenes with drawn swords, as likely as not, one on each side of the door." "You don't think," said Jill, "it might be . . . you know . . . that horrid thing we saw?" "Tash himself?" whispered Tirian.

"There's no knowing. But courage, child: we are all between the paws of the true Aslan."

Then a most surprising thing happened. Ginger the Cat said in a cool, clear voice, not at all as if he was excited, "I'll go in, if you like."

Every creature turned and fixed its eyes on the Cat. "Mark their subtleties, Sire," said Poggin to the King. "This cursed cat is in the plot, in the very center of it. Whatever is in the stable will not hurt him, I'll be bound. Then Ginger will come out again and say that he has seen some wonder."

But Tirian had no time to answer him. The Ape was calling the Cat to come forward. "Hoho!" said the Ape. "So you, a pert Puss, would look upon him face to face. Come on, then! I'll open the door for you. Don't blame me if he scares the whiskers off your face. That's your affair."

And the Cat got up and came out of its

place in the crowd, walking primly and daintily, with its tail in the air, not one hair on its sleek coat out of place. It came on till it had passed the fire and was so close that Tirian, from where he stood with his shoulder against the end-wall of the stable, could look right into its face. Its big green eyes never blinked. ("Cool as a cucumber," muttered Eustace. "*It* knows it has nothing to fear.") The Ape, chuckling and making faces, shuffled across beside the Cat: put up his paw: drew the bolt and opened the door. Tirian thought he could hear the Cat purring as it walked into the dark doorway.

"Aii-aii-aouwee!—" The most horrible caterwaul you ever heard made everyone jump. You have been wakened yourself by cats quarreling or making love on the roof in the middle of the night: you know the sound.

This was worse. The Ape was knocked head over heels by Ginger coming back out of the

135

stable at top speed. If you had not known he was a cat, you might have thought he was a ginger-colored streak of lightning. He shot across the open grass, back into the crowd. No one wants to meet a cat in that state. You could see animals getting out of his way to left and right. He dashed up a tree, whisked round, and hung head downward. His tail was bristled out till it was nearly as thick as his whole body: his eyes were like saucers of green fire: along his back every single hair stood on end.

"I'd give my beard," whispered Poggin, "to know whether that brute is only acting or whether it has really found something in there that frightened it!"

"Peace, friend," said Tirian, for the Captain and the Ape were also whispering and he wanted to hear what they said. He did not succeed, except that he heard the Ape once more whimpering "My head, my head," but he got the idea that those two were almost as puzzled by the cat's behavior as himself.

"Now, Ginger," said the Captain. "Enough of that noise. Tell them what thou hast seen."

"Aii—Aii—Aaow—Awah," screamed the Cat.

"Art thou not called a *Talking* Beast?" said the Captain. "Then hold thy devilish noise and talk."

What followed was rather horrible. Tirian felt quite certain (and so did the others) that the Cat was trying to say something: but nothing came out of his mouth except the ordinary, ugly cat-noises you might hear from any angry or frightened old Tom in a backyard in England. And the longer he caterwauled the less like a Talking Beast he looked. Uneasy whimperings and little sharp squeals broke out from among the other Animals.

"Look, look!" said the voice of the Bear. "It can't talk. It has forgotten how to talk! It has gone back to being a dumb beast. Look at its face." Everyone saw that it was true. And then the greatest terror of all fell upon those Narnians. For every one of them had been taught—when only a chick or a puppy or a cub—how Aslan at the beginning of the world had turned the beasts of Narnia into Talking Beasts and warned them that if they weren't good they might one day be turned back again and be like the poor witless animals one meets in other countries. "And now it is coming upon us," they moaned.

"Mercy! Mercy!" wailed the Beasts. "Spare us, Lord Shift, stand between us and Aslan, you must always go in and speak to him for us. We daren't, we daren't."

Ginger disappeared further up into the tree.

No one ever saw him again.

Tirian stood with his hand on his sword-hilt and his head bowed. He was dazed with the horrors of that night. Sometimes he thought it would be best to draw his sword at once and rush upon the Calormenes: then next moment he thought it would be better to wait and see what new turn affairs might take. And now a new turn came.

"My Father," came a clear, ringing voice from the left of the crowd. Tirian knew at once that it was one of the Calormenes speaking, for in The Tisroc's army the common soldiers call the officers "My Master" but the officers call their senior officers "My Father." Jill and Eustace didn't know this but, after looking this way and that, they saw the speaker, for of course people at the sides of the crowd were easier to see than people in the middle where the glare of the fire made all beyond it look rather black. He was young and tall and slender, and even rather beautiful in the dark, haughty, Calormene way.

"My Father," he said to the Captain, "I also desire to go in."

"Peace, Emeth," said the Captain. "Who called thee to counsel? Does it become a boy to speak?"

"My Father," said Emeth. "Truly I am younger than thou, yet I also am of the blood of the Tarkaans even as thou art, and I also am the servant of Tash. Therefore . . ."

"Silence," said Rishda Tarkaan. "Am I not thy Captain? Thou hast nothing to do with this stable. It is for the Narnians."

"Nay, my Father," answered Emeth. "Thou hast said that their Aslan and our Tash are all one. And if that is the truth, then Tash himself is in yonder. And how then sayest thou that I have nothing to do with him? For gladly would I die a thousand deaths if I might look once on the face of Tash."

"Thou art a fool and understandest nothing," said Rishda Tarkaan. "These be high matters."

Emeth's face grew sterner. "Is it then not true that Tash and Aslan are all one?" he asked. "Has the Ape lied to us?"

"Of course they're all one," said the Ape.

"Swear it, Ape," said Emeth.

"Oh dear!" whimpered Shift, "I wish you'd all stop bothering me. My head does ache. Yes, yes, I swear it."

"Then, my Father," said Emeth, "I am utterly determined to go in."

"Fool," began Rishda Tarkaan, but at once the Dwarfs began shouting: "Come along, Darkie. Why don't you let him in? Why do you let Narnians in and keep your own people out?

What have you got in there that you don't want your own men to meet?"

Tirian and his friends could only see the back of Rishda Tarkaan, so they never knew what his face looked like as he shrugged his shoulders and said, "Bear witness all that I am guiltless of this young fool's blood. Get thee in, rash boy, and make haste."

Then, just as Ginger had done, Emeth came walking forward into the open strip of grass between the bonfire and the stable. His eyes were shining, his face very solemn, his hand was on his sword-hilt, and he carried his head high. Jill felt like crying when she looked at his face. And Jewel whispered in the King's ear, "By the

Lion's Mane, I almost love this young warrior, Calormene though he be. He is worthy of a better god than Tash."

"I do wish we knew what is really inside there," said Eustace.

Emeth opened the door and went in, into the black mouth of the stable. He closed the door behind him. Only a few moments passed— but it seemed longer—before the door opened again. A figure in Calormene armor reeled out, fell on its back, and lay still: the door closed behind it. The Captain leaped toward it and bent down to stare at its face. He gave a start of surprise. Then he recovered himself and turned to the crowd, crying out:

"The rash boy has had his will. He has looked on Tash and is dead. Take warning, all of you."

"We will, we will," said the poor Beasts. But Tirian and his friends stared first at the dead Calormene and then at one another. For they, being so close, could see what the crowd, being further off and beyond the fire, could not see: this dead man was not Emeth. He was quite different: an older man, thicker and not so tall, with a big beard.

"Ho-ho-ho," chuckled the Ape. "Any more? Anyone else want to go in? Well, as you're all shy, I'll choose the next. You, you Boar! On you

141

come. Drive him up, Calormenes. He *shall* see Tashlan face to face."

"O-o-mph," grunted the Boar, rising heavily to his feet. "Come on, then. Try my tusks."

When Tirian saw that brave Beast getting ready to fight for its life—and Calormene soldiers beginning to close in on him with their drawn scimitars—and no one going to its help—something seemed to burst inside him. He no longer cared if this was the best moment to interfere or not.

"Swords out," he whispered to the others. "Arrow on string. Follow."

Next moment the astonished Narnians saw seven figures leap forth in front of the stable, four of them in shining mail. The King's sword flashed in the firelight as he waved it above his head and cried in a great voice:

"Here stand I, Tirian of Narnia, in Aslan's name, to prove with my body that Tash is a foul fiend, the Ape a manifold traitor, and these Calormenes worthy of death. To my side, all true Narnians. Would you wait till your new masters have killed you all one by one?"

11

THE PACE QUICKENS

Quick as lightning, Rishda Tarkaan leaped back out of reach of the King's sword. He was no coward, and would have fought single-handed against Tirian and the Dwarf if need were. But he could not take on the Eagle and the Unicorn as well. He knew how Eagles can fly into your face and peck at your eyes and blind you with their wings. And he had heard from his father (who had met Narnians in battle) that no man, except with arrows, or a long spear, can match a Unicorn, for it rears on its hind legs as it falls upon you and then you have its hoofs and its horn and its teeth to deal with all at once. So he rushed into the crowd and stood calling out:

"To me, to me, warriors of The Tisroc, may-he-live-forever. To me, all loyal Narnians, lest the wrath of Tashlan fall upon you!"

While this was happening two other things happened as well. The Ape had not realized his danger as quickly as the Tarkaan. For a second or so he remained squatting beside the fire staring at the newcomers. Then Tirian rushed upon the wretched creature, picked it up by the scruff of the neck, and dashed back to the stable shouting, "Open the door!" Poggin opened it. "Go and drink your own medicine, Shift!" said Tirian and hurled the Ape through into the darkness. But as the Dwarf banged the door shut again, a blinding greenish-blue light shone out from the inside of the stable, the earth shook, and there was a strange noise—a clucking and screaming as if it was the hoarse voice of some monstrous bird. The Beasts moaned and howled and called out "Tashlan! Hide us from him!" and many fell down, and many hid their faces in their wings or paws. No one except Farsight the Eagle, who has the best eyes of all living things, noticed the face of Rishda Tarkaan at that moment. And from what Farsight saw there he knew at once that Rishda was just as surprised, and nearly frightened, as everyone else. "There goes one," thought Farsight, "who has called on

gods he does not believe in. How will it be with him if they have really come?"

The third thing—which also happened at the same moment—was the only really beautiful thing that night. Every single Talking Dog in the whole meeting (there were fifteen of them) came bounding and barking joyously to the King's side. They were mostly great big dogs with thick shoulders and heavy jaws. Their coming was like the breaking of a great wave on the sea-beach: it nearly knocked you down. For though they were Talking Dogs they were just as doggy as they could be: and they all stood up and put their front paws on the shoulders of the humans and licked their faces, all saying at once: "Welcome! Welcome! We'll help, we'll help, help, help. Show us how to help, show us how, how. How-how-how?"

It was so lovely that it made you want to cry. This, at last, was the sort of thing they had been hoping for. And when, a moment later, several little animals (mice and moles and a squirrel or so) came pattering up, squealing with joy, and saying "See, see. We're here," and when, after that, the Bear and the Boar came too, Eustace began to feel that perhaps, after all, everything might be going to come right. But Tirian gazed round and saw how very few of the animals had moved.

"To me! to me!" he called. "Have you all

turned cowards since I was your King?"

"We daren't," whimpered dozens of voices. "Tashlan would be angry. Shield us from Tashlan."

"Where are all the Talking Horses?" asked Tirian.

"We've seen, we've seen," squealed the Mice. "The Ape has made them work. They're all tied—down at the bottom of the hill."

"Then all you little ones," said Tirian, "you nibblers and gnawers and nutcrackers, away with you as fast as you can scamper and see if the Horses are on our side. And if they are, get your teeth into the ropes and gnaw till the Horses are free and bring them hither."

"With a good will, Sire," came the small voices, and with a whisk of tails those sharp-eyed and sharp-toothed folk were off. Tirian smiled for mere love as he saw them go. But it was already time to be thinking of other things. Rishda Tarkaan was giving his orders.

"Forward," he said. "Take all of them alive if you can and hurl them into the stable or drive them into it. When they are all in we will put fire to it and make them an offering to the great god Tash."

"Ha!" said Farsight to himself. "So that is how he hopes to win Tash's pardon for his unbelief."

The enemy line—about half of Rishda's force—was now moving forward, and Tirian had barely time to give his orders.

"Out on the left, Jill, and try to shoot all you may before they reach us. Boar and Bear next to her. Poggin on my left, Eustace on my right. Hold the right wing, Jewel. Stand by him, Puzzle, and use your hoofs. Hover and strike, Farsight. You Dogs, just behind us. Go in among them after the sword-play has begun. Aslan to our aid!"

Eustace stood with his heart beating terribly, hoping and hoping that he would be brave. He had never seen anything (though he had seen both a dragon and a sea-serpent) that made his blood run so cold as that line of dark-faced bright-eyed men. There were fifteen Calormenes, a Talking Bull of Narnia, Slinkey the Fox, and Wraggle the Satyr. Then he heard twang-and-zipp on his left and one Calormene fell: then twang-and-zipp again and the Satyr was down. "Oh, well done, daughter!" came Tirian's voice; and then the enemy were upon them.

Eustace could never remember what happened in the next two minutes. It was all like a dream (the sort you have when your temperature is over 100) until he heard Rishda Tarkaan's voice calling out from the distance:

"Retire. Back hither and re-form."

Then Eustace came to his senses and saw the Calormenes scampering back to their friends. But not all of them. Two lay dead, pierced by Jewel's horn, one by Tirian's sword. The Fox lay dead at his own feet, and he wondered if it was he who had killed it. The Bull also was down, shot through the eye by an arrow from Jill and gashed in his side by the Boar's tusk. But our side had its losses too. Three dogs were killed and a fourth was hobbling behind the line on three legs and whimpering. The Bear lay on the ground, moving feebly. Then it mumbled in its throaty voice, bewildered to the last, "I—I don't—understand," laid its big head down on the grass as quietly as a child going to sleep, and never moved again.

In fact, the first attack had failed. Eustace didn't seem able to be glad about it: he was so terribly thirsty and his arm ached so.

As the defeated Calormenes went back to their commander, the Dwarfs began jeering at them.

"Had enough, Darkies?" they yelled. "Don't you like it? Why doesn't your great Tarkaan go and fight himself instead of sending you to be killed? Poor Darkies!"

"Dwarfs," cried Tirian. "Come here and use your swords, not your tongues. There is still time. Dwarfs of Narnia! You can fight well, I know. Come back to your allegiance."

"Yah!" sneered the Dwarfs. "Not likely. You're just as big humbugs as the other lot. We don't want any Kings. The Dwarfs are for the Dwarfs. Boo!"

Then the Drum began: not a Dwarf drum this time, but a big bull's hide Calormene drum. The children from the very first hated the sound. *Boom—boom—ba-ba-boom* it went. But they would have hated it far worse if they had known what it meant. Tirian did. It meant that there were other Calormene troops somewhere near and that Rishda Tarkaan was calling them to his aid. Tirian and Jewel looked at one another sadly. They had just begun to hope that they might win that night: but it would be all over with them if new enemies appeared.

Tirian gazed despairingly round. Several Narnians were standing with the Calormenes, whether through treachery or in honest fear of "Tashlan." Others were sitting still, staring, not likely to join either side. But there were fewer animals now: the crowd was much smaller. Clearly, several of them had just crept quietly away during the fighting.

Boom—boom—ba-ba-boom went the horrible drum. Then another sound began to mix with it. "Listen!" said Jewel: and then "Look!"

said Farsight. A moment later there was no doubt what it was. With a thunder of hoofs, with tossing heads, widened nostrils, and waving manes, over a score of Talking Horses of Narnia came charging up the hill. The gnawers and nibblers had done their work.

Poggin the Dwarf and the children opened their mouths to cheer but that cheer never came. Suddenly the air was full of the sound of twanging bow-strings and hissing arrows. It was the Dwarfs who were shooting and—for a moment Jill could hardly believe her eyes—they were shooting the Horses. Dwarfs are deadly archers. Horse after Horse rolled over. Not one of those noble Beasts ever reached the King.

"Little *Swine*," shrieked Eustace, dancing in his rage. "Dirty, filthy, treacherous little brutes." Even Jewel said, "Shall I run after those Dwarfs, Sire, and spit ten of them on my horn at each plunge?" But Tirian with his face as stern as stone, said, "Stand fast, Jewel. If you must weep, sweetheart" (this was to Jill), "turn your face aside and see you wet not your bow-string. And peace, Eustace. Do not scold, like a kitchen-girl. No warrior scolds. Courteous words or else hard knocks are his only language."

But the Dwarfs jeered back at Eustace. "That was a surprise for you, little boy, eh? Thought we were on *your* side, did you? No fear.

We don't want any Talking Horses. We don't want you to win any more than the other gang. You can't take *us* in. The Dwarfs are for the Dwarfs."

Rishda Tarkaan was still talking to his men, doubtless making arrangements for the next attack and probably wishing he had sent his whole force into the first. The drum boomed on. Then, to their horror, Tirian and his friends heard, far fainter as if from a long way off, an answering drum. Another body of Calormenes had heard Rishda's signal and were coming to support him. You would not have known from Tirian's face that he had now given up all hope.

"Listen," he whispered in a matter-of-fact voice, "we must attack now, before yonder miscreants are strengthened by their friends."

"Bethink you, Sire," said Poggin, "that here we have the good wooden wall of the stable at our backs. If we advance, shall we not be encircled and get sword-points between our shoulders?"

"I would say as you do, Dwarf," said Tirian. "Were it not their very plan to force us into the stable? The further we are from its deadly door, the better."

"The King is right," said Farsight. "Away from this accursed stable, and whatever goblin lives inside it, at all costs."

"Yes, do let's," said Eustace. "I'm coming to hate the very sight of it."

"Good," said Tirian. "Now look yonder to our left. You see a great rock that gleams white like marble in the firelight. First we will fall upon those Calormenes. You, maiden, shall move out on our left and shoot as fast as ever you may into their ranks: and you, Eagle, fly at their faces from the right. Meanwhile, we others will be charging them. When we are so close, Jill, that you can no longer shoot at them for fear of striking us, go back to the white rock and wait. You others, keep your ears wide even in the fighting. We must put them to flight in a few minutes or else not at all, for we are fewer than they. As soon as I call *Back*, then rush to join Jill at the white rock, where we shall have protection behind us and can breathe awhile. Now, be off, Jill."

Feeling terribly alone, Jill ran out about twenty feet, put her right leg back and her left leg forward, and set an arrow to her string. She wished her hands were not shaking so. "That's a rotten shot!" she said as her first arrow sped toward the enemy and flew over their heads. But she had another on the string next moment: she knew that speed was what mattered. She saw something big and black darting into the faces of the Calormenes. That was Farsight. First one man, and then another, dropped his sword and put up both his hands to defend his eyes. Then one of her own arrows hit a man, and another hit a Narnian wolf, who had, it seemed, joined the enemy. But she had been shooting only for a few seconds when she had to stop. With a flash of swords and of the Boar's tusks and Jewel's horn, and with deep baying from the dogs, Tirian and his party were rushing on their enemies, like men in a hundred yards' race. Jill was astonished to see how unprepared the Calormenes seemed to be. She did not realize that this was the result of her work and the Eagle's. Very few troops can keep on looking steadily to the front if they are getting arrows in their faces from one side and being pecked by an eagle on the other.

"Oh well done. *Well* done!" shouted Jill. The King's party were cutting their way right into the enemy. The Unicorn was tossing men as you'd toss hay on a fork. Even Eustace seemed to Jill (who after all didn't know very much about swordsmanship) to be fighting brilliantly. The Dogs were at the Calormenes' throats. It was going to work! It was victory at last— With a horrible, cold shock Jill noticed a strange thing. Though Calormenes were falling at each Narnian sword-stroke, they never seemed to get any fewer. In fact, there were actually more of them now than when the fight began. There were more every second. They were running up from every side. They were new Calormenes. These new ones had spears. There was such a crowd of them that she could hardly see her own friends. Then she heard Tirian's voice crying:

"Back! To the rock!"

The enemy had been reinforced. The drum had done its work.

THROUGH THE
STABLE DOOR

Jill ought to have been back at the white rock
already but she had quite forgotten that part of
her orders in the excitement of watching the
fight. Now she remembered. She turned at once
and ran to it, and arrived there barely a second
before the others. It thus happened that all of
them, for a moment, had their backs to the enemy. They all wheeled round the moment they
had reached it. A terrible sight met their eyes.

A Calormene was running toward the stable
door carrying something that kicked and struggled. As he came between them and the fire

they could see clearly both the shape of the man and the shape of what he carried. It was Eustace.

Tirian and the Unicorn rushed out to rescue him. But the Calormene was now far nearer to the door than they. Before they had covered half the distance he had flung Eustace in and shut the door on him. Half a dozen more Calormenes had run up behind him. They formed a line on the open space before the stable. There was no getting at it now.

Even then Jill remembered to keep her face turned aside, well away from her bow. "Even if I can't stop blubbing, I *won't* get my string wet," she said.

"'Ware arrows," said Poggin suddenly.

Everyone ducked and pulled his helmet well over his nose. The Dogs crouched behind. But though a few arrows came their way it soon became clear that they were not being shot at. Griffle and his Dwarfs were at their archery again. This time they were coolly shooting at the Calormenes.

"Keep it up, boys!" came Griffle's voice. "All together. Carefully. We don't want Darkies any more than we want Monkeys—or Lions—or Kings. The Dwarfs are for the Dwarfs."

Whatever else you may say about Dwarfs, no one can say they aren't brave. They could easily have got away to some safe place. They preferred to stay and kill as many of both sides as they could, except when both sides were kind enough to save them trouble by killing one another. They wanted Narnia for their own.

What perhaps they had not taken into account was that the Calormenes were mail-clad and the Horses had had no protection. Also the Calormenes had a leader. Rishda Tarkaan's voice cried out:

"Thirty of you keep watch on those fools by the white rock. The rest, after me, that we may teach these sons of earth a lesson."

Tirian and his friends, still panting from their fight and thankful for a few minutes' rest, stood and looked on while the Tarkaan led his men against the Dwarfs. It was a strange scene by now. The fire had sunk lower: the light it gave was now less and of a darker red. As far as one could see, the whole place of assembly was now empty except for the Dwarfs and the Calormenes. In that light one couldn't make out much of what was happening. It sounded as if the Dwarfs were putting up a good fight. Tirian could hear Griffle using dreadful language, and every now and then the Tarkaan calling, "Take all you can alive! Take them alive!"

Whatever that fight may have been like, it did not last long. The noise of it died away.

Then Jill saw the Tarkaan coming back to the stable: eleven men followed him, dragging eleven bound Dwarfs. (Whether the others had all been killed, or whether some of them had got away, was never known.)

"Throw them into the shrine of Tash," said Rishda Tarkaan.

And when the eleven Dwarfs, one after the other, had been flung or kicked into that dark doorway and the door had been shut again, he bowed low to the stable and said:

"These also are for thy burnt offering, Lord Tash."

And all the Calormenes banged the flats of their swords on their shields and shouted, "Tash! Tash! The great god Tash! Inexorable Tash!" (There was no nonsense about "Tashlan" now.)

The little party by the white rock watched these doings and whispered to one another. They had found a trickle of water coming down the rock and all had drunk eagerly—Jill and Poggin and the King in their hands, while the four-footed ones lapped from the little pool which it had made at the foot of the stone. Such was their thirst that it seemed the most delicious drink they had ever had in their lives, and while they were drinking they were perfectly happy and could not think of anything else.

"I feel in my bones," said Poggin, "that we

shall all, one by one, pass through that dark door before morning. I can think of a hundred deaths I would rather have died."

"It is indeed a grim door," said Tirian. "It is more like a mouth."

"Oh, can't we do *anything* to stop it?" said Jill in a shaken voice.

"Nay, fair friend," said Jewel, nosing her gently. "It may be for us the door to Aslan's country and we shall sup at his table tonight."

Rishda Tarkaan turned his back on the stable and walked slowly to a place in front of the white rock.

"Hearken," he said. "If the Boar and the Dogs and the Unicorn will come over to me and put themselves in my mercy, their lives shall be spared. The Boar shall go to a cage in The Tisroc's garden, the Dogs to The Tisroc's kennels, and the Unicorn, when I have sawn his horn off, shall draw a cart. But the Eagle, the children, and he who was the King shall be offered to Tash this night."

The only answer was growls.

"Get on, warriors," said the Tarkaan. "Kill the beasts, but take the two-legged ones alive."

And then the last battle of the last King of Narnia began.

What made it hopeless, even apart from the numbers of the enemy, was the spears. The

Calormenes who had been with the Ape almost from the beginning had had no spears: that was because they had come into Narnia by ones and twos, pretending to be peaceful merchants, and of course they had carried no spears for a spear is not a thing you can hide. The new ones must have come in later, after the Ape was already strong and they could march openly. The spears made all the difference. With a long spear you can kill a boar before you are in reach of his tusks and a unicorn before you are in reach of his horn; if you are very quick and keep your head. And now the leveled spears were closing in on Tirian and his last friends. Next minute they were all fighting for their lives.

In a way it wasn't quite so bad as you might think. When you are using every muscle to the full—ducking under a spear-point here, leaping over it there, lunging forward, drawing back, wheeling round—you haven't much time to feel either frightened or sad. Tirian knew he could do nothing for the others now; they were all doomed together. He vaguely saw the Boar go down on one side of him, and Jewel fighting furiously on the other. Out of the corner of one eye he saw, but only just saw, a big Calormene pulling Jill away somewhere by her hair. But he hardly thought about any of these things. His only thought now was to sell his life as dearly as he could. The worst of it was that he couldn't keep to the position in which he had started, under the white rock. A man who is fighting a dozen enemies at once must take his chances wherever he can; must dart in wherever he sees an enemy's breast or neck unguarded. In a very few strokes this may get you quite a distance from the spot where you began. Tirian soon found that he was getting further and further to the right, nearer to the stable. He had a vague idea in his mind that there was some good reason for keeping away from it. But he couldn't now remember what the reason was. And anyway, he couldn't help it.

All at once everything came quite clear. He found he was fighting the Tarkaan himself. The bonfire (what was left of it) was straight in front. He was in fact fighting in the very doorway of the stable, for it had been opened and two Calormenes were holding the door, ready to slam it shut the moment he was inside. He remembered everything now, and he realized that the enemy had been edging him to the stable on purpose ever since the fight began. And while he was thinking this he was still fighting the Tarkaan as hard as he could.

A new idea came into Tirian's head. He dropped his sword, darted forward, in under the sweep of the Tarkaan's scimitar, seized his enemy by the belt with both hands, and jumped back into the stable, shouting:

"Come in and meet Tash yourself!"

There was a deafening noise. As when the Ape had been flung in, the earth shook and there was a blinding light.

The Calormene soldiers outside screamed, "Tash, Tash!" and banged the door. If Tash wanted their own Captain, Tash must have him. They, at any rate, did not want to meet Tash.

For a moment or two Tirian did not know where he was or even who he was. Then he steadied himself, blinked, and looked around. It was not dark inside the stable, as he had expected. He was in strong light: that was why he was blinking.

He turned to look at Rishda Tarkaan, but Rishda was not looking at him. Rishda gave a great wail and pointed; then he put his hands before his face and fell flat, face downward, on the ground. Tirian looked in the direction where the Tarkaan had pointed. And then he understood.

A terrible figure was coming toward them. It was far smaller than the shape they had seen from the Tower, though still much bigger than a man, and it was the same. It had a vulture's head and four arms. Its beak was open and its eyes blazed. A croaking voice came from its beak.

"Thou hast called me into Narnia, Rishda Tarkaan. Here I am. What hast thou to say?"

But the Tarkaan neither lifted his face from the ground nor said a word. He was shaking like a man with a bad hiccup. He was brave enough

in battle: but half his courage had left him earlier that night when he first began to suspect that there might be a real Tash. The rest of it had left him now.

With a sudden jerk—like a hen stooping to pick up a worm—Tash pounced on the miserable Rishda and tucked him under the upper of his two right arms. Then Tash turned his head sidewise to fix Tirian with one of his terrible eyes: for of course, having a bird's head, he couldn't look at you straight.

But immediately, from behind Tash, strong and calm as the summer sea, a voice said:

"Begone, Monster, and take your lawful prey to your own place: in the name of Aslan and Aslan's great Father the Emperor-over-the-Sea."

The hideous creature vanished, with the Tarkaan still under its arm. And Tirian turned to see who had spoken. And what he saw then set his heart beating as it had never beaten in any fight.

Seven Kings and Queens stood before him, all with crowns on their heads and all in glittering clothes, but the Kings wore fine mail as well and had their swords drawn in their hands. Tirian bowed courteously and was about to speak when the youngest of the Queens laughed. He stared hard at her face, and then gasped with amazement, for he knew her. It was

Jill: but not Jill as he had last seen her, with her face all dirt and tears and an old drill dress half slipping off one shoulder. Now she looked cool and fresh, as fresh as if she had just come from bathing. And at first he thought she looked older, but then didn't, and he could never make up his mind on that point. And then he saw that the youngest of the Kings was Eustace: but he also was changed as Jill was changed.

Tirian suddenly felt awkward about coming among these people with the blood and dust and sweat of a battle still on him. Next moment he realized that he was not in that state at all. He was fresh and cool and clean, and dressed in such clothes as he would have worn for a great feast at Cair Paravel. (But in Narnia your good clothes were never your uncomfortable ones. They knew how to make things that felt

beautiful as well as looking beautiful in Narnia: and there was no such thing as starch or flannel or elastic to be found from one end of the country to the other.)

"Sire," said Jill coming forward and making a beautiful curtsey, "let me make you known to Peter the High King over all Kings in Narnia."

Tirian had no need to ask which was the High King, for he remembered his face (though here it was far nobler) from his dream. He stepped forward, sank on one knee and kissed Peter's hand.

"High King," he said. "You are welcome to me."

And the High King raised him and kissed him on both cheeks as a High King should. Then he led him to the eldest of the Queens—but even she was not old, and there were no gray hairs on her head and no wrinkles on her cheek—and said, "Sir, this is that Lady Polly who came into Narnia on the First Day, when Aslan made the trees grow and the Beasts talk." He brought him next to a man whose golden beard flowed over his breast and whose face was full of wisdom. "And this," he said, "is the Lord Digory who was with her on that day. And this is my brother, King Edmund: and this my sister, the Queen Lucy."

"Sir," said Tirian, when he had greeted all

these. "If I have read the chronicle aright, there should be another. Has not your Majesty two sisters? Where is Queen Susan?"

"My sister Susan," answered Peter shortly and gravely, "is no longer a friend of Narnia."

"Yes," said Eustace, "and whenever you've tried to get her to come and talk about Narnia or do anything about Narnia, she says, 'What wonderful memories you have! Fancy your still thinking about all those funny games we used to play when we were children.'"

"Oh Susan!" said Jill. "She's interested in nothing nowadays except nylons and lipstick and invitations. She always was a jolly sight too keen on being grown-up."

"Grown-up, indeed," said the Lady Polly. "I wish she *would* grow up. She wasted all her school time wanting to be the age she is now, and she'll waste all the rest of her life trying to stay that age. Her whole idea is to race on to the silliest time of one's life as quick as she can and then stop there as long as she can."

"Well, don't let's talk about that now," said Peter. "Look! Here are lovely fruit-trees. Let us taste them."

And then, for the first time, Tirian looked about him and realized how very queer this adventure was.

13

HOW THE DWARFS REFUSED TO BE TAKEN IN

Tirian had thought—or he would have thought if he had time to think at all—that they were inside a little thatched stable, about twelve feet long and six feet wide. In reality they stood on grass, the deep blue sky was overhead, and the air which blew gently on their faces was that of a day in early summer. Not far away from them rose a grove of trees, thickly leaved, but under every leaf there peeped out the gold or faint yellow or purple or glowing red of fruits such as no one has seen in our world. The fruit made Tirian feel that it must be autumn but there was something in the feel of the air that told him it could not be later than June. They all moved toward the trees.

Everyone raised his hand to pick the fruit he best liked the look of, and then everyone paused for a second. This fruit was so beautiful that each felt "It can't be meant for me . . . surely we're not allowed to pluck it."

"It's all right," said Peter. "I know what we're all thinking. But I'm sure, quite sure, we needn't. I've a feeling we've got to the country where everything is allowed."

"Here goes, then!" said Eustace. And they all began to eat.

What was the fruit like? Unfortunately no one can describe a taste. All I can say is that, compared with those fruits, the freshest grapefruit you've ever eaten was dull, and the juiciest orange was dry, and the most melting pear was hard and woody, and the sweetest wild strawberry was sour. And there were no seeds or stones, and no wasps. If you had once eaten that fruit, all the nicest things in this world would taste like medicines after it. But I can't describe it. You can't find out what it is like unless you can get to that country and taste it for yourself.

When they had eaten enough, Eustace said to King Peter, "You haven't yet told us how you got here. You were just going to, when King

Tirian turned up."

"There's not much to tell," said Peter. "Edmund and I were standing on the platform and we saw your train coming in. I remember thinking it was taking the bend far too fast. And I remember thinking how funny it was that our people were probably in the same train though Lucy didn't know about it—"

"Your people, High King?" said Tirian.

"I mean my Father and Mother—Edmund's and Lucy's and mine."

"Why were they?" asked Jill. "You don't mean to say *they* know about Narnia?"

"Oh no, it had nothing to do with Narnia. They were on their way to Bristol. I'd only heard they were going that morning. But Edmund said they'd be bound to be going by that train." (Edmund was the sort of person who knows about railways.)

"And what happened then?" said Jill.

"Well, it's not very easy to describe, is it, Edmund?" said the High King.

"Not very," said Edmund. "It wasn't at all like that other time when we were pulled out of our own world by Magic. There was a frightful roar and something hit me with a bang, but it didn't hurt. And I felt not so much scared as— well, excited. Oh—and this is one queer thing. I'd had a rather sore knee, from a hack at rugger.

I noticed it had suddenly gone. And I felt very light. And then—here we were."

"It was much the same for us in the railway carriage," said the Lord Digory, wiping the last traces of the fruit from his golden beard. "Only I think you and I, Polly, chiefly felt that we'd been unstiffened. You youngsters won't understand. But we stopped feeling old."

"Youngsters, indeed!" said Jill. "I don't believe you two really are much older than we are here."

"Well if we aren't, we have been," said the Lady Polly.

"And what has been happening since you got here?" asked Eustace.

"Well," said Peter, "for a long time (at least I suppose it was a long time) nothing happened. Then the door opened—"

"The door?" said Tirian.

"Yes," said Peter. "The door you came in—or came out—by. Have you forgotten?"

"But where is it?"

"Look," said Peter and pointed.

Tirian looked and saw the queerest and most ridiculous thing you can imagine. Only a few yards away, clear to be seen in the sunlight, there stood up a rough wooden door and, round it, the framework of the doorway: nothing else, no walls, no roof. He walked toward it, bewildered, and the others followed, watching to see what he would do. He walked round to the other side of the door. But it looked just the same from the other side: he was still in the open air, on a summer morning. The door was simply standing up by itself as if it had grown there like a tree.

"Fair Sir," said Tirian to the High King, "this is a great marvel."

"It is the door you came through with that Calormene five minutes ago," said Peter smiling.

"But did I not come in out of the wood into the stable? Whereas this seems to be a door leading from nowhere to nowhere."

"It looks like that if you walk *round* it," said Peter. "But put your eye to that place where there is a crack between two of the planks and look *through*."

Tirian put his eye to the hole. At first he could see nothing but blackness. Then, as his eyes grew used to it, he saw the dull red glow of a bonfire that was nearly going out, and above that, in a black sky, stars. Then he could see dark figures moving about or standing between him and the fire: he could hear them talking and their voices were like those of Calormenes. So he knew that he was looking out through the stable door into the darkness of Lantern Waste where he had fought his last battle. The men were discussing whether to go in and look for Rishda Tarkaan (but none of them wanted to do that) or to set fire to the stable.

He looked round again and could hardly believe his eyes. There was the blue sky overhead, and grassy country spreading as far as he could see in every direction, and his new friends all round him laughing.

"It seems, then," said Tirian, smiling him-

self, "that the stable seen from within and the stable seen from without are two different places."

"Yes," said the Lord Digory. "Its inside is bigger than its outside."

"Yes," said Queen Lucy. "In our world too, a stable once had something inside it that was bigger than our whole world." It was the first time she had spoken, and from the thrill in her voice, Tirian now knew why. She was drinking everything in even more deeply than the others. She had been too happy to speak. He wanted to hear her speak again, so he said:

"Of your courtesy, Madam, tell on. Tell me your whole adventure."

"After the shock and the noise," said Lucy, "we found ourselves here. And we wondered at the door, as you did. Then the door opened for the first time (we saw darkness through the doorway when it did) and there came through a big man with a naked sword. We saw by his arms that he was a Calormene. He took his stand beside the door with his sword raised, resting on his shoulder, ready to cut down anyone who came through. We went to him and spoke to him, but we thought he could neither see nor hear us. And he never looked round on the sky and the sunlight and the grass: I think he couldn't see them either. So then we waited a long time. Then we heard the bolt being drawn on the other side of the door. But the man didn't get ready to strike with his sword till he could see who was coming in. So we supposed he had been told to strike some and spare others. But at the very moment when the door opened, all of a sudden Tash was there, on this side of the door; none of us saw where he came from. And through the door there came a big Cat. It gave one look at Tash and ran for its life: just in time, for he pounced at it and the door hit his beak as it was shut. The man could see Tash. He turned very pale and bowed down before the Monster: but it vanished away.

"Then we waited a long time again. At last the door opened for the third time and there came in a young Calormene. I liked him. The sentinel at the door started, and looked very surprised, when he saw him. I think he'd been expecting someone quite different—"

"I see it all now," said Eustace (he had the bad habit of interrupting stories). "The Cat was to go in first and the sentry had orders to do him no harm. Then the Cat was to come out and say he'd seen their beastly Tashlan and *pretend* to be frightened to scare the other Animals. But what Shift never guessed was that the real Tash would turn up; so Ginger came out really frightened. And after that, Shift would send in anyone he wanted to get rid of and the sentry would kill them.

"And—"

"Friend," said Tirian softly, "you hinder the lady in her tale."

"Well," said Lucy, "the sentry was surprised. That gave the other man just time to get on guard. They had a fight. He killed the sentry and flung him outside the door. Then he came walking slowly forward to where we were. He could see us, and everything else. We tried to talk to him but he was rather like a man in a trance. He kept on saying Tash, Tash, where is Tash? I go to Tash. So we gave it up and he went away somewhere—over there. I liked him. And after that . . . ugh!" Lucy made a face.

"After that," said Edmund, "someone flung a monkey through the door. And Tash was there again. My sister is so tender-hearted she doesn't like to tell you that Tash made one peck and the Monkey was gone!"

"Serve him right!" said Eustace. "All the same, I hope he'll disagree with Tash too."

"And after that," said Edmund, "came about a dozen Dwarfs: and then Jill, and Eustace, and last of all yourself."

"I hope Tash ate the Dwarfs too," said Eustace. "Little swine."

"No, he didn't," said Lucy. "And don't be

horrid. They're still here. In fact you can see them from here. And I've tried and tried to make friends with them but it's no use."

"*Friends* with them!" cried Eustace. "If you knew how those Dwarfs have been behaving!"

"Oh stop it, Eustace," said Lucy. "Do come and see them. King Tirian, perhaps *you* could do something with them."

"I can feel no great love for Dwarfs today," said Tirian. "Yet at your asking, Lady, I would do a greater thing than this."

Lucy led the way and soon they could all see the Dwarfs. They had a very odd look. They weren't strolling about or enjoying themselves (although the cords with which they had been tied seemed to have vanished) nor were they lying down and having a rest. They were sitting very close together in a little circle facing one another. They never looked round or took any notice of the humans till Lucy and Tirian were almost near enough to touch them. Then the Dwarfs all cocked their heads as if they couldn't see anyone but were listening hard and trying to guess by the sound what was happening.

"Look out!" said one of them in a surly voice. "Mind where you're going. Don't walk into our faces!"

"All right!" said Eustace indignantly. "We're

not blind. We've got eyes in our heads."

"They must be darn good ones if you can see in here," said the same Dwarf whose name was Diggle.

"In where?" asked Edmund.

"Why you bone-head, in *here* of course," said Diggle. "In this pitch-black, poky, smelly little hole of a stable."

"Are you blind?" said Tirian.

"Ain't we all blind in the dark!" said Diggle.

"But it isn't dark, you poor stupid Dwarfs," said Lucy. "Can't you see? Look up! Look round! Can't you see the sky and the trees and the flowers? Can't you see *me*?"

"How in the name of all Humbug can I see what ain't there? And how can I see you any more than you can see me in this pitch darkness?"

"But I *can* see you," said Lucy. "I'll prove I can see you. You've got a pipe in your mouth."

"Anyone that knows the smell of baccy could tell that," said Diggle.

"Oh the poor things! This is dreadful," said Lucy. Then she had an idea. She stooped and picked some wild violets. "Listen, Dwarf," she said. "Even if your eyes are wrong, perhaps your nose is all right: can you smell *that*?" She leaned across and held the fresh, damp flowers to

Diggle's ugly nose. But she had to jump back quickly in order to avoid a blow from his hard little fist.

"None of that!" he shouted. "How dare you! What do you mean by shoving a lot of filthy stable-litter in my face? There was a thistle in it too. It's like your sauce! And who are you, anyway?"

"Earth-man," said Tirian, "she is the Queen Lucy, sent hither by Aslan out of the deep past. And it is for her sake alone that I, Tirian your lawful King, do not cut all your heads from your shoulders, proved and twice-proved traitors that you are."

"Well if that doesn't beat everything!" exclaimed Diggle. "How *can* you go on talking all that rot? Your wonderful Lion didn't come and help you, did he? Thought not. And now—even now—when you've been beaten and shoved into this black hole, just the same as the rest of us, you're still at your old game. Starting a new lie! Trying to make us believe we're none of us shut up, and it ain't dark, and heaven knows what."

"There *is* no black hole, save in your own fancy, fool," cried Tirian. "Come *out* of it." And, leaning forward, he caught Diggle by the belt and the hood and swung him right out of the circle of Dwarfs. But the moment Tirian put him down, Diggle darted back to his place among the others, rubbing his nose and howling:

"Ow! Ow! What d'you do that for! Banging my face against the wall. You've nearly broken my nose."

"Oh dear!" said Lucy. "What *are* we to do for them?"

"Let 'em alone," said Eustace: but as he spoke the earth trembled. The sweet air grew suddenly sweeter. A brightness flashed behind them. All turned. Tirian turned last because he was afraid. There stood his heart's desire, huge and real, the golden Lion, Aslan himself, and already the others were kneeling in a circle round his forepaws and burying their hands and faces in his mane as he stooped his great head to touch them with his tongue. Then he fixed his eyes upon Tirian, and Tirian came near, trembling, and flung himself at the Lion's feet, and the Lion kissed him and said, "Well done, last of the Kings of Narnia who stood firm at the darkest hour."

"Aslan," said Lucy through her tears, "could you—will you—do something for these poor Dwarfs?"

"Dearest," said Aslan, "I will show you both what I can, and what I cannot, do." He came close to the Dwarfs and gave a low growl: low, but it set all the air shaking. But the Dwarfs said to one another, "Hear that? That's the gang at the other end of the stable. Trying to frighten us. They do it with a machine of some kind. Don't take any notice. They won't take *us* in again!"

Aslan raised his head and shook his mane. Instantly a glorious feast appeared on the Dwarfs' knees: pies and tongues and pigeons and trifles and ices, and each Dwarf had a goblet of good wine in his right hand. But it wasn't much use. They began eating and drinking greedily enough, but it was clear that they couldn't taste it properly. They thought they were eating and drinking only the sort of things you might find in a stable. One said he was trying to eat hay and another said he had got a bit of an old turnip and a third said he'd found a raw cabbage leaf. And they raised golden goblets of rich red

wine to their lips and said "Ugh! Fancy drinking dirty water out of a trough that a donkey's been at! Never thought we'd come to this." But very soon every Dwarf began suspecting that every other Dwarf had found something nicer than he had, and they started grabbing and snatching, and went on to quarreling, till in a few minutes there was a free fight and all the good food was smeared on their faces and clothes or trodden under foot. But when at last they sat down to nurse their black eyes and their bleeding noses, they all said:

"Well, at any rate there's no Humbug here. We haven't let anyone take us in. The Dwarfs are for the Dwarfs."

"You see," said Aslan. "They will not let us help them. They have chosen cunning instead of belief. Their prison is only in their own

minds, yet they are in that prison; and so afraid of being taken in that they cannot be taken out. But come, children. I have other work to do."

He went to the Door and they all followed him. He raised his head and roared, "Now it is time!" then louder, "Time!"; then so loud that it could have shaken the stars, "TIME." The Door flew open.

NIGHT FALLS
ON NARNIA

They all stood beside Aslan, on his right side, and looked through the open doorway.

The bonfire had gone out. On the earth all was blackness: in fact you could not have told that you were looking into a wood if you had not seen where the dark shapes of the trees ended and the stars began. But when Aslan had roared yet again, out on their left they saw another black shape. That is, they saw another patch where there were no stars: and the patch rose up higher and higher and became the shape of a man, the hugest of all giants. They all knew

Narnia well enough to work out where he must be standing. He must be on the high moorlands that stretch away to the North beyond the River Shribble. Then Jill and Eustace remembered how once long ago, in the deep caves beneath those moors, they had seen a great giant asleep and been told that his name was Father Time, and that he would wake on the day the world ended.

"Yes," said Aslan, though they had not spoken. "While he lay dreaming his name was Time. Now that he is awake he will have a new one."

Then the great giant raised a horn to his mouth. They could see this by the change of the black shape he made against the stars. After that—quite a bit later, because sound travels so slowly—they heard the sound of the horn: high and terrible, yet of a strange, deadly beauty.

Immediately the sky became full of shooting stars. Even one shooting star is a fine thing to see; but these were dozens, and then scores, and then hundreds, till it was like silver rain: and it went on and on. And when it had gone on for some while, one or two of them began to think that there was another dark shape against the sky as well as the giant's. It was in a different place, right overhead, up in the very roof of the sky as you might call it. "Perhaps it is a cloud," thought Edmund. At any rate, there were no stars there: just blackness. But all around, the downpour of stars went on. And then the starless patch began to grow, spreading further and further out from the center of the sky. And presently a quarter of the whole sky was black, and then a half, and at last the rain of shooting stars was going on only low down near the horizon.

With a thrill of wonder (and there was some terror in it too) they all suddenly realized what was happening. The spreading blackness was not a cloud at all: it was simply emptiness. The black part of the sky was the part in which there were no stars left. All the stars were falling: Aslan had called them home.

The last few seconds before the rain of stars had quite ended were very exciting. Stars began falling all round them. But stars in that world are not the great flaming globes they are in ours. They are people (Edmund and Lucy had once met one). So now they found showers of glittering people, all with long hair like burning silver and spears like white-hot metal, rushing down to them out of the black air, swifter than falling stones. They made a hissing noise as they landed and burnt the grass. And all these stars glided past them and stood somewhere behind, a little to the right.

This was a great advantage, because otherwise, now that there were no stars in the sky, everything would have been completely dark and you could have seen nothing. As it was, the crowd of stars behind them cast a fierce, white light over their shoulders. They could see mile upon mile of Narnian woods spread out before them, looking as if they were floodlit. Every bush and almost every blade of grass had its black shadow behind it. The edge of every leaf stood out so sharp that you'd think you could cut your finger on it.

On the grass before them lay their own shadows. But the great thing was Aslan's shadow. It streamed away to their left, enormous and very terrible. And all this was under a sky that would now be starless forever.

The light from behind them (and a little to their right) was so strong that it lit up even the slopes of the Northern Moors. Something was moving there. Enormous animals were crawling and sliding down into Narnia: great dragons and giant lizards and featherless birds with wings like bats' wings. They disappeared into the woods and for a few minutes there was silence. Then there came—at first from very far off—sounds of wailing and then, from every direction, a rustling and a pattering and a sound of wings. It came nearer and nearer. Soon one could distinguish the scamper of little feet from the padding of big paws, and the clack-clack of light little hoofs from the thunder of great ones. And then one could see thousands of pairs of eyes gleaming. And at last, out of the shadow of the trees, racing up the hill for dear life, by thousands and by millions, came all kinds of creatures—Talking Beasts, Dwarfs, Satyrs, Fauns, Giants, Calormenes, men from Archenland, Monopods, and strange unearthly things from the remote islands or the unknown Western lands. And all these ran up to the doorway where Aslan stood.

This part of the adventure was the only one which seemed rather like a dream at the time and rather hard to remember properly afterward. Especially, one couldn't say how long it had taken. Sometimes it seemed to have lasted only a few minutes, but at others it felt as if it might have gone on for years. Obviously, unless either the Door had grown very much larger or the creatures had suddenly grown as small as gnats, a crowd like that couldn't ever have tried to get through it. But no one thought about that sort of thing at the time.

The creatures came rushing on, their eyes brighter and brighter as they drew nearer and nearer to the standing Stars. But as they came right up to Aslan one or other of two things happened to each of them. They all looked

straight in his face, I don't think they had any choice about that. And when some looked, the expression of their faces changed terribly—it was fear and hatred: except that, on the faces of Talking Beasts, the fear and hatred lasted only for a fraction of a second. You could see that they suddenly ceased to be *Talking* Beasts. They were just ordinary animals. And all the creatures who looked at Aslan in that way swerved to their right, his left, and disappeared into his huge black shadow, which (as you have heard) streamed away to the left of the doorway. The children never saw them again. I don't know what became of them. But the others looked in the face of Aslan and loved him, though some of them were very frightened at the same time. And all these came in at the Door, in on Aslan's right. There were some queer specimens among them. Eustace even recognized one of those very Dwarfs who had helped to shoot the Horses. But he had no time to wonder about that sort of thing (and anyway it was no business of his) for a great joy put everything else out of his head. Among the happy creatures who now came crowding round Tirian and his friends were all those whom they had thought dead. There was Roonwit the Centaur and Jewel the Unicorn and the good Boar and the good Bear, and Farsight the Eagle, and the dear Dogs and the

Horses, and Poggin the Dwarf.

"Further in and higher up!" cried Roonwit and thundered away in a gallop to the West. And though they did not understand him, the words somehow set them tingling all over. The Boar grunted at them cheerfully. The Bear was just going to mutter that he still didn't understand, when he caught sight of the fruit-trees behind them. He waddled to those trees as fast as he could and there, no doubt, found something he understood very well. But the Dogs remained, wagging their tails, and Poggin remained, shaking hands with everyone and grinning all over his honest face. And Jewel leaned his snowy white head over the King's shoulder and the King whispered in Jewel's ear. Then everyone turned his attention again to what could be seen through the Doorway.

The Dragons and Giant Lizards now had Narnia to themselves. They went to and fro tearing up the trees by the roots and crunching them up as if they were sticks of rhubarb. Minute by minute the forests disappeared. The whole country became bare and you could see all sorts of things about its shape—all the little humps and hollows—which you had never noticed before. The grass died. Soon Tirian found that he was looking at a world of bare rock and earth. You could hardly believe that anything had ever lived there. The monsters themselves grew old and lay down and died. Their flesh shriveled up and the bones appeared: soon they were only huge skeletons that lay here and there on the dead rock, looking as if they had died thousands of years ago. For a long time everything was still.

At last something white—a long, level line of whiteness that gleamed in the light of the standing stars—came moving toward them from the Eastern end of the world. A widespread noise broke the silence: first a murmur then a rumble, then a roar. And now they could see what it was that was coming, and how fast it came. It was a foaming wall of water. The sea was rising. In that tree-less world you could see it very well. You could see all the rivers getting wider and the lakes getting larger, and separate lakes joining into one, and valleys turning into new lakes, and hills turning into islands, and then those islands vanishing. And the high moors to their left and the higher mountains to their right crumbled and slipped down with a roar and a splash into the mounting water; and the water came swirling up to the very threshold of the Doorway (but never passed it) so that the foam splashed about Aslan's forefeet. All now was level water from where they stood to where the waters met the sky.

And out there it began to grow light. A streak of dreary and disastrous dawn spread along the horizon, and widened and grew brighter, till in the end they hardly noticed the light of the stars who stood behind them. At last the sun came up. When it did, the Lord Digory and the Lady Polly looked at one another and gave a little nod: those two, in a different world, had once seen a dying sun, and so they knew at once that this sun also was dying. It was three times—twenty times—as big as it ought to be, and very dark red. As its rays fell upon the great Time-giant, he turned red too: and in the reflection of that sun the whole waste of shoreless waters looked like blood.

Then the Moon came up, quite in her wrong position, very close to the sun, and she also looked red. And at the sight of her the sun began shooting out great flames, like whiskers or snakes of crimson fire, toward her. It is as if he were an octopus trying to draw her to himself in his tentacles. And perhaps he did draw her. At any rate she came to him, slowly at first, but then more and more quickly, till at last his long flames licked round her and the two ran together and became one huge ball like a burning coal. Great lumps of fire came dropping out of it into the sea and clouds of steam rose up.

Then Aslan said, "Now make an end."

The giant threw his horn into the sea. Then he stretched out one arm—very black it looked, and thousands of miles long—across the sky till his hand reached the Sun. He took the Sun and squeezed it in his hand as you would squeeze an orange. And instantly there was total darkness.

Everyone except Aslan jumped back from the ice-cold air which now blew through the Doorway. Its edges were already covered with icicles.

"Peter, High King of Narnia," said Aslan. "Shut the Door."

Peter, shivering with cold, leaned out into the darkness and pulled the Door to. It scraped over ice as he pulled it. Then, rather clumsily (for even in that moment his hands had gone numb and blue) he took out a golden key and locked it.

They had seen strange things enough through that Doorway. But it was stranger than any of them to look round and find themselves in warm daylight, the blue sky above them, flowers at their feet, and laughter in Aslan's eyes.

He turned swiftly round, crouched lower, lashed himself with his tail and shot away like a golden arrow.

"Come further in! Come further up!" he shouted over his shoulder. But who could keep up with him at that pace? They set out walking Westward to follow him.

"So," said Peter, "night falls on Narnia. What, Lucy! You're not *crying*? With Aslan ahead, and all of us here?"

"Don't try to stop me, Peter," said Lucy, "I am sure Aslan would not. I am sure it is not wrong to mourn for Narnia. Think of all that lies dead and frozen behind that door."

"Yes and I *did* hope," said Jill, "that it might go on forever. I knew *our* world couldn't. I did think Narnia might."

"I saw it begin," said the Lord Digory. "I did not think I would live to see it die."

"Sirs," said Tirian. "The ladies do well to weep. See, I do so myself. I have seen my mother's death. What world but Narnia have I ever known? It were no virtue, but great discourtesy, if we did not mourn."

They walked away from the Door and away from the Dwarfs who still sat crowded together in their imaginary stable. And as they went they talked to one another about old wars and old peace and ancient Kings and all the glories of Narnia.

The Dogs were still with them. They joined in the conversation but not very much because they were too busy racing on ahead and racing back and rushing off to sniff at smells in the

grass till they made themselves sneeze. Suddenly they picked up a scent which seemed to excite them very much. They all started arguing about it — "Yes it is — No it isn't — That's just what I said — anyone can smell what *that* is — Take your great nose out of the way and let someone else smell."

"What is it, cousins?" said Peter.

"A Calormene, Sire," said several Dogs at once.

"Lead on to him, then," said Peter. "Whether he meets us in peace or war, he shall be welcome."

The Dogs darted on ahead and came back a moment later, running as if their lives depended on it, and barking loudly to say that it really was a Calormene. (Talking Dogs, just like the common ones, behave as if they thought whatever they are doing at the moment immensely important.)

The others followed where the Dogs led them and found a young Calormene sitting under a chestnut tree beside a clear stream of water. It was Emeth. He rose at once and bowed gravely.

"Sir," he said to Peter, "I know not whether you are my friend or my foe, but I should count it my honor to have you for either. Has not one of the poets said that a noble friend is the best gift and a noble enemy the next best?"

"Sir," said Peter, "I do not know that there need be any war between you and us."

"Do tell us who you are and what's happened to you," said Jill.

"If there's going to be a story, let's all have a drink and sit down," barked the Dogs. "We're quite blown."

"Well of course you will be if you keep tearing about the way you have done," said Eustace.

So the humans sat down on the grass. And when the Dogs had all had a very noisy drink out of the stream they all sat down, bolt upright, panting, with their tongues hanging out of their heads a little on one side to hear the story. But Jewel remained standing, polishing his horn against his side.

FURTHER UP AND FURTHER IN

"Know, O warlike Kings," said Emeth, "and you, O ladies whose beauty illuminates the universe, that I am Emeth, the seventh son of Harpa Tarkaan of the city of Tehishbaan, Westward beyond the desert. I came lately into Narnia with nine and twenty others under the command of Rishda Tarkaan. Now when I first heard that we should march upon Narnia I rejoiced; for I had heard many things of your Land and desired greatly to meet you in battle. But when I found that we were to go in disguised as merchants (which is a shameful dress for a warrior and the son of a Tarkaan) and to work by lies and trickery, then my joy departed from me. And most of all when I found we must wait upon a Monkey, and when it began to be said that Tash and Aslan were one, then the world became dark in my eyes. For always since I was a boy I have served Tash and my great desire was to know more of him, if it might be, to look upon his face. But the name of Aslan was hateful to me.

"And, as you have seen, we were called together outside the straw-roofed hovel, night after night, and the fire was kindled, and the Ape brought forth out of the hovel something upon four legs that I could not well see. And the people and the Beasts bowed down and did honor to it. But I thought, the Tarkaan is deceived by the Ape: for this thing that comes out of the stable is neither Tash nor any other god. But when I watched the Tarkaan's face, and marked every word that he said to the Monkey, then I changed my mind: for I saw that the Tarkaan did not believe in it himself. And then I understood that he did not believe in Tash at all: for if he had, how could he dare to mock him?

"When I understood this, a great rage fell upon me and I wondered that the true Tash did not strike down both the Monkey and the Tarkaan with fire from heaven. Nevertheless I hid my anger and held my tongue and waited to see how it would end. But last night, as some of you know, the Monkey brought not forth the yellow thing but said that all who desired to look upon Tashlan—for so they mixed the two words to pretend that they were all one—must pass one by one into the hovel. And I said to myself, Doubtless this is some other deception. But when the Cat had followed in and had come out again in a madness of terror, then I said to myself, Surely the true Tash, whom they called on without knowledge or belief, has now come among us, and will avenge himself. And though my heart was turned into water inside me because of the greatness and terror of Tash, yet my desire was stronger than my fear, and I put force upon my knees to stay them from trembling, and on my teeth that they should not chatter, and resolved to look upon the face of Tash though he should slay me. So I offered myself to go into the hovel; and the Tarkaan, though unwillingly, let me go.

"As soon as I had gone in at the door, the first wonder was that I found myself in this great sunlight (as we all are now) though the inside of the hovel had looked dark from outside. But I had no time to marvel at this, for immediately I was forced to fight for my head against one of our own men. As soon as I saw him I understood that the Monkey and the Tarkaan had set him there to slay any who came in if he were not in their secrets: so that this man also was a liar and a mocker and no true servant of Tash. I had the better will to fight him; and having slain the villain, I cast him out behind me through the door.

"Then I looked about me and saw the sky and the wide lands and smelled the sweetness. And I said, By the Gods, this is a pleasant place: it may be that I am come into the country of Tash. And I began to journey into the strange country and to seek him.

"So I went over much grass and many flowers and among all kinds of wholesome and delectable trees till lo! in a narrow place between two rocks there came to meet me a great Lion. The speed of him was like the ostrich, and his size was an elephant's; his hair was like pure gold and the brightness of his eyes like gold that is liquid in the furnace. He was more terrible than the Flaming Mountain of Lagour, and in beauty he surpassed all that is in the world even as the rose in bloom surpasses the dust of the desert. Then I fell at his feet and thought, Surely this is the hour of death, for the Lion (who is worthy of all honor) will know that I have served Tash all my days and not him. Nevertheless, it is better to see the Lion and die than to be Tisroc of the world and live and not to have seen him. But the Glorious One bent down his golden head and touched my forehead with his tongue and said, Son, thou art welcome. But I said, Alas, Lord, I am no son of thine but the servant of Tash. He answered, Child, all the service thou hast done to Tash, I account as service done to me. Then by reasons of my great desire for wisdom and understanding, I overcame my fear and questioned the Glorious One and said, Lord, is it then true, as the Ape said, that thou and Tash are one? The Lion growled so that the earth shook (but his wrath was not against me) and said, It is false. Not because he and I are one, but because we are opposites, I take to me the services which thou hast done to him. For I and he are of such different kinds that no service which is vile can be done to me, and none which is not vile can be done to him. Therefore if any man swear by Tash and keep his oath for the oath's sake, it is by me that he has truly sworn, though he know it not, and it is I who reward him. And if any man do a cruelty in my name, then, though he says the name Aslan, it is Tash whom he serves and by Tash his deed is accepted. Dost thou understand, Child? I said, Lord, thou knowest how much I understand. But I said also (for the truth constrained me), Yet I have been seeking Tash all my days. Beloved, said the Glorious One, unless thy desire had been for me thou wouldst not have sought so long and so truly. For all find what they truly seek.

"Then he breathed upon me and took away the trembling from my limbs and caused me to stand upon my feet. And after that, he said not much but that we should meet again, and I must go further up and further in. Then he turned him about in a storm and flurry of gold and was gone suddenly.

"And since then, O Kings and Ladies, I have been wandering to find him and my happiness is so great that it even weakens me like a wound. And this is the marvel of marvels, that he called me Beloved, me who am but as a dog—"

"Eh? What's that?" said one of the Dogs.

"Sir," said Emeth. "It is but a fashion of speech which we have in Calormen."

"Well, I can't say it's one I like very much," said the Dog.

"He doesn't mean any harm," said an older Dog. "After all, *we* call our puppies *Boys* when they don't behave properly."

"So we do," said the first Dog. "Or *girls*."

"S-s-sh!" said the Old Dog. "That's not a nice word to use. Remember where you are."

"Look!" said Jill suddenly. Someone was coming, rather timidly, to meet them; a graceful creature on four feet, all silvery-gray. And they stared at him for a whole ten seconds before five

or six voices said all at once, "Why, it's old Puzzle!" They had never seen him by daylight with the lion-skin off, and it made an extraordinary difference. He was himself now: a beautiful donkey with such a soft, gray coat and such a gentle, honest face that if you had seen him you would have done just what Jill and Lucy did—rushed forward and put your arms round his neck and kissed his nose and stroked his ears.

When they asked him where he had been he said he had come in at the door along with all the other creatures but he had—well, to tell the truth, he had been keeping out of their way as much as he could; and out of Aslan's way. For the sight of the real Lion had made him so ashamed of all that nonsense about dressing up in a lion-skin that he did not know how to look anyone in the face. But when he saw that all his friends were going away Westward, and after he had had a mouthful or so of grass ("And I've never tasted such good grass in my life," said Puzzle), he plucked up his courage and followed. "But what I'll do if I really have to meet Aslan, I'm sure I don't know," he added.

"You'll find it will be all right when you really do," said Queen Lucy.

Then they all went forward together, always Westward, for that seemed to be the direction Aslan had meant when he cried out, "Further up and further in." Many other creatures were slowly moving the same way, but that grassy country was very wide and there was no crowding.

It still seemed to be early, and the morning freshness was in the air. They kept on stopping to look round and to look behind them, partly because it was so beautiful but partly also because there was something about it which they could not understand.

"Peter," said Lucy, "where is this, do you suppose?"

"I don't know," said the High King. "It reminds me of somewhere but I can't give it a name. Could it be somewhere we once stayed for a holiday when we were very, very small?"

"It would have to have been a jolly good holiday," said Eustace. "I bet there isn't a country like this anywhere in *our* world. Look at the colors! You couldn't get a blue like the blue on those mountains in our world."

"Is it not Aslan's country?" said Tirian.

"Not like Aslan's country on top of that mountain beyond the Eastern end of the world," said Jill. "I've been there."

"If you ask me," said Edmund, "it's like somewhere in the Narnian world. Look at those mountains ahead—and the big ice-mountains beyond them. Surely they're rather like the mountains we used to see from Narnia, the ones up Westward beyond the Waterfall?"

"Yes, so they are," said Peter. "Only these are bigger."

"I don't think *those* ones are so very like anything in Narnia," said Lucy. "But look there." She pointed Southward to their left, and everyone stopped and turned to look. "Those hills," said Lucy, "the nice woody ones and the blue ones behind—aren't they very like the Southern border of Narnia?"

"Like!" cried Edmund after a moment's silence. "Why, they're exactly like. Look, there's Mount Pire with his forked head, and there's the pass into Archenland and everything!"

"And yet they're not like," said Lucy. "They're different. They have more colors on them and they look further away than I remembered and they're more . . . more . . . oh, I don't know . . ."

"More like the real thing," said the Lord Digory softly.

Suddenly Farsight the Eagle spread his wings, soared thirty or forty feet up into the air, circled round and then alighted on the ground.

"Kings and Queens," he cried, "we have all been blind. We are only beginning to see where we are. From up there I have seen it all— Ettinsmuir, Beaversdam, the Great River, and

Cair Paravel still shining on the edge of the
Eastern Sea. Narnia is not dead. This is Narnia."

"But how can it be?" said Peter. "For Aslan
told us older ones that we should never return to
Narnia, and here we are."

"Yes," said Eustace. "And we saw it all destroyed and the sun put out."

"And it's all so different," said Lucy.

"The Eagle is right," said the Lord Digory.
"Listen, Peter. When Aslan said you could
never go back to Narnia, he meant the Narnia
you were thinking of. But that was not the real
Narnia. That had a beginning and an end. It
was only a shadow or a copy of the real Narnia
which has always been here and always will be
here: just as our own world, England and all, is
only a shadow or copy of something in Aslan's

real world. You need not mourn over Narnia, Lucy. All of the old Narnia that mattered, all the dear creatures, have been drawn into the real Narnia through the Door. And of course it is different; as different as a real thing is from a shadow or as waking life is from a dream." His voice stirred everyone like a trumpet as he spoke these words: but when he added under his breath "It's all in Plato, all in Plato: bless me, what *do* they teach them at these schools!" the older ones laughed. It was so exactly like the sort of thing they had heard him say long ago in that other world where his beard was gray instead of golden. He knew why they were laughing and joined in the laugh himself. But very quickly they all became grave again: for, as you know, there is a kind of happiness and wonder that makes you serious. It is too good to waste on jokes.

It is as hard to explain how this sunlit land was different from the old Narnia as it would be to tell you how the fruits of that country taste. Perhaps you will get some idea of it if you think like this. You may have been in a room in which there was a window that looked out on a lovely bay of the sea or a green valley that wound away among mountains. And in the wall of that room opposite to the window there may have been a looking-glass. And as you turned away from the window you suddenly caught sight of that sea or that valley, all over again, in the looking-glass. And the sea in the mirror, or the valley in the mirror, were in one sense just the same as the real ones: yet at the same time they were somehow different—deeper, more wonderful, more like places in a story: in a story you have never heard but very much want to know. The difference between the old Narnia and the new Narnia was like that. The new one was a deeper country: every rock and flower and blade of grass looked as if it meant more. I can't describe it any better than that: if you ever get there you will know what I mean.

It was the Unicorn who summed up what everyone was feeling. He stamped his right forehoof on the ground and neighed, and then cried:

"I have come home at last! This is my real country! I belong here. This is the land I have been looking for all my life, though I never knew it till now. The reason why we loved the old Narnia is that it sometimes looked a little like this. Bree-hee-hee! Come further up, come further in!"

He shook his mane and sprang forward into a great gallop—a Unicorn's gallop, which, in our world, would have carried him out of sight in a few moments. But now a most strange thing happened. Everyone else began to run, and they found, to their astonishment, that they could keep up with him: not only the Dogs and the humans but even fat little Puzzle and short-legged Poggin the Dwarf. The air flew in their faces as if they were driving fast in a car without a windscreen. The country flew past as if they were seeing it from the windows of an express train. Faster and faster they raced, but no one got hot or tired or out of breath.

16

FAREWELL TO
SHADOWLANDS

If one could run without getting tired, I don't
think one would often want to do anything else.
But there might be special reasons for stopping,
and it was a special reason which made Eustace
presently shout:

"I say! Steady! Look what we're coming to!"

And well he might. For now they saw before
them Caldron Pool and beyond the Pool the
high unclimbable cliffs and, pouring down the
cliffs, thousands of tons of water every second,
flashing like diamonds in some places and dark,
glassy green in others, the Great Waterfall; and

already the thunder of it was in their ears.

"Don't stop! Further up and further in," called Farsight, tilting his flight a little upward.

"It's all very well for *him*," said Eustace, but Jewel also cried out:

"Don't stop. Further up and further in! Take it in your stride."

His voice could only just be heard above the roar of the water but next moment everyone saw that he had plunged into the Pool. And helter-skelter behind him, with splash after splash, all the others did the same. The water was not bitingly cold as all of them (and especially Puzzle) expected, but of a delicious foamy coolness. They all found they were swimming straight for the Waterfall itself.

"This is absolutely crazy," said Eustace to Edmund.

"I know. And yet—" said Edmund.

"Isn't it wonderful?" said Lucy. "Have you noticed one can't feel afraid, even if one wants to? Try it."

"By Jove, neither one can," said Eustace after he had tried.

Jewel reached the foot of the Waterfall first, but Tirian was only just behind him. Jill was last, so she could see the whole thing better than the others. She saw something white moving steadily up the face of the Waterfall. That white thing was the Unicorn. You couldn't tell whether he was swimming or climbing, but he moved on, higher and higher. The point of his horn divided the water just above his head, and it cascaded out in two rainbow-colored streams all round his shoulders. Just behind him came King Tirian. He moved his legs and arms as if he were swimming, but he moved straight upward: as if one could swim up the wall of a house.

What looked funniest was the Dogs. During the gallop they had not been at all out of breath, but now, as they swarmed and wriggled upwards, there was plenty of spluttering and sneezing among them; that was because they would keep on barking, and every time they barked they got their mouths and noses full of water. But before Jill had time to notice all these things fully, she was going up the Waterfall herself. It was the sort of thing that would have been quite impossible in our world. Even if you hadn't been drowned, you would have been smashed to pieces by the terrible weight of water against the countless jags of rock. But in that world you could do it. You went on, up and up, with all kinds of reflected lights flashing at you from the water and all manner of colored stones flashing through it, till it seemed as if you were climbing up light itself—and always higher and higher till the sense of height would have terrified you if you could be terrified, but later it was only gloriously exciting. And then at last one came to the lovely, smooth green curve in which the water poured over the top and found that one was out on the level river above the Waterfall. The current was racing away behind you, but you were such a wonderful swimmer that you could make headway against it. Soon they were all on the bank, dripping but happy.

A long valley opened ahead and great snow-mountains, now much nearer, stood up against the sky.

"Further up and further in," cried Jewel and instantly they were off again.

They were out of Narnia now and up into the Western Wild which neither Tirian nor Peter nor even the Eagle had ever seen before. But the Lord Digory and the Lady Polly had. "Do you remember? Do you remember?" they said—and said it in steady voices too, without panting, though the whole party was now running faster than an arrow flies.

"What, Lord?" said Tirian. "Is it then true, as stories tell, that you two journeyed here on the very day the world was made?"

"Yes," said Digory, "and it seems to me as if it were only yesterday."

"And on a flying horse?" asked Tirian. "Is that part true?"

"Certainly," said Digory. But the Dogs barked, "Faster, faster!"

So they ran faster and faster till it was more like flying than running, and even the Eagle overhead was going no faster than they. And they went through winding valley after winding valley and up the steep sides of hills and, faster than ever, down the other side, following the river and sometimes crossing it and skimming across mountain lakes as if they were living speedboats, till at last at the far end of one long lake which looked as blue as a turquoise, they saw a smooth green hill. Its sides were as steep as the sides of a pyramid and round the very top of it ran a green wall: but above the wall rose the branches of trees whose leaves looked like silver and their fruit like gold.

"Further up and further in!" roared the Unicorn, and no one held back. They charged straight at the foot of the hill and then found themselves running up it almost as water from a broken wave runs up a rock out at the point of some bay. Though the slope was nearly as steep as the roof of a house and the grass was smooth as a bowling green, no one slipped. Only when they had reached the very top did they slow up; that was because they found themselves facing great golden gates. And for a moment none of them was bold enough to try if the gates would open. They all felt just as they had felt about the fruit—"Dare we? Is it right? Can it be meant for *us*?"

But while they were standing thus a great horn, wonderfully loud and sweet, blew from somewhere inside that walled garden and the gates swung open.

Tirian stood holding his breath and wondering who would come out. And what came was the last thing he had expected: a little, sleek, bright-eyed Talking Mouse with a red feather stuck in a circlet on its head and its left paw resting on a long sword. It bowed, a most beautiful bow, and said in its shrill voice:

"Welcome, in the Lion's name. Come further up and further in."

Then Tirian saw King Peter and King Edmund and Queen Lucy rush forward to kneel down and greet the Mouse and they all cried out "Reepicheep!" And Tirian breathed fast with the sheer wonder of it, for now he knew that he was looking at one of the great heroes of Narnia, Reepicheep the Mouse who had fought at the great Battle of Beruna and afterward sailed to the World's end with King Caspian the Seafarer. But before he had had much time to think of this he felt two strong arms thrown about him and felt a bearded kiss on his cheeks and heard a well remembered voice saying:

"What, lad? Art thicker and taller since I last touched thee!"

It was his own father, the good King Erlian: but not as Tirian had seen him last when they brought him home pale and wounded from his fight with the giant, nor even as Tirian remembered him in his later years when he was a gray-headed warrior. This was his father, young and merry, as he could just remember him from very early days when he himself had been a little boy playing games with his father in the castle garden at Cair Paravel, just before bedtime on summer evenings. The very smell of the bread-and-milk he used to have for supper came back to him.

Jewel thought to himself, "I will leave them

to talk for a little and then I will go and greet the good King Erlian. Many a bright apple has he given me when I was but a colt." But next moment he had something else to think of, for out of the gateway there came a horse so mighty and noble that even a Unicorn might feel shy in its presence: a great winged horse. It looked a moment at the Lord Digory and the Lady Polly and neighed out "What, cousins!" and they both shouted "Fledge! Good old Fledge!" and rushed to kiss it.

But by now the Mouse was again urging them to come in. So all of them passed in through the golden gates, into the delicious smell that blew toward them out of that garden and into the cool mixture of sunlight and shadow under the trees, walking on springy turf that was all dotted with white flowers. The very first thing which struck everyone was that the place was far larger than it had seemed from outside. But no one had time to think about that for people were coming up to meet the newcomers from every direction.

Everyone you had ever heard of (if you knew the history of those countries) seemed to be there. There was Glimfeather the Owl and Puddleglum the Marsh-wiggle, and King Rilian the Disenchanted, and his mother the Star's daughter and his great father Caspian himself.

And close beside him were the Lord Drinian and the Lord Berne and Trumpkin the Dwarf and Truffle-hunter the good Badger with Glenstorm the Centaur and a hundred other heroes of the great War of Deliverance. And then from another side came Cor the King of Archenland with King Lune his father and his wife Queen Aravis and the brave Prince Corin Thunder-Fist, his brother, and Bree the Horse and Hwin the Mare. And then—which was a wonder beyond all wonders to Tirian—there came from further away in the past, the two good Beavers and Tumnus the Faun. And there was greeting and kissing and hand-shaking and old jokes revived, (you've no idea how good an old joke sounds when you take it out again after a rest of five or six hundred years) and the whole company moved forward to the center of the orchard where the Phoenix sat in a tree and looked down upon them all, and at the foot of that tree were two thrones and in those two thrones a King and Queen so great and beautiful that everyone bowed down before them. And well they might, for these two were King Frank and Queen Helen from whom all the most ancient Kings of Narnia and Archenland are descended. And Tirian felt as you would feel if you were brought before Adam and Eve in all their glory.

About half an hour later—or it might have been half a hundred years later, for time there is not like time here—Lucy stood with her dear friend, her oldest Narnian friend, the Faun Tumnus, looking down over the wall of that garden, and seeing all Narnia spread out below. But when you looked down you found that this hill was much higher than you had thought: it sank down with shining cliffs, thousands of feet below them and trees in that lower world looked no bigger than grains of green salt. Then she turned inward again and stood with her back to the wall and looked at the garden.

"I see," she said at last, thoughtfully. "I see now. This garden is like the stable. It is far bigger inside than it was outside."

"Of course, Daughter of Eve," said the Faun. "The further up and the further in you go, the bigger everything gets. The inside is larger than the outside."

Lucy looked hard at the garden and saw that it was not really a garden but a whole world, with its own rivers and woods and sea and mountains. But they were not strange: she knew them all.

"I see," she said. "This is still Narnia, and more real and more beautiful than the Narnia down below, just as *it* was more real and more beautiful than the Narnia outside the stable door! I see . . . world within world, Narnia within Narnia. . . ."

"Yes," said Mr. Tumnus, "like an onion: except that as you continue to go in and in, each circle is larger than the last."

And Lucy looked this way and that and soon found that a new and beautiful thing had happened to her. Whatever she looked at, however far away it might be, once she had fixed her eyes steadily on it, became quite clear and close as if she were looking through a telescope. She could see the whole Southern desert and beyond it the great city of Tashbaan: to Eastward she could see Cair Paravel on the edge of the sea and the very window of the room that had once been her own. And far out to sea she could discover the islands, islands after islands to the end of the world, and, beyond the end, the huge mountain which they had called Aslan's country. But now she saw that it was part of a great chain of mountains which ringed round the whole world. In front of her it seemed to come quite close. Then she looked to her left and saw what she took to be a great bank of brightly colored cloud, cut off from them by a gap. But she looked harder and saw that it was not a cloud at all but a real land. And when she had fixed her eyes on one particular spot of it, she at once cried out, "Peter! Edmund! Come and look!

Come quickly." And they came and looked, for their eyes also had become like hers.

"Why!" exclaimed Peter. "It's England. And that's the house itself—Professor Kirk's old home in the country where all our adventures began!"

"I thought that house had been destroyed," said Edmund.

"So it was," said the Faun. "But you are now looking at the England within England, the real England just as this is the real Narnia. And in that inner England no good thing is destroyed."

Suddenly they shifted their eyes to another spot, and then Peter and Edmund and Lucy gasped with amazement and shouted out and began waving: for there they saw their own father and mother, waving back at them across the great, deep valley. It was like when you see people waving at you from the deck of a big ship when you are waiting on the quay to meet them.

"How can we get at them?" said Lucy.

"That is easy," said Mr. Tumnus. "That country and this country—all the *real* countries—are only spurs jutting out from the great mountains of Aslan. We have only to walk along the ridge, upward and inward, till it joins on. And listen! There is King Frank's horn: we must all go up."

And soon they found themselves all walking

together—and a great, bright procession it was—up toward mountains higher than you could see in this world even if they were there to be seen. But there was no snow on those mountains: there were forests and green slopes and sweet orchards and flashing waterfalls, one above the other, going up forever. And the land they were walking on grew narrower all the time, with a deep valley on each side: and across that valley the land which was the real England grew nearer and nearer.

The light ahead was growing stronger. Lucy saw that a great series of many-colored cliffs led up in front of them like a giant's staircase. And then she forgot everything else, because Aslan himself was coming, leaping down from cliff to cliff like a living cataract of power and beauty.

And the very first person whom Aslan called to him was Puzzle the Donkey. You never saw a donkey look feebler and sillier than Puzzle did as he walked up to Aslan, and he looked, beside Aslan, as small as a kitten looks beside a St. Bernard. The Lion bowed down his head and whispered something to Puzzle at which his long ears went down, but then he said something else at which the ears perked up again. The humans couldn't hear what he had said either time. Then Aslan turned to them and said:

"You do not yet look so happy as I mean you to be."

Lucy said, "We're so afraid of being sent away, Aslan. And you have sent us back into our own world so often."

"No fear of that," said Aslan. "Have you not guessed?"

Their hearts leaped and a wild hope rose within them.

"There *was* a real railway accident," said Aslan softly. "Your father and mother and all of you are—as you used to call it in the Shadowlands—dead. The term is over: the holidays have begun. The dream is ended: this is the morning."

And as He spoke He no longer looked to them like a lion; but the things that began to happen after that were so great and beautiful that I cannot write them. And for us this is the end of all the stories, and we can most truly say that they all lived happily ever after. But for them it was only the beginning of the real story. All their life in this world and all their adventures in Narnia had only been the cover and the title page: now at last they were beginning Chapter One of the Great Story which no one on earth has read: which goes on forever: in which every chapter is better than the one before.

10677778

THE HORSE
AND
HIS BOY

———◆———

Mt. Pire

Anvard

narrow gorge

DESER

Rock

N
W E
S

The CHRONICLES *of* NARNIA

The CHRONICLES of NARNIA

C. S. LEWIS

BOOK 3

THE HORSE
AND
HIS BOY

Illustrated by Pauline Baynes

HarperTrophy
A Division of HarperCollinsPublishers

"Narnia" is a trademark of C.S. Lewis (Pte) Limited.
"The Chronicles of Narnia" is a U.S. Registered Trademark of C.S. Lewis (Pte) Limited.

The Horse and His Boy
Copyright © 1954 by C.S. Lewis (Pte) Limited
Copyright renewed 1982 by C.S. Lewis (Pte) Limited
All rights reserved. No part of this book may be used or reproduced in any
manner whatsoever without written permission except in the case of brief
quotations embodied in critical articles and reviews. Printed in the United States of
America. For information address HarperCollins Children's Books, a division of
HarperCollins Publishers, 10 East 53rd Street, New York, NY 10022.

Library of Congress Cataloging-in-Publication Data
Lewis, C. S. (Clive Staples), 1898–1963.
  The horse and his boy / C. S. Lewis ; illustrated by Pauline Baynes.
    p.   cm. — (The Chronicles of Narnia ; bk. 3)
  Summary: A boy and a talking horse share an adventurous and dangerous journey to
Narnia to warn of invading barbarians.
  ISBN 0-06-023488-1. — ISBN 0-06-023489-X (lib. bdg.)
  ISBN 0-06-447106-3 (pbk.)
  [1. Fantasy.]   I. Baynes, Pauline, ill.   II. Title.   III. Series: Lewis, C. S. (Clive
Staples), 1898–1963.   Chronicles of Narnia   (HarperCollins (Firm)) ; bk. 3.
PZ7.L58474Ho   1994   93-14300
[Fic]—dc20   CIP
                                                                          AC

Typography by Nicholas Krenitsky
❖
First Harper Trophy Edition, 1994

To David and Douglas Gresham

CAST OF CHARACTERS

ASLAN. The King, Lord of the whole wood, and son of the Emperor across the Sea. Aslan is the Lion, the Great Lion. He comes and goes as and when he pleases; he comes to overthrow the witch and save Narnia. Aslan appears in all seven books.

DIGORY KIRKE. Digory was there at the very beginning in *The Magician's Nephew*, and he is also in *The Lion, the Witch and the Wardrobe*. If it were not for Digory's courage, we might never have heard of Narnia. Find out why in *The Magician's Nephew*.

POLLY PLUMMER. Polly is the first person to leave our world. She and Digory take part in the very beginning of everything in *The Magician's Nephew*.

JADIS. The last Queen of Charn, which she herself destroyed. Jadis arrives in Narnia with Digory and Polly in *The Magician's Nephew* and has taken over the land as the White Witch in *The Lion, the Witch and the Wardrobe*. Completely evil, she is also very dangerous, even in *The Silver Chair*.

UNCLE ANDREW. Mr. Andrew Ketterley thinks he is a magician, but like all who meddle with magic, he doesn't really know what he is doing. The results are dire in *The Magician's Nephew*.

THE PEVENSIES.

Peter Pevensie, King Peter the Magnificent, the High King

Susan Pevensie, Queen Susan the Gentle

Edmund Pevensie, King Edmund the Just

Lucy Pevensie, Queen Lucy the Valiant

The four Pevensies, brothers and sisters, visited Narnia at the time of the winter rule of the White Witch. They remained there for many Narnian years and established the Golden Age of Narnia. Peter is the oldest, followed by Susan, then Edmund and Lucy. They are all in *The Lion, the Witch and the Wardrobe* and *Prince Caspian*. Edmund and Lucy are also in *The Voyage of the Dawn Treader*; Edmund, Lucy, and Susan appear in *The Horse and His Boy*; and Peter, Edmund, and Lucy appear in *The Last Battle*.

SHASTA. There is a mystery about this adopted son of a Calormene fisherman. He is not what he seems, as he himself discovers in *The Horse and His Boy*.

BREE. This great war horse is also unusual. He was kidnapped as a foal from the forests of Narnia and sold as a slave-horse in Calormen, a country across Archenland and far to the south of Narnia. His real adventures begin when he tries to escape in *The Horse and His Boy*.

ARAVIS. Aravis is a Tarkheena, a Calormene

noblewoman, but even so she has many good points, and they come to light in *The Horse and His Boy*.

HWIN. Hwin is a good-natured, sensible horse. Another slave taken from Narnia, she and Aravis become friends in *The Horse and His Boy*.

PRINCE CASPIAN. He is the nephew of King Miraz and is known as Caspian the Tenth, Son of Caspian, and the True King of Narnia (King of Old Narnians). He is also called a Telmarine of Narnia, Lord of Cair Paravel, and Emperor of the Lone Islands. He appears in *Prince Caspian*, *The Voyage of the Dawn Treader*, *The Silver Chair*, and *The Last Battle*.

MIRAZ. Miraz is a Telmarine from the land of Telmar, far beyond the Western Mountains (originally the ancestors of the Telmarines came from our world), and the usurper of the throne of Narnia in *Prince Caspian*.

REEPICHEEP. Reepicheep is the Chief Mouse. He is the self-appointed humble servant to Prince Caspian, and perhaps the most valiant knight in all of Narnia. His chivalry is unsurpassed, as also are his courage and skill with the sword. Reepicheep appears in *Prince Caspian*, *The Voyage of the Dawn Treader*, and *The Last Battle*.

EUSTACE CLARENCE SCRUBB. Eustace is a cousin of the Pevensie family whom Edmund

and Lucy must go and visit. He finds Narnia something of a shock. He appears in *The Voyage of the* Dawn Treader, *The Silver Chair,* and *The Last Battle.*

JILL POLE. Jill is the heroine of *The Silver Chair;* she goes to Narnia with Eustace on his second Narnian adventure. She also comes to aid Narnia in *The Last Battle.*

PRINCE RILIAN. The son of King Caspian the Tenth, Rilian is the lost Prince of Narnia; find him in *The Silver Chair.*

PUDDLEGLUM. Puddleglum is a Marsh-wiggle from the Eastern Marshes of Narnia. He is tall, and his very serious demeanor masks a true heart of great courage. He appears in *The Silver Chair* and *The Last Battle.*

KING TIRIAN. Noble and brave, Tirian is the last King of Narnia. He and his friend Jewel, a Unicorn, fight *The Last Battle.*

SHIFT. An old and ugly Ape, Shift decides that he should be in charge of Narnia and starts things that he can't stop in *The Last Battle.*

PUZZLE. Puzzle, a donkey, never meant any harm—you see, he's not really very clever. And Shift deceives him in *The Last Battle.*

CONTENTS

1

HOW SHASTA SET OUT
ON HIS TRAVELS

This is the story of an adventure that happened
in Narnia and Calormen and the lands between,
in the Golden Age when Peter was High King in
Narnia and his brother and his two sisters were
King and Queens under him.

In those days, far south in Calormen on a
little creek of the sea, there lived a poor fisherman called Arsheesh, and with him there lived a
boy who called him Father. The boy's name was
Shasta. On most days Arsheesh went out in his
boat to fish in the morning, and in the afternoon he harnessed his donkey to a cart and

loaded the cart with fish and went a mile or so southward to the village to sell it. If it had sold well he would come home in a moderately good temper and say nothing to Shasta, but if it had sold badly he would find fault with him and perhaps beat him. There was always something to find fault with for Shasta had plenty of work to do, mending and washing the nets, cooking the supper, and cleaning the cottage in which they both lived.

Shasta was not at all interested in anything that lay south of his home because he had once or twice been to the village with Arsheesh and he knew that there was nothing very interesting there. In the village he only met other men who were just like his father—men with long, dirty robes, and wooden shoes turned up at the toe, and turbans on their heads, and beards, talking to one another very slowly about things that sounded dull. But he was very interested in everything that lay to the North because no one ever went that way and he was never allowed to go there himself. When he was sitting out of doors mending the nets, and all alone, he would often look eagerly to the North. One could see nothing but a grassy slope running up to a level ridge and beyond that the sky with perhaps a few birds in it.

Sometimes if Arsheesh was there Shasta

would say, "O my Father, what is there beyond that hill?" And then if the fisherman was in a bad temper he would box Shasta's ears and tell him to attend to his work. Or if he was in a peaceable mood he would say, "O my son, do not allow your mind to be distracted by idle questions. For one of the poets has said, 'Application to business is the root of prosperity, but those who ask questions that do not concern them are steering the ship of folly toward the rock of indigence.'"

Shasta thought that beyond the hill there must be some delightful secret which his father wished to hide from him. In reality, however, the fisherman talked like this because he didn't know what lay to the North. Neither did he care. He had a very practical mind.

One day there came from the South a stranger who was unlike any man that Shasta had seen before. He rode upon a strong dappled horse with flowing mane and tail and his stirrups and bridle were inlaid with silver. The spike of a helmet projected from the middle of his silken turban and he wore a shirt of chain mail. By his side hung a curving scimitar, a round shield studded with bosses of brass hung at his back, and his right hand grasped a lance. His face was dark, but this did not surprise Shasta because all the people of Calormen are like that;

what did surprise him was the man's beard which was dyed crimson, and curled and gleaming with scented oil. But Arsheesh knew by the gold on the stranger's bare arm that he was a Tarkaan or great lord, and he bowed kneeling before him till his beard touched the earth and made signs to Shasta to kneel also.

The stranger demanded hospitality for the night which of course the fisherman dared not refuse. All the best they had was set before the Tarkaan for supper (and he didn't think much of it) and Shasta, as always happened when the fisherman had company, was given a hunk of bread and turned out of the cottage. On these occasions he usually slept with the donkey in its little thatched stable. But it was much too early to go to sleep yet, and Shasta, who had never learned that it is wrong to listen behind doors, sat down with his ear to a crack in the wooden wall of the cottage to hear what the grown-ups were talking about. And this is what he heard.

"And now, O my host," said the Tarkaan, "I have a mind to buy that boy of yours."

"O my master," replied the fisherman (and Shasta knew by the wheedling tone the greedy look that was probably coming into his face as he said it), "what price could induce your servant, poor though he is, to sell into slavery his only child and his own flesh? Has not one of the poets said, 'Natural affection is stronger than soup and offspring more precious than carbuncles?'"

"It is even so," replied the guest dryly. "But another poet has likewise said, 'He who attempts to deceive the judicious is already baring his own back for the scourge.' Do not load your aged mouth with falsehoods. This boy is manifestly no son of yours, for your cheek is as dark as mine but the boy is fair and white like the accursed but beautiful barbarians who inhabit the remote North."

"How well it was said," answered the fisherman, "that Swords can be kept off with shields but the Eye of Wisdom pierces through every defense! Know then, O my formidable guest, that because of my extreme poverty I have never married and have no child. But in that same year in which the Tisroc (may he live forever) began his august and beneficent reign, on a night when the moon was at her full, it pleased the gods to deprive me of my sleep. Therefore I arose from my bed in this hovel and went forth to the beach to refresh myself with looking upon the water and the moon and breathing the cool air. And presently I heard a noise as of oars coming to me across the water and then, as it were, a weak cry. And shortly after, the tide brought to the land a little boat in which there was nothing but a man lean with extreme hunger and thirst who seemed to have died but a few moments before (for he was still warm), and an empty water-skin, and a child, still living. 'Doubtless,' said I, 'these unfortunates have escaped from the wreck of a great ship, but by the admirable designs of the gods, the elder has starved himself to keep the child alive and has perished in sight of land.' Accordingly, remembering how the gods never fail to reward those who befriend the destitute, and being moved by compassion (for your servant is a man of tender heart)—"

"Leave out all these idle words in your own praise," interrupted the Tarkaan. "It is enough to know that you took the child—and have had ten times the worth of his daily bread out of him in labor, as anyone can see. And now tell me at once what price you put on him, for I am wearied with your loquacity."

"You yourself have wisely said," answered Arsheesh, "that the boy's labor has been to me of inestimable value. This must be taken into account in fixing the price. For if I sell the boy I must undoubtedly either buy or hire another to do his work."

"I'll give you fifteen crescents for him," said the Tarkaan.

"Fifteen!" cried Arsheesh in a voice that was something between a whine and a scream.

"Fifteen! For the prop of my old age and the delight of my eyes! Do not mock my gray beard, Tarkaan though you be. My price is seventy."

At this point Shasta got up and tiptoed away. He had heard all he wanted, for he had often listened when men were bargaining in the village and knew how it was done. He was quite certain that Arsheesh would sell him in the end for something much more than fifteen crescents and much less than seventy, but that he and the Tarkaan would take hours in getting to an agreement.

You must not imagine that Shasta felt at all as you and I would feel if we had just overheard our parents talking about selling us for slaves. For one thing, his life was already little better than slavery; for all he knew, the lordly stranger on the great horse might be kinder to him than Arsheesh. For another, the story about his own discovery in the boat had filled him with excitement and with a sense of relief. He had often been uneasy because, try as he might, he had never been able to love the fisherman, and he knew that a boy ought to love his father. And now, apparently, he was no relation to Arsheesh at all. That took a great weight off his mind. "Why, I might be anyone!" he thought. "I might be the son of a Tarkaan myself—or the son of the Tisroc (may he live forever)—or of a god!"

He was standing out in the grassy place before the cottage while he thought these things. Twilight was coming on apace and a star or two was already out, but the remains of the sunset could still be seen in the west. Not far away the stranger's horse, loosely tied to an iron ring in the wall of the donkey's stable, was grazing. Shasta strolled over to it and patted its neck. It went on tearing up the grass and took no notice of him.

Then another thought came into Shasta's mind. "I wonder what sort of a man that Tarkaan is," he said out loud. "It would be splendid if he was kind. Some of the slaves in a great lord's house have next to nothing to do. They wear lovely clothes and eat meat every day. Perhaps he'd take me to the wars and I'd save his life in a battle and then he'd set me free and adopt me as his son and give me a palace and a chariot and a suit of armor. But then he might be a horrid cruel man. He might send me to work on the fields in chains. I wish I knew. How can I know? I bet this horse knows, if only he could tell me."

The Horse had lifted its head. Shasta stroked its smooth-as-satin nose and said, "I wish *you* could talk, old fellow."

And then for a second he thought he was dreaming, for quite distinctly, though in a low voice, the Horse said, "But I can."

Shasta stared into its great eyes and his own grew almost as big, with astonishment.

"How ever did *you* learn to talk?" he asked.

"Hush! Not so loud," replied the Horse. "Where I come from, nearly all the animals talk."

"Wherever is that?" asked Shasta.

"Narnia," answered the Horse. "The happy land of Narnia—Narnia of the heathery mountains and the thymy downs, Narnia of the many rivers, the plashing glens, the mossy caverns and the deep forests ringing with the hammers of the Dwarfs. Oh the sweet air of Narnia! An hour's life there is better than a thousand years in Calormen." It ended with a whinny that sounded very like a sigh.

"How did you get here?" said Shasta.

"Kidnapped," said the Horse. "Or stolen, or captured—whichever you like to call it. I was only a foal at the time. My mother warned me not to range the Southern slopes, into Archenland and beyond, but I wouldn't heed her. And by the Lion's Mane I have paid for my folly. All these years I have been a slave to humans, hiding my true nature and pretending to be dumb and witless like *their* horses."

"Why didn't you tell them who you were?"

"Not such a fool, that's why. If they'd once

found out I could talk they would have made a show of me at fairs and guarded me more carefully than ever. My last chance of escape would have been gone."

"And why—" began Shasta, but the Horse interrupted him.

"Now look," it said, "we mustn't waste time on idle questions. You want to know about my master the Tarkaan Anradin. Well, he's bad. Not too bad to me, for a war horse costs too much to be treated very badly. But you'd better be lying dead tonight than go to be a human slave in his house tomorrow."

"Then I'd better run away," said Shasta, turning very pale.

"Yes, you had," said the Horse. "But why not run away with me?"

"Are you going to run away too?" said Shasta.

"Yes, if you'll come with me," answered the Horse. "This is the chance for both of us. You see if I run away without a rider, everyone who sees me will say 'Stray horse' and be after me quick as he can. With a rider I've a chance to get through. That's where you can help me. On the other hand, you can't get very far on those two silly legs of yours (what absurd legs humans have!) without being overtaken. But on me you can outdistance any other horse in this country.

That's where I can help you. By the way, I suppose you know how to ride?"

"Oh yes, of course," said Shasta. "At least, I've ridden the donkey."

"Ridden the *what?*" retorted the Horse with extreme contempt. (At least, that is what he meant. Actually it came out in a sort of neigh— "Ridden the wha-ha-ha-ha-ha." Talking horses always sound more horsey in accent when they are angry.)

"In other words," it continued, "you *can't* ride. That's a drawback. I'll have to teach you as we go along. If you can't ride, can you fall?"

"I suppose anyone can fall," said Shasta.

"I mean can you fall and get up again without crying and mount again and fall again and yet not be afraid of falling?"

"I—I'll try," said Shasta.

"Poor little beast," said the Horse in a gentler tone. "I forget you're only a foal. We'll make a fine rider of you in time. And now—we mustn't start until those two in the hut are asleep. Meantime we can make our plans. My Tarkaan is on his way North to the great city, to Tashbaan itself and the court of the Tisroc—"

"I say," put in Shasta in rather a shocked voice, "oughtn't you to say 'May he live forever'?"

"Why?" asked the Horse. "I'm a free

Narnian. And why should I talk slaves' and fools' talk? I don't want him to live forever, and I know that he's not going to live forever whether I want him to or not. And I can see you're from the free North too. No more of this Southern jargon between you and me! And now, back to our plans. As I said, my human was on his way North to Tashbaan."

"Does that mean we'd better go to the South?"

"I think not," said the Horse. "You see, he thinks I'm dumb and witless like his other horses. Now if I really were, the moment I got loose I'd go back home to my stable and paddock; back to his palace which is two days' journey South. That's where he'll look for me. He'd never dream of my going on North on my own. And anyway he will probably think that someone in the last village who saw him ride through has followed us here and stolen me."

"Oh hurrah!" said Shasta. "Then we'll go North. I've been longing to go to the North all my life."

"Of course you have," said the Horse. "That's because of the blood that's in you. I'm sure you're true Northern stock. But not too loud. I should think they'd be asleep soon now."

"I'd better creep back and see," suggested Shasta.

"That's a good idea," said the Horse. "But take care you're not caught."

It was a good deal darker now and very silent except for the sound of the waves on the beach, which Shasta hardly noticed because he had been hearing it day and night as long as he could remember. The cottage, as he approached it, showed no light. When he listened at the front there was no noise. When he went round to the only window, he could hear, after a second or two, the familiar noise of the old fisherman's squeaky snore. It was funny to think that if all went well he would never hear it again. Holding his breath and feeling a little bit sorry, but much less sorry than he was glad, Shasta glided away over the grass and went to the donkey's stable, groped along to a place he knew where the key was hidden, opened the door and found the Horse's saddle and bridle which had been locked up there for the night. He bent forward and kissed the donkey's nose. "I'm sorry we can't take *you*," he said.

"There you are at last," said the Horse when he got back to it. "I was beginning to wonder what had become of you."

"I was getting your things out of the stable," replied Shasta. "And now, can you tell me how to put them on?"

For the next few minutes Shasta was at

work, very cautiously to avoid jingling, while the Horse said things like, "Get that girth a bit tighter," or "You'll find a buckle lower down," or "You'll need to shorten those stirrups a good bit." When all was finished it said:

"Now; we've got to have reins for the look of the thing, but you won't be using them. Tie them to the saddle-bow: very slack so that I can do what I like with my head. And, remember— you are not to touch them."

"What are they for, then?" asked Shasta.

"Ordinarily they are for directing me," replied the Horse. "But as I intend to do all the directing on this journey, you'll please keep your hands to yourself. And there's another thing. I'm not going to have you grabbing my mane."

"But I say," pleaded Shasta. "If I'm not to hold on by the reins or by your mane, what *am* I to hold on by?"

"You hold on with your knees," said the Horse. "That's the secret of good riding. Grip my body between your knees as hard as you like; sit straight up, straight as a poker; keep your elbows in. And by the way, what did you do with the spurs?"

"Put them on my heels, of course," said Shasta. "I do know that much."

"Then you can take them off and put them in the saddle-bag. We may be able to sell them when we get to Tashbaan. Ready? And now I think you can get up."

"Ooh! You're a dreadful height," gasped Shasta after his first, and unsuccessful, attempt.

"I'm a horse, that's all," was the reply. "Anyone would think I was a haystack from the way you're trying to climb up me! There, that's better. Now sit *up* and remember what I told you about your knees. Funny to think of me who has led cavalry charges and won races having a potato sack like you in the saddle! However, off we go." It chuckled, not unkindly.

And it certainly began their night journey with great caution. First of all it went just south of the fisherman's cottage to the little river which there ran into the sea, and took care to leave in the mud some very plain hoof-marks pointing South. But as soon as they were in the middle of the ford it turned upstream and waded till they were about a hundred yards farther inland than the cottage. Then it selected a nice gravelly bit of bank which would take no footprints and came out on the Northern side. Then, still at a walking pace, it went Northward till the cottage, the one tree, the donkey's stable, and the creek—everything, in fact, that Shasta had ever known—had sunk out of sight in the gray summer-night darkness. They had been going uphill and now were at the top of the ridge—that ridge which had always been the boundary of Shasta's known world. He could not see what was ahead except that it was all open and grassy. It looked endless: wild and lonely and free.

"I say!" observed the Horse. "What a place for a gallop, eh?"

"Oh don't let's," said Shasta. "Not yet. I don't know how to—please, Horse. I don't know your name."

"Breehy-hinny-brinny-hoohy-hah," said the Horse.

"I'll never be able to say that," said Shasta. "Can I call you Bree?"

"Well, if it's the best you can do, I suppose you must," said the Horse. "And what shall I call you?"

"I'm called Shasta."

"Hm," said Bree. "Well, now, there's a name that's *really* hard to pronounce. But now about this gallop. It's a good deal easier than trotting if you only knew, because you don't have to rise and fall. Grip with your knees and keep your eyes straight ahead between my ears. Don't look at the ground. If you think you're going to fall just grip harder and sit up straighter. Ready? Now: for Narnia and the North."

2

A WAYSIDE ADVENTURE

It was nearly noon on the following day when Shasta was wakened by something warm and soft moving over his face. He opened his eyes and found himself staring into the long face of a horse; its nose and lips were almost touching his. He remembered the exciting events of the previous night and sat up. But as he did so he groaned.

"Ow, Bree," he gasped. "I'm so sore. All over. I can hardly move."

"Good morning, small one," said Bree. "I was afraid you might feel a bit stiff. It can't be the falls. You didn't have more than a dozen or so, and it was all lovely, soft springy turf that must have been almost a pleasure to fall on. And the only one that might have been nasty was broken by that gorse bush. No: it's the riding itself that comes hard at first. What about breakfast? I've had mine."

"Oh bother breakfast. Bother everything," said Shasta. "I tell you I can't move." But the horse nuzzled at him with its nose and pawed him gently with a hoof till he had to get up. And then he looked about him and saw where they were. Behind them lay a little copse. Before them the turf, dotted with white flowers, sloped down to the brow of a cliff. Far below them, so that the sound of the breaking waves was very faint, lay the sea. Shasta had never seen it from such a height and never seen so much of it before, nor dreamed how many colors it had. On either hand the coast stretched away, headland after headland, and at the points you could see the white foam running up the rocks but making no noise because it was so far off. There were gulls flying overhead and the heat shivered on the ground; it was a blazing day. But what Shasta chiefly noticed was the air. He couldn't think what was missing, until at last he realized that there was no smell of fish in it. For of course, neither in the cottage nor among the nets, had he ever been away from that smell in his life.

And this new air was so delicious, and all his old life seemed so far away, that he forgot for a moment about his bruises and his aching muscles and said:

"I say, Bree, didn't you say something about breakfast?"

"Yes, I did," answered Bree. "I think you'll find something in the saddle-bags. They're over there on that tree where you hung them up last night—or early this morning, rather."

They investigated the saddle-bags and the results were cheering—a meat pasty, only slightly stale, a lump of dried figs and another lump of green cheese, a little flask of wine, and some money; about forty crescents in all, which was more than Shasta had ever seen.

While Shasta sat down—painfully and cautiously—with his back against a tree and started on the pasty, Bree had a few more mouthfuls of grass to keep him company.

"Won't it be stealing to use the money?" asked Shasta.

"Oh," said the Horse, looking up with its mouth full of grass, "I never thought of that. A free horse and a talking horse mustn't steal, of course. But I think it's all right. We're prisoners and captives in enemy country. That money is booty, spoil. Besides, how are we to get any food for you without it? I suppose, like all humans, you won't eat natural food like grass and oats."

"I can't."

"Ever tried?"

"Yes, I have. I can't get it down at all. You couldn't either if you were me."

"You're rum little creatures, you humans," remarked Bree.

When Shasta had finished his breakfast (which was by far the nicest he had ever eaten), Bree said, "I think I'll have a nice roll before we put on that saddle again." And he proceeded to do so. "That's good. That's very good," he said, rubbing his back on the turf and waving all four legs in the air. "You ought to have one too, Shasta," he snorted. "It's most refreshing."

But Shasta burst out laughing and said, "You do look funny when you're on your back!"

"I look nothing of the sort," said Bree. But then suddenly he rolled round on his side, raised his head and looked hard at Shasta, blowing a little.

"Does it really look funny?" he asked in an anxious voice.

"Yes, it does," replied Shasta. "But what does it matter?"

"You don't think, do you," said Bree, "that it might be a thing *talking* horses never do—a silly, clownish trick I've learned from the dumb ones? It would be dreadful to find, when I get back to

Narnia, that I've picked up a lot of low, bad habits. What do you think, Shasta? Honestly, now. Don't spare my feelings. Should you think the real, free horses—the talking kind—do roll?"

"How should I know? Anyway I don't think I should bother about it if I were you. We've got to get there first. Do you know the way?"

"I know my way to Tashbaan. After that comes the desert. Oh, we'll manage the desert somehow, never fear. Why, we'll be in sight of the Northern mountains then. Think of it! To Narnia and the North! Nothing will stop us then. But I'd be glad to be past Tashbaan. You and I are safer away from cities."

"Can't we avoid it?"

"Not without going a long way inland, and that would take us into cultivated land and main roads; and I wouldn't know the way. No, we'll just have to creep along the coast. Up here on the downs we'll meet nothing but sheep and rabbits and gulls and a few shepherds. And by the way, what about starting?"

Shasta's legs ached terribly as he saddled Bree and climbed into the saddle, but the Horse was kindly to him and went at a soft pace all afternoon. When evening twilight came they dropped by steep tracks into a valley and found a village. Before they got into it Shasta dismounted and entered it on foot to buy a loaf and some onions and radishes. The Horse trotted round by the fields in the dusk and met Shasta at the far side. This became their regular plan every second night.

These were great days for Shasta, and every day better than the last as his muscles hardened and he fell less often. Even at the end of his training Bree still said he sat like a bag of flour in the saddle. "And even if it was safe, young 'un, I'd be ashamed to be seen with you on the main road." But in spite of his rude words Bree was a patient teacher. No one can teach riding so well as a horse. Shasta learned to trot, to canter, to jump, and to keep his seat even when Bree pulled up suddenly or swung unexpectedly to the left or the right—which, as Bree told him, was a thing you might have to do at any moment in a battle. And then of course Shasta begged to be told of the battles and wars in which Bree had carried the Tarkaan. And Bree would tell of forced marches and the fording of swift rivers, of charges and of fierce fights between cavalry and cavalry when the war horses fought as well as the men, being all fierce stallions, trained to bite and kick, and to rear at the right moment so that the horse's weight as well as the rider's would come down on an enemy's crest in the stroke of sword or battle-axe. But Bree did not want to talk about the wars as often as Shasta wanted to hear about them. "Don't speak of them, youngster," he would say. "They were only the Tisroc's wars and I fought in them as a slave and a dumb beast. Give me the Narnian wars where I shall fight as a free Horse among my own people! Those will be wars worth talking about. Narnia and the North! Bra-ha-ha! Broo hoo!"

Shasta soon learned, when he heard Bree talking like that, to prepare for a gallop.

After they had traveled on for weeks and weeks past more bays and headlands and rivers and villages than Shasta could remember, there came a moonlit night when they started their journey at evening, having slept during the day. They had left the downs behind them and were crossing a wide plain with a forest about half a mile away on their left. The sea, hidden by low sandhills, was about the same distance on their right. They had jogged along for about an hour, sometimes trotting and sometimes walking, when Bree suddenly stopped.

"What's up?" said Shasta.

"S-s-ssh!" said Bree, craning his neck round and twitching his ears. "Did you hear something? Listen."

"It sounds like another horse—between us and the wood," said Shasta after he had listened for about a minute.

"It *is* another horse," said Bree. "And that's what I don't like."

"Isn't it probably just a farmer riding home late?" said Shasta with a yawn.

"Don't tell me!" said Bree. "*That's* not a farmer's riding. Nor a farmer's horse either. Can't you tell by the sound? That's quality, that horse is. And it's being ridden by a real horseman. I tell you what it is, Shasta. There's a Tarkaan under the edge of that wood. Not on his war horse—it's too light for that. On a fine blood mare, I should say."

"Well, it's stopped now, whatever it is," said Shasta.

"You're right," said Bree. "And why should he stop just when we do? Shasta, my boy, I do believe there's someone shadowing us at last."

"What shall we do?" said Shasta in a lower whisper than before. "Do you think he can see us as well as hear us?"

"Not in this light so long as we stay quite still," answered Bree. "But look! There's a cloud coming up. I'll wait till that gets over the moon. Then we'll get off to our right as quietly as we can, down to the shore. We can hide among the sandhills if the worst comes to the worst."

They waited till the cloud covered the moon and then, first at a walking pace and afterward at a gentle trot, made for the shore.

The cloud was bigger and thicker than it had looked at first and soon the night grew very dark. Just as Shasta was saying to himself, "We must be nearly at those sandhills by now," his heart leaped into his mouth because an appalling noise had suddenly risen out of the darkness ahead; a long snarling roar, melancholy and utterly savage. Instantly Bree swerved round and began galloping inland again as fast as he could gallop.

"What is it?" gasped Shasta.

"Lions!" said Bree, without checking his pace or turning his head.

After that there was nothing but sheer galloping for some time. At last they splashed across a wide, shallow stream and Bree came to a stop on the far side. Shasta noticed that he was trembling and sweating all over.

"That water may have thrown the brute off our scent," panted Bree when he had partly got his breath again. "We can walk for a bit now."

As they walked Bree said, "Shasta, I'm ashamed of myself. I'm just as frightened as a common, dumb Calormene horse. I am really. I don't feel like a Talking Horse at all. I don't mind swords and lances and arrows but I can't bear—those creatures. I think I'll trot for a bit."

About a minute later, however, he broke into a gallop again, and no wonder. For the roar broke out again, this time on their left from the direction of the forest.

"Two of them," moaned Bree.

When they had galloped for several minutes without any further noise from the lions Shasta said, "I say! That other horse is galloping beside us now. Only a stone's throw away."

"All the b-better," panted Bree. "Tarkaan on it—will have a sword—protect us all."

"But, Bree!" said Shasta. "We might just as well be killed by lions as caught. Or I might. They'll hang me for horse-stealing." He was feeling less frightened of lions than Bree because he had never met a lion; Bree had.

Bree only snorted in answer but he did sheer away to his right. Oddly enough the other horse seemed also to be sheering away to the left, so that in a few seconds the space between them had widened a good deal. But as soon as it did so there came two more lions' roars, immediately after one another, one on the right and the other on the left, the horses began drawing nearer together. So, apparently, did the lions. The roaring of the brutes on each side was horribly close and they seemed to be keeping up with the galloping horses quite easily. Then the cloud rolled away. The moonlight, astonishingly bright, showed up everything almost as if it were broad day. The two horses and two riders were galloping neck to neck and knee to knee just as if they were in a race. Indeed Bree said (afterward) that a finer race had never been seen in Calormen.

Shasta now gave himself up for lost and began to wonder whether lions killed you quickly or played with you as a cat plays with a mouse and how much it would hurt. At the same time (one sometimes does this at the most frightful moments) he noticed everything. He saw that the other rider was a very small, slender person, mail-clad (the moon shone on the mail) and riding magnificently. He had no beard.

Something flat and shining was spread out

before them. Before Shasta had time even to guess what it was there was a great splash and he found his mouth half full of salt water. The shining thing had been a long inlet of the sea. Both horses were swimming and the water was up to Shasta's knees. There was an angry roaring behind them and looking back Shasta saw a great, shaggy, and terrible shape crouched on the water's edge; but only one. "We must have shaken off the other lion," he thought.

The lion apparently did not think its prey worth a wetting; at any rate it made no attempt to take to the water in pursuit. The two horses, side by side, were now well out into the middle of the creek and the opposite shore could be clearly seen. The Tarkaan had not yet spoken a word. "But he will," thought Shasta. "As soon as we have landed. What am I to say? I must begin thinking out a story."

Then, suddenly, two voices spoke at his side.

"Oh, I *am* so tired," said the one. "Hold your tongue, Hwin, and don't be a fool," said the other.

"I'm dreaming," thought Shasta. "I could have sworn that other horse spoke."

Soon the horses were no longer swimming but walking and soon with a great sound of water running off their sides and tails and with a great crunching of pebbles under eight hoofs, they came out on the farther beach of the inlet. The Tarkaan, to Shasta's surprise, showed no wish to ask questions. He did not even look at Shasta but seemed anxious to urge his horse straight on. Bree, however, at once shouldered himself in the other horse's way.

"Broo-hoo-hah!" he snorted. "Steady there! I *heard* you, I did. There's no good pretending, Ma'am. *I* heard you. You're a Talking Horse, a Narnian horse just like me."

"What's it got to do with you if she is?" said the strange rider fiercely, laying hand on sword-hilt. But the voice in which the words were spoken had already told Shasta something.

"Why, it's only a girl!" he exclaimed.

"And what business is it of yours if I am *only* a girl?" snapped the stranger. "You're probably only a boy: a rude, common little boy—a slave probably, who's stolen his master's horse."

"That's all *you* know," said Shasta.

"He's not a thief, little Tarkheena," said Bree. "At least, if there's been any stealing, you might just as well say I stole *him*. And as for its not being my business, you wouldn't expect me to pass a lady of my own race in this strange country without speaking to her? It's only natural I should."

"I think it's very natural too," said the mare.

31

"I wish you'd hold your tongue, Hwin," said the girl. "Look at the trouble you've got us into."

"I don't know about trouble," said Shasta. "You can clear off as soon as you like. We shan't keep you."

"No, you shan't," said the girl.

"What quarrelsome creatures these humans are," said Bree to the mare. "They're as bad as mules. Let's try to talk a little sense. I take it, ma'am, your story is the same as mine? Captured in early youth—years of slavery among the Calormenes?"

"Too true, sir," said the mare with a melancholy whinny.

"And now, perhaps—escape?"

"Tell him to mind his own business, Hwin," said the girl.

"No, I won't, Aravis," said the mare putting her ears back. "This is my escape just as much as yours. And I'm sure a noble war horse like this is not going to betray us. We are trying to escape, to get to Narnia."

"And so, of course, are we," said Bree. "Of course you guessed that at once. A little boy in rags riding (or trying to ride) a war horse at dead of night couldn't mean anything but an escape of some sort. And, if I may say so, a high-born Tarkheena riding alone at night—dressed up in her brother's armor—and very anxious for everyone to mind their own business and ask her no questions—well, if that's not fishy, call me a cob!"

"All right then," said Aravis. "You've guessed it. Hwin and I are running away. We are trying to get to Narnia. And now, what about it?"

"Why, in that case, what is to prevent us all going together?" said Bree. "I trust, Madam Hwin, you will accept such assistance and protection as I may be able to give you on the journey?"

"Why do you keep talking to my horse instead of to me?" asked the girl.

"Excuse me, Tarkheena," said Bree (with just the slightest backward tilt of his ears), "but that's Calormene talk. We're free Narnians, Hwin and I, and I suppose, if you're running away to Narnia, you want to be one too. In that case Hwin isn't *your* horse any longer. One might just as well say you're *her* human."

The girl opened her mouth to speak and then stopped. Obviously she had not quite seen it in that light before.

"Still," she said after a moment's pause, "I don't know that there's so much point in all going together. Aren't we more likely to be noticed?"

"Less," said Bree; and the mare said, "Oh

do let's. I should feel much more comfortable. We're not even certain of the way. I'm sure a great charger like this knows far more than we do."

"Oh come on, Bree," said Shasta, "and let them go their own way. Can't you see they don't want us?"

"We do," said Hwin.

"Look here," said the girl. "I don't mind going with *you*, Mr. War Horse, but what about this boy? How do I know he's not a spy?"

"Why don't you say at once that you think I'm not good enough for you?" said Shasta.

"Be quiet, Shasta," said Bree. "The Tarkheena's question is quite reasonable. I'll vouch for the boy, Tarkheena. He's been true to me and a good friend. And he's certainly either a Narnian or an Archenlander."

"All right, then. Let's go together." But she didn't say anything to Shasta and it was obvious that she wanted Bree, not him.

"Splendid!" said Bree. "And now that we've got the water between us and those dreadful animals, what about you two humans taking off our saddles and our all having a rest and hearing one another's stories."

Both the children unsaddled their horses and the horses had a little grass and Aravis produced rather nice things to eat from her saddle-bag. But Shasta sulked and said No thanks, and that he wasn't hungry. And he tried to put on what he thought very grand and stiff manners, but as a fisherman's hut is not usually a good place for learning grand manners, the result was dreadful. And he half knew that it wasn't a success and then became sulkier and more awkward than ever. Meanwhile the two horses were getting on splendidly. They remembered the very same places in Narnia—"the grasslands up above Beaversdam" and found that they were some sort of second cousins once removed. This made things more and more uncomfortable for the humans until at last Bree said, "And now, Tarkheena, tell us your story. And don't hurry it—I'm feeling comfortable now."

Aravis immediately began, sitting quite still and using a rather different tone and style from her usual one. For in Calormen, story-telling (whether the stories are true or made up) is a thing you're taught, just as English boys and girls are taught essay writing. The difference is that people want to hear the stories, whereas I never heard of anyone who wanted to read the essays.

3

AT THE GATES OF TASHBAAN

"My name," said the girl at once, "is Aravis Tarkheena and I am the only daughter of Kidrash Tarkaan, the son of Rishti Tarkaan, the son of Kidrash Tarkaan, the son of Ilsombreh Tisroc, the son of Ardeeb Tisroc who was descended in a right line from the god Tash. My father is the lord of the province of Calavar and is one who has the right of standing on his feet in his shoes before the face of Tisroc himself (may he live forever). My mother (on whom be the peace of the gods) is dead and my father has married another wife. One of my brothers has fallen in battle against the rebels in the far west and the other is a child. Now it came to pass that my father's wife, my stepmother, hated me, and the sun appeared dark in her eyes as long as I lived in my father's house. And so she persuaded my father to promise me in marriage to Ahoshta Tarkaan. Now this Ahoshta is of base birth, though in these latter years he has won the favor of the Tisroc (may he live forever) by flattery and evil counsels, and is now made a Tarkaan and the lord of many cities and is likely to be chosen as the Grand Vizier when the present Grand Vizier dies. Moreover he is at least sixty years old and has a hump on his back and his face resembles that of an ape. Nevertheless my father, because of the wealth and power of this Ahoshta, and being persuaded by his wife, sent messengers offering me in marriage, and the offer was favorably accepted and Ahoshta sent word that he would marry me this very year at the time of high summer.

"When this news was brought to me the sun appeared dark in my eyes and I laid myself on my bed and wept for a day. But on the second day I rose up and washed my face and caused my mare Hwin to be saddled and took with me a sharp dagger which my brother had carried in the western wars and rode out alone. And when my father's house was out of sight and I was come to a green open place in a certain wood where there were no dwellings of men, I dismounted from Hwin my mare and took out the dagger. Then I parted my clothes where I thought the readiest way lay to my heart and I prayed to all the gods that as soon as I was dead I might find myself with my brother. After that I shut my eyes and my teeth and prepared to drive the dagger into my heart. But before I had done so, this mare spoke with the voice of one of the daughters of men and said, 'O my mistress, do not by any means destroy yourself, for if you live you may yet have good fortune but all the dead are dead alike.'"

"I didn't say it half so well as that," muttered the mare.

"Hush, Ma'am, hush," said Bree, who was thoroughly enjoying the story. "She's telling it in the grand Calormene manner and no story-teller in a Tisroc's court could do it better. Pray go on, Tarkheena."

"When I heard the language of men uttered by my mare," continued Aravis, "I said to my-self, the fear of death has disordered my reason and subjected me to delusions. And I became full of shame for none of my lineage ought to fear death more than the biting of a gnat. Therefore I addressed myself a second time to the stabbing, but Hwin came near to me and put her head in between me and the dagger and discoursed to me most excellent reasons and rebuked me as a mother rebukes her daughter. And now my wonder was so great that I forgot about killing myself and about Ahoshta and said, 'O my mare, how have you learned to speak like one of the daughters of men?' And Hwin told me what is known to all this company, that in Narnia there are beasts that talk, and how she herself was stolen from thence when she was a little foal. She told me also of the woods and waters of Narnia and the castles and the great ships, till I said, 'In the name of Tash and Azaroth and Zardeenah, Lady of the Night, I have a great wish to be in that country of Narnia.' 'O my mistress,' answered the mare, 'if you were in Narnia you would be happy, for in that land no maiden is forced to marry against her will.'

"And when we had talked together for a great time hope returned to me and I rejoiced that I had not killed myself. Moreover it was agreed between Hwin and me that we should steal ourselves away together and we planned it in this fashion. We returned to my father's house and I put on my gayest clothes and sang and danced before my father and pretended to be delighted with the marriage which he had prepared for me. Also I said to him, 'O my father and O the delight of my eyes, give me your license and permission to go with one of my maidens alone for three days into the woods to do secret sacrifices to Zardeenah, Lady of the Night and of Maidens, as is proper and customary for damsels when they must bid farewell to the service of Zardeenah and prepare themselves for marriage.' And he answered, 'O my daughter and O the delight of my eyes, so it shall be.'

"But when I came out from the presence of my father I went immediately to the oldest of his slaves, his secretary, who had dandled me on his knees when I was a baby and loved me more than the air and the light. And I swore him to be secret and begged him to write a certain letter for me. And he wept and implored me to change my resolution but in the end he said, 'To hear is to obey,' and did all my will. And I sealed the letter and hid it in my bosom."

"But what was in the letter?" asked Shasta.

"Be quiet, youngster," said Bree. "You're spoiling the story. She'll tell us all about the letter in the right place. Go on, Tarkheena."

"Then I called the maid who was to go with me to the woods and perform the rites of Zardeenah and told her to wake me very early in the morning. And I became merry with her and gave her wine to drink; but I had mixed such things in her cup that I knew she must sleep for

41

a night and a day. As soon as the household of my father had committed themselves to sleep I arose and put on an armor of my brother's which I always kept in my chamber in his memory. I put into my girdle all the money I had and certain choice jewels and provided myself also with food, and saddled the mare with my own hands and rode away in the second watch of the night. I directed my course not to the woods where my father supposed I would go but north and east to Tashbaan.

"Now for three days and more I knew that my father would not seek me, being deceived by the words I had said to him. And on the fourth day we arrived at the city of Azim Balda. Now Azim Balda stands at the meeting of many roads and from it the posts of the Tisroc (may he live forever) ride on swift horses to every part of the empire: and it is one of the rights and privileges of the greater Tarkaans to send messages by them. I therefore went to the Chief of the Messengers in the House of Imperial Posts in Azim Balda and said, 'O dispatcher of messages, here is a letter from my uncle Ahoshta Tarkaan to Kidrash Tarkaan lord of Calavar. Take now these five crescents and cause it to be sent to him.' And the Chief of the Messengers said, 'To hear is to obey.'

"This letter was feigned to be written by

Ahoshta and this was the signification of the writing: 'Ahoshta Tarkaan to Kidrash Tarkaan, salutation and peace. In the name of Tash the irresistible, the inexorable. Be it known to you that as I made my journey toward your house to perform the contract of marriage between me and your daughter Aravis Tarkheena, it pleased fortune and the gods that I fell in with her in the forest when she had ended the rites and sacrifices of Zardeenah according to the custom of maidens. And when I learned who she was, being delighted with her beauty and discretion, I became inflamed with love and it appeared to me that the sun would be dark to me if I did not marry her at once. Accordingly I prepared the necessary sacrifices and married your daughter the same hour that I met her and have returned

with her to my own house. And we both pray and charge you to come hither as speedily as you may that we may be delighted with your face and speech; and also that you may bring with you the dowry of my wife, which, by reason of my great charges and expenses, I require without delay. And because thou and I are brothers I assure myself that you will not be angered by the haste of my marriage which is wholly occasioned by the great love I bear your daughter. And I commit you to the care of all the gods.'

"As soon as I had done this I rode on in all haste from Azim Balda, fearing no pursuit and expecting that my father, having received such a letter, would send messages to Ahoshta or go to him himself, and that before the matter was discovered I should be beyond Tashbaan. And that is the pith of my story until this very night when I was chased by lions and met you at the swimming of the salt water."

"And what happened to the girl—the one you drugged?" asked Shasta.

"Doubtless she was beaten for sleeping late," said Aravis coolly. "But she was a tool and spy of my stepmother's. I am very glad they should beat her."

"I say, that was hardly fair," said Shasta.

"I did not do any of these things for the sake of pleasing *you*," said Aravis.

"And there's another thing I don't understand about that story," said Shasta. "You're not grown up, I don't believe you're any older than I am. I don't believe you're as old. How could you be getting married at your age?"

Aravis said nothing, but Bree said at once, "Shasta, don't display your ignorance. They're always married at that age in the great Tarkaan families."

Shasta turned very red (though it was hardly light enough for the others to see this) and felt snubbed. Aravis asked Bree for his story. Bree told it, and Shasta thought that he put in a great deal more than he needed about the falls and the bad riding. Bree obviously thought it very funny, but Aravis did not laugh. When Bree had finished they all went to sleep.

Next day all four of them, two horses and two humans, continued their journey together. Shasta thought it had been much pleasanter when he and Bree were on their own. For now it was Bree and Aravis who did nearly all the talking. Bree had lived a long time in Calormen and had always been among Tarkaans and Tarkaans' horses, and so of course he knew a great many of the same people and places that Aravis knew. She would always be saying things like, "But if you were at the fight of Zulindreh you would have seen my cousin Alimash," and Bree would answer, "Oh, yes, Alimash, he was only captain of the chariots, you know. I don't quite hold with chariots or the kind of horses who draw chariots. That's not real cavalry. But he is a worthy nobleman. He filled my nosebag with sugar after the taking of Teebeth." Or else Bree would say, "I was down at the lake of Mezreel that summer," and Aravis would say, "Oh, Mezreel! I had a friend there, Lasaraleen Tarkheena. What a delightful place it is. Those gardens, and the Valley of the Thousand Perfumes!" Bree was not in the least trying to leave Shasta out of things, though Shasta sometimes nearly thought he was. People who know a lot of the same things can hardly help talking about them, and if you're there you can hardly help feeling that you're out of it.

Hwin the mare was rather shy before a great war horse like Bree and said very little. And Aravis never spoke to Shasta at all if she could help it.

Soon, however, they had more important things to think of. They were getting near Tashbaan. There were more, and larger, villages, and more people on the roads. They now did nearly all their traveling by night and hid as best they could during the day. And at every halt they argued and argued about what they were to do when they reached Tashbaan. Everyone had been putting off this difficulty, but now it could be put off no longer. During these discussions Aravis became a little, a very little, less unfriendly to Shasta; one usually gets on better with people when one is making plans than when one is talking about nothing in particular.

Bree said the first thing now to do was to fix a place where they would all promise to meet on the far side of Tashbaan even if, by any ill luck, they got separated in passing the city. He said the best place would be the Tombs of the Ancient Kings on the very edge of the desert. "Things like great stone beehives," he said, "you can't possibly miss them. And the best of it is that none of the Calormenes will go near them because they think the place is haunted by ghouls and are afraid of it." Aravis asked if it wasn't really haunted by ghouls. But Bree said he was a free Narnian horse and didn't believe in these Calormene tales. And then Shasta said he wasn't a Calormene either and didn't care a straw about these old stories of ghouls. This wasn't quite true. But it rather impressed Aravis (though at the moment it annoyed her too) and of course she said she didn't mind any number of ghouls either. So it was settled that the Tombs should be their assembly place on the other side of Tashbaan, and everyone felt they were getting on very well till Hwin humbly pointed out that the real problem was not where they should go when they had got through Tashbaan but how they were to get through it.

"We'll settle that tomorrow, Ma'am," said Bree. "Time for a little sleep now."

But it wasn't easy to settle. Aravis's first suggestion was that they should swim across the river below the city during the night and not go into Tashbaan at all. But Bree had two reasons against this. One was that the river-mouth was very wide and it would be far too long a swim for Hwin to do, especially with a rider on her back. (He thought it would be too long for himself too, but he said much less about that.) The other was that it would be full of shipping and of course anyone on the deck of a ship who saw two horses swimming past would be almost certain to be inquisitive.

Shasta thought they should go up the river above Tashbaan and cross it where it was narrower. But Bree explained that there were gardens and pleasure houses on both banks of the river for miles and that there would be Tarkaans and Tarkheenas living in them and riding about the roads and having water parties on the river. In fact it would be the most likely place in the world for meeting someone who would recognize Aravis or even himself.

"We'll have to have a disguise," said Shasta.

Hwin said it looked to her as if the safest thing was to go right through the city itself from gate to gate because one was less likely to be noticed in the crowd. But she approved of the idea of disguise as well. She said, "Both the humans will have to dress in rags and look like peasants or slaves. And all Aravis's armor and our saddles and things must be made into bundles and put on our backs, and the children must pretend to drive us and people will think we're only pack-horses."

"My dear Hwin!" said Aravis rather scornfully. "As if anyone could mistake Bree for anything but a war horse however you disguised him!"

"I should think not, indeed," said Bree, snorting and letting his ears go ever so little back.

"I know it's not a *very* good plan," said Hwin. "But I think it's our only chance. And we haven't been groomed for ages and we're not looking quite ourselves (at least, I'm sure I'm not). I do think if we get well plastered with mud and go along with our heads down as if we're tired and lazy—and don't lift our hoofs hardly at all—we might not be noticed. And our tails ought to be cut shorter: not neatly, you know, but all ragged."

"My dear Madam," said Bree. "Have you

pictured to yourself how very disagreeable it would be to arrive in Narnia in *that* condition?"

"Well," said Hwin humbly (she was a very sensible mare), "the main thing is to get there."

Though nobody much liked it, it was Hwin's plan which had to be adopted in the end. It was a troublesome one and involved a certain amount of what Shasta called stealing, and Bree called "raiding." One farm lost a few sacks that evening and another lost a coil of rope the next: but some tattered old boy's clothes for Aravis to wear had to be fairly bought and paid for in a village. Shasta returned with them in triumph just as evening was closing in. The others were waiting for him among the trees at the foot of a low range of wooded hills which lay right across their path. Everyone was feeling excited because this was the last hill; when they reached the ridge at the top they would be looking down on Tashbaan. "I do wish we were safely past it," muttered Shasta to Hwin. "Oh I do, I do," said Hwin fervently.

That night they wound their way through the woods up to the ridge by a woodcutter's track. And when they came out of the woods at the top they could see thousands of lights in the valley down below them. Shasta had had no notion of what a great city would be like and it frightened him. They had their supper and the children got some sleep. But the horses woke them very early in the morning.

The stars were still out and the grass was terribly cold and wet, but daybreak was just beginning, far to their right across the sea. Aravis went a few steps away into the wood and came back looking odd in her new, ragged clothes and carrying her real ones in a bundle. These, and her armor and shield and scimitar and the two saddles and the rest of the horses' fine furnishings were put into the sacks. Bree and Hwin had already got themselves as dirty and bedraggled as they could and it remained to shorten their tails. As the only tool for doing this was Aravis's scimitar, one of the packs had to be undone again in order to get it out. It was a longish job and rather hurt the horses.

"My word!" said Bree, "if I wasn't a Talking Horse what a lovely kick in the face I could give you! I thought you were going to cut it, not pull it out. That's what it feels like."

But in spite of the semi-darkness and cold fingers all was done in the end, the big packs bound on the horses, the rope halters (which they were now wearing instead of bridles and reins) in the children's hands, and the journey began.

"Remember," said Bree. "Keep together if we possibly can. If not, meet at the Tombs of the

Ancient Kings, and whoever gets there first must wait for the others."

"And remember," said Shasta. "Don't you two horses forget yourselves and start *talking*, whatever happens."

4

SHASTA FALLS IN WITH
THE NARNIANS

At first Shasta could see nothing in the valley below him but a sea of mist with a few domes and pinnacles rising from it; but as the light increased and the mist cleared away he saw more and more. A broad river divided itself into two streams and on the island between them stood the city of Tashbaan, one of the wonders of the world. Round the very edge of the island, so that the water lapped against the stone, ran high walls strengthened with so many towers that he soon gave up trying to count them. Inside the walls the island rose in a hill and every bit of that hill, up to the Tisroc's palace and the great temple of Tash at the top, was completely covered with buildings—terrace above terrace, street above street, zigzag roads or huge flights of steps bordered with orange trees and lemon trees, roof-gardens, balconies, deep archways, pillared colonnades, spires, battlements, minarets, pinnacles. And when at last the sun rose out of the sea and the great silver-plated dome of the temple flashed back its light, he was almost dazzled.

"Get on, Shasta," Bree kept saying.

The river banks on either side of the valley were such a mass of gardens that they looked at first like forest, until you got closer and saw the white walls of innumerable houses peeping out from beneath the trees. Soon after that, Shasta noticed a delicious smell of flowers and fruit. About fifteen minutes later they were down among them, plodding on a level road with white walls on each side and trees bending over the walls.

"I say," said Shasta in an awed voice. "This is a wonderful place!"

"I daresay," said Bree. "But I wish we were safely through it and out at the other side. Narnia and the North!"

At that moment a low, throbbing noise began which gradually swelled louder and louder

till the whole valley seemed to be swaying with it. It was a musical noise, but so strong and solemn as to be a little frightening.

"That's the horns blowing for the city gates to be open," said Bree. "We shall be there in a minute. Now, Aravis, do droop your shoulders a bit and step heavier and try to look less like a princess. Try to imagine you've been kicked and cuffed and called names all your life."

"If it comes to that," said Aravis, "what about you drooping your head a bit more and arching your neck a bit less and trying to look less like a war horse?"

"Hush," said Bree. "Here we are."

And they were. They had come to the river's edge and the road ahead of them ran along a many-arched bridge. The water danced brightly in the early sunlight; away to their right nearer the river's mouth, they caught a glimpse of ships' masts. Several other travelers were before them on the bridge, mostly peasants driving laden donkeys and mules or carrying baskets on their heads. The children and horses joined the crowd.

"Is anything wrong?" whispered Shasta to Aravis, who had an odd look on her face.

"Oh it's all very well for *you*," whispered Aravis rather savagely. "What would *you* care about Tashbaan? But I ought to be riding in on a litter with soldiers before me and slaves behind, and perhaps going to a feast in the Tisroc's palace (may he live forever)—not sneaking in like this. It's different for you."

Shasta thought all this very silly.

At the far end of the bridge the walls of the city towered high above them and the brazen gates stood open in the gateway which was really wide but looked narrow because it was so very high. Half a dozen soldiers, leaning on their spears, stood on each side. Aravis couldn't help thinking, "They'd all jump to attention and salute me if they knew whose daughter I am." But the others were only thinking of how they'd get through and hoping the soldiers would not ask any questions. Fortunately they did not. But one of them picked a carrot out of a peasant's basket and threw it at Shasta with a rough laugh, saying:

"Hey! Horse-boy! You'll catch it if your master finds you've been using his saddle-horse for pack work."

This frightened him badly for of course it showed that no one who knew anything about horses would mistake Bree for anything but a charger.

"It's my master's orders, so there!" said Shasta. But it would have been better if he had held his tongue for the soldier gave him a box on the side of his face that nearly knocked him down and said, "Take that, you young filth, to teach you how to talk to freemen." But they all slunk into the city without being stopped. Shasta cried only a very little; he was used to hard knocks.

Inside the gates Tashbaan did not at first seem so splendid as it had looked from a distance. The first street was narrow and there were hardly any windows in the walls on each side. It was much more crowded than Shasta had expected: crowded partly by the peasants (on their way to market) who had come in with them, but also with water sellers, sweetmeat sellers, porters, soldiers, beggars, ragged children, hens, stray dogs, and barefooted slaves. What you would chiefly have noticed if you had been there was the smells, which came from un-washed people, unwashed dogs, scent, garlic, onions, and the piles of refuse which lay every-where.

Shasta was pretending to lead but it was really Bree who knew the way and kept guiding him by little nudges with his nose. They soon turned to the left and began going up a steep hill. It was much fresher and pleasanter, for the road was bordered by trees and there were houses only on the right side; on the other they looked out over the roofs of houses in the lower town and could see some way up the river. Then they went round a hairpin bend to their right and continued rising. They were zigzagging up to the center of Tashbaan. Soon they came to finer streets. Great statues of the gods and he-roes of Calormen—who are mostly impressive rather than agreeable to look at—rose on shin-ing pedestals. Palm trees and pillared arcades cast shadows over the burning pavements. And through the arched gateways of many a palace Shasta caught sight of green branches, cool fountains, and smooth lawns. It must be nice in-side, he thought.

At every turn Shasta hoped they were get-ting out of the crowd, but they never did. This made their progress very slow, and every now and then they had to stop altogether. This usually happened because a loud voice shouted out "Way, way, way for the Tarkaan," or "for the Tarkheena," or "for the fifteenth Vizier," or "for the Ambassador," and everyone in the crowd would crush back against the walls; and above their heads Shasta would sometimes see the great lord or lady for whom all the fuss was being made, lolling upon a litter which four or even six gigantic slaves carried on their bare shoulders. For in Tashbaan there is only one traffic regulation, which is that everyone who is less important has to get out of the way for everyone who is more important; unless you want a cut from a whip or punch from the butt end of a spear.

It was in a splendid street very near the top of the city (the Tisroc's palace was the only thing above it) that the most disastrous of these stoppages occurred.

"Way! Way! Way!" came the voice. "Way for the White Barbarian King, the guest of the Tisroc (may he live forever)! Way for the Narnian lords."

Shasta tried to get out of the way and to make Bree go back. But no horse, not even a Talking Horse from Narnia, backs easily. And a woman with a very edgy basket in her hands, who was just behind Shasta, pushed the basket hard against his shoulders, and said, "Now then!

Who are you shoving!" And then someone else jostled him from the side and in the confusion of the moment he lost hold of Bree. And then the whole crowd behind him became so stiffened and packed tight that he couldn't move at all. So he found himself, unintentionally, in the first row and had a fine sight of the party that was coming down the street.

It was quite unlike any other party they had seen that day. The crier who went before it shouting "Way, way!" was the only Calormene in it. And there was no litter; everyone was on foot. There were about half a dozen men and Shasta had never seen anyone like them before. For one thing, they were all as fair-skinned as himself, and most of them had fair hair. And they were not dressed like men of Calormen. Most of them had legs bare to the knee. Their tunics were of fine, bright, hardy colors—woodland green, or gay yellow, or fresh blue. Instead of turbans they wore steel or silver caps, some of them set with jewels, and one with little wings on each side. A few were bare-headed. The swords at their sides were long and straight, not curved like Calormene scimitars. And instead of being grave and mysterious like most Calormenes, they walked with a swing and let their arms and shoulders go free, and chatted and laughed. One was whistling. You could see that they were ready to be friends with anyone who was friendly and didn't give a fig for anyone who wasn't. Shasta thought he had never seen anything so lovely in his life.

But there was not time to enjoy it for at once a really dreadful thing happened. The leader of the fair-headed men suddenly pointed at Shasta, cried out, "There he is! There's our runaway!" and seized him by the shoulder. Next moment he gave Shasta a smack—not a cruel one to make you cry but a sharp one to let you know you are in disgrace—and added, shaking:

"Shame on you, my lord! Fie for shame! Queen Susan's eyes are red with weeping because of you. What! Truant for a whole night! Where have you been?"

Shasta would have darted under Bree's body and tried to make himself scarce in the crowd if he had had the least chance; but the fair-haired men were all round him by now and he was held firm.

Of course his first impulse was to say that he was only poor Arsheesh the fisherman's son and that the foreign lord must have mistaken him for someone else. But then, the very last thing he wanted to do in that crowded place was to start explaining who he was and what he was doing. If he started on that, he would soon be

asked where he had got his horse from, and who
Aravis was—and then, good-bye to any chance
of getting through Tashbaan. His next impulse
was to look at Bree for help. But Bree had no intention of letting all that crowd know that he
could talk, and stood looking just as stupid as a
horse can. As for Aravis, Shasta did not even
dare to look at her for fear of drawing attention.
And there was no time to think, for the leader
of the Narnians said at once:

"Take one of his little lordship's hands,
Peridan, of your courtesy, and I'll take the other.
And now, on. Our royal sister's mind will be
greatly eased when she sees our young scape-
grace safe in our lodging."

And so, before they were half-way through
Tashbaan, all their plans were ruined, and without even a chance to say good-bye to the others
Shasta found himself being marched off among
strangers and quite unable to guess what might
be going to happen next. The Narnian King—
for Shasta began to see by the way the rest spoke
to him that he must be a king—kept on asking
him questions; where he had been, how he had
got out, what he had done with his clothes, and
didn't he know that he had been very naughty.
Only the king called it "naught" instead of
naughty.

And Shasta said nothing in answer, because

he couldn't think of anything to say that would not be dangerous.

"What! All mum?" asked the king. "I must plainly tell you, prince, that this hangdog silence becomes one of your blood even less than the scape itself. To run away might pass for a boy's frolic with some spirit in it. But the king's son of Archenland should avouch his deed; not hang his head like a Calormene slave."

This was very unpleasant, for Shasta felt all the time that this young king was the very nicest kind of grown-up and would have liked to make a good impression on him.

The strangers led him—held tightly by both hands—along a narrow street and down a flight of shallow stairs and then up another to a wide doorway in a white wall with two tall, dark cypress trees, one on each side of it. Once through the arch, Shasta found himself in a courtyard which was also a garden. A marble basin of clear water in the center was kept continually rippling by the fountain that fell into it. Orange trees grew round it out of smooth grass, and the four white walls which surrounded the lawn were covered with climbing roses. The noise and dust and crowding of the streets seemed suddenly far away. He was led rapidly across the garden and then into a dark doorway. The crier remained outside. After that they took him along a corridor, where the stone floor felt beautifully cool to his hot feet, and up some stairs. A moment later he found himself blinking in the light of a big, airy room with wide open windows, all looking North so that no sun came in. There was a carpet on the floor more wonderfully colored than anything he had ever seen and his feet sank down into it as if he were treading in thick moss. All round the walls there were low sofas with rich cushions on them, and the room seemed to be full of people; very queer people some of them, thought Shasta. But he had no time to think of that before the most beautiful lady he had ever seen rose from her place and threw her arms round him and kissed him, saying:

"Oh Corin, Corin, how could you? And thou and I such close friends ever since thy mother died. And what should I have said to thy royal father if I came home without thee? Would have been a cause almost of war between Archenland and Narnia which are friends time out of mind. It was naught, playmate, very naught of thee to use us so."

"Apparently," thought Shasta to himself, "I'm being mistaken for a prince of Archenland, wherever that is. And these must be Narnians. I wonder where the real Corin is?" But these thoughts did not help him say anything out loud.

"Where hast been, Corin?" said the lady, her hands still on Shasta's shoulders.

"I—I don't know," stammered Shasta.

"There it is, Susan," said the King. "I could get no tale out of him, true or false."

"Your Majesties! Queen Susan! King Edmund!" said a voice: and when Shasta turned to look at the speaker he nearly jumped out of his skin with surprise. For this was one of those queer people whom he had noticed out of the corner of his eye when he first came into the room. He was about the same height as Shasta himself. From the waist upward he was like a man, but his legs were hairy like a goat's, and shaped like a goat's and he had goat's hoofs and a tail. His skin was rather red and he had curly hair and a short pointed beard and two little horns. He was in fact a Faun, which is a creature Shasta had never seen a picture of or even heard of. And if you've read a book called *The Lion, the Witch and the Wardrobe*, you may like to know that this was the very same Faun, Tumnus by name, whom Queen Susan's sister Lucy had met on the very first day when she found her way into Narnia. But he was a good deal older now for by this time Peter and Susan and

Edmund and Lucy had been Kings and Queens of Narnia for several years.

"Your Majesties," he was saying, "His little Highness has had a touch of the sun. Look at him! He is dazed. He does not know where he is."

Then of course everyone stopped scolding Shasta and asking him questions and he was made much of and laid on a sofa and cushions were put under his head and he was given iced sherbet in a golden cup to drink and told to keep very quiet.

Nothing like this had ever happened to Shasta in his life before. He had never even imagined lying on anything so comfortable as that sofa or drinking anything so delicious as that sherbet. He was still wondering what had

happened to the others and how on earth he was going to escape and meet them at the Tombs, and what would happen when the real Corin turned up again. But none of these worries seemed so pressing now that he was comfortable. And perhaps, later on, there would be nice things to eat!

Meanwhile the people in that cool airy room were very interesting. Besides the Faun there were two Dwarfs (a kind of creature he had never seen before) and a very large Raven. The rest were all humans; grown-ups, but young, and all of them, both men and women, had nicer faces and voices than most Calormenes. And soon Shasta found himself taking an interest in the conversation. "Now, Madam," the King was saying to Queen Susan (the lady who had kissed Shasta). "What think you? We have been in this city fully three weeks. Have you yet settled in your mind whether you will marry this dark-faced lover of yours, this Prince Rabadash, or no?"

The lady shook her head. "No, brother," she said, "not for all the jewels in Tashbaan." ("Hullo!" thought Shasta. "Although they're king and queen, they're brother and sister, not married to one another.")

"Truly, sister," said the King, "I should have loved you the less if you had taken him. And I tell you that at the first coming of the Tisroc's ambassadors into Narnia to treat of this marriage, and later when the Prince was our guest at Cair Paravel, it was a wonder to me that ever you could find it in your heart to show him so much favor."

"That was my folly, Edmund," said Queen Susan, "of which I cry you mercy. Yet when he was with us in Narnia, truly this Prince bore himself in another fashion than he does now in Tashbaan. For I take you all to witness what marvelous feats he did in that great tournament and hastilude which our brother the High King made for him, and how meekly and courteously he consorted with us the space of seven days. But here, in his own city, he has shown another face."

"Ah!" croaked the Raven. "It is an old saying: See the bear in his own den before you judge of his conditions."

"That's very true, Sallowpad," said one of the Dwarfs. "And another is, Come, live with me and you'll know me."

"Yes," said the King. "We have now seen him for what he is: that is, a most proud, bloody, luxurious, cruel, and self-pleasing tyrant."

"Then in the name of Aslan," said Susan, "let us leave Tashbaan this very day."

"There's the rub, sister," said Edmund. "For

now I must open to you all that has been growing in my mind these last two days and more.
Peridan, of your courtesy look to the door and
see that there is no spy upon us. All well? So.
For now we must be secret."

Everyone had begun to look very serious.
Queen Susan jumped up and ran to her brother.
"Oh, Edmund," she cried. "What is it? There is
something dreadful in your face."

5

PRINCE CORIN

"My dear sister and very good Lady," said King Edmund, "you must now show your courage. For I tell you plainly we are in no small danger."

"What is it, Edmund?" asked the Queen.

"It is this," said Edmund. "I do not think we shall find it easy to leave Tashbaan. While the Prince had hope that you would take him, we were honored guests. But by the Lion's Mane, I think that as soon as he has your flat denial we shall be no better than prisoners."

One of the Dwarfs gave a low whistle.

"I warned your Majesties, I warned you," said Sallowpad the Raven. "Easily in but not easily out, as the lobster said in the lobster pot!"

"I have been with the Prince this morning," continued Edmund. "He is little used (more's the pity) to having his will crossed. And he is very chafed at your long delays and doubtful answers. This morning he pressed very hard to know your mind. I put it aside—meaning at the same time to diminish his hopes—with some light common jests about women's fancies, and hinted that his suit was likely to be cold. He grew angry and dangerous. There was a sort of threatening, though still veiled under a show of courtesy, in every word he spoke."

"Yes," said Tumnus. "And when I supped with the Grand Vizier last night, it was the same. He asked me how I liked Tashbaan. And I (for I could not tell him I hated every stone of it and I would not lie) told him that now, when high summer was coming on, my heart turned to the cool woods and dewy slopes of Narnia. He gave a smile that meant no good and said, 'There is nothing to hinder you from dancing there again, little goatfoot; *always provided you leave us in exchange a bride for our prince.*'"

"Do you mean he would make me his wife by force?" exclaimed Susan.

"That's my fear, Susan," said Edmund. "Wife: or slave which is worse."

"But how can he? Does the Tisroc think our

brother the High King would suffer such an out-rage?"

"Sire," said Peridan to the King. "They would not be so mad. Do they think there are no swords and spears in Narnia?"

"Alas," said Edmund. "My guess is that the Tisroc has very small fear of Narnia. We are a little land. And little lands on the borders of a great empire were always hateful to the lords of the great empire. He longs to blot them out, gobble them up. When first he suffered the Prince to come to Cair Paravel as your lover, sister, it may be that he was only seeking an occasion against us. Most likely he hopes to make one mouthful of Narnia and Archenland both."

"Let him try," said the second Dwarf. "At sea we are as big as he is. And if he assaults us by land, he has the desert to cross."

"True, friend," said Edmund. "But is the desert a sure defense? What does Sallowpad say?"

"I know that desert well," said the Raven. "For I have flown above it far and wide in my younger days" (you may be sure that Shasta pricked up his ears at this point). "And this is certain; that if the Tisroc goes by the great oasis he can never lead a great army across it into Archenland. For though they could reach the oasis by the end of their first day's march, yet the springs there would be too little for the thirst of all those soldiers and their beasts. But there is another way."

Shasta listened more attentively still.

"He that would find that way," said the Raven, "must start from the Tombs of the Ancient Kings and ride northwest so that the double peak of Mount Pire is always straight ahead of him. And so, in a day's riding or a little more, he shall come to the head of a stony valley, which is so narrow that a man might be within a furlong of it a thousand times and never know that it was there. And looking down this valley he will see neither grass nor water nor anything else good. But if he rides on down it he will come to a river and can ride by the water all the way into Archenland."

"And do the Calormenes know of this Western way?" asked the Queen.

"Friends, friends," said Edmund, "what is the use of all this discourse? We are not asking whether Narnia or Calormen would win if war arose between them. We are asking how to save the honor of the Queen and our own lives out of this devilish city. For though my brother, Peter the High King, defeated the Tisroc a dozen times over, yet long before that day our throats would be cut and the Queen's grace would be the wife, or more likely, the slave, of this prince."

"We have our weapons, King," said the first Dwarf. "And this is a reasonably defensible house."

"As to that," said the King, "I do not doubt that every one of us would sell our lives dearly in the gate and they would not come at the Queen but over our dead bodies. Yet we should be merely rats fighting in a trap when all's said."

"Very true," croaked the Raven. "These last stands in a house make good stories, but nothing ever came of them. After their first repulses the enemy always set the house on fire."

"I am the cause of all this," said Susan, bursting into tears. "Oh, if only I had never left Cair Paravel. Our last happy day was before those ambassadors came from Calormen. The Moles were planting an orchard for us . . . oh . . . oh." And she buried her face in her hands and sobbed.

"Courage, Su, courage," said Edmund. "Remember—but what is the matter with *you*, Master Tumnus?" For the Faun was holding both his horns with his hands as if he were trying to keep his head on by them and writhing to and fro as if he had a pain in his inside.

"Don't speak to me, don't speak to me," said Tumnus. "I'm thinking. I'm thinking so that I can hardly breathe. Wait, wait, do wait."

There was a moment's puzzled silence and then the Faun looked up, drew a long breath, mopped its forehead and said:

"The only difficulty is how to get down to our ship—with some stores, too—without being seen and stopped."

"Yes," said a Dwarf dryly. "Just as the beggar's only difficulty about riding is that he has no horse."

"Wait, wait," said Mr. Tumnus impatiently. "All we need is some pretext for going down to our ship today and taking stuff on board."

"Yes," said King Edmund doubtfully.

"Well, then," said the Faun, "how would it be if your majesties bade the Prince to a great banquet to be held on board our own galleon, the *Splendor Hyaline*, tomorrow night? And let the message be worded as graciously as the Queen can contrive without pledging her honor: so as to give the Prince a hope that she is weakening."

"This is very good counsel, Sire," croaked the Raven.

"And then," continued Tumnus excitedly, "everyone will expect us to be going down to the ship all day, making preparations for our guests. And let some of us go to the bazaars and spend every minim we have at the fruiterers and the sweetmeat sellers and the wine merchants, just as we would if we were really giving a feast. And let us order magicians and jugglers and dancing girls and flute players, all to be on board tomorrow night."

"I see, I see," said King Edmund, rubbing his hands.

"And then," said Tumnus, "we'll all be on board tonight. And as soon as it is quite dark—"

"Up sails and out oars—!" said the King.

"And so to sea," cried Tumnus, leaping up and beginning to dance.

"And our nose Northward," said the first Dwarf.

"Running for home! Hurrah for Narnia and the North!" said the other.

"And the Prince waking next morning and finding his birds flown!" said Peridan, clapping his hands.

"Oh Master Tumnus, dear Master Tumnus," said the Queen, catching his hands and swinging with him as he danced. "You have saved us all."

"The Prince will chase us," said another lord, whose name Shasta had not heard.

"That's the least of my fears," said Edmund. "I have seen all the shipping in the river and there's no tall ship of war nor swift galley there. I wish he may chase us! For the *Splendor Hyaline*

could sink anything he has to send after her—if we were overtaken at all."

"Sire," said the Raven. "You shall hear no better plot than the Faun's though we sat in council for seven days. And now, as we birds say, nests before eggs. Which is as much as to say, let us all take our food and then at once be about our business."

Everyone arose at this and the doors were opened and the lords and the creatures stood aside for the King and Queen to go out first. Shasta wondered what he ought to do, but Mr. Tumnus said, "Lie there, your Highness, and I will bring you up a little feast to yourself in a few moments. There is no need for you to move until we are all ready to embark." Shasta laid his head down again on the pillows and soon he was alone in the room.

"This is perfectly dreadful," thought Shasta. It never came into his head to tell these Narnians the whole truth and ask for their help. Having been brought up by a hard, closefisted man like Arsheesh, he had a fixed habit of never telling grown-ups anything if he could help it: he thought they would always spoil or stop whatever you were trying to do. And he thought that even if the Narnian King might be friendly to the two horses, because they were Talking Beasts of Narnia, he would hate Aravis, because she was a Calormene, and either sell her for a slave or send her back to her father. As for himself, "I simply daren't tell them I'm not Prince Corin *now*," thought Shasta. "I've heard all their plans. If they knew I wasn't one of themselves, they'd never let me out of this house alive. They'd be afraid I'd betray them to the Tisroc. They'd kill me. And if the real Corin turns up, it'll all come out, and they *will*!" He had, you see, no idea of how noble and free-born people behave.

"What am I to do? What am I to do?" he kept saying to himself. "What—hullo, here comes that goaty little creature again."

The Faun trotted in, half dancing, with a tray in its hands which was nearly as large as itself. This he set on an inlaid table beside Shasta's sofa, and sat down himself on the carpeted floor with his goaty legs crossed.

"Now, princeling," he said. "Make a good dinner. It will be your last meal in Tashbaan."

It was a fine meal after the Calormene fashion. I don't know whether you would have liked it or not, but Shasta did. There were lobsters, and salad, and snipe stuffed with almonds and truffles, and a complicated dish made of chicken livers and rice and raisins and nuts, and there were cool melons and gooseberry fools and mulberry fools, and every kind of nice thing that can be made with ice. There was also a little flagon of the sort of wine that is called "white" though it is really yellow.

While Shasta was eating, the good little Faun, who thought he was still dazed with sunstroke, kept talking to him about the fine times he would have when they all got home; about his good old father King Lune of Archenland and the little castle where he lived on the

southern slopes of the pass. "And don't forget," said Mr. Tumnus, "that you are promised your first suit of armor and your first war horse on your next birthday. And then your Highness will begin to learn how to tilt and joust. And in a few years, if all goes well, King Peter has promised your royal father that he himself will make you Knight at Cair Paravel. And in the meantime there will be plenty of comings and goings between Narnia and Archenland across the neck of the mountains. And of course you remember you have promised to come for a whole week to stay with me for the Summer Festival, and there'll be bonfires and all-night dances of Fauns and Dryads in the heart of the woods and, who knows?—we might see Aslan himself!"

When the meal was over the Faun told Shasta to stay quietly where he was. "And it wouldn't do you any harm to have a little sleep," he added. "I'll call you in plenty of time to get on board. And then, Home. Narnia and the North!"

Shasta had so enjoyed his dinner and all the things Tumnus had been telling him that when he was left alone his thoughts took a different turn. He only hoped now that the real Prince Corin would not turn up until it was too late and that he would be taken away to Narnia by ship. I am afraid he did not think at all of what might happen to the real Corin when he was left behind in Tashbaan. He was a little worried about Aravis and Bree waiting for him at the Tombs. But then he said to himself, "Well, how can I help it?" and, "Anyway, that Aravis thinks she's too good to go about with me, so she can jolly well go alone," and at the same time he couldn't help feeling that it would be much nicer going to Narnia by sea than toiling across the desert.

When he had thought all this he did what I expect you would have done if you had been up very early and had a long walk and a great deal of excitement and then a very good meal, and were lying on a sofa in a cool room with no noise in it except when a bee came buzzing in through the wide open windows. He fell asleep.

What woke him was a loud crash. He jumped up off the sofa, staring. He saw at once from the mere look of the room—the lights and shadows all looked different—that he must have slept for several hours. He saw also what had made the crash: a costly porcelain vase which had been standing on the windowsill lay on the floor broken into about thirty pieces. But he hardly noticed all these things. What he did notice was two hands gripping the windowsill from outside. They gripped harder and harder (get-

ting white at the knuckles) and then up came a head and a pair of shoulders. A moment later there was a boy of Shasta's own age sitting astride the sill with one leg hanging down inside the room.

Shasta had never seen his own face in a looking-glass. Even if he had, he might not have realized that the other boy was (at ordinary times) almost exactly like himself. At the moment this boy was not particularly like anyone for he had the finest black eye you ever saw, and a tooth missing, and his clothes (which must have been splendid ones when he put them on) were torn and dirty, and there was both blood and mud on his face.

"Who are you?" said the boy in a whisper.

"Are you Prince Corin?" said Shasta.

"Yes, of course," said the other. "But who are you?"

"I'm nobody, nobody in particular, I mean," said Shasta. "King Edmund caught me in the street and mistook me for you. I suppose we must look like one another. Can I get out the way you've got in?"

"Yes, if you're any good at climbing," said Corin. "But why are you in such a hurry? I say: we ought to be able to get some fun out of this being mistaken for one another."

"No, no," said Shasta. "We must change places at once. It'll be simply frightful if Mr. Tumnus comes back and finds us both here. I've had to pretend to be you. And you're starting tonight—secretly. And where were you all this time?"

"A boy in the street made a beastly joke about Queen Susan," said Prince Corin, "so I knocked him down. He ran howling into a house and his big brother came out. So I knocked the big brother down. Then they all followed me until we ran into three old men with spears who are called the Watch. So I fought the Watch and they knocked me down. It was getting dark by now. Then the Watch took me along to lock me up somewhere. So I asked them if they'd like a stoup of wine and they said they didn't mind if they did. Then I took them to a wine shop and got them some and they all sat down and drank till they fell asleep. I thought it was time for me to be off so I came out quietly and then I found the first boy—the one who had started all the trouble— still hanging about. So I knocked him down again. After that I climbed up a pipe onto the roof of a house and lay quiet till it began to get light this morning. Ever since that I've been finding my way back. I say, is there anything to drink?"

"No, I drank it," said Shasta. "And now, show me how you got in. There's not a minute to lose. You'd better lie down on the sofa and pretend—but I forgot. It'll be no good with all those bruises and black eye. You'll just have to tell them the truth, once I'm safely away."

"What else did you think I'd be telling them?" asked the Prince with a rather angry look. "And who are *you*?"

"There's no time," said Shasta in a frantic whisper. "I'm a Narnian, I believe; something Northern anyway. But I've been brought up all my life in Calormen. And I'm escaping: across the desert; with a talking Horse called Bree. And now, quick! How do I get away?"

"Look," said Corin. "Drop from this window

onto the roof of the verandah. But you must do it lightly, on your toes, or someone will hear you. Then along to your left and you can get up to the top of that wall if you're any good at all as a climber. Then along the wall to the corner. Drop onto the rubbish heap you will find outside, and there you are."

"Thanks," said Shasta, who was already sitting on the sill. The two boys were looking into each other's faces and suddenly found that they were friends.

"Good-bye," said Corin. "And *good* luck. I do hope you get safe away."

"Good-bye," said Shasta. "I say, you have been having some adventures."

"Nothing to yours," said the Prince. "Now drop; lightly—I say," he added as Shasta dropped. "I hope we meet in Archenland. Go to my father King Lune and tell him you're a friend of mine. Look out! I hear someone coming."

6

SHASTA AMONG THE TOMBS

Shasta ran lightly along the roof on tiptoes. It felt hot to his bare feet. He was only a few seconds scrambling up the wall at the far end and when he got to the corner he found himself looking down into a narrow, smelly street, and there was a rubbish heap against the outside of the wall just as Corin had told him. Before jumping down he took a rapid glance round him to get his bearings. Apparently he had now come over the crown of the island-hill on which Tashbaan is built. Everything sloped away before him, flat roofs below flat roofs, down to the towers and battlements of the city's Northern wall. Beyond that was the river and beyond the river a short slope covered with gardens. But beyond that again there was something he had never seen the like of—a great yellowish-gray thing, flat as a calm sea, and stretching for miles. On the far side of it were huge blue things, lumpy but with jagged edges, and some of them with white tops. "The desert! the mountains!" thought Shasta.

He jumped down onto the rubbish and began trotting along downhill as fast as he could in the narrow lane, which soon brought him into a wider street where there were more people. No one bothered to look at a little ragged boy running along on bare feet. Still, he was anxious and uneasy till he turned a corner and there saw the city gate in front of him. Here he was pressed and jostled a bit, for a good many other people were also going out; and on the bridge beyond the gate the crowd became quite a slow procession, more like a queue than a crowd. Out there, with clear running water on each side, it was deliciously fresh after the smell and heat and noise of Tashbaan.

When once Shasta had reached the far end of the bridge he found the crowd melting away; everyone seemed to be going either to the left or right along the river bank. He went straight ahead up a road that did not appear to be much used, between gardens. In a few paces he was alone, and a few more brought him to the top of the slope. There he stood and stared. It was like coming to the end of the world for all the grass stopped quite suddenly a few feet before him and the sand began: endless level sand like on a sea shore but a bit rougher because it was never wet. The mountains, which now looked further off than before, loomed ahead. Greatly to his relief he saw, about five minutes' walk away on his left, what must certainly be the Tombs, just as Bree had described them; great masses of moul- dering stone shaped like gigantic beehives, but a little narrower. They looked very black and

grim, for the sun was now setting right behind them.

He turned his face West and trotted toward the Tombs. He could not help looking out very hard for any sign of his friends, though the setting sun shone in his face so that he could see hardly anything. "And anyway," he thought, "of course they'll be round on the far side of the farthest Tomb, not this side where anyone might see them from the city."

There were about twelve Tombs, each with a low arched doorway that opened into absolute blackness. They were dotted about in no kind of order, so that it took a long time, going round this one and going round that one, before you could be sure you had looked round every side of every tomb. This was what Shasta had to do. There was nobody there.

It was very quiet here out on the edge of the desert; and now the sun had really set.

Suddenly from somewhere behind him there came a terrible sound. Shasta's heart gave a great jump and he had to bite his tongue to keep himself from screaming. Next moment he realized what it was: the horns of Tashbaan blowing for the closing of the gates. "Don't be a silly little coward," said Shasta to himself. "Why, it's only the same noise you heard this morning." But there is a great difference be-

tween a noise heard letting you in with your
friends in the morning, and a noise heard alone
at nightfall, shutting you out. And now that the
gates were shut he knew there was no chance of
the others joining him that evening. "Either
they're shut up in Tashbaan for the night,"
thought Shasta, "or else they've gone on without me. It's just the sort of thing that Aravis
would do. But Bree wouldn't. Oh, he wouldn't—
now, would he?"

In this idea about Aravis Shasta was once
more quite wrong. She was proud and could be
hard enough but she was as true as steel and
would never have deserted a companion,
whether she liked him or not.

Now that Shasta knew he would have to
spend the night alone (it was getting darker
every minute) he began to like the look of the
place less and less. There was something very
uncomfortable about those great, silent shapes
of stone. He had been trying his hardest for a
long time not to think of ghouls: but he couldn't
keep it up any longer.

"Ow! Ow! Help!" he shouted suddenly, for
at that very moment he felt something touch his
leg. I don't think anyone can be blamed for
shouting if something comes up from behind
and touches him; not in such a place and at such
a time, when he is frightened already. Shasta at

any rate was too frightened to run. Anything would be better than being chased round and round the burial place of the Ancient Kings with something he dared not look at behind him. Instead, he did what was really the most sensible thing he could do. He looked round; and his heart almost burst with relief. What had touched him was only a cat.

The light was too bad now for Shasta to see much of the cat except that it was big and very solemn. It looked as if it might have lived for long, long years among the Tombs, alone. Its eyes made you think it knew secrets it would not tell.

"Puss, puss," said Shasta. "I suppose you're not a *talking* cat."

The cat stared at him harder than ever. Then it started walking away, and of course Shasta followed it. It led him right through the tombs and out on the desert side of them. There it sat down bolt upright with its tail curled round its feet and its face set toward the desert and toward Narnia and the North, as still as if it were watching for some enemy. Shasta lay down beside it with his back against the cat and his face toward the Tombs, because if one is nervous there's nothing like having your face toward the danger and having something warm and solid at your back. The sand wouldn't have seemed very comfortable to you, but Shasta had been sleeping on the ground for weeks and hardly noticed it. Very soon he fell asleep, though even in his dreams he went on wondering what had happened to Bree and Aravis and Hwin.

He was wakened suddenly by a noise he had never heard before. "Perhaps it was only a nightmare," said Shasta to himself. At the same moment he noticed that the cat had gone from his back, and he wished it hadn't. But he lay quite still without even opening his eyes because he felt sure he would be more frightened if he sat up and looked round at the Tombs and the loneliness: just as you or I might lie still with bedclothes over our heads. But then the noise came again—a harsh, piercing cry from behind him out of the desert. Then of course he had to open his eyes and sit up.

The moon was shining brightly. The Tombs—far bigger and nearer than he had thought they would be—looked gray in the moonlight. In fact, they looked horribly like huge people, draped in gray robes that covered their heads and faces. They were not at all nice things to have near you when spending a night alone in a strange place. But the noise had come from the opposite side, from the desert. Shasta had to turn his back on the Tombs (he didn't like that much) and stare out across the level sand. The wild cry rang out again.

"I hope it's not more lions," thought Shasta. It was in fact not very like the lion's roars he had heard on the night when they met Hwin and Aravis, and was really the cry of a jackal. But of course Shasta did not know this. Even if he had known, he would not have wanted very much to meet a jackal.

The cries rang out again and again. "There's more than one of them, whatever they are," thought Shasta. "And they're coming nearer."

I suppose that if he had been an entirely sensible boy he would have gone back through the Tombs nearer to the river where there were houses, and wild beasts would be less likely to come. But then there were (or he thought there were) the ghouls. To go back through the Tombs would mean going past those dark openings in the Tombs; and what might come out of them? It may have been silly, but Shasta felt he had rather risk the wild beasts. Then, as the cries came nearer and nearer, he began to change his mind.

He was just going to run for it when suddenly, between him and the desert, a huge animal bounded into view. As the moon was behind it, it looked quite black, and Shasta did not know what it was, except that it had a very big, shaggy head and went on four legs. It did not seem to have noticed Shasta, for it suddenly stopped, turned its head toward the desert, and let out a roar which re-echoed through the Tombs and seemed to shake the sand under Shasta's feet. The cries of the other creatures suddenly stopped and he thought he could hear feet scampering away. Then the great beast turned to examine Shasta.

"It's a lion, I know it's a lion," thought Shasta. "I'm done. I wonder will it hurt much. I wish it was over. I wonder does anything happen to people after they're dead. O-o-oh! Here it comes!" And he shut his eyes and teeth tight.

But instead of teeth and claws he only felt something warm lying down at his feet. And when he opened his eyes he said, "Why, it's not nearly as big as I thought! It's only half the size. No, it isn't even quarter the size. I do declare it's only the cat!! I must have dreamed all that about its being as big as a horse."

And whether he really had been dreaming or not, what was now lying at his feet, and staring him out of countenance with its big, green, unwinking eyes, was the cat; though certainly one of the largest cats he had ever seen.

"Oh, Puss," gasped Shasta. "I *am* so glad to see you again. I've been having such horrible dreams." And he at once lay down again, back to back with the cat as they had been at the beginning of the night. The warmth from it spread all over him.

"I'll never do anything nasty to a cat again as long as I live," said Shasta, half to the cat and half to himself. "I did once, you know. I threw stones at a half-starved mangy old stray. Hey! Stop that." For the cat had turned round and given him a scratch. "None of that," said Shasta. "It isn't as if you could understand what I'm saying." Then he dozed off.

Next morning when he woke, the cat was gone, the sun was already up, and the sand hot. Shasta, very thirsty, sat up and rubbed his eyes. The desert was blindingly white and, though there was a murmur of noises from the city behind him, where he sat everything was perfectly still. When he looked a little left and west, so that the sun was not in his eyes, he could see the mountains on the far side of the desert, so sharp and clear that they looked only a stone's throw away. He particularly noticed one blue height that divided into two peaks at the top and decided that it must be Mount Pire. "That's our direction, judging by what the Raven said," he thought, "so I'll just make sure of it, so as not to waste any time when the others show up." So he made a good, deep straight furrow with his foot pointing exactly to Mount Pire.

The next job, clearly, was to get something

to eat and drink. Shasta trotted back through the Tombs—they looked quite ordinary now and he wondered how he could ever have been afraid of them—and down into the cultivated land by the river's side. There were a few people about but not very many, for the city gates had been open several hours and the early morning crowds had already gone in. So he had no difficulty in doing a little "raiding" (as Bree called it). It involved a climb over a garden wall and the results were three oranges, a melon, a fig or two, and a pomegranate. After that, he went down to the river bank, but not too near the bridge, and had a drink. The water was so nice that he took off his hot, dirty clothes and had a dip; for of course Shasta, having lived on the shore all his life, had learned to swim almost as soon as he had learned to walk. When he came out he lay on the grass looking across the water at Tashbaan—all the splendor and strength and glory of it. But that made him remember the dangers of it too. He suddenly realized that the others might have reached the Tombs while he was bathing ("and gone on without me, as likely as not"), so he dressed in a fright and tore back at such speed that he was all hot and thirsty when he arrived and so the good of his bathe was gone.

Like most days when you are alone and

waiting for something this day seemed about a hundred hours long. He had plenty to think of, of course, but sitting alone, just thinking, is pretty slow. He thought a good deal about the Narnians and especially about Corin. He wondered what had happened when they discovered the boy who had been lying on the sofa and hearing all their secret plans wasn't really Corin at all. It was very unpleasant to think of all those nice people imagining him a traitor.

But as the sun slowly, slowly climbed up to the top of the sky and then slowly, slowly began going downward to the West, and no one came and nothing at all happened, he began to get more and more anxious. And of course he now realized that when they arranged to wait for one another at the Tombs no one had said anything about How Long. He couldn't wait here for the rest of his life! And soon it would be dark again, and he would have another night just like last night. A dozen different plans went through his head, all wretched ones, and at last he fixed on the worst plan of all. He decided to wait till it was dark and then go back to the river and steal as many melons as he could carry and set out for Mount Pire alone, trusting for his direction to the line he had drawn that morning in the sand. It was a crazy idea and if he had read as many books as you have about journeys over deserts he would never have dreamed it. But Shasta had read no books at all.

Before the sun set something did happen. Shasta was sitting in the shadow of one of the Tombs when he looked up and saw two horses coming toward him. Then his heart gave a great leap, for he recognized them as Bree and Hwin. But the next moment his heart went down into his toes again. There was no sign of Aravis. The Horses were being led by a strange man, an armed man pretty handsomely dressed like an upper slave in a great family. Bree and Hwin were no longer got up like pack-horses, but saddled and bridled. And what could it all mean? "It's a trap," thought Shasta. "Somebody has caught Aravis and perhaps they've tortured her and she's given the whole thing away. They want me to jump out and run up and speak to Bree, and then I'll be caught too! And yet if I don't, I may be losing my only chance to meet the others. Oh I do wish I knew what had happened." And he skulked behind the Tomb, looking out every few minutes, and wondering which was the least dangerous thing to do.

ARAVIS IN TASHBAAN

What had really happened was this. When Aravis saw Shasta hurried away by the Narnians and found herself alone with two horses who (very wisely) wouldn't say a word, she never lost her head even for a moment. She grabbed Bree's halter and stood still, holding both the horses; and though her heart was beating as hard as a hammer, she did nothing to show it. As soon as the Narnian lords had passed she tried to move on again. But before she could take a step, another crier ("Bother all these people," thought Aravis) was heard shouting out, "Way, way, way! Way for the Tarkheena Lasaraleen!" and

immediately, following the crier, came four armed slaves and then four bearers carrying a litter which was all a-flutter with silken curtains and all a-jingle with silver bells and which scented the whole street with perfumes and flowers. After the litter, female slaves in beautiful clothes, and then a few grooms, runners, pages, and the like. And now Aravis made her first mistake.

She knew Lasaraleen quite well—almost as if they had been at school together—because they had often stayed in the same houses and been to the same parties. And Aravis couldn't help looking up to see what Lasaraleen looked like now that she was married and a very great person indeed.

It was fatal. The eyes of the two girls met. And immediately Lasaraleen sat up in the litter and burst out at the top of her voice.

"Aravis! What on earth are you doing here? Your father—"

There was not a moment to lose. Without a second's delay Aravis let go the Horses, caught the edge of the litter, swung herself up beside Lasaraleen and whispered furiously in her ear.

"Shut up! Do you hear! Shut up. You must hide me. Tell your people—"

"But darling—" began Lasaraleen in the same loud voice. (She didn't in the least mind making people stare; in fact she rather liked it.)

"Do what I tell you or I'll never speak to you again," hissed Aravis. "Please, please be quick, Las. It's frightfully important. Tell your people to bring those two horses along. Pull all the curtains of the litter and get away somewhere where I can't be found. And do *hurry*."

"All right, darling," said Lasaraleen in her lazy voice. "Here. Two of you take the Tarkheena's horses." (This was to the slaves.) "And now home. I say, darling, do you think we really want the curtains drawn on a day like this? I mean to say—"

But Aravis had already drawn the curtains, enclosing Lasaraleen and herself in a rich and scented, but rather stuffy, kind of tent.

"I mustn't be seen," she said. "My father doesn't know I'm here. I'm running away."

"My dear, how perfectly thrilling," said Lasaraleen. "I'm dying to hear all about it. Darling, you're sitting on my dress. Do you mind? That's better. It is a new one. Do you like it? I got it at—"

"Oh, Las, do be serious," said Aravis. "Where is my father?"

"Didn't you know?" said Lasaraleen. "He's here, of course. He came to town yesterday and is asking about you everywhere. And to think of you and me being here together and his not knowing anything about it! It's the funniest thing I ever heard." And she went off into giggles. She always had been a terrible giggler, as Aravis now remembered.

"It isn't funny at all," she said. "It's dreadfully serious. Where can you hide me?"

"No difficulty at all, my dear girl," said Lasaraleen. "I'll take you home. My husband's away and no one will see you. Phew! It's not much fun with the curtains drawn. I want to see people. There's no point in having a new dress on if one's to go about shut up like this."

"I hope no one heard you when you shouted out to me like that," said Aravis.

"No, no, of course, darling," said Lasaraleen absentmindedly. "But you haven't even told me yet what you think of the dress."

"Another thing," said Aravis. "You must tell your people to treat those two horses very respectfully. That's part of the secret. They're really Talking Horses from Narnia."

"Fancy!" said Lasaraleen. "How exciting! And oh, darling, have you seen the barbarian queen from Narnia? She's staying in Tashbaan at present. They say Prince Rabadash is madly in love with her. There have been the most wonderful parties and hunts and things all this last fortnight. I can't see that she's so very pretty myself. But some of the Narnian *men* are lovely. I was taken out on a river party the day before yesterday, and I was wearing my—"

"How shall we prevent your people telling everyone that you've got a visitor—dressed like a beggar's brat—in your house? It might so easily get round to my father."

"Now don't keep fussing, there's a dear," said Lasaraleen. "We'll get you some proper clothes in a moment. And here we are!"

The bearers had stopped and the litter was being lowered. When the curtains had been drawn Aravis found that she was in a courtyard-garden very like the one that Shasta had been taken into a few minutes earlier in another part of the city. Lasaraleen would have gone indoors at once but Aravis reminded her in a frantic whisper to say something to the slaves about not telling anyone of their mistress's strange visitor.

"Sorry, darling, it had gone right out of my head," said Lasaraleen. "Here. All of you. And you, doorkeeper. No one is to be let out of the house today. And anyone I catch talking about this young lady will be first beaten to death and then burned alive and after that be kept on bread and water for six weeks. There."

Although Lasaraleen had said she was dying to hear Aravis's story, she showed no sign of really wanting to hear it at all. She was, in fact, much better at talking than at listening. She insisted on Aravis having a long and luxurious bath (Calormene baths are famous) and then dressing her up in the finest clothes before she would let her explain anything. The fuss she made about choosing the dresses nearly drove Aravis mad. She remembered now that Lasaraleen had always been like that, interested in clothes and parties and gossip. Aravis had always been more interested in bows and arrows and horses and dogs and swimming. You will guess that each thought the other silly. But

when at last they were both seated after a meal (it was chiefly of the whipped cream and jelly and fruit and ice sort) in a beautiful pillared room (which Aravis would have liked better if Lasaraleen's spoiled pet monkey hadn't been climbing about it all the time) Lasaraleen at last asked her why she was running away from home.

When Aravis had finished telling her story, Lasaraleen said, "But, darling, why *don't* you marry Ahoshta Tarkaan? Everyone's crazy about him. My husband says he is beginning to be one of the greatest men in Calormen. He has just been made Grand Vizier now old Axartha has died. Didn't you know?"

"I don't care. I can't stand the sight of him," said Aravis.

"But, darling, only think! Three palaces, and one of them that beautiful one down on the lake at Ilkeen. Positively ropes of pearls, I'm told. Baths of asses' milk. And you'd see such a lot of *me*."

"He can keep his pearls and palaces as far as I'm concerned," said Aravis.

"You always *were* a queer girl, Aravis," said Lasaraleen. "What more *do* you want?"

In the end, however, Aravis managed to make her friend believe that she was in earnest and even to discuss plans. There would be no difficulty now about getting the two horses out of the North gate and then on to the Tombs. No one would stop or question a groom in fine clothes leading a war horse and a lady's saddle horse down to the river, and Lasaraleen had plenty of grooms to send. It wasn't so easy to decide what to do about Aravis herself. She suggested that she could be carried out in the litter with the curtains drawn. But Lasaraleen told her that litters were only used in the city and the sight of one going out through the gate would be certain to lead to questions.

When they had talked for a long time—and it was all the longer because Aravis found it hard to keep her friend to the point—at last Lasaraleen clapped her hands and said, "Oh, I have an idea. There is *one* way of getting out of the city without using the gates. The Tisroc's garden (may he live forever!) runs right down to the water and there is a little water-door. Only for the palace people of course—but then you know, dear" (here she tittered a little) "we almost *are* palace people. I say, it is lucky for you that you came to *me*. The dear Tisroc (may he live forever!) is *so* kind. We're asked to the palace almost every day and it is like a second home. I love all the dear princes and princesses and I positively *adore* Prince Rabadash. I might run in and see any of the palace ladies at any hour of the day or night. Why shouldn't I slip in with you, after dark, and let you out by the water-door? There are always a few punts and things tied up outside it. And even if we were caught—"

"All would be lost," said Aravis.

"Oh darling, don't get so excited," said Lasaraleen. "I was going to say, even if we were caught everyone would only say it was one of my mad jokes. I'm getting quite well known for them. Only the other day—do listen, dear, this is frightfully funny—"

"I meant, all would be lost *for me*," said Aravis a little sharply.

"Oh—ah—yes—I *do* see what you mean, darling. Well, can you think of any better plan?"

Aravis couldn't, and answered, "No. We'll have to risk it. When can we start?"

"Oh, not tonight," said Lasaraleen. "Of course not tonight. There's a great feast on tonight (I must start getting my hair done for it in a few minutes) and the whole place will be a blaze of lights. And such a crowd too! It would have to be tomorrow night."

This was bad news for Aravis, but she had to make the best of it. The afternoon passed very slowly and it was a relief when Lasaraleen went out to the banquet, for Aravis was very tired of her giggling and her talk about dresses and parties, weddings and engagements and scandals. She went to bed early and that part she did enjoy: it was so nice to have pillows and sheets again.

But the next day passed very slowly. Lasaraleen wanted to go back on the whole arrangement and kept on telling Aravis that Narnia was a country of perpetual snow and ice inhabited by demons and sorcerers, and she was mad to think of going there. "And with a peasant boy, too!" said Lasaraleen. "Darling, think of it! It's not Nice." Aravis had thought of it a good deal, but she was so tired of Lasaraleen's silliness by now that, for the first time, she began to think that traveling with Shasta was really rather more fun than fashionable life in Tashbaan. So she only replied, "You forget that I'll be nobody, just like him, when we get to Narnia. And anyway, I promised."

"And to think," said Lasaraleen, almost crying, "that if only you had sense you could be the wife of a Grand Vizier!" Aravis went away to have a private word with the horses.

"You must go with a groom a little before sunset down to the Tombs," she said. "No more of those packs. You'll be saddled and bridled again. But there'll have to be food in Hwin's saddle-bags and a full water-skin behind yours, Bree. The man has orders to let you both have a good long drink at the far side of the bridge."

"And then, Narnia and the North!" whispered Bree. "But what if Shasta is not at the Tombs."

"Wait for him of course," said Aravis. "I hope you've been quite comfortable."

"Never better stabled in my life," said Bree. "But if the husband of that tittering Tarkheena friend of yours is paying his head groom to get the best oats, then I think the head groom is cheating him."

Aravis and Lasaraleen had supper in the pillared room.

About two hours later they were ready to start. Aravis was dressed to look like a superior slave-girl in a great house and wore a veil over her face. They had agreed that if any questions were asked Lasaraleen would pretend that Aravis was a slave she was taking as a present to one of the princesses.

The two girls went out on foot. A very few minutes brought them to the palace gates. Here there were of course soldiers on guard but the officer knew Lasaraleen quite well and called his men to attention and saluted. They passed at once into the Hall of Black Marble. A fair number of courtiers, slaves and others were still moving about here but this only made the two girls less conspicuous. They passed on into the Hall of Pillars and then into the Hall of Statues and down the colonnade, passing the great beaten-copper doors of the throne room. It was all magnificent beyond description; what they could see of it in the dim light of the lamps.

Presently they came out into the garden-court which sloped downhill in a number of terraces. On the far side of that they came to the Old Palace. It had already grown almost quite dark and they now found themselves in a maze of corridors lit only by occasional torches fixed in brackets to the walls. Lasaraleen halted at a place where you had to go either left or right.

"Go on, do go on," whispered Aravis, whose heart was beating terribly and who still felt that her father might run into them at any corner.

"I'm just wondering . . ." said Lasaraleen. "I'm not absolutely sure which way we go from here. I *think* it's the left. Yes, I'm almost sure it's the left. What fun this is!"

They took the left hand way and found themselves in a passage that was hardly lighted at all and which soon began going down steps.

"It's all right," said Lasaraleen. "I'm sure we're right now. I remember these steps." But at that moment a moving light appeared ahead. A second later there appeared from round a distant corner, the dark shapes of two men walking backward and carrying tall candles. And of course it is only before royalties that people walk backward. Aravis felt Lasaraleen grip her arm—that sort of sudden grip which is almost a pinch and which means that the person who is gripping you is very frightened indeed. Aravis thought it odd that Lasaraleen should be so afraid of the Tisroc if he were really such a friend of hers, but there was no time to go on thinking. Lasaraleen was hurrying her back to the top of the steps, on tiptoes, and groping wildly along the wall.

"Here's a door," she whispered. "Quick."

They went in, drew the door softly behind them, and found themselves in pitch darkness. Aravis could hear by Lasaraleen's breathing that she was terrified.

"Tash preserve us!" whispered Lasaraleen. "What *shall* we do if he comes in here. Can we hide?"

There was a soft carpet under their feet. They groped forward into the room and blundered onto a sofa.

"Let's lie down behind it," whimpered Lasaraleen. "Oh, I *do* wish we hadn't come."

There was just room between the sofa and the curtained wall and the two girls got down. Lasaraleen managed to get the better position and was completely covered. The upper part of Aravis's face stuck out behind the sofa, so that if anyone came into that room with a light and happened to look in exactly the right place they would see her. But of course, because she was wearing a veil, what they saw would not at once look like a forehead and a pair of eyes. Aravis shoved desperately to try and make Lasaraleen give her a little more room. But Lasaraleen, now quite selfish in her panic, fought back and pinched her feet. They gave it up and lay still, panting a little. Their own breath seemed dreadfully noisy, but there was no other noise.

"Is it safe?" said Aravis at last in the tiniest possible whisper.

"I—I—*think* so," began Lasaraleen. "But my poor nerves—" and then came the most terrible noise they could have heard at that moment: the noise of the door opening. And then came light. And because Aravis couldn't get her head any further in behind the sofa, she saw everything.

First came the two slaves (deaf and dumb, as Aravis rightly guessed, and therefore used at the most secret councils) walking backward and carrying the candles. They took up their stand one at each end of the sofa. This was a good thing, for of course it was now harder for anyone to see Aravis once a slave was in front of her and she was looking between his heels. Then came an old man, very fat, wearing a curious pointed cap by which she immediately knew that he was the Tisroc. The least of the jewels with which he was covered was worth more than all the clothes and weapons of the Narnian lords put together: but he was so fat and such a mass of frills and pleats and bobbles and buttons and tassels and talismans that Aravis couldn't help thinking the Narnian fashions (at any rate for men) looked nicer. After him came a tall young man with a feathered and jeweled turban on his head and an ivory-sheathed scimitar at his side. He seemed very excited and his eyes and teeth flashed fiercely in the candlelight. Last of all came a little hump-backed, wizened old man in whom she recognized with a shudder the new Grand Vizier and her own betrothed husband, Ahoshta Tarkaan himself.

As soon as all three had entered the room and the door was shut, the Tisroc seated himself on the divan with a sigh of contentment, the young man took his place, standing before him, and the Grand Vizier got down on his knees and elbows and laid his face flat on the carpet.

IN THE HOUSE OF THE TISROC

"**O**h-my-father-and-oh-the-delight-of-my eyes," began the young man, muttering the words very quickly and sulkily and not at all as if the Tisroc *were* the delight of his eyes. "May you live forever, but you have utterly destroyed me. If you had given me the swiftest of the galleys at sunrise when I first saw that the ship of the accursed barbarians was gone from her place I would perhaps have overtaken them. But you persuaded me to send first and see if they had not merely moved round the point into better anchorage. And now the whole day has been wasted. And they are gone—gone—out of my reach! The false jade, the—" and here he added a great many descriptions of Queen Susan which would not look at all nice in print. For of course this young man was Prince Rabadash and of course the false jade was Susan of Narnia.

"Compose yourself, O my son," said the Tisroc. "For the departure of guests makes a wound that is easily healed in the heart of a judicious host."

"But I *want* her," cried the Prince. "I must have her. I shall die if I do not get her—false, proud, black-hearted daughter of a dog that she is! I cannot sleep and my food has no savor and my eyes are darkened because of her beauty. I must have the barbarian queen."

"How well it was said by a gifted poet," observed the Vizier, raising his face (in a somewhat dusty condition) from the carpet, "that deep drafts from the fountain of reason are desirable in order to extinguish the fire of youthful love."

This seemed to exasperate the Prince. "Dog," he shouted, directing a series of well-aimed kicks at the hindquarters of the Vizier, "do not dare to quote the poets to me. I have had maxims and verses flung at me all day and I can endure them no more." I am afraid Aravis did not feel at all sorry for the Vizier.

The Tisroc was apparently sunk in thought,

but when, after a long pause, he noticed what was happening, he said tranquilly:

"My son, by all means desist from kicking the venerable and enlightened Vizier: for as a costly jewel retains its value even if hidden in a dung-hill, so old age and discretion are to be respected even in the vile persons of our subjects. Desist therefore, and tell us what you desire and propose."

"I desire and propose, O my father," said Rabadash, "that you immediately call out your invincible armies and invade the thrice-accursed land of Narnia and waste it with fire and sword and add it to your illimitable empire, killing their High King and all of his blood except the queen Susan. For I must have her as my wife, though she shall learn a sharp lesson first."

"Understand, O my son," said the Tisroc, "that no words you can speak will move me to open war against Narnia."

"If you were not my father, O ever-living Tisroc," said the Prince, grinding his teeth, "I should say that was the word of a coward."

"And if you were not my son, O most inflammable Rabadash," replied his father, "your life would be short and your death slow when you had said it." (The cool, placid voice in which he spoke these words made Aravis's blood run cold.)

"But why, O my father," said the Prince—this time in a much more respectful voice, "why should we think twice about punishing Narnia any more than about hanging an idle slave or sending a worn-out horse to be made into dog's-meat? It is not the fourth size of one of your least provinces. A thousand spears could conquer it in five weeks. It is an unseemly blot on the skirts of your empire."

"Most undoubtedly," said the Tisroc. "These little barbarian countries that call themselves *free* (which is as much as to say, idle, disordered, and unprofitable) are hateful to the gods and to all persons of discernment."

"Then why have we suffered such a land as Narnia to remain thus long unsubdued?"

"Know, O enlightened Prince," said the Grand Vizier, "that until the year in which your exalted father began his salutary and unending reign, the land of Narnia was covered with ice and snow and was moreover ruled by a most powerful enchantress."

"This I know very well, O loquacious Vizier," answered the Prince. "But I know also that the enchantress is dead. And the ice and snow have vanished, so that Narnia is now wholesome, fruitful, and delicious."

"And this change, O most learned Prince, has doubtless been brought to pass by the powerful incantations of those wicked persons who now call themselves kings and queens of Narnia."

"I am rather of the opinion," said Rabadash, "that it has come about by the alteration of the stars and the operation of natural causes."

"All this," said the Tisroc, "is a question for the disputations of learned men. I will never believe that so great an alteration, and the killing of the old enchantress, were effected without the aid of strong magic. And such things are to be expected in that land, which is chiefly inhabited by demons in the shape of beasts that talk like men, and monsters that are half man and half beast. It is commonly reported that the High King of Narnia (whom may the gods utterly reject) is supported by a demon of hideous aspect and irresistible maleficence who appears in the shape of a Lion. Therefore the attacking of Narnia is a dark and doubtful enterprise, and I am determined not to put my hand out farther than I can draw it back."

"How blessed is Calormen," said the Vizier, popping up his face again, "on whose ruler the gods have been pleased to bestow prudence and circumspection! Yet as the irrefutable and sapient Tisroc has said it is very grievous to be constrained to keep our hands off such a dainty dish as Narnia. Gifted was that poet who said—" but at this point Ahoshta noticed an impatient movement of the Prince's toe and became suddenly silent.

"It is very grievous," said the Tisroc in his deep, quiet voice. "Every morning the sun is darkened in my eyes, and every night my sleep is the less refreshing, because I remember that Narnia is still free."

"O my father," said Rabadash. "How if I show you a way by which you can stretch out your arm to take Narnia and yet draw it back unharmed if the attempt prove unfortunate?"

"If you can show me that, O Rabadash," said the Tisroc, "you will be the best of sons."

"Hear then, O father. This very night and in this hour I will take but two hundred horse and ride across the desert. And it shall seem to all men that you know nothing of my going. On the second morning I shall be at the gates of King Lune's castle of Anvard in Archenland. They are at peace with us and unprepared and I shall take Anvard before they have bestirred themselves. Then I will ride through the pass above Anvard and down through Narnia to Cair Paravel. The High King will not be there; when I left them he was already preparing a raid against the giants on his northern border. I shall find Cair Paravel, most likely with open gates, and ride in. I shall exercise prudence and courtesy and spill as little Narnian blood as I can. And what then remains but to sit there till the *Splendor Hyaline* puts in, with Queen Susan on board, catch my strayed bird as she sets foot ashore, swing her into the saddle, and then ride, ride, ride back to Anvard?"

"But is it not probable, O my son," said the Tisroc, "that at the taking of the woman either King Edmund or you will lose his life?"

"They will be a small company," said Rabadash, "and I will order ten of my men to disarm and bind him: restraining my vehement desire for his blood so that there shall be no deadly cause of war between you and the High King."

"And how if the *Splendor Hyaline* is at Cair Paravel before you?"

"I do not look for that with these winds, O my father."

"And lastly, O my resourceful son," said the Tisroc, "you have made clear how all this might give you the barbarian woman, but not how it helps me to the overthrowing of Narnia."

"O my father, can it have escaped you that though I and my horsemen will come and go through Narnia like an arrow from a bow, yet we shall have Anvard for ever? And when you hold Anvard you sit in the very gate of Narnia, and your garrison in Anvard can be increased by little and little till it is a great host."

"It is spoken with understanding and foresight. But how do I draw back my arm if all this miscarries?"

"You shall say that I did it without your knowledge and against your will, and without your blessing, being constrained by the violence of my love and the impetuosity of youth."

"And how if the High King then demands that we send back the barbarian woman, his sister?"

"O my father, be assured that he will not. For though the fancy of a woman has rejected this marriage, the High King Peter is a man of prudence and understanding who will in no way wish to lose the high honor and advantage of being allied to our House and seeing his nephew and grand nephew on the throne of Calormen."

"He will not see that if I live forever as is no doubt your wish," said the Tisroc in an even drier voice than usual.

"And also, O my father and O the delight of my eyes," said the Prince, after a moment of awkward silence, "we shall write letters as if from the Queen to say that she loves me and has no desire to return to Narnia. For it is well known that women are as changeable as weathercocks. And even if they do not wholly believe the letters, they will not dare to come to Tashbaan in arms to fetch her."

"O enlightened Vizier," said the Tisroc, "bestow your wisdom upon us concerning this strange proposal."

"O eternal Tisroc," answered Ahoshta, "the strength of paternal affection is not unknown to me and I have often heard that sons are in the eyes of their fathers more precious than carbuncles. How then shall I dare freely to unfold to you my mind in a matter which may imperil the life of this exalted Prince?"

"Undoubtedly you will dare," replied the Tisroc. "Because you will find that the dangers of not doing so are at least equally great."

"To hear is to obey," moaned the wretched man. "Know then, O most reasonable Tisroc, in the first place, that the danger of the Prince is not altogether so great as might appear. For the gods have withheld from the barbarians the light of discretion, as that their poetry is not, like ours, full of choice apophthegms and useful maxims, but is all of love and war. Therefore nothing will appear to them more noble and admirable than such a mad enterprise as this of—ow!" For the Prince, at the word "mad," had kicked him.

"Desist, O my son," said the Tisroc. "And you, estimable Vizier, whether he desists or not, by no means allow the flow of your eloquence to be interrupted. For nothing is more suitable to persons of gravity and decorum than to endure minor inconveniences with constancy."

"To hear is to obey," said the Vizier, wriggling himself round a little so as to get his hinder parts further away from Rabadash's toe. "Nothing, I say, will seem as pardonable, if not estimable, in their eyes as this—er—hazardous attempt, especially because it is undertaken for the love of a woman. Therefore, if the Prince by misfortune fell into their hands, they would assuredly not kill him. Nay, it may even be, that though he failed to carry off the queen, yet the sight of his great valor and of the extremity of his passion might incline her heart to him."

"This is a good point, old babbler," said

Rabadash. "Very good, however it came into your ugly head."

"The praise of my masters is the light of my eyes," said Ahoshta. "And secondly, O Tisroc, whose reign must and shall be interminable, I think that with the aid of the gods it is very likely that Anvard will fall into the Prince's hands. And if so, we have Narnia by the throat."

There was a long pause and the room became so silent that the two girls hardly dared to breathe. At last the Tisroc spoke.

"Go, my son," he said. "And do as you have said. But expect no help nor countenance from me. I will not avenge you if you are killed and I will not deliver you if the barbarians cast you into prison. And if, either in success or failure, you shed a drop more than you need of Narnian noble blood and open war arises from it, my favor shall never fall upon you again and your next brother shall have your place in Calormen. Now go. Be swift, secret, and fortunate. May the strength of Tash the inexorable, the irresistible be in your sword and lance."

"To hear is to obey," cried Rabadash, and after kneeling for a moment to kiss his father's hands he rushed from the room. Greatly to the disappointment of Aravis, who was now horribly cramped, the Tisroc and the Vizier remained.

"O Vizier," said the Tisroc, "is it certain that no living soul knows of this council we three have held here tonight?"

"O my master," said Ahoshta, "it is not possible that any should know. For that very reason I proposed, and you in your infallible wisdom agreed, that we should meet here in the Old Palace where no council is ever held and none of the household has any occasion to come."

"It is well," said the Tisroc. "If any man knew, I would see to it that he died before an hour had passed. And do you also, O prudent Vizier, forget it. I sponge away from my own heart and from yours all knowledge of the Prince's plans. He is gone without my knowl-

edge or my consent, I know not whither, because of his violence and the rash and disobedient disposition of youth. No man will be more astonished than you and I to hear that Anvard is in his hands."

"To hear is to obey," said Ahoshta.

"That is why you will never think even in your secret heart that I am the hardest hearted of fathers who thus send my first-born son on an errand so likely to be his death; pleasing as it must be to you who do not love the Prince. For I see into the bottom of your mind."

"O impeccable Tisroc," said the Vizier. "In comparison with you I love neither the Prince nor my own life nor bread nor water nor the light of the sun."

"Your sentiments," said the Tisroc, "are elevated and correct. I also love none of these things in comparison with the glory and strength of my throne. If the Prince succeeds, we have Archenland, and perhaps hereafter Narnia. If he fails—I have eighteen other sons and Rabadash, after the manner of the eldest sons of kings, was beginning to be dangerous. More than five Tisrocs in Tashbaan have died before their time because their eldest sons, enlightened princes, grew tired of waiting for their throne. He had better cool his blood abroad than boil it in inaction here. And now, O excellent Vizier, the excess of my paternal anxiety inclines me to sleep. Command the musicians to my chamber. But before you lie down, call back the pardon we wrote for the third cook. I feel within me the manifest prognostics of indigestion."

"To hear is to obey," said the Grand Vizier. He crawled backward on all fours to the door, rose, bowed, and went out. Even then the Tisroc remained seated in silence on the divan till Aravis almost began to be afraid that he had dropped asleep. But at last with a great creaking and sighing he heaved up his enormous body, signed to the slaves to precede him with the lights, and went out. The door closed behind him, the room was once more totally dark, and the two girls could breathe freely again.

9

ACROSS THE DESERT

"How dreadful! How perfectly dreadful!" whimpered Lasaraleen. "Oh darling, I *am* so frightened. I'm shaking all over. Feel me."

"Come on," said Aravis, who was trembling herself. "They've gone back to the new palace. Once we're out of this room we're safe enough. But it's wasted a terrible time. Get me down to that water-gate as quick as you can."

"Darling, how *can* you?" squeaked Lasaraleen. "I can't do anything—not now. My poor nerves! No: we must just lie still a bit and then go back."

"Why back?" asked Aravis.

"Oh, you don't understand. You're so unsympathetic," said Lasaraleen, beginning to cry. Aravis decided it was no occasion for mercy.

"Look here!" she said, catching Lasaraleen and giving her a good shake. "If you say another word about going back, and if you don't start taking me to that water-gate at once—do you know what I'll do? I'll rush out into that passage and scream. Then we'll both be caught."

"But we shall both be k-k-killed!" said Lasaraleen. "Didn't you hear what the Tisroc (may he live forever) said?"

"Yes, and I'd sooner be killed than married to Ahoshta. So come on."

"Oh you *are* unkind," said Lasaraleen. "And I in such a state!"

But in the end she had to give in to Aravis. She led the way down the steps they had already descended, and along another corridor and so finally out into the open air. They were now in the palace garden which sloped down in terraces to the city wall. The moon shone brightly. One of the drawbacks about adventures is that when you come to the most beautiful places you are often too anxious and hurried to appreciate them; so that Aravis (though she remembered them years later) had only a vague impression of gray lawns, quietly bubbling fountains, and the long black shadows of cypress trees.

When they reached the very bottom and the wall rose frowning above them, Lasaraleen was shaking so that she could not unbolt the gate. Aravis did it. There, at last, was the river, full of reflected moonlight, and a little landing stage and a few pleasure boats.

"Good-bye," said Aravis, "and thank you. I'm sorry if I've been a pig. But think what I'm flying from!"

"Oh Aravis darling," said Lasaraleen. "Won't you change your mind? Now that you've seen what a very great man Ahoshta is!"

"Great man!" said Aravis. "A hideous groveling slave who flatters when he's kicked but treasures it all up and hopes to get his own back by egging on that horrible Tisroc to plot his son's death. Faugh! I'd sooner marry my father's scullion than a creature like that."

"Oh Aravis, Aravis! How can you say such dreadful things; and about the Tisroc (may he live forever) too. It must be right if *he's* going to do it!"

"Good-bye," said Aravis, "and I thought your dresses lovely. And I think your house is lovely too. I'm sure you'll have a lovely life— though it wouldn't suit me. Close the door softly behind me."

She tore herself away from her friend's affectionate embraces, stepped into a punt, cast off, and a moment later was out in midstream with a huge real moon overhead and a huge reflected moon down, deep down, in the river. The air was fresh and cool and as she drew near the farther bank she heard the hooting of an owl. "Ah! That's better!" thought Aravis. She had always lived in the country and had hated every minute of her time in Tashbaan.

When she stepped ashore she found herself in darkness for the rise of the ground, and the trees, cut off the moonlight. But she managed to find the same road that Shasta had found, and came just as he had done to the end of the grass and the beginning of the sand, and looked (like him) to her left and saw the big, black Tombs. And now at last, brave girl though she was, her heart quailed. Supposing the others weren't there! Supposing the ghouls were! But she stuck out her chin (and a little bit of her tongue too) and went straight toward them.

But before she had reached them she saw Bree and Hwin and the groom.

"You can go back to your mistress now," said Aravis (quite forgetting that he couldn't, until the city gates opened next morning). "Here is money for your pains."

"To hear is to obey," said the groom, and at once set off at a remarkable speed in the direction of the city. There was no need to tell him to make haste: he also had been thinking a good deal about ghouls.

For the next few seconds Aravis was busy kissing the noses and patting the necks of Hwin and Bree just as if they were quite ordinary horses.

"And here comes Shasta! Thanks be to the Lion!" said Bree.

Aravis looked round, and there, right enough, was Shasta who had come out of hiding the moment he saw the groom going away.

"And now," said Aravis. "There's not a moment to lose." And in hasty words she told them about Rabadash's expedition.

"Treacherous hounds!" said Bree, shaking his mane and stamping his hoof. "An attack in time of peace, without defiance sent! But we'll grease his oats for him. We'll be there before he is."

"Can we?" said Aravis, swinging herself into Hwin's saddle. Shasta wished he could mount like that.

"Brooh-hoo!" snorted Bree. "Up you get, Shasta. Can we! And with a good start too!"

"He said he was going to start at once," said Aravis.

"That's how humans talk," said Bree. "But you don't get a company of two hundred horse and horsemen watered and victualed and armed and saddled and started all in a minute. Now: what's our direction? Due North?"

"No," said Shasta. "I know about that. I've drawn a line. I'll explain later. Bear a bit to our left, both you horses. Ah—here it is!"

"Now," said Bree. "All that about galloping for a day and a night, like in stories, can't really be done. It must be walk and trot: but brisk trots and short walks. And whenever we walk you two humans can slip off and walk too. Now. Are you ready, Hwin? Off we go. Narnia and the North!"

At first it was delightful. The night had now been going on for so many hours that the sand had almost finished giving back all the sun-heat it had received during the day, and the air was cool, fresh, and clear. Under the moonlight the sand, in every direction and as far as they could see, gleamed as if it were smooth water or a great silver tray. Except for the noise of Bree's and Hwin's hoofs there was not a sound to be heard. Shasta would nearly have fallen asleep if he had not had to dismount and walk every now and then.

This seemed to last for hours. Then there came a time when there was no longer any moon. They seemed to ride in the dead darkness for hours and hours. And after that there came a moment when Shasta noticed that he could see

Bree's neck and head in front of him a little more clearly than before; and slowly, very slowly, he began to notice the vast gray flatness on every side. It looked absolutely dead, like something in a dead world; and Shasta felt quite terribly tired and noticed that he was getting cold and that his lips were dry. And all the time the squeak of the leather, the jingle of the bits, and the noise of the hoofs—not *Propputty-propputty* as it would be on a hard road, but *Thubbudy-thubbudy* on the dry sand.

At last, after hours of riding, far away on his right there came a single long streak of paler gray, low down on the horizon. Then a streak of red. It was the morning at last, but without a single bird to sing about it. He was glad of the walking bits now, for he was colder than ever.

Then suddenly the sun rose and everything changed in a moment. The gray sand turned yellow and twinkled as if it was strewn with diamonds. On their left the shadows of Shasta and Hwin and Bree and Aravis, enormously long, raced beside them. The double peak of Mount Pire, far ahead, flashed in the sunlight and Shasta saw they were a little out of the course. "A bit left, a bit left," he sang out. Best of all, when you looked back, Tashbaan was already small and remote. The Tombs were quite invisible: swallowed up in that single, jagged-edge hump which was the city of the Tisroc. Everyone felt better.

But not for long. Though Tashbaan looked very far away when they first saw it, it refused to look any further away as they went on. Shasta gave up looking back at it, for it only gave him the feeling that they were not moving at all. Then the light became a nuisance. The glare of the sand made his eyes ache: but he knew he mustn't shut them. He must screw them up and keep looking on ahead at Mount Pire and shouting out directions. Then came the heat. He noticed it for the first time when he had to dismount and walk: as he slipped down to the sand the heat from it struck up into his face as if from the opening of an oven door. Next time it was worse. But the third time, as his bare feet touched the sand he screamed with pain and got one foot back in the stirrup and the other half over Bree's back before you could have said knife.

"Sorry, Bree," he gasped. "I can't walk. It burns my feet." "Of course!" panted Bree. "Should have thought of that myself. Stay on. Can't be helped."

"It's all right for *you*," said Shasta to Aravis who was walking beside Hwin. "You've got shoes on."

Aravis said nothing and looked prim. Let's

hope she didn't mean to, but she did.

On again, trot and walk and trot, jingle-jingle-jingle, squeak-squeak-squeak, smell of hot horse, smell of hot self, blinding glare, headache. And nothing at all different for mile after mile. Tashbaan would never look any further away. The mountains would never look any nearer. You felt this had been going on for always—jingle-jingle-jingle, squeak-squeak-squeak, smell of hot horse, smell of hot self.

Of course one tried all sorts of games with oneself to try to make the time pass: and of course they were all no good. And one tried very hard not to think of drinks—iced sherbet in a palace at Tashbaan, clear spring water tinkling with a dark earthy sound, cold, smooth milk just creamy enough and not too creamy—and the harder you tried not to think, the more you thought.

At last there was something different—a mass of rock sticking up out of the sand about fifty yards long and thirty feet high. It did not cast much shadow, for the sun was now very high, but it cast a little. Into that shade they crowded. There they ate some food and drank a little water. It is not easy giving a horse a drink out of a skin bottle, but Bree and Hwin were clever with their lips. No one had anything like enough. No one spoke. The Horses were flecked with foam and their breathing was noisy. The children were pale.

After a very short rest they went on again. Same noises, same smells, same glare, till at last their shadows began to fall on their right, and then got longer and longer till they seemed to stretch out to the Eastern end of the world. Very slowly the sun drew nearer to the Western horizon. And now at last he was down and, thank goodness, the merciless glare was gone, though the heat coming up from the sand was still as bad as ever. Four pairs of eyes were looking out eagerly for any sign of the valley that Sallowpad the Raven had spoken about. But, mile after mile, there was nothing but level sand. And now the day was quite definitely done, and most of the stars were out, and still the Horses thundered on and the children rose and sank in their saddles, miserable with thirst and weariness. Not till the moon had risen did Shasta—in the strange, barking voice of someone whose mouth is perfectly dry—shout out:

"There it is!"

There was no mistaking it now. Ahead, and a little to their right, there was at last a slope: a slope downward and hummocks of rock on each side. The Horses were far too tired to speak but they swung round toward it and in a minute or two they were entering the gully. At first it was worse in there than it had been out in the open desert, for there was a breathless stuffiness between the rocky walls and less moonlight. The slope continued steeply downward and the rocks on either hand rose to the height of cliffs. Then they began to meet vegetation—prickly cactus-like plants and coarse grass of the kind that would prick your fingers. Soon the horse-hoofs were falling on pebbles and stones instead of sand. Round every bend of the valley—and it

had many bends—they looked eagerly for water. The Horses were nearly at the end of their strength now, and Hwin, stumbling and panting, was lagging behind Bree. They were almost in despair before at last they came to a little muddiness and a tiny trickle of water through softer and better grass. And the trickle became a brook, and the brook became a stream with bushes on each side, and the stream became a river and there came (after more disappointments than I could possibly describe) a moment when Shasta, who had been in a kind of doze, suddenly realized that Bree had stopped and found himself slipping off. Before them a little cataract of water poured into a broad pool: and both the Horses were already in the pool with their heads down, drinking, drinking, drinking. "O-o-oh," said Shasta and plunged in—it was about up to his knees—and stooped his head right into the cataract. It was perhaps the loveliest moment in his life.

It was about ten minutes later when all four of them (the two children wet nearly all over) came out and began to notice their surroundings. The moon was now high enough to peep down into the valley. There was soft grass on both sides of the river, and beyond the grass, trees and bushes sloped up to the bases of the cliffs. There must have been some wonderful

flowering shrubs hidden in that shadowy undergrowth for the whole glade was full of the coolest and most delicious smells. And out of the darkest recess among the trees there came a sound Shasta had never heard before—a nightingale.

Everyone was much too tired to speak or eat. The Horses, without waiting to be unsaddled, lay down at once. So did Aravis and Shasta.

About ten minutes later the careful Hwin said, "But we mustn't go to sleep. We've got to keep ahead of that Rabadash."

"No," said Bree very slowly. "Mustn't go sleep. Just a little rest."

Shasta knew (for a moment) that they

would all go to sleep if he didn't get up and do something about it, and felt that he ought to. In fact he decided that he would get up and persuade them to go on. But presently; not yet: not just yet . . .

Very soon the moon shone and the nightingale sang over two horses and two human children, all fast asleep.

It was Aravis who awoke first. The sun was already high in the heavens and the cool morning hours were already wasted. "It's my fault," she said to herself furiously as she jumped up and began rousing the others. "One wouldn't expect Horses to keep awake after a day's work like that, even if they *can* talk. And of course that Boy wouldn't; he's had no decent training. But *I* ought to have known better."

The others were dazed and stupid with the heaviness of their sleep.

"Heigh-ho—broo-hoo," said Bree. "Been sleeping in my saddle, eh? I'll never do that again. Most uncomfortable—"

"Oh come on, come on," said Aravis. "We've lost half the morning already. There isn't a moment to spare."

"A fellow's got to have a mouthful of grass," said Bree.

"I'm afraid we can't wait," said Aravis.

"What's the terrible hurry?" said Bree.

"We've crossed the desert, haven't we?"

"But we're not in Archenland yet," said Aravis. "And we've got to get there before Rabadash."

"Oh, we must be miles ahead of him," said Bree. "Haven't we been coming a shorter way? Didn't that Raven friend of yours say this was a short cut, Shasta?"

"He didn't say anything about *shorter*," answered Shasta. "He only said *better*, because you got to a river this way. If the oasis is due North of Tashbaan, then I'm afraid this may be longer."

"Well I can't go on without a snack," said Bree. "Take my bridle off, Shasta."

"P-please," said Hwin, very shyly, "I feel just like Bree that I *can't* go on. But when Horses have humans (with spurs and things) on their backs, aren't they often made to go on when they're feeling like this? and then they find they can. I m-mean—oughtn't we to be able to do more even, now that we're free. It's all for Narnia."

"I think, Ma'am," said Bree very crushingly, "that I know a little more about campaigns and forced marches and what a horse can stand than you do."

To this Hwin made no answer, being, like most highly bred mares, a very nervous and gentle person who was easily put down. In reality she was quite right, and if Bree had had a Tarkaan on his back at that moment to make him go on, he would have found that he was good for several hours' hard going. But one of the worst results of being a slave and being forced to do things is that when there is no one to force you any more you find you have almost lost the power of forcing yourself.

So they had to wait while Bree had a snack and a drink, and of course Hwin and the children had a snack and a drink too. It must have been nearly eleven o'clock in the morning before they finally got going again. And even then Bree took things much more gently than yesterday. It was really Hwin, though she was the weaker and more tired of the two, who set the pace.

The valley itself, with its brown, cool river, and grass and moss and wild flowers and rhododendrons, was such a pleasant place that it made you want to ride slowly.

10

THE HERMIT OF THE SOUTHERN MARCH

After they had ridden for several hours down the valley, it widened out and they could see what was ahead of them. The river which they had been following here joined a broader river, wide and turbulent, which flowed from their left to their right, toward the east. Beyond this new river a delightful country rose gently in low hills, ridge beyond ridge, to the Northern Mountains themselves. To the right there were rocky pinnacles, one or two of them with snow clinging to the ledges. To the left, pine-clad slopes, frowning cliffs, narrow gorges, and blue peaks stretched away as far as the eye could reach. He could no longer make out Mount Pire. Straight ahead the mountain range sank to a wooded saddle which of course must be the pass from Archenland into Narnia.

"Broo-hoo-hoo, the North, the green North!" neighed Bree: and certainly the lower hills looked greener and fresher than anything that Aravis and Shasta, with their southern-bred eyes, had ever imagined. Spirits rose as they clattered down to the water's-meet of the two rivers.

The eastern-flowing river, which was pouring from the higher mountains at the western end of the range, was far too swift and too broken with rapids for them to think of swimming it; but after some casting about, up and down the bank, they found a place shallow enough to wade. The roar and clatter of water, the great swirl against the horses' fetlocks, the cool, stirring air and the darting dragonflies filled Shasta with a strange excitement.

"Friends, we are in Archenland!" said Bree proudly as he splashed and churned his way out on the Northern bank. "I think that river we've just crossed is called the Winding Arrow."

"I hope we're in time," murmured Hwin.

Then they began going up, slowly and zigzagging a good deal, for the hills were steep. It was all open, park-like country with no roads or houses in sight. Scattered trees, never thick enough to be a forest, were everywhere. Shasta, who had lived all his life in an almost treeless grassland, had never seen so many or so many kinds. If you had been there you would probably have known (he didn't) that he was seeing oaks, beeches, silver birches, rowans, and sweet chestnuts. Rabbits scurried away in every direction as they advanced, and presently they saw a whole herd of fallow deer making off among the trees.

"Isn't it simply glorious!" said Aravis.

At the first ridge Shasta turned in the saddle and looked back. There was no sign of Tashbaan; the desert, unbroken except by the narrow green crack which they had traveled down, spread to the horizon.

"Hullo!" he said suddenly. "What's that?"

"What's what?" said Bree, turning round. Hwin and Aravis did the same.

"That," said Shasta, pointing. "It looks like smoke. Is it a fire?"

"Sand-storm, I should say," said Bree.

"Not much wind to raise it," said Aravis.

"Oh!" exclaimed Hwin. "Look! There are things flashing in it. Look! They're helmets—and armor. And it's moving: moving this way."

"By Tash!" said Aravis. "It's the army. It's Rabadash."

"Of course it is," said Hwin. "Just what I was afraid of. Quick! We must get to Anvard before it." And without another word she whisked round and began galloping North. Bree tossed his head and did the same.

"Come *on*, Bree, come on," yelled Aravis over her shoulder.

This race was very grueling for the Horses. As they topped each ridge they found another valley and another ridge beyond it; and though they knew they were going in more or less the right direction, no one knew how far it was to Anvard. From the top of the second ridge Shasta looked back again. Instead of a dust-cloud well out in the desert he now saw a black, moving mass, rather like ants, on the far bank of the Winding Arrow. They were doubtless looking for a ford.

"They're on the river!" he yelled wildly.

"Quick! Quick!" shouted Aravis. "We might as well not have come at all if we don't reach Anvard in time. Gallop, Bree, gallop. Remember you're a war horse."

It was all Shasta could do to prevent himself from shouting out similar instructions; but he thought, "The poor chap's doing all he can already," and held his tongue. And certainly both Horses were doing, if not all they could, all they thought they could; which is not quite the same thing. Bree had caught up with Hwin and they thundered side by side over the turf. It didn't look as if Hwin could possibly keep it up much longer.

At that moment everyone's feelings were completely altered by a sound from behind. It was not the sound they had been expecting to hear—the noise of hoofs and jingling armor, mixed, perhaps, with Calormene battle-cries. Yet Shasta knew it at once. It was the same snarling roar he had heard that moonlit night when they first met Aravis and Hwin. Bree knew it too. His eyes gleamed red and his ears lay flat back on his skull. And Bree now discovered that he had not really been going as fast—not quite as fast—as he could. Shasta felt the change at once. Now they were really going all out. In a few seconds they were well ahead of Hwin.

"It's not fair," thought Shasta. "I *did* think we'd be safe from lions here!"

He looked over his shoulder. Everything was only too clear. A huge tawny creature, its body low to the ground, like a cat streaking across the lawn to a tree when a strange dog has got into the garden, was behind them. And it was nearer every second and half second.

He looked forward again and saw something which he did not take in, or even think about. Their way was barred by a smooth green wall about ten feet high. In the middle of that wall there was a gate, open. In the middle of the gateway stood a tall man, dressed, down to his bare feet, in a robe colored like autumn leaves, leaning on a straight staff. His beard fell almost to his knees.

Shasta saw all this in a glance and looked back again. The lion had almost got Hwin now. It was making snaps at her hind legs, and there was no hope now in her foam-flecked, wide-eyed face.

"Stop," bellowed Shasta in Bree's ear. "Must go back. Must help!"

Bree always said afterward that he never

heard, or never understood this; and as he was in general a very truthful horse we must accept his word.

Shasta slipped his feet out of the stirrups, slid both his legs over on the left side, hesitated for one hideous hundredth of a second, and jumped. It hurt horribly and nearly winded him; but before he knew how it hurt him he was staggering back to help Aravis. He had never done anything like this in his life before and hardly knew why he was doing it now.

One of the most terrible noises in the world, a horse's scream, broke from Hwin's lips. Aravis was stooping low over Hwin's neck and seemed to be trying to draw her sword. And now all three—Aravis, Hwin, and the lion—were almost on top of Shasta. Before they reached him,

the lion rose on its hind legs, larger than you would have believed a lion could be, and jabbed at Aravis with its right paw. Shasta could see all the terrible claws extended. Aravis screamed and reeled in the saddle. The lion was tearing her shoulders. Shasta, half mad with horror, managed to lurch toward the brute. He had no weapon, not even a stick or a stone. He shouted out, idiotically, at the lion as one would at a dog. "Go home! Go home!" For a fraction of a second he was staring right into its wide-opened, raging mouth. Then, to his utter astonishment, the lion, still on its hind legs, checked itself suddenly, turned head over heels, picked itself up, and rushed away.

Shasta did not for a moment suppose it had gone for good. He turned and raced for the gate in the green wall which, now for the first time, he remembered seeing. Hwin, stumbling and nearly fainting, was just entering the gate: Aravis still kept her seat but her back was covered with blood.

"Come in, my daughter, come in," the robed and bearded man was saying, and then, "Come in, my son," as Shasta panted up to him. He heard the gate closed behind him; and the bearded stranger was already helping Aravis off her horse.

They were in a wide and perfectly circular

enclosure, protected by a high wall of green turf. A pool of perfectly still water, so full that the water was almost exactly level with the ground, lay before him. At one end of the pool, completely overshadowing it with its branches, there grew the hugest and most beautiful tree that Shasta had ever seen. Beyond the pool was a little low house of stone roofed with deep and ancient thatch. There was a sound of bleating and over at the far side of the enclosure there were some goats. The level ground was completely covered with the finest grass.

"Are—are—are you," panted Shasta. "Are you King Lune of Archenland?"

The old man shook his head. "No," he replied in a quiet voice, "I am the Hermit of the Southern March. And now, my son, waste no time on questions, but obey. This damsel is wounded. Your horses are spent. Rabadash is at this moment finding a ford over the Winding Arrow. If you run now, without a moment's rest, you will still be in time to warn King Lune."

Shasta's heart fainted at these words for he felt he had no strength left. And he writhed inside at what seemed the cruelty and unfairness of the demand. He had not yet learned that if you do one good deed your reward usually is to be set to do another and harder and better one. But all he said out loud was:

"Where is the King?"

The Hermit turned and pointed with his staff. "Look," he said. "There is another gate, right opposite to the one you entered by. Open it and go straight ahead: always straight ahead, over level or steep, over smooth or rough, over dry or wet. I know by my art that you will find King Lune straight ahead. But run, run: always run."

Shasta nodded his head, ran to the northern gate and disappeared beyond it. Then the Hermit took Aravis, whom he had all this time been supporting with his left arm, and half led, half carried her into the house. After a long time he came out again.

"Now, cousins," he said to the Horses. "It is your turn."

Without waiting for an answer—and indeed they were too exhausted to speak—he took the bridles and saddles off both of them. Then he rubbed them both down, so well that a groom in a King's stable could not have done it better.

"There, cousins," he said, "dismiss it all from your minds and be comforted. Here is water and there is grass. You shall have a hot mash when I have milked my other cousins, the goats."

"Sir," said Hwin, finding her voice at last, "will the Tarkheena live? Has the lion killed her?"

"I who know many present things by my art," replied the Hermit with a smile, "have yet little knowledge of things future. Therefore I do not know whether any man or woman or beast in the whole world will be alive when the sun sets tonight. But be of good hope. The damsel is likely to live as long as any her age."

When Aravis came to herself she found that she was lying on her face on a low bed of extraordinary softness in a cool, bare room with walls of undressed stone. She couldn't understand why she had been laid on her face; but when she tried to turn and felt the hot, burning pains all over her back, she remembered, and realized why. She couldn't understand what delightfully springy stuff the bed was made of, because it was made of heather (which is the best bedding) and heather was a thing she had never seen or heard of.

The door opened and the Hermit entered, carrying a large wooden bowl in his hand. After carefully setting this down, he came to the bedside, and asked:

"How do you find yourself, my daughter?"

"My back is very sore, father," said Aravis, "but there is nothing else wrong with me."

He knelt beside her, laid his hand on her forehead, and felt her pulse.

"There is no fever," he said. "You will do

well. Indeed there is no reason why you should not get up tomorrow. But now, drink this."

He fetched the wooden bowl and held it to her lips. Aravis couldn't help making a face when she tasted it, for goats' milk is rather a shock when you are not used to it. But she was very thirsty and managed to drink it all and felt better when she had finished.

"Now, my daughter, you may sleep when you wish," said the Hermit. "For your wounds are washed and dressed and though they smart they are no more serious than if they had been the cuts of a whip. It must have been a very strange lion; for instead of catching you out of the saddle and getting his teeth into you, he has only drawn his claws across your back. Ten scratches: sore, but not deep or dangerous."

"I say!" said Aravis. "I *have* had luck."

"Daughter," said the Hermit, "I have now lived a hundred and nine winters in this world and have never yet met any such thing as Luck. There is something about all this that I do not understand: but if ever we need to know it, you may be sure that we shall."

"And what about Rabadash and his two hundred horse?" asked Aravis.

"They will not pass this way, I think," said the Hermit. "They must have found a ford by now well to the east of us. From there they will try to ride straight to Anvard."

"Poor Shasta!" said Aravis. "Has he far to go? Will he get there first?"

"There is good hope of it," said the old man.

Aravis lay down again (on her side this time) and said, "Have I been asleep for a long time? It seems to be getting dark."

The Hermit was looking out of the only window, which faced north. "This is not the darkness of night," he said presently. "The clouds are falling down from Stormness Head. Our foul weather always comes from there in these parts. There will be thick fog tonight."

Next day, except for her sore back, Aravis felt so well that after breakfast (which was porridge and cream) the Hermit said she could get up. And of course she at once went out to speak to the Horses. The weather had changed and the whole of that green enclosure was filled, like a great green cup, with sunlight. It was a very peaceful place, lonely and quiet.

Hwin at once trotted across to Aravis and gave her a horse-kiss.

"But where's Bree?" said Aravis when each had asked after the other's health and sleep.

"Over there," said Hwin, pointing with her nose to the far side of the circle. "And I wish you'd come and talk to him. There's something wrong, I can't get a word out of him."

They strolled across and found Bree lying with his face toward the wall, and though he must have heard them coming, he never turned his head or spoke a word.

"Good morning, Bree," said Aravis. "How are you this morning?"

Bree muttered something that no one could hear.

"The Hermit says that Shasta probably got to King Lune in time," continued Aravis, "so it looks as if all our troubles are over. Narnia, at last, Bree!"

"I shall never see Narnia," said Bree in a low voice.

"Aren't you well, Bree dear?" said Aravis.

Bree turned round at last, his face mournful as only a horse's can be.

"I shall go back to Calormen," he said.

"What?" said Aravis. "Back to slavery!"

"Yes," said Bree. "Slavery is all I'm fit for. How can I ever show my face among the free Horses of Narnia?—I who left a mare and a girl and a boy to be eaten by lions while I galloped all I could to save my own wretched skin!"

"We all ran as hard as we could," said Hwin.

"Shasta didn't!" snorted Bree. "At least he ran in the right direction: ran *back*. And that is what shames me most of all. I, who called myself a war horse and boasted of a hundred fights, to be beaten by a little human boy—a child, a mere foal, who had never held a sword nor had any good nurture or example in his life!"

"I know," said Aravis. "I felt just the same. Shasta was marvelous. I'm just as bad as you, Bree. I've been snubbing him and looking down on him ever since you met us and now he turns out to be the best of us all. But I think it would be better to stay and say we're sorry than to go back to Calormen."

"It's all very well for you," said Bree. "You haven't disgraced yourself. But I've lost everything."

"My good Horse," said the Hermit, who had approached them unnoticed because his bare feet made so little noise on that sweet, dewy grass. "My good Horse, you've lost nothing but your self-conceit. No, no, cousin. Don't put back your ears and shake your mane at me. If you are really so humbled as you sounded a minute ago, you must learn to listen to sense. You're not quite the great Horse you had come to think, from living among poor dumb horses. Of course you were braver and cleverer than *them*. You could hardly help being that. It doesn't follow that you'll be anyone very special in Narnia. But as long as you know you're nobody very special, you'll be a very decent sort of Horse, on the whole, and taking one thing with another. And now, if you and my other four-footed cousin will come round to the kitchen door we'll see about the other half of that mash."

11

THE UNWELCOME
FELLOW TRAVELER

When Shasta went through the gate he found a slope of grass and a little heather running up before him to some trees. He had nothing to think about now and no plans to make: he had only to run, and that was quite enough. His limbs were shaking, a terrible stitch was beginning in his side, and the sweat that kept dropping into his eyes blinded them and made them smart. He was unsteady on his feet too, and more than once he nearly turned his ankle on a loose stone.

The trees were thicker now than they had

yet been and in the more open spaces there was bracken. The sun had gone in without making it any cooler. It had become one of those hot, gray days when there seem to be twice as many flies as usual. Shasta's face was covered with them; he didn't even try to shake them off—he had too much else to do.

Suddenly he heard a horn—not a great throbbing horn like the horns of Tashbaan but a merry call, Ti-ro-to-to-ho! Next moment he came out into a wide glade and found himself in a crowd of people.

At least, it looked a crowd to him. In reality there were about fifteen or twenty of them, all gentlemen in green hunting-dress, with their horses; some in the saddle and some standing by their horses' heads. In the center someone was holding the stirrup for a man to mount. And the man he was holding it for was the jolliest, fat, apple-cheeked, twinkling-eyed King you could imagine.

As soon as Shasta came in sight this King forgot all about mounting his horse. He spread out his arms to Shasta, his face lit up, and he cried out in a great, deep voice that seemed to come from the bottom of his chest:

"Corin! My son! And on foot, and in rags! What—"

"No," panted Shasta, shaking his head. "Not Prince Corin. I—I—know I'm like him . . . saw

165

his Highness in Tashbaan . . . sent his greetings."

The King was staring at Shasta with an extraordinary expression on his face.

"Are you K-King Lune?" gasped Shasta.
And then, without waiting for an answer, "Lord
King—fly—Anvard—shut the gates—enemies
upon you—Rabadash and two hundred horse."

"Have you assurance of this, boy?" asked
one of the other gentlemen.

"My own eyes," said Shasta. "I've seen
them. Raced them all the way from Tashbaan."

"On foot?" said the gentleman, raising his
eyebrows a little.

"Horses—with the Hermit," said Shasta.

"Question him no more, Darrin," said King
Lune. "I see truth in his face. We must ride for
it, gentlemen. A spare horse there, for the boy.
You can ride fast, friend?"

For answer Shasta put his foot in the stirrup
of the horse which had been led toward him and
a moment later he was in the saddle. He had
done it a hundred times with Bree in the last
few weeks, and his mounting was very different
now from what it had been on that first night
when Bree had said that he climbed up a horse
as if he were climbing a haystack.

He was pleased to hear the Lord Darrin say
to the King, "The boy has a true horseman's

seat, Sire. I'll warrant there's noble blood in him."

"His blood, aye, there's the point," said the King. And he stared hard at Shasta again with that curious expression, almost a hungry expression, in his steady gray eyes.

But by now the whole party was moving off at a brisk canter. Shasta's seat was excellent but he was sadly puzzled what to do with his reins, for he had never touched the reins while he was on Bree's back. But he looked very carefully out of the corners of his eyes to see what the others were doing (as some of us have done at parties when we weren't quite sure which knife or fork we were meant to use) and tried to get his fingers right. But he didn't dare to try really directing the horse; he trusted it would follow the rest. The horse was of course an ordinary horse, not a Talking Horse; but it had quite wits enough to realize that the strange boy on its back had no whip and no spurs and was not really master of the situation. That was why Shasta soon found himself at the tail end of the procession.

Even so, he was going pretty fast. There were no flies now and the air in his face was delicious. He had got his breath back too. And his errand had succeeded. For the first time since the arrival at Tashbaan (how long ago it seemed!) he was beginning to enjoy himself.

He looked up to see how much nearer the mountain tops had come. To his disappointment he could not see them at all: only a vague grayness, rolling down toward them. He had never been in mountain country before and was surprised. "It's a cloud," he said to himself, "a cloud coming down. I see. Up here in the hills one is really in the sky. I shall see what the inside of a cloud is like. What fun! I've often wondered." Far away on his left and a little behind him, the sun was getting ready to set.

They had come to a rough kind of road by now and were making very good speed. But Shasta's horse was still the last of the lot. Once or twice when the road made a bend (there was now continuous forest on each side of it) he lost sight of the others for a second or two.

Then they plunged into the fog, or else the fog rolled over them. The world became gray. Shasta had not realized how cold and wet the inside of a cloud would be; nor how dark. The gray turned to black with alarming speed.

Someone at the head of the column winded the horn every now and then, and each time the sound came from a little farther off. He couldn't see any of the others now, but of course he'd be able to as soon as he got round the next bend. But when he rounded it he still couldn't see them. In fact he could see nothing at all. His horse was walking now. "Get on, Horse, get on," said Shasta. Then came the horn, very faint. Bree had always told him that he must keep his heels well turned out, and Shasta had got the idea that something very terrible would happen if he dug his heels into a horse's sides. This seemed to him an occasion for trying it. "Look here, Horse," he said, "if you don't buck up, do you know what I'll do? I'll dig my heels into you. I really will." The horse, however, took no notice of this threat. So Shasta settled himself firmly in the saddle, gripped with his knees, clenched his teeth, and punched both the horse's sides with his heels as hard as he could.

The only result was that the horse broke into a kind of pretense of a trot for five or six paces and then subsided into a walk again. And now it was quite dark and they seemed to have given up blowing that horn. The only sound was a steady drip-drip from the branches of the trees.

"Well, I suppose even a walk will get us somewhere sometime," said Shasta to himself. "I only hope I shan't run into Rabadash and his people."

He went on for what seemed like a long time, always at a walking pace. He began to hate that horse, and he was also beginning to feel very hungry.

Presently he came to a place where the road

divided into two. He was just wondering which led to Anvard when he was startled by a noise from behind him. It was the noise of trotting horses. "Rabadash!" thought Shasta. He had no way of guessing which road Rabadash would take. "But if I take one," said Shasta to himself, "he *may* take the other: and if I stay at the crossroads I'm *sure* to be caught." He dismounted and led his horse as quickly as he could along the right-hand road.

The sound of the cavalry grew rapidly nearer and in a minute or two Shasta realized that they were at the crossroads. He held his breath, waiting to see which way they would take.

There came a low word of command "Halt!" then a moment of horsey noises—nostrils blowing, hoofs pawing, bits being champed, necks being patted. Then a voice spoke.

"Attend, all of you," it said. "We are now within a furlong of the castle. Remember your orders. Once we are in Narnia, as we should be by sunrise, you are to kill as little as possible. On this venture you are to regard every drop of Narnian blood as more precious than a gallon of your own. On *this* venture, I say. The gods will send us a happier hour and then you must leave nothing alive between Cair Paravel and the Western Waste. But we are not yet in Narnia.

Here in Archenland it is another thing. In the assault on this castle of King Lune's, nothing matters but speed. Show your mettle. It must be mine within an hour. And if it is, I give it all to you. I reserve no booty for myself. Kill me every barbarian male within its walls, down to the child that was born yesterday, and everything else is yours to divide as you please—the women, the gold, the jewels, the weapons, and the wine. The man that I see hanging back when we come to the gates shall be burned alive. In the name of Tash the irresistible, the inexorable—forward!"

With a great cloppitty-clop the column began to move, and Shasta breathed again. They had taken the other road.

Shasta thought they took a long time going past, for though he had been talking and thinking about "two hundred horse" all day, he had not realized how many they really were. But at last the sound died away and once more he was alone amid the drip-drip from the trees.

He now knew the way to Anvard but of course he could not now go there: that would only mean running into the arms of Rabadash's troopers. "What on earth am I to do?" said Shasta to himself. But he remounted his horse and continued along the road he had chosen, in the faint hope of finding some cottage where he might ask for shelter and a meal. He had thought, of course, of going back to Aravis and Bree and Hwin at the hermitage, but he couldn't because by now he had not the least idea of the direction.

"After all," said Shasta, "this road is bound to get somewhere."

But that all depends on what you mean by somewhere. The road kept on getting to somewhere in the sense that it got to more and more trees, all dark and dripping, and to colder and colder air. And strange, icy winds kept blowing the mist past him though they never blew it away. If he had been used to mountain country he would have realized that this meant he was now very high up—perhaps right at the top of the pass. But Shasta knew nothing about mountains.

"I *do* think," said Shasta, "that I must be the most unfortunate boy that ever lived in the whole world. Everything goes right for everyone except me. Those Narnian lords and ladies got safe away from Tashbaan; I was left behind. Aravis and Bree and Hwin are all as snug as anything with that old Hermit: of course I was the one who was sent on. King Lune and his people must have got safely into the castle and shut the gates long before Rabadash arrived, but I get left out."

And being very tired and having nothing inside him, he felt so sorry for himself that the tears rolled down his cheeks.

What put a stop to all this was a sudden fright. Shasta discovered that someone or somebody was walking beside him. It was pitch dark and he could see nothing. And the Thing (or Person) was going so quietly that he could hardly hear any footfalls. What he could hear was breathing. His invisible companion seemed to breathe on a very large scale, and Shasta got the impression that it was a very large creature. And he had come to notice this breathing so gradually that he had really no idea how long it had been there. It was a horrible shock.

It darted into his mind that he had heard long ago that there were giants in these Northern countries. He bit his lip in terror. But now that he really had something to cry about, he stopped crying.

The Thing (unless it was a Person) went on beside him so very quietly that Shasta began to hope he had only imagined it. But just as he was becoming quite sure of it, there suddenly came a deep, rich sigh out of the darkness beside him. That couldn't be imagination! Anyway, he had felt the hot breath of that sigh on his chilly left hand.

If the horse had been any good—or if he

had known how to get any good out of the horse—he would have risked everything on a breakaway and a wild gallop. But he knew he couldn't make that horse gallop. So he went on at a walking pace and the unseen companion walked and breathed beside him. At last he could bear it no longer.

"Who are you?" he said, scarcely above a whisper.

"One who has waited long for you to speak," said the Thing. Its voice was not loud, but very large and deep.

"Are you—are you a giant?" asked Shasta.

"You might call me a giant," said the Large Voice. "But I am not like the creatures you call giants."

"I can't see you at all," said Shasta, after staring very hard. Then (for an even more terrible idea had come into his head) he said, almost in a scream, "You're not—not something *dead*, are you? Oh please—please do go away. What harm have I ever done you? Oh, I am the unluckiest person in the whole world!"

Once more he felt the warm breath of the Thing on his hand and face. "There," it said, "that is not the breath of a ghost. Tell me your sorrows."

Shasta was a little reassured by the breath:

so he told how he had never known his real father or mother and had been brought up sternly by the fisherman. And then he told the story of his escape and how they were chased by lions and forced to swim for their lives; and of all their dangers in Tashbaan and about his night among the tombs and how the beasts howled at him out of the desert. And he told about the heat and thirst of their desert journey and how they were almost at their goal when another lion chased them and wounded Aravis. And also, how very long it was since he had had anything to eat.

"I do not call you unfortunate," said the Large Voice.

"Don't you think it was bad luck to meet so many lions?" said Shasta.

"There was only one lion," said the Voice.

"What on earth do you mean? I've just told you there were at least two the first night, and—"

"There was only one: but he was swift of foot."

"How do you know?"

"I was the lion." And as Shasta gaped with open mouth and said nothing, the Voice continued. "I was the lion who forced you to join with Aravis. I was the cat who comforted you among the houses of the dead. I was the lion who drove the jackals from you while you slept. I was the lion who gave the Horses the new strength of fear for the last mile so that you should reach King Lune in time. And I was the lion you do not remember who pushed the boat in which you lay, a child near death, so that it came to shore where a man sat, wakeful at midnight, to receive you."

"Then it was you who wounded Aravis?"

"It was I."

"But what for?"

"Child," said the Voice, "I am telling you your story, not hers. I tell no one any story but his own."

"Who *are* you?" asked Shasta.

"Myself," said the Voice, very deep and low so that the earth shook: and again "Myself," loud and clear and gay: and then the third time "Myself," whispered so softly you could hardly hear it, and yet it seemed to come from all round you as if the leaves rustled with it.

Shasta was no longer afraid that the Voice belonged to something that would eat him, nor that it was the voice of a ghost. But a new and different sort of trembling came over him. Yet he felt glad too.

The mist was turning from black to gray and from gray to white. This must have begun to happen some time ago, but while he had been talking to the Thing he had not been noticing anything else. Now, the whiteness around him became a shining whiteness; his eyes began to blink. Somewhere ahead he could hear birds singing. He knew the night was over at last. He could see the mane and ears and head of his horse quite easily now. A golden light fell on them from the left. He thought it was the sun.

He turned and saw, pacing beside him, taller than the horse, a Lion. The horse did not seem to be afraid of it or else could not see it. It was from the Lion that the light came. No one ever saw anything more terrible or beautiful.

Luckily Shasta had lived all his life too far south in Calormen to have heard the tales that were whispered in Tashbaan about a dreadful Narnian demon that appeared in the form of a lion. And of course he knew none of the true stories about Aslan, the great Lion, the son of the Emperor-over-the-sea, the King above all High Kings in Narnia. But after one glance at the Lion's face he slipped out of the saddle and fell at its feet. He couldn't say anything but then he didn't want to say anything, and he knew he needn't say anything.

The High King above all kings stooped toward him. Its mane, and some strange and solemn perfume that hung about the mane, was all round him. It touched his forehead with its tongue. He lifted his face and their eyes met. Then instantly **the pale brightness** of the mist and the fiery brightness of the Lion rolled themselves together into a swirling glory and gathered themselves up and disappeared. He was alone with the horse on a grassy hillside under a blue sky. And there were birds singing.

12

SHASTA IN NARNIA

"**W**as it all a dream?" wondered Shasta. But it couldn't have been a dream for there in the grass before him he saw the deep, large print of the Lion's front right paw. It took one's breath away to think of the weight that could make a footprint like that. But there was something more remarkable than the size about it. As he looked at it, water had already filled the bottom of it. Soon it was full to the brim, and then overflowing, and a little stream was running downhill, past him, over the grass.

Shasta stooped and drank—a very long drink—and then dipped his face in and splashed his head. It was extremely cold, and clear as glass, and refreshed him very much. After that he stood up, shaking the water out of his ears and flinging the wet hair back from his forehead, and began to take stock of his surroundings.

Apparently it was still very early morning. The sun had only just risen, and it had risen out of the forests which he saw low down and far away on his right. The country which he was looking at was absolutely new to him. It was a green valley-land dotted with trees through which he caught the gleam of a river that wound away roughly to the Northwest. On the far side of the valley there were high and even rocky hills, but they were lower than the mountains he had seen yesterday. Then he began to guess where he was. He turned and looked behind him and saw that the slope on which he was standing belonged to a range of far higher mountains.

"I see," said Shasta to himself. "Those are the big mountains between Archenland and Narnia. I was on the other side of them yesterday. I must have come through the pass in the night. What luck that I hit it!—at least it wasn't luck at all really, it was *Him*. And now I'm in Narnia."

He turned and unsaddled his horse and took

off its bridle—"Though you *are* a perfectly horrid horse," he said. It took no notice of this remark and immediately began eating grass. That horse had a very low opinion of Shasta.

"I wish I could eat grass!" thought Shasta. "It's no good going back to Anvard, it'll all be besieged. I'd better get lower down into the valley and see if I can get anything to eat."

So he went on downhill (the thick dew was cruelly cold to his bare feet) till he came into a wood. There was a kind of track running through it and he had not followed this for many minutes when he heard a thick and rather wheezy voice saying to him:

"Good morning, neighbor."

Shasta looked round eagerly to find the speaker and presently saw a small, prickly person with a dark face who had just come out from among the trees. At least, it was small for a person but very big indeed for a hedgehog, which was what it was.

"Good morning," said Shasta. "But I'm not a neighbor. In fact I'm a stranger in these parts."

"Ah?" said the Hedgehog inquiringly.

"I've come over the mountains—from Archenland, you know."

"Ah, Archenland," said the Hedgehog. "That's a terrible long way. Never been there myself."

"And I think, perhaps," said Shasta, "someone ought to be told that there's an army of savage Calormenes attacking Anvard at this very moment."

"You don't say so!" answered the Hedgehog. "Well, think of that. And they do say that Calormen is hundreds and thousands of miles away, right at the world's end, across a great sea of sand."

"It's not nearly as far as you think," said Shasta. "And oughtn't something to be done about this attack on Anvard? Oughtn't your High King to be told?"

"Certain sure, something ought to be done about it," said the Hedgehog. "But you see I'm just on my way to bed for a good day's sleep. Hullo, neighbor!"

The last words were addressed to an immense biscuit-colored rabbit whose head had just popped up from somewhere beside the path. The Hedgehog immediately told the Rabbit what it had just learned from Shasta. The Rabbit agreed that this was very remarkable news and that somebody ought to tell someone about it with a view to doing something.

And so it went on. Every few minutes they were joined by other creatures, some from the branches overhead and some from little underground houses at their feet, till the party con-

sisted of five rabbits, a squirrel, two magpies, a goat-foot faun, and a mouse, who all talked at the same time and all agreed with the Hedgehog. For the truth was that in that golden age when the Witch and the Winter had gone and Peter the High King ruled at Cair Paravel, the smaller woodland people of Narnia were so safe and happy that they were getting a little careless.

Presently, however, two more practical people arrived in the little wood. One was a Red Dwarf whose name appeared to be Duffle. The other was a stag, a beautiful lordly creature with wide liquid eyes, dappled flanks and legs so thin and graceful that they looked as if you could break them with two fingers.

"Lion alive!" roared the Dwarf as soon as he had heard the news. "And if that's so, why are we all standing still, chattering? Enemies at Anvard! News must be sent to Cair Paravel at once. The army must be called out. Narnia must go to the aid of King Lune."

"Ah!" said the Hedgehog. "But you won't find the High King at the Cair. He's away to the North trouncing those giants. And talking of giants, neighbors, that puts me in mind—"

"Who'll take our message?" interrupted the Dwarf. "Anyone here got more speed than me?"

"I've got speed," said the Stag. "What's my message? How many Calormenes?"

"Two hundred: under Prince Rabadash. And—" But the Stag was already away—all four legs off the ground at once, and in a moment its white stern had disappeared among the remoter trees.

"Wonder where he's going," said a Rabbit. "He won't find the High King at Cair Paravel, you know."

"He'll find Queen Lucy," said Duffle. "And then—hullo! What's wrong with the Human? It looks pretty green. Why, I do believe it's quite faint. Perhaps it's mortal hungry. When did you last have a meal, youngster?"

"Yesterday morning," said Shasta weakly.

"Come on, then, come on," said the Dwarf, at once throwing his thick little arms round Shasta's waist to support him. "Why, neighbors, we ought all to be ashamed of ourselves! You come with me, lad. Breakfast! Better than talking."

With a great deal of bustle, muttering reproaches to itself, the Dwarf half led and half supported Shasta at a great speed further into the wood and a little downhill. It was a longer walk than Shasta wanted at that moment and his legs had begun to feel very shaky before they came out from the trees onto bare hillside. There they found a little house with a smoking chimney and an open door, and as they came to the doorway Duffle called out:

"Hey, brothers! A visitor for breakfast."

And immediately, mixed with a sizzling sound, there came to Shasta a simply delightful smell. It was one he had never smelled in his life before, but I hope you have. It was, in fact, the smell of bacon and eggs and mushrooms all frying in a pan.

"Mind your head, lad," said Duffle a moment too late, for Shasta had already bashed his forehead against the low lintel of the door. "Now," continued the Dwarf, "sit you down. The table's a bit low for you, but then the stool's low too. That's right. And here's porridge—and here's a jug of cream—and here's a spoon."

By the time Shasta had finished his porridge, the Dwarf's two brothers (whose names were Rogin and Bricklethumb) were putting the dish of bacon and eggs and mushrooms, and the coffeepot and the hot milk, and the toast, on the table.

It was all new and wonderful to Shasta for Calormene food is quite different. He didn't even know what the slices of brown stuff were, for he had never seen toast before. He didn't know what the yellow soft thing they smeared on the toast was, because in Calormen you nearly always get oil instead of butter. And the house itself was quite different from the dark, frowsty, fish-smelling hut of Arsheesh and from the pillared and carpeted halls in the palaces of Tashbaan. The roof was very low, and everything was made of wood, and there was a cuckoo-clock and a red-and-white checked tablecloth and a bowl of wild flowers and little curtains on the thick-paned windows. It was also rather troublesome having to use dwarf cups and plates and knives and forks. This meant that helpings were very small, but then there were a great many helpings, so that Shasta's plate or cup was being filled every moment, and every moment the Dwarfs themselves were saying, "Butter, please," or "Another cup of coffee," or "I'd like a few more mushrooms," or "What about frying another egg or so?" And when at last they had all eaten as much as they possibly could the three Dwarfs drew lots for who would do the washing-up, and Rogin was the unlucky one. Then Duffle and Bricklethumb took Shasta outside to a bench which ran against the cottage wall, and they all stretched out their legs and gave a great sigh of contentment and the two Dwarfs lit their pipes. The dew was off the grass now and the sun was warm; indeed, if there hadn't been a light breeze, it would have been too hot.

"Now, Stranger," said Duffle, "I'll show you the lie of the land. You can see nearly all South Narnia from here, and we're rather proud of the view. Right away on your left, beyond those near hills, you can just see the Western Mountains. And that round hill away on your right is called the Hill of the Stone Table. Just beyond—"

But at that moment he was interrupted by a snore from Shasta who, what with his night's journey and his excellent breakfast, had gone fast asleep. The kindly Dwarfs, as soon as they noticed this, began making signs to each other not to wake him, and indeed did so much whispering and nodding and getting up and tiptoeing away that they certainly would have

waked him if he had been less tired.

He slept pretty well nearly all day but woke up in time for supper. The beds in that house were all too small for him but they made him a fine bed of heather on the floor, and he never stirred or dreamed all night. Next morning they had just finished breakfast when they heard a shrill, exciting sound from outside.

"Trumpets!" said all the Dwarfs, as they and Shasta all came running out.

The trumpets sounded again: a new noise to Shasta, not huge and solemn like the horns of Tashbaan nor gay and merry like King Lune's hunting horn, but clear and sharp and valiant. The noise was coming from the woods to the East, and soon there was a noise of horse-hoofs

mixed with it. A moment later the head of the column came into sight.

First came the Lord Peridan on a bay horse carrying the great banner of Narnia—a red lion on a green ground. Shasta knew him at once. Then came three people riding abreast, two on great chargers and one on a pony. The two on the chargers were King Edmund and a fair-haired lady with a very merry face who wore a helmet and a mail shirt and carried a bow across her shoulder and a quiver full of arrows at her side. ("The Queen Lucy," whispered Duffle.) But the one on the pony was Corin. After that came the main body of the army: men on ordinary horses, men on Talking Horses (who didn't mind being ridden on proper occasions, as when

Narnia went to war), centaurs, stern, hard-bitten bears, great Talking Dogs, and last of all six giants. For there are good giants in Narnia. But though he knew they were on the right side Shasta at first could hardly bear to look at them; there are some things that take a lot of getting used to.

Just as the King and Queen reached the cottage and the Dwarfs began making low bows to them, King Edmund called out:

"Now, friends! Time for a halt and a morsel!" and at once there was a great bustle of people dismounting and haversacks being opened and conversation beginning when Corin came running up to Shasta and seized both his hands and cried:

"What! *You* here! So you got through all right? I *am* glad. Now we shall have some sport. And isn't it luck! We only got into the harbor at Cair Paravel yesterday morning and the very first person who met us was Chervy the Stag with this news of an attack on Anvard. Don't you think—"

"Who is your Highness's friend?" said King Edmund who had just got off his horse.

"Don't you see, Sire?" said Corin. "It's my double: the boy you mistook me for at Tashbaan."

"Why, so he is your double," exclaimed

Queen Lucy. "As like as two twins. This is a marvelous thing."

"Please, your Majesty," said Shasta to King Edmund, "I was no traitor, really I wasn't. And I couldn't help hearing your plans. But I'd never have dreamed of telling them to your enemies."

"I know now that you were no traitor, boy," said King Edmund, laying his hand on Shasta's head. "But if you would not be taken for one, another time try not to hear what's meant for other ears. But all's well."

After that there was so much bustle and talk and coming and going that Shasta for a few minutes lost sight of Corin and Edmund and Lucy. But Corin was the sort of boy whom one is sure to hear of pretty soon and it wasn't very long before Shasta heard King Edmund saying in a loud voice:

"By the Lion's Mane, prince, this is too much! Will your Highness never be better? You are more of a heart's-scald than our whole army together! I'd as lief have a regiment of hornets in my command as you."

Shasta wormed his way through the crowd and there saw Edmund, looking very angry indeed, Corin looking a little ashamed of himself, and a strange Dwarf sitting on the ground making faces. A couple of fauns had apparently just been helping it out of its armor.

"If I had but my cordial with me," Queen Lucy was saying, "I could soon mend this. But the High King has so strictly charged me not to carry it commonly to the wars and to keep it only for great extremities!"

What had happened was this. As soon as Corin had spoken to Shasta, Corin's elbow had been plucked by a Dwarf in the army called Thornbut.

"What is it, Thornbut?" Corin had said.

"Your Royal Highness," said Thornbut, drawing him aside, "our march today will bring us through the pass and right to your royal father's castle. We may be in battle before night."

"I know," said Corin. "Isn't it splendid!"

"Splendid or not," said Thornbut, "I have the strictest orders from King Edmund to see to it that your Highness is not in the fight. You will be allowed to see it, and that's treat enough for your Highness's little years."

"Oh what nonsense!" Corin burst out. "Of course I'm going to fight. Why, the Queen Lucy's going to be with the archers."

"The Queen's grace will do as she pleases," said Thornbut. "But you are in my charge. Either I must have your solemn and princely word that you'll keep your pony beside mine— not half a neck ahead—till I give your Highness leave to depart: or else—it is his Majesty's word—we must go with our wrists tied together like two prisoners."

"I'll knock you down if you try to bind me," said Corin.

"I'd like to see your Highness do it," said the Dwarf.

That was quite enough for a boy like Corin and in a second he and the Dwarf were at it hammer and tongs. It would have been an even match for, though Corin had longer arms and more height, the Dwarf was older and tougher. But it was never fought out (that's the worst of fights on a rough hillside) for by very bad luck Thornbut trod on a loose stone, came flat down on his nose, and found when he tried to get up that he had sprained his ankle: a real excruciating sprain which would keep him from walking or riding for at least a fortnight.

"See what your Highness has done," said King Edmund. "Deprived us of a proved warrior on the very edge of battle."

"I'll take his place, Sire," said Corin.

"Pshaw," said Edmund. "No one doubts your courage. But a boy in battle is a danger only to his own side."

At that moment the King was called away to attend to something else, and Corin, after apologizing handsomely to the Dwarf, rushed up to Shasta and whispered:

"Quick. There's a spare pony now, and the Dwarf's armor. Put it on before anyone notices."

"What for?" said Shasta.

"Why, so that you and I can fight in the battle of course! Don't you want to?"

"Oh—ah, yes, of course," said Shasta. But he hadn't been thinking of doing so at all, and began to get a most uncomfortable prickly feeling in his spine.

"That's right," said Corin. "Over your head. Now the sword-belt. But we must ride near the tail of the column and keep as quiet as mice. Once the battle begins everyone will be far too busy to notice us."

13

THE FIGHT AT ANVARD

By about eleven o'clock the whole company was once more on the march, riding westward with the mountains on their left. Corin and Shasta rode right at the rear with the Giants immediately in front of them. Lucy and Edmund and Peridan were busy with their plans for the battle and though Lucy once said, "But where is his goosecap Highness?" Edmund only replied, "Not in the front, and that's good news enough. Leave well alone."

Shasta told Corin most of his adventures and explained that he had learned all his riding from a horse and didn't really know how to use the reins. Corin instructed him in this, besides telling him all about their secret sailing from Tashbaan.

"And where is the Queen Susan?"

"At Cair Paravel," said Corin. "She's not like Lucy, you know, who's as good as a man, or at any rate as good as a boy. Queen Susan is more like an ordinary grown-up lady. She doesn't ride to the wars, though she is an excellent archer."

The hillside path which they were following became narrower all the time and the drop on their right hand became steeper. At last they were going in single file along the edge of the precipice and Shasta shuddered to think that he had done the same last night without knowing it. "But of course," he thought, "I was quite safe. That is why the Lion kept on my left. He was between me and the edge all the time."

Then the path went left and south away from the cliff and there were thick woods on both sides of it and they went steeply up and up into the pass. There would have been a splendid view from the top if it were open ground but among all those trees you could see nothing— only, every now and then, some huge pinnacle of rock above the treetops, and an eagle or two wheeling high up in the blue air.

"They smell battle," said Corin, pointing at

the birds. "They know we're preparing a feed for them."

Shasta didn't like this at all.

When they had crossed the neck of the pass and come a good deal lower they reached more open ground and from here Shasta could see all Archenland, blue and hazy, spread out below him and even (he thought) a hint of the desert beyond it. But the sun, which had perhaps two hours or so to go before it set, was in his eyes and he couldn't make things out distinctly.

Here the army halted and spread out in a line, and there was a great deal of rearranging. A whole detachment of very dangerous-looking Talking Beasts whom Shasta had not noticed before and who were mostly of the cat kind (leopards, panthers, and the like) went padding and growling to take up their positions on the left. The giants were ordered to the right, and before going there they all took off something they had been carrying on their backs and sat down for a moment. Then Shasta saw that what they had been carrying and were now putting on were pairs of boots: horrid, heavy, spiked boots which came up to their knees. Then they sloped their huge clubs over their shoulders and marched to their battle position. The archers, with Queen Lucy, fell to the rear and you could first see them bending their bows and then hear the twang-twang as they tested the strings. And wherever you looked you could see people tightening girths, putting on helmets, drawing swords, and throwing cloaks to the ground. There was hardly any talking now. It was very solemn and very dreadful. "I'm in for it now—I really am in for it now," thought Shasta. Then there came noises far ahead: the sound of many men shouting and a steady thud-thud-thud.

"Battering ram," whispered Corin. "They're battering the gate."

Even Corin looked quite serious now.

"Why doesn't King Edmund get *on?*" he said. "I can't stand this waiting about. Chilly too."

Shasta nodded: hoping he didn't look as frightened as he felt.

The trumpet at last! On the move now—now trotting—the banner streaming out in the wind. They had topped a low ridge now, and below them the whole scene suddenly opened out; a little, many-towered castle with its gate toward them. No moat, unfortunately, but of course the gate shut and the portcullis down. On the walls they could see, like little white dots, the faces of the defenders. Down below, about fifty of the Calormenes, dismounted, were steadily swinging a great tree trunk against the gate. But at once the scene changed. The main bulk of Rabadash's men had been on foot ready to assault the gate. But now he had seen the Narnians sweeping down the ridge. There is no doubt those Calormenes are wonderfully trained. It seemed to Shasta only a second before a whole line of the enemy were on horseback again, wheeling round to meet them, swinging toward them.

And now a gallop. The ground between the two armies grew less every moment. Faster, faster. All swords out now, all shields up to the nose, all prayers said, all teeth clenched. Shasta was dreadfully frightened. But it suddenly came into his head, "If you funk this, you'll funk every battle all your life. Now or never."

But when at last the two lines met he had really very little idea of what happened. There was a frightful confusion and an appalling noise. His sword was knocked clean out of his hand

pretty soon. And he'd got the reins tangled somehow. Then he found himself slipping. Then a spear came straight at him and as he ducked to avoid it he rolled right off his horse, bashed his left knuckles terribly against someone else's armor, and then—

But it is no use trying to describe the battle from Shasta's point of view; he understood too little of the fight in general and even of his own part in it. The best way I can tell you what really happened is to take you some miles away to where the Hermit of the Southern March sat gazing into the smooth pool beneath the spreading tree, with Bree and Hwin and Aravis beside him.

For it was in this pool that the Hermit looked when he wanted to know what was going on in the world outside the green walls of his hermitage. There, as in a mirror, he could see, at certain times, what was going on in the streets of cities far farther south than Tashbaan, or what ships were putting into Redhaven in the remote Seven Isles, or what robbers or wild beasts stirred in the great Western forests between Lantern Waste and Telmar. And all this day he had hardly left his pool, even to eat or drink, for he knew that great events were on foot in Archenland. Aravis and the Horses gazed into it too. They could see it was a magic pool: instead of reflecting the tree and the sky it revealed cloudy and colored shapes moving, always moving, in its depths. But they could see nothing clearly. The Hermit could and from time to time he told them what he saw. A little while before Shasta rode into his first battle, the Hermit had begun speaking like this:

"I see one—two—three eagles wheeling in the gap by Stormness Head. One is the oldest of all eagles. He would not be out unless battle was at hand. I see him wheel to and fro, peering down sometimes at Anvard and sometimes to the east, behind Stormness. Ah—I see now what Rabadash and his men have been so busy at all day. They have felled and lopped a great tree and they are now coming out of the woods carrying it as a ram. They have learned something from the failure of last night's assault. He would have been wiser if he had set his men to making ladders: but it takes too long and he is impatient. Fool that he is! He ought to have ridden back to Tashbaan as soon as the first attack failed, for his whole plan depended on speed and surprise. Now they are bringing their ram into position. King Lune's men are shooting hard from the walls. Five Calormenes have fallen: but not many will. They have their shields above their heads. Rabadash is giving his orders now. With him are his most trusted lords, fierce

Tarkaans from the eastern provinces. I can see their faces. There is Corradin of Castle Tormunt, and Azrooh, and Chlamash, and Ilgamuth of the twisted lip, and a tall Tarkaan with a crimson beard—"

"By the Mane, my old master Anradin!" said Bree.

"S-s-sh," said Aravis.

"Now the ram has started. If I could hear as well as see, what a noise that would make! Stroke after stroke: and no gate can stand it forever. But wait! Something up by Stormness has scared the birds. They're coming out in masses. And wait again . . . I can't see yet . . . ah! Now I can. The whole ridge, up on the east, is black with horsemen. If only the wind would catch that standard and spread it out. They're over the ridge now, whoever they are. Aha! I've seen the banner now. Narnia, Narnia! It's the red lion. They're in full career down the hill now. I can see King Edmund. There's a woman behind among the archers. Oh!—"

"What is it?" asked Hwin breathlessly.

"All his Cats are dashing out from the left of the line."

"Cats?" said Aravis.

"Great cats, leopards and such," said the Hermit impatiently. "I see, I see. The Cats are coming round in a circle to get at the horses of the dismounted men. A good stroke. The Calormene horses are mad with terror already. Now the Cats are in among them. But Rabadash has re-formed his line and has a hundred men in the saddle. They're riding to meet the Narnians. There's only a hundred yards between the two lines now. Only fifty. I can see King Edmund, I can see the Lord Peridan. There are two mere children in the Narnian line. What can the King be about to let them into the battle? Only ten yards—the lines have met. The Giants on the Narnian right are doing wonders . . . but one's down . . . shot through the eye, I suppose. The center's all a muddle. I can see more on the left. There are the two boys again. Lion alive! one is Prince Corin. The other, like him as two peas. It's your little Shasta. Corin is fighting like a man. He's killed a Calormene. I can see a bit of the center now. Rabadash and Edmund almost met then, but the press has separated them—"

"What about Shasta?" said Aravis.

"Oh the fool!" groaned the Hermit. "Poor, brave little fool. He knows nothing about this work. He's making no use at all of his shield. His whole side's exposed. He hasn't the faintest idea what to do with his sword. Oh, he's remembered it now. He's waving it wildly about . . . nearly cut his own pony's head off, and he will in a moment if he's not careful. It's been knocked out of his hand now. It's mere murder sending a child into the battle; he can't live five minutes. Duck, you fool—oh, he's down."

"Killed?" asked three voices breathlessly.

"How can I tell?" said the Hermit. "The Cats have done their work. All the riderless horses are dead or escaped now: no retreat for the Calormenes on *them*. Now the Cats are turning back into the main battle. They're leaping on the rams-men. The ram is down. Oh, good! good! The gates are opening from the inside: there's going to be a sortie. The first three are out. It's King Lune in the middle: the brothers Dar and Darrin on each side of him. Behind them are Tran and Shar and Cole with his brother Colin. There are ten—twenty—nearly thirty of them out by now. The Calormen line is being forced back upon them. King Edmund is dealing marvelous strokes. He's just slashed Corradin's head off. Lots of Calormenes have thrown down their arms and are running for the woods. Those that remain are hard pressed. The Giants are closing in on the right—Cats on the left—King Lune from their rear. The Calormenes are a little knot now, fighting back to back. Your Tarkaan's down, Bree. Lune and Azrooh are fighting hand to hand; the King looks like winning—the King is keeping it up well—the King has won. Azrooh's down. King

Edmund's down—no, he's up again: he's at it with Rabadash. They're fighting in the very gate of the castle. Several Calormenes have surrendered. Darrin has killed Ilgamuth. I can't see what's happened to Rabadash. I think he's dead, leaning against the castle wall, but I don't know. Chlamash and King Edmund are still fighting but the battle is over everywhere else. Chlamash has surrendered. The battle *is* over. The Calormenes are utterly defeated."

When Shasta fell off his horse he gave himself up for lost. But horses, even in battle, tread on human beings very much less than you would suppose. After a very horrible ten minutes or so Shasta realized suddenly that there were no longer any horses stamping about in the immediate neighborhood and that the noise (for there were still a good many noises going on) was no longer that of a battle. He sat up and stared about him. Even he, little as he knew of battles, could soon see that the Archenlanders and Narnians had won. The only living Calormenes he could see were prisoners, the castle gates were wide open, and King Lune and King Edmund were shaking hands across the battering ram. From the circle of lords and warriors around them there arose a sound of breathless and excited, but obviously cheerful conversation. And then, suddenly, it all united and

swelled into a great roar of laughter.

Shasta picked himself up, feeling uncommonly stiff, and ran toward the sound to see what the joke was. A very curious sight met his eyes. The unfortunate Rabadash appeared to be suspended from the castle walls. His feet, which were about two feet from the ground, were kicking wildly. His chain-shirt was somehow hitched up so that it was horribly tight under the arms and came halfway over his face. In fact he looked just as a man looks if you catch him in the very act of getting into a stiff shirt that is a little too small for him. As far as could be made out afterward (and you may be sure the story was well talked over for many a day) what had happened was something like this. Early in the battle one of the Giants had made an unsuccessful stamp at Rabadash with his spiked boot: unsuccessful because it didn't crush Rabadash, which was what the Giant had intended, but not quite useless because one of the spikes tore the chain mail, just as you or I might tear an ordinary shirt. So Rabadash, by the time he encountered Edmund at the gate, had a hole in the back of his hauberk. And when Edmund pressed him back nearer and nearer to the wall, he jumped up on a mounting block and stood there raining down blows on Edmund from above. But then, finding that this position, by raising him above the heads of everyone else, made him a mark for every arrow from the Narnian bows, he decided to jump down again. And he meant to look and sound—no doubt for a moment he *did* look and sound—very grand and very dreadful as he jumped, crying, "The bolt of Tash falls from above." But he had to jump sideways because the crowd in front of him left him no landing place in that direction. And then, in the neatest way you could wish, the tear in the back of his hauberk caught on a hook in the wall. (Ages ago this hook had had a ring in it for tying horses to.) And there he found himself, like a piece of washing hung up to dry, with everyone laughing at him.

"Let me down, Edmund," howled Rabadash. "Let me down and fight me like a king and a man; or if you are too great a coward to do that, kill me at once."

"Certainly," began King Edmund, but King Lune interrupted.

"By your Majesty's good leave," said King Lune to Edmund. "Not so." Then turning to Rabadash he said, "Your royal Highness, if you had given that challenge a week ago, I'll answer for it there was no one in King Edmund's dominion, from the High King down to the smallest Talking Mouse, who would have refused it. But by attacking our castle of Anvard in time of peace without defiance sent, you have proved yourself no knight, but a traitor, and one rather to be whipped by the hangman than to be suffered to cross swords with any person of honor. Take him down, bind him, and carry him within till our pleasure is further known."

Strong hands wrenched Rabadash's sword from him and he was carried away into the castle, shouting, threatening, cursing, and even crying. For though he could have faced torture he couldn't bear being made ridiculous. In

Tashbaan everyone had always taken him seriously.

At that moment Corin ran up to Shasta, seized his hand and started dragging him toward King Lune. "Here he is, Father, here he is," cried Corin.

"Aye, and here *thou* art, at last," said the King in a very gruff voice. "And hast been in the battle, clean contrary to your obedience. A boy to break a father's heart! At your age a rod to your breech were fitter than a sword in your fist, ha!" But everyone, including Corin, could see that the King was very proud of him.

"Chide him no more, Sire, if it please you," said Lord Darrin. "His Highness would not be your son if he did not inherit your conditions. It

would grieve your Majesty more if he had to be reproved for the **opposite fault**."

"Well, well," grumbled the King. "We'll pass it over for this time. And now—"

What came next surprised Shasta as much as anything that had ever happened to him in his life. He found himself suddenly embraced in a bear-like hug by King Lune and kissed on both cheeks. Then the King set him down again and said, "Stand here together, boys, and let all the court see you. Hold up your heads. Now, gentlemen, look on them both. Has any man any doubts?"

And still Shasta could not understand why everyone stared at him and at Corin nor what all the cheering was about.

14

HOW BREE BECAME A
WISER HORSE

We must now return to Aravis and the Horses.
The Hermit, watching his pool, was able to tell
them that Shasta was not killed or even seriously wounded, for he saw him get up and saw
how affectionately he was greeted by King Lune.
But as he could only see, not hear, he did not
know what anyone was saying and, once the
fighting had stopped and the talking had begun,
it was not worthwhile looking in the pool any
longer.

Next morning, while the Hermit was
indoors, the three of them discussed what

they should do next.

"I've had enough of this," said Hwin. "The Hermit has been very good to us and I'm very much obliged to him I'm sure. But I'm getting as fat as a pet pony, eating all day and getting no exercise. Let's go on to Narnia."

"Oh not today, Ma'am," said Bree. "I wouldn't hurry things. Some other day, don't you think?"

"We must see Shasta first and say good-bye to him—and—and apologize," said Aravis.

"Exactly!" said Bree with great enthusiasm. "Just what I was going to say."

"Oh, of course," said Hwin. "I expect he is in Anvard. Naturally we'd look in on him and say good-bye. But that's on our way. And why shouldn't we start at once? After all, I thought it was Narnia we all wanted to get to?"

"I suppose so," said Aravis. She was beginning to wonder what exactly she would do when she got there and was feeling a little lonely.

"Of course, of course," said Bree hastily. "But there's no need to rush things, if you know what I mean."

"No, I don't know what you mean," said Hwin. "Why don't you want to go?"

"M-m-m, broo-hoo," muttered Bree. "Well, don't you see, Ma'am—it's an important occasion—returning to one's own country—entering society—the best society—it is so essential to make a good impression—not perhaps looking quite ourselves, yet, eh?"

Hwin broke out into a horse-laugh. "It's your tail, Bree! I see it all now. You want to wait till your tail's grown again! And we don't even know if tails are worn long in Narnia. Really, Bree, you're as vain as that Tarkheena in Tashbaan!"

"You *are* silly, Bree," said Aravis.

"By the Lion's Mane, Tarkheena, I'm nothing of the sort," said Bree indignantly. "I have a proper respect for myself and for my fellow horses, that's all."

"Bree," said Aravis, who was not very interested in the cut of his tail, "I've been wanting to ask you something for a long time. Why do you keep swearing *By the Lion* and *By the Lion's Mane*? I thought you hated lions."

"So I do," answered Bree. "But when I speak of *the* Lion of course I mean Aslan, the great deliverer of Narnia who drove away the Witch and the Winter. All Narnians swear by *him*."

"But is he a lion?"

"No, no, of course not," said Bree in a rather shocked voice.

"All the stories about him in Tashbaan say he is," replied Aravis. "And if he isn't a lion why do you call him a lion?"

"Well, you'd hardly understand that at your age," said Bree. "And I was only a little foal when I left so I don't quite fully understand it myself."

(Bree was standing with his back to the green wall while he said this, and the other two were facing him. He was talking in rather a superior tone with his eyes half shut; that was why he didn't see the changed expression in the faces of Hwin and Aravis. They had good reason to have open mouths and staring eyes; because while Bree spoke they saw an enormous lion leap up from outside and balance itself on top of the green wall; only it was a brighter yellow and it was bigger and more beautiful and more alarming than any lion they had ever seen. And at once it jumped down inside the wall and began approaching Bree from behind. It made no noise at all. And Hwin and Aravis couldn't make any noise themselves, no more than if they were frozen.)

"No doubt," continued Bree, "when they speak of him as a Lion they only mean he's as strong as a lion or (to our enemies, of course) as fierce as a lion. Or something of that kind. Even a little girl like you, Aravis, must see that it would be quite absurd to suppose he is a *real* lion. Indeed it would be disrespectful. If he was a lion he'd have to be a Beast just like the rest of us. Why!" (and here Bree began to laugh) "If he was a lion he'd have four paws, and a tail, and *Whiskers*! . . . Aie, ooh, hoo-hoo! Help!"

For just as he said the word *Whiskers*, one of Aslan's had actually tickled his ear. Bree shot away like an arrow to the other side of the enclosure and there turned; the wall was too high for him to jump and he could fly no farther. Aravis and Hwin both started back. There was about a second of intense silence.

Then Hwin, though shaking all over, gave a strange little neigh and trotted across to the Lion.

"Please," she said, "you're so beautiful. You may eat me if you like. I'd sooner be eaten by you than fed by anyone else."

"Dearest daughter," said Aslan, planting a lion's kiss on her twitching, velvet nose, "I knew you would not be long in coming to me. Joy shall be yours."

Then he lifted his head and spoke in a louder voice.

"Now, Bree," he said, "you poor, proud, frightened Horse, draw near. Nearer still, my son. Do not dare not to dare. Touch me. Smell me. Here are my paws, here is my tail, these are my whiskers. I am a true Beast."

"Aslan," said Bree in a shaken voice, "I'm afraid I must be rather a fool."

"Happy the Horse who knows that while he is still young. Or the Human either. Draw near, Aravis my daughter. See! My paws are velveted. You will not be torn this time."

"This time, sir?" said Aravis.

"It was I who wounded you," said Aslan. "I am the only lion you met in all your journeyings. Do you know why I tore you?"

"No, sir."

"The scratches on your back, tear for tear, throb for throb, blood for blood, were equal to the stripes laid on the back of your stepmother's slave because of the drugged sleep you cast upon her. You needed to know what it felt like."

"Yes, sir. Please—"

"Ask on, my dear," said Aslan.

"Will any more harm come to her by what I did?"

"Child," said the Lion, "I am telling you your story, not hers. No one is told any story but their own." Then he shook his head and spoke in a lighter voice.

"Be merry, little ones," he said. "We shall meet soon again. But before that you will have another visitor." Then in one bound he reached the top of the wall and vanished from their sight.

Strange to say, they felt no inclination to talk to one another about him after he had gone. They all moved slowly away to different parts of the quiet grass and there paced to and fro, each alone, thinking.

About half an hour later the two Horses were summoned to the back of the house to eat something nice that the Hermit had got ready for them and Aravis, still walking and thinking, was startled by the harsh sound of a trumpet outside the gate.

"Who is there?" said Aravis.

"His Royal Highness Prince Cor of Archenland," said a voice from outside.

Aravis undid the door and opened it, drawing back a little way to let the strangers in.

Two soldiers with halberds came first and took their stand at either side of the entry. Then followed a herald, and the trumpeter.

"His Royal Highness Prince Cor of Archenland desires an audience of the Lady Aravis," said the Herald. Then he and the trumpeter drew aside and bowed and the soldiers saluted and the Prince himself came in. All his attendants withdrew and closed the gate behind them.

The Prince bowed, and a very clumsy bow for a Prince it was. Aravis curtsied in the Calormene style (which is not at all like ours) and did it very well because, of course, she had been taught how. Then she looked up and saw

what sort of person this Prince was.

She saw a mere boy. He was bare-headed and his fair hair was encircled with a very thin band of gold, hardly thicker than a wire. His upper tunic was of white cambric, as fine as a handkerchief, so that the bright red tunic beneath it showed through. His left hand, which rested on his enameled sword hilt, was bandaged.

Aravis looked twice at his face before she gasped and said, "Why! It's Shasta!"

Shasta all at once turned very red and began speaking very quickly. "Look here, Aravis," he said, "I do hope you won't think I'm got up like this (and the trumpeter and all) to try to impress you or make out that I'm different or any rot of that sort. Because I'd far rather have come in my old clothes, but they're burnt now, and my father said—"

"Your father?" said Aravis.

"Apparently King Lune is my father," said Shasta. "I might really have guessed it. Corin being so like me. We were twins, you see. Oh, and my name isn't Shasta, it's Cor."

"Cor is a nicer name than Shasta," said Aravis.

"Brothers' names run like that in Archenland," said Shasta (or Prince Cor as we must now call him). "Like Dar and Darrin, Cole and Colin and so on."

"Shasta—I mean Cor," said Aravis. "No, shut up. There's something I've got to say at once. I'm sorry I've been such a pig. But I did change before I knew you were a Prince, honestly I did: when you went back, and faced the Lion."

"It wasn't really going to kill you at all, that Lion," said Cor.

"I know," said Aravis, nodding. Both were still and solemn for a moment as each saw that the other knew about Aslan.

Suddenly Aravis remembered Cor's bandaged hand. "I say!" she cried, "I forgot! You've been in a battle. Is that a wound?"

"A mere scratch," said Cor, using for the first time a rather lordly tone. But a moment later he burst out laughing and said, "If you want to know the truth, it isn't a proper wound at all. I only took the skin off my knuckles just as any clumsy fool might do without going near a battle."

"Still you were in the battle," said Aravis. "It must have been wonderful."

"It wasn't at all like what I thought," said Cor.

"But Sha—Cor, I mean—you haven't told me anything yet about King Lune and how he found out who you were."

"Well, let's sit down," said Cor. "For it's rather a long story. And by the way, Father's an absolute brick. I'd be just as pleased—or very nearly—at finding he's my father even if he wasn't a king. Even though Education and all sorts of horrible things are going to happen to me. But you want the story. Well, Corin and I were twins. And about a week after we were both born, apparently, they took us to a wise old Centaur in Narnia to be blessed or something. Now this Centaur was a prophet as a good many Centaurs are. Perhaps you haven't seen any Centaurs yet? There were some in the battle yesterday. Most remarkable people, but I can't say I feel quite at home with them yet. I say, Aravis, there are going to be a lot of things to get used to in these Northern countries."

"Yes, there are," said Aravis. "But get on with the story."

"Well, as soon as he saw Corin and me, it seems this Centaur looked at me and said, A day will come when that boy will save Archenland from the deadliest danger in which ever she lay. So of course my Father and Mother were very pleased. But there was someone present who wasn't. This was a chap called Lord Bar who had been Father's Lord Chancellor. And apparently he'd done something wrong—*bezzling* or some word like that—I didn't understand that part very well—and Father had had to dismiss him. But nothing else was done to him and he was allowed to go on living in Archenland. But he must have been as bad as he could be, for it came out afterward he had been in the pay of

the Tisroc and had sent a lot of secret information to Tashbaan. So as soon as he heard I was going to save Archenland from a great danger he decided I must be put out of the way. Well, he succeeded in kidnapping me (I don't exactly know how) and rode away down the Winding Arrow to the coast. He'd had everything prepared and there was a ship manned with his own followers lying ready for him and he put out to sea with me on board. But Father got wind of it, though not quite in time, and was after him as quickly as he could. The Lord Bar was already at sea when Father reached the coast, but not out of sight. And Father was embarked in one of his own warships within twenty minutes.

"It must have been a wonderful chase. They were six days following Bar's galleon and brought her to battle on the seventh. It was a great sea-fight (I heard a lot about it yesterday evening) from ten o'clock in the morning till sunset. Our people took the ship in the end. But I wasn't there. The Lord Bar himself had been killed in the battle. But one of his men said that, early that morning, as soon as he saw he was certain to be overhauled, Bar had given me to one of his knights and sent us both away in the ship's boat. And that boat was never seen again. But of course that was the same boat that Aslan (he seems to be at the back of all the stories) pushed ashore at the right place for Arsheesh to pick me up. I wish I knew that knight's name, for he must have kept me alive and starved himself to do it."

"I suppose Aslan would say that was part of someone else's story," said Aravis.

"I was forgetting that," said Cor.

"And I wonder how the prophecy will work out," said Aravis, "and what the great danger is that you're to save Archenland from."

"Well," said Cor rather awkwardly, "they seem to think I've done it already."

Aravis clapped her hands. "Why, of course!" she said. "How stupid I am. And how wonderful! Archenland can never be in much greater danger than it was when Rabadash had crossed the Arrow with his two hundred horse and you hadn't yet got through with your message. Don't you feel proud?"

"I think I feel a bit scared," said Cor.

"And you'll be living in Anvard now," said Aravis rather wistfully.

"Oh!" said Cor. "I'd nearly forgotten what I came about. Father wants you to come and live with us. He says there's been no lady in the court (they call it the court, I don't know why) since Mother died. Do, Aravis. You'll like Father—

and Corin. They're not like me; they've been properly brought up. You needn't be afraid that—"

"Oh stop it," said Aravis, "or we'll have a real fight. Of course I'll come."

"Now let's go and see the Horses," said Cor.

There was a great and joyous meeting between Bree and Cor, and Bree, who was still in a rather subdued frame of mind, agreed to set out for Anvard at once: he and Hwin would cross into Narnia on the following day. All four bade an affectionate farewell to the Hermit and promised that they would soon visit him again. By about the middle of the morning they were on their way. The Horses had expected that Aravis and Cor would ride, but Cor explained that except in war, where everyone must do what he can do best, no one in Narnia or Archenland ever dreamed of mounting a Talking Horse.

This reminded poor Bree again of how little he knew about Narnian customs and what dreadful mistakes he might make. So while Hwin strolled along in a happy dream, Bree got more nervous and more self-conscious with every step he took.

"Buck up, Bree," said Cor. "It's far worse for me than for you. You aren't going to be *educated*. I shall be learning reading and writing and heraldry and dancing and history and music while you'll be galloping and rolling on the hills of Narnia to your heart's content."

"But that's just the point," groaned Bree. "*Do* Talking Horses roll? Supposing they don't? I can't bear to give it up. What do you think, Hwin?"

"I'm going to roll anyway," said Hwin. "I don't suppose any of them will care two lumps of sugar whether you roll or not."

"Are we near that castle?" said Bree to Cor.

"Round the next bend," said the Prince.

"Well," said Bree, "I'm going to have a good one now: it may be the last. Wait for me a minute."

It was five minutes before he rose again,

blowing hard and covered with bits of bracken.

"Now I'm ready," he said in a voice of profound gloom. "Lead on, Prince Cor, Narnia and the North."

But he looked more like a horse going to a funeral than a long-lost captive returning to home and freedom.

15

RABADASH THE RIDICULOUS

The next turn of the road brought them out from among the trees and there, across green lawns, sheltered from the north wind by the high wooded ridge at its back, they saw the castle of Anvard. It was very old and built of a warm, reddish-brown stone.

Before they had reached the gate King Lune came out to meet them, not looking at all like Aravis's idea of a king and wearing the oldest of old clothes; for he had just come from making a round of the kennels with his Huntsman and had only stopped for a moment to wash his doggy hands. But the bow with which he greeted Aravis as he took her hand would have been stately enough for an Emperor.

"Little lady," he said, "we bid you very heartily welcome. If my dear wife were still alive we could make you better cheer but could not do it with a better will. And I am sorry that you have had misfortunes and been driven from your father's house, which cannot but be a grief to you. My son Cor has told me about your adventures together and all your valor."

"It was he who did all that, Sir," said Aravis. "Why, he rushed at a lion to save me."

"Eh, what's that?" said King Lune, his face brightening. "I haven't heard that part of the story."

Then Aravis told it. And Cor, who had very much wanted the story to be known, though he felt he couldn't tell it himself, didn't enjoy it so much as he had expected, and indeed felt rather foolish. But his father enjoyed it very much indeed and in the course of the next few weeks told it to so many people that Cor wished it had never happened.

Then the King turned to Hwin and Bree and was just as polite to them as to Aravis, and asked them a lot of questions about their families and where they had lived in Narnia before they had been captured. The Horses were rather tongue-tied for they weren't yet used to being talked to as equals by Humans—grown-up Humans, that is. They didn't mind Aravis and Cor.

Presently Queen Lucy came out from the castle and joined them and King Lune said to Aravis, "My dear, here is a loving friend of our house, and she has been seeing that your apartments are put to rights for you better than I could have done it."

"You'd like to come and see them, wouldn't you?" said Lucy, kissing Aravis. They liked each other at once and soon went away together to talk about Aravis's bedroom and Aravis's boudoir and about getting clothes for her, and all the sort of things girls do talk about on such an occasion.

After lunch, which they had on the terrace (it was cold birds and cold game pie and wine and bread and cheese), King Lune ruffled up his brow and heaved a sigh and said, "Heigh-ho! We have still that sorry creature Rabadash on our hands, my friends, and must needs resolve what to do with him."

Lucy was sitting on the King's right and Aravis on his left. King Edmund sat at one end of the table and the Lord Darrin faced him at the other. Dar and Peridan and Cor and Corin were on the same side as the King.

"Your Majesty would have a perfect right to strike off his head," said Peridan. "Such an assault as he made puts him on a level with assassins."

"It is very true," said Edmund. "But even a traitor may mend. I have known one that did." And he looked very thoughtful.

"To kill this Rabadash would go near to raising war with the Tisroc," said Darrin.

"A fig for the Tisroc," said King Lune. "His strength is in numbers and numbers will never cross the desert. But I have no stomach for killing men (even traitors) in cold blood. To have cut his throat in battle would have eased my heart mightily: but this is a different thing."

"By my counsel," said Lucy, "your Majesty shall give him another trial. Let him go free on strait promise of fair dealing in the future. It may be that he will keep his word."

"Maybe Apes will grow honest, Sister," said Edmund. "But, by the Lion, if he breaks it again, may it be in such time and place that any of us could swap off his head in clean battle."

"It shall be tried," said the King: and then to one of the attendants, "Send for the prisoner, friend."

Rabadash was brought before them in chains. To look at him anyone would have supposed that he had passed the night in a noisome dungeon without food or water; but in reality he had been shut up in quite a comfortable room and provided with an excellent supper. But as he was sulking far too furiously to touch the supper and had spent the whole night stamping and roaring and cursing, he naturally did not now look his best.

"Your royal Highness needs not to be told," said King Lune, "that by the law of nations as well as by all reasons of prudent policy, we have as good right to your head as ever one mortal man had against another. Nevertheless, in consideration of your youth and the ill nurture, devoid of all gentilesse and courtesy, which you have doubtless had in the land of slaves and tyrants, we are disposed to set you free, unharmed, on these conditions: first, that—"

"Curse you for a barbarian dog!" spluttered Rabadash. "Do you think I will even hear your conditions? Faugh! You talk very largely of nurture and I know not what. It's easy, to a man in chains, ha! Take off these vile bonds, give me a sword, and let any of you who dares then debate with me."

Nearly all the lords sprang to their feet, and Corin shouted:

"Father! Can I *box* him? Please."

"Peace! Your Majesties! My Lords!" said King Lune. "Have we no more gravity among us than to be so chafed by the taunt of a pajock? Sit down, Corin, or shalt leave the table. I ask your Highness again, to hear our conditions."

"I hear no conditions from barbarians and sorcerers," said Rabadash. "Not one of you dare touch a hair of my head. Every insult you have heaped on me shall be paid with oceans of Narnian and Archenlandish blood. Terrible shall the vengeance of the Tisroc be: even now. But kill me, and the burnings and torturings in these northern lands shall become a tale to frighten the world a thousand years hence. Beware! Beware! Beware! The bolt of Tash falls from above!"

"Does it ever get caught on a hook halfway?" asked Corin.

"Shame, Corin," said the King. "Never taunt a man save when he is stronger than you: then, as you please."

"Oh you foolish Rabadash," sighed Lucy.

Next moment Cor wondered why everyone at the table had risen and was standing perfectly still. Of course he did the same himself. And then he saw the reason. Aslan was among them though no one had seen him coming. Rabadash started as the immense shape of the Lion paced softly in between him and his accusers.

"Rabadash," said Aslan. "Take heed. Your doom is very near, but you may still avoid it.

Forget your pride (what have you to be proud of?) and your anger (who has done you wrong?) and accept the mercy of these good kings."

Then Rabadash rolled his eyes and spread out his mouth into a horrible, long mirthless grin like a shark, and wagged his ears up and down (anyone can learn how to do this if they take the trouble). He had always found this very effective in Calormen. The bravest had trembled when he made these faces, and ordinary people had fallen to the floor, and sensitive people had often fainted. But what Rabadash hadn't realized is that it is very easy to frighten people who know you can have them boiled alive the moment you give the word. The grimaces didn't look at all alarming in Archenland; indeed Lucy only thought Rabadash was going to be sick.

"Demon! Demon! Demon!" shrieked the Prince. "I know you. You are the foul fiend of Narnia. You are the enemy of the gods. Learn who *I* am, horrible phantasm. I am descended from Tash, the inexorable, the irresistible. The curse of Tash is upon you. Lightning in the shape of scorpions shall be rained on you. The mountains of Narnia shall be ground into dust. The—"

"Have a care, Rabadash," said Aslan quietly. "The doom is nearer now: it is at the door; it has lifted the latch."

"Let the skies fall," shrieked Rabadash. "Let the earth gape! Let blood and fire obliterate the world! But be sure I will never desist till I have dragged to my palace by her hair the barbarian queen, the daughter of dogs, the—"

"The hour has struck," said Aslan: and Rabadash saw, to his supreme horror, that everyone had begun to laugh.

They couldn't help it. Rabadash had been wagging his ears all the time and as soon as Aslan said, "The hour has struck!" the ears began to change. They grew longer and more pointed and soon were covered with gray hair. And while everyone was wondering where they had seen ears like that before, Rabadash's face began to change too. It grew longer, and thicker at the top and larger eyed, and the nose sank back into the face (or else the face swelled out and became all nose) and there was hair all over it. And his arms grew longer and came down in front of him till his hands were resting on the ground: only they weren't hands, now, they were hoofs. And he was standing on all fours, and his clothes disappeared, and everyone laughed louder and louder (because they couldn't help it) for now what had been Rabadash was, simply and unmistakably, a donkey. The terrible thing was that his human speech lasted just a moment longer than his human shape, so that when he realized the change that was coming over him, he screamed out:

"Oh, not a Donkey! Mercy! If it were even a horse—e'en—a—hor—eeh—auh, eeh-auh." And so the words died away into a donkey's bray.

"Now hear me, Rabadash," said Aslan. "Justice shall be mixed with mercy. You shall not always be an Ass."

At this of course the Donkey twitched its ears forward—and that also was so funny that everybody laughed all the more. They tried not to, but they tried in vain.

"You have appealed to Tash," said Aslan. "And in the temple of Tash you shall be healed. You must stand before the altar of Tash in Tashbaan at the great Autumn Feast this year and there, in the sight of all Tashbaan, your ass's shape will fall from you and all men will know you for Prince Rabadash. But as long as you live, if ever you go more than ten miles away from the great temple in Tashbaan you shall instantly become again as you now are. And from that second change there will be no return."

There was a short silence and then they all stirred and looked at one another as if they were waking from sleep. Aslan was gone. But there was a brightness in the air and on the grass, and a joy in their hearts, which assured them that he had been no dream: and anyway, there was the donkey in front of them.

King Lune was the kindest-hearted of men and on seeing his enemy in this regrettable condition he forgot all his anger.

"Your royal Highness," he said, "I am most truly sorry that things have come to this extremity. Your Highness will bear witness that it was none of our doing. And of course we shall be delighted to provide your Highness with shipping back to Tashbaan for the—er—treatment which Aslan has prescribed. You shall have every comfort which your Highness's

situation allows: the best of the cattle-boats—
the freshest carrots and thistles—"

But a deafening bray from the Donkey and a
well-aimed kick at one of the guards made it
clear that these kindly offers were ungratefully
received.

And here, to get him out of the way, I'd better finish off the story of Rabadash. He (or it)
was duly sent back by boat to Tashbaan and
brought into the temple of Tash at the great
Autumn Festival, and then he became a man
again. But of course four or five thousand people
had seen the transformation and the affair could
not possibly be hushed up. And after the old
Tisroc's death when Rabadash became Tisroc in
his place he turned out the most peaceable
Tisroc Calormen had ever known. This was because, not daring to go more than ten miles from
Tashbaan, he could never go on a war himself:
and he didn't want his Tarkaans to win fame in
the wars at his expense, for that is the way
Tisrocs get overthrown. But though his reasons
were selfish, it made things much more comfortable for all the smaller countries round
Calormen. His own people never forgot that he
had been a donkey. During his reign, and to his
face, he was called Rabadash the Peacemaker,
but after his death and behind his back he was
called Rabadash the Ridiculous, and if you look

him up in a good History of Calormen (try the local library) you will find him under that name. And to this day in Calormene schools, if you do anything unusually stupid, you are very likely to be called "a second Rabadash."

Meanwhile at Anvard everyone was very glad that he had been disposed of before the real fun began, which was a grand feast held that evening on the lawn before the castle, with dozens of lanterns to help the moonlight. And the wine flowed and tales were told and jokes were cracked, and then silence was made and the King's poet with two fiddlers stepped out into the middle of the circle. Aravis and Cor prepared themselves to be bored, for the only poetry they knew was the Calormene kind, and you know now what that was like. But at the very first scrape of the fiddles a rocket seemed to go up inside their heads, and the poet sang the great old lay of Fair Olvin and how he fought the Giant Pire and turned him into stone (and that is the origin of Mount Pire—it was a two-headed Giant) and won the Lady Liln for his bride; and when it was over they wished it was going to begin again. And though Bree couldn't sing he told the story of the fight of Zalindreh. And Lucy told again (they had all, except Aravis and Cor, heard it many times but they all wanted it again) the tale of the Wardrobe and how she and King Edmund and Queen Susan and Peter the High King had first come into Narnia.

And presently, as was certain to happen sooner or later, King Lune said it was time for young people to be in bed. "And tomorrow, Cor," he added, "shalt come over all the castle with me and see the estres and mark all its strength and weakness: for it will be thine to guard when I'm gone."

"But Corin will be the King then, Father," said Cor.

"Nay, lad," said King Lune, "thou art my heir. The crown comes to thee."

"But I don't want it," said Cor. "I'd far rather—"

"'Tis no question what thou wantest, Cor, nor I either. 'Tis in the course of law."

"But if we're twins we must be the same age."

"Nay," said the King with a laugh. "One must come first. Art Corin's elder by full twenty minutes. And his better too, let's hope, though that's no great mastery." And he looked at Corin with a twinkle in his eyes.

"But, Father, couldn't you make whichever you like to be the next King?"

"No. The king's under the law, for it's the law makes him a king. Hast no more power to start away from thy crown than any sentry from his post."

"Oh dear," said Cor. "I don't want to at all. And Corin—I am most dreadfully sorry. I never dreamed my turning up was going to chisel you out of your kingdom."

"Hurrah! Hurrah!" said Corin. "I shan't have to be King. I shan't have to be King. I'll always be a prince. It's princes have all the fun."

"And that's truer than thy brother knows, Cor," said King Lune. "For this is what it means to be a king: to be first in every desperate attack and last in every desperate retreat, and when there's hunger in the land (as must be now and then in bad years) to wear finer clothes and laugh louder over a scantier meal than any man in your land."

When the two boys were going upstairs to bed Cor again asked Corin if nothing could be done about it. And Corin said:

"If you say another word about it, I'll—I'll knock you down."

It would be nice to end the story by saying that after that the two brothers never disagreed about anything again, but I am afraid it would not be true. In reality they quarreled and fought just about as often as any other two boys would, and all their fights ended (if they didn't begin) with Cor getting knocked down. For though, when they had both grown up and become swordsmen, Cor was the more dangerous man in battle, neither he nor anyone else in the North Countries could ever equal Corin as a boxer. That was how he got his name of Corin Thunder-Fist; and how he performed his great exploit against the Lapsed Bear of Stormness, which was really a Talking Bear but had gone back to Wild Bear habits. Corin climbed up to its lair on the Narnian side of Stormness one winter day when the snow was on the hills and boxed it without a time-keeper for thirty-three rounds. And at the end it couldn't see out of its eyes and became a reformed character.

Aravis also had many quarrels (and, I'm afraid, even fights) with Cor, but they always made it up again: so that years later, when they were grown up, they were so used to quarreling and making up again that they got married so as to go on doing it more conveniently. And after King Lune's death they made a good King and Queen of Archenland and Ram the Great, the most famous of all the kings of Archenland, was their son. Bree and Hwin lived happily to a great age in Narnia and both got married but not to one another. And there weren't many months in which one or both of them didn't come trotting over the pass to visit their friends at Anvard.

THE LION, THE WITCH
AND
THE WARDROBE

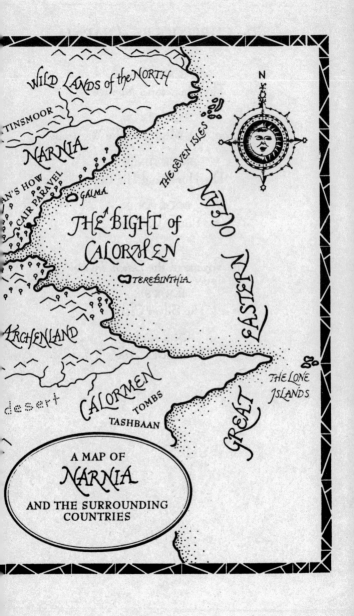

A MAP OF
NARNIA
AND THE SURROUNDING
COUNTRIES

The CHRONICLES *of* NARNIA

The CHRONICLES *of* NARNIA

C. S. LEWIS

BOOK 2

THE LION, THE WITCH
AND
THE WARDROBE

Illustrated by Pauline Baynes

HarperTrophy
A Division of HarperCollins*Publishers*

The HarperCollins editions of The Chronicles of Narnia have been renumbered in compliance with the original wishes of the author, C. S. Lewis. This is the first time the series has appeared in this order in the United States.

"Narnia" is a trademark of C. S. Lewis (Pte) Limited.
"The Chronicles of Narnia" is a U.S. Registered Trademark of
C. S. Lewis (Pte) Limited.

The Lion, the Witch and the Wardrobe
Copyright © 1950 by C.S. Lewis (Pte) Limited
Copyright renewed 1978 by C.S. Lewis (Pte) Limited
All rights reserved. No part of this book may be used or reproduced in any manner whatsoever without written permission except in the case of brief quotations embodied in critical articles and reviews. Printed in the United States of America. For information address HarperCollins Children's Books, a division of HarperCollins Publishers, 10 East 53rd Street, New York, NY 10022.

Library of Congress Cataloging-in-Publication Data
Lewis, C. S. (Clive Staples), 1898–1963.
    The lion, the witch and the wardrobe / C. S. Lewis ; illustrated by Pauline Baynes.
        p.   cm. — (The Chronicles of Narnia ; bk. 2)
    Summary: Four English schoolchildren find their way through the back of a wardrobe into the magic land of Narnia and assist Aslan, the golden lion, to triumph over the White Witch, who has cursed the land with eternal winter.
    ISBN 0-06-023481-4. — ISBN 0-06-023482-2 (lib. bdg.)
    ISBN 0-06-447104-7 (pbk.)
    [1. Fantasy.]   I. Baynes, Pauline, ill.   II. Title.   III. Series: Lewis, C. S. (Clive Staples), 1898–1963. Chronicles of Narnia (HarperCollins (Firm)) ; bk. 2.
PZ7.L58474Li   1994   93-8889
[Fic]—dc20   CIP
                                                                                      AC

Typography by Nicholas Krenitsky
❖

To Lucy Barfield

My Dear Lucy,
I wrote this story for you, but when I began it I had not realized that girls grow quicker than books. As a result you are already too old for fairy tales, and by the time it is printed and bound you will be older still. But some day you will be old enough to start reading fairy tales again. You can then take it down from some upper shelf, dust it, and tell me what you think of it. I shall probably be too deaf to hear, and too old to understand a word you say, but I shall still be

your affectionate Godfather,
C. S. Lewis

CAST OF CHARACTERS

ASLAN. The King, Lord of the whole wood, and son of the Emperor across the Sea. Aslan is the Lion, the Great Lion. He comes and goes as and when he pleases; he comes to overthrow the witch and save Narnia. Aslan appears in all seven books.

DIGORY KIRKE. Digory was there at the very beginning in *The Magician's Nephew*, and he is also in *The Lion, the Witch and the Wardrobe*. If it were not for Digory's courage, we might never have heard of Narnia. Find out why in *The Magician's Nephew*.

POLLY PLUMMER. Polly is the first person to leave our world. She and Digory take part in the very beginning of everything in *The Magician's Nephew*.

JADIS. The last Queen of Charn, which she herself destroyed. Jadis arrives in Narnia with Digory and Polly in *The Magician's Nephew* and has taken over the land as the White Witch in *The Lion, the Witch and the Wardrobe*. Completely evil, she is also very dangerous, even in *The Silver Chair*.

UNCLE ANDREW. Mr. Andrew Ketterley thinks he is a magician, but like all who meddle with magic, he doesn't really know what he is doing. The results are dire in *The Magician's Nephew*.

THE PEVENSIES.

Peter Pevensie, King Peter the Magnificent, the High King

Susan Pevensie, Queen Susan the Gentle

Edmund Pevensie, King Edmund the Just

Lucy Pevensie, Queen Lucy the Valiant

The four Pevensies, brothers and sisters, visited Narnia at the time of the winter rule of the White Witch. They remained there for many Narnian years and established the Golden Age of Narnia. Peter is the oldest, followed by Susan, then Edmund and Lucy. They are all in *The Lion, the Witch and the Wardrobe* and *Prince Caspian*. Edmund and Lucy are also in *The Voyage of the* Dawn Treader; Edmund, Lucy, and Susan appear in *The Horse and His Boy*; and Peter, Edmund, and Lucy appear in *The Last Battle*.

SHASTA. There is a mystery about this adopted son of a Calormene fisherman. He is not what he seems, as he himself discovers in *The Horse and His Boy*.

BREE. This great war horse is also unusual. He was kidnapped as a foal from the forests of Narnia and sold as a slave-horse in Calormen, a country across Archenland and far to the south of Narnia. His real adventures begin when he tries to escape in *The Horse and His Boy*.

ARAVIS. Aravis is a Tarkheena, a Calormene

noblewoman, but even so she has many good points, and they come to light in *The Horse and His Boy*.

HWIN. Hwin is a good-natured, sensible horse. Another slave taken from Narnia, she and Aravis become friends in *The Horse and His Boy*.

PRINCE CASPIAN. He is the nephew of King Miraz and is known as Caspian the Tenth, Son of Caspian, and the True King of Narnia (King of Old Narnians). He is also called a Telmarine of Narnia, Lord of Cair Paravel, and Emperor of the Lone Islands. He appears in *Prince Caspian*, *The Voyage of the Dawn Treader*, *The Silver Chair*, and *The Last Battle*.

MIRAZ. Miraz is a Telmarine from the land of Telmar, far beyond the Western Mountains (originally the ancestors of the Telmarines came from our world), and the usurper of the throne of Narnia in *Prince Caspian*.

REEPICHEEP. Reepicheep is the Chief Mouse. He is the self-appointed humble servant to Prince Caspian, and perhaps the most valiant knight in all of Narnia. His chivalry is unsurpassed, as also are his courage and skill with the sword. Reepicheep appears in *Prince Caspian*, *The Voyage of the Dawn Treader*, and *The Last Battle*.

EUSTACE CLARENCE SCRUBB. Eustace is a cousin of the Pevensie family whom Edmund

and Lucy must go and visit. He finds Narnia something of a shock. He appears in *The Voyage of the Dawn Treader*, *The Silver Chair*, and *The Last Battle*.

JILL POLE. Jill is the heroine of *The Silver Chair*; she goes to Narnia with Eustace on his second Narnian adventure. She also comes to aid Narnia in *The Last Battle*.

PRINCE RILIAN. The son of King Caspian the Tenth, Rilian is the lost Prince of Narnia; find him in *The Silver Chair*.

PUDDLEGLUM. Puddleglum is a Marsh-wiggle from the Eastern Marshes of Narnia. He is tall, and his very serious demeanor masks a true heart of great courage. He appears in *The Silver Chair* and *The Last Battle*.

KING TIRIAN. Noble and brave, Tirian is the last King of Narnia. He and his friend Jewel, a Unicorn, fight *The Last Battle*.

SHIFT. An old and ugly Ape, Shift decides that he should be in charge of Narnia and starts things that he can't stop in *The Last Battle*.

PUZZLE. Puzzle, a donkey, never meant any harm—you see, he's not really very clever. And Shift deceives him in *The Last Battle*.

CONTENTS

LUCY LOOKS INTO
A WARDROBE

Once there were four children whose names were Peter, Susan, Edmund and Lucy. This story is about something that happened to them when they were sent away from London during the war because of the air-raids. They were sent to the house of an old Professor who lived in the heart of the country, ten miles from the nearest railway station and two miles from the nearest post office. He had no wife and he lived in a very large house with a housekeeper called Mrs. Macready and three servants. (Their names were Ivy, Margaret and Betty, but they do not come into the story much.) He himself was a very old man with shaggy white hair which grew over most of his face as well as on his head, and they liked him almost at once; but on the first evening when he came out to meet them at the front door he was so odd-looking that Lucy (who was the youngest) was a little afraid of him, and Edmund (who was the next youngest) wanted to laugh and had to keep on pretending he was blowing his nose to hide it.

As soon as they had said good night to the Professor and gone upstairs on the first night, the boys came into the girls' room and they all talked it over.

"We've fallen on our feet and no mistake," said Peter. "This is going to be perfectly splendid. That old chap will let us do anything we like."

"I think he's an old dear," said Susan.

"Oh, come off it!" said Edmund, who was tired and pretending not to be tired, which always made him bad-tempered. "Don't go on talking like that."

"Like what?" said Susan; "and anyway, it's time you were in bed."

"Trying to talk like Mother," said Edmund. "And who are you to say when I'm to go to bed? Go to bed yourself."

"Hadn't we all better go to bed?" said Lucy.

"There's sure to be a row if we're heard talking here."

"No, there won't," said Peter. "I tell you this is the sort of house where no one's going to mind what we do. Anyway, they won't hear us. It's about ten minutes' walk from here down to that dining room, and any amount of stairs and passages in between."

"What's that noise?" said Lucy suddenly. It was a far larger house than she had ever been in before and the thought of all those long passages and rows of doors leading into empty rooms was beginning to make her feel a little creepy.

"It's only a bird, silly," said Edmund.

"It's an owl," said Peter. "This is going to be a wonderful place for birds. I shall go to bed now. I say, let's go and explore tomorrow. You might find anything in a place like this. Did you see those mountains as we came along? And the woods? There might be eagles. There might be stags. There'll be hawks."

"Badgers!" said Lucy.

"Foxes!" said Edmund.

"Rabbits!" said Susan.

But when next morning came there was a steady rain falling, so thick that when you looked out of the window you could see neither the mountains nor the woods nor even the stream in the garden.

"Of course it *would* be raining!" said Edmund. They had just finished their breakfast with the Professor and were upstairs in the room he had set apart for them—a long, low room with two windows looking out in one direction and two in another.

"Do stop grumbling, Ed," said Susan. "Ten to one it'll clear up in an hour or so. And in the meantime we're pretty well off. There's a wireless and lots of books."

"Not for me," said Peter; "I'm going to explore in the house."

Everyone agreed to this and that was how the adventures began. It was the sort of house that you never seem to come to the end of, and it was full of unexpected places. The first few doors they tried led only into spare bedrooms, as everyone had expected that they would; but soon they came to a very long room full of pictures and there they found a suit of armor; and after that was a room all hung with green, with a harp in one corner; and then came three steps down and five steps up, and then a kind of little upstairs hall and a door that led out onto a balcony, and then a whole series of rooms that led into each other and were lined with books—most of them very old books and some bigger than a Bible in a church. And shortly after that they looked into a room that was quite empty except for one big wardrobe; the sort that has a looking-glass in the door. There was nothing else in the room at all except a dead blue-bottle on the window-sill.

"Nothing there!" said Peter, and they all trooped out again—all except Lucy. She stayed behind because she thought it would be worth while trying the door of the wardrobe, even though she felt almost sure that it would be locked. To her surprise it opened quite easily, and two moth-balls dropped out.

Looking into the inside, she saw several coats hanging up—mostly long fur coats. There was nothing Lucy liked so much as the smell and feel of fur. She immediately stepped into the

wardrobe and got in among the coats and rubbed her face against them, leaving the door open, of course, because she knew that it is very foolish to shut oneself into any wardrobe. Soon she went further in and found that there was a second row of coats hanging up behind the first one. It was almost quite dark in there and she kept her arms stretched out in front of her so as not to bump her face into the back of the wardrobe. She took a step further in—then two or three steps—always expecting to feel wood-work against the tips of her fingers. But she could not feel it.

"This must be a simply enormous wardrobe!" thought Lucy, going still further in and pushing the soft folds of the coats aside to make room for her. Then she noticed that there was something crunching under her feet. "I wonder is that more moth-balls?" she thought, stooping down to feel it with her hand. But instead of feeling the hard, smooth wood of the floor of the wardrobe, she felt something soft and powdery and extremely cold. "This is very queer," she said, and went on a step or two further.

Next moment she found that what was rub-bing against her face and hands was no longer soft fur but something hard and rough and even prickly. "Why, it is just like branches of trees!" exclaimed Lucy. And then she saw that there was a light ahead of her; not a few inches away where the back of the wardrobe ought to have been, but a long way off. Something cold and soft was falling on her. A moment later she found that she was standing in the middle of a wood at night-time with snow under her feet and snowflakes falling through the air.

Lucy felt a little frightened, but she felt very inquisitive and excited as well. She looked back over her shoulder and there, between the dark tree-trunks, she could still see the open doorway of the wardrobe and even catch a glimpse of the empty room from which she had set out. (She had, of course, left the door open, for she knew that it is a very silly thing to shut oneself into a wardrobe.) It seemed to be still daylight there. "I can always get back if anything goes wrong," thought Lucy. She began to walk forward, crunch-crunch over the snow and through the wood toward the other light. In about ten minutes she reached it and found it was a lamp-post. As she stood looking at it, wondering why there was a lamp-post in the middle of a wood and wondering what to do next, she heard a pitter patter of feet coming toward her. And soon after that a very strange person stepped out from among the trees into the light of the lamp-post.

He was only a little taller than Lucy herself and he carried over his head an umbrella, white

with snow. From the waist upward he was like a man, but his legs were shaped like a goat's (the hair on them was glossy black) and instead of feet he had goat's hoofs. He also had a tail, but Lucy did not notice this at first because it was neatly caught up over the arm that held the umbrella so as to keep it from trailing in the snow. He had a red woollen muffler round his neck and his skin was rather reddish too. He had a strange, but pleasant little face, with a short pointed beard and curly hair, and out of the hair there stuck two horns, one on each side of his forehead. One of his hands, as I have said, held the umbrella: in the other arm he carried several brown-paper parcels. What with the parcels and the snow it looked just as if he had been doing his Christmas shopping. He was a Faun. And when he saw Lucy he gave such a start of surprise that he dropped all his parcels.

"Goodness gracious me!" exclaimed the Faun.

2

WHAT LUCY
FOUND THERE

"Good evening," said Lucy. But the Faun was so busy picking up its parcels that at first it did not reply. When it had finished it made her a little bow.

"Good evening, good evening," said the Faun. "Excuse me—I don't want to be inquisitive—but should I be right in thinking that you are a Daughter of Eve?"

"My name's Lucy," said she, not quite understanding him.

"But you are—forgive me—you are what they call a girl?" asked the Faun.

"Of course I'm a girl," said Lucy.

"You are in fact Human?"

"Of course I'm human," said Lucy, still a little puzzled.

"To be sure, to be sure," said the Faun. "How stupid of me! But I've never seen a Son of Adam or a Daughter of Eve before. I am delighted. That is to say—" and then it stopped as if it had been going to say something it had not intended but had remembered in time. "Delighted, delighted," it went on. "Allow me to introduce myself. My name is Tumnus."

"I am very pleased to meet you, Mr. Tumnus," said Lucy.

"And may I ask, O Lucy Daughter of Eve," said Mr. Tumnus, "how you have come into Narnia?"

"Narnia? What's that?" said Lucy.

"This is the land of Narnia," said the Faun, "where we are now; all that lies between the lamp-post and the great castle of Cair Paravel on the eastern sea. And you—you have come from the wild woods of the west?"

"I—I got in through the wardrobe in the spare room," said Lucy.

"Ah!" said Mr. Tumnus in a rather melancholy voice, "if only I had worked harder at geography when I was a little Faun, I should no doubt know all about those strange countries. It is too late now."

"But they aren't countries at all," said Lucy, almost laughing. "It's only just back there—at least—I'm not sure. It is summer there."

"Meanwhile," said Mr. Tumnus, "it is winter in Narnia, and has been for ever so long, and we shall both catch cold if we stand here talking in the snow. Daughter of Eve from the far land of Spare Oom where eternal summer reigns around the bright city of War Drobe, how would it be if you came and had tea with me?"

"Thank you very much, Mr. Tumnus," said Lucy. "But I was wondering whether I ought to be getting back."

"It's only just round the corner," said the Faun, "and there'll be a roaring fire—and toast—and sardines—and cake."

"Well, it's very kind of you," said Lucy. "But I shan't be able to stay long."

"If you will take my arm, Daughter of Eve," said Mr. Tumnus, "I shall be able to hold the umbrella over both of us. That's the way. Now—off we go."

And so Lucy found herself walking through the wood arm in arm with this strange creature as if they had known one another all their lives.

They had not gone far before they came to a

place where the ground became rough and there were rocks all about and little hills up and little hills down. At the bottom of one small valley Mr. Tumnus turned suddenly aside as if he were going to walk straight into an unusually large rock, but at the last moment Lucy found he was leading her into the entrance of a cave. As soon as they were inside she found herself blinking in the light of a wood fire. Then Mr. Tumnus stooped and took a flaming piece of wood out of the fire with a neat little pair of tongs, and lit a lamp. "Now we shan't be long," he said, and immediately put a kettle on.

Lucy thought she had never been in a nicer place. It was a little, dry, clean cave of reddish stone with a carpet on the floor and two little chairs ("one for me and one for a friend," said Mr. Tumnus) and a table and a dresser and a mantelpiece over the fire and above that a picture of an old Faun with a gray beard. In one corner there was a door which Lucy thought must lead to Mr. Tumnus's bedroom, and on one wall was a shelf full of books. Lucy looked at these while he was setting out the tea things. They had titles like *The Life and Letters of Silenus* or *Nymphs and Their Ways* or *Men, Monks, and Gamekeepers; a Study in Popular Legend* or *Is Man a Myth?*

"Now, Daughter of Eve!" said the Faun.

And really it was a wonderful tea. There was a nice brown egg, lightly boiled, for each of them, and then sardines on toast, and then buttered toast, and then toast with honey, and then a sugar-topped cake. And when Lucy was tired of eating, the Faun began to talk. He had wonderful tales to tell of life in the forest. He told about the midnight dances and how the Nymphs who lived in the wells and the Dryads

who lived in the trees came out to dance with the Fauns; about long hunting parties after the milk-white stag who could give you wishes if you caught him; about feasting and treasure-seeking with the wild Red Dwarfs in deep mines and caverns far beneath the forest floor; and then about summer when the woods were green and old Silenus on his fat donkey would come to visit them, and sometimes Bacchus himself, and then the streams would run with wine instead of water and the whole forest would give itself up to jollification for weeks on end. "Not that it isn't always winter now," he added gloomily. Then to cheer himself up he took out from its case on the dresser a strange little flute that looked as if it were made of straw and began to play. And the tune he played made Lucy want to cry and laugh and dance and go to sleep all at the same time. It must have been hours later when she shook herself and said:

"Oh, Mr. Tumnus—I'm so sorry to stop you, and I do love that tune—but really, I must go home. I only meant to stay for a few minutes."

"It's no good *now*, you know," said the Faun, laying down its flute and shaking its head at her very sorrowfully.

"No good?" said Lucy, jumping up and feeling rather frightened. "What do you mean? I've got to go home at once. The others will be wondering what has happened to me." But a moment later she asked, "Mr. Tumnus! Whatever is the matter?" for the Faun's brown eyes had filled with tears and then the tears began trickling down its cheeks, and soon they were running off the end of its nose; and at last it covered its face with its hands and began to howl.

"Mr. Tumnus! Mr. Tumnus!" said Lucy in great distress. "Don't! Don't! What is the matter? Aren't you well? Dear Mr. Tumnus, do tell me what is wrong." But the Faun continued sobbing as if its heart would break. And even when Lucy went over and put her arms round him and lent him her handkerchief, he did not stop. He merely took the handkerchief and kept on using it, wringing it out with both hands whenever it got too wet to be any more use, so that presently Lucy was standing in a damp patch.

"Mr. Tumnus!" bawled Lucy in his ear, shaking him. "Do stop. Stop it at once! You ought to be ashamed of yourself, a great big Faun like you. What on earth are you crying about?"

"Oh—oh—oh!" sobbed Mr. Tumnus, "I'm crying because I'm such a bad Faun."

"I don't think you're a bad Faun at all," said Lucy. "I think you are a very good Faun. You are the nicest Faun I've ever met."

"Oh—oh—you wouldn't say that if you knew," replied Mr. Tumnus between his sobs. "No, I'm a bad Faun. I don't suppose there ever was a worse Faun since the beginning of the world."

"But what have you done?" asked Lucy.

"My old father, now," said Mr. Tumnus; "that's his picture over the mantelpiece. He would never have done a thing like this."

19

"A thing like what?" said Lucy.

"Like what I've done," said the Faun. "Taken service under the White Witch. That's what I am. I'm in the pay of the White Witch."

"The White Witch? Who is she?"

"Why, it is she that has got all Narnia under her thumb. It's she that makes it always winter. Always winter and never Christmas; think of that!"

"How awful!" said Lucy. "But what does she pay *you* for?"

"That's the worst of it," said Mr. Tumnus with a deep groan. "I'm a kidnapper for her, that's what I am. Look at me, Daughter of Eve. Would you believe that I'm the sort of Faun to meet a poor innocent child in the wood, one that had never done me any harm, and pretend to be friendly with it, and invite it home to my cave, all for the sake of lulling it asleep and then handing it over to the White Witch?"

"No," said Lucy. "I'm sure you wouldn't do anything of the sort."

"But I have," said the Faun.

"Well," said Lucy rather slowly (for she wanted to be truthful and yet not be too hard on him), "well, that was pretty bad. But you're so sorry for it that I'm sure you will never do it again."

"Daughter of Eve, don't you understand?"

said the Faun. "It isn't something I have done. I'm doing it now, this very moment."

"What do you mean?" cried Lucy, turning very white.

"You are the child," said Tumnus. "I had orders from the White Witch that if ever I saw a Son of Adam or a Daughter of Eve in the wood, I was to catch them and hand them over to her. And you are the first I ever met. And I've pretended to be your friend and asked you to tea, and all the time I've been meaning to wait till you were asleep and then go and tell *Her*."

"Oh, but you won't, Mr. Tumnus," said Lucy. "You won't, will you? Indeed, indeed you really mustn't."

"And if I don't," said he, beginning to cry again, "she's sure to find out. And she'll have my tail cut off, and my horns sawn off, and my beard plucked out, and she'll wave her wand over my beautiful cloven hoofs and turn them into horrid solid hoofs like a wretched horse's. And if she is extra and specially angry she'll turn me into stone and I shall be only a statue of a Faun in her horrible house until the four thrones at Cair Paravel are filled—and goodness knows when that will happen, or whether it will ever happen at all."

"I'm very sorry, Mr. Tumnus," said Lucy. "But please let me go home."

"Of course I will," said the Faun. "Of course I've got to. I see that now. I hadn't known what Humans were like before I met you. Of course I can't give you up to the Witch; not now that I know you. But we must be off at once. I'll see you back to the lamp-post. I suppose you can find your own way from there back to Spare Oom and War Drobe?"

"I'm sure I can," said Lucy.

"We must go as quietly as we can," said Mr. Tumnus. "The whole wood is full of *her* spies. Even some of the trees are on her side."

They both got up and left the tea things on the table, and Mr. Tumnus once more put up his umbrella and gave Lucy his arm, and they went out into the snow. The journey back was not at all like the journey to the Faun's cave; they stole along as quickly as they could, without speaking a word, and Mr. Tumnus kept to the darkest places. Lucy was relieved when they reached the lamp-post again.

"Do you know your way from here, Daughter of Eve?" said Tumnus.

Lucy looked very hard between the trees and could just see in the distance a patch of light that looked like daylight. "Yes," she said, "I can see the wardrobe door."

"Then be off home as quick as you can," said the Faun, "and—c-can you ever forgive me for what I meant to do?"

"Why, of course I can," said Lucy, shaking him heartily by the hand. "And I do hope you won't get into dreadful trouble on my account."

"Farewell, Daughter of Eve," said he. "Perhaps I may keep the handkerchief?"

"Rather!" said Lucy, and then ran toward the far-off patch of daylight as quickly as her legs would carry her. And presently instead of rough branches brushing past her she felt coats, and instead of crunching snow under her feet she felt wooden boards, and all at once she found herself jumping out of the wardrobe into the same empty room from which the whole adventure had started. She shut the wardrobe door tightly behind her and looked around, panting for breath. It was still raining and she could hear the voices of the others in the passage.

"I'm here," she shouted. "I'm here. I've come back, I'm all right."

EDMUND AND
THE WARDROBE

Lucy ran out of the empty room into the passage and found the other three.

"It's all right," she repeated, "I've come back."

"What on earth are you talking about, Lucy?" asked Susan.

"Why," said Lucy in amazement, "haven't you all been wondering where I was?"

"So you've been hiding, have you?" said Peter. "Poor old Lu, hiding and nobody noticed! You'll have to hide longer than that if you want people to start looking for you."

"But I've been away for hours and hours," said Lucy.

The others all stared at one another.

"Batty!" said Edmund, tapping his head. "Quite batty."

"What do you mean, Lu?" asked Peter.

"What I said," answered Lucy. "It was just after breakfast when I went into the wardrobe, and I've been away for hours and hours, and had tea, and all sorts of things have happened."

"Don't be silly, Lucy," said Susan. "We've only just come out of that room a moment ago, and you were there then."

"She's not being silly at all," said Peter, "she's just making up a story for fun, aren't you, Lu? And why shouldn't she?"

"No, Peter, I'm not," she said. "It's—it's a magic wardrobe. There's a wood inside it, and it's snowing, and there's a Faun and a Witch and it's called Narnia; come and see."

The others did not know what to think, but Lucy was so excited that they all went back with her into the room. She rushed ahead of them, flung open the door of the wardrobe and cried, "Now! go in and see for yourselves."

"Why, you goose," said Susan, putting her head inside and pulling the fur coats apart, "it's just an ordinary wardrobe; look! there's the back of it."

Then everyone looked in and pulled the coats apart; and they all saw—Lucy herself saw—a perfectly ordinary wardrobe. There was no wood and no snow, only the back of the wardrobe, with hooks on it. Peter went in and rapped his knuckles on it to make sure that it was solid.

"A jolly good hoax, Lu," he said as he came out again; "you have really taken us in, I must admit. We half-believed you."

"But it wasn't a hoax at all," said Lucy, "really and truly. It was all different a moment ago. Honestly it was. I promise."

"Come, Lu," said Peter, "that's going a bit far. You've had your joke. Hadn't you better drop it now?"

Lucy grew very red in the face and tried to say something, though she hardly knew what she was trying to say, and burst into tears.

For the next few days she was very miserable. She could have made it up with the others quite easily at any moment if she could have brought herself to say that the whole thing was only a story made up for fun. But Lucy was a very truthful girl and she knew that she was really in the right; and she could not bring herself to say this. The others who thought she was telling a lie, and a silly lie too, made her very unhappy. The two elder ones did this without meaning to do it, but Edmund could be spiteful, and on this occasion he was spiteful. He sneered and jeered at Lucy and kept on asking her if she'd found any other new countries in other cupboards all over the house. What made it worse was that these days ought to have been delightful. The weather was fine and they were out of doors from morning to night, bathing, fishing, climbing trees, and lying in the heather. But Lucy could not properly enjoy any of it. And so things went on until the next wet day.

That day, when it came to the afternoon and there was still no sign of a break in the weather, they decided to play hide-and-seek. Susan was "It" and as soon as the others scattered to hide, Lucy went to the room where the wardrobe was. She did not mean to hide in the wardrobe, because she knew that would only set the others talking again about the whole wretched business. But she did want to have one more look inside it; for by this time she was beginning to wonder herself whether Narnia and the Faun had not been a dream. The house was so large and complicated and full of hiding-places that she thought she would have time to have one look into the wardrobe and then hide somewhere else. But as soon as she reached it she heard steps in the passage outside, and then there was nothing for it but to jump into the wardrobe and hold the door closed behind her. She did not shut it properly because she knew that it is very silly to shut oneself into a wardrobe, even if it is not a magic one.

Now the steps she had heard were those of Edmund; and he came into the room just in time to see Lucy vanishing into the wardrobe. He at once decided to get into it himself—not because he thought it a particularly good place to hide but because he wanted to go on teasing her about her imaginary country. He opened the door. There were the coats hanging up as usual, and a smell of mothballs, and darkness and silence, and no sign of Lucy. "She thinks I'm Susan come to catch her," said Edmund to himself, "and so she's keeping very quiet in at the

back." He jumped in and shut the door, forgetting what a very foolish thing this is to do. Then he began feeling about for Lucy in the dark. He had expected to find her in a few seconds and was very surprised when he did not. He decided to open the door again and let in some light. But he could not find the door either. He didn't like this at all and began groping wildly in every direction; he even shouted out, "Lucy! Lu! Where are you? I know you're here."

There was no answer and Edmund noticed that his own voice had a curious sound—not the sound you expect in a cupboard, but a kind of open-air sound. He also noticed that he was unexpectedly cold; and then he saw a light.

"Thank goodness," said Edmund, "the door must have swung open of its own accord." He forgot all about Lucy and went toward the light, which he thought was the open door of the wardrobe. But instead of finding himself stepping out into the spare room he found himself stepping out from the shadow of some thick dark fir trees into an open place in the middle of a wood.

There was crisp, dry snow under his feet and more snow lying on the branches of the trees. Overhead there was a pale blue sky, the sort of sky one sees on a fine winter day in the morning. Straight ahead of him he saw between the

tree-trunks the sun, just rising, very red and clear. Everything was perfectly still, as if he were the only living creature in that country. There was not even a robin or a squirrel among the trees, and the wood stretched as far as he could see in every direction. He shivered.

He now remembered that he had been looking for Lucy; and also how unpleasant he had been to her about her "imaginary country" which now turned out not to have been imaginary at all. He thought that she must be somewhere quite close and so he shouted, "Lucy! Lucy! I'm here too—Edmund."

There was no answer.

"She's angry about all the things I've been saying lately," thought Edmund. And though he did not like to admit that he had been wrong, he also did not much like being alone in this strange, cold, quiet place; so he shouted again.

"I say, Lu! I'm sorry I didn't believe you. I see now you were right all along. Do come out. Make it Pax."

Still there was no answer.

"Just like a girl," said Edmund to himself, "sulking somewhere, and won't accept an apology." He looked round him again and decided he did not much like this place, and had almost made up his mind to go home, when he heard, very far off in the wood, a sound of bells. He listened and the sound came nearer and nearer and at last there swept into sight a sledge drawn by two reindeer.

The reindeer were about the size of Shetland ponies and their hair was so white that even the snow hardly looked white compared with them; their branching horns were gilded and shone like something on fire when the sunrise caught them. Their harness was of scarlet leather and covered with bells. On the sledge, driving the reindeer, sat a fat dwarf who would have been about three feet high if he had been standing. He was dressed in polar bear's fur and on his head he wore a red hood with a long gold tassel hanging down from its point; his huge beard covered his knees and served him instead of a rug. But behind him, on a much higher seat in the middle of the sledge sat a very different person—a great lady, taller than any woman that Edmund had ever seen. She also was covered in white fur up to her throat and held a long straight golden wand in her right hand and wore a golden crown on her head. Her face was

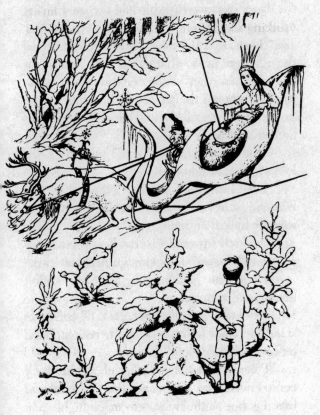

white—not merely pale, but white like snow or paper or icing-sugar, except for her very red mouth. It was a beautiful face in other respects, but proud and cold and stern.

The sledge was a fine sight as it came sweeping toward Edmund with the bells jingling and the dwarf cracking his whip and the snow flying up on each side of it.

"Stop!" said the Lady, and the dwarf pulled the reindeer up so sharp that they almost sat down. Then they recovered themselves and stood champing their bits and blowing. In the frosty air the breath coming out of their nostrils looked like smoke.

"And what, pray, are you?" said the Lady, looking hard at Edmund.

"I'm—I'm—my name's Edmund," said Edmund rather awkwardly. He did not like the way she looked at him.

The Lady frowned. "Is that how you address a Queen?" she asked, looking sterner than ever.

"I beg your pardon, your Majesty, I didn't know," said Edmund.

"Not know the Queen of Narnia?" cried she. "Ha! You shall know us better hereafter. But I repeat—what are you?"

"Please, your Majesty," said Edmund, "I don't know what you mean. I'm at school—at least I was—it's the holidays now."

TURKISH DELIGHT

"But what *are* you?" said the Queen again. "Are you a great overgrown dwarf that has cut off its beard?"

"No, your Majesty," said Edmund, "I never had a beard, I'm a boy."

"A boy!" said she. "Do you mean you are a Son of Adam?"

Edmund stood still, saying nothing. He was too confused by this time to understand what the question meant.

"I see you are an idiot, whatever else you may be," said the Queen. "Answer me, once and for all, or I shall lose my patience. Are you human?"

"Yes, your Majesty," said Edmund.

"And how, pray, did you come to enter my dominions?"

"Please, your Majesty, I came in through a wardrobe."

"A wardrobe? What do you mean?"

"I—I opened a door and just found myself here, your Majesty," said Edmund.

"Ha!" said the Queen, speaking more to herself than to him. "A door. A door from the world of men! I have heard of such things. This may wreck all. But he is only one, and he is easily dealt with." As she spoke these words she rose from her seat and looked Edmund full in the face, her eyes flaming; at the same moment she raised her wand. Edmund felt sure that she was going to do something dreadful but he seemed unable to move. Then, just as he gave himself up for lost, she appeared to change her mind.

"My poor child," she said in quite a different voice, "how cold you look! Come and sit with me here on the sledge and I will put my mantle round you and we will talk."

Edmund did not like this arrangement at all but he dared not disobey; he stepped onto the sledge and sat at her feet, and she put a fold of her fur mantle round him and tucked it well in.

"Perhaps something hot to drink?" said the Queen. "Should you like that?"

"Yes please, your Majesty," said Edmund, whose teeth were chattering.

The Queen took from somewhere among her wrappings a very small bottle which looked as if it were made of copper. Then, holding out her arm, she let one drop fall from it onto the snow beside the sledge. Edmund saw the drop for a second in mid-air, shining like a diamond. But the moment it touched the snow there was a hissing sound and there stood a jeweled cup full of something that steamed. The dwarf immediately took this and handed it to Edmund with a bow and a smile; not a very nice smile. Edmund felt much better as he began to sip the hot drink. It was something he had never tasted before, very sweet and foamy and creamy, and it

warmed him right down to his toes.

"It is dull, Son of Adam, to drink without eating," said the Queen presently. "What would you like best to eat?"

"Turkish Delight, please, your Majesty," said Edmund.

The Queen let another drop fall from her bottle onto the snow, and instantly there appeared a round box, tied with green silk ribbon, which, when opened, turned out to contain several pounds of the best Turkish Delight. Each piece was sweet and light to the very center and Edmund had never tasted anything more delicious. He was quite warm now, and very comfortable.

While he was eating the Queen kept asking him questions. At first Edmund tried to remember that it is rude to speak with one's mouth full, but soon he forgot about this and thought only of trying to shovel down as much Turkish Delight as he could, and the more he ate the more he wanted to eat, and he never asked himself why the Queen should be so inquisitive. She got him to tell her that he had one brother and two sisters, and that one of his sisters had already been in Narnia and had met a Faun there, and that no one except himself and his brother and his sisters knew anything about Narnia. She seemed especially interested in the fact that there were four of them, and kept on coming back to it. "You are sure there are just four of you?" she asked. "Two Sons of Adam and two Daughters of Eve, neither more nor less?" and Edmund, with his mouth full of Turkish Delight, kept on saying, "Yes, I told you that before," and forgetting to call her "Your Majesty," but she didn't seem to mind now.

At last the Turkish Delight was all finished and Edmund was looking very hard at the empty box and wishing that she would ask him whether he would like some more. Probably the Queen knew quite well what he was thinking; for she knew, though Edmund did not, that this was enchanted Turkish Delight and that anyone who had once tasted it would want more and more of it, and would even, if they were allowed, go on eating it till they killed themselves. But she did not offer him any more. Instead, she said to him,

"Son of Adam, I should so much like to see your brother and your two sisters. Will you bring them to see me?"

"I'll try," said Edmund, still looking at the empty box.

"Because, if you did come again—bringing them with you of course—I'd be able to give you some more Turkish Delight. I can't do it now, the magic will only work once. In my own house it would be another matter."

"Why can't we go to your house now?" said Edmund. When he had first got onto the sledge he had been afraid that she might drive away with him to some unknown place from which he would not be able to get back; but he had forgotten about that fear now.

"It is a lovely place, my house," said the Queen. "I am sure you would like it. There are whole rooms full of Turkish Delight, and what's more, I have no children of my own. I want a nice boy whom I could bring up as a Prince and who would be King of Narnia when I am gone. While he was Prince he would wear a gold crown and eat Turkish Delight all day long; and you are much the cleverest and handsomest young man I've ever met. I think I would like to make you the Prince—some day, when you bring the others to visit me."

"Why not now?" said Edmund. His face had become very red and his mouth and fingers were sticky. He did not look either clever or handsome, whatever the Queen might say.

"Oh, but if I took you there now," said she, "I shouldn't see your brother and your sisters. I very much want to know your charming relations. You are to be the Prince and—later on—the King; that is understood. But you must have courtiers and nobles. I will make your brother a

Duke and your sisters Duchesses."

"There's nothing special about *them*," said Edmund, "and, anyway, I could always bring them some other time."

"Ah, but once you were in my house," said the Queen, "you might forget all about them. You would be enjoying yourself so much that you wouldn't want the bother of going to fetch them. No. You must go back to your own country now and come to me another day, *with them*, you understand. It is no good coming without them."

"But I don't even know the way back to my own country," pleaded Edmund.

"That's easy," answered the Queen. "Do you see that lamp?" She pointed with her wand and Edmund turned and saw the same lamp-post under which Lucy had met the Faun. "Straight on, beyond that, is the way to the World of Men. And now look the other way"—here she pointed in the opposite direction—"and tell me if you can see two little hills rising above the trees."

"I think I can," said Edmund.

"Well, my house is between those two hills. So next time you come you have only to find the lamp-post and look for those two hills and walk through the wood till you reach my house. But remember—you must bring the others with you. I might have to be very angry with you if you came alone."

"I'll do my best," said Edmund.

"And, by the way," said the Queen, "you needn't tell them about me. It would be fun to keep it a secret between us two, wouldn't it? Make it a surprise for them. Just bring them along to the two hills—a clever boy like you will easily think of some excuse for doing that—and when you come to my house you could just say 'Let's see who lives here' or something like that. I am sure that would be best. If your sister has met one of the Fauns, she may have heard strange stories about me—nasty stories that might make her afraid to come to me. Fauns will say anything, you know, and now—"

"Please, please," said Edmund suddenly, "please couldn't I have just one piece of Turkish Delight to eat on the way home?"

"No, no," said the Queen with a laugh, "you must wait till next time." While she spoke, she signaled to the dwarf to drive on, but as the sledge swept away out of sight, the Queen waved to Edmund, calling out, "Next time! Next time! Don't forget. Come soon."

Edmund was still staring after the sledge when he heard someone calling his own name, and looking round he saw Lucy coming toward him from another part of the wood.

"Oh, Edmund!" she cried. "So you've got in too! Isn't it wonderful, and now—"

"All right," said Edmund, "I see you were right and it is a magic wardrobe after all. I'll say I'm sorry if you like. But where on earth have you been all this time? I've been looking for you everywhere."

"If I'd known you had got in I'd have waited for you," said Lucy, who was too happy and excited to notice how snappishly Edmund spoke or how flushed and strange his face was. "I've been having lunch with dear Mr. Tumnus, the Faun, and he's very well and the White Witch has done nothing to him for letting me go, so he thinks she can't have found out and perhaps everything is going to be all right after all."

"The White Witch?" said Edmund; "who's she?"

"She is a perfectly terrible person," said Lucy. "She calls herself the Queen of Narnia though she has no right to be queen at all, and all the Fauns and Dryads and Naiads and Dwarfs and Animals—at least all the good ones—simply hate her. And she can turn people into stone and do all kinds of horrible things. And she has made a magic so that it is always winter in Narnia—always winter, but it never gets to Christmas. And she drives about on a sledge, drawn by reindeer, with her wand in her hand

and a crown on her head."

Edmund was already feeling uncomfortable from having eaten too many sweets, and when he heard that the Lady he had made friends with was a dangerous witch he felt even more uncomfortable. But he still wanted to taste that Turkish Delight again more than he wanted anything else.

"Who told you all that stuff about the White Witch?" he asked.

"Mr. Tumnus, the Faun," said Lucy.

"You can't always believe what Fauns say," said Edmund, trying to sound as if he knew far more about them than Lucy.

"Who said so?" asked Lucy.

"Everyone knows it," said Edmund; "ask anybody you like. But it's pretty poor sport standing here in the snow. Let's go home."

"Yes, let's," said Lucy. "Oh, Edmund, I *am* glad you've got in too. The others will have to believe in Narnia now that both of us have been there. What fun it will be!"

But Edmund secretly thought that it would not be as good fun for him as for her. He would have to admit that Lucy had been right, before all the others, and he felt sure the others would all be on the side of the Fauns and the animals; but he was already more than half on the side of the Witch. He did not know what he would say, or how he would keep his secret once they were all talking about Narnia.

By this time they had walked a good way. Then suddenly they felt coats around them instead of branches and next moment they were both standing outside the wardrobe in the empty room.

"I say," said Lucy, "you do look awful, Edmund. Don't you feel well?"

"I'm all right," said Edmund, but this was not true. He was feeling very sick.

"Come on then," said Lucy, "let's find the others. What a lot we shall have to tell them! And what wonderful adventures we shall have now that we're all in it together."

5

BACK ON THIS SIDE
OF THE DOOR

Because the game of hide-and-seek was still going on, it took Edmund and Lucy some time to find the others. But when at last they were all together (which happened in the long room, where the suit of armor was), Lucy burst out:

"Peter! Susan! It's all true. Edmund has seen it too. There *is* a country you can get to through the wardrobe. Edmund and I both got in. We met one another in there, in the wood. Go on, Edmund; tell them all about it."

"What's all this about, Ed?" said Peter.

And now we come to one of the nastiest

things in this story. Up to that moment Edmund had been feeling sick, and sulky, and annoyed with Lucy for being right, but he hadn't made up his mind what to do. When Peter suddenly asked him the question he decided all at once to do the meanest and most spiteful thing he could think of. He decided to let Lucy down.

"Tell us, Ed," said Susan.

And Edmund gave a very superior look as if he were far older than Lucy (there was really only a year's difference) and then a little snigger and said, "Oh, yes, Lucy and I have been playing—pretending that all her story about a country in the wardrobe is true. Just for fun, of course. There's nothing there really."

Poor Lucy gave Edmund one look and rushed out of the room.

Edmund, who was becoming a nastier person every minute, thought that he had scored a great success, and went on at once to say, "There she goes again. What's the matter with her? That's the worst of young kids, they always—"

"Look here," said Peter, turning on him savagely, "shut up! You've been perfectly beastly to Lu ever since she started this nonsense about the wardrobe, and now you go playing games with her about it and setting her off again. I believe you did it simply out of spite."

"But it's all nonsense," said Edmund, very taken aback.

"Of course it's all nonsense," said Peter, "that's just the point. Lu was perfectly all right when we left home, but since we've been down here she seems to be either going queer in the head or else turning into a most frightful liar. But whichever it is, what good do you think you'll do by jeering and nagging at her one day and encouraging her the next?"

"I thought—I thought," said Edmund; but he couldn't think of anything to say.

"You didn't think anything at all," said Peter; "it's just spite. You've always liked being beastly to anyone smaller than yourself; we've seen that at school before now."

"Do stop it," said Susan; "it won't make things any better having a row between you two. Let's go and find Lucy."

It was not surprising that when they found Lucy, a good deal later, everyone could see that she had been crying. Nothing they could say to her made any difference. She stuck to her story and said:

"I don't care what you think, and I don't care what you say. You can tell the Professor or you can write to Mother or you can do anything

THE LION, THE WITCH AND THE WARDROBE

you like. I know I've met a Faun in there and—I wish I'd stayed there and you are all beasts, beasts."

It was an unpleasant evening. Lucy was miserable and Edmund was beginning to feel that his plan wasn't working as well as he had expected. The two older ones were really beginning to think that Lucy was out of her mind. They stood in the passage talking about it in whispers long after she had gone to bed.

The result was the next morning they decided that they really would go and tell the whole thing to the Professor. "He'll write to Father if he thinks there is really something wrong with Lu," said Peter; "it's getting beyond us." So they went and knocked at the study door, and the Professor said "Come in," and got up and found chairs for them and said he was quite at their disposal. Then he sat listening to them with the tips of his fingers pressed together and never interrupting, till they had finished the whole story. After that he said nothing for quite a long time. Then he cleared his throat and said the last thing either of them expected:

"How do you know," he asked, "that your sister's story is not true?"

"Oh, but—" began Susan, and then stopped. Anyone could see from the old man's face that he was perfectly serious. Then Susan pulled herself together and said, "But Edmund said they had only been pretending."

"That is a point," said the Professor, "which certainly deserves consideration; very careful consideration. For instance—if you will excuse me for asking the question—does your experience lead you to regard your brother or your sister as the more reliable? I mean, which is the more truthful?"

"That's just the funny thing about it, sir," said Peter. "Up till now, I'd have said Lucy every time."

"And what do you think, my dear?" said the Professor, turning to Susan.

"Well," said Susan, "in general, I'd say the same as Peter, but this couldn't be true—all this about the wood and the Faun."

"That is more than I know," said the Professor, "and a charge of lying against someone whom you have always found truthful is a very serious thing; a very serious thing indeed."

"We were afraid it mightn't even be lying," said Susan; "we thought there might be something wrong with Lucy."

"Madness, you mean?" said the Professor quite coolly. "Oh, you can make your minds easy about that. One has only to look at her and talk to her to see that she is not mad."

"But then," said Susan, and stopped. She

had never dreamed that a grown-up would talk like the Professor and didn't know what to think.

"Logic!" said the Professor half to himself. "Why don't they teach logic at these schools? There are only three possibilities. Either your sister is telling lies, or she is mad, or she is telling the truth. You know she doesn't tell lies and it is obvious that she is not mad. For the moment then and unless any further evidence turns up, we must assume that she is telling the truth."

Susan looked at him very hard and was quite sure from the expression on his face that he was not making fun of them.

"But how could it be true, sir?" said Peter.

"Why do you say that?" asked the Professor.

"Well, for one thing," said Peter, "if it was real why doesn't everyone find this country every time they go to the wardrobe? I mean, there was nothing there when we looked; even Lucy didn't pretend there was."

"What has that to do with it?" said the Professor.

"Well, sir, if things are real, they're there all the time."

"Are they?" said the Professor; and Peter did not know quite what to say.

"But there was no time," said Susan. "Lucy

had had no time to have gone anywhere, even if there was such a place. She came running after us the very moment we were out of the room. It was less than a minute, and she pretended to have been away for hours."

"That is the very thing that makes her story so likely to be true," said the Professor. "If there really is a door in this house that leads to some other world (and I should warn you that this is a very strange house, and even I know very little

53

about it)—if, I say, she had got into another world, I should not be at all surprised to find that the other world had a separate time of its own; so that however long you stayed there it would never take up any of *our* time. On the other hand, I don't think many girls of her age would invent that idea for themselves. If she had been pretending, she would have hidden for a reasonable time before coming out and telling her story."

"But do you really mean, sir," said Peter, "that there could be other worlds—all over the place, just round the corner—like that?"

"Nothing is more probable," said the Professor, taking off his spectacles and beginning to polish them, while he muttered to himself, "I wonder what they *do* teach them at these schools."

"But what are we to do?" said Susan. She felt that the conversation was beginning to get off the point.

"My dear young lady," said the Professor, suddenly looking up with a very sharp expression at both of them, "there is one plan which no one has yet suggested and which is well worth trying."

"What's that?" said Susan.

"We might all try minding our own busi-

ness," said he. And that was the end of that conversation.

After this things were a good deal better for Lucy. Peter saw to it that Edmund stopped jeering at her, and neither she nor anyone else felt inclined to talk about the wardrobe at all. It had become a rather alarming subject. And so for a time it looked as if all the adventures were coming to an end; but that was not to be.

This house of the Professor's—which even he knew so little about—was so old and famous that people from all over England used to come and ask permission to see over it. It was the sort of house that is mentioned in guide books and even in histories; and well it might be, for all manner of stories were told about it, some of them even stranger than the one I am telling you now. And when parties of sightseers arrived and asked to see the house, the Professor always gave them permission, and Mrs. Macready, the housekeeper, showed them round, telling them about the pictures and the armor, and the rare books in the library. Mrs. Macready was not fond of children, and did not like to be interrupted when she was telling visitors all the things she knew. She had said to Susan and Peter almost on the first morning (along with a good many other instructions), "And please remember you're to keep out of the way whenever I'm taking a party over the house."

"Just as if any of us would *want* to waste half the morning trailing round with a crowd of strange grown-ups!" said Edmund, and the other three thought the same. That was how the adventures began for the second time.

A few mornings later Peter and Edmund were looking at the suit of armor and wondering if they could take it to bits when the two girls rushed into the room and said, "Look out! Here comes the Macready and a whole gang with her."

"Sharp's the word," said Peter, and all four made off through the door at the far end of the room. But when they had got out into the Green Room and beyond it, into the Library, they suddenly heard voices ahead of them, and realized that Mrs. Macready must be bringing her party of sightseers up the back stairs—instead of up the front stairs as they had expected. And after that—whether it was that they lost their heads, or that Mrs. Macready was trying to catch them, or that some magic in the house had come to life and was chasing them into Narnia—they seemed to find themselves being followed everywhere, until at last Susan said, "Oh bother those trippers! Here—let's get into the Wardrobe Room till they've passed. No one will follow us in there." But the moment they were inside they heard voices in the passage—and then someone fumbling at the door—and then they saw the handle turning.

"Quick!" said Peter, "there's nowhere else," and flung open the wardrobe. All four of them bundled inside it and sat there, panting, in the dark. Peter held the door closed but did not shut it; for, of course, he remembered, as every sensible person does, that you should never never shut yourself up in a wardrobe.

6

INTO THE FOREST

"I wish the Macready would hurry up and take all these people away," said Susan presently, "I'm getting horribly cramped."

"And what a filthy smell of camphor!" said Edmund.

"I expect the pockets of these coats are full of it," said Susan, "to keep away moths."

"There's something sticking into my back," said Peter.

"And isn't it cold?" said Susan.

"Now that you mention it, it is cold," said Peter, "and hang it all, it's wet too. What's the matter with this place? I'm sitting on something wet. It's getting wetter every minute." He struggled to his feet.

"Let's get out," said Edmund, "they've gone."

"O-o-oh!" said Susan suddenly, and everyone asked her what was the matter.

"I'm sitting against a tree," said Susan, "and look! It's getting light—over there."

"By jove, you're right," said Peter, "and look there—and there. It's trees all round. And this wet stuff is snow. Why, I do believe we've got into Lucy's wood after all."

And now there was no mistaking it, and all four children stood blinking in the daylight of a winter day. Behind them were coats hanging on pegs, in front of them were snow-covered trees.

Peter turned at once to Lucy.

"I apologize for not believing you," he said, "I'm sorry. Will you shake hands?"

"Of course," said Lucy, and did.

"And now," said Susan, "what do we do next?"

"Do?" said Peter, "why, go and explore the wood, of course."

"Ugh!" said Susan, stamping her feet, "it's pretty cold. What about putting on some of these coats?"

"They're not ours," said Peter doubtfully.

"I am sure nobody would mind," said Susan;

"it isn't as if we wanted to take them out of the house; we shan't take them even out of the wardrobe."

"I never thought of that, Su," said Peter. "Of course, now you put it that way, I see. No one could say you had bagged a coat as long as you leave it in the wardrobe where you found it. And I suppose this whole country is in the wardrobe."

They immediately carried out Susan's very sensible plan. The coats were rather too big for them so that they came down to their heels and looked more like royal robes than coats when they had put them on. But they all felt a good deal warmer and each thought the others looked better in their new getups and more suitable to the landscape.

"We can pretend we are Arctic explorers," said Lucy.

"This is going to be exciting enough without pretending," said Peter, as he began leading the way forward into the forest. There were heavy darkish clouds overhead and it looked as if there might be more snow before night.

"I say," began Edmund presently, "oughtn't we to be bearing a bit more to the left, that is, if we are aiming for the lamp-post?" He had forgotten for the moment that he must pretend never to have been in the wood before. The

moment the words were out of his mouth he realized that he had given himself away. Everyone
stopped; everyone stared at him. Peter whistled.

"So you really were here," he said, "that
time Lu said she'd met you in here—and you
made out she was telling lies."

There was a dead silence. "Well, of all
the poisonous little beasts—" said Peter, and
shrugged his shoulders and said no more. There
seemed, indeed, no more to say, and presently
the four resumed their journey; but Edmund was
saying to himself, "I'll pay you all out for this,
you pack of stuck-up, self-satisfied prigs."

"Where *are* we going anyway?" said Susan,
chiefly for the sake of changing the subject.

"I think Lu ought to be the leader," said
Peter; "goodness knows she deserves it. Where
will you take us, Lu?"

"What about going to see Mr. Tumnus?" said
Lucy. "He's the nice Faun I told you about."

Everyone agreed to this and off they went
walking briskly and stamping their feet. Lucy
proved a good leader. At first she wondered
whether she would be able to find the way, but
she recognized an odd-looking tree on one place
and a stump in another and brought them on to
where the ground became uneven and into the
little valley and at last to the very door of Mr.

Tumnus's cave. But there a terrible surprise awaited them.

The door had been wrenched off its hinges and broken to bits. Inside, the cave was dark and cold and had the damp feel and smell of a place that had not been lived in for several days. Snow had drifted in from the doorway and was heaped on the floor, mixed with something black, which turned out to be the charred sticks and ashes from the fire. Someone had apparently flung it about the room and then stamped it out. The crockery lay smashed on the floor and the picture of the Faun's father had been slashed into shreds with a knife.

"This is a pretty good washout," said Edmund; "not much good coming here."

"What is this?" said Peter, stooping down. He had just noticed a piece of paper which had

been nailed through the carpet to the floor.

"Is there anything written on it?" asked Susan.

"Yes, I think there is," answered Peter, "but I can't read it in this light. Let's get out into the open air."

They all went out in the daylight and crowded round Peter as he read out the following words:

The former occupant of these premises, the Faun Tumnus, is under arrest and awaiting his trial on a charge of High Treason against her Imperial Majesty Jadis, Queen of Narnia, Chatelaine of Cair Paravel, Empress of the Lone Islands, etc., also of comforting her said Majesty's enemies, harboring spies and fraternizing with Humans.

signed MAUGRIM, *Captain of the Secret Police,*
LONG LIVE THE QUEEN!

The children stared at each other.

"I don't know that I'm going to like this place after all," said Susan.

"Who is this Queen, Lu?" said Peter. "Do you know anything about her?"

"She isn't a real queen at all," answered Lucy; "she's a horrible witch, the White Witch. Everyone—all the wood people—hate her. She has made an enchantment over the whole country so that it is always winter here and never Christmas."

"I—I wonder if there's any point in going on," said Susan. "I mean, it doesn't seem particularly safe here and it looks as if it won't be much fun either. And it's getting colder every minute, and we've brought nothing to eat. What about just going home?"

"Oh, but we can't, we can't," said Lucy suddenly; "don't you see? We can't just go home, not after this. It is all on my account that the poor Faun has got into this trouble. He hid me from the Witch and showed me the way back. That's what it means by comforting the Queen's enemies and fraternizing with Humans. We simply must try to rescue him."

"A lot *we* could do!" said Edmund, "when we haven't even got anything to eat!"

"Shut up—you!" said Peter, who was still very angry with Edmund. "What do you think, Susan?"

"I've a horrid feeling that Lu is right," said Susan. "I don't want to go a step further and I wish we'd never come. But I think we must try to do something for Mr. Whatever-his-name-is—I mean the Faun."

"That's what I feel too," said Peter. "I'm worried about having no food with us. I'd vote for going back and getting something from the larder, only there doesn't seem to be any certainty of getting into this country again when once you've got out of it. I think we'll have to go on."

"So do I," said both the girls.

"If only we knew where the poor chap was imprisoned!" said Peter.

They were all still wondering what to do next, when Lucy said, "Look! There's a robin, with such a red breast. It's the first bird I've seen here. I say!—I wonder can birds talk in Narnia? It almost looks as if it wanted to say something to us." Then she turned to the Robin and said, "Please, can you tell us where Tumnus the Faun has been taken to?" As she said this she took a step toward the bird. It at once flew away but only as far as to the next tree. There it perched and looked at them very hard as if it understood all they had been saying. Almost without noticing that they had done so, the four children went a step or two nearer to it. At this the Robin flew away again to the next tree and once more looked at them very hard. (You couldn't have found a robin with a redder chest or a brighter eye.)

"Do you know," said Lucy, "I really believe he means us to follow him."

"I've an idea he does," said Susan. "What do you think, Peter?"

"Well, we might as well try it," answered Peter.

The Robin appeared to understand the matter thoroughly. It kept going from tree to tree, always a few yards ahead of them, but always so near that they could easily follow it. In this way it led them on, slightly downhill. Wherever the Robin alighted a little shower of snow would fall off the branch. Presently the clouds parted overhead and the winter sun came out and the snow all around them grew dazzlingly bright. They had been traveling in this way for about half an hour, with the two girls in front, when Edmund said to Peter, "if you're not still too high and mighty to talk to me, I've something to say which you'd better listen to."

"What is it?" asked Peter.

"Hush! Not so loud," said Edmund; "there's no good frightening the girls. But have you realized what we're doing?"

"What?" said Peter, lowering his voice to a whisper.

"We're following a guide we know nothing about. How do we know which side that bird is on? Why shouldn't it be leading us into a trap?"

"That's a nasty idea. Still—a robin, you know. They're good birds in all the stories I've ever read. I'm sure a robin wouldn't be on the wrong side."

"If it comes to that, which *is* the right side? How do we know that the Fauns are in the right and the Queen (yes, I know we've been *told* she's a witch) is in the wrong? We don't really know anything about either."

"The Faun saved Lucy."

"He *said* he did. But how do we know? And there's another thing too. Has anyone the least idea of the way home from here?"

"Great Scott!" said Peter, "I hadn't thought of that."

"And no chance of dinner either," said Edmund.

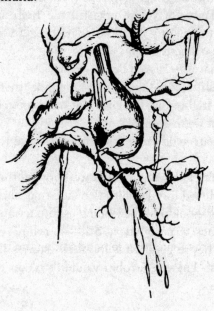

7

A DAY WITH THE
BEAVERS

While the two boys were whispering behind,
both the girls suddenly cried "Oh!" and stopped.

"The robin!" cried Lucy, "the robin. It's
flown away." And so it had—right out of sight.

"And now what are we to do?" said
Edmund, giving Peter a look which was as much
as to say "What did I tell you?"

"Sh! Look!" said Susan.

"What?" said Peter.

"There's something moving among the trees
over there to the left."

They all stared as hard as they could, and no one felt very comfortable.

"There it goes again," said Susan presently.

"I saw it that time too," said Peter. "It's still there. It's just gone behind that big tree."

"What is it?" asked Lucy, trying very hard not to sound nervous.

"Whatever it is," said Peter, "it's dodging us. It's something that doesn't want to be seen."

"Let's go home," said Susan. And then, though nobody said it out loud, everyone suddenly realized the same fact that Edmund had whispered to Peter at the end of the last chapter. They were lost.

"What's it like?" said Lucy.

"It's—it's a kind of animal," said Susan; and then, "Look! Look! Quick! There it is."

They all saw it this time, a whiskered furry face which had looked out at them from behind a tree. But this time it didn't immediately draw back. Instead, the animal put its paw against its mouth just as humans put their finger on their lips when they are signaling to you to be quiet. Then it disappeared again. The children all stood holding their breath.

A moment later the stranger came out from behind the tree, glanced all round as if it were afraid someone was watching, said "Hush," made signs to them to join it in the thicker bit

of wood where it was standing, and then once more disappeared.

"I know what it is," said Peter; "it's a beaver. I saw the tail."

"It wants us to go to it," said Susan, "and it is warning us not to make a noise."

"I know," said Peter. "The question is, are we to go to it or not? What do you think, Lu?"

"I think it's a nice beaver," said Lucy.

"Yes, but how do we *know*?" said Edmund.

"Shan't we have to risk it?" said Susan. "I mean, it's no good just standing here and I feel I want some dinner."

At this moment the Beaver again popped its head out from behind the tree and beckoned earnestly to them.

"Come on," said Peter, "let's give it a try. All

keep close together. We ought to be a match for one beaver if it turns out to be an enemy."

So the children all got close together and walked up to the tree and in behind it, and there, sure enough, they found the Beaver; but it still drew back, saying to them in a hoarse throaty whisper, "Further in, come further in. Right in here. We're not safe in the open!" Only when it had led them into a dark spot where four trees grew so close together that their boughs met and the brown earth and pine nee-

dles could be seen underfoot because no snow had been able to fall there, did it begin to talk to them.

"Are you the Sons of Adam and the Daughters of Eve?" it said.

"We're some of them," said Peter.

"S-s-s-sh!" said the Beaver, "not so loud please. We're not safe even here."

"Why, who are you afraid of?" said Peter. "There's no one here but ourselves."

"There are the trees," said the Beaver. "They're always listening. Most of them are on our side, but there *are* trees that would betray us to *her*; you know who I mean," and it nodded its head several times.

"If it comes to talking about sides," said Edmund, "how do we know you're a friend?"

"Not meaning to be rude, Mr. Beaver," added Peter, "but you see, we're strangers."

"Quite right, quite right," said the Beaver. "Here is my token." With these words it held up to them a little white object. They all looked at it in surprise, till suddenly Lucy said, "Oh, of course. It's my handkerchief—the one I gave to poor Mr. Tumnus."

"That's right," said the Beaver. "Poor fellow, he got wind of the arrest before it actually happened and handed this over to me. He said that if anything happened to him I must meet you here and take you on to—" Here the Beaver's voice sank into silence and it gave one or two very mysterious nods. Then signaling to the children to stand as close around it as they possibly could, so that their faces were actually tickled by its whiskers, it added in a low whisper—

"They say Aslan is on the move—perhaps has already landed."

And now a very curious thing happened. None of the children knew who Aslan was any more than you do; but the moment the Beaver had spoken these words everyone felt quite different. Perhaps it has sometimes happened to you in a dream that someone says something which you don't understand but in the dream it feels as if it had some enormous meaning—either a terrifying one which turns the whole dream into a nightmare or else a lovely meaning too lovely to put into words, which makes the dream so beautiful that you remember it all your life and are always wishing you could get into that dream again. It was like that now. At the name of Aslan each one of the children felt something jump in its inside. Edmund felt a sensation of mysterious horror. Peter felt suddenly brave and adventurous. Susan felt as if some delicious smell or some delightful strain of music had just floated by her. And Lucy got the feeling you have when you wake up in the morning and realize that it is the beginning of the holidays or the beginning of summer.

"And what about Mr. Tumnus?" said Lucy; "where is he?"

"S-s-s-sh," said the Beaver, "not here. I must bring you where we can have a real talk and also dinner."

No one except Edmund felt any difficulty about trusting the beaver now, and everyone, including Edmund, was very glad to hear the word "dinner." They therefore all hurried along behind their new friend who led them at a surprisingly quick pace, and always in the thickest parts of the forest, for over an hour. Everyone was feeling very tired and very hungry when suddenly the trees began to get thinner in front of them and the ground to fall steeply downhill. A minute later they came out under the open sky (the sun was still shining) and found themselves looking down on a fine sight.

They were standing on the edge of a steep, narrow valley at the bottom of which ran—at least it would have been running if it hadn't been frozen—a fairly large river. Just below them a dam had been built across this river, and when they saw it everyone suddenly remembered that of course beavers are always making dams and felt quite sure that Mr. Beaver had made this one. They also noticed that he now had a sort of modest expression on his face—the sort of look people have when you are visiting a garden they've made or reading a story they've written. So it was only common politeness when Susan said, "What a lovely dam!" And Mr. Beaver didn't say "Hush" this time but "Merely a trifle! Merely a trifle! And it isn't really finished!"

Above the dam there was what ought to have been a deep pool but was now, of course, a level floor of dark green ice. And below the dam, much lower down, was more ice, but instead of being smooth this was all frozen into the foamy and wavy shapes in which the water had been rushing along at the very moment when the frost came. And where the water had been trickling over and spurting through the dam there was now a glittering wall of icicles, as if the side of the dam had been covered all over with flowers and wreaths and festoons of the purest sugar. And out in the middle, and partly on top of the dam was a funny little house shaped rather like an enormous beehive and from a hole in the roof smoke was going up, so that when you saw it (especially if you were hungry) you at once thought of cooking and became hungrier than you were before.

That was what the others chiefly noticed, but Edmund noticed something else. A little

lower down the river there was another small river which came down another small valley to join it. And looking up that valley, Edmund could see two small hills, and he was almost sure they were the two hills which the White Witch had pointed out to him when he parted from her at the lamp-post that other day. And then between them, he thought, must be her palace, only a mile off or less. And he thought about Turkish Delight and about being a King ("And I wonder how Peter will like that?" he asked himself) and horrible ideas came into his head.

"Here we are," said Mr. Beaver, "and it looks as if Mrs. Beaver is expecting us. I'll lead the way. But be careful and don't slip."

The top of the dam was wide enough to walk on, though not (for humans) a very nice place to walk because it was covered with ice, and though the frozen pool was level with it on one side, there was a nasty drop to the lower river on the other. Along this route Mr. Beaver led them in single file right out to the middle where they could look a long way up the river and a long way down it. And when they had reached the middle they were at the door of the house.

"Here we are, Mrs. Beaver," said Mr. Beaver, "I've found them. Here are the Sons and Daughters of Adam and Eve"—and they all went in.

The first thing Lucy noticed as she went in was a burring sound, and the first thing she saw was a kind-looking old she-beaver sitting in the corner with a thread in her mouth working busily at her sewing machine, and it was from it that the sound came. She stopped her work and got up as soon as the children came in.

"So you've come at last!" she said, holding out both her wrinkled old paws. "At last! To think that ever I should live to see this day! The potatoes are on boiling and the kettle's singing and I daresay, Mr. Beaver, you'll get us some fish."

"That I will," said Mr. Beaver, and he went

out of the house (Peter went with him), and across the ice of the deep pool to where he had a little hole in the ice which he kept open every day with his hatchet. They took a pail with them. Mr. Beaver sat down quietly at the edge of the hole (he didn't seem to mind it being so chilly), looked hard into it, then suddenly shot in his paw, and before you could say Jack Robinson had whisked out a beautiful trout. Then he did it all over again until they had a fine catch of fish.

Meanwhile the girls were helping Mrs. Beaver to fill the kettle and lay the table and cut

the bread and put the plates in the oven to heat and draw a huge jug of beer for Mr. Beaver from a barrel which stood in one corner of the house, and to put on the frying-pan and get the dripping hot. Lucy thought the Beavers had a very snug little home though it was not at all like Mr. Tumnus's cave. There were no books or pictures, and instead of beds there were bunks, like on board ship, built into the wall. And there were hams and strings of onions hanging from the roof, and against the walls were gum boots and oilskins and hatchets and pairs of shears and spades and trowels and things for carrying mortar in and fishing-rods and fishing-nets and sacks. And the cloth on the table, though very clean, was very rough.

Just as the frying-pan was nicely hissing Peter and Mr. Beaver came in with the fish which Mr. Beaver had already opened with his knife and cleaned out in the open air. You can think how good the new-caught fish smelled while they were frying and how the hungry children longed for them to be done and how very much hungrier still they had become before Mr. Beaver said, "Now we're nearly ready." Susan drained the potatoes and then put them all back in the empty pot to dry on the side of the range while Lucy was helping Mrs. Beaver to dish up the trout, so that in a very few minutes everyone was drawing up their stools (it was all three-legged stools in the Beavers' house except for Mrs. Beaver's own special rocking chair beside the fire) and preparing to enjoy themselves. There was a jug of creamy milk for the children (Mr. Beaver stuck to beer) and a great big lump of deep yellow butter in the middle of the table

from which everyone took as much as he wanted to go with his potatoes, and all the children thought—and I agree with them—that there's nothing to beat good freshwater fish if you eat it when it has been alive half an hour ago and has come out of the pan half a minute ago. And when they had finished the fish Mrs. Beaver brought unexpectedly out of the oven a great and gloriously sticky marmalade roll, steaming hot, and at the same time moved the kettle onto the fire, so that when they had finished the marmalade roll the tea was made and ready to be poured out. And when each person had got his (or her) cup of tea, each person shoved back his (or her) stool so as to be able to lean against the wall and gave a long sigh of contentment.

"And now," said Mr. Beaver, pushing away his empty beer mug and pulling his cup of tea toward him, "if you'll just wait till I've got my pipe lit up and going nicely—why, now we can get to business. It's snowing again," he added, cocking his eye at the window. "That's all the better, because it means we shan't have any visitors; and if anyone should have been trying to follow you, why he won't find any tracks."

8

WHAT HAPPENED
AFTER DINNER

"And now," said Lucy, "do please tell us what's happened to Mr. Tumnus."

"Ah, that's bad," said Mr. Beaver, shaking his head. "That's a very, very bad business. There's no doubt he was taken off by the police. I got that from a bird who saw it done."

"But where's he been taken to?" asked Lucy.

"Well, they were heading northward when they were last seen and we all know what that means."

"No, *we* don't," said Susan. Mr. Beaver shook his head in a very gloomy fashion.

"I'm afraid it means they were taking him to her House," he said.

"But what'll they do to him, Mr. Beaver?" gasped Lucy.

"Well," said Mr. Beaver, "you can't exactly say for sure. But there's not many taken in there that ever comes out again. Statues. All full of statues they say it is—in the courtyard and up the stairs and in the hall. People she's turned"— (he paused and shuddered) "turned into stone."

"But, Mr. Beaver," said Lucy, "can't we—I mean we *must* do something to save him. It's too dreadful and it's all on my account."

"I don't doubt you'd save him if you could, dearie," said Mrs. Beaver, "but you've no chance of getting into that House against her will and ever coming out alive."

"Couldn't we have some stratagem?" said Peter. "I mean couldn't we dress up as something, or pretend to be—oh, peddlers or anything—or watch till she was gone out—or—oh, hang it all, there must be *some* way. This Faun saved my sister at his own risk, Mr. Beaver. We can't just leave him to be—to be—to have that done to him."

"It's no good, Son of Adam," said Mr. Beaver, "no good *your* trying, of all people. But now that Aslan is on the move—"

"Oh, yes! Tell us about Aslan!" said several voices at once; for once again that strange feeling—like the first signs of spring, like good news, had come over them.

"Who is Aslan?" asked Susan.

"Aslan?" said Mr. Beaver. "Why, don't you know? He's the King. He's the Lord of the whole wood, but not often here, you understand. Never in my time or my father's time. But the word has reached us that he has come back. He is in Narnia at this moment. He'll settle the White Queen all right. It is he, not you, that will save Mr. Tumnus."

"She won't turn him into stone too?" said Edmund.

"Lord love you, Son of Adam, what a simple thing to say!" answered Mr. Beaver with a great laugh. "Turn *him* into stone? If she can stand on her two feet and look him in the face it'll be the most she can do and more than I expect of her. No, no. He'll put all to rights as it says in an old rhyme in these parts:

Wrong will be right, when Aslan comes in sight,
At the sound of his roar, sorrows will be no more,
When he bares his teeth, winter meets its death,
And when he shakes his mane, we shall have
   spring again.

You'll understand when you see him."

"But shall we see him?" asked Susan.

"Why, Daughter of Eve, that's what I brought you here for. I'm to lead you where you shall meet him," said Mr. Beaver.

"Is—is he a man?" asked Lucy.

"Aslan a man!" said Mr. Beaver sternly. "Certainly not. I tell you he is the King of the wood and the son of the great Emperor-beyond-the-Sea. Don't you know who is the King of Beasts? Aslan is a lion—*the* Lion, the great Lion."

"Ooh!" said Susan, "I'd thought he was a man. Is he—quite safe? I shall feel rather nervous about meeting a lion."

"That you will, dearie, and no mistake," said Mrs. Beaver; "if there's anyone who can appear before Aslan without their knees knocking, they're either braver than most or else just silly."

"Then he isn't safe?" said Lucy.

"Safe?" said Mr. Beaver; "don't you hear what Mrs. Beaver tells you? Who said anything about safe? 'Course he isn't safe. But he's good. He's the King, I tell you."

"I'm longing to see him," said Peter, "even if I do feel frightened when it comes to the point."

"That's right, Son of Adam," said Mr. Beaver, bringing his paw down on the table with a crash that made all the cups and saucers rattle.

"And so you shall. Word has been sent that you *are* to meet him, tomorrow if you can, at the Stone Table."

"Where's that?" said Lucy.

"I'll show you," said Mr. Beaver. "It's down the river, a good step from here. I'll take you to it!"

"But meanwhile what about poor Mr. Tumnus?" said Lucy.

"The quickest way you can help him is by going to meet Aslan," said Mr. Beaver, "once he's with us, then we can begin doing things. Not that we don't need you too. For that's another of the old rhymes:

> When Adam's flesh and Adam's bone
> Sits at Cair Paravel in throne,
> The evil time will be over and done.

So things must be drawing near their end now he's come and you've come. We've heard of Aslan coming into these parts before—long ago, nobody can say when. But there's never been any of your race here before."

"That's what I don't understand, Mr. Beaver," said Peter, "I mean isn't the Witch herself human?"

"She'd like us to believe it," said Mr. Beaver, "and it's on that that she bases her claim to be

Queen. But she's no Daughter of Eve. She comes of your father Adam's"—(here Mr. Beaver bowed) "your father Adam's first wife, her they called Lilith. And she was one of the Jinn. That's what she comes from on one side. And on the other she comes of the giants. No, no, there isn't a drop of real human blood in the Witch."

"That's why she's bad all through, Mr. Beaver," said Mrs. Beaver.

"True enough, Mrs. Beaver," replied he, "there may be two views about humans (meaning no offense to the present company). But there's no two views about things that look like humans and aren't."

"I've known good Dwarfs," said Mrs. Beaver.

"So've I, now you come to speak of it," said her husband, "but precious few, and they were the ones least like men. But in general, take my advice, when you meet anything that's going to be human and isn't yet, or used to be human once and isn't now, or ought to be human and isn't, you keep your eyes on it and feel for your hatchet. And that's why the Witch is always on the lookout for any humans in Narnia. She's been watching for you this many a year, and if she knew there were four of you she'd be more dangerous still."

"What's that to do with it?" asked Peter.

"Because of another prophecy," said Mr. Beaver. "Down at Cair Paravel—that's the castle on the seacoast down at the mouth of this river which ought to be the capital of the whole country if all was as it should be—down at Cair Paravel there are four thrones and it's a saying in Narnia time out of mind that when two Sons of Adam and two Daughters of Eve sit in those four thrones, then it will be the end not only of the White Witch's reign but of her life, and that is why we had to be so cautious as we came along, for if she knew about you four, your lives wouldn't be worth a shake of my whiskers!"

All the children had been attending so hard to what Mr. Beaver was telling them that they had noticed nothing else for a long time. Then during the moment of silence that followed his last remark, Lucy suddenly said:

"I say—where's Edmund?"

There was a dreadful pause, and then everyone began asking "Who saw him last? How long has he been missing? Is he outside?" and then all rushed to the door and looked out. The snow was falling thickly and steadily, the green ice of the pool had vanished under a thick white blanket, and from where the little house stood in the center of the dam you could hardly see either bank. Out they went, plunging well over their ankles into the soft new snow, and went round

the house in every direction. "Edmund! Edmund!" they called till they were hoarse. But the silently falling snow seemed to muffle their voices and there was not even an echo in answer.

"How perfectly dreadful!" said Susan as they at last came back in despair. "Oh, how I wish we'd never come."

"What on earth are we to do, Mr. Beaver?" said Peter.

"Do?" said Mr. Beaver, who was already putting on his snow-boots, "do? We must be off at once. We haven't a moment to spare!"

"We'd better divide into four search parties," said Peter, "and all go in different directions. Whoever finds him must come back here at once and——"

"Search parties, Son of Adam?" said Mr.

Beaver; "what for?"

"Why, to look for Edmund, of course!"

"There's no point in looking for him," said Mr. Beaver.

"What do you mean?" said Susan. "He can't be far away yet. And we've got to find him. What do you mean when you say there's no use looking for him?"

"The reason there's no use looking," said Mr. Beaver, "is that we know already where he's gone!" Everyone stared in amazement. "Don't you understand?" said Mr. Beaver. "He's gone to *her*, to the White Witch. He has betrayed us all."

"Oh, surely—oh, really!" said Susan; "he can't have done that."

"Can't he?" said Mr. Beaver, looking very hard at the three children, and everything they wanted to say died on their lips, for each felt suddenly quite certain inside that this was exactly what Edmund had done.

"But will he know the way?" said Peter.

"Has he been in this country before?" asked Mr. Beaver. "Has he ever been here alone?"

"Yes," said Lucy, almost in a whisper. "I'm afraid he has."

"And did he tell you what he'd done or who he'd met?"

"Well, no, he didn't," said Lucy.

"Then mark my words," said Mr. Beaver, "he has already met the White Witch and joined her side, and been told where she lives. I didn't like to mention it before (he being your brother and all) but the moment I set eyes on that brother of yours I said to myself 'Treacherous.' He had the look of one who has been with the Witch and eaten her food. You can always tell them if you've lived long in Narnia; something about their eyes."

"All the same," said Peter in a rather choking sort of voice, "we'll still have to go and look for him. He is our brother after all, even if he is rather a little beast. And he's only a kid."

"Go to the Witch's House?" said Mrs. Beaver. "Don't you see that the only chance of saving either him or yourselves is to keep away from her?"

"How do you mean?" said Lucy.

"Why, all she wants is to get all four of you (she's thinking all the time of those four thrones at Cair Paravel). Once you were all four inside her House her job would be done—and there'd be four new statues in her collection before you'd had time to speak. But she'll keep him alive as long as he's the only one she's got, because she'll want to use him as a decoy; as bait to catch the rest of you with."

"Oh, can *no* one help us?" wailed Lucy.

"Only Aslan," said Mr. Beaver, "we must go on and meet him. That's our only chance now."

"It seems to me, my dears," said Mrs. Beaver, "that it is very important to know just *when* he slipped away. How much he can tell her depends on how much he heard. For instance, had we started talking of Aslan before he left? If not, then we may do very well, for she won't know that Aslan has come to Narnia, or that we are meeting him, and will be quite off her guard as far as *that* is concerned."

"I don't remember his being here when we were talking about Aslan—" began Peter, but Lucy interrupted him.

"Oh yes, he was," she said miserably; "don't you remember, it was he who asked whether the Witch couldn't turn Aslan into stone too?"

"So he did, by Jove," said Peter; "just the sort of thing he would say, too!"

"Worse and worse," said Mr. Beaver, "and the next thing is this. Was he still here when I told you that the place for meeting Aslan was the Stone Table?"

And of course no one knew the answer to this question.

"Because, if he was," continued Mr. Beaver, "then she'll simply sledge down in that direction and get between us and the Stone Table and catch us on our way down. In fact we shall be cut off from Aslan."

"But that isn't what she'll do first," said Mrs. Beaver, "not if I know her. The moment that Edmund tells her that we're all here she'll set out to catch us this very night, and if he's been gone about half an hour, she'll be here in about another twenty minutes."

"You're right, Mrs. Beaver," said her husband, "we must all get away from here. There's not a moment to lose."

IN THE WITCH'S HOUSE

And now of course you want to know what had happened to Edmund. He had eaten his share of the dinner, but he hadn't really enjoyed it because he was thinking all the time about Turkish Delight—and there's nothing that spoils the taste of good ordinary food half so much as the memory of bad magic food. And he had heard the conversation, and hadn't enjoyed it much either, because he kept on thinking that the others were taking no notice of him and trying to give him the cold shoulder. They weren't, but he imagined it. And then he had listened until Mr. Beaver told them about Aslan and until he had heard the whole arrangement for meeting Aslan at the Stone Table. It was then that he began very quietly to edge himself under the curtain which hung over the door. For the mention of Aslan gave him a mysterious and horrible feeling just as it gave the others a mysterious and lovely feeling.

Just as Mr. Beaver had been repeating the rhyme about *Adam's flesh and Adam's bone* Edmund had been very quietly turning the doorhandle; and just before Mr. Beaver had begun telling them that the White Witch wasn't really human at all but half a Jinn and half a giantess, Edmund had got outside into the snow and cautiously closed the door behind him.

You mustn't think that even now Edmund was quite so bad that he actually wanted his brother and sisters to be turned into stone. He did want Turkish Delight and to be a Prince (and later a King) and to pay Peter out for calling him a beast. As for what the Witch would do with the others, he didn't want her to be particularly nice to them—certainly not to put them on the same level as himself; but he managed to believe, or to pretend he believed, that she wouldn't do anything very bad to them, "Because," he said to himself, "all these people who say nasty things about her are her enemies and probably half of it isn't true. She was jolly nice to me, anyway, much nicer than they are. I expect she is the rightful Queen really. Anyway, she'll be better than that awful Aslan!" At least, that was the excuse he made in his own mind for what he was doing. It wasn't a very good excuse, however, for deep down inside him he really knew that the White Witch was bad and cruel.

The first thing he realized when he got outside and found the snow falling all round him, was that he had left his coat behind in the Beavers' house. And of course there was no chance of going back to get it now. The next thing he realized was that the daylight was almost gone, for it had been nearly three o'clock when they sat down to dinner and the winter days were short. He hadn't reckoned on this; but he had to make the best of it. So he turned up his collar and shuffled across the top of the dam (luckily it wasn't so slippery since the snow had fallen) to the far side of the river.

It was pretty bad when he reached the far side. It was growing darker every minute and what with that and the snowflakes swirling all round him he could hardly see three feet ahead. And then too there was no road. He kept slipping into deep drifts of snow, and skidding on frozen puddles, and tripping over fallen tree-trunks, and sliding down steep banks, and

barking his shins against rocks, till he was wet and cold and bruised all over. The silence and the loneliness were dreadful. In fact I really think he might have given up the whole plan and gone back and owned up and made friends with the others, if he hadn't happened to say to himself, "When I'm King of Narnia the first thing I shall do will be to make some decent roads." And of course that set him off thinking about being a King and all the other things he would do and this cheered him up a good deal. He had just settled in his mind what sort of palace he would have and how many cars and all about his private cinema and where the principal railways would run and what laws he would make against beavers and dams and was putting the finishing touches to some schemes for keeping Peter in his place, when the weather changed. First the snow stopped. Then a wind sprang up and it became freezing cold. Finally, the clouds rolled away and the moon came out. It was a full moon and, shining on all that snow, it made everything almost as bright as day—only the shadows were rather confusing.

He would never have found his way if the moon hadn't come out by the time he got to the other river—you remember he had seen (when they first arrived at the Beavers') a smaller river flowing into the great one lower down. He now reached this and turned to follow it up. But the little valley down which it came was much steeper and rockier than the one he had just left and much overgrown with bushes, so that he could not have managed it at all in the dark. Even as it was, he got wet through for he had to stoop under branches and great loads of snow came sliding off onto his back. And every time this happened he thought more and more how he hated Peter—just as if all this had been Peter's fault.

But at last he came to a part where it was more level and the valley opened out. And there, on the other side of the river, quite close to him, in the middle of a little plain between two hills, he saw what must be the White Witch's House. And the moon was shining brighter than ever. The House was really a small castle. It seemed to be all towers; little towers

with long pointed spires on them, sharp as needles. They looked like huge dunce's caps or sorcerer's caps. And they shone in the moonlight and their long shadows looked strange on the snow. Edmund began to be afraid of the House.

But it was too late to think of turning back now. He crossed the river on the ice and walked up to the House. There was nothing stirring; not the slightest sound anywhere. Even his own feet made no noise on the deep newly fallen snow. He walked on and on, past corner after corner of the House, and past turret after turret to find the door. He had to go right round to the far side before he found it. It was a huge arch but the great iron gates stood wide open.

Edmund crept up to the arch and looked inside into the courtyard, and there he saw a sight that nearly made his heart stop beating. Just inside the gate, with the moonlight shining on it, stood an enormous lion crouched as if it was ready to spring. And Edmund stood in the shadow of the arch, afraid to go on and afraid to go back, with his knees knocking together. He stood there so long that his teeth would have been chattering with cold even if they had not been chattering with fear. How long this really lasted I don't know, but it seemed to Edmund to last for hours.

Then at last he began to wonder why the lion was standing so still—for it hadn't moved one inch since he first set eyes on it. Edmund now ventured a little nearer, still keeping in the shadow of the arch as much as he could. He now saw from the way the lion was standing that it couldn't have been looking at him at all. ("But supposing it turns its head?" thought Edmund.) In fact it was staring at something else—namely a little dwarf who stood with his back to it about four feet away. "Aha!" thought Edmund. "When it springs at the dwarf then will be my chance to escape." But still the lion never moved, nor did the dwarf. And now at last Edmund remembered what the others had said about the White Witch turning people into stone. Perhaps this was only a stone lion. And as soon as he had

thought of that he noticed that the lion's back and the top of its head were covered with snow. Of course it must be only a statue! No living animal would have let itself get covered with snow. Then very slowly and with his heart beating as if it would burst, Edmund ventured to go up to the lion. Even now he hardly dared to touch it, but at last he put out his hand, very quickly, and did. It was cold stone. He had been frightened of a mere statue!

The relief which Edmund felt was so great that in spite of the cold he suddenly got warm all over right down to his toes, and at the same time there came into his head what seemed a perfectly lovely idea. "Probably," he thought, "this is the great Lion Aslan that they were all talking about. She's caught him already and turned him into stone. So *that's* the end of all their fine ideas about him! Pooh! Who's afraid of Aslan?"

And he stood there gloating over the stone lion, and presently he did something very silly and childish. He took a stump of lead pencil out of his pocket and scribbled a moustache on the lion's upper lip and then a pair of spectacles on its eyes. Then he said, "Yah! Silly old Aslan! How do you like being a stone? You thought yourself mighty fine, didn't you?" But in spite of the scribbles on it the face of the great stone beast still looked so terrible, and sad, and noble, staring up in the moonlight, that Edmund didn't really get any fun out of jeering at it. He turned away and began to cross the courtyard.

As he got into the middle of it he saw that there were dozens of statues all about—standing here and there rather as the pieces stand on a chessboard when it is halfway through the game. There were stone satyrs, and stone wolves, and bears and foxes and cat-a-mountains of stone. There were lovely stone

shapes that looked like women but who were really the spirits of trees. There was the great shape of a centaur and a winged horse and a long lithe creature that Edmund took to be a dragon. They all looked so strange standing there perfectly life-like and also perfectly still, in the bright cold moonlight, that it was eerie work crossing the courtyard. Right in the very middle stood a huge shape like a man, but as tall as a tree, with a fierce face and a shaggy beard and a great club in its right hand. Even though he knew that it was only a stone giant and not a live one, Edmund did not like going past it.

He now saw that there was a dim light showing from a doorway on the far side of the courtyard. He went to it, there was a flight of stone steps going up to an open door. Edmund went up them. Across the threshold lay a great wolf.

"It's all right, it's all right," he kept saying to himself; "it's only a stone wolf. It can't hurt me," and he raised his leg to step over it. Instantly the huge creature rose, with all the hair bristling along its back, opened a great, red mouth and said in a growling voice:

"Who's there? Who's there? Stand still, stranger, and tell me who you are."

"If you please, sir," said Edmund, trembling so that he could hardly speak, "my name is

Edmund, and I'm the Son of Adam that Her Majesty met in the wood the other day and I've come to bring her the news that my brother and sisters are now in Narnia—quite close, in the Beavers' house. She—she wanted to see them."

"I will tell Her Majesty," said the Wolf. "Meanwhile, stand still on the threshold, as you value your life." Then it vanished into the house.

Edmund stood and waited, his fingers aching with cold and his heart pounding in his chest, and presently the gray wolf, Maugrim, the Chief of the Witch's Secret Police, came bounding back and said, "Come in! Come in! Fortunate favorite of the Queen—or else not so fortunate."

And Edmund went in, taking great care not to tread on the Wolf's paws.

He found himself in a long gloomy hall with many pillars, full, as the courtyard had been, of statues. The one nearest the door was a little faun with a very sad expression on its face, and Edmund couldn't help wondering if this might be Lucy's friend. The only light came from a single lamp and close beside this sat the White Witch.

"I'm come, your Majesty," said Edmund, rushing eagerly forward.

"How dare you come alone?" said the Witch

in a terrible voice. "Did I not tell you to bring the others with you?"

"Please, your Majesty," said Edmund, "I've done the best I can. I've brought them quite close. They're in the little house on top of the dam just up the river—with Mr. and Mrs. Beaver."

A slow cruel smile came over the Witch's face.

"Is this all your news?" she asked.

"No, your Majesty," said Edmund, and proceeded to tell her all he had heard before leaving the Beavers' house.

"What! Aslan?" cried the Queen, "Aslan! Is this true? If I find you have lied to me—"

"Please, I'm only repeating what they said," stammered Edmund.

But the Queen, who was no longer attending to him, clapped her hands. Instantly the same dwarf whom Edmund had seen with her before appeared.

"Make ready our sledge," ordered the Witch, "and use the harness without bells."

THE SPELL BEGINS
TO BREAK

Now we must go back to Mr. and Mrs. Beaver and the three other children. As soon as Mr. Beaver said, "There's no time to lose," everyone began bundling themselves into coats, except Mrs. Beaver, who started picking up sacks and laying them on the table and said: "Now, Mr. Beaver, just reach down that ham. And here's a packet of tea, and there's sugar, and some matches. And if someone will get two or three loaves out of the crock over there in the corner."

"What *are* you doing, Mrs. Beaver?" exclaimed Susan.

"Packing a load for each of us, dearie," said Mrs. Beaver very coolly. "You didn't think we'd set out on a journey with nothing to eat, did you?"

"But we haven't time!" said Susan, buttoning the collar of her coat. "She may be here any minute."

"That's what I say," chimed in Mr. Beaver.

"Get along with you all," said his wife. "Think it over, Mr. Beaver. She can't be here for quarter of an hour at least."

"But don't we want as big a start as we can possibly get," said Peter, "if we're to reach the Stone Table before her?"

"You've got to remember *that*, Mrs. Beaver," said Susan. "As soon as she has looked in here and finds we're gone she'll be off at top speed."

"That she will," said Mrs. Beaver. "But we can't get there before her whatever we do, for she'll be on a sledge and we'll be walking."

"Then—have we no hope?" said Susan.

"Now don't you get fussing, there's a dear," said Mrs. Beaver, "but just get half a dozen clean handkerchiefs out of the drawer. 'Course we've got a hope. We can't get there *before* her but we can keep under cover and go by ways she won't expect and perhaps we'll get through."

"That's true enough, Mrs. Beaver," said her husband. "But it's time we were out of this."

"And don't *you* start fussing either, Mr. Beaver," said his wife. "There. That's better. There's five loads and the smallest for the smallest of us: that's you, my dear," she added, looking at Lucy.

"Oh, do please come on," said Lucy.

"Well, I'm nearly ready now," answered Mrs. Beaver at last, allowing her husband to help her into her snow-boots. "I suppose the sewing machine's too heavy to bring?"

"Yes. It *is*," said Mr. Beaver. "A great deal too heavy. And you don't think you'll be able to use it while we're on the run, I suppose?"

"I can't abide the thought of that Witch fiddling with it," said Mrs. Beaver, "and breaking it or stealing it, as likely as not."

"Oh, please, please, please, do hurry!" said

the three children. And so at last they all got outside and Mr. Beaver locked the door ("It'll delay her a bit," he said) and they set off, all carrying their loads over their shoulders.

The snow had stopped and the moon had come out when they began their journey. They went in single file—first Mr. Beaver, then Lucy, then Peter, then Susan, and Mrs. Beaver last of all. Mr. Beaver led them across the dam and on to the right bank of the river and then along a very rough sort of path among the trees right down by the river-bank. The sides of the valley, shining in the moonlight, towered up far above them on either hand. "Best keep down here as much as possible," he said. "She'll have to keep to the top, for you couldn't bring a sledge down here."

It would have been a pretty enough scene to look at it through a window from a comfortable armchair; and even as things were, Lucy enjoyed it at first. But as they went on walking and walking—and walking—and as the sack she was carrying felt heavier and heavier, she began to wonder how she was going to keep up at all. And she stopped looking at the dazzling brightness of the frozen river with all its waterfalls of ice and at the white masses of the tree-tops and the great glaring moon and the countless stars and could only watch the little short legs of Mr. Beaver going pad-pad-pad-pad through the snow in front of her as if they were never going to stop. Then the moon disappeared and the snow began to fall once more. And at last Lucy was so tired that she was almost asleep and walking at the same time when suddenly she found that Mr. Beaver had turned away from the river-bank to the right and was leading them steeply uphill into the very thickest bushes. And then as she came fully awake she found that Mr. Beaver was just vanishing into a little hole in the bank which had been almost hidden under the bushes until you were quite on top of it. In fact, by the time she realized what was happening, only his short flat tail was showing.

Lucy immediately stooped down and crawled in after him. Then she heard noises of scrambling and puffing and panting behind her and in a moment all five of them were inside.

"Wherever is this?" said Peter's voice, sounding tired and pale in the darkness. (I hope you know what I mean by a voice sounding pale.)

"It's an old hiding-place for beavers in bad times," said Mr. Beaver, "and a great secret. It's not much of a place but we must get a few hours' sleep."

"If you hadn't all been in such a plaguey fuss when we were starting, I'd have brought some pillows," said Mrs. Beaver.

It wasn't nearly such a nice cave as Mr. Tumnus's, Lucy thought—just a hole in the ground but dry and earthy. It was very small so that when they all lay down they were all a bundle of clothes together, and what with that and being warmed up by their long walk they were really rather snug. If only the floor of the cave had been a little smoother! Then Mrs. Beaver handed round in the dark a little flask out of which everyone drank something—it made one cough and splutter a little and stung the throat, but it also made you feel deliciously warm after you'd swallowed it—and everyone went straight to sleep.

It seemed to Lucy only the next minute (though really it was hours and hours later) when she woke up feeling a little cold and dreadfully stiff and thinking how she would like a hot bath. Then she felt a set of long whiskers tickling her cheek and saw the cold daylight coming in through the mouth of the cave. But immediately after that she was very wide awake indeed, and so was everyone else. In fact they were all sitting up with their mouths and eyes wide open listening to a sound which was the very sound they'd all been thinking of (and sometimes imagining they heard) during their walk last night. It was a sound of jingling bells.

Mr. Beaver was out of the cave like a flash the moment he heard it. Perhaps you think, as Lucy thought for a moment, that this was a very silly thing to do? But it was really a very sensible one. He knew he could scramble to the top of the bank among bushes and brambles without being seen; and he wanted above all things to see which way the Witch's sledge went. The others all sat in the cave waiting and wondering. They waited nearly five minutes. Then they heard something that frightened them very much. They heard voices. "Oh," thought Lucy, "he's been seen. She's caught him!" Great was their surprise when a little later, they heard Mr. Beaver's voice calling to them from just outside the cave.

"It's all right," he was shouting. "Come out, Mrs. Beaver. Come out, Sons and Daughters of Adam. It's all right! It isn't *Her*!" This was bad grammar of course, but that is how beavers talk when they are excited; I mean, in Narnia—in our world they usually don't talk at all.

So Mrs. Beaver and the children came bundling out of the cave, all blinking in the daylight, and with earth all over them, and looking very frowsty and unbrushed and uncombed and with the sleep in their eyes.

"Come on!" cried Mr. Beaver, who was almost dancing with delight. "Come and see! This is a nasty knock for the Witch! It looks as if her power is already crumbling."

"What *do* you mean, Mr. Beaver?" panted Peter as they all scrambled up the steep bank of the valley together.

"Didn't I tell you," answered Mr. Beaver, "that she'd made it always winter and never Christmas? Didn't I tell you? Well, just come and see!"

And then they were all at the top and did see.

It *was* a sledge, and it *was* reindeer with bells on their harness. But they were far bigger than the Witch's reindeer, and they were not white but brown. And on the sledge sat a person whom everyone knew the moment they set eyes on him. He was a huge man in a bright red robe (bright as hollyberries) with a hood that had fur inside it and a great white beard that fell like a foamy waterfall over his chest. Everyone knew him because, though you see people of his sort only in Narnia, you see pictures of them and hear them talked about even in our world— the world on this side of the wardrobe door. But when you really see them in Narnia it is rather different. Some of the pictures of Father Christmas in our world make him look only funny and jolly. But now that the children actually stood looking at him they didn't find it quite like that. He was so big, and so glad, and so real, that they all became quite still. They felt very glad, but also solemn.

"I've come at last," said he. "She has kept me out for a long time, but I have got in at last. Aslan is on the move. The Witch's magic is weakening."

And Lucy felt running through her that deep shiver of gladness which you only get if you are being solemn and still.

"And now," said Father Christmas, "for your presents. There is a new and better sewing machine for you, Mrs. Beaver. I will drop it in your house as I pass."

"If you please, sir," said Mrs. Beaver, making a curtsey. "It's locked up."

"Locks and bolts make no difference to me," said Father Christmas. "And as for you, Mr. Beaver, when you get home you will find your dam finished and mended and all the leaks stopped and a new sluice-gate fitted."

Mr. Beaver was so pleased that he opened his mouth very wide and then found he couldn't say anything at all.

"Peter, Adam's Son," said Father Christmas.

"Here, sir," said Peter.

"These are your presents," was the answer,

"and they are tools not toys. The time to use them is perhaps near at hand. Bear them well." With these words he handed to Peter a shield and a sword. The shield was the color of silver and across it there ramped a red lion, as bright as a ripe strawberry at the moment when you pick it. The hilt of the sword was of gold and it had a sheath and a sword belt and everything it needed, and it was just the right size and weight for Peter to use. Peter was silent and solemn as he received these gifts, for he felt they were a very serious kind of present.

"Susan, Eve's Daughter," said Father Christmas. "These are for you," and he handed her a bow and a quiver full of arrows and a little ivory horn. "You must use the bow only in great need," he said, "for I do not mean you to fight in the battle. It does not easily miss. And when you put this horn to your lips and blow it, then, wherever you are, I think help of some kind will come to you."

Last of all he said, "Lucy, Eve's Daughter," and Lucy came forward. He gave her a little bottle of what looked like glass (but people said afterward that it was made of diamond) and a small dagger. "In this bottle," he said, "there is a cordial made of the juice of one of the fire-flowers that grow in the mountains of the sun. If you or any of your friends is hurt, a few drops of this will restore them. And the dagger is to defend yourself at great need. For you also are not to be in the battle."

"Why, sir?" said Lucy. "I think—I don't know—but I think I could be brave enough."

"That is not the point," he said. "But battles are ugly when women fight. And now"—here he suddenly looked less grave—"here is something for the moment for you all!" and he brought out (I suppose from the big bag at his back, but nobody quite saw him do it) a large tray containing five cups and saucers, a bowl of lump sugar, a jug of cream, and a great big teapot all sizzling and piping hot. Then he cried out "Merry Christmas! Long live the true King!" and cracked his whip, and he and the reindeer and the sledge and all were out of sight before anyone realized that they had started.

Peter had just drawn his sword out of its sheath and was showing it to Mr. Beaver, when Mrs. Beaver said:

"Now then, now then! Don't stand talking there till the tea's got cold. Just like men. Come and help to carry the tray down and we'll have breakfast. What a mercy I thought of bringing the bread-knife."

So down the steep bank they went and back to the cave, and Mr. Beaver cut some of the bread and ham into sandwiches and Mrs. Beaver poured out the tea and everyone enjoyed themselves. But long before they had finished enjoying themselves Mr. Beaver said, "Time to be moving on now."

11

ASLAN IS NEARER

Edmund meanwhile had been having a most disappointing time. When the dwarf had gone to get the sledge ready he expected that the Witch would start being nice to him, as she had been at their last meeting. But she said nothing at all. And when at last Edmund plucked up his courage to say, "Please, your Majesty, could I have some Turkish Delight? You—you—said—" she answered, "Silence, fool!" Then she appeared to change her mind and said, as if to herself, "And yet it will not do to have the brat fainting on the way," and once more clapped her hands. Another dwarf appeared.

"Bring the human creature food and drink," she said.

The dwarf went away and presently returned bringing an iron bowl with some water in it and an iron plate with a hunk of dry bread on it. He grinned in a repulsive manner as he set them down on the floor beside Edmund and said:

"Turkish Delight for the little Prince. Ha! Ha! Ha!"

"Take it away," said Edmund sulkily. "I don't want dry bread." But the Witch suddenly turned on him with such a terrible expression on her face that he apologized and began to nibble at

the bread, though it was so stale he could hardly get it down.

"You may be glad enough of it before you taste bread again," said the Witch.

While he was still chewing away the first dwarf came back and announced that the sledge was ready. The White Witch rose and went out, ordering Edmund to go with her. The snow was again falling as they came into the courtyard, but she took no notice of that and made Edmund sit beside her on the sledge. But before they drove off she called Maugrim and he came bounding like an enormous dog to the side of the sledge.

"Take with you the swiftest of your wolves and go at once to the house of the Beavers," said the Witch, "and kill whatever you find there. If they are already gone, then make all speed to the Stone Table, but do not be seen. Wait for me there in hiding. I meanwhile must go many miles to the West before I find a place where I can drive across the river. You may overtake these humans before they reach the Stone Table. You will know what to do if you find them!"

"I hear and obey, O Queen," growled the Wolf, and immediately he shot away into the snow and darkness, as quickly as a horse can gallop. In a few minutes he had called another wolf and was with him down on the dam and sniffing at the Beavers' house. But of course they found it empty. It would have been a dreadful thing for the Beavers and the children if the night had remained fine, for the wolves would then have been able to follow their trail—and ten to one would have overtaken them before they had got to the cave. But now that the snow had begun again the scent was cold and even the footprints were covered up.

Meanwhile the dwarf whipped up the reindeer, and the Witch and Edmund drove out under the archway and on and away into the darkness and the cold. This was a terrible journey for Edmund, who had no coat. Before they had been going quarter of an hour all the front of him was covered with snow—he soon stopped trying to shake it off because, as quickly as he did that, a new lot gathered, and he was so tired. Soon he was wet to the skin. And oh, how miserable he was! It didn't look now as if the Witch intended to make him a King. All the things he had said to make himself believe that she was good and kind and that her side was really the right side sounded to him silly now. He would have given anything to meet the others at this moment—even Peter! The only way to comfort himself now was to try to believe that the whole thing was a dream and that he might wake up at any moment. And as they went on, hour after hour, it did come to seem like a dream.

This lasted longer than I could describe even if I wrote pages and pages about it. But I will skip on to the time when the snow had stopped and the morning had come and they were racing along in the daylight. And still they went on and on, with no sound but the everlasting swish of the snow and the creaking of the reindeer's harness. And then at last the Witch said, "What have we here? Stop!" and they did.

How Edmund hoped she was going to say something about breakfast! But she had stopped for quite a different reason. A little way off at the foot of a tree sat a merry party, a squirrel and his wife with their children and two satyrs and a dwarf and an old dog-fox, all on stools round a table. Edmund couldn't quite see what they were eating, but it smelled lovely and there seemed to be decorations of holly and he wasn't at all sure that he didn't see something like a plum pudding. At the moment when the sledge stopped, the Fox, who was obviously the oldest person present, had just risen to its feet, holding a glass in its right paw as if it was going to say something. But when the whole party saw the sledge stopping and who was in it, all the gaiety went out of their faces. The father squirrel stopped eating with his fork halfway to his mouth and one of the satyrs stopped with its fork actually in its mouth, and the baby squirrels squeaked with terror.

"What is the meaning of this?" asked the Witch Queen. Nobody answered.

"Speak, vermin!" she said again. "Or do you want my dwarf to find you a tongue with his whip? What is the meaning of all this gluttony, this waste, this self-indulgence? Where did you get all these things?"

"Please, your Majesty," said the Fox, "we were given them. And if I might make so bold as to drink your Majesty's very good health—"

"Who gave them to you?" said the Witch.

"F-F-F-Father Christmas," stammered the Fox.

"What?" roared the Witch, springing from the sledge and taking a few strides nearer to the

terrified animals. "He has not been here! He cannot have been here! How dare you—but no. Say you have been lying and you shall even now be forgiven."

At that moment one of the young squirrels lost its head completely.

"He has—he has—he has!" it squeaked, beating its little spoon on the table. Edmund saw the Witch bite her lips so that a drop of blood appeared on her white cheek. Then she raised her wand. "Oh, don't, don't, please don't," shouted Edmund, but even while he was shouting she had waved her wand and instantly where the merry party had been there were only statues of creatures (one with its stone fork fixed forever halfway to its stone mouth) seated round a stone table on which there were stone plates and a stone plum pudding.

"As for you," said the Witch, giving

Edmund a stunning blow on the face as she re-mounted the sledge, "let that teach you to ask favor for spies and traitors. Drive on!" And Edmund for the first time in this story felt sorry for someone besides himself. It seemed so pitiful to think of those little stone figures sitting there all the silent days and all the dark nights, year after year, till the moss grew on them and at last even their faces crumbled away.

Now they were steadily racing on again. And soon Edmund noticed that the snow which splashed against them as they rushed through it was much wetter than it had been all last night. At the same time he noticed that he was feeling much less cold. It was also becoming foggy. In fact every minute it grew foggier and warmer. And the sledge was not running nearly as well as it had been running up till now. At first he thought this was because the reindeer were tired, but soon he saw that that couldn't be the real reason. The sledge jerked, and skidded and kept on jolting as if it had struck against stones. And however the dwarf whipped the poor rein-deer the sledge went slower and slower. There also seemed to be a curious noise all round them, but the noise of their driving and jolting and the dwarf's shouting at the reindeer pre-vented Edmund from hearing what it was, until suddenly the sledge stuck so fast that it wouldn't go on at all. When that happened there was a moment's silence. And in that silence Edmund could at last listen to the other noise properly. A strange, sweet, rustling, chattering noise—and yet not so strange, for he'd heard it before—if only he could remember where! Then all at once he did remember. It was the noise of running water. All round them though out of sight, there were streams, chattering, murmuring, bubbling, splashing and even (in the distance) roaring. And his heart gave a great leap (though he hardly knew why) when he realized that the frost was over. And much nearer there was a drip-drip-drip from the branches of all the trees. And then, as he looked at one tree he saw a great load of snow slide off it and for the first time since he had entered Narnia he saw the dark green of a fir tree. But he hadn't time to listen or watch any longer, for the Witch said:

"Don't sit staring, fool! Get out and help."

And of course Edmund had to obey. He stepped out into the snow—but it was really only slush by now—and began helping the dwarf to get the sledge out of the muddy hole it had got into. They got it out in the end, and by being very cruel to the reindeer the dwarf managed to get it on the move again, and they drove a little further. And now the snow was really melting in earnest and patches of green grass were beginning to appear in every direction. Unless you have looked at a world of snow as long as Edmund had been looking at it, you will hardly be able to imagine what a relief those green patches were after the endless white. Then the sledge stopped again.

"It's no good, your Majesty," said the dwarf. "We can't sledge in this thaw."

"Then we must walk," said the Witch.

"We shall never overtake them walking," growled the dwarf. "Not with the start they've got."

"Are you my councillor or my slave?" said the Witch. "Do as you're told. Tie the hands of the human creature behind it and keep hold of the end of the rope. And take your whip. And

cut the harness of the reindeer; they'll find their own way home."

The dwarf obeyed, and in a few minutes Edmund found himself being forced to walk as fast as he could with his hands tied behind him. He kept on slipping in the slush and mud and wet grass, and every time he slipped the dwarf gave him a curse and sometimes a flick with the whip. The Witch walked behind the dwarf and kept on saying, "Faster! Faster!"

Every moment the patches of green grew bigger and the patches of snow grew smaller. Every moment more and more of the trees shook off their robes of snow. Soon, wherever you looked, instead of white shapes you saw the dark green of firs or the black prickly branches of bare oaks and beeches and elms. Then the mist turned from white to gold and presently cleared away altogether. Shafts of delicious sunlight struck down onto the forest floor and overhead you could see a blue sky between the tree tops.

Soon there were more wonderful things happening. Coming suddenly round a corner into a glade of silver birch trees Edmund saw the ground covered in all directions with little yellow flowers—celandines.

The noise of water grew louder. Presently they actually crossed a stream. Beyond it they found snowdrops growing.

"Mind your own business!" said the dwarf when he saw that Edmund had turned his head to look at them; and he gave the rope a vicious jerk.

But of course this didn't prevent Edmund from seeing. Only five minutes later he noticed a dozen crocuses growing round the foot of an old tree—gold and purple and white. Then came a sound even more delicious than the sound of the water. Close beside the path they were following a bird suddenly chirped from the branch of a tree. It was answered by the chuckle of another bird a little further off. And then, as if that had been a signal, there was chattering and chirruping in every direction, and then a moment of full song, and within five minutes the whole wood was ringing with birds' music, and wherever Edmund's eyes turned he saw birds alighting on branches, or sailing overhead or chasing one another or having their little quar-

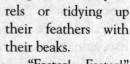

rels or tidying up their feathers with their beaks.

"Faster! Faster!" said the Witch.

There was no trace of the fog now. The sky became bluer

and bluer, and now there were white clouds hurrying across it from time to time. In the wide glades there were primroses. A light breeze sprang up which scattered drops of moisture from the sway-  ing branches and carried cool, delicious scents against the faces of the travelers. The trees began to come fully alive. The larches and birches were covered with green, the laburnums with gold. Soon the beech trees had put forth their delicate, transparent leaves. As the travelers walked under them the light also became green. A bee buzzed across their path.

"This is no thaw," said the dwarf, suddenly stopping. "This is *Spring*. What are we to do? Your winter has been destroyed, I tell you! This is Aslan's doing."

"If either of you mentions that name again," said the Witch, "he shall instantly be killed."

PETER'S FIRST BATTLE

While the Dwarf and the White Witch were saying this, miles away the Beavers and the children were walking on hour after hour into what seemed a delicious dream. Long ago they had left the coats behind them. And by now they had even stopped saying to one another, "Look! there's a kingfisher," or "I say, bluebells!" or "What was that lovely smell?" or "Just listen to that thrush!" They walked on in silence drinking it all in, passing through patches of warm sunlight into cool, green thickets and out again into wide mossy glades where tall elms raised the leafy roof far overhead, and then into dense masses of flowering currant and among hawthorn bushes where the sweet smell was almost overpowering.

They had been just as surprised as Edmund when they saw the winter vanishing and the whole wood passing in a few hours or so from January to May. They hadn't even known for certain (as the Witch did) that this was what would happen when Aslan came to Narnia. But they all knew that it was her spells which had produced the endless winter; and therefore they all knew when this magic spring began that something had gone wrong, and badly wrong, with the Witch's schemes. And after the thaw had been going on for some time they all realized that the Witch would no longer be able to use her sledge. After that they didn't hurry so much and they allowed themselves more rests and longer ones. They were pretty tired by now of course; but not what I'd call bitterly tired— only slow and feeling very dreamy and quiet inside as one does when one is coming to the end of a long day in the open. Susan had a slight blister on one heel.

They had left the course of the big river some time ago; for one had to turn a little to the right (that meant a little to the south) to reach the place of the Stone Table. Even if this had not been their way they couldn't have kept to the river valley once the thaw began, for with all that melting snow the river was soon in flood—a wonderful, roaring, thundering yellow flood—and their path would have been under water.

And now the sun got low and the light got redder and the shadows got longer and the flowers began to think about closing.

"Not long now," said Mr. Beaver, and began leading them uphill across some very deep, springy moss (it felt nice under their tired feet) in a place where only tall trees grew, very wide apart. The climb, coming at the end of the long day, made them all pant and blow. And just as Lucy was wondering whether she could really get to the top without another long rest, suddenly they *were* at the top. And this is what they saw.

They were on a green open space from which you could look down on the forest spreading as far as one could see in every direction—except right ahead. There, far to the East, was something twinkling and moving. "By gum!" whispered Peter to Susan, "the sea!" In the very middle of this open hilltop was the Stone Table. It was a great grim slab of gray stone supported on four upright stones. It looked very old; and it was cut all over with strange lines and figures that might be the letters of an unknown language. They gave you a curious feeling when you looked at them. The next thing they saw was a pavilion pitched on one side of the open place. A wonderful pavilion it was—and especially now when the light of the setting sun fell upon it—with sides of what looked like yellow silk and cords of crimson and tent-pegs of ivory; and high above it on a pole a banner which bore a red rampant lion fluttering in the breeze which was blowing in their faces from the far-off sea. While they were looking at this they heard a sound of music on their right; and turning in that direction they saw what they had come to see.

Aslan stood in the center of a crowd of creatures who had grouped themselves round him in the shape of a half-moon. There were Tree-Women there and Well-Women (Dryads and Naiads as they used to be called in our world) who had stringed instruments; it was they who had made the music. There were four great centaurs. The horse part of them was like huge English farm horses, and the man part was like stern but beautiful giants. There was also a unicorn, and a bull with the head of a man, and a pelican, and an eagle, and a great Dog. And next to Aslan stood two leopards of whom one carried his crown and the other his standard.

But as for Aslan himself, the Beavers and

the children didn't know what to do or say when they saw him. People who have not been in Narnia sometimes think that a thing cannot be good and terrible at the same time. If the children had ever thought so, they were cured of it now. For when they tried to look at Aslan's face they just caught a glimpse of the golden mane and the great, royal, solemn, overwhelming eyes; and then they found they couldn't look at him and went all trembly.

"Go on," whispered Mr. Beaver.

"No," whispered Peter, "you first."

"No, Sons of Adam before animals," whispered Mr. Beaver back again.

"Susan," whispered Peter, "what about you? Ladies first."

"No, you're the eldest," whispered Susan. And of course the longer they went on doing this the more awkward they felt. Then at last Peter realized that it was up to him. He drew his sword and raised it to the salute and hastily saying to the others "Come on. Pull yourselves together," he advanced to the Lion and said:

"We have come—Aslan."

"Welcome, Peter, Son of Adam," said Aslan. "Welcome, Susan and Lucy, Daughters of Eve. Welcome He-Beaver and She-Beaver."

His voice was deep and rich and somehow took the fidgets out of them. They now felt glad and quiet and it didn't seem awkward to them to stand and say nothing.

"But where is the fourth?" asked Aslan.

"He has tried to betray them and joined the White Witch, O Aslan," said Mr. Beaver. And then something made Peter say,

"That was partly my fault, Aslan. I was angry with him and I think that helped him to go wrong."

And Aslan said nothing either to excuse Peter or to blame him but merely stood looking at him with his great unchanging eyes. And it seemed to all of them that there was nothing to be said.

"Please—Aslan," said Lucy, "can anything be done to save Edmund?"

"All shall be done," said Aslan. "But it may be harder than you think." And then he was silent again for some time. Up to that moment Lucy had been thinking how royal and strong and peaceful his face looked; now it suddenly came into her head that he looked sad as well. But next minute that expression was quite gone. The Lion shook his mane and clapped his paws together ("Terrible paws," thought Lucy, "if he didn't know how to velvet them!") and said,

"Meanwhile, let the feast be prepared. Ladies, take these Daughters of Eve to the pavilion and minister to them."

When the girls had gone Aslan laid his paw—and though it was velveted it was very heavy—on Peter's shoulder and said, "Come, Son of Adam, and I will show you a far-off sight of the castle where you are to be King."

And Peter with his sword still drawn in his hand went with the Lion to the eastern edge of the hilltop. There a beautiful sight met their eyes. The sun was setting behind their backs. That meant that the whole country below them lay in the evening light—forest and hills and valleys and, winding away like a silver snake, the lower part of the great river. And beyond all this, miles away, was the sea, and beyond the sea the sky, full of clouds which were just turning rose color with the reflection of the sunset. But just where the land of Narnia met the sea—in fact, at the mouth of the great river—there was something on a little hill, shining. It was shining because it was a castle and of course the sunlight was reflected from all the windows which looked toward Peter and the sunset; but to Peter it looked like a great star resting on the seashore.

"That, O Man," said Aslan, "is Cair Paravel of the four thrones, in one of which you must sit as King. I show it to you because you are the firstborn and you will be High King over all the rest."

And once more Peter said nothing, for at that moment a strange noise woke the silence suddenly. It was like a bugle, but richer.

"It is your sister's horn," said Aslan to Peter in a low voice; so low as to be almost a purr, if it is not disrespectful to think of a Lion purring.

For a moment Peter did not understand. Then, when he saw all the other creatures start forward and heard Aslan say with a wave of his paw, "Back! Let the Prince win his spurs," he did understand, and set off running as hard as he could to the pavilion. And there he saw a dreadful sight.

The Naiads and Dryads were scattering in every direction. Lucy was running toward him as fast as her short legs would carry her and her face was as white as paper. Then he saw Susan make a dash for a tree, and swing herself up, followed by a huge gray beast. At first Peter thought it was a bear. Then he saw that it looked like an Alsatian, though it was far too big to be a dog. Then he realized that it was a wolf—a wolf standing on its hind legs, with its front paws against the tree-trunk, snapping and snarling. All the hair on its back stood up on end. Susan had not been able to get higher than the second big branch. One of her legs hung down so that her foot was only an inch or two above the snapping teeth. Peter wondered why she did not get higher or at least take a better grip; then he realized that she was just going to faint and that if she fainted she would fall off.

Peter did not feel very brave; indeed, he felt he was going to be sick. But that made no difference to what he had to do. He rushed straight up to the monster and aimed a slash of his sword at its side. That stroke never reached the Wolf. Quick as lightning it turned round, its eyes flaming, and its mouth wide open in a howl of anger. If it had not been so angry that it simply had to howl it would have got him by the throat at once. As it was—though all this happened too quickly for Peter to think at all—he had just time to duck down and plunge his sword, as hard as he could, between the brute's forelegs into its heart. Then came a horrible, confused moment like something in a nightmare. He was tugging and pulling and the Wolf seemed neither alive nor dead, and its bared teeth knocked against his forehead, and everything was blood and heat and hair. A moment later he found that the monster lay dead and he had drawn his sword out of it and was straightening his back and rubbing the sweat off his face and out of his eyes. He felt tired all over.

Then, after a bit, Susan came down the tree. She and Peter felt pretty shaky when they met and I won't say there wasn't kissing and crying on both sides. But in Narnia no one thinks any the worse of you for that.

"Quick! Quick!" shouted the voice of Aslan. "Centaurs! Eagles! I see another wolf in the thickets. There—behind you. He has just darted away. After him, all of you. He will be going to his mistress. Now is your chance to find the Witch and rescue the fourth Son of Adam." And instantly with a thunder of hoofs and beating of wings a dozen or so of the swiftest creatures disappeared into the gathering darkness.

Peter, still out of breath, turned and saw Aslan close at hand.

"You have forgotten to clean your sword," said Aslan.

It was true. Peter blushed when he looked at the bright blade and saw it all smeared with the Wolf's hair and blood. He stooped down and wiped it quite clean on the grass, and then wiped it quite dry on his coat.

"Hand it to me and kneel, Son of Adam," said Aslan. And when Peter had done so he struck him with the flat of the blade and said, "Rise up, Sir Peter Wolf's-Bane. And, whatever happens, never forget to wipe your sword."

13

DEEP MAGIC FROM THE DAWN OF TIME

Now we must get back to Edmund. When he had been made to walk far further than he had ever known that anybody *could* walk, the Witch at last halted in a dark valley all overshadowed with fir trees and yew trees. Edmund simply sank down and lay on his face doing nothing at all and not even caring what was going to happen next provided they would let him lie still. He was too tired even to notice how hungry and thirsty he was. The Witch and the dwarf were talking close beside him in low tones.

"No," said the dwarf, "it is no use now, O

Queen. They must have reached the Stone Table by now."

"Perhaps the Wolf will smell us out and bring us news," said the Witch.

"It cannot be good news if he does," said the dwarf.

"Four thrones in Cair Paravel," said the Witch. "How if only three were filled? That would not fulfill the prophecy."

"What difference would that make now that *He* is here?" said the dwarf. He did not dare, even now, to mention the name of Aslan to his mistress.

"He may not stay long. And then—we would fall upon the three at Cair."

"Yet it might be better," said the dwarf, "to keep this one" (here he kicked Edmund) "for bargaining with."

"Yes! and have him rescued," said the Witch scornfully.

"Then," said the dwarf, "we had better do what we have to do at once."

"I would like to have done it on the Stone Table itself," said the Witch. "That is the proper place. That is where it has always been done before."

"It will be a long time now before the Stone Table can again be put to its proper use," said the dwarf.

"True," said the Witch; and then, "Well, I will begin."

At that moment with a rush and a snarl a Wolf rushed up to them.

"I have seen them. They are all at the Stone Table, with Him. They have killed my captain, Maugrim. I was hidden in the thickets and saw it all. One of the Sons of Adam killed him. Fly! Fly!"

"No," said the Witch. "There need be no flying. Go quickly. Summon all our people to meet me here as speedily as they can. Call out the giants and the werewolves and the spirits of those trees who are on our side. Call the Ghouls, and the Boggles, the Ogres, and the Minotaurs. Call the Cruels, the Hags, the Specters, and the people of the Toadstools. We will fight. What? Have I not still my wand? Will not their ranks turn into stone even as they come on? Be off quickly, I have a little thing to finish here while you are away."

The great brute bowed its head, turned, and galloped away.

"Now!" said she, "we have no table—let me see. We had better put it against the trunk of a tree."

Edmund found himself being roughly forced to his feet. Then the dwarf set him with his back against a tree and bound him fast. He saw the

Witch take off her outer mantle. Her arms were bare underneath it and terribly white. Because they were so very white he could see them, but he could not see much else, it was so dark in this valley under the dark trees.

"Prepare the victim," said the Witch. And the dwarf undid Edmund's collar and folded back his shirt at the neck. Then he took Edmund's hair and pulled his head back so that he had to raise his chin. After that Edmund heard a strange noise—whizz—whizz—whizz. For a moment he couldn't think what it was. Then he realized. It was the sound of a knife being sharpened.

At that very moment he heard loud shouts from every direction—a drumming of hoofs and a beating of wings—a scream from the Witch—confusion all round him. And then he found he was being untied. Strong arms were round him

and he heard big, kind voices saying things like—

"Let him lie down—give him some wine— drink this—steady now—you'll be all right in a minute."

Then he heard the voices of people who were not talking to him but to one another. And they were saying things like "Who's got the Witch?" "I thought you had her." "I didn't see her after I knocked the knife out of her hand—I was after the dwarf—do you mean to say she's escaped?" "—A chap can't mind everything at once—what's that? Oh, sorry, it's only an old stump!" But just at this point Edmund went off in a dead faint.

Presently the centaurs and unicorns and deer and birds (they were of course the rescue party which Aslan had sent in the last chapter) all set off to go back to the Stone Table, carrying Edmund with them. But if they could have seen what happened in that valley after they had gone, I think they might have been surprised.

It was perfectly still and presently the moon grew bright; if you had been there you would have seen the moonlight shining on an old tree- stump and on a fair-sized boulder. But if you had gone on looking you would gradually have be- gun to think there was something odd about both the stump and the boulder. And next you would have thought that the stump did look really remarkably like a little fat man crouching on the ground. And if you had watched long enough you would have seen the stump walk across to the boulder and the boulder sit up and begin talking to the stump; for in reality the stump and the boulder were simply the Witch and the dwarf. For it was part of her magic that she could make things look like what they aren't, and she had the presence of mind to do so at the very moment when the knife was knocked out of her hand. She had kept hold of her wand, so it had been kept safe, too.

When the other children woke up next morning (they had been sleeping on piles of cushions in the pavilion) the first thing they heard—from Mrs. Beaver—was that their brother had been rescued and brought into camp late last night; and was at that moment with Aslan. As soon as they had breakfasted they all went out, and there they saw Aslan and Edmund walking together in the dewy grass, apart from the rest of the court. There is no need to tell you (and no one ever heard) what Aslan was saying, but it was a conversation which Edmund never forgot. As the others drew nearer Aslan turned to meet them, bringing Edmund with him.

"Here is your brother," he said, "and—there is no need to talk to him about what is past."

Edmund shook hands with each of the others and said to each of them in turn, "I'm sorry," and everyone said, "That's all right." And then everyone wanted very hard to say something which would make it quite clear that they were all friends with him again—something ordinary and natural—and of course no one could think of anything in the world to say. But before they had time to feel really awkward one of the leopards approached Aslan and said,

"Sire, there is a messenger from the enemy who craves audience."

"Let him approach," said Aslan.

The leopard went away and soon returned leading the Witch's dwarf.

"What is your message, Son of Earth?" asked Aslan.

"The Queen of Narnia and Empress of the Lone Islands desires a safe conduct to come and speak with you," said the dwarf, "on a matter which is as much to your advantage as to hers."

"Queen of Narnia, indeed!" said Mr. Beaver. "Of all the cheek—"

"Peace, Beaver," said Aslan. "All names will soon be restored to their proper owners. In the meantime we will not dispute about them. Tell your mistress, Son of Earth, that I grant her safe conduct on condition that she leaves her wand behind her at that great oak."

This was agreed to and two leopards went back with the dwarf to see that the conditions were properly carried out. "But supposing she turns the two leopards into stone?" whispered Lucy to Peter. I think the same idea had occurred to the leopards themselves; at any rate, as they walked off their fur was all standing up on their backs and their tails were bristling—like a cat's when it sees a strange dog.

"It'll be all right," whispered Peter in reply. "He wouldn't send them if it weren't."

A few minutes later the Witch herself walked out on to the top of the hill and came straight across and stood before Aslan. The three children who had not seen her before felt shudders running down their backs at the sight of her face; and there were low growls among all the animals present. Though it was bright sunshine everyone felt suddenly cold. The only two people present who seemed to be quite at their ease were Aslan and the Witch herself. It was the oddest thing to see those two faces—the golden face and the dead-white face—so close together. Not that the Witch looked Aslan exactly in his eyes; Mrs. Beaver particularly noticed this.

"You have a traitor there, Aslan," said the Witch. Of course everyone present knew that she meant Edmund. But Edmund had got past thinking about himself after all he'd been through and after the talk he'd had that morning. He just went on looking at Aslan. It didn't seem to matter what the Witch said.

"Well," said Aslan. "His offense was not against you."

"Have you forgotten the Deep Magic?" asked the Witch.

"Let us say I have forgotten it," answered Aslan gravely. "Tell us of this Deep Magic."

"Tell you?" said the Witch, her voice growing suddenly shriller. "Tell you what is written on that very Table of Stone which stands beside us? Tell you what is written in letters deep as a spear is long on the fire-stones on the Secret Hill? Tell you what is engraved on the scepter of the Emperor-beyond-the-Sea? You at least know the Magic which the Emperor put into Narnia at the very beginning. You know that every traitor belongs to me as my lawful prey and that for every treachery I have a right to a kill."

"Oh," said Mr. Beaver. "So *that's* how you came to imagine yourself a queen—because you were the Emperor's hangman. I see."

"Peace, Beaver," said Aslan, with a very low growl.

"And so," continued the Witch, "that human creature is mine. His life is forfeit to me. His blood is my property."

"Come and take it then," said the Bull with the man's head in a great bellowing voice.

"Fool," said the Witch with a savage smile that was almost a snarl, "do you really think your master can rob me of my rights by mere force? He knows the Deep Magic better than that. He knows that unless I have blood as the Law says all Narnia will be overturned and perish in fire and water."

"It is very true," said Aslan, "I do not deny it."

"Oh, Aslan!" whispered Susan in the Lion's ear, "can't we— I mean, you won't, will you? Can't we do something about the Deep Magic? Isn't there something you can work against it?"

"Work against the Emperor's Magic?" said Aslan, turning to her with something like a frown on his face. And nobody ever made that suggestion to him again.

Edmund was on the other side of Aslan, looking all the time at Aslan's face. He felt a choking feeling and wondered if he ought to say something; but a moment later he felt that he was not expected to do anything except to wait, and do what he was told.

"Fall back, all of you," said Aslan, "and I will talk to the Witch alone."

They all obeyed. It was a terrible time this—waiting and wondering while the Lion and the Witch talked earnestly together in low voices. Lucy said, "Oh, Edmund!" and began to cry. Peter stood with his back to the others looking out at the distant sea. The Beavers stood holding each other's paws with their heads bowed. The centaurs stamped uneasily with their hoofs. But everyone became perfectly still in the end, so that you noticed even small sounds like a bumble-bee flying past, or the birds in the forest down below them, or the wind rustling the leaves. And still the talk between Aslan and the White Witch went on.

At last they heard Aslan's voice, "You can all come back," he said. "I have settled the matter. She has renounced the claim on your brother's blood." And all over the hill there was a noise as if everyone had been holding their breath and had now begun breathing again, and then a murmur of talk.

The Witch was just turning away with a look of fierce joy on her face when she stopped and said,

"But how do I know this promise will be kept?"

"Haa-a-arrh!" roared Aslan, half rising from his throne; and his great mouth opened wider and wider and the roar grew louder and louder, and the Witch, after staring for a moment with her lips wide apart, picked up her skirts and fairly ran for her life.

14

THE TRIUMPH OF
THE WITCH

As soon as the Witch had gone Aslan said,
"We must move from this place at once, it will
be wanted for other purposes. We shall encamp
tonight at the Fords of Beruna."

Of course everyone was dying to ask him
how he had arranged matters with the witch;
but his face was stern and everyone's ears were
still ringing with the sound of his roar and so
nobody dared.

After a meal, which was taken in the open
air on the hill-top (for the sun had got strong by
now and dried the grass), they were busy for a

while taking the pavilion down and packing things up. Before two o'clock they were on the march and set off in a northeasterly direction, walking at an easy pace for they had not far to go.

During the first part of the journey Aslan explained to Peter his plan of campaign. "As soon as she has finished her business in these parts," he said, "the Witch and her crew will almost certainly fall back to her House and prepare for a siege. You may or may not be able to cut her off and prevent her from reaching it." He then went on to outline two plans of battle—one for fighting the Witch and her people in the wood and another for assaulting her castle. And all the time he was advising Peter how to conduct the operations, saying things like, "You must put your Centaurs in such and such a place" or "You must post scouts to see that she doesn't do so-and-so," till at last Peter said,

"But you will be there yourself, Aslan."

"I can give you no promise of that," answered the Lion. And he continued giving Peter his instructions.

For the last part of the journey it was Susan and Lucy who saw most of him. He did not talk very much and seemed to them to be sad.

It was still afternoon when they came down to a place where the river valley had widened out and the river was broad and shallow. This was the Fords of Beruna and Aslan gave orders to halt on this side of the water. But Peter said,

"Wouldn't it be better to camp on the far side—for fear she should try a night attack or anything?"

Aslan, who seemed to have been thinking about something else, roused himself with a shake of his magnificent mane and said, "Eh? What's that?" Peter said it all over again.

"No," said Aslan in a dull voice, as if it didn't matter. "No. She will not make an attack tonight." And then he sighed deeply. But presently he added, "All the same it was well thought of. That is how a soldier ought to think. But it doesn't really matter." So they proceeded to pitch their camp.

Aslan's mood affected everyone that evening. Peter was feeling uncomfortable too at the idea of fighting the battle on his own; the news that Aslan might not be there had come as a great shock to him. Supper that evening was a quiet meal. Everyone felt how different it had been last night or even that morning. It was as if the good times, having just begun, were already drawing to their end.

This feeling affected Susan so much that she couldn't get to sleep when she went to bed. And after she had lain counting sheep and turning over and over she heard Lucy give a long sigh and turn over just beside her in the darkness.

"Can't you get to sleep either?" said Susan.

"No," said Lucy. "I thought you were asleep. I say, Susan!"

"What?"

"I've a most horrible feeling—as if something were hanging over us."

"Have you? Because, as a matter of fact, so have I."

"Something about Aslan," said Lucy. "Either some dreadful thing is going to happen to him, or something dreadful that he's going to do."

"There's been something wrong with him all afternoon," said Susan. "Lucy! What was that he said about not being with us at the battle? You don't think he could be stealing away and leaving us tonight, do you?"

"Where is he now?" said Lucy. "Is he here in the pavilion?"

"I don't think so."

"Susan! let's go outside and have a look round. We might see him."

"All right. Let's," said Susan; "we might just as well be doing that as lying awake here."

Very quietly the two girls groped their way among the other sleepers and crept out of the tent. The moonlight was bright and everything was quite still except for the noise of the river chattering over the stones. Then Susan suddenly caught Lucy's arm and said, "Look!" On the far side of the camping ground, just where the trees began, they saw the Lion slowly walking away from them into the wood. Without a word they both followed him.

He led them up the steep slope out of the river valley and then slightly to the right—apparently by the very same route which they had used that afternoon in coming from the Hill of the Stone Table. On and on he led them, into dark shadows and out into pale moonlight, getting their feet wet with the heavy dew. He looked somehow different from the Aslan they knew. His tail and his head hung low and he walked slowly as if he were very, very tired. Then, when they were crossing a wide open place where there were no shadows for them to hide in, he stopped and looked round. It was no good trying to run away so they came toward him. When they were closer he said,

"Oh, children, children, why are you following me?"

"We couldn't sleep," said Lucy—and then felt sure that she need say no more and that Aslan knew all they had been thinking.

"Please, may we come with you—wherever you're going?" asked Susan.

"Well—" said Aslan, and seemed to be thinking. Then he said, "I should be glad of company tonight. Yes, you may come, if you will promise to stop when I tell you, and after that leave me to go on alone."

"Oh, thank you, thank you. And we will," said the two girls.

Forward they went again and one of the girls walked on each side of the Lion. But how slowly he walked! And his great, royal head drooped so that his nose nearly touched the grass. Presently he stumbled and gave a low moan.

"Aslan! Dear Aslan!" said Lucy, "what is wrong? Can't you tell us?"

"Are you ill, dear Aslan?" asked Susan.

"No," said Aslan. "I am sad and lonely. Lay your hands on my mane so that I can feel you are there and let us walk like that."

And so the girls did what they would never have dared to do without his permission, but what they had longed to do ever since they first saw him—buried their cold hands in the beautiful sea of fur and stroked it and, so doing, walked with him. And presently they saw that they were going with him up the slope of the hill on which the Stone Table stood. They went up at the side where the trees came furthest up, and when they got to the last tree (it was one that had some bushes about it) Aslan stopped and said,

"Oh, children, children. Here you must stop. And whatever happens, do not let yourselves be seen. Farewell."

And both the girls cried bitterly (though they hardly knew why) and clung to the Lion and kissed his mane and his nose and his paws and his great, sad eyes. Then he turned from them and walked out on to the top of the hill. And Lucy and Susan, crouching in the bushes, looked after him and this is what they saw.

A great crowd of people were standing all round the Stone Table and though the moon was shining many of them carried torches which burned with evil-looking red flames and black smoke. But such people! Ogres with monstrous teeth, and wolves, and bull-headed men; spirits of evil trees and poisonous plants; and other creatures whom I won't describe because if I did the grown-ups would probably not let you read this book—Cruels and Hags and Incubuses, Wraiths, Horrors, Efreets, Sprites, Orknies, Wooses, and Ettins. In fact here were all those who were on the Witch's side and whom the Wolf had summoned at her command. And right in the middle, standing by the Table, was the Witch herself.

A howl and a gibber of dismay went up from the creatures when they first saw the great Lion pacing toward them, and for a moment even the Witch herself seemed to be struck with fear. Then she recovered herself and gave a wild, fierce laugh.

"The fool!" she cried. "The fool has come. Bind him fast."

Lucy and Susan held their breaths waiting for Aslan's roar and his spring upon his enemies. But it never came. Four Hags, grinning and leering, yet also (at first) hanging back and half afraid of what they had to do, had approached him. "Bind him, I say!" repeated the White Witch. The Hags made a dart at him and shrieked with triumph when they found that he made no resistance at all. Then others—evil dwarfs and apes—rushed in to help them, and between them they rolled the huge Lion over on his back and tied all his four paws together, shouting and cheering as if they had done something brave, though, had the Lion chosen, one of those paws could have been the death of them all. But he made no noise, even when the enemies, straining and tugging, pulled the cords so tight that they cut into his flesh. Then they began to drag him toward the Stone Table.

"Stop!" said the Witch. "Let him first be shaved."

Another roar of mean laughter went up from her followers as an ogre with a pair of shears came forward and squatted down by Aslan's head. Snip-snip-snip went the shears and masses of curling gold began to fall to the ground. Then the ogre stood back and the children, watching from their hiding-place, could see the face of Aslan looking all small and different without its mane. The enemies also saw the difference.

"Why, he's only a great cat after all!" cried one.

"Is *that* what we were afraid of?" said another.

And they surged round Aslan, jeering at him, saying things like "Puss, Puss! Poor Pussy," and "How many mice have you caught today, Cat?" and "Would you like a saucer of milk, Pussums?"

"Oh, how *can* they?" said Lucy, tears streaming down her cheeks. "The brutes, the brutes!" for now that the first shock was over the shorn face of Aslan looked to her braver, and more beautiful, and more patient than ever.

"Muzzle him!" said the Witch. And even now, as they worked about his face putting on the muzzle, one bite from his jaws would have cost two or three of them their hands. But he never moved. And this seemed to enrage all that rabble. Everyone was at him now. Those who had been afraid to come near him even after he was bound began to find their courage, and for a few minutes the two girls could not even see him—so thickly was he surrounded by the whole crowd of creatures kicking him, hitting him, spitting on him, jeering at him.

At last the rabble had had enough of this. They began to drag the bound and muzzled Lion to the Stone Table, some pulling and some pushing. He was so huge that even when they got him there it took all their efforts to hoist him onto the surface of it. Then there was more tying and tightening of cords.

"The cowards! The cowards!" sobbed Susan. "Are they *still* afraid of him, even now?"

When once Aslan had been tied (and tied so that he was really a mass of cords) on the flat stone, a hush fell on the crowd. Four Hags, holding four torches, stood at the corners of the Table. The Witch bared her arms as she had bared them the previous night when it had been Edmund instead of Aslan. Then she began to whet her knife. It looked to the children, when the gleam of the torchlight fell on it, as if the knife were made of stone, not of steel, and it was of a strange and evil shape.

At last she drew near. She stood by Aslan's head. Her face was working and twitching with passion, but his looked up at the sky, still quiet, neither angry nor afraid, but a little sad. Then, just before she gave the blow, she stooped down and said in a quivering voice,

"And now, who has won? Fool, did you think that by all this you would save the human traitor? Now I will kill you instead of him as our pact was and so the Deep Magic will be appeased. But when you are dead what will prevent me from killing him as well? And who will take him out of my hand *then*? Understand that you have given me Narnia forever, you have lost your own life and you have not saved his. In that knowledge, despair and die."

The children did not see the actual moment of the killing. They couldn't bear to look and had covered their eyes.

15

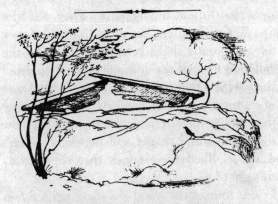

DEEPER MAGIC
FROM BEFORE THE
DAWN OF TIME

While the two girls still crouched in the bushes with their hands over their faces, they heard the voice of the Witch calling out,

"Now! Follow me all and we will set about what remains of this war! It will not take us long to crush the human vermin and the traitors now that the great Fool, the great Cat, lies dead."

At this moment the children were for a few seconds in very great danger. For with wild cries and a noise of skirling pipes and shrill horns blowing, the whole of that vile rabble came sweeping off the hilltop and down the slope right past their hiding-place. They felt the Specters go by them like a cold wind and they felt the ground shake beneath them under the galloping feet of the Minotaurs; and overhead there went a flurry of foul wings and a blackness of vultures and giant bats. At any other time they would have trembled with fear; but now the sadness and shame and horror of Aslan's death so filled their minds that they hardly thought of it.

As soon as the wood was silent again Susan and Lucy crept out onto the open hilltop. The moon was getting low and thin clouds were passing across her, but still they could see the shape of the Lion lying dead in his bonds. And down they both knelt in the wet grass and kissed his cold face and stroked his beautiful fur—what was left of it—and cried till they could cry no more. And then they looked at each other and held each other's hands for mere loneliness and cried again; and then again were silent. At last Lucy said,

"I can't bear to look at that horrible muzzle. I wonder could we take it off?"

So they tried. And after a lot of working at it (for their fingers were cold and it was now the darkest part of the night) they succeeded. And

when they saw his face with- out it they burst out crying again and kissed it and fondled it and wiped away the blood and the foam as well as they could. And it was all more lonely and hopeless and horrid than I know how to describe.

"I wonder could we untie him as well?" said Susan presently. But the enemies, out of pure spitefulness, had drawn the cords so tight that the girls could make nothing of the knots.

I hope no one who reads this book has been quite as miserable as Susan and Lucy were that night; but if you have been—if you've been up all night and cried till you have no more tears left in you—you will know that there comes in the end a sort of quietness. You feel as if nothing was ever going to happen again. At any rate that was how it felt to these two. Hours and hours seemed to go by in this dead calm, and they hardly noticed that they were getting colder and colder. But at last Lucy noticed two other things. One was that the sky on the east side of the hill was a little less dark than it had been an hour ago. The other was some tiny movement going on in the grass at her feet. At first she took no interest in this. What did it matter? Nothing mattered now! But at last she saw that whatever-it-was had begun to move up the upright stones of the Stone Table. And now whatever-they-were were moving about on Aslan's body. She peered closer. They were little gray things.

"Ugh!" said Susan from the other side of the Table. "How beastly! There are horrid little mice crawling over him. Go away, you little beasts." And she raised her hand to frighten them away.

"Wait!" said Lucy, who had been looking at them more closely still. "Can you see what they're doing?"

Both girls bent down and stared.

"I do believe—" said Susan. "But how queer! They're nibbling away at the cords!"

"That's what I thought," said Lucy. "I think

they're friendly mice. Poor little things—they don't realize he's dead. They think it'll do some good untying him."

It was quite definitely lighter by now. Each of the girls noticed for the first time the white face of the other. They could see the mice nibbling away; dozens and dozens, even hundreds, of little field mice. And at last, one by one, the ropes were all gnawed through.

The sky in the east was whitish by now and the stars were getting fainter—all except one very big one low down on the eastern horizon. They felt colder than they had been all night. The mice crept away again.

The girls cleared away the remains of the gnawed ropes. Aslan looked more like himself without them. Every moment his dead face looked nobler, as the light grew and they could see it better.

175

In the wood behind them a bird gave a chuckling sound. It had been so still for hours and hours that it startled them. Then another bird answered it. Soon there were birds singing all over the place.

It was quite definitely early morning now, not late night.

"I'm so cold," said Lucy.

"So am I," said Susan. "Let's walk about a bit."

They walked to the eastern edge of the hill and looked down. The one big star had almost disappeared. The country all looked dark gray, but beyond, at the very end of the world, the sea showed pale. The sky began to turn red. They walked to and fro more times than they could count between the dead Aslan and the eastern ridge, trying to keep warm; and oh, how tired their legs felt. Then at last, as they stood for a moment looking out toward the sea and Cair Paravel (which they could now just make out) the red turned to gold along the line where the sea and the sky met and very slowly up came the edge of the sun. At that moment they heard from behind them a loud noise—a great cracking, deafening noise as if a giant had broken a giant's plate.

"What's that?" said Lucy, clutching Susan's arm.

"I—I feel afraid to turn round," said Susan; "something awful is happening."

"They're doing something worse to *Him*," said Lucy. "Come on!" And she turned, pulling Susan round with her.

The rising of the sun had made everything look so different—all colors and shadows were changed—that for a moment they didn't see the important thing. Then they did. The Stone Table was broken into two pieces by a great crack that ran down it from end to end; and there was no Aslan.

"Oh, oh, oh!" cried the two girls, rushing back to the Table.

"Oh, it's *too* bad," sobbed Lucy; "they might have left the body alone."

"Who's done it?" cried Susan. "What does it mean? Is it more magic?"

"Yes!" said a great voice behind their backs.

"It is more magic." They looked round. There, shining in the sunrise, larger than they had seen him before, shaking his mane (for it had apparently grown again) stood Aslan himself.

"Oh, Aslan!" cried both the children, staring up at him, almost as much frightened as they were glad.

"Aren't you dead then, dear Aslan?" said Lucy.

"Not now," said Aslan.

"You're not—not a—?" asked Susan in a shaky voice. She couldn't bring herself to say the word *ghost*. Aslan stooped his golden head and licked her forehead. The warmth of his breath and a rich sort of smell that seemed to hang about his hair came all over her.

"Do I look it?" he said.

"Oh, you're real, you're real! Oh, Aslan!" cried Lucy, and both girls flung themselves upon him and covered him with kisses.

"But what does it all mean?" asked Susan when they were somewhat calmer.

"It means," said Aslan, "that though the Witch knew the Deep Magic, there is a magic deeper still which she did not know. Her knowledge goes back only to the dawn of time. But if she could have looked a little further back, into the stillness and the darkness before Time dawned, she would have read there a different incantation. She would have known that when a willing victim who had committed no treachery was killed in a traitor's stead, the Table would crack and Death itself would start working backward. And now—"

"Oh yes. Now?" said Lucy, jumping up and clapping her hands.

"Oh, children," said the Lion, "I feel my strength coming back to me. Oh, children, catch me if you can!" He stood for a second, his eyes very bright, his limbs quivering, lashing himself with his tail. Then he made a leap high over their heads and landed on the other side of the Table. Laughing, though she didn't know why, Lucy scrambled over it to reach him. Aslan leaped again. A mad chase began. Round and round the hilltop he led them, now hopelessly out of their reach, now letting them almost catch his tail, now diving between them, now tossing them in the air with his huge and beautifully velveted paws and catching them again, and now stopping unexpectedly so that all three of them rolled over together in a happy laughing heap of fur and arms and legs. It was such a romp as no one has ever had except in Narnia; and whether it was more like playing with a thunderstorm or playing with a kitten Lucy could never make up her mind. And the funny thing was that when all three finally lay together panting in the sun the girls no longer felt in the least tired or hungry or thirsty.

"And now," said Aslan presently, "to business. I feel I am going to roar. You had better put your fingers in your ears."

And they did. And Aslan stood up and when he opened his mouth to roar his face became so terrible that they did not dare to look at it. And they saw all the trees in front of him bend before the blast of his roaring as grass bends in a meadow before the wind. Then he said,

"We have a long journey to go. You must ride on me." And he crouched down and the children climbed onto his warm, golden back, and Susan sat first, holding on tightly to his mane and Lucy sat behind holding on tightly to Susan. And with a great heave he rose underneath them and then shot off, faster than any horse could go, down hill and into the thick of the forest.

That ride was perhaps the most wonderful thing that happened to them in Narnia. Have you ever had a gallop on a horse? Think of that; and then take away the heavy noise of the hoofs and the jingle of the bits and imagine instead the almost noiseless padding of the great paws. Then imagine instead of the black or gray or chestnut back of the horse the soft roughness of golden fur, and the mane flying back in the wind. And then imagine you are going about twice as fast as the fastest racehorse. But this is a mount that doesn't need to be guided and never grows tired. He rushes on and on, never missing his footing, never hesitating, threading his way with perfect skill between tree trunks, jumping over bush and briar and the smaller streams, wading the larger, swimming the largest of all. And you are riding not on a road nor in a park nor even on the downs, but right across Narnia, in spring, down solemn avenues of beech and across sunny glades of oak, through wild orchards of snow-white cherry trees, past roaring waterfalls and mossy rocks and echoing caverns, up windy slopes alight with gorse bushes, and across the shoulders of heathery mountains and along giddy ridges and down, down, down again into wild valleys and out into acres of blue flowers.

It was nearly midday when they found themselves looking down a steep hillside at a castle—a little toy castle it looked from where they stood—which seemed to be all pointed towers. But the Lion was rushing down at such a speed that it grew larger every moment and before they had time even to ask themselves what it was they were already on a level with it. And now it no longer looked like a toy castle but rose frowning in front of them. No face looked over the battlements and the gates were fast shut. And Aslan, not at all slacking his pace, rushed straight as a bullet toward it.

"The Witch's home!" he cried. "Now, children, hold tight."

Next moment the whole world seemed to turn upside down, and the children felt as if they had left their insides behind them; for the Lion had gathered himself together for a greater leap than any he had yet made and jumped—or you may call it flying rather than jumping—right over the castle wall. The two girls, breathless but unhurt, found themselves tumbling off his back in the middle of a wide stone courtyard full of statues.

WHAT HAPPENED ABOUT THE STATUES

"What an extraordinary place!" cried Lucy. "All those stone animals—and people too! It's—it's like a museum."

"Hush," said Susan, "Aslan's doing something."

He was indeed. He had bounded up to the stone lion and breathed on him. Then without waiting a moment he whisked round—almost as if he had been a cat chasing its tail—and breathed also on the stone dwarf, which (as you remember) was standing a few feet from the lion with his back to it. Then he pounced on a tall stone dryad which stood beyond the dwarf, turned rapidly aside to deal with a stone rabbit on his right, and rushed on to two centaurs. But at that moment Lucy said,

"Oh, Susan! Look! Look at the lion."

I expect you've seen someone put a lighted match to a bit of newspaper which is propped up in a grate against an unlit fire. And for a second nothing seems to have happened; and then you notice a tiny streak of flame creeping along the edge of the newspaper. It was like that now. For a second after Aslan had breathed upon him the stone lion looked just the same. Then a tiny streak of gold began to run along his white marble back—then it spread—then the color seemed to lick all over him as the flame licks all over a bit of paper—then, while his hindquarters were still obviously stone, the lion shook his mane and all the heavy, stone folds rippled into living hair. Then he opened a great red mouth, warm and living, and gave a prodigious yawn. And now his hind legs had come to life. He lifted one of them and scratched himself. Then, having caught sight of Aslan, he went bounding after him and frisking round him whimpering with delight and jumping up to lick his face.

Of course the children's eyes turned to follow the lion; but the sight they saw was so wonderful that they soon forgot about *him*.

Everywhere the statues were coming to life. The courtyard looked no longer like a museum; it looked more like a zoo. Creatures were running after Aslan and dancing round him till he was almost hidden in the crowd. Instead of all that deadly white the courtyard was now a blaze of colors; glossy chestnut sides of centaurs, indigo horns of unicorns, dazzling plumage of birds, reddy-brown of foxes, dogs and satyrs, yellow stockings and crimson hoods of dwarfs; and the birch-girls in silver, and the beech-girls in fresh, transparent green, and the larch-girls in green so bright that it was almost yellow. And instead of the deadly silence the whole place rang with the sound of happy roarings, brayings, yelpings, barkings, squealings, cooings, neighings, stampings, shouts, hurrahs, songs and laughter.

"Oh!" said Susan in a different tone. "Look! I wonder—I mean, is it safe?"

Lucy looked and saw that Aslan had just breathed on the feet of the stone giant.

"It's all right!" shouted Aslan joyously. "Once the feet are put right, all the rest of him will follow."

"That wasn't exactly what I meant," whispered Susan to Lucy. But it was too late to do anything about it now even if Aslan would have listened to her. The change was already creeping up the Giant's legs. Now he was moving his feet.

A moment later he lifted the club off his shoulder, rubbed his eyes and said,

"Bless me! I must have been asleep. Now! Where's that dratted little Witch that was running about on the ground. Somewhere just by my feet it was." But when everyone had shouted up to him to explain what had really happened, and when the Giant had put his hand to his ear and got them to repeat it all again so that at last he understood, then he bowed down till his head was no further off than the top of a haystack and touched his cap repeatedly to Aslan, beaming all over his honest ugly face. (Giants of any sort are now so rare in England and so few giants are good-tempered that ten to one you have never seen a giant when his face is beaming. It's a sight well worth looking at.)

"Now for the inside of this house!" said Aslan. "Look alive, everyone. Up stairs and down stairs and in my lady's chamber! Leave no corner unsearched. You never know where some poor prisoner may be concealed."

And into the interior they all rushed and for several minutes the whole of that dark, horrible, fusty old castle echoed with the opening of windows and with everyone's voices crying out at once, "Don't forget the dungeons— Give us a hand with this door!— Here's another little winding stair— Oh! I say. Here's a poor kangaroo. Call Aslan— Phew! How it smells in here— Look out for trap-doors— Up here! There are a whole lot more on the landing!" But the best of all was when Lucy came rushing upstairs shouting out,

"Aslan! Aslan! I've found Mr. Tumnus. Oh, do come quick."

A moment later Lucy and the little Faun were holding each other by both hands and dancing round and round for joy. The little chap was none the worse for having been a statue and was of course very interested in all she had to tell him.

But at last the ransacking of the Witch's fortress was ended. The whole castle stood empty with every door and window open and the light and the sweet spring air flooding in to all the dark and evil places which needed them so badly. The whole crowd of liberated statues surged back into the courtyard. And it was then that someone (Tumnus, I think) first said,

"But how are we going to get out?" for Aslan had got in by a jump and the gates were still locked.

"That'll be all right," said Aslan; and then, rising on his hind-legs, he bawled up at the Giant. "Hi! You up there," he roared. "What's your name?"

"Giant Rumblebuffin, if it please your

honor," said the Giant, once more touching his cap.

"Well then, Giant Rumblebuffin," said Aslan, "just let us out of this, will you?"

"Certainly, your honor. It will be a pleasure," said Giant Rumblebuffin. "Stand well away from the gates, all you little 'uns." Then he strode to the gate himself and bang—bang—bang—went his huge club. The gates creaked at the first blow, cracked at the second, and shivered at the third. Then he tackled the towers on each side of them and after a few minutes of crashing and thudding both the towers and a good bit of the wall on each side went thundering down in a mass of hopeless rubble; and when the dust cleared it was odd, standing in that dry, grim, stony yard, to see through the gap all the grass and waving trees and sparkling streams of the forest, and the blue hills beyond that and beyond them the sky.

"Blowed if I ain't all in a muck sweat," said the Giant, puffing like the largest railway engine. "Comes of being out of condition. I suppose neither of you young ladies has such a thing as a pocket-handkerchee about you?"

"Yes, I have," said Lucy, standing on tip-toes and holding her handkerchief up as far as she could reach.

"Thank you, Missie," said Giant Rumblebuffin, stooping down. Next moment Lucy got rather a fright for she found herself caught up in mid-air between the Giant's finger and thumb. But just as she was getting near his face he suddenly started and then put her gently back on the ground muttering, "Bless me! I've picked up the little girl instead. I beg your pardon, Missie, I thought you *was* the handkerchee!"

"No, no," said Lucy laughing, "here it is!" This time he managed to get it but it was only about the same size to him that a saccharine tablet would be to you, so that when she saw him solemnly rubbing it to and fro across his great red face, she said, "I'm afraid it's not much use to you, Mr. Rumblebuffin."

"Not at all. Not at all," said the giant politely. "Never met a nicer handkerchee. So fine, so handy. So—I don't know how to describe it."

"What a nice giant he is!" said Lucy to Mr. Tumnus.

"Oh yes," replied the Faun. "All the Buffins always were. One of the most respected of all the giant families in Narnia. Not very clever, perhaps (I never knew a giant that was), but an old family. With traditions, you know. If he'd been the other sort she'd never have turned him into stone."

At this point Aslan clapped his paws

together and called for silence.

"Our day's work is not yet over," he said, "and if the Witch is to be finally defeated before bedtime we must find the battle at once."

"And join in, I hope, sir!" added the largest of the Centaurs.

"Of course," said Aslan. "And now! Those who can't keep up—that is, children, dwarfs, and small animals—must ride on the backs of those who can—that is, lions, centaurs, unicorns, horses, giants and eagles. Those who are good with their noses must come in the front with us lions to smell out where the battle is. Look lively and sort yourselves."

And with a great deal of bustle and cheering they did. The most pleased of the lot was the other lion who kept running about everywhere pretending to be very busy but really in order to say to everyone he met, "Did you hear what he said? *Us Lions*. That means him and me. *Us Lions*. That's what I like about Aslan. No side, no stand-off-ishness. *Us Lions*. That meant him and me." At least he went on saying this till Aslan had loaded him up with three dwarfs, one dryad, two rabbits, and a hedgehog. That steadied him a bit.

When all were ready (it was a big sheepdog who actually helped Aslan most in getting them

sorted into their proper order) they set out
through the gap in the castle wall. At first the
lions and dogs went nosing about in all directions. But then suddenly one great hound
picked up the scent and gave a bay. There was
no time lost after that. Soon all the dogs and
lions and wolves and other hunting animals
were going at full speed with their noses to the
ground, and all the others, streaked out for
about half a mile behind them, were following
as fast as they could. The noise was like an
English fox-hunt only better because every now
and then with the music of the hounds was
mixed the roar of the other lion and sometimes
the far deeper and more awful roar of Aslan
himself. Faster and faster they went as the scent
became easier and easier to follow. And then,
just as they came to the last curve in a narrow,
winding valley, Lucy heard above all these
noises another noise—a different one, which

gave her a queer feeling inside. It was a noise of shouts and shrieks and of the clashing of metal against metal.

Then they came out of the narrow valley and at once she saw the reason. There stood Peter and Edmund and all the rest of Aslan's army fighting desperately against the crowd of horrible creatures whom she had seen last night; only now, in the daylight, they looked even stranger and more evil and more deformed. There also seemed to be far more of them. Peter's army—which had their backs to her— looked terribly few. And there were statues dotted all over the battlefield, so apparently the Witch had been using her wand. But she did not seem to be using it now. She was fighting with her stone knife. It was Peter she was fighting— both of them going at it so hard that Lucy could hardly make out what was happening; she only

saw the stone knife and Peter's sword flashing so quickly that they looked like three knives and three swords. That pair were in the center. On each side the line stretched out. Horrible things were happening wherever she looked.

"Off my back, children," shouted Aslan. And they both tumbled off. Then with a roar that shook all Narnia from the western lamp-post to the shores of the eastern sea the great beast flung himself upon the White Witch. Lucy saw her face lifted toward him for one second with an expression of terror and amazement. Then Lion and Witch had rolled over together but with the Witch underneath; and at the same moment all war-like creatures whom Aslan had led from the Witch's house rushed madly on the enemy lines, dwarfs with their battleaxes, dogs with teeth, the Giant with his club (and his feet also crushed dozens of the foe), unicorns with their horns, centaurs with swords and hoofs. And Peter's tired army cheered, and the newcomers roared, and the enemy squealed and gibbered till the wood re-echoed with the din of that onset.

17

THE HUNTING OF THE WHITE STAG

The battle was all over a few minutes after their arrival. Most of the enemy had been killed in the first charge of Aslan and his companions; and when those who were still living saw that the Witch was dead they either gave themselves up or took to flight. The next thing that Lucy knew was that Peter and Aslan were shaking hands. It was strange to her to see Peter looking as he looked now—his face was so pale and stern and he seemed so much older.

"It was all Edmund's doing, Aslan," Peter was saying. "We'd have been beaten if it hadn't been for him. The Witch was turning our troops into stone right and left. But nothing would stop him. He fought his way through three ogres to where she was just turning one of your leopards into a statue. And when he reached her he had sense to bring his sword smashing down on her wand instead of trying to go for her directly and simply getting made a statue himself for his pains. That was the mistake all the rest were making. Once her wand was broken we began to have some chance—if we hadn't lost so many already. He was terribly wounded. We must go and see him."

They found Edmund in charge of Mrs. Beaver a little way back from the fighting line. He was covered with blood, his mouth was open, and his face a nasty green color.

"Quick, Lucy," said Aslan.

And then, almost for the first time, Lucy remembered the precious cordial that had been given her for a Christmas present. Her hands trembled so much that she could hardly undo the stopper, but she managed it in the end and poured a few drops into her brother's mouth.

"There are other people wounded," said Aslan while she was still looking eagerly into Edmund's pale face and wondering if the cordial would have any result.

"Yes, I know," said Lucy crossly. "Wait a minute."

"Daughter of Eve," said Aslan in a graver voice, "others also are at the point of death. Must *more* people die for Edmund?"

"I'm sorry, Aslan," said Lucy, getting up and going with him. And for the next half-hour they were busy—she attending to the wounded while he restored those who had been turned into stone. When at last she was free to come back to Edmund she found him standing on his feet and not only healed of his wounds but looking better than she had seen him look—oh, for ages; in fact ever since his first term at that horrid school which was where he had begun to go wrong. He had become his real old self again and could look you in the face. And there on the field of battle Aslan made him a knight.

"Does he know," whispered Lucy to Susan, "what Aslan did for him? Does he know what the arrangement with the Witch really was?"

"Hush! No. Of course not," said Susan.

"Oughtn't he to be told?" said Lucy.

"Oh, surely not," said Susan. "It would be too awful for him. Think how you'd feel if you were he."

"All the same I think he ought to know,"

said Lucy. But at that moment they were interrupted.

That night they slept where they were. How
Aslan provided food for them all I don't know;
but somehow or other they found themselves all
sitting down on the grass to a fine high tea at
about eight o'clock. Next day they began
marching eastward down the side of the great
river. And the next day after that, at about
teatime, they actually reached the mouth. The
castle of Cair Paravel on its little hill towered up
above them; before them were the sands, with
rocks and little pools of salt water, and seaweed,
and the smell of the sea and long miles of
bluish-green waves breaking for ever and ever
on the beach. And oh, the cry of the seagulls!
Have you heard it? Can you remember?

That evening after tea the four children all managed to get down to the beach again and get their shoes and stockings off and feel the sand between their toes. But next day was more solemn. For then, in the Great Hall of Cair Paravel—that wonderful hall with the ivory roof and the west wall hung with peacock's feathers and the eastern door which looks towards the sea, in the presence of all their friends and to the sound of trumpets, Aslan solemnly crowned them and led them to the four thrones amid deafening shouts of, "Long Live King Peter! Long Live Queen Susan! Long Live King Edmund! Long Live Queen Lucy!"

"Once a king or queen in Narnia, always a king or queen. Bear it well, Sons of Adam! Bear it well, Daughters of Eve!" said Aslan.

And through the eastern door, which was wide open, came the voices of the mermen and the mermaids swimming close to the shore and singing in honor of their new Kings and Queens.

So the children sat on their thrones and scepters were put into their hands and they gave rewards and honors to all their friends, to Tumnus the Faun, and to the Beavers, and Giant Rumblebuffin, to the leopards, and the good centaurs, and the good dwarfs, and to the lion. And that night there was a great feast in Cair Paravel, and revelry and dancing, and gold flashed and wine flowed, and answering to the music inside, but stranger, sweeter, and more piercing, came the music of the sea people.

But amid all these rejoicings Aslan himself quietly slipped away. And when the Kings and Queens noticed that he wasn't there they said nothing about it. For Mr. Beaver had warned them, "He'll be coming and going," he had said. "One day you'll see him and another you won't. He doesn't like being tied down—and of course he has other countries to attend to. It's quite all right. He'll often drop in. Only you mustn't press him. He's wild, you know. Not like a *tame* lion."

And now, as you see, this story is nearly (but not quite) at an end. These two Kings and two Queens governed Narnia well, and long and happy was their reign. At first much of their time was spent in seeking out the remnants of the White Witch's army and destroying them, and indeed for a long time there would be news of evil things lurking in the wilder parts of the forest—a haunting here and a killing there, a glimpse of a werewolf one month and a rumor of a hag the next. But in the end all that foul brood was stamped out. And they made good laws and kept the peace and saved good trees from being unnecessarily cut down, and liberated young dwarfs and young satyrs from being sent to school, and generally stopped busybodies and interferers and encouraged ordinary people who wanted to live and let live. And they drove back the fierce giants (quite a different sort from Giant Rumblebuffin) on the north of Narnia when these ventured across the frontier. And they entered into friendship and alliance with countries beyond the sea and paid them visits of state and received visits of state from them. And they themselves grew and changed as the years passed over them. And Peter became a tall and deep-chested man and a great warrior, and he was called King Peter the Magnificent. And Susan grew into a tall and gracious woman with black hair that fell almost to her feet and the kings of the countries beyond the sea began to send ambassadors asking for her hand in marriage. And she was called Susan the Gentle. Edmund was a graver and quieter man than Peter, and great in council and judgment. He was called King Edmund the Just. But as for Lucy, she was always gay and golden-haired, and all princes in those parts desired her to be their Queen, and her own people called her Queen Lucy the Valiant.

So they lived in great joy and if ever they remembered their life in this world it was only as one remembers a dream. And one year it fell out that Tumnus (who was a middle-aged Faun by now and beginning to be stout) came down river and brought them news that the White Stag had once more appeared in his parts—the White Stag who would give you wishes if you caught him. So these two Kings and two Queens with the principal members of their court, rode a-hunting with horns and hounds in the Western Woods to follow the White Stag. And they had not hunted long before they had a sight of him. And he led them a great pace over rough and smooth and through thick and thin, till the horses of all the courtiers were tired out and only these four were still following. And they saw the stag enter into a thicket where their horses could not follow. Then said King Peter (for they talked in quite a different style now, having been Kings and Queens for so long), "Fair Consorts, let us now alight from our horses and follow this beast into the thicket; for

in all my days I never hunted a nobler quarry."

"Sir," said the others, "even so let us do."

So they alighted and tied their horses to trees and went on into the thick wood on foot. And as soon as they had entered it Queen Susan said,

"Fair friends, here is a great marvel for I seem to see a tree of iron."

"Madam," said King Edmund, "if you look well upon it you shall see it is a pillar of iron with a lantern set on the top thereof."

"By the Lion's Mane, a strange device," said King Peter, "to set a lantern here where the trees cluster so thick about it and so high above it that if it were lit it should give light to no man!"

"Sir," said Queen Lucy. "By likelihood when this post and this lamp were set here there were smaller trees in the place, or fewer, or none. For this is a young wood and the iron post is old." And they stood looking upon it. Then said King Edmund,

"I know not how it is, but this lamp on the post worketh upon me strangely. It runs in my mind that I have seen the like before; as it were in a dream, or in the dream of a dream."

"Sir," answered they all, "it is even so with us also."

"And more," said Queen Lucy, "for it will not go out of my mind that if we pass this post and lantern either we shall find strange adventures or else some great change of our fortunes."

"Madam," said King Edmund, "the like foreboding stirreth in my heart also."

"And in mine, fair brother," said King Peter.

"And in mine too," said Queen Susan. "Wherefore by my counsel we shall lightly return to our horses and follow this White Stag no further."

"Madam," said King Peter, "therein I pray thee to have me excused. For never since we four were Kings and Queens in Narnia have we set our hands to any high matter, as battles, quests, feats of arms, acts of justice, and the like, and then given over; but always what we have taken in hand, the same we have achieved."

"Sister," said Queen Lucy, "my royal brother speaks rightly. And it seems to me we should be shamed if for any fearing or foreboding we turned back from following so noble a beast as now we have in chase."

"And so say I," said King Edmund. "And I have such desire to find the signification of this thing that I would not by my good will turn back for the richest jewel in all Narnia and all the islands."

"Then in the name of Aslan," said Queen Susan, "if ye will all have it so, let us go on and take the adventure that shall fall to us."

So these Kings and Queens entered the thicket, and before they had gone a score of paces they all remembered that the thing they had seen was called a lamp-post, and before they had gone twenty more they noticed that they were making their way not through branches but through coats. And next moment they all came tumbling out of a wardrobe door into the empty room, and they were no longer Kings and Queens in their hunting array but just Peter, Susan, Edmund and Lucy in their old clothes. It was the same day and the same hour of the day on which they had all gone into the wardrobe to hide. Mrs. Macready and the visitors were still talking in the passage; but luckily they never came into the empty room and so the children weren't caught.

And that would have been the very end of the story if it hadn't been that they felt they really must explain to the Professor why four of the coats out of his wardrobe were missing. And the Professor, who was a very remarkable man, didn't tell them not to be silly or not to tell lies, but believed the whole story. "No," he said, "I don't think it will be any good trying to go back through the wardrobe door to get the coats. You won't get into Narnia again by *that* route. Nor would the coats be much use by now if you did!

Eh? What's that? Yes, of course you'll get back to Narnia again someday. Once a King in Narnia, always a King in Narnia. But don't go trying to use the same route twice. Indeed, don't *try* to get there at all. It'll happen when you're not looking for it. And don't talk too much about it even among yourselves. And don't mention it to anyone else unless you find that they've had adventures of the same sort themselves. What's that? How will you know? Oh, you'll *know* all right. Odd things they say—even their looks—will let the secret out. Keep your eyes open. Bless me, what *do* they teach them at these schools?"

And that is the very end of the adventure of the wardrobe. But if the Professor was right it was only the beginning of the adventures of Narnia.